ZOGARTH

THE PRIMAL HUNTER

BOOK SEVEN

THE PRIMAL HUNTER 7
©2023 ZOGARTH

Aethon Books
www.aethonbooks.com

Print and eBook formatting by Josh Hayes. Artwork provided by Antti Hakosaari.

Published by Aethon Books LLC.

ALSO BY ZOGARTH

PREVIOUSLY ON THE PRIMAL HUNTER

Back from the Treasure Hunt, Jake was reminded by his brother Caleb that he is a kind of shitty son for never visiting his parents since the integration. Having no real argument against that – besides not wanting to make the long trip, but seriously, that's a weak excuse to not visit your parents for such a long period – he finally gets his shit together and goes on a road trip.

Arriving in Skyggen, where his parents and brother had settled down, Jake spent two weeks of quality time with his family before it was time to participate in the Auction event that would directly follow the Treasure Hunt. An event that would once more gather all the influential individuals of Earth.

The auction turns out to be very much a mixed bag, with more disappointments than pleasant surprises. At least initially. That is how auctions tend to work, after all. The bad stuff comes first, with the best saved for last, and even if Jake did buy a few of the lower-rarity items, he primarily sold the things he had obtained in the Treasure Hunt, raking in the big bucks.

Luckily, despite the utterly boring auction of low-level crap, Jake still does something productive with his time: alchemy. He also sadly did have to talk with a few people, but he pretty much delegated all work to Miranda and Sultan – the City Lord of his city, Haven, and Haven's resident shady merchant.

When the good stuff arrived, Jake bought a few items of note. The most important of which was a quiver and bow, a nice vest for Sylphie that doubled as a spatial storage, and finally, an item called Soul

Renewal with the ability to fully heal any soul it's used on, no matter the damage.

This item was clearly designed with the Sword Saint in mind to heal him up after using his Transcendence at the end of the Treasure Hunt, but due to the stubbornness of the old man and Jake really wanting the Soul Renewal for something that was totally a good idea, Jake ends up getting it.

As for his brilliant idea?

To revive the King of the Forest that nearly killed him as the final boss of the Tutorial, because what could possibly go wrong? Well, Jake at least had the foresight to not do it inside a major city but out in the middle of nowhere.

The revival proves to be a great success, and after discussing the logistics of Jake effectively "owning" the Unique Lifeform due to their peculiar connection, they do what any two normal people do after one has revived the other and have a fight that destroys most of the local landscape.

After that, the King of the Forest, who has now chosen to be called the Fallen King, goes his own way as Jake proceeds with his own plan: to make a new cool melee weapon with some of all the cool shit he'd picked up recently.

During the Treasure Hunt, Jake obtained the item known as the Root of Eternal Resentment, an artifact filled with insane quantities of curse energy, as well as a Chimeric weapon made from combining all the vampire boss weapons. Jake, being the smart boy he is, decides that taking all this curse energy and jamming it into his already existing curse weapon – the Scimitar of Hunger - while also combining it with the Chimeric weapon and a bunch of other high-rarity things is a great idea, and nothing could possibly go wrong, right?

From there, things went wrong.

It turns out there was a bit more curse energy than Jake was capable of handling... actually, scratch that, more than Earth was capable of handling. From his semi-failed ritual to create his new weapon, curse energy emanated and affected the entire planet with a curse of hunger, making the restaurant industry boom while making Casper, the only person on Earth who actually knew shit about curses, facepalm an unhealthy number of times.

Meanwhile, as the rest of the world was experiencing a global crisis, Jake was underground in a large termite hive, not entirely in a stable mental state, desperately trying to sate his own hunger by constantly laughtering monsters to absorb their energies. Descending deeper and deeper, Jake killed anything in his path, as he did all he could to feed the cursed monstrosity he had created by throwing nearly every single valuable thing he owned into the hungering cursed weapon to try and sate it. This served both as a great way to clean out his inventory as well as a way to make the cursed weapon of pure hunger a little less likely to realize that eating Jake to death was a valid option.

After a long time and many dead termites, Jake finally succeeds in merging his cursed scimitar, the Chimera weapon, and the curse energy in the Root of Eternal Resentment, creating a mythical weapon named Eternal Hunger – the first item on Earth above legendary rarity ever created. This gave him not only a new title that makes it easier to craft similar high-rarity items in the future but also a damn sweet new weapon that can change its shape as Jake desires while stealing resources from anything it hits, and should he kill anything, he would even absorb its soul. A definitely-not ominous weapon that Villy thought suited him nicely as the totally-not-evil Chosen of the Malefic Viper.

Diving deeper and wanting to feed the still-hungry Eternal Hunger – hence the name - Jake proceeded to slaughter more and more termites. The further he descended, the more powerful foes he encountered, until soon he found himself facing peak D-grade opponents. Jake, feeling like a big, strong boy after making his new weapon, decides that now is a great time to have his first encounter with a C-grade in the wild. Breaking into the Termite Hive Queen's, well, hive, Jake began his plans of fumigating the place. The Hive Queen proved an annoying foe due to her durability and healing skills, but Jake has confidence that he will win given enough time.

Now, this is where Jake discovered a super funny fact that most people don't know. Most eusocial (insects that make big hives that work as one large entity) usually only have a queen and then a bunch of drones, soldiers, etc., but termites are pretty unique in the insect world in that they also have kings. A termite king will mate with the Queen throughout his life and is considered the second-most important member of any colony. Termite kings are larger than other termites and tend to have a dark color, and when one exterminates a hive, it is important to kill both the king and the Queen.

In the post-system world, the hive also happened to have both a king and a queen... resulting in Jake being in a very precarious situation. While the Queen had a path focused on healing and reproduction, the Termite King was the exact opposite. It was a being that existed only to protect the hive, and with a level even higher than the Queen, Jake had no choice but to try and get away and hide. Especially after he fails to penetrate the exoskeleton of this termite, nearly losing his life in the process.

Barely escaping by upgrading his stealth skill and bunkering down within a tunnel, Jake only gets away because the C-grade cannot ascend above ground due to system restriction and because it has matters to attend to deep beneath the earth. As for what it had to attend to? Well, that will be revealed in a later book.

Anyway, after Jake screwed up Earth enough by making a potentially cataclysmic cursed weapon and barely avoiding getting killed by an insect, he was happy to hear that a monument that would allow him to tap into his identity as the Chosen of the Malefic Viper had been built. This would give him the opportunity to teleport away from not just Earth but the 93rd universe, straight to the Order of the Malefic Viper.

Before going there, he does a quick pit-stop at Villy's to practice controlling his Shroud of the Primordial a bit – the legendary skill he received when the Malefic Viper blessed him. After spending just fourteen years in time-dilation learning the magical version of creating a fake ID, Jake is ready to go to the Order, where he can surely keep his identity as the Chosen of the Malefic Viper hidden for at least that long, right?

...right?

After a quick trip back to Earth to pick up some people he wants to bring along to the Order, such as Reika and a few alchemists from the Noboru Clan the Sword Saint is the leader of, Jake heads off to the Order.

However, before he was even allowed to join this super exclusive club his buddy was the leader of, Jake had to do an entry test. Well, alright, if he wasn't so damn steadfast on keeping his identity as Villy's Chosen a secret, he would have just waltzed in there on a red carpet, but where would the fun in that be? No, doing the same entrance test everyone else would do was definitely the way to go.

What followed was Jake doing different tests while being told in only slightly kinder words that he was pretty good at some things when it came to alchemy but was shit in most areas. His general knowledge of how to alchemy was utterly lacking, with his foundation shaky at best.

Good thing he had come to join an academy that taught alchemy then, right?

After completing all of the tests that are actually related to alchemy, he just has one more. Because what good alchemy academy doesn't have a combat test? In fact, what teaching institution worth its salt doesn't have a combat test?

This combat test required Jake to beat progressively harder opponents with difficulty scaled to his own level, which resulted in it being a complete cakewalk. That is until he gets to the final challenge, where he faces an image of the Lord Protector himself. Of course, he only actually faces a D-grade version back when the Lord Protector was only a dumb Two-Headed Hydra. That doesn't mean the fight is easy, though, as the Hydra eats all his arrows and gives Jake a good beating until he suddenly has a flash of enlightenment.

Using that enlightenment, he triggers a vision with Path of the Heretic-Chosen by consuming two of its use-charges. In the vision, Jake sees the Malefic Viper as an S-grade fight against another S-grade human. Throughout the fight, the Viper is arrogant and believes himself superior as he beats down the human, who Jake learns is the future Primordial known as Valdemar. Yet no matter how many times Valdemar is beaten down, he gets back up and eventually turns the tables as he rips out a fang from the Viper's draconic mouth and declares his weapon the "fang of man," as he nearly kills the Viper and forces him to retreat.

Jake, being inspired by the absolute badassery of his fellow man, is inspired and forms his own Fang of Man skill, making his melee fighting prowess far superior. With renewed vigor, he faces the Hydra once more, and with great confidence, the timer of the test expires, and Jake fails to slay his foe.

Ah, but don't worry, he'll have his rematch in... not this book. Maybe book 8? Anyway, moving on.

Having successfully joined the academy belonging to the Order of the Malefic Viper, Jake receives not only a cool new mansion and a token Villy has rigged to have infinite Academy Credits so he can take any lessons he wants to, but he even gets an elf slave!

Yeah, Jake is not a fan of that one and has a heated discussion with the Viper. Jake is put between a rock and a hard place where he feels like there are no good choices but ultimately decides that the best course of action is to have his first – and the only one he will ever have

– slave become strong enough to join the Order on her own merits so he can safely set her free.

Meira, his new slave, has quite a hard time adapting to this weird new master of hers, especially with Jake being very adamant she is not allowed to ever call him master or anything like that. However, Jake has confidence that she will learn not only independence but that Meira can become her entirely own person given enough time. As the author, I can confirm Jake will eventually be proven correct.

With all that slave business hopefully handled, Jake tried to enjoy his school life. He goes to a few lessons and learns about Soulflames – a way to enhance your Alchemical Flame – general alchemy stuff, is hit on by dragon ladies, meets new people, and does all the other usual school stuff one would expect.

He even tries to enjoy his school life while beginning to shore up many of his weaknesses as an alchemist. Too bad he still had to deal with actually being social at the Order, even if he tries his best not to.

Anyway, book 6 was a long one, and I sure hope I didn't miss anything important! Not that this book is that much shorter...

Now! Back to Jake and his evil snake order school shenanigans!

CHAPTER 1

SLOW AND STEADY WINS THE RACE

J ake read the book in his bed as he went over the information in a crystal he had gained from the prior day's lesson. Finding everything to be in order, he nodded along. Then, with a wave of his hand, he destroyed the crystal and scattered the dust with a blast of destructive arcane mana. After all, the fellow student he had gained it from had asked him to.

Well over a month had passed since Jake had entered the Order of the Malefic Viper, and honestly? Things were going well. He had expected way more Bloodline trouble or people trying to start shit with him, but so far, everyone had been perfectly civil. Okay, he'd had a run-in with one moron in a lesson where they had to spar. The dude had been an overly confident asshole when he was clearly wrong, but Jake had chosen to be gracious and not assume malice where it may just be ignorance.

However, he wasn't the one making the most progress. As he sat on the bed, he heard a knock on the door, and he opened it to a far more kept-together elf in a white dress.

She slightly bowed. "Sir, I have brought the book you requested from the Order Library."

"Thanks, Meira," Jake said with a smile as he got off the bed and went over to accept the book. Meira smiled in response as she gave it to him. "Any issues getting it?"

"None. The librarian was very helpful there." She bowed again. "I shall return to my studies if there is no other matter Sir needs me to take care of?"

"There isn't. How are the lessons going, by the way?" Jake already knew the answer for the most part.

"I am doing my utmost and believe I am making acceptable progress," Meira answered with a small, embarrassed smile. Jake just smirked a bit in response as he finally allowed her to scurry away.

Meira was surely embarrassed because a teacher had sent her back with a letter of recommendation to her "sponsor." It was a letter that would allow Meira to attend another lesson taught by the same teacher for a heavy discount. The letter was addressed to Jake and had some assumptions within he had cracked up over. However, the crux of it was that Meira was quite a talented healer and had a great talent for metaphysiology—the study of the metaphysical body.

The letter had assumed Meira was an employee of Jake or perhaps just a follower of his. From what Jake had gathered, no one Meira had met during any lessons had even the slightest clue she was a slave or even a servant. As for the lesson, Jake had already allowed her to go; it wasn't even a question to him. But that she had even asked and expressed interest was huge progress.

Her coming out and saying she had a preference or a wish was something the Meira of one month ago would never have done. She would've just done whatever Jake wanted, never voicing her own thoughts. There was also the huge thing of her now calling him "Sir," and she didn't stumble over her words to avoid calling him the banned M-word.

It was slow but steady progress, and in the end, the best method to have her get more comfortable was simply time. She also smiled more and didn't seem as nervous as before.

The only place with absolutely no progress was in the department of randomly visiting gods, AKA Viper visits. The closest to progress there was her being able to leave the area whenever he visited without passing out. Half the time, at least.

Jake himself had also made good progress. He had only gained a single level in his profession, bringing him to level 152, which came from him experimenting a bit in his own time. While that seemed slow —and was, compared to Jake's old progress—it was considered good in the Order. In fact, Jake had come to learn that leveling fast was viewed as a fool's game, and he kind of understood why. There was no reason to try and rush through D-grade in a handful of years when you had millennia. Not that Jake would ever take that long—not unless Villy came up with another practice lesson like with Shroud.

As for what he had learned... Well, a lot, most of it the most basic here was in any subject. One such area was flasks, where Jake had finally made a few, even if they were quite honestly crap.

[flask of Minor Poison Resistance (Inferior)] – *A flask giving minor poison resistance against most forms of toxins for a duration of thirty (30) minutes.*
Requirements: *D-grade*

[flask of Fortified Mana(Inferior)] – *A flask increasing maximum mana by 50 for a duration of thirty (30) minutes.*
Requirements: *D-grade*

The first gave so little poison resistance it was inconsequential, and it worked before his Palate, as they had overlapping effects. So unless Jake made a way better version, it did nothing for him besides preventing him from consuming another flask for a full day, as that was the cooldown.

The flask of Fortified Mana was even worse, as there was once more overlap with his mask. As his mask increased mana by 25%, the flask served no purpose, since he had already reached the "cap" of how much he could increase it. He had considered making some for health, but that would take a while to learn. Overall, there were many different flasks Jake was working on, but he quickly concluded it would take a long time to learn to craft the useful ones.

There was also the problem of Jake being unable to make any flasks for those below D-grade, no matter how shit they were. This was what Villy had talked about when it came to Records, and apparently, his Myth Originator title just made it worse. So, yeah, he could make flasks no one wanted, not even himself.

Not to misunderstand, flasks could be great. They fell into a category a bit like his own Arcane Awakening and functioned as temporary boosting items. The best ones came with drawbacks, especially those circumventing the equipment stat cap from gear. In fact, there was a lot of overlap between equipment and flasks. If Jake had a helm that granted him super fire magic resistance, he could not drink a flask giving him even more fire resistance. However, he could drink a flask that gave him general magic resistance or, instead of resisting fire magic, gave him a temporary anti-fire shield with a set absorption amount that didn't take any advantage of his fire resistance. So, yeah,

if you had the right flask for the right situation, they could b
amazing.

And this was a great segue, because the biggest competitor for flask
when it came to alchemical products were pills. Pills were actually a big
competitor to, like... everything. Pills could take so many damn forms
and do pretty much everything there was, for one simple reason that
honestly sounded so dumb Jake hadn't believed it when the teacher
said it the first time:

*"Pills are just potions, elixirs, flasks, or whatever else liquid product
condensed and turned into a solid form. The crafting method differs, but
ultimately the same concepts apply, and the system recognizes them as
equivalent. A healing pill will trigger the usual potion cooldown, a stat-
increasing pill will count the same as any elixir, and a pill increasing
your Strength temporarily will share all cooldowns and limits as a flask."*

So... yeah. This meant Jake had no interest in becoming a pill-
focused alchemist, even if pills had some advantages, such as their
smaller form factor and their far longer shelf life, but it often came at
the cost of a near-negligible reduction in effect and a small increase in
cost.

Besides that, he truly dove into the world of poisons. Neurotoxins
were, of course, something he researched, but he'd also learned to make
poison of different affinities, and he had two new types of poison he
would be moving forward with and actively using in combat when he
felt comfortable enough with their potency.

The first of which was one making full use of Jake's dark affinity.

[Dark Shade Poison (Common)] – A poison with dark
affinity properties, infecting and corroding the energies of the
target. Any target infected by Dark Shade Venom will suffer
reduced Perception and damage. This poison is incredibly
difficult to detect and heal, but deals nearly no damage and is
easily cleansed by certain types of magic.

This type of poison was incredibly valuable in prolonged battles
and against certain foes. It was an insidious poison that would dig deep
and slip into every bit of the target, and most importantly, it was
incredibly difficult to get rid of once infected. This did have some
hidden benefits that were a primary reason Jake was so excited to
learn it.

Sense of the Malefic Viper allowed Jake to feel his own poison better, especially when it was within a target. This poison would function as a scanner of sorts and allow Jake to easily keep track of a foe even if they didn't notice they were infected. He was already theorizing an even better version made solely as a tracking poison, but that was a good ways away.

The second was a type of poison Jake dearly needed.

[Draining Lightning Poison (Inferior)] – A poison with lightning-affinity properties, dealing significant damage and draining the mana of any entity it comes into contact with. This poison is incredibly fast-acting and will often expend all its potency within moments.

Jake still remembered the first time he had set foot upon the cloud island with Hawkie. How he had been utterly embarrassed by what was quite honestly a weak elemental and been forced to learn some basic magic to have a fighting chance. Back then, none of his poison had worked, as he'd only known Hemotoxin and Necrotic Poison and they only worked on biological beings. His blood was the best thing he'd had, and even that wasn't good.

Even before coming to the Order, that hadn't changed in the least, and even after Fangs upgraded and he got the better venom, it was still ultimately reliant on his blood. If Jake met an elemental or even something like the Altmar Census Golem, he was in for a bad time.

This type of poison changed that. The lightning affinity was the bane of mana and consumed it actively. Jake remembered briefly talking to his brother about it, and he did know that Caleb's dark lightning didn't drain just mana, but all resources the target possessed. Jake was not going for that, as while it drained everything, that meant the potency was spread out.

What Jake wanted was pure lightning intent on only draining mana. A poison that would be effective against mana barriers and elementals alike. Of course, if he faced a lightning elemental, he would still be in for a bad time, but he was confident in working up another poison to fight those.

Jake had also dabbled in many other areas to shore up weaknesses, and he was still in the early stages, but every day was rapid progress.

However, there was one area in which Jake had made no progress. There was a type of poison Jake had wanted to make for a good while, and he'd believed he would be able to do it by now, but no matter what he did, it just never worked out.

Arcane poison still eluded him. The problem was in the very essence of Jake's affinity. His affinity was one of balancing destruction and stability, controlling that equilibrium or willingly leaning into one part nearly entirely.

The key to his issues was in the word control. His affinity needed constant control, or it would be either pure stability or pure destruction. No in-between. It worked due to Jake influencing the energy with his will, but what happened when it became an object? Well, it either turned into what was basically crystalized mana, or it drained itself instantly by turning into pure destructive energy.

No matter what he tried, he had found no solution. He did find it a bit weird he could make arcane mana potions, but quickly discovered the reason... He didn't, really? It did contain his arcane energy in a stable form, but the moment he ingested it, it once more came under the control of his will and thus functioned as expected.

Well, this did mean he could maybe make an arcane poison that could only poison himself, but he didn't see any use for this. Okay, Jake had to confess he had tried to see if he could make a cheat to regen mana through Palate or something, but it had resulted in Jake still dealing more damage than he regenerated.

Jake hadn't had any lessons in formations or anything related to awakening the Pollendust Bee Queen yet, either, and he had yet to touch any combat classes. There were only so many hours in a day, and Jake was swarmed as it was. He did have a plan in mind, and as he finished lessons, he opened up his schedule. It was often a bad idea for him to continue in the same lane before fully digesting what he learned. Hence, he planned on beginning lessons in formations and one on refining Beastcores once he was done with the one on making pills and the two on flasks.

And that was about it for Jake's time in the Academy so far. He had been busy, but so had everyone. However, soon there would be a small break-day of sorts for many of them, as an event was coming up: The World Congress.

It was a bit odd, but every World Congress was at the same time. Jake had considered this weird as hell, because he clearly remembered it being triggered by a hundred claimed Pylons back then on Earth, and it wasn't like every planet of the 93rd Universe claimed a hundred at the same time.

Well, it turned out the one hundred claimed just meant you got the announcement seven days early. He discovered others had only gotten he notification a day before with not even a hundred claimed yet, with other planets getting the notification weeks before. This was primarily for planets with far more sapient life than Earth.

The reason why this mattered now was that Jake had gotten a nice little system announcement.

Announcement to all Nobles: The Second World Congress will commence in 24 hours. Any noble in possession of or ruling a Pylon can attend, as well as any participant of the First World Congress. Due to your presence in another universe, it is not possible to bring any representatives with you. If accepted, you will be teleported once the World Congress commences.

It was a bit longer and had some fluff, but in essence, Jake was golden and could attend without leaving the Order. He had already had a brief talk with Miranda, and she'd confirmed she could bring along people and would have Lillian and Neil come with her once again. Neil for space-mage business, Lillian for Miranda-helping business.

With the upcoming World Congress, many from the 93rd Universe were making preparations, but someone had also taken the chance now that many were free. Irin, the succubus, had sent Jake an invitation at the behest of this person. The organizer was someone pretty unknown to Jake, but he was pretty sure it was that human-elven pair, based on Irin's description.

That's right—it was his first official party after entering the Order.

Chapter 2

Party Prepping

Jake had done something he had never thought he would do. I
fact, he was pretty sure no one would have ever thought th
current situation playing out was possible.

He stood in a dressing room as an elf wearing a fancy rob
scrutinized his appearance and talked to an attendant about getting
new type of cloth Jake had never heard of. The attendant quickly ra
for it as the tailor spoke.

"No, no, you need something to truly bring forth that ferociou
look of yours," the elf said with much fervor. "One that can emphasiz
those wonderful eyes and mask properly!"

"I did like the first set quite a bit, and to truly show his personalit
and interests, how about embroidering the cloak with mushroor
symbols?" a fourth person said. It was a scalekin with dark green scale
and a cheeky smile that looked on as Jake was getting outfitted.

"Yeah, that is never going to happen," Jake said instantly.

"I must agree; it would not at all go with his style!" the tailor saic
fully backing up Jake. A smart man, it seemed.

The scalekin, who also happened to be the leader of the Order an
a Primordial, just scuffed in disappointment as he held up both hi
hands. "Fine, but at least keep the snake symbol on the back of th
robe."

"Naturally—anything else would be blasphemous, as he holds th
Blessing of the Malefic One!" the tailor said, looking at Villy wit
offense.

"Yeah, Villy, don't act all blasphemous," Jake agreed teasingly.

"I would never!" Villy practically yelled. "None is greater than the magnificent Malefic Viper! I cannot imagine anyone acting blasphemously, or, even worse, heretically towards such a being!"

This earned a satisfied nod from the tailor. "Well said! But who would even dare to be a heretic?" He shook his head, chuckling.

Villy and Jake exchanged a look and a smile just as the attendant returned, bringing a rectangular piece of cloth. It was to be made into some kind of shawl, but Jake quickly rejected it. The tailor was a bit disappointed, but he relented by agreeing to go with what he called a "warrior look" rather than a sophisticated hidden hunter with a slight desert theme.

As for how Jake had ended up in this situation... well, the answer naturally lay with a certain snake god. Villy had told Jake he needed to look "proper dapper" if he was going to his first party, and that he should go out and get a new party outfit.

Jake had agreed, as, quite frankly, he did feel a bit out of place, always wearing his full equipment no matter where he went. While it didn't exactly attract attention, since most people honestly dressed weirdly, he would prefer to wear something more casual at times. He was lucky he at least wore lighter armor, as he could already imagine if he was a warrior walking around in full plate armor going to lessons— something he had seen dozens of times within the Order.

The set he was getting currently consisted of a pair of nice dress pants and a weird shirt. He called it weird because, while it had buttons, it also didn't have buttons. Whenever he closed a button, the cloth just melded together, while it stayed visible and open if he opened one. It was odd.

Over that, he wore a weird mix of a trenchcoat and a normal cloak with a large motif of a snake on the back. He'd come to learn only those with a Blessing were allowed to even have this specific symbol on their clothes, and the tailor was visibly excited at being allowed to make such a piece of clothing.

His shoes were the biggest thing that needed changing, at least according to the tailor. Jake didn't know why old, scuffed leather boots weren't in fashion, but they clearly didn't sit well with the fancy elf. He looked like Jake was committing some cardinal sin just by wearing them, especially when Jake said he had originally planned to wear them to a social function.

The entire set wasn't actually considered equipment, even if it was high quality. If he wanted to have it be made into actual equipment

giving stats and such, he would have to pay extra, as the items would
need further energy infusion and crafting time.

By paying extra, Jake naturally meant having Villy pay extra. Not
that Jake was poor, but more on that later.

He exited the shop looking pretty good, in his own opinion, even if
he did have to discuss getting a hood added to go with the mask. Yes, he
would keep using the mask. The compromise they reached was the
hood becoming able to meld into the neck of the coat. Jake still had no
idea what kind of sorcery was going on, especially since it wasn't even
considered equipment.

"The life as a sugar daddy is hard," Villy said, sighing as they
entered the street.

"Poor you," Jake said with a smirk. "I have to ask, are you planning
on attending the party too?"

"Nah, that honestly sounds boring. While it may look like I enjoy
fucking with people for my own entertainment, I only bother to mess
with people I find entertaining to do so with. A bunch of random D-
grades does not fall into that category." Villy shook his head.

"Huh, not even that guy you gave a Divine Blessing? I assume you
did have some interest in him." Jake knew Divine Blessings were
considered high-tier, so Jake would find it weird if Villy had just given
it out willy-nilly.

"Not particularly, no. He is a good seed, but is ultimately just one
gamble of many. If he manages to reach A-grade or maybe S-grade, I
probably will begin paying attention, but he isn't worth my time as he
is right now. Chances are he will die before I bother."

"You say that talking to a mere D-grade," Jake chuckled as the two
of them reached a wall with a teleportation gateway in it. They were
scattered throughout the entire city and were honestly just so damn
convenient.

"No, I am talking to a friend," Villy answered. He did sigh and look
a bit more serious as they went through the gateway, appearing in
Jake's mansion. "I am currently just running with the assumption you
will become a god and thus immortal, and with that assumption in
mind, treating the current you as immortal already makes sense,
doesn't it? And who's got time to bother with mortals?"

"A bold assumption, based on what you yourself said in the past
about the chances anyone has of reaching godhood." Jake shook his
head. "Not that I necessarily disagree. Dying to old age certainly
doesn't seem like a possibility."

"Exactly, and gods can die fighting too, so it's the same thing, right? You are just a bit more fragile, that's all." The snake god laughed. "Speaking of being fragile, I have an appointment with Duskleaf, and he is gonna get mad if he finds out I split my attention between the two of you and didn't fully assist in his experiment..."

Jake looked at Villy with exaggerated surprise. "You actually have productive things to do? Also, how is Duskleaf fragile?"

"How is going shopping for new clothes not productive and imperative to running the Order of the Malefic Viper? No, let me rephrase that. How is making sure my Chosen presents himself the best he can not important? As for Duskleaf, well, his poor ego would suffer, so that counts as fragile."

"Yeah yeah, now get going," Jake said, waving his hand. "I have to leave soon, too, but need to make my gift first."

"Sure thing—see you around," Villy said as he disappeared.

Why did we bother using gates when he can just teleport us around casually? Jake questioned as the god left.

A few seconds passed before he saw a head peek out down the large entry hall. Meira had finally dared come out, having no doubt been waiting for the Viper to leave.

"Hey, Meira, did you get the ingredients I asked for?"

As she had seen the coast was clear, she came out, went up to Jake, and summoned three glass boxes with herbs in each. "Yes! They were all widely available."

Meira had summoned the items out of her spatial necklace, as, of course, Jake had gotten her one of those. Seeing her try and stuff items into a damn oversized satchel just got silly. She had protested a bit, to begin with, but Jake had insisted. Besides, he had found out he was loaded.

You see, not all Credits were created equal. Or, well, all Credits were... aside from the Credits of the 93rd Universe. Jake could not have Credits transferred to him, but he could spend them. At the same time, the Credits from his universe apparently were incredibly valuable for those walking a merchant path due to opportunities given by the integration. Especially merchant gods. This meant that the Order offered the transfer of Credits to contribution points of AC at a way higher rate for those of the 93rd Universe.

Jake's Credits had roughly a one-to-one hundred exchange rate compared with other types of Credits. Jake had found the rate a bit weird in that it was so straightforward, but Villy had told him the exchange rate was set by what was essentially a council of merchant gods or something to make sure competition didn't go crazy. Yep, it appeared the entire multiversal financial industry was effectively run by an oligopoly of powerful gods.

The ingredients he had asked Meira to help him procure were for a very specific kind of poison that one just had to bring when invited to a social function within the Order. Anything besides bringing a good bottle of tasty poison would just be straight-up rude.

Jake went into his laboratory after swiftly changing out of his new clothes and back into his usual getup, then did some alchemy for the next one and a half hours. He had been mentally planning this poison since the moment he got the invitation, and he was already looking forward to the effects it would have. Of course, he didn't try to make it lethal, but it surely wouldn't be a good time if their Palate was lacking.

Once he was done, he quickly got on his dapper outfit and prepared himself to go. He went to the living room, where Meira was already waiting, and flopped down on a couch. Jake sighed a bit as he looked up at the floor.

"Is anything the matter, Sir?" Meira asked.

"You know... I was the type to never want to go to the bar after a house party ended, but instead just head home and chill... and as I sit here, I remember why," Jake said.

Meira went over and sat across from him, waiting for him to continue talking.

"I don't like it. I don't like these damn social events that you can't avoid getting into. I always feel out of place, like my presence is somehow contrary to what the event is all about. There are so many norms, spoken and unspoken, making it feel like an arena with poorly defined playing rules."

Meira just sat there, listening patiently.

"Only after the system arrived did I begin to understand why I always felt so out of place... Well, one of the reasons anyway. You see, my Bloodline is quite peculiar... I am quite peculiar. I don't tend to deal well with rules in general, and reflecting back on everything before the system arrived, I understand that it wasn't just dealing with rules, but dealing with rules set by those I considered my lessers. Subconsciously, at least, I viewed them as such. Like I was surrounded by weaklings who told me how to behave. Of course, it wasn't like that, but that is another part of me. I tend to boil things down till they become simple to the point of oversimplification, even in too-complex situations."

"Sir, if I may?" Meira finally said.

"Yeah?" Jake asked, feeling a bit embarrassed at his ramblings.

"Norms and rules only apply to those they are applicable to," Meira said encouragingly. "I do not know how the world worked before, but at least everywhere I have been, the norms and rules are decided by those with the power to do so. If you are strong enough, no one complains. So Sir shouldn't worry, but just act like himself, and if any such norms are broken by doing so... well, then, Sir can just change the norm."

Jake listened to her words and smiled a bit. "You do make it sound simple. While I am sure people like the Viper can do that, I am not quite there yet unless I want to reveal my identity. I have no interest in leveraging that unless I have to."

"Sir is plenty strong on his own," Meira said assuredly.

He knew she didn't truly know how strong he was. She probably didn't even know his level, yet she seemed so convinced in her belief. It was a bit flattering, and Jake had to be honest—it did help cheer him up a little bit.

"Well, complaining won't change the fact that I am going." Jake ultimately just sighed. This was just like every time he'd had to go to a gathering before the system, where he always considered just canceling last minute. Usually, he at least had Miranda to lean on and shield him, but here he would go alone. Reika was the only one he truly knew there, and he knew she had enough to deal with herself.

Meira shifted in her seat, clearly still feeling his discomfort. "Sir, is there anything I can do to assist?"

That part of her had never changed. In fact, it had gotten worse. In any situation where any issue existed, Meira always felt like she had to be the one to fix it. If she could or not didn't matter, as she would at least ask if there was anything she could do.

Taking Meira along to the party was obviously not an option. She was not from the 93rd Universe, and he was sure she would be even more out of place than himself. Jake wasn't a saint, but he sure wouldn't put her through that.

"Just your encouragement is good enough." Jake smiled at her as he got up. He stretched his back as he finally stopped delaying more than necessary and headed for the hall with the gateway circle on it.

Meira followed him, trying to be encouraging. When he looked at her, he honestly found his own social discomfort silly. She'd had to deal with being thrown into an entirely different world where she suddenly served the Chosen of the Malefic Viper, with the god himself sometimes coming by. She'd had to deal with knowing Jake was both a heretic and a Chosen while also just learning how to deal with Jake as a person.

Jake could deal with a damn Academy party if she could do that.

Let's go, Jake thought as he activated the gateway. With a final "good luck!" from Meira, Jake went through.

He appeared in a massive hall already filled with people, and as Jake looked about, something quickly became clear: This wasn't just a party for the new members of the 93rd Universe, but something far more, as he felt over a hundred C-grade auras scattered throughout the utterly humongous hall.

As he stood there, someone approached him, and Jake turned to see Irin. She wore a low-cut red dress that actually managed to cover more than her usual outfit, if barely.

"I am glad you could make it, and may I say, you are looking even better than usual," she said flirtatiously.

Jake regarded Irin and smiled beneath his mask. "Thanks, you look great too. Now, this is quite a gathering, but can I ask you just one thing?"

He knew *exactly* what he needed.

"Where is the alcohol?"

CHAPTER 3

THE POWER OF BOOZE

Reika hadn't even considered if she should go to the social gathering or not. It was a natural choice, and she understood that this party was as much networking as it was an actual celebration of sorts. She had talked a lot with many of her fellow students and slowly ingratiated herself with some who had more talented and higher-rated comrades.

The reason why this meeting was held now and not earlier was due to many outside observers wanting to get an idea of the new students. They wanted to see how they performed in the first classes, what they showed talent in, and if some were worthy of picking up and cultivating.

That's right—this entire party was one big recruitment drive. Representatives of factions of the Order were present in droves, along with several auxiliary factions working with the Order. They were all talking with those from the 93rd Universe they found worth talking to.

There were also other new students present, but the representatives showed less interest in them. Reika knew that individuals from new universes had some special properties, such as their Tongue of the Myriad Races, as well as apparently a boost in Records. Or, more accurately, a boost in that they were all Forerunners, automatically giving a good dose of Records right off the bat. This was what had allowed even the untalented and unmotivated back on Earth to get level 50 or so with little effort. Needless to say, this boost of Records was far from enough to be helpful in the long run, but it could be built upon with momentum. They lacked the boost of Records one got from powerful parents, but the ones from the new universe were considered better in many ways.

Then, of course, there was the fact many factions wanted a foothold in the new universe. It was something that was usually not that big of a priority in the early days for many factions, but this time it was different. Because according to the rumors, the Chosen of the Malefic One belonged to the new universe.

Jake's existence made it essential for them to establish themselves in hopes of assisting him in the early days. They would gladly do this if it meant getting in the good graces of the Malefic One and his Chosen, even if it took sacrifices and much work.

Now, talking about Jake... Reika had said she hadn't even considered if she should go before the event, but currently, she was seriously doubting her own decision-making skills. Reika herself had wanted to make allies. She knew that Jake was talented in areas she was not, but she was confident in her social skills after lots of practice in her younger days.

So how the hell had Jake turned out to get along so damn well with bloody everyone?

"Ya know, I just don't get it; why does Palate make shit taste better?" Jake loudly complained as he swung a bottle around. "This one's got literal shit in it!"

"It's from mushroom extra—"

"Literal. Shit," Jake interrupted some poor early D-grade who tried to correct him.

"True!" a scaled dragonkin beside him said. "I grew up eating that garbage every damn day; no way I am now drinking it!"

The scalekin was perhaps the most popular figure present, with Jake hiding his identity. It was the one who carried the Divine Blessing —Draskil—and he was currently bonding with Jake over their shared hate for mushrooms, even though Draskil seemed to despise moss more than fungi.

They were surrounded by a whole crowd of primarily scalekin who had all gathered when Jake and Draskil, for some god-forsaken reason, decided that throwing acid to test the other's scales was a funny side activity. To make it worse, both began laughing when Draskil's entire arm fell off from getting corroded through.

Then, for good measure, Jake did the same shit and poured acid over his own arm. It ended up still hanging on by a few centimeters of flesh as Jake celebrated loudly.

And yes, they were both smashed. Reika had been afraid Jake would reveal something he shouldn't, but nothing like that had happened so far. Plenty of things Reika thought Jake should not do had happened, but it wasn't like she could tell him what to do…

Either way, it turned out that while Jake had not really made any connections with the more humanoid races, he sure was a hit among the more monstrous ones.

"Wait, you were scared of the sun?" Jake laughed as Draskil made his confession.

"All three of 'em!" the dragonkin responded with laughter. "You try and live underground and then suddenly get functional eyes and seek out the surface, only to see three massive balls of fire! Down below, fire usually meant lava, and lava meant you were about to get roasted!"

"Wait, I thought you were blind?" Molemen were blind, right? Jake was pretty sure of that.

"To light, not heat," Draskil corrected as he took a huge chug of a bottle. Putting it down, he looked straight at Jake. "Why the mask?"

"Loot from probably the strongest foe I've ever fought," Jake responded in a serious tone.

"Hm, a treant of sorts?"

"Something far more powerful than that." Jake smirked below his mask. Even while pretty smashed, his brain still worked well enough to not share stuff like that.

"Fine, keep your secrets." Draskil shrugged as he raised his bottle again. "Cheers to powerful foes and the bounty from their kills!"

"Cheers!" Jake and dozens of scalekin all around them said as they drank.

Honestly, Draskil was a pretty cool dude. He could also hold his alcohol quite well, and Jake felt happy he had finally found a match.

Draskil had originally struck Jake as the silent type, but he had quickly come to learn it wasn't quite like that. Draskil and Jake were very similar in that they both didn't really like large social settings. Jake due to how he was, and Draskil due to the way he had lived his life so far as a solitary survivor. Molemen were a nomadic race that lived underground and had to always travel for food. They had been far more intelligent than any animal on Earth besides humans, but were still not at the level of men. Perhaps at the level of ten to eleven-year-olds.

The now-dragonkin had been a bit special, in that he had been smarter than his brethren. This meant he had been shunned and forced to survive on his own for his entire life. He'd had to scour for food himself, and had eventually begun looting caravans of his brethren to survive. His experience had allowed him to prevail right off the bat during the tutorial and get to where he was today.

Jake was a bit surprised at how loose Draskil's tongue was after getting a few drinks in, but he soon realized he had just finally loosened up. He wasn't the type to care about secrets, even if he was clearly a prideful man. Draskil had only spoken to a handful so far, and with Jake the most, as the dragonkin had more or less confessed that he only viewed Jake as a proper equal because, to quote, "I feel it in my bones you are strong."

On the note of alcohol, Palate worked weird with it. It eliminated some parts of it while allowing other parts to function. This meant Jake was drunk; he knew that. But he also knew he was drunk, and his thought process and mind were only semi-affected. That is why he could be both clear-headed and feel the joy of alcohol at the same time, almost like he could switch back and forth at will. He was sure he could reach a level of intoxication where that was no longer the case—a few passed-out scalekin sitting slumped in chairs proved this—but so far, Jake was far off that.

What did consistently work was Jake feeling way calmer and soothed overall. Also, he didn't know why, but he really jelled with these scalekin as they all drank and celebrated. Jake knew they were there for Draskil to begin with, but eventually, Jake became included.

He did also do some politics after he found out it was a political party thing. He got a bunch of contact numbers, including those of several brewers who had helped supply alcohol to the party. Yes, that counted as valuable networking too.

Anyway, around four hours had passed since Jake arrived, and finally it seemed like everyone had come. People had been delayed due to them having lessons or other engagements to handle first. With that, it seemed like the host would finally make their appearance.

"A belated welcome to everyone!" a voice suddenly rang out, getting the attention of everyone. In the middle of the hall, on a podium of newly raised stone, stood the elf-and-human pair Jake had seen on the first day he went to the Academy.

[Human – lvl 161]

[Elf – lvl 167]

The human had gained two levels, and the elf one. The elf was a woman who looked a bit like Meira but with long red hair, while the human had a strong build and generally what Jake guessed would be described as "heroic" features. They looked like a couple out of some fantasy game or movie, and it turned out they were.

"At the request of many of the wonderful sponsors of this gathering and influential factions within the Order, we are holding this get-together to not only get to bond with one another, but to make new friends among those already established in this universe," the human began. "Allow me to first introduce myself. I am King Aiborn of the Twinsoul Kingdom, and beside me is my wife, Queen Eilenria. As many likely can guess, we come from a planet where elves and humans have lived in coexistence for centuries already, and we are more than happy to see the Order also be like that."

Jake was already beginning to feel bored as he looked at Draskil, who also just grinned and shook his head. Who cared if they were kings and queens or whatever? He was pretty damn sure they didn't have the nobility titles from the system.

"With the advent of change—both for us as individuals, as well as for our universe—I hope that today can be the foundation of a strong working relationship for the future. For not only our own factions back home, but the Order and those we ally with to get footholds within the new frontier that is our world!"

He said it all with much fervor, and Jake did see that some were touched. He also clearly felt the human had some hefty social skills bordering on mental manipulation. Not that anyone minded—not even Jake. There seemed to be a general agreement that if you were weak enough to get influenced, good riddance.

Next up to speak was the elf-queen lady, who also clearly possessed some potent leadership skills. Even better than the human's.

"The Twinsoul Kingdom has already made partnerships, and we are certain there is power in numbers. Not a single force in this room will stand a chance in the 93rd Universe against powerful factions like the Holy Church, Altmar Empire, Valhal, or any other large faction I am certain have already begun planting their roots. The ectognamorphs have already begun their conquests, the Starborne empires have made preparations, and the Endless Steppe armies have banded together... Even the demon empires and automatons stand ready to grasp this new unconquered territory. Not a single faction is uninterested in claiming their own piece of the pie.

"That is why it is imperative that we each at least secure our own planets. To do that, you will need allies, and as our universe opens up gradually, we will become able to rely on these allies more and more. So, please, I plead to all of you: For the sake of the Order and our own futures in the 93rd Universe, let today, before the Second World Congress, be the day we all stand side by side!"

Jake just sat back and listened to the impassioned speech. While he was certain a few were moved, he was most certainly not. Her flowery words were nice enough, but it was clear they wanted to make themselves and their own little kingdom a center point of this new alliance of sorts.

He also saw a small group of Risen standing by themselves, all sneering a bit. Among them were two C-grades and all of the students who had arrived from the 93rd Universe. They were naturally looking down at this entire display, and Jake had also noted the lack of mention of the entire Risen faction.

As Jake had already come to learn with the whole Emberflight debacle, the Order didn't truly function as a traditional faction for the vast majority of members. More an overall alliance of different factions who all worked with or for the Order or were subservient to it. This did mean one could be part of the Order and the Altmar Empire or many other factions. One didn't even need to view the Viper as the greatest of all the gods—just one of the greatest.

This philosophy did have some factions it didn't jell with. The Court of Shadows was one, as were many others in the multiverse, and the Holy Church was an exclusive faction. High-ranking members of pretty much any faction would also belong exclusively to that one faction.

Jake was certain the Order worked as it did due to Villy's entire philosophy on freedom. How it was the most important thing to have agency and control your own path. So, of course he didn't bother to have a faction that locked people in—at least, not as a requirement.

The Order did have core members. These were the members of the different Halls, of which there was only one currently. This is where one found the true believers of the Malefic Viper and the individuals who had pledged their lives to the Order. They were the leading faction within the Order and had the backing of Villy himself, though, in reality, it had been Snappy fulfilling that role for the longest time.

Draskil, who sat with Jake, also didn't bother with the human and elf much besides the basic level courtesy of not interrupting. From their earlier conversation, Draskil was already dedicated to the Order and had no interest in joining any other faction, no matter what.

By now, most knew this, but there was still the occasional hopeful. The queen-and-king pair kept talking a bit more about the power of unity and the importance of conquering through the World Congress before spreading out and making allies. They first greeted and talked with those who went up to them, but soon enough, they set their sights on where Jake and Draskil were sitting and drinking together.

For the third time in a short while, the dragonkin and human exchanged a glance, as they knew what was coming. The elf-and-human pair was even joined by a few representatives from different factions, most of them lower-rung ones who no doubt wanted some of that Divine Blessing clout.

Oh, boy, here we go again, Jake thought as he and Draskil shared another drink before more political bullshit arrived.

Chapter 4

Outed

Ah, politics. Jake hated doing it with a passion, which was why he always outsourced it whenever possible. He hadn't liked it before the system either. He wasn't talking about the large political things like elections and such, but the small political maneuvering everyone did in their daily lives.

One example was making friends with certain other employees for their positions and then leveraging that friendship whenever needed. Jake knew it was almost expected that managers made friends with certain people in the HR department so they had an ally to back them up on most issues.

People also did this with their bosses. In fact, the best example was how everyone was always way nicer to their boss than any other "equal" employee. How if the boss didn't like anyone, everyone else also ostracized that employee to stay in the good graces of their glorious leader. Anyone who chose to show sympathy would naturally fall into the same camp as the pariah and be shunned themselves.

Jake had always hated this. Ass-lickers and sycophants who he didn't doubt would throw their own mother under a bus for a promotion and a pat on the back from boss almighty. He knew their look, and as he saw the approaching crowd, he recognized it all too well.

Many plans were being formed in his mind on how to handle them. On the one hand, he knew offending them could lead to trouble down the road—not just for him, but also Miranda and others—but on the other hand, he really didn't wanna deal with them. Instead, he preferred to set a hard line in the sand.

Luckily for him, Draskil didn't have any of Jake's reservations.

"The fuck you two want?" he aggressively asked the collection of humans, elves, and a few beastkin coming over.

"I apologize, Lord Draskil. We did not mean to disturb you. We merely meant to ask if we could borrow Lord Hunter for a minute to discu—"

"No, fuck off, we're busy," Draskil sneered as he stared them down. Jake just kept his mouth shut, and when they looked at him, he shrugged powerlessly while inwardly wanting to give the dragonkin a high-five.

"Please, I promise to be brief," the human insisted again, but Draskil was having none of it.

"Are you blind? We are drinking, so if you want to talk, grab a drink and sit down or leave us be."

Well, okay, that wasn't exactly what Jake had planned, but he guessed it would be an okay compromise. Also, he needed an opportunity to give his gift, so maybe it would work out? His only problem was that he hadn't really seen anyone give anything either—besides the boot-lickers—so he wasn't really sure if he even wanted to.

The human-and-elf pair exchanged a glance before eventually moving to sit down. However, behind them, an early C-grade elf suddenly stopped them by raising his hand.

"Young man, showing courtesy is a virtue," the elf said—not to Jake, but Draskil. "There is no need for such an attitude, and you would do well to correct it."

The dragonkin stood up and stared at the C-grade dead in the eye. "And you would do well to know when you are out of your league."

An aura descended as Draskil let his presence loose, and Jake had to raise an eyebrow and keep himself calm. He clenched his fists a bit as his instincts made it clear... Draskil had gotten stronger. Jake had seen him as only slightly stronger when they entered the Order, but he was now far more powerful... and he even had a feeling that initial evaluations had been slightly off.

"Oh, yeah... I guess I never told you," Villy's voice suddenly intruded. *"The dragonkin killed his version of Snappy, and he isn't really an alchemist at all. He is just a being of pure slaughter."*

Jake didn't react outwardly, but inwardly he processed the information. Draskil beating his version of Snappy meant he'd killed one at level 190, thirty levels above the one Jake had fought. Even if Jake believed he would have a chance now against the 160 one, he knew he would be utterly outclassed against one at level 190.

And Jake was also very sure that a level 190 Snappy would have been able to utterly destroy most early C-grades... especially if they were someone clearly not combat-focused, like the C-grade attendant that had come with the human and elf.

Killing intent mixed with an odd feeling of emptiness rolled across the hall from Draskil as he towered over the elf who had seemed so confident before. However, the moment Draskil released his power, the elf clearly realized he had fucked up.

"Please do not misunderstand; I merely meant tha—"

A claw flew out and grasped the C-grade by the face before he could react. The moment he did so, Jake felt another presence appear —one that had been observing them from the start—and a scaled figure teleported into his sphere.

Draskil looked over at the newcomer and let go of the stupid attendant, who fell to the floor with blood running down his face from the claws digging in. The scaled figure saw this, nodded, and was gone as quickly as he'd appeared.

It seemed that even Draskil would back down when a random A-grade popped in.

However, even then, Draskil had established himself as the dominant party. Jake got up and put a hand on Draskil's shoulder. "Chill and sit down. Ignore the morons of the world."

Draskil turned his head and looked at Jake before just smirking and sitting back down casually like nothing had ever happened.

Jake followed suit, but not before telling the elf-and-human pair, "I have no interest in aligning myself with any faction. Oh, and trust me, the competition you would have to beat if I was interested isn't in your league. As for your whole idea of an alliance, I shall let time decide if that ever becomes a necessity. However, as things are back on my home-world, things are a bit too complicated for the likes of you two to get involved."

The two of them looked at him briefly before nodding in understanding and turning to leave again. The C-grade representative also left in embarrassment as Jake sat his ass back down and turned to Draskil.

"See, that is how rejection is gracefully done," Jake scolded the brute dragonkin.

"Words when actions are more effective." Draskil just shook his head.

Jake smirked as he held out his hand towards a bottle of beer on the table and spoke, **"Come."**

The bottle moved on its own, flying into Jake's hand. Jake was still far too weak to use Words of Power for anything useful in combat, but it was still a fun technique. "Behold, the power of words."

"Words of Power," Draskil corrected.

"And Words of Power is the power of words," Jake countered.

The two of them chuckled a bit as they each enjoyed their drinks. Jake finally decided to ask something he now wondered about after seeing the display against the C-grade.

"You killed any C-grades yet?"

Draskil looked at Jake and raised an eyebrow. "Plenty."

"At what level were you when you killed your first?"

Somewhat suspicious, Drasil said, "173 or 174. Why?"

Jake laughed it off. "Just curious. Relax, I am not looking for a dick-measuring contest."

"Why would the size of one's genitalia matter when killing?" Draskil asked with genuine confusion.

Jake just shook his head in response. "Not going to explain that one to you."

Mainly because he couldn't. Who had even come up with such a stupid saying and concept anyway?

Poor Draskil looked confused for a few moments before shrugging it off and continuing to drink. The two of them relaxed a bit more and talked about good fights they'd had in the past, and Jake came to learn that he and Draskil were both sole survivors of their tutorials, though for different reasons.

In Jake's, everyone had been officially "killed," and it'd been a shit-show, while Draskil had killed everyone else in his tutorial. One thing was for sure: Draskil was not a kindhearted dragonkin, and his path so far had been one where he killed most others who got in his way. He did own a Pylon and had a position similar to Jake's, but he'd apparently had to go through three City Lords before he got one who didn't get ambitious or try to backstab him. Jake had really gotten lucky with Miranda, now that he thought about it.

As they talked, more people kept arriving at the gathering, and political maneuvering was ongoing all around. They just had their own corner where they chilled with other scalekin who sometimes joined in, and Jake learned a lot about the different kinds of scalekins, a race far more diverse than humans.

This kept on until Jake felt a familiar presence approach. Two of them, in fact. One was Irin, but she looked a bit nervous as she walked beside another figure Jake had met with not that long ago. The dragonkin Helen had also decided to pay a visit.

Jake glanced at Draskil to see if he would toss them away again, but he just stared at their approach. He seemed almost transfixed, still staring when they made it over and greeted them.

"Lord Hunter, Lord Draskil, I have brought Lady Helenstromoz Emberflight, who decided to grace this lowly event with her presence," Irin said.

Jake at first thought it was done sarcastically, but she was one hundred percent sincere. The dragon lady had some social standing; that was for sure.

Jake just greeted her with a nod. "We meet again."

"Indeed we do, Patriarch Hunter," she said with a meaningful smile.

Jake's smile instantly faded, as she had spoken loud enough for Draskil and Irin as well as several scalekin to hear. Irin looked at Jake with surprise, and Draskil looked bewildered for a moment before it also clicked in his head.

Calling out his Bloodline like that was honestly a bit of a dick move.

He looked at her and shook his head. "A bit petty, isn't it? Just because I rejected you once, you come to cause trouble like a little girl who didn't get what she wanted the first time around?"

It was entirely possible she wanted to keep up a façade of ignorance, grace, and civility, but Jake didn't. He knew his Bloodline would be shared eventually, but to openly out him like this just wasn't okay and wasn't going to fly.

Helen frowned at Jake's word but chose to act ignorant as predicted. "I am uncertain what you mean? If I remember correctly, our last meeting ended with you taking time to think about the offer."

"You got a Bloodline?" Draskil butted in before Jake could answer Helen.

"Yep," Jake quickly answered, then turned back to Helen. "And that thinking period is now over. I honestly liked the straightforward approach the first time around, but this manipulative bullshit isn't acceptable."

Helen looked surprised at Jake's outright refusal and attitude. She stared at him in disbelief for a moment, then said, "Very well. I can see I engaged you at a bad time, and you seem to have had a bit too much to drink. Let us have this discussion in a more private setting the next time? We could even go to the local Emberflight Sanctum to—"

"I think I made my answer clear?"

"I shall choose to allow you to keep considering the offer," Helen said as she promptly turned and teleported away, turning into flames and disappearing through a gate.

Did she just run away to get the last word? Now that is petty, Jake scoffed internally as he shook his head and took another drink of his beer.

Irin and Draskil both stared at him, then looked towards the direction Helen had gone.

"Uhm, Lord Hunter..." Irin began. "Do you know who the young mistress is?"

Jake shrugged. "A little girl with personality issues because Daddy gave her everything she wanted growing up?"

Draskil chuckled, but Irin looked grave. "She is the young mistress of the Emberflight Clan, born with a unique and very powerful Bloodline. She is already being nurtured by several S-grades, with even some gods paying attention... Offending her and making an enemy of a Dragonflight isn't wise. I would try to mend the relationship if possible."

"While I appreciate the advice and understand it comes from a place of concern, it is unnecessary," Jake answered.

"Did that lass want to have your hatchlings?" Draskil suddenly asked out of the blue.

Jake and Irin were both taken aback, as Draskil looked like the question was completely innocent. Jake wasn't sure what to say, but he chose to just be honest. "There indeed were talks of 'procuring' my Bloodline, and that she would be involved isn't out of the question. But I have no interest at all—not with her or anyone."

"A shame; she looks very breedable." Draskil shrugged. "But seeing as you aren't going for her, can I? She looks like she would give powerful hatchlings. Don't worry—wouldn't go for it if you had already claimed her as your mate."

Jake looked at Draskil for a moment, deciding then and there to never talk relationships with the guy. "No comments."

"Great." He smiled, but it quickly turned to a frown. "Not that I know how to contact her."

He then looked towards Irin, who shook her head. "I do not have any way of contacting her. I only met her just now as she arrived at the venue."

Before Draskil even looked over, Jake answered, "This is your issue to deal with, buddy."

While Jake didn't care about Helen, he wasn't going to just give out the contact information of others without consent, no matter how little he liked them. Besides, he now knew he had a whole other problem to deal with as Irin finally returned her attention to him.

"So... a Bloodline?"

"It is what it is." Jake shrugged.

"A beneficial one, too, based on the actions of the Emberflight."

Jake knew he didn't need to answer, as the actions of Helen had all but confirmed it. He also knew denying he had a Bloodline would be a waste of time, as someone present was bound to report it to some superiors or backers or something who could send someone to check. Instead, he decided to just own up to it and go with the old illusion of it being a presence-based one.

Through his Sphere of Perception, he had already seen several individuals take out their tokens after Helen had arrived and outed him. Many reports had already been sent out, and Jake knew that before long, the existence of his Bloodline and the fact that the Emberflight deemed it valuable would be spread far and wide.

I need some more beer...

CHAPTER 5

POLITICAL MANEUVERING & PREPERATIONS

Jake couldn't help but reflect on what exactly Helen and the Emberflight Clan had tried to accomplish by outing him. It was clearly a tactic of theirs, and Jake seriously doubted it was something the young mistress had suddenly decided on doing herself. It was deliberate and with a goal.

Irin decided to stick around Jake and Draskil, so he asked her some roundabout questions to get an idea, and he came to a rather quick understanding. In fact, Irin straight-up told him that he would probably be smart to make sure he had some kind of backing after today. Not to avoid getting kidnapped or some other stuff, but for anyone to want to back him.

When Jake said he already had a backer, Irin nodded in understanding and said, "Being pieces in the games of the powerhouses is never fun."

Jake had taken a bit to understand, but it soon clicked... The Emberflight hadn't done what they did today to get a response out of Jake; they wanted one out of his backer.

They were running with the assumption Jake had a powerful backer behind him, and that backer had to have influence over Jake, right? Helen showing up to a public meeting with several representatives from factions also clearly communicated the Emberflight Clan was interested in Jake, which would lead to two potential outcomes.

If a stronger faction became aware of Jake through the actions of the Emberflight, it would only reflect well on them. They would lose nothing besides recruiting Jake, something they maybe didn't view as that high of a priority or as having that high of a probability. Or maybe they just didn't think a more powerful faction would bother.

The weaker factions would back off to not offend the Dragonflight or potentially harm a future working relationship. Jake had gathered that the Emberflight truly was considered a top-tier faction of the multiverse. They were not a peak-tier such as the Holy Church, Court of Shadows, or Altmar Empire, but were still not easily offended by any but the biggest of players.

They had just made one miscalculation... The Order of the Malefic Viper was considered a peak faction. The power of a faction was not decided by their size or area of influence, but by their power. More accurately, the power of the god at its helm.

Now, if he thought about it, they had clearly never considered it possible the Malefic Viper was his backer. That made sense, as that was so astronomically unlikely. What they'd probably believed was that Jake had a powerful S-grade master who was a member of the Order. Either a true member part of a Hall or a normal member, but either way, this backer or master would no doubt view Jake as a way to get in the good graces of another faction. Why else would an S-grade bother with a weak D-grade whose biggest redeeming feature was his Bloodline?

The backer would be made to choose, and the Emberflight was confident. Of course, not choosing would be an issue too. It would result in Jake being hounded until he made his position clear, and the backer would also find himself revealed soon enough and under pressure. Perhaps not directly, but indirectly. Moreover, this backer would get nothing out of Jake if he didn't become part of a larger faction.

All of this boiled down to the basic assumption that Jake was nothing more than a chess piece in the game of powerful experts. A chess piece holding a valuable commodity to be traded away sooner or later, with the backer being the primary decider of how this would be done. This was naturally completely wrong, but if that was what they believed, the Emberflight Clan's actions made a bit more sense. They'd never considered if offending Jake mattered or not, and even if they offended his backer, it would just be a measly S-grade.

Irin's initial interpretation of the situation seemed to be identical to Jake's, and she even admitted something as they spoke. "I will be honest: My clan was interested in potentially recruiting you as an auxiliary member even before the Bloodline. Just due to the fact you had a Blessing, we believed it worth it. Now, with a Bloodline and a Dragonflight showing interest, I firmly believe they will back off. Our Matriarch is only A-grade, so offending the Emberflight Clan simply isn't something we can afford."

Draskil had just shrugged, as his input boiled down to not caring about factions at all besides the Order of the Malefic Viper. The guy really looked up to Villy and was a true believer.

So... to summarize, the Emberflight Clan believed that what they had done today would put pressure on Jake and his backer to decide on a faction to join. As the backer would pick the faction that could offer the most, the Emberflight naturally assumed they were a popular choice.

Too bad for them. They were as wrong as could be, and Jake decided to stay away from any factions for now. Did he have the choice of joining the Order of the Malefic Viper for real in one of the Halls? Sure, but he also had the choice of just going, "Oh, by the way, Chosen of the Viper right here" to get everyone off his back. If he said that, Jake would be viewed as not only a true member of the Order, but the most important member besides a few people.

"Villy, any thoughts?" Jake asked after reaching his own conclusion.

"On what?" the god answered promptly.

"You know... the Emberflight putting pressure on me, my Bloodline being public knowledge within a few days, and the issues that are to follow?" he asked, knowing full well the Viper knew all this.

"Oh. That. Seems like a you-problem, last time I checked."

"So you would be fine with me revealing my identity as your Chosen and using that to make everyone back off and be treated like the second coming of you?"

"Jake, Jake, Jake. I was always fine with that. I wanted to help you hide your identity for your own sake, not mine. I picked you as my Chosen, and of course, I stand by that choice. One day it will be revealed no matter what, and when you choose to do so is up to you and you alone. You can invoke my name whenever you feel like it, as long as you want to deal with what it will bring. I will support you far more openly if you choose this—not that I think it will be needed or even wanted."

Jake was silent for a bit. *"So, just for advice, then... Any way to get around this entire Bloodline thing without revealing myself as your Chosen and not joining a faction outright?"*

"Plenty of ways. All for you to discover yourself." The god's presence slowly faded away.

This left Jake sitting with his own thoughts as he pondered a solution. Because damn, did he need one. He felt hundreds of gazes upon him at nearly all times from attendants all around, as well as other students who looked like they *really* wanted to go up and talk to him.

Right now, he had Draskil as a shield, as the dragonkin had shown himself to be less than approachable. He tolerated the presence of the scalekin groupies and Irin, but Jake knew that protection would only last for this party, so for now, he just leaned back and enjoyed his drink.

Irin still seemed genuinely concerned and continued to talk to Jake until he shot the topic down and told her to relax. He didn't know why she cared, but he did appreciate her advice, some of which even went against the interests of her clan.

With the matter shelved, the rest of the party went by as Jake just sat back and drank with his new dragonkin buddy and Irin, who decided to stick around throughout the entire day. Politics went on all around them, but they managed to make their small oasis of relaxation where the words "World Congress" weren't mentioned at least every second sentence.

Not that Jake had forgotten. In only a few hours, it would be World Congress time.

Jacob sat at the high seat of the massively expanded conference room. Golden projections of men and women lined the seats all around the room, all of them nobles of different kinds, with many of them being City Lords.

By now, the Holy Church controlled close to a hundred Pylons of Civilization. They had more people within their territories than any other faction on the planet, and their strength had only consolidated and grown. Yet they knew they still faced many challenges on Earth.

The Great Famine, as the crisis was dubbed, had been a major setback. No one knew what had been the cause of the event, and even Jacob's divination skill always came up blank. This made him believe it had somehow been system-imposed.

Certain members of the Church who specialized in curses had come forward and said they'd felt a powerful pulse of curse energy that day. The Church had looked into it, but it didn't appear the Risen had done anything, as Casper was naturally the first suspect when it came to anything curse-related.

In the end, they quickly shut down all theories that this event had been manmade or even caused by any being on Earth. The power involved—if it truly had been caused by an individual—would be very concerning. That was why they had officially stated it was system-caused, the same as most other factions.

Because the alternative would only cause panic.

Jacob shook his head as all the seats were finally filled. This would be the last meeting before the World Congress and had all of the people present who would attend.

The Augur stood up and regarded them all with a bright smile.

"Welcome to the assembly where we will discuss the Holy Church's approach in the Second World Congress."

A Congress Jacob firmly believed they would gain more influence in than any other faction.

--

Miyamoto stood covered in sweat as he swung his blade again and again. The pressure upon him was unlike anything a human could normally survive, but he persisted as the nearly twenty mages all around him focused on the formation beneath his feet.

Soon enough, they ran out of mana, the pressure disappeared, and an attendant walked up to him with a towel.

"Thank you," he said as he wiped his face clean. The rest of the sweat turned into droplets that floated off his body and formed a small bubble of water that rapidly evaporated.

"Patriarch, are you ready to meet the ministers?" another attendant came and asked. Several more also entered to help the mages out of the courtyard to recover.

"Lead the way." Miyamoto smiled as he got handed a robe to cover his bare upper body. As he walked, a certain vampire also appeared and walked beside him. "It will be interesting to see what this World Congress is all about."

The former Monarch of Blood, Iskar, was a constant companion for Miyamoto and seemed especially interested in the political side of things. Far more so than the Sword Saint had ever thought. His vast knowledge had helped in places nobody in the Noboru clan had ever expected, and by now, Iskar was beginning to hold some influence.

He also helped by training those who had chosen to become vampires. It wasn't many so far, but a few hundred who felt stuck in their paths or simply hadn't found a place they felt they belonged had chosen to embrace vampirism. The clan had a stringent screening process, and far from everyone was allowed to choose this path.

"The World Congress always comes as an impetus of change for our small planet, so I too hold interest in what it will bring," Miyamoto said to the vampire.

The two entered a large meeting hall with all those present from the Miyamoto Clan who would attend. They had shown up either in person or communicated from afar, some only using voice due to the distance.

The Noboru Clan was ready for whatever was to come, and with their expansion, the Sword Saint believed they should now be the second-largest faction after the Holy Church.

Valhal, the Court of Shadows, the Risen, Haven, and a plethora of other factions made their preparations for the upcoming World Congress. This time, they knew what to expect and were far more ready than the last time. Plans and strategies were made, and new forces would participate that had never been there before. Alliances had been struck between factions all across the planet.

Arthur, Jacob's father and the leader of a large alliance, was one such force, its true power unknown to the other factions. In pure numbers, perhaps their alliance could even match the Holy Church, while they had many experts who had before never worked with others and chosen to stay independent.

Eron, whose plans were similarly unknown, also prepared, as even he understood the importance of the World Congress.

Every single force on Earth, small or large, prepared. Nearly everyone who had gotten the invitation planned to attend, and they all were ready...

Not knowing that there was one more faction. One that no one but a single person on Earth was even aware of. And it was questionable if even he had predicted what was to happen.

The mountain range spanned into the horizon as winged beasts patrolled the area. To one side were infinite mountains, the other the endless ocean. Monsters of legends and myths converged on a certain mountaintop, and even the oceanic creatures made their appearance to show respect.

Powerful beast lords—creatures no human on Earth would feel confident challenging—all gathered around that mountain. Atop it stood a structure of what looked like golden wood. A testament to the monster that lived there, and one whom they all feared.

On Earth, beasts had fought for territory, and this area was one of the most sought-after. It led into the human lands while still connecting to the ocean, and was part of the area C-grades were allowed to roam freely at the current time.

A land of death for most humans... yet on the mountain, several buildings had been raised. A small city was under construction in the valley below, with no beasts harassing the humans working away. Occasionally, a human would look towards the peak above, awed by the golden temple and the Lord who lived up there... No, the King.

System notifications were not a new thing. Quests were not new, but this was indeed a first. With an ivory claw, the Unique Lifeform waved his hand to open the door, and he stared out over the land that was his.

Behind him stood two humans who were to assist in this "World Congress" that was to come.

The Fallen King had to admit, it did indeed seem interesting.

Chapter 6

Presence of a King

J ake returned to his mansion half an hour before the World Congress to do some last-second preparations. He'd already had a talk with Miranda using her communication skill and agreed on a few minor things.

Contrary to the first time, where Jake had barely made it, he didn't rush this time. He took a shower after the party and sobered up, smiling at remembering it. Draskil and he had been drinking until Jake had to leave, at which point Draskil also couldn't be arsed to stay any longer.

Meira was at a lesson still, so Jake just sat in the living room in meditation until the system notification appeared. He accepted it instantly. His vision went black, and he was teleported to who-knows-where—the location of the World Congress.

Jake opened his eyes and found himself in a familiar room. Somewhat familiar, at least, as it had now expanded significantly. People teleported in all around him, and in only a few seconds, it was clear that far more than the hundred or so cities would be present this time around.

Miranda popped in right next to Jake, with Lillian and Neil following soon after.

"Hey, guys and gals," Jake greeted them with a smile. Not that they could see it; Jake would be mask-on for this Congress, just like the last one.

"New outfit?" Miranda asked, looking him over.

Jake was still wearing the party clothes, as they seemed more fitting for this kind of event than his combat getup. "Yep. What do you think?"

"Looks good, even if the snake motif is a bit on the nose and really advertising you are related to the Order of the Malefic Viper. Not that doing so is a bad thing." She smiled. "And good to see you again. I gather it goes well at the Order?"

"Eh, it's a bit so-so. Lots of annoying political stuff, same as everywhere, but I made some new friends and am learning a lot. You should come by at some point."

"I honestly have no need to. I am being taught using my Dreams of the Verdant Lagoon skill every chance I get, which I would argue is more effective in many ways due to the time dilation. Even if I can't do anything there besides talk, at my current level of knowledge, that is what I need most. I don't doubt I will go in the future, but the time isn't right yet."

Jake nodded in understanding, and before he could check in with Lillian and Neil, the system notification appeared.

Welcome to the Second World Congress of Earth.

The World Congress is an opportunity for the newly integrated denizens of Earth to establish political connections and an arena for discussion, voting, and international politics that can impact the planet as a whole. Note that no fighting will be allowed during the World Congress. Each booth has an aura that will offer privacy to each city.

During the Second World Congress, two votes will be held with one four-hour intermission between each to discuss the proposal, after which a vote will be held. The total length of the World Congress will be six hours.

The first vote will be held in one hour and pertain to the election of a World Leader. The World Leader will automatically have their noble rank advance one stage (up to the limit of King). Becoming a World Leader requires more than 60% of the total votes.

For a moment, Jake thought it was identical to the message they'd gotten during the First World Congress, but he quickly noted three small differences. The first was the number of total votes only being two, which also decreased the duration of the event, and the disclaimer of sorts about those with the nobility rank of King not getting it upgraded.

Jake wondered why this was relevant for a moment as he looked across the room. He saw Jacob, Caleb, Casper, Priscilla, the Sword Saint, Carmen, Eron, and everyone else he knew appear on their respective platforms. He even saw Arthur appear on a lower-ranked platform.

Overall, Jake counted perhaps three thousand total booths, which meant three thousand claimed Pylons. Their planet had truly expanded in this time, and it was entirely possible many Pylons had been claimed with the owners not participating. However, one thing was off. Jake was not the only one to notice it, either, as Jacob also looked confused when he saw the layout of the room.

The elevation of the platforms was based on the occupant's nobility rank. Jake himself stood higher than everyone else, even if he did see some had managed to upgrade their nobility ranks above that of Lord in the lower rungs.

However… there was one platform that was above all others. Larger than all others. All attention was gathered on it as, suddenly, an aura appeared on top of it. A golden wave swept through the entire hall, and Jake felt himself subtly being suppressed in power.

A figure rose, and Jake felt his mask faintly resonate with the being that had appeared. Jake was surprised and instantly used Identify on the willow figure of the former King of the Forest, who had somehow shown up in the World Congress.

[Fallen King – lvl 191]

Jake's eyes opened wide, and he instantly felt the mood of the room shift. If during the First World Congress it had been Jake who suppressed all others and set the mood, then it was clear the King would do that this time.

He instantly also got another thought as he checked the voting rules of the World Congress.

Voting rules of the World Congress:

The number of available votes is based on the nobility rank of the attending members. The number of votes per nobility rank is as follows:

King: 1000
Prince: 250
Duke: 100
Marquiss: 25
Earl: 10
Viscount: 5
Baron: 3
Lord: 1

The noble in question may distribute their votes as they choose if there are multiple options. The noble may abstain from voting. Votes are final and cannot be appealed. Any agreements will come into effect until the next World Congress or if all included parties choose to revoke it. All tie-breakers will be decided by the highest-ranking noble present at the World Congress.

Well, fuck, Jake thought as he saw the massive number of votes the King had available. It was honestly insane, and Jake felt like something was entirely wrong and unbalanced. Jake had talked to the King and knew he had the nobility title, but this wasn't what he had expected.

The entire hall was silent, just staring up at the King. He guessed many were faster than him at checking the voting rules and seeing that the situation truly wasn't what anyone had expected. The carefully laid plans of all factions, including the ones he and Miranda had made, were instantly made null due to the appearance of one Unique Lifeform.

"Introductions are in order," the King's voice echoed out in Jake's—and no doubt everyone else's—mind. *"I am known as the Fallen King: A Unique Lifeform born in another world, brought here by certain circumstances. I believe this saying would be considered cliche, but I come in peace."*

Jake was a bit surprised at the King not instantly proclaiming himself the superior being and telling them all to bow in reverence, but instead acting... reasonable? What the hell was he planning?

"Fallen King..." Jacob muttered aloud. "You being here should not be possible."

"Augur, what else but the impossible is expected of a being such as I?" the King answered, making Jake feel more at ease. The King still had an ego the size of the sun. *"I am a born King, my nobility more rightful than anyone else present."*

Jacob frowned at the response. Everyone else was silent before the Sword Saint stepped forward and spoke, "Fallen King, I can't help but notice you do not come alone?"

That was when Jake actually paid attention to the two people the King had brought along: A man and a woman, both clearly human. The King actually stood a step back as the two introduced themselves.

"I am the local mayor of a yet-to-be-named city under the control of the Fallen King, and this is the representative of our newly established crafting guild," the woman said. "We were all wanderers in an especially dangerous part of the planet, quite a bit away from any larger settlement, but were eventually recruited by the King to inhabit his lands. Currently, we are rapidly constructing our territory, but we already have tens of thousands who have sought refuge under our banner."

"A bit convenient, isn't it?" Carmen said. "A monster appears out of nothing and is suddenly all friendly to humans without anyone knowing before now. Excuse me if I find it a little suspicious."

The King turned to her. *"Do not think me foolish enough to believe I am almighty. I have learned that humans are not a race to ever underestimate, and I do not plan to do so. In fact, I want humanity to prosper on this planet more than ever before, and I believe I can make that possible."*

"How so?" the Sword Saint asked.

"Through power and my existence as neither beast nor human. I have observed the antagonistic relationship and believe this conflict will only escalate. Beasts desire the resources of humans, while humans desire the resources provided by slaying beasts. It is an unavoidable circle of slaughter, but one I believe can be managed. Sapient beasts are plentiful, and many of them do not desire conflict, and as long as humanity and the sapients work together, the feral can be controlled. But to make this happen, an entity needs to function as a mediator. One that cares not for humans, beasts, elementals, or monsters, but at the same time cares for all of them equally. Something... Unique."

Jake finally understood what was going on.

The Fallen King was actually throwing his hat in the ring to become World Leader. The vote would take place in an hour, and he had already taken the opportunity to voice his stance and make a proposal to humanity.

"Which naturally begs the question... if you don't care for any party, what is in it for you to act as this mediator?" Jacob asked. He seemed oddly thrown off, and Jake could feel his old boss really struggling internally as he tried to grasp the situation.

"A silly question you should have realized already. I am a King. I am a ruler. To rule is my Path, simple as that. A world that is not wrought by unnecessary war will reward me more, and I am not blind to the benefits humanity can bring. I even chose to harbor humans and defend them out of purely selfish ambition. I desire what humans can create. Their minds and their ingenuity. I will have to look far to find beasts worth a proper conversation, while in any human settlement, I can find plenty of minds worth sparring with."

He really had all the answers. Jake was surprised to see this side of the King. He knew the King wasn't stupid from their talks after he had awakened the Unique Lifeform, but he did not expect a being such as the King to understand things such as diplomacy and acting with moderation. The King was still overbearing, sure, but not to the point of putting everyone off. Jake also felt a very subtle aura, making it clear the King had actual leadership skills and talents most city leaders possessed.

"You are aiming for World Leader?" a man from the back suddenly asked. Jake turned and saw it was Jacob's father, Arthur, who had finally decided to join the conversation.

"None is more qualified. While you may believe you are here to elect a leader of humanity, you are selecting the leader of the entire world. Unless you plan to suppress or annihilate all other races but your own, you will need to compromise. I am a being in the middle that can serve as that compromise."

"In other words, you want us to subjugate ourselves to an unknown lifeform that has suddenly appeared?"

"An oversimplified interpretation I do not fully agree with. What is the difference between subjugating yourself to another human or me? Unless you insist on trying to claim racial superiority, in which case I must disappoint. None are superior to I." That good-old arrogance was shining through.

Not that anyone who knew anything about Unique Lifeforms could object. It was a statement one could argue was objective as Unique Lifeforms being peak creatures of the multiverse.

"No, I believe you oversimplify," Arthur argued. "No one said a monarchal structure is the only valid one. We are gathered here today as a congress. Why should a single being be granted power over all others? In our old world, we had democracy. Each individual held power, and everyone could vote equally. This ideology was tried and tested as superior to any individual leader for more reasons than any of us have time to hear."

"An interesting idea. However, it relies on assumptions no longer applicable. Equality is nothing but a dream and an ideology that can only exist if the strong permit it. Power rules all in this world, whether you like it or not. Even if you try to change such a system, you need the power to do so."

It was a conversation Jake was pretty sure he had heard before, and one where he honestly didn't bother picking a side. However, he had to admit that organizations with solo leaders were the norm in the multiverse, even if exceptions did exist. For those exceptions, it was only that way because everyone was equal in power or because the strongest member allowed it to be so.

"But it should be obvious that any World Leader elected will not deal with every issue or even have an opinion. I am not rejecting the concept of voting or having representations. I am merely saying to have one being act as the backing and facilitator of these decisions. This individual will only have the interests of the people in mind, as ruling through tyranny is simply inefficient. Unless, of course, that individual belongs to a faction with an ideology they wish to enact upon the world. Such as the will of a god." The last remarks were clearly calling out nearly all of the major forces on Earth.

This led to some discussion, and the conversation was officially derailed. Like before, the independent factions weren't a big fan of organizations like the Holy Church coming in and ruling the planet for some new god. This was a conflict that had been ongoing since Earth was integrated, and one Jake doubted would end anytime soon.

Jake and everyone from Haven had been silent so far, but the three of them had looked at him a bit weirdly ever since the King appeared. The reason was obvious, and soon enough, the question also came as one of the leaders of a religious faction tried to refocus the talks.

"I just have one burning question," Jacob said as he finally mentioned the elephant in the room. One most had been waiting to ask but had held their tongue on as the flow of conversation was led elsewhere.

"Why do you wear the same mask as Lord Thayne? What is your relationship?"

CHAPTER 7

DISCUSSING THE FUTURE OF EARTH

Now, honestly, Jake felt really put on the spot. He had just dealt with the damn Bloodline debacle at the Order, and had believed this entire World Congress would be a relaxing time where he could chill with friends and do some voting and stuff. You know, something to enjoy a little.

But no, the King had to show up and make everything incredibly complicated, so instead of getting a nice and relaxing break, Jake went straight from the frying pan and into the fire.

Everyone looked back and forth between the King and Jake. Perhaps some had not noticed it to begin with, but the two masks did look exactly the same. Which made sense, because the mask Jake wore on his face was kind of a clone of the King, as far as Jake knew. In fact, it was the "real" body Jake always had on his face, while the King before him was... well, also the real body.

Yeah, Jake still wasn't sure exactly how it worked.

However, before the King answered the crowd, Jake addressed what had been burning in his mind. Not openly, but directed only at the King. He reached out mentally, and the King responded as he made a telepathic bridge.

"I thought you said you couldn't surpass me in level?" Jake said immediately.

"I did, but it appears I miscalculated, even if I just now learned you are, in fact, below me in level. You see, I assumed my Soulspace would surpass yours in power if my level did, and the two would have to be roughly equal, but it was clear my assumptions were wrong somewhere.

Parts of me wondered what would happen if I surpassed your level, but my Soulspace never surpassed yours. I primarily assumed I would hit a wall, so I kept slaughtering and claiming my land as I waited for that to happen. It never did. Ah, but I am certain that advancing in grade before you will be impossible, so do not dally."

The exchange between the King and Jake was nearly instantaneous due to its telepathic nature, so in the view of everyone else present, the King and Jake had just stared at each other for a moment before the Unique Lifeform answered Jacob's question.

"He is why I am fallen," the King said simply.

Jacob, who seemed to have managed to collect himself a bit, continued down this line of questioning. "I may be incorrect, but you were formerly known as the King of the Forest, the final opponent of the tutorial that Lord Thayne and I were in?"

"Correct," the King answered.

"In which case, how are you alive? To my knowledge, he gained the title of Progenitor through slaying you."

Jake once more had attention gathered on him, and he seriously considered if he should talk about it now. Well, the King was handling it so far, so maybe he should just let him do the talking—eh, telepathy.

"We Unique Lifeforms have our own ways of survival... and can I not ask you the same?" the King said, doing some good-old whataboutism. *"To my knowledge, you were slain too during the tutorial but had methods to stay alive. The same is true for the Risen and that other mage. There are endless methods to survive, so do you truly find it that surprising?"*

The revelation that Jacob had died brought attention to him. Surviving death was an odd concept to most, and Jake actually had a feeling it made Jacob appear better. However, it also sought to derail the conversation, something Jacob was clearly not willing to allow.

"This answers how you met, not why you are standing where you are today or the nature of your relationship with Lord Thayne," Jacob stated.

"I believe the simplest answer would be that the Hunter is my bane. If you wish for a balancing scale on this planet, he can fulfill that role, as even now, I hold no confidence in surviving if he sought to end my reign."

Jake was kind of happy he had shut up, as the King was seriously spinning the truth. Jake understood why, too... There were plenty of skills to discern truths, and even if they didn't work fully, they at least had to have partial effects. Downright lying would probably trigger them, at least. Of course, it was also possible the King was partly truthful for some other reason.

Jacob looked at Jake with questioning eyes, and Jake decided to also be truthful. "I have killed the King once, and I can do it again. Trust me, it wouldn't even be a fight; I know his weakness."

Hey, it wasn't a lie? It was Jake being one hundred percent honest and not at all obscuring the truth.

Carmen suddenly raised her hand and asked, "If what you are saying is true, wouldn't that just mean picking you effectively puts Jake in charge?"

"Yes and no," the King answered. *"It would give him veto, yes, but calling him in charge would be inaccurate, as the Hunter cares not for leadership of any kind. Merely look at who truly leads his city currently. His position would be comparable to that, except I would not seek to make decisions benefiting him, but everyone under my rule."*

"Let us say we do believe everything you said," Arthur put in, rejoining the conversation. "Let us assume you do have the wellbeing of this planet in mind. Choosing to elect you World Leader within an hour of meeting you... Doesn't that sound like a hasty and unwise choice?"

"It does, and it would confirm you are all incompetent leaders and not worth respecting in the long term," the King answered, getting a varied response. Some looked offended, others looked like everything suddenly made sense, and people like Jake didn't quite have time to get what the King was playing at before he continued after an adequately long dramatic pause.

"Which is why I would advocate for not selecting one during this vote. By my estimates, I hold roughly a fourth or a fifth of the total votes by myself, meaning that if I do not vote for anyone, their chances of being elected are slim. I am also aware that no other faction would have the votes even without my presence here. No, I come today to open up a line of communication and a chance to prove my competency. Let me also make it clear, no King rules alone. Even if I do ultimately get elected, none will lose their positions unless deemed incompetent, as I see no purpose in ruining what already works, and I am also acutely aware that hostile takeovers would mean war with many factions."

Miranda nodded along, seeming to agree with the King for the most part. There also didn't seem to be much resistance, and a few new players even joined the conversation.

"The Risen do agree that a time to prove oneself is necessary,"

Priscilla said. "We are not opposed, as we believe inclusivity is key to a well-functioning society. I just want to confirm if the Fallen King has any thoughts on the Risen?"

"None in particular. Any creature with a soul is living in my eyes, and I shall confess, I do not even possess the usual sensory organs of you humans or Risen. To me, you all look alike aside from some faint differences in energy signatures."

This again got a varied response. Some humans seemed to frown—especially many of those associated with the Holy Church and independent factions. Jake did notice Arthur didn't seem to hold any strong opinion on the Risen, which at least was a good sign. Jacob's dad likely represented more Pylons than anyone else, and Jake wagered the man could be quite influential when he wanted to.

"What are your thoughts on this, Lord Thayne?" Arthur suddenly asked as he looked at Jake.

Being put on the spot again, Jake took a moment to think before he answered, "Who leads Earth or not really isn't that big of a concern to me. In my eyes, the multiverse is far larger than this planet, and even if Earth will forever be my home, I only consider Haven truly mine. So as long as whatever faction or individual gets elected leaves Haven alone and lets it stay neutral, I truly don't care."

"You have no interest in spreading the influence of the Order of the Malefic Viper?" Jacob's dad further questioned.

"None whatsoever," Jake answered truthfully. "Neither does the Malefic Viper. Not to be an ass, but the Viper has made it pretty clear he cares little for a small planet such as Earth. He cares about individuals and not dead rock, if it comes down to things. Ultimately, the Order is the kind of organization that doesn't recruit by taking over territory, but by people coming to join it. If the Order does take over a territory, it wouldn't be through me trying to weasel my way into becoming World Leader, but by overwhelming force."

Miranda decided to also finally join the conversation, adding, "I also want to point out that Haven is still only in possession of a single Pylon, and has thus far made no efforts to expand except the natural growth of said Pylon. Haven is still open to members of any faction to visit, and besides some basic rules, we welcome everyone. The only religious institution we have is a temple where anyone is allowed to place a statue as long as it passes some basic evaluations. All of this is to say, Haven truly has no desire to reach for more power or influence besides being a neutral force that hopes our independence can be respected no matter who becomes World Leader."

It wasn't anything new, and Jake knew she had emphasized this repeatedly when talking to other factions. But, hey, reemphasizing was always good, especially with new people present.

"There is just one issue," Caleb said, also bringing himself and the Court of Shadows into play. "As of now, we are only a single planet, and while this vote may only appear to pertain to Earth, we must acknowledge that is only for now. In the context of the old world, a country was just a piece of land on a single planet, but in the multiverse, countries expand across entire star sectors."

Jake frowned at this as he understood the implications.

Caleb continued, voicing exactly what Jake had just realized. "So let's say any single faction is elected World Leader and agrees to leave every other faction alone to act independently while not allowing them to continue to expand. What happens in a few hundred years? What happens when the entire solar system is conquered? When, in times to come, potentially entire parts of the galaxy are conquered? Even if a small piece of land such as Haven remains, it will be cut off. Defensive formations covering the entire country will isolate them, and I see no scenario where a true multiversal kingdom will allow so many factions to have teleportation arrays placed in its heart. Especially not opposing factions such as the Risen and Holy Church."

"Isn't this putting the cart before the horse?" Arthur argued from afar. "You postulate a scenario so far off I don't see why it is relevant to discuss at the current time."

"So far off?" Caleb said. "No, this is all within our near futures. The timescale of the multiverse moves differently from what we are used to. Every single person in this room will live hundreds of years more unless killed. Within that time, this entire planet will surely be conquered, and whatever factions accomplish this will surely seek to expand."

"What are you arguing, then?" Arthur asked. "That we all just fully submit to one faction?"

"No, I am not proposing any solutions, just pointing out problems. No matter who wins, the Court of Shadow will likely stay. As a known faction or an unknown one, we tend to be good at staying in the shadows. It's kind of what we do." Caleb shrugged. "I just don't wanna see my home planet fall into civil war and would prefer to stay in the light. At least partly."

"All issues I believe there will be found solutions to in due time," the

King said, reentering the discussion. *"However, to propose one solution is to have borderline no protection besides the sheer knowledge this area is inhabited by so many powerful factions. I can understand why the Holy Church and Risen would have issues coexisting, but even so, no war shall begin. If war means not only offending one opposing faction, but all those present on the planet along with so many prolific individuals, not even the Church or Risen would risk conflict. Additionally, this shall natu-rally serve as an aegis for the weaker factions, as the aggression of any large force to usurp a smaller one will be frowned upon."*

Caleb shrugged again. "Maybe, maybe not. I still see it being incredibly risky if any faction can just teleport people in."

"They would be able to anyway, or do you truly believe any organiza-tion anyone on this planet can establish in a few centuries can match even a fraction of a true power of the multiverse?" the King said. *"No, we would be crushed if any truly powerful and ancient being decided to descend. Unless, of course, they fear an equally or more powerful entity descending in response."*

"Making Earth such a place of high tension with so many innocent and uninvolved citizens living here seems unwise, and almost like we are disregarding their presence," Jacob said.

"It is also high tension to attempt to force everyone into one ideology. No conquest of a planet ever ends peacefully. Augur, you know as well as I that if the Holy Church were to act according to their usual modus operandi, this planet would become a homogenous society not by under-standing and inclusion, but by forced assimilation and cleansing." It was more or less a direct jab at the Church; however, he also further added, *"Not that I hold much faith in any other organization or faction of the multiverse to do much better. The Court would lock the planet down and use it to recruit new assassins. In an ideal situation, the Risen would attune the entire planet to their own magic, and Valhal would turn it into nothing more than a massive hunting ground on which everything is killed before rebuilding from the ruins, just to take a few examples."*

"What about us?" the Sword Saint asked with a smile.

"You, I know little about. However, the Noboru Clan, as you call yourself, has the massive issue of being nothing more than a fledgling faction that will be gobbled up by other forces regardless of your wishes. Even if you seek to stay independent, this can only happen if another faction allows it. Granted, I will not argue that the god who blessed you won't choose to intervene and act as a shield, but in that case, what makes you different from someone like the Hunter? Naturally, all of this

assumes the Noboru Clan is truly virtuous and seeks only the best for everyone—something I doubt, based on the history of this world."

The Sword Saint just nodded in response. "Arguing against history and your ignorance of my faction seems futile, and I will not claim any faction perfect. On the note of gods, am I correct to assume Unique Lifeforms are unable to be blessed?"

It was a question many already knew the answer to. Jake, of course, did. Jacob likely did, as well as many leaders of major factions. However, many didn't, and while Jake wasn't sure if the old man knew, the question would still serve as a clarification for everyone.

"That is correct. Unique Lifeforms are unable to obtain the Blessings of gods, for we need no guidance nor to be shown a Path. We are to forge our own or die trying to realize what we were born to be." The King's answer was fittingly arrogant. Almost prideful at being unable to be blessed.

The old man nodded and stated a conclusion that was pretty obviously eventual. "For the vote of World Leader, the Noboru Clan will choose to vote for ourselves with the goal of electing no one."

"The Court shall do the same," Caleb quickly added.

"Us too," Miranda said, Jake naturally not disagreeing.

"Very well." Jacob nodded.

The rest of the congress quickly followed suit, and it became clear no World Leader would be chosen during the Second World Congress.

CHAPTER 8

PATHS TO A BETTER FUTURE

Results: No individual obtained at least 60% of the total votes. No World Leader will be elected during this World Congress. Note that a World Leader must be elected within the first 3 World Congresses.

The vote had ended as everyone expected. Jake had decided to just vote for Neil for fun, getting a weird look from the guy afterward. It had actually gone about as Miranda had theorized before they entered the World Congress, with, of course, the small change of the King being present.

Miranda had not believed any World Leader would be elected due to how many dissenting opinions still existed. The Noboru Clan and Holy Church alone opposed the other gaining power, the Risen wanted neither but preferred the Noboru Clan, the independents wanted neither of them, and Valhal wanted who-knows-what.

The Court of Shadows and Haven didn't really matter much anymore, voting-wise, as they were beaten out by sheer numbers. However, their opinions could still sway some, and not having their support would potentially only lead to trouble down the line. The same was true for Eron, who had been oddly silent since the entire event began, almost hiding away.

Determining who was happy or not with this conclusion wasn't hard to do. The Holy Church seemed disappointed, and the Noboru Clan also appeared to hope that they would have won the vote. In fact, Jake got the feeling the Noboru Clan and many of the independents associated with Arthur had made some kind of agreement.

However, it seemed like most had assumed this vote would end in no winner as a foregone conclusion. Getting sixty percent of the votes was no easy task, and no faction had confidence in achieving it as things currently were on Earth. In fact, Jake was unsure a real agreement of more than sixty percent would ever be reached.

That was why both he and Miranda had agreed that all of this was just planting the seeds of the next World Congress, where, according to the rules, a World Leader had to be selected. No one knew how the next election would work, but the best guess was that the winner would simply be the individual with the most votes.

With the end of the first vote, a new one instantly began. Jake had wondered what the next vote would be about. A new shop of some kind? A system event? Something entirely different? Well, it sure did turn out to be different than Jake had expected.

The second vote of the World Congress will relate to allowing those who have yet to find their Path to do so.

As the world progresses and many begin to find their footing, some stumble as they fail to find their Path. They reach an impasse as their progress stops and their motivation dies. This event is one that will allow those who faltered to reignite their inner fire and discover their true Path. At the same time, members of the World Congress can decide in which direction they wish for their planet to go.

The voting options are as follows:
1. Paths of the Unusual Unions
2. Paths of the Heretical Few
3. Paths of the Devoted Ones
4. Paths of the Lonely Souls
5. Paths of the Independent Worlds
6. Paths of the Recognized Supremes
7. Paths of the Submissive Realists

Additionally, an event known as the Path of Myriad Choices will open up for those overqualified to participate in this system event. This event will allow qualifying participants to explore another potential Path they may have followed and seek inspiration from it, or perhaps choose to change their Path entirely. Further information on how to qualify for this event will follow.

All of these events will potentially allow participants to change their current class, profession, or race based on the nature of their experiences during the event.

Voting will begin in: 3:59:59

Jake carefully read it over, and he had to admit... it was not what he expected. He also tried to poke the options a bit, fishing for a response, but it did nothing. In other words, they would have to vote purely based on the names of the seven paths and what they could deduce from them.

The entire congress hall was silent as everyone read the options and description. Jake frowned further as he understood what this was about and how it wasn't directed at him besides that extra event. Jake knew his own Path, and this event seemed to be aimed at those who didn't. It was an event to boost not only the elite, but everyone.

Out of the corner of his eye, he saw Jacob smile, the Sword Saint nod in approval, and many of those at the independent factions looking on with great interest. Jake was still interested, as he wanted to see what that extra event, Path of Myriad Choices, was all about.

"Interesting proposition by the system," the King said, being the first to speak. *"Alas, a vote in which I will recuse myself from participating, even if I do have my own opinions on the matter. This seems to be for you humans more than anyone else, and no matter the choice, it will benefit other races if they can participate."*

Jacob chose to take the opportunity to follow up. "Rather than argue what is the best choice, can we agree to exclude some initially? I believe there are some that should naturally be disregarded."

"Why? Becoming a planet of heretics seems like a great way to get it blown up," Carmen joked in response.

"Indeed it would be. Hence why I believe it's a natural one to exclude. While we have no details on each option, I also believe excluding Paths of the Lonely Souls, just based on the name, would be wise. Humans—or beasts, for that matter—do better in groups than on their lonesome, and this entire scenario is clearly aimed at the masses and not the powerful individuals. The lonely souls have already found their paths; they do not need this." His words primarily received approving nods.

"The independent factions would also vote to exclude the third, sixth, and seventh option for obvious reasons," Arthur argued.

"Devoted Ones reeks of recognizing a single religion or turning our world into a theocracy. Recognized Supremes appears like one where the paths are all about assisting those already at the top, and the seventh option should be excluded by name alone."

"There is more to devotion than recognition of a god," Jacob said as a counterargument. "It can be a devotion to a good life or the community. Even if it is aimed at factions with religious leanings, that does not necessarily mean it is only for them."

"I don't remember you being openly ignorant to reality," Arthur answered as he looked sharply at Jacob. "I am more surprised you didn't argue for selecting Submissive Realists, as that seems to describe the Holy Church more than anything."

"Submission is a choice that should not be made out of fear or recognizing it as the only realistic option remaining, so naturally, I disagree with that option. I am surprised you didn't instantly argue that we should choose the Lonely Souls options. You seem to have quite the talent for pushing people away." Jacob finished with a smile. You know, the kind of smile that wasn't really a smile.

Jake felt like this pretty much confirmed there was some kind of beef between the two of them. This was a bit surprising, as Jake remembered the father and son seeming quite close before the system. Did Arthur just not agree with Jacob taking up the mantle of Augur? Or was Jacob disappointed Arthur directly opposed him?

"Independent Worlds and Unusual Unions," the Sword Saint cut in, stopping the two men from airing their personal grievances. "I do believe there is much positive to be said about independence, but so is there for unions. To call the current situation on Earth an unusual union would not necessarily be an incorrect description. The only question is, is what we are seeing on Earth truly a union or merely a temporary moment of peace? Not that Independent Worlds is that much better, as many of us are independent forces as it stands."

"This vote is clearly as much about what we want Earth to become as what it currently is," Caleb said. "The Court of Shadows has little input on these options, but the prior conversation about the future of Earth is very relevant. Do we want it to be an unusual union of forces, or an independent entity capable of functioning regardless of the factions? In many ways, was the goal not to become an independent world through an unusual union, mixing the two a bit?"

"That is one interpretation," Priscilla said. "The Independent Worlds choice can also have an emphasis on the 'worlds' part. As it currently exists, Earth is but one world, but there are ways to make several smaller dimensions or even small worlds within the same area. I do find it entirely possible this choice is not about uniting the factions in any way, but instead having each capable of properly isolating themselves."

"Fair enough," Caleb relented with a nod. "In that case, is that truly something we want? It would also inevitably result in only one faction ruling the true space of Earth with little interaction between each force."

"It is a safer choice, if that is truly what it is about, but we also have to question what exactly these Paths will be about and what the majority of the denizens of Earth would resonate with," Jacob said, reentering the conversation. He was clearly done with the useless bickering with his father, and besides the two throwing sharp looks at one another, they stayed civil.

Definitely something there, Jake thought, nodding. Now, what was Jake's opinion on this vote? Well, to be perfectly honest, he didn't really care much. He was clearly also the only one who would even be fine with the heretic choice. Speaking of which, it was interesting the system even offered such a path. Then again, it was just one extreme end of the spectrum, and so far, it felt like the system was impartial on the topic.

Miranda also began participating, and although Jake listened in, he ultimately knew this truly didn't concern him. As Jacob had said, this choice was as much about what would resonate with those of Earth, and Jake hadn't even been on the planet for the last couple of months. He would leave again the moment this World Congress ended, assuming where he currently was could even be considered on Earth.

To believe he had any fucking clue what those who couldn't find their Path needed or wanted to "pull themselves up by their bootstraps" would be stupid even for him. Jake was privileged and knew his own Path already nearly perfectly, and he had his own goals. In almost all ways, this entire vote had nothing to do with him.

Luckily, it appeared the discussions soon reached an impasse, and it was decided that the factions would spread out and have some more intimate discussions and deal-making. It was also an excuse to have all the space mages group up and discuss space-mage stuff, and likewise for the merchants. Lillian went with the merchants, and Neil was, of course, a space mage.

Miranda went over to the Sword Saint right away, and Jake considered what his plans were for a moment before he decided to head over to the only other person who looked about as bored as he was: Carmen.

Also, he had noticed her throwing him the occasional glance during the meeting. She looked like she wanted to talk to him, and as he had nothing better to do, why not?

Jake went up to her and waved. "Long time, no see."

"Hey," Carmen greeted in return. "How is Sylphie?"

He should have known. Sylphie had talked about Carmen a few times, calling her the "nice punchy lady," and it seemed like Carmen also liked Sylphie equally.

"She is doing fine," Jake answered with a smile. "Had some fun doing a dungeon and is otherwise just flying around in the forest and hunting things. That, or she is hanging out with her parents, probably still hunting things for some quality family time."

"Her parents?" Carmen asked, interested.

Jake realized Carmen truly only knew Sylphie from the Treasure Hunt, and seeing how they had the time...

"Oh, boy, let me tell you about the time I was attacked and taught how to fly by a random hawk just after getting my wings, and said hawk decided to bring me to his and his mate's nest to make a super baby hawk."

The two of them ended up heading for Haven's booth and isolating it, just chatting while everyone else was working. Jake had considered doing alchemy during this period, but he was currently working on poisons, so he wasn't sure he could attempt to concoct something during the World Congress lest the fumes count as attacking others.

Carmen also shared what she had been up to in recent times. Primarily that she had focused on her profession like so many others and was currently forging her "weapons."

Jake was a bit confused at what the weaponless fighter meant until she took out a dagger and jammed it down onto her own palm, only for the blade to be deflected, unable to even scratch the skin. "The Path I walk is one where my body becomes my weapon. I am good at punching people—that is all I am good at—and while I could use gloves before to somewhat alleviate damage to my fists, I recently became able to refine them."

"Wait, how strong can you make them?" Jake inquired.

"Remembering your battle with the Sword Saint at the end of the

Treasure Hunt, I am pretty sure I would be able to directly block the blade with my fist once refinement is complete," she explained with a confident smile.

"How exactly does it work? And... well, can I do it too?"

Yeah, Jake was shameless, so what? Seriously, he had his gloves, which became incredibly durable when infused with mana, but the mana expenditure was great and only grew the more powerful a blow he blocked. To passively have his hands be as tough as an actual weapon? Oh, boy, he could only imagine his Touch of the Malefic Viper-powered punches.

"Well, probably not," she explained, putting a damper on Jake's hopes and dreams. "It is tied to my profession and is expensive as fuck. Moreover, it doesn't work if I use weapons."

"Well, that's too bad. Speaking of which, what god is it that blessed you?" He didn't actually know, and it was time to finally ask.

"Well, Gudrun. It was first another guy who seemed cool enough, but he quickly said I didn't really fit his teaching anyway, so instead, I got blessed by Gudrun. She is apparently the wife of the bigshot of Valhal, Valdemar. Gotta be honest—doesn't feel good to be tossed from god to god like that, but Gudrun has been great so far, even if she is a bit hands-off, and I mainly get advice from C-grades these days through some rituals from my profession."

"Huh. Gotta say, sure are a lot of Primordials hanging around Earth." Jake chuckled a bit.

Carmen snickered. "All your fault, oh mighty Chosen of the evil ancient snake god."

"Hey, it is what it is. He is a friend, and that is that." He shrugged.

"Sure." Carmen just shook her head, changing the topic. "Remember when you said you owed me a favor after that thing with Limit Break during the Treasure Hunt... Were you serious?"

Jake sure did remember, and he nodded. "As long as it isn't anything ludicrous."

"You are a hunter, right? Do you know how to track people? Not now, but when I am done with my refinement, and you got time."

"I can do a bit of tracking, but it really depends. I do have a tracking skill, and my Perception is decent enough. Moreover, I am always up for a challenge. Why? What do you need to track?"

"Not a what, but who... I wanted to ask your help to track down my family. I think it is about time for a proper reunion." Carmen gave Jake an odd smile that he wasn't quite sure what to make of.

CHAPTER 9

A GOOD CHAT & HIDDEN AGENDAS

J ake knew he wasn't exactly a tracker. He could track a little, and his senses were sharper than ever. With some clues, his tracking skill would allow him to chase mana signatures and other signs, though, of course, there were many who were significantly more qualified. Jacob was probably the best on the planet, but there had to be many more who were far more effective than Jake. Something he felt like he did need to voice.

"While I can track, I am not exactly good at it compared to others. I am sure you can ask some seer or something who is far better at it."

It was primarily that she wanted to find her family, which meant it was solely a tracking job. Jake had kind of assumed she needed help tracking some powerful beast or something, but if it was just some humans, she could find far better. Jake had kind of assumed she'd asked him because fighting strong stuff would be involved.

"I am already on it, and have worked with some to boil down the general area," she said. "However, it looks like they are on the other side of a large body of water. Based on some space mages from Midtgaard, it is probably around where that guy Arthur and many of the independent factions are located." Carmen's explanation still didn't address one key point.

"I am still sure you can find better once you get there, and if you wanted assistance getting across this body of water, you could have just asked for that," Jake answered a bit suspiciously.

Carmen just sighed. "Yeah, but I want someone to help who isn't affiliated with Valhal or anything like that. This is purely a personal thing."

Jake finally nodded. "Okay, fine. Do you have any plans on when you want to go and how we are supposed to get there? You know, all the logistics."

"No fucking idea quite yet, but from what I hear, the space mages in a nearby port-city should soon have a circle up and running. Once that works, I can get word to Miranda, and she can contact you about getting to the port? It will be a bit from Haven, but hopefully the teleportation network will reach there by then, making the journey not too annoying. I know you are currently busy elsewhere, but you can return to our universe, right?"

"I can." Jake nodded. "How do you know I am not on Earth currently? And does everyone know?"

"Miranda told me, and no, I don't think others know. Apparently, you are super hard to track. Ah, but don't blame her for telling me. She did it after getting permission from those gods who blessed her. By the way, how does that work? I thought you could only be blessed by one god at a time."

"A mix of god stuff and system fuckery, I reckon," Jake answered incredibly accurately.

"Makes sense," Carmen nodded, not a hint of sarcasm in her voice. Well, it made as much sense as any other answer. "We have an agreement, then? I will tell Miranda, and then she will send a response back? Don't worry, I already got ways of contacting her. Or, well, she's got ways of contacting me with her weird witchy magic."

"Miranda does have weird witchy magic," Jake said, nodding in understanding.

He had to admit he had no fucking clue how any of her skills worked. Despite learning a bit about formations and such, he only came to realize her magic was even more complicated and reliant on an entirely different school of thought than the kind of magic he wanted to learn.

The two of them kept talking a bit longer about random stuff, and Jake learned how Carmen was taught. Apparently, she could set up virtual battlefields of some sort and fight echoes of individuals located pretty much anywhere, even in other universes. The echoes had corresponding magic circles on their end set up by Valhal to facilitate all this, with Carmen essentially being a summoner. These echoes couldn't actually interact with anything non-simulated outside the battlefield, but it was still an incredibly valuable tool.

Valhal was an organization all about war. Not just the act of fighting but war as a concept, which had also led to Valdemar being called the God of War. Legends spawned from war, the songs of bards, the concept of morale, armies clashing, celebrating after a victory, or dealing with the emotions after a lost battle—all of this was part of what Valhal stood for, and in many ways, they were a truly neutral faction in the multiverse in that they didn't have any enemies.

Because an enemy would mean war, and Valhal had never lost a war. The mere thought of Valhal declaring war on a faction was almost like a scary story one would tell their kids. Stories such as Valdemar picking up his axe and leading what was known as a Warband into battle. Individuals of all grades, hundreds of gods, descending all at once with no regard for their lives, caring for nothing but a good battle and dying with honor.

Other factions were constantly at war. The Holy Church and the Ghostlands—the land of the Risen—were embroiled in fighting. Several factions who weren't fans of the Court of Shadows had declared war against the assassins. Jake also learned that the Automata and the Endless Empire were at war, and had been for the last thirty eras. The Endless Empire was a faction Jake had never heard of before; it consisted of some of the most powerful ectognamorphs in existence, led by a large coalition of powerful Hive Queens—Insect Queens who had ascended to godhood and commanded armies of unprecedented scale. They were, in general, incredibly warlike, as they viewed it as a healthy way to constantly thin their herds and grow in power by weeding out the weak.

Yet not even they wanted a war with Valhal.

And if Jake was being honest, he totally understood why. It was a bit similar to why no one wanted conflict with the Order of the Malefic Viper. Most wars only involved the mortals, but if Valhal went to war, they pulled out all the stops and made it a war where one side was annihilated. Meanwhile, Villy would ensure that even if the other side won, it would bring so much devastation and death upon them it wouldn't be worth it.

The reason for this was simple enough... Villy didn't care about having a controlled war, and Valhal viewed war as something where a side had to win. They still wanted to battle, of course, and members of Valhal were primarily known as incredibly powerful mercenaries who joined the side they agreed with the most in a conflict. Carmen even told Jake it often happened that two members of Valhal found themselves facing each other on a battlefield. The result of that would nearly always be one of them dead and the other one having a toast for the fallen comrade he had just slain.

So, yeah, Valhal was a paradise for battle maniacs, and Jake felt like he would have fit in pretty damn well. Carmen also seemed happy with it and had an interesting perspective on fighting former comrades or people from the same faction.

"Fighting is fighting. I used to do boxing, and it was normal to fight friends or former colleagues. I was in quite a small town with only one noteworthy gym, and in tournaments I often ended up fighting people I had trained with and gotten along with before. That didn't mean I would show the slightest restraint in the ring, though. The same is true for the warriors of Valhal... In fact, holding back when you see another member on the opposing side would just be disrespectful. Valdemar allegedly once said that dying in battle is an honorable death, and an honorable death is a good death. A good death means it was a worthy life, and all worthy lives are worth celebrating and remembering."

Jake had once more found himself nodding along. He'd had a lot of rather infantile views on honor in his early days of the system. He remembered burying the guy Nicholas, as he had put up a good fight, and he had refused to loot entire beast corpses, as he found it disrespectful. His opinion had eventually been refined, and Jake now no longer cared as much about a concept such as honor. He had his own rules of sorts, and while those rules might be considered honorable by some, Jake didn't particularly care.

They did agree on a good death being a worthwhile death. Jake viewed dying to anything other than a good fight as a nightmare. Carmen was like him, also a battle maniac, and as they talked, they both looked back on the fight with the Monarch of Blood fondly, even if Carmen had found the conclusion of it incredibly frustrating.

"By the way, is it fine for us to talk in here?" Jake asked, jokingly adding, People may start rumors we are plotting an alliance or something. Not that I am complaining. I am sure Miranda will view this as good diplomatic work."

"Nah, who cares? Sven also kept insisting I should get closer to Haven and the old swordsman, so I guess this counts." She shrugged.

"Where is Sven, by the way?" Jake asked. He wasn't at the World Congress, which was a bit weird.

"In a dungeon, I think? He entered with his party a good while ago and has yet to get out. Who knows? Maybe they all died." Carmen just shrugged. "Not sure if people can enter the World Congress if they are in a dungeon or if they were just too busy doing other stuff. He is there with a party of five, and he would only bring one of them if he went to the World Congress, so bailing on more than half the party would also be a shitty move. Sven had at least made plans in case he and the others would not be back in time."

"Huh." Jake nodded. "You done the dungeon? Is it any good?"

Yeah, probably not the part he was supposed to bite onto. Jake hadn't found any good dungeons in a while, and he knew his class was probably going to get a bit behind his profession if he kept focusing on alchemy within the Order. So a good dungeon would be a great way to catch up on some levels.

"Eh, I have been in there once but didn't clear it," she said. "It seemed okayish. It was a plant dungeon, and most of the enemies were around level 140. It was not that hard, honestly, and I saw nothing that could take down Sven and his party at all, but it was large and annoying to navigate, as the entire dungeon seemed to rearrange itself constantly with a lot of ambush predators lurking about."

"Aight." Jake nodded, not sure if he wanted to do that dungeon even if he could. 140 was way too low for him, though it was possible more powerful foes would appear further in.

"Speaking of challenges... how the hell did you beat that masked monster?" Carmen finally asked.

"Oh, man, that is a long story, but to make it short, a bunch of overpowered bullshit items meant to specifically counter him, a lot of luck, me being awesome, and then another massive dose of luck to tie it all together," Jake semi-joked.

"And you are confident in winning again? I will be honest; I don't trust that masked freak for even a second. He may have the King title, but that doesn't make him a good leader. Shit, you are an Earl, and I wouldn't want you leading even a children's football team." Carmen shook her head.

"Hurtful, but yes, I am confident in bringing down the King if he gets out of control," Jake confirmed.

Carmen nodded. "For the record, I am also a Viscount, but that doesn't mean I think for even a second I can lead."

"I guess the primary qualifier for being a noble so far is one's ability to kill stuff," Jake joked.

"Kind of fucked up, when you think about it," Carmen noted.

"Sure is."

Greg kept an eye on the booth and noticed that the female leader of Valhal and the Chosen of the Malefic Viper hadn't exited for a long time. He wondered what their meeting was about as he tried to comprehend the web of deceit and planning this Chosen had deployed.

Before the system, Greg had worked as a professional investigator running his own online blog, where he'd uncovered corruption and government secrets. Some people had called him a nutjob, but Greg knew one couldn't trust the masses of sheep who were always blind to the truth and willingly rejected what was right before their eyes.

Many people thought this Lord Thayne was a simple man, but Greg knew differently. The masked man was far from simple, and only wished to be perceived as such as he puppeteered the City Leader behind the scenes.

Lord Thayne, if that was truly his real identity, also hid from all kinds of scouting at all times. None of Greg's investigation skills worked, and no divinations or tracking spells had worked when Greg had sought assistance.

Greg had worked in the industry long enough to know that only people who had something to hide would go that far to hide it. It was obvious, and Greg wanted to get to the bottom of it even if it was the last thing he did. His former colleagues and friends had all called him paranoid and said he was overthinking things, but could they not connect the dots? All of them led to the same source: the Chosen.

The Augur was the former "boss" of the Chosen. Greg was sure it was backward, but their connection was obvious. The same was true for the influential undead called Casper. They clearly had some kind of relation, and Lord Thayne had influence over him.

Not to get started on the fact that his brother was the leader of the Court of Shadows. The Sword Saint was friendly with him—something Greg theorized was due to the old man also recognizing the threat this man posed to their planet.

Valhal had clearly already fallen under their thumb, based on how that woman Carmen had submitted herself and sought him out. He'd even heard odd rumors that the Chosen had used animals to get closer to her, which he would have found questionable if not for all of the other extreme methods the man—if he was a man—had prepared.

And now... now this Fallen King had suddenly appeared. Finally, he had revealed another of his many hidden cards. A powerful lifeform to function as his puppet to lead the planet into the destiny the Chosen, and perhaps even the evil god known as the Malefic Viper, desired.

To Greg, the most maddening thing was that no one else could see this. How no one else could put all the data together and reach the same conclusion that the monster known as Lord Thayne was a true master manipulator. A puppeteer of unholy talent and power who controlled nearly every faction from the shadows.

No... maybe people knew but feared speaking it. Maybe the Chosen was so talented that any who realized or spoke openly were removed from existence. His brother did lead a cult of assassins.

As an investigator, Greg had covered many things throughout his life. Uncovered secrets hidden by the elites. But he had never faced anything as intricate, as grand, as the web of lies and pure manipulation the Chosen had spun. Lord Thayne was no doubt the most cunning individual Greg had ever come across... perhaps the most cunning throughout human history.

It was intimidating.

He had already noticed the fallout and influence this "man" had over others. Greg had noticed that a lot of people had stopped talking to him, complaining that he spoke of nothing but his "mad conspiracy theory," and while some would write that off as Greg just being annoying to be around, Greg knew better. They feared the knowledge he held and what dangers it could bring them.

But Greg would keep fighting. He would prove the truth to everyone else on Earth... He just hoped that the Chosen wouldn't realize his grand design before it was too late.

However... he first had to find out what this grand design even was.

Chapter 10

A Case of Bad Communication

The hours quickly passed as Jake just sat back and chatted with Carmen. After a while, the two of them went to talk a bit with the old man too, but he was busy being the leader of the Noboru Clan and all that. Honestly, Jake wasn't a big fan of this entire World Congress, as there were two votes that didn't matter at all to him personally. He was also annoyed at so many people staring at him constantly, including this guy who kept trying to be sneaky about it and even used some weird scouting skills.

Nevertheless, he was still glad he had attended due to the appearance of the King, and he still had a good talk with Carmen, but he sure wouldn't classify it as productive or a good way to spend his time. Once the political maneuvering was coming to an end, Jake gathered with Miranda and Lillian again, with Neil still busy with other space mages, having occupied a booth by themselves while not allowing others to interfere.

"So, what is the expected outcome of the vote?" Jake asked Miranda once in their properly isolated booth. "And what should I vote for?"

"This one is hard," Miranda said, shaking her head. "Many want the Independent Worlds, some want the Devoted Ones. Many also want the Unusual Unions, but it is honestly hard to get a feel for the room, and many keep their cards close to their chest. I have a feeling no one can truly know before all the votes are cast."

"What do you want?"

"Honestly, if I am truthful, the Paths of the Recognized Supremes will probably be best for Haven, considering your presence and just overall what we are going for as a city. We focus on the powerful and the influential, not the masses. Most who want to live in Haven are those who do know their Path already, and those who don't would probably do best by taking advantage of your Records, or maybe even the Records of Arnold or me."

"I have a feeling not many other factions shared this sentiment," Jake said, shaking his head.

"No. In fact, it was futile to even bring up, so I didn't. The second best would probably be Unusual Unions, based on the general interpretation of it, and that is a fine choice for us. It is also a popular one. It may even be the most popular."

"So, we voting for it?" Jake asked

Miranda nodded. "I believe that would be the wisest."

"You talked to the King about it?" Hey, a thousand extra votes were always welcome.

"I only heard that he would abstain... Jake, what exactly is your relationship with that... thing?" she asked a bit nervously. "You told me about your tutorial, and I have put together that was the former King of the Forest, but didn't you kill him? And if you did kill him, how did he come back to life?"

"Remember that Soul Renewal from the Auction event? Well, the King managed to survive by hiding a bit of his soul within my mask that I got as loot from him, and using the Soul Renewal, I then healed that part to fully revive the King, who has now changed from the King of the Forest into the Fallen King. I am pretty sure the name change is due to some Unique Lifeform stuff."

"Wait... why would you go so far to resurrect a Unique Lifeform that you have slain?" Miranda said as she looked at Jake critically. "The mere fact the King didn't try to kill you off the bat is already a miracle, and who is to say he won't try and get rid of you subtly now? Moreover, even if he leaves you alone, what exactly do you have to gain besides putting an extremely powerful new contender into play on Earth, that may or may not negatively affect Haven and everyone else?"

All good questions Jake honestly had no answer to. He was silent for a time before answering, "I did not know about the nobility title before the resurrection, and as for what I get out of it... well, a good fight for one, and as I still have the mask, I made a gamble it would improve the item. Even though it didn't turn out that way, I don't regret resurrecting him. I don't think he is an enemy—let me just say that—as he can't really kill me or make me too pissed for reasons I won't share."

"It was questionable at best." Miranda just sighed. "You took a massive gamble... Wait... the King was resurrected shortly after the Auction, wasn't he?"

"Yeah?"

"How long after?"

"Not that long," Jake explained somewhat defensively. "It was shortly after I left for the Insect Plains I decided to do it. I did think enough to do it outside the city, and away from any settlements in case things went south."

Miranda frowned deeply. "That is about the time the Great Famine arrived... Could it have been a response somehow to the King's reawakening? The timing seems too convenient."

"Great Famine?" Jake asked, confused. He hadn't heard of this.

"You know, when everyone suddenly became gluttonous," Miranda said, making Jake realize what she was talking about.

Now that he remembered... he had never told anyone he did that. Based on Miranda's words, he also seriously doubted if he should tell anyone he did. Well... anyone besides Miranda and Lillian. Miranda was the City Leader and blessed by those Verdant Witches, and Lillian was bound by a contract, so it was all good, right? Not that he really wanted to explain it.

"I may or may not know how it happened..." Jake said a bit meekly as he explained what had happened while making Cursed Hunger.

Miranda looked at him, surprised in the beginning, then frowning, and finally looking rather pissed. "What the hell were you even thinking?" she eventually blurted out when Jake was about done explaining how he had gotten the curse under control. He didn't go into details, but Miranda clearly knew enough about curses to know how risky it was.

"I was confident I could make it work... and that even if I fucked up, I could handle the consequences," Jake said, defending himself.

"Based on what? Pure ego? Jake, that was not risky; that was just downright moronic. The amount of energy in that curse was not something you could have any reasonable confidence level in handling. And then you even decide to seal away a portion of the curse within your own soul... It is just a matter of time before it awakens some kind of ego or basic instinct if you keep it in there."

Now Jake really didn't want to share that Eternal Hunger already had this basic instinct and had taken the form of a chimera within his Truesoul. Though, to be fair, that wasn't Jake's fault, but that of the Chimera Weapon he had used as a base to fuse the curse into.

"I know it was risky, but I had my reasons to be confident, okay?" Jake said a tad sternly. "While I will admit I did not know the global effects my crafting session would have, and that large parts of the crafting process were unintentional, I will not apologize for the outcome."

"What Miranda is trying to say is that your stunt had a negative effect on every single individual and faction on the planet, and that if it was discovered you or Haven were in any way involved with it, our diplomatic situation on Earth would become a lot more complicated," Lillian said. "Our talks of neutrality would go right out the window, as we had effectively just launched unprovoked attacks on every other faction. Intentionally or not. And to do something so massive and then not inform us of any of that is a shitty thing to do if you expect us to handle Haven. What if someone knew it was you? In fact, does that Risen Casper not know? He asked how you were doing as if a bit worried just now, and considering his proficiency in curses, it wouldn't be surprising he put two and two together. Not to mention how your friend Casper nearly got blamed for what you did."

Jake stood with his mouth open as he took the words in. He wanted to argue, but didn't really come up with any good arguments that wouldn't make him come off as either an idiot or an apathetic asshole.

"Jake, I don't care much what you did, but that you didn't at least inform us you would do it, or even just give a quick update after the fact," Miranda added further. "Even if it hadn't helped us, it would have allowed us not to spend time and resources trying to discover the source. A single sentence could have saved everyone from a lot of work and even allowed us to potentially help obscure what had happened if someone came close to finding out. I had an idea it was maybe you behind it, but when you never mentioned it, it made me reconsider. The only thing you told me back then was that you were 'handling it,' or something to that effect."

He felt more and more shitty as she went on. It really felt like he got scolded, and the worst part was that he had fucked up.

The weekly meetings he and Miranda had held in the start had stopped all of this from happening. She had always been updated about what he was doing, and Jake had been updated on everything related to Haven. But recently, they had drifted a bit apart, with Jake having so many of his own goals and his presence in Haven no longer being a necessity.

"I fucked up," Jake said. "Sorry... Yeah, it just slips my mind. It is no excuse, but I tend to just focus on other things and not even think about informing you unless directly asked or anything like that..."

That they hadn't even talked about the Great Famine properly was an obvious sign of bad communication. Miranda had known a bit, but Jake had been dismissive back then and hadn't wanted to explain, as he'd been busy dealing with the curse. He had just brushed her off to deal with it and then never brought up the topic again, and Miranda had no doubt felt his unwillingness to talk about the topic.

"Would it be possible to reinstate those weekly meetings?" Jake finally asked. "I know it is a bit harder, but if you can contact me with that ritual, can't we set something up? If you need materials to do the ritual, I will naturally cover the cost."

Miranda smiled a touch as she answered, "I think the weekly meetings are a good idea. We can even make them monthly or biweekly if we are busy. As for covering costs, those altars from Yalsten more than cover everything."

"We got an agreement, then." Jake nodded. "And while we wait for the vote result... let me tell you about the newest drama in the Order of the Malefic Viper."

Jake decided this would be a good time to finally mention one secret he had kept from them both so far: The fact that he had a Bloodline. The entire Order would soon know, and it would be odd for Miranda not to. He would still keep all details a secret, but he did reveal he had one and that it was related to presences. He even used it to explain away some of how he controlled the cursed weapon.

She was surprisingly not very surprised. In fact, she said she had already guessed he had something like that, especially as she knew Eron had a Bloodline and that Jake seemed to "get along" well with him, if that was the right phrase.

Overall, Jake realized how dumb it was that they had never actually discussed it before, but it was good to get it all out in the open. She did show quite some schadenfreude when Jake told her about the many people who would be hounding him in the Order, but she also gave him one good piece of advice.

"You need to move the target off your own back, and the fact everyone believes you have a backer is a great way to do that. Just make it clear that you cannot make the decision on your own, but need the permission or maybe even command of your mysterious backer. Make it clear that convincing you is a waste of their time and that they should aim to convince the backer instead, as without his involvement, you are unable to choose."

"But my backer is the Viper..." Jake began as it clicked. "Who no one can discover, and even if they think they find out, they won't actually believe it possible for the Malefic Viper to be my backer. So I would just put them all on a wild goose chase while everyone else leaves me alone to not further annoy me."

"Which will at the very least buy you some time until they find out your backer is too hard to find, begin to believe you somehow never had one, or do realize it is the Viper, in which case I am sure you have progressed enough to handle that," Miranda said. "I am certain it will leak at some point either way."

Man, those meetings were going to be a good thing. Jake wanted to ask her about Meira, too, but was interrupted as the system said they only had a minute left to vote.

"Unusual Unions?" he quickly asked.

Miranda nodded, and Jake placed all his votes on it. A minute swiftly passed as the second and only "real" vote of the Second World Congress ended.

The vote for Paths has concluded!
With 32% of the total votes, the chosen System Event is the Paths of the Unusual Unions.
The event will begin in 1 month (30 days), and all eligible participants will be invited at that time. Additional information will follow.

It was short and simple with nothing concrete. A bit like the Treasure Hunt. It seemed that the votes had been damn tight, with the winner only taking 32%. It was clear many factions had tried to go for something else. The overall percentage of actual votes probably also went down due to the King abstaining. Either way, this was not an event Jake would participate in, but the next one sure was.

System Announcement

Quest Received: The Call of the Exalted Prima

As the world progresses, the Prima Watcher of Earth has been observing. Soon the Seat of the Exalted Prima shall appear on Earth and invite in all those who have managed to form keys to allow their entry. Anyone entering the Seat of the Exalted Prima can participate in the Path of Myriad Choices event, as well as gain access to the other benefits offered within the Seat of the Exalted Prima.

Beware, however, for the Seat holds dangers that the current warriors of Earth may not be ready to face yet. Should they unleash this danger and come out victorious, it shall reward the entire planet, while should they fail, it may fall to ruin.

The Seat of the Exalted Prima will appear on Earth in three months (90 days). Be prepared.

Objective: Obtain a Key of the Exalted Prima by combining three Key Fragments of the Exalted Prima.
Current progress: 2/3 Key Fragments of the Exalted Prima

Jake read it over and only thought for a moment before he pulled out two small items he hadn't thought about for a very long time.

[Key Fragment of the Exalted Prima (Unique)] – A key fragment to the Seat of the Exalted Prima. Collect three fragments to form the Key of the Exalted Prima to gain access.

Well, then, I guess Prima-hunting season just started.

CHAPTER 11

THE RIGHT PATH

"Do you have any of those keys?" Miranda asked Jake once she had also read the message. It appeared she had gotten the quest too.

"Nope, but I got two fragments, so I think I can get one more quite easily," Jake answered. "But, hey, we got the vote we wanted. Well, kind of wanted."

"It is indeed one of the better options, though, to be fair, most would be good options," Miranda said, nodding approvingly.

"Speaking of options," Jake said as he removed the isolation from their booth to hear all the discussion going around in the hall.

"This is a blatant attempt at forced integration!" someone yelled.

"It says Unusual Unions, not Forced Integrations," another guy yelled. "A union takes at least two willing parties to function."

"Mere semantics," the first guy said. "Unions can be forced as much as they can be voluntary, and for a union to function, the parties need some level of equality!"

"Then work on getting good enough to be recognized as at least worth looking at and stop being shit?" Carmen said, suddenly joining the discussion.

Jake couldn't help but smirk at the bickering going on. People unsatisfied with the vote appeared to be aplenty, but that only made sense considering the low percentage that the winning choice had. He didn't really bother listening in much, as he noted there was an hour till the Second World Congress would end.

Ten or so more minutes passed with senseless bickering and useless complaining until, finally, the conversation switched a bit towards the quest. It was a quest that it appeared far from everyone had gotten. In fact, it looked like the vast majority of cities had several, if not all, members not receiving the quest, based on their confused responses.

While they talked, Jake and a few others made eye contact as they gathered. They had an hour, and the quest contained things that pertained to them all collectively. They decided to gather on the platform of Sanctdomo, and Jake saw that even the Fallen King decided to float down from his mighty booth and join the lower rungs of nobility.

Jake, Jacob, Bertram, Fallen King, Carmen, Sword Saint, Casper, and even Eron came together to discuss it. It was the group that had also faced the Monarch of Blood, plus Jacob. Eron looked a bit out of place, too, as he stood as far from the Fallen King as he possibly could —something they all noticed.

"Relax, human, I do not seek to end your life despite your past transgression of overstepping your boundaries," the Fallen King said to Eron, the man freezing up a little.

That was when Jake understood why Eron was afraid of the Fallen King. It was the same reason the man didn't want to mess with Sultan... They countered him. The King more than anyone else.

The Fallen King could kill him. Permanently. Jake had theorized Eron more or less had an infinite health pool, but even an infinite health pool wouldn't matter if you had your soul crushed. It was the difference between someone slowly draining the water from a jug and someone just smashing the jug altogether. The King could attack the container of health while everyone else only attacked the inside.

"I apologize for past misunderstandings," Eron said as he bowed. "I misread the situation and allowed curiosity to get the better of me, and for that, I seek your forgiveness."

Jake felt like the apology was a bit out of character. Like it was practiced somehow. However, it appeared the King truly didn't care, as he waved his ivory claw dismissively.

"An action done cannot be retracted, only acknowledged as misguided or wrong. I accept your apology and wish not to dwell on it further than is necessary." At least the King's outright dismissal meant the group could finally move on to the real topic at hand.

"So, let's do a tally," Carmen said. "How many keys or fragments do you all have? I got two fragments."

"One fragment," Bertram said. "Others in Sanctdomo or the Church may have more. We will do a survey when we return."

"Zero fragments or keys," Eron said with a tone that made it clear he had never cared about collecting them.

"One key, two fragments," the Sword Saint answered. "I know others in the clan may have a fragment or two more."

"Two fragments," Jake answered, feeling a bit embarrassed answering after the Sword Saint had flexed on all of them.

"One key, zero fragments," the King said, making Jake feel even worse. The damn Unique Lifeform had gathered more than Jake had in a few months. Damn.

"A single fragment," Caleb said, making him a little happy his little brother hadn't beat him.

"In any case, it looks like most of us, if not all, are going to attend this event," the Sword Saint said with a smile. "Assuming a few people here can scrounge together the fragments."

The last part was said primarily towards Jake for some reason, despite others having less than him.

"I am just wondering," Jacob said, "how many people will each key give access to? Only one seems unrealistic, and an entire city would also be too much."

"Maybe just a party of five, like a dungeon?" Carmen said.

"Potentially." Jacob nodded. "However, even that would be low unless this event is truly aimed at the elite and the elite only. Additionally, these creatures with Prima in their name are not that easy to find, but I believe it will be possible to locate quite a few."

That was when Jake realized something. While he had confidence in killing Primas, he still needed to find them. Meanwhile, he had a living cheat in front of him when it came to finding stuff. Something he clearly knew.

"I shall focus my efforts on locating these Primas and ensuring that we can get as many keys as possible in the next three months"—Jacob smiled—"for all of us. The vote was for us to become an Unusual Union, was it not?"

"And I assume you are doing this out of the kindness of your heart?" Caleb asked with a wry smile.

"Now, while there may be much kindness in my actions, using my divination abilities does not come cheap for me," Jacob said, returning the smile in kind. "I simply cannot justify sacrificing for others and burdening my faction without proper cause."

"Man, you remind me of those damn soothsayers on the streets looking for naïve tourists," Carmen commented.

"Except my abilities are real," Jacob answered. "We can discuss potential partnerships for any who wishes to enter one. I will be in Sanctdomo waiting."

"Sure, that sounds like a good idea; let me just enter a city that literally burns me while within it," Casper said sarcastically.

That turned the mood a bit awkward; Jake hadn't known the Risen got burned by entering a holy city. It was almost like those old tropes. "Better avoid holy water," Jake joked.

"Well, yeah, holy-affinity liquid does sound like an idiotic thing to touch," Casper said with a deadpan face.

"Anyway, it's been nice seeing you all again," Carmen said as she turned to the Fallen King. "Besides maybe you, as I am still not sure if you are some evil entity who plans to lead the world into ruin."

"I believe such a thing would be meaningless, and I would face all those gathered here—something I neither have interest in doing nor believe is a wise choice," the King answered, not properly getting Carmen was semi-joking. *"Not that more than the Hunter is needed..."*

"Yeah, if he gets out of line, I got this," Jake said as he gave a thumbs-up. "His weakness is so obvious you will all kick yourselves for not realizing it earlier."

"Overwhelming power?" Casper asked.

"That would work," Jake said.

The mood after that was a bit more relaxed, as Carmen left and the former King of the Forest disappeared soon after. Eron left hastily, too, as he still seemed uncomfortable after spending time around the King. Caleb and the Sword Saint also bailed, as they had some stuff to attend to, leaving only Jake, Bertram, Jacob, and Casper.

That was when Jacob said something Jake had not seen coming.

"Casper, the Holy Church is going to advocate for the expulsion of the Risen from Earth and not allow them into any kind of unions. It may result in an outright attack with the goal of pushing you off the planet or annihilating you outright."

"Huh?" Casper said, surprised.

"The Holy Pantheon is determined," Jacob explained. "They place a lot of importance on Earth due to the presence of so many powerful factions here. The Court of Shadows, Valhal, the Chosen of the Malefic Viper, someone with a Divine Blessing given by Stormild, another by Aeon, and of course a Transcendent... now also a Unique Lifeform. To give up the planet would be moronic. The Church can accept the presence of all these, but the Risen are the mortal enemies of the Church, and coexistence is not acceptable to the leadership at all."

Jake also stood surprised, as Jacob had just said a lot of things he had not expected to come out of the Augur and leader of the Holy Church on Earth.

"Why are you...?" Casper asked, equally confused.

"Within a system event such as this, we are entirely cut off from the rest of the multiverse. There are no observers, and they have no control over us, so I need to say it here where we can speak truly freely. You need to be prepared, Casper. And while I am the leader of the Holy Church on Earth, I am not the leader of the faction. My protests will do nothing but make me lose influence, and it may even result in losing my position."

Casper frowned. "Still doesn't answer why you are telling me all this to begin with."

"Because I'm not a complete asshole, and even with my position in the Church, I don't need to agree with everything that is happening. Publicly, I will need to be against the Risen and even lead a campaign against them, but privately I honestly don't care. In fact, if I actively helped to destroy a friend, that would go directly against my Path." Jacob sighed. "Casper, you may now be Risen, but you are still a friend and the same lazy employee who spent more time complaining about being unable to get a good date than actually working."

"Now that is just harsh..."

"You once told me you liked hanging out with Jake because he couldn't get a girl either," Jacob continued.

"Wait, what?" Jake blurted out.

"It wasn't like that!" Casper said, embarrassed. "You know, I just liked hanging out with someone who didn't always go on and on about their perfect relationships."

"Anyway, Casper, I just wanted to warn you," Jacob went on. "Be ready, for something will come. The Church will soon likely order assassins to go after you and other influential people, spread more propaganda against you, and try to insert people into your cities to cause civil unrest. In fact, many are already in your cities. Once the universe opens up more and people can be brought here, forces will likely descend. Even if it isn't possible to bring outside help, the forces of the Holy Church grow every day."

"Will the Church really go to war?" Jake asked. "Don't they fear the consequences?"

"There will be a justification. Perhaps claims they are killing and forcing people to become undead. That they murder the living to fuel themselves. Essentially, slander to make the living side against them. At the same time, they assume you and others will stay out of it as the Malefic One never tended to get involved in other conflicts. He isn't involved in the one that is currently going on. As for Valhal and the Court of Shadows, it is entirely possible they will be hired. For Valhal, we just need to hire individuals as mercenaries, and the upper echelon of the Church may negotiate with the Court of Shadows and force your brother to side with us."

Casper looked grave for a moment, then sighed. "Thanks for the heads-up."

Jacob nodded. "Just take care of yourself. Please don't spread anything about our talk. Needless to say, this is not approved by the Church in any way and may even be considered treacherous."

The last part was also partly directed at Jake, and he, of course, nodded.

Casper also nodded as he muttered, "Well... I guess I need to speed up that project a bit."

William sat in meditation atop the block of metal, slowly absorbing the energy within. He was thrown out of meditation and lost his focus when the system message suddenly appeared and informed him that he had just received a quest.

"Master?" he asked as he felt the presence of Eversmile descend upon his mind. It felt like his head was on fire from the pressure, but he resisted and gritted his teeth as his master spoke.

"Such an event is not right for you. Seeing a second potential Path will only confuse you and risk making you stray from your current one. The right one. I have said it before, but all these system events are nothing more than distractions that will ruin you down the line. Just keep walking the Path paved before you, and you will find what you seek, my dear disciple."

William felt the presence disappear again as he breathed out in relief. He tasted a bit of blood in his mouth, and his eyes were red from the stress. Talking with his master was no easy feat, but a necessary one. His master always gave him advice on what was best for him, and had already led him towards several opportunities. Nevermore was just one of many, and when he had stood before the Judge from the Court of Shadows and been superior, it had proven his Path was the correct one.

He still didn't know exactly what his Path was or where it would lead him. However, he had not been led astray so far, and Kimmie and little Seo had also been able to live peaceful lives in a small city he had claimed.

Not that there weren't setbacks. Recently, the Unique Lifeform from their tutorial had appeared and settled close to the area William usually worked in, creating some issues. The monster had dominated a huge region, far larger than he believed humanity knew, and the monsters William had gotten close to were now doubtful if they should also join this Fallen King. While this might be a wrench in the works, William also believed it an opportunity. He and this Unique Lifeform had a shared enemy, after all.

Stretching a bit, he decided to get up from the slab of metal. He needed a few more skill upgrades and to make some more preparations before he was ready to make the final push to C-grade. He had already made so many preparations, and he would have nothing get in his way. Because while William knew little of what Master wanted, he did know that he and Master had one shared goal:

To overcome the karmic curse laid upon William by the one who had slain him.

CHAPTER 12

GOLDEN OPPORTUNITIES ONLY A MORON WOULD WASTE

Jake spent the rest of the World Congress chatting with a few people, including checking in with the Sword Saint to tell him that Reika was doing fine at the Order. He had expected Arthur to talk to him at some point, but it never happened. Jacob's dad had approached nearly every other faction but had stayed clear of Haven for some reason.

The last five minutes were spent chatting with Miranda as they set up a time for the next meeting. They had to plan it around Jake's lessons, but also Miranda's meetings and work. Scheduling was hard work.

As Jake just waited to be transported out, he mentally went over his near-future plans. Participating in the Path of Myriad Choices event was going to happen, so he needed another fragment before that. He also had a current list of classes in the Order he wanted to finish before heading back to Earth.

On that subject, he had to figure out how easy it was to travel between Earth and the Order, so he would have to chat with Villy about that. As things currently were, he couldn't stray far from Haven if he wanted to be able to return to the Order on short notice, and he naturally couldn't attend classes back on Earth or make use of other benefits the Order offered. Those teleportation gates in the Order were fancy, but not fancy enough to work cross-universe.

Hopefully, the Viper would have some convenient method to allow Jake easy travel. His ideal situation would include being able to both attend lessons he wanted and going to Earth whenever, while also being able to leave Haven to head out and hunt. He even had another plan.

Carmen had asked him to help her track down some family members, and while he did want to help, he had little confidence. So... wasn't Prima hunting a good opportunity? He could use the hunting trip to improve his tracking skill and get another Prima under his belt to complete the key. Win-win right there.

With those thoughts, Jake said his temporary goodbyes to Miranda and Lillian. Neil was still holed up with other space mages, with no one daring to interrupt their work.

Thus the World Congress ended, and Jake's vision flashed for a moment before he found himself back on the couch in the living room of the mansion.

"Eik!" Meira yelped, sitting right beside him and having jumped away the moment he teleported back in. She looked at him in fright before she finally calmed down and got off the couch. "Sir, I did not know you were returning so soon!"

"Pretty sure nobody knew how long it would be." Jake shrugged. To be fair, he had told Meira he would probably be gone for around ten hours, as that was how long the First World Congress had taken, so he was back four hours early.

As for why she was sitting on the couch? He wasn't sure. She usually resided in her own residence when preparing for lessons or meditating, and it wasn't like she had any work in the main mansions. Chores like cleaning weren't a thing in magical mansions.

"But it is good you are here," Jake said. "Things are ramping up a bit back on Earth, and I will need to return pretty soon, so I will be around less than before. I still plan on attending some of the lessons, but not as many. I just need to find a good way to travel back and forth first."

Meira seemed a tad disappointed but didn't voice her thoughts. "I shall make sure the mansion and the gardens remain in perfect condition so Sir can return at any time without discomfort."

It was a nice roundabout way for her to say that he should keep coming to the mansion. She also seemed to have one more thought. "Shall I also end my currently planned lessons?"

"No, of course not," Jake said, shaking his head. "Keep going as before; you have full access. Keep learning and improving as much as you can, okay? Don't worry; I will be sure to check up on you once in a while, and you are also to select new lessons yourself if you run out."

That was one thing Jake had learned... Meira borderline needed him to check up on her. It wasn't that she wouldn't do any work if he didn't, but that she seemed to have some odd mindset where if Jake didn't see and recognize her results, she didn't make any progress.

Meira nodded enthusiastically at his words, and Jake dismissed her with a look they both knew: He was about to talk to Villy, and she didn't want to be anywhere near when that happened due to the god's tendency to descend with mildly alcoholic beverages.

Once she was gone, Jake opened his mouth. "Hey, Vil—"

"Sup." A god popped into existence right in front of him, sitting on another couch. Two glasses filled with some weird blue liquid already sat on the coffee table between them.

"Done with the World Congress," Jake said casually as he gave Villy a quick breakdown of what had happened: The King's appearance, the vote for no World Leader, and then the second vote and the quest he'd received right after.

Villy silently listened and nodded along here and there. When Jake finished, the Viper took a quick sip of the drink, Jake mimicking his actions. It tasted a bit of strawberry despite the blue color.

"That no World Leader was elected makes sense, as it would be hard for your planet to select a single uniting leader without a huge war first," Villy said.

"Just to make sure, you aren't advocating I should take up the position?" Jake asked.

"No, quite the opposite. Doing so would be a waste of time and likely set you down a path where nobility holds a great impact. You would be required to participate in certain things, and while that isn't an issue currently, it would just be an annoyance down the line. You would waste a lot of time on things I know you have no interest in, and for what? To lead a small planet? Even if the influence expands and you take over the galaxy, so what? Become a god, and you can waltz into most empires, kill a god or two, and bam—you own a country larger than the budding kingdom on Earth instantly."

"Well, I still kind of care about the planet and have friends and family there," Jake said. "Abandoning them outright is not an option."

"So, just make that known and ensure whoever is in power knows you have that viewpoint, and that all hell will break loose if they go after anyone close to you. If push comes to shove, evacuate those you care about. Bring them here or somewhere else of your choosing if the hotly contested territory of Earth isn't worth the real estate. You could then even choose to make Earth an example of what happens when someone makes you an enemy. Quite a common tactic, that one. Or, you know, just put someone loyal or at least not antagonistic in charge."

"Sounds like you are suggesting I put in Miranda or the Fallen King," Jake said.

"Or most others, honestly," Villy said. "Not many on Earth view you as an enemy, and the only problem is that many of your friends and family belong to factions that are not exactly on friendly terms. But it is up to you; I have no skin in the game."

"Yeah, I guess I will figure it out." Jake nodded. "So, the system event?"

Villy turned a bit more serious. "This is not a normal event; just know that. The ability to change one's Path is not at all simple, and especially the opportunity to experience a secondary one is once-in-a-lifetime. Needless to say, I would heavily advise you to do it; only a moron wouldn't. However, I am also very interested in this Seat of the Exalted Prima."

"How so?" Jake asked. He had just assumed it was some place on Earth that would appear as part of the system event. Maybe some kind of hidden world like Yalsten?

"The Primas existed on Earth from the start," Villy explained. "A Watcher of Earth... This feels like part of something bigger. Moreover, I have heard some rumors that other factions have investigated it already and come up short. What little they have found points to this Exalted Prima not being something simple at all, and these Seats of the Exalted Prima are appearing on every planet with sufficient life across your entire universe."

"Is that abnormal? I would reckon system events appear for everyone."

"It is just the entire way it is designed." The Viper shook his head. "A Seat of something is often only the first stage. An introduction of what is to come."

"You sound like you have an idea what it may be all about?" Jake asked.

"I do, but I won't share more than I already have. Just focus on the events as represented and participate in all those you can. All of these system events are golden opportunities to a new universe, and missing even a single one is a huge waste."

"I have been thinking," Jake began. "How hard are titles to obtain?

I got one from the tutorial and one from the Treasure Hunt, all giving percentage stat increases, so won't someone who has done dozens of these events just be downright overpowered for their level?"

"They would be," the Viper agreed as he grinned. "Such as the Chosen sitting right in front of me. You underestimate how hard titles are to obtain. Every single chance to get one is an unmissable event. This even ignores the massive amount of Records associated with every title gained from these events."

"How rare are system events outside of system integrations?"

"Rare, but it, of course, varies. Some are small, some are large, some can be attended at all times, some are time-limited, but most are once-in-forever. Many titles do exist that just give minor benefits with no percentage increases, but perhaps a few stat points or other small bonuses. Some titles are gained by everyone, such as the evolution titles and the dungeon-related ones. Not that it matters much. As you are right now, you are well ahead of the curve, and if you just keep doing as you are right now, you will stay ahead."

"I do feel like my level has stagnated a little, though," Jake admitted. "Many people at the World Congress were catching up."

It was the truth. Especially someone like the King. Jake and the King had been at the same level only a few months ago, but now the Unique Lifeform had him beaten badly. Jake knew the reasons why, as he was shoring up weaknesses and "solidifying his fundamentals," as people kept saying, but it still felt bad.

"You haven't stagnated. Trust me. Stagnation is when you stop gaining levels at all, or it becomes difficult and takes a long-ass time for every one of them. Level-up rates also vary. You will come to experience that as you shore up your weaknesses and shortcomings, the levels will come to you faster and easier, and you won't hit a wall. Many of those who rush their levels will hit a wall or end up taking a worse evolution."

"So, you are saying the Fallen King will be in trouble?" Jake asked a bit teasingly.

"Maybe," Villy said, fully serious. "Even a Unique Lifeforms will reach walls and have to overcome challenges. Every evolution is difficult for them, and if they fail to live up to expectations, they will be stuck in their current grades forever. No one has an easy path to godhood; all need to struggle."

Jake sighed. "Guess I do feel a bit better now."

"Ah, but I would advise you to begin to get some levels under your belt. You are so far off stagnation as you are right now that it isn't a worry. While it is true that rushing might bite you in the ass, that will only happen to you if you overdo it. So I think it is time for you to make a push in levels. Meanwhile, I will work on a better solution for when you go to Earth and back here."

Jake didn't even have to ask. He had planned on asking for a better teleportation solution, but the Viper had clearly inferred this from the talk before.

"One that can work outside of Haven?" Jake asked.

"Well, that is the plan. Your little friend I blessed will need to help, though. I still need that monument as a beacon, so I guess it is time to put him to work again." Villy smirked.

"Wait, what has Chris even been doing all this time?"

"Eh, a bit of maintenance work, I guess? I don't really bother with him." The Viper shrugged. "Jake, after my return, I gave out Blessings in the millions. I don't keep track of every minor insignificant character."

"No, I am just saying, the guy was lost, and you put him on a Path," Jake argued. "Only feels right to take some responsibility."

"Then bring him to the Order once he is done with his tasks on Earth." Villy just shrugged again. "Here, he can find plenty of things to do. He still needs to remain in your little city for now, but in the future, just bring him along."

"Alright." Originally, he hadn't wanted to bring Chris as he went to do alchemy, but by now, he realized it wouldn't matter. Even as a Builder, Chris could easily find his place in the Order. "Now, with all of that settled, I guess it is time to get some alchemy done."

Jake only had lessons for the next week. After that, he hadn't booked more, as he had predicted the World Congress would lead to some changes. Even the rest of this week's lessons didn't really require his attendance. There were so many lessons that it didn't matter when Jake took them or even if he delayed. He also had infinite Academy Credits, so he didn't care about missing stuff.

"Just one piece of advice," Villy said. "Pay a visit to the Nalkar House."

"The vampires?" Jake asked as he remembered. "The High-tier Token."

He instantly took it out, and the Viper nodded.

[High-tier Alchemy Token of the Malefic Order (Legendary)] —
A token created by the Order of the Malefic Viper. This token represents a

deal made with the Nalkar vampire line to grant a set number of the
Nalkar Clan vampires membership to the Order, and includes a set
number of benefits. This token has never been turned in, and doing so
may lead to certain rewards. Gives off an aura that encourages growth in
toxic alchemical products.

"If you are going to do a leveling push, you need materials. You obtained that token yourself, so go exchange it with the Nalkar House. Trust me, they will be more than happy to." Villy finished with a mischievous smile.

Jake suddenly remembered the original plan to use this token when he originally entered the Academy as a cover of sorts. It turned out that was utterly unnecessary due to the plans the Viper had made and how the Order worked. Jake had just been swept up by everything and completely forgotten it. Reika had obviously forgotten, too, making him feel a bit better about it.

"Well, then, I guess it is time to visit a vampire house."

CHAPTER 13

VAMPIRE VISIT

Ah, vampires. If any race had been truly marginalized and suppressed throughout the history of the multiverse, it was them. The Risen and Holy Church both hated them, and most humans, elves, and other humanoids also weren't fans due to the racial skills they possessed.

For a good reason, too. Vampires had the ability to drain the lifeforce of others. In fact, they had to do this due to a massive drawback associated with their race: the lack of natural regeneration.

Pretty much all other races could live without any kind of sustenance until they died of age after reaching a certain grade. You could put Jake in a box, and he would keep living until he ran out of lifespan. If you took the same box and put a vampire in it, the vampire would eventually die due to starvation simply due to passive energy expenditure. They did have some racial skills to alleviate this drawback, such as the Eternal Slumber skill, but it wasn't perfect, and there were many times Eternal Slumber truly did turn out to be an eternal rest.

Now, the usual way to drain lifeforce for a vampire was through drinking blood. It was easy and straightforward, but it had the issue of harming the victim that was used as food quite a lot, and could easily result in a casualty. Even if the target didn't die, they would lose resources, and continued exposure to vampires would result in a temporary reduction in stats and prolonged periods of weakness. It was like Jake overdrawing his own body with Arcane Awakening, except far worse, and items or extremely skilled and specialized healers were often required to fix the ailment.

Jake had already learned all of this during his time in Yalsten, and he had now learned even more by reading a few basic tomes on vampires that were already present in his library. He had even called Meira, who had given him quite the negative input, if he said so himself.

"Vampires are always part of powerful families and really ward their legacies and power. They also buy a lot of slaves to use as food and simply for pleasure. The most positive outcome for a slave sent to a vampire house is the vampires liking the taste of their blood and deciding to use them for crafting blood potions. Well, they would also get really lucky and one day become a vampire themselves... if that is even considered a better fate."

So, yeah, Meira wasn't a fan. Yet she didn't seem alarmed or surprised when Jake said he would go and visit the Nalkar House. Jake learned the reason for this was quite simple: There was no way they would ever dare drink a single drop of his blood. No, not because he was blessed by the Viper or had a backer or something like that, but because drinking his blood would be what in the vampire world was known as a very bad time.

You see, it turned out that drinking from someone with highly toxic blood—courtesy of Blood of the Malefic Viper—wasn't the most pleasant experience. It involved a lot of corroded flesh and overall just made the entire action futile, as the vampire would lose more blood energy than they would gain.

The polar opposite of someone like Jake were slaves or servants bred to be used as food. Viewed as livestock or pets, these people were trained and nurtured all their lives to be valuable blood banks. It was somehow a recognized Path of the system, and they even had skills and professions focused on providing better and more tasty blood while not being susceptible to the weakness after a vampire used them.

For classes, they tended to still have one focused on combat, but nearly always of the physical variety for better stat distributions. These were also specialized and worked in synergy with vampires, making them potential soldiers.

The classification for the weaker and less-recognized ones was Blood Thrall. Blood Servant was then used for the more qualified and influential non-vampires, and finally, the Blood Disciples. Blood Disciples were those who had the potential of joining the main family and becoming vampires themselves.

Jake had decided to read a bit more up on modern vampirism, as he didn't wanna go in with knowledge many eras old from Yalsten. In fact, it was a bit funny to read the books from Yalsten and compare them with more modern ones. One difference was that in Yalsten, merely consuming health and herb-based potions was considered adequate to regenerate blood energy, but in modern times, consuming such potions was only done in combat.

The Path of vampirism was inherently tied to the consumption of blood and life, so to try and substitute it was to stray from that Path. Short term, it didn't matter, but long term, the effects on Records became significant. Maybe some vampires in Yalsten knew this, as they still kept live humanoids to drink from, but Jake knew only the elite were able to indulge in this. Keeping the fact that using health potions was harmful in the long run secret made sense if the supply was limited and used to quell dissent.

Now, needless to say, Jake wasn't a big fan of how vampires did things. He could totally understand why many races and factions distrusted or were outright antagonistic towards a race that literally required the subjugation and consumption of other humanoid races. The worst part was that it had to be humanoid. Beast blood and such only worked for vampiric beasts, and often the best blood was that of the race from which you'd transformed. Human-turned-vampire would do best drinking from a human, and so on and so forth.

At the same time, Jake also saw the vampires take some level of responsibility. One big thing was how few there were, even with their ability to transform others. The Risen more or less had an open-door policy for any living who wanted to become a Risen, but for vampires, it was far different. You had to be part of a family or be hunted down and slain, as they did not want rogue vampires out there. They cared a lot for lineage, and the only way for an outsider to become a vampire was to join the family as a powerful expert deemed worthy, or to be a Blood Thrall that managed to climb to Blood Disciple and then be gifted vampirism.

This did result in the average vampire being far more powerful than most other humanoid races, but it also meant they were more restrained and fewer in number. They were careful and wanted to avoid vampires causing trouble. The vampire families associated with the Order of the Malefic Viper were also incredibly loyal, with not a single family having left. Ever.

So, yeah, to conclude, the vampires were truly a mixed bag of evil nature, loyalty, and odd social dynamics where family was everything.

That entire thing where only the talented could become vampires also led to every natural-born vampire being the child of talented individuals. The weakest vampires were born at D-grade, the majority in C-grade, and the Nalkar House, as an example, had four S-grades and dozens of A-grades currently alive. This did not sound like a lot for a "faction," but one had to remember this was merely a faction connected to the Order and did not contain all Nalkar vampires that existed. They were also just one of six houses.

Anyway, their strength meant they had resources, and Jake needed resources. As he researched them, he also concluded that him going there and receiving benefits would help obscure who his backer was, maybe even making some factions assume the Nalkar House or a member from there backed him.

Getting there also wasn't as simple as merely taking a teleportation gate. Jake had to put in a request to be able to enter their area, as it was always sealed off, which had given him even more time to consider his approach once he got there.

It had only taken him half a day to hear back and get a positive affirmation that he could come, which also unlocked his token and allowed him to teleport to them. He got no other information besides an approval, and the second he got it, Jake headed off.

He didn't wear his fancy party clothes, instead staying in his good-old combat outfit. Jake didn't think he would get into a fight, but he wanted to be in what he felt most comfortable with.

Jake used the token on the teleportation wall in his mansion, and after a brief goodbye to Meira, he stepped through, finding himself in an entirely new area. Jake stepped out of a large rectangular monument in the middle of what looked like a city square, and he instantly felt hundreds of eyes land upon him.

Through his sphere, he spotted dozens of individuals staring at the newcomer. All of them were either elves, humans, a few beastkin, or some mixed races. Compared to everywhere else in the Order, there was a distinct lack of any scalekin. No vampires either.

All of the people around him looked relatively normal, and the entire place seemed like the outer area of a large medieval city. The only thing really distinguishing this place from anywhere else was the oddly familiar sky. It was red, and something that looked like the Blood Moon the Monarch of Blood had summoned using the divine artifact hung in the sky above.

Before Jake had any time to figure out where to go, a dark red swirl appeared in front of Jake as a humanoid form condensed from mist. It was a young man that looked about Jake's own age, with black hair and one of those slightly androgynous yet also often-considered-handsome faces. However, the most striking feature was the two red eyes that met Jake's.

[Vampire – lvl ???]

It was undoubtedly a C-grade, and Jake had a feeling that he was not a weak one. The vampire looked at Jake briefly before smiling, revealing his fangs. "Welcome to our humble abode, Hunter. I am Alcor, and I am to act as guide without you becoming too uncomfortable."

The moment the vampire had appeared, Jake felt all the people observing back away while bowing deeply. The vampire Alcor didn't even recognize their existence, just looking at Jake. The vampire also let his aura really go off, as if trying to assess Jake.

Jake smiled in response, not getting intimidated. "I would sure hope for a pleasant stay."

"Then it seems my job will be easier. Now, follow me; the Patriarch is ready to see you." Alcor opened his hand to reveal a rune of blood that then conjured a frame of red mist. The center of the frame took on a mirror-like surface before it condensed into a gate.

Jake looked at the spooky-looking mirror portal for a moment before stepping through. He felt no sense of danger from it, and quite frankly, the C-grade wouldn't need to use weird tricks if he wanted to kill Jake.

The other side of the portal revealed a giant, fully furnished hall, and Jake instantly felt dozens of auras far more powerful than his. At least twenty C-grades, and one that was far above anyone else present. Below a god... but not by far.

Jake turned and looked at the figure, who gave off an aura that seemed to almost tinge the very atmosphere around him red.

He looked a lot like Alcor, but was middle-aged and wore an old-timey suit. He had a well-kept beard and the same deep red eyes. The vampire was currently sitting on a large lounge chair with two barely dressed women standing at his side—an elf and a human, both C-grade.

"Hunter... What a peculiar name, but not one chosen out of pure hubris, I believe," the vampire said in a deep tone as he got up and began walking towards Jake. "All wish to be the hunter in any situation, but never the prey. And as you stand here, I come to believe that you do indeed adopt this trait, at least in concept. Immune to presences of those stronger... unwilling to recognize himself as potential prey before a predator. You are a hunter indeed, with all the bravado that comes with it, young Bloodline Patriarch."

Jake looked at the vampire, who stopped right in front of him. He was a good head taller than Jake and looked down at him, feeling Jake out just as his junior had done mere minutes ago.

"You seem to have done your research," Jake said, as he clearly didn't need to explain who he was.

When he had sent his message to the Nalkar House, he had only informed them that he had obtained an old item related to their lineage and the Order. He had not gone into any specific details, but it was evident that they had looked into him before inviting him over.

"I do appreciate the luck involved in me living through the phase of a new integration," the vampire said. "Always such an exciting time, bringing about change like never before. The Order itself has changed more than I thought possible with the return of the Malefic One." Taking a few steps back and walking towards his seat, he asked in a searching tone, "A truly momentous and equally surprising event, do you not agree?"

Jake felt the subtle waves of mental energy in the air. They were ever so slightly affecting him, but more than that, reading him. He only felt them due to how on-alert he was and his sphere, making it clear the vampire had no intention of revealing his actions.

Alcor, the young vampire, just stood back with his head lowered, same as everyone else.

"I don't believe many would call the return of a Primordial anything less than momentous," Jake answered.

"But not surprising?" the vampire said with an inquisitive look.

"Of course it was, but why would it be more surprising than other events? We natives of new universes know nothing of the rest of the multiverse upon integration. The mere existence of gods was a massive surprise." He was only speaking only the truth.

Something the vampire recognized as he nodded. "Perhaps as difficult as it is for me to recognize the possibility of a creature not living with the system." He sighed. "I am Fairleigh, current Patriarch of the Nalkar House. I do believe we skipped the formal introduction, did we not? Now, tell me, Hunter the hunter, what is it you bring from your nascent universe you claim is related to my lineage?"

Without any further ado, Jake pulled out the High-Tier Alchemy Token of the Malefic Viper.

Fairleigh looked at it deeply for a few moments before he sighed. "Such items truly belong in the annals of history. They come from a time when we vampires were on our way to becoming a truly multiversal force. Able to stand toe-to-toe with the Holy Church and the Risen." With a melancholic tone, he added, "Yet it is also a reminder that the Malefic One and his Order were our allies, even in those times. Where did you acquire it?"

"During a system event, I went to a world once known as Yalsten. An old, hidden world once inhabited and ruled by vampires. It had been destroyed due to its isolation, but the system does as the system does and brought back the Yalsten of many, many eras ago. I found this specific token in a vault set up by the Nalkar of Yalsten—one created with the hope of passing down some of their treasures. When I got the treasure, I was asked by a projection left behind to have positive inclinations towards the Nalkar, so here I am."

"A hunter that also keeps his word, it seems. Very well. If you treat me with honesty, I shall return the favor. Now, tell me, what is it you desire of us in exchange for an old relic of the past?"

CHAPTER 14

THE SENTIMENT OF VAMPIRES

J ake had many questions and doubts as he stood before the vampire. First of all, why was the Patriarch of the Nalkar Family there, and not just some lower-level leader? Heck, why was there a leader to begin with? Even if Jake assumed the vampires just placed a lot of importance on history and lineage, this still seemed like overkill.

Based on the line of questioning, it was possible they suspected him of being more than he represented himself as. The poking into his views on the Viper's return seemed very deliberate, as if they wanted him to reveal something, but even that made little sense. If Jake was the Chosen, would using lie-detection and trying to make him reveal his identity be a smart choice, not just one that would piss him off?

No matter the case, the Patriarch was willing to negotiate, and he did seem interested in the Alchemy Token.

"An old relic, perhaps, but still one that would be honored," Jake answered. "The Order of the Malefic Viper would undoubtedly adhere to its promise, making it more than just an interesting trinket."

"While true, we do not need such a token to enter the Order anymore. It was of a time when we Nalkar were spread all over the multiverse, and to enter the Order was a sign of success. Now, all the Nalkar able to join are members already, making the primary function of the token null."

Jake couldn't really argue with the fact that they could enter without the token, but he still knew the vampire wanted it. The current act of downplaying the value of the Alchemy Token was only proof to Jake that the Nalkar were interested. If they weren't, why bother and not just buy it cheaply, telling Jake to bugger off if he refused? At least, that was what Jake was banking on.

"In that case, perhaps it would be better to save it and find Nalkar unassociated with the Order," Jake said, sighing as he faked disappointment.

Fairleigh looked at Jake and smiled. "Please, let us stay in the realm of honesty. While that was no outright lie, we are both aware of the value such an item holds to my family. Even if it is not purely based on the benefits it offers, but the sentimental value. In fact... come, let me show you something."

Jake couldn't even resist; he was forcefully teleported and appeared within a massive chamber of sorts. On a second look, it reminded him more of a museum, with glass containers and complicated magic arrays guarding many mundane items spread throughout.

"Remembering history has always been important to our kin," Fairleigh explained. "Perhaps we merely enjoy living in the glory of the past, or maybe it is a way to not repeat our mistakes. Either way, we preserve and we collect. That token you hold may not be a treasure to most, but to us, it is invaluable."

Looking around, Jake saw a lot of rather, well, boring items. One area had a dining set sealed away, another section was filled with old paintings and pictures, and a third contained bookshelves stacked upon bookshelves with old books in them.

"We have items from all eras, even some from before our fall," he continued. "In fact, we value anything from before then, as it speaks of what once was, and the Records it contains matter. Perhaps not to you or anyone else not of our lineage, but to us, there is power in history." He then went over and pointed out what looked like a fountain pen. "This pen was used by a scholar of the Sixth Era to write letters back to his family. It managed to reach epic rarity back in the day but has returned to a mundane item after this long. Items such as that Alchemy Token have yet to return to mundanity but still contain such powerful Records, making them even more valuable."

Jake nodded along, unable to help but think about the ludicrous amount of resources expelled by that one chamber he was in. It was humongous, larger than any museum Jake had ever seen or heard of on Earth. At the same time, it was incredibly densely packed, with every single item sealed away with incredibly powerful and intricate formations. These formations were able to freeze time itself for the item and prevent them from turning to dust through the passage of time.

"Tell me, do you find our obsession with the past foolish?" the vampire finally asked him.

"No, not really." Jake shrugged. He had never been the type himself to collect old antiques or care much for cultural inheritances, but he knew it was a perfectly normal hobby. "Even on my planet before the system arrived, we collected pieces of history, families had heirlooms they warded with their lives, and I know of at least one old man who picked up an old heirloom his clan possessed and turned it into a monstrous weapon."

"But you seem to not personally share the sentiment?"

"No." Jake shook his head. "While I do understand placing sentimental value on objects, I rarely do it. Not that I entirely avoid it... I still have the first potions I ever crafted stowed away, and all the equipment I wear I earned myself one way or another. I do value these items more than they are necessarily worth, and value some more than others, but that is due to the story of how I got them."

The vampire nodded. "An understandable view for a hunter. Now, tell me, what kind of compensation are you seeking in return for the token? It cannot merely be the extra alchemical ingredient associated with enrollment. If it was, you would have no need to come here."

"I am in need of alchemical ingredients of higher value, most specifically ones of the hemotoxic variety," Jake said. Vampires were damn good at Hemotoxins. A massive surprise that vampires, wielding blood magic and using blood energy, were good at blood poisons.

"And?" Fairleigh asked.

Jake took out his second item, his necklace, by un-fusing it from his body and holding it up. "I need this improved. I know the Nalkar family has long been part of the Order, so I assume I am correct when I believe you can do this?"

[Prodigious Alchemist's Necklace of Holding (Epic)] - An amulet awarded to a prodigious young alchemist upon completion of a trial. An ornate creation of high craftsmanship made of metal attuned to the space affinity, holding a spacegem in place. Allows the user to store items in a small pocket dimension found within the gem. Due to the nature of the gemstone used, living, non-sentient entities can be stored without harmful side effects in temporal suspension. **Enchantments:** *Alchemist's Spatial Storage.* **+25 Wisdom.**

Requirements: Soulbound.

It was the first piece of epic equipment Jake had gotten, and probably still one of his best items to date. In terms of sheer usefulness and convenience, it was at the top, as nothing beat spatial storages. However, Jake was also acutely aware that the item had fallen off big time. The stats it gave had been great when Jake was level 26, but now? Now they were irrelevant.

He could probably have gotten a better spatial storage, even one that featured the same Alchemist's Spatial Storage enchantment. Maybe not as good, but at least close. It had to be noted that each person could only hold one spatial storage item under normal circumstances, so Jake couldn't have swapped for another without choosing to "unbind" his Prodigious Alchemist's Necklace of Holding. Now, even if it was Soulbound, this wouldn't destroy the item but just make it completely inert. Of course, it would still be Soulbound, as one couldn't get rid of that connection without breaking the item altogether.

So, yeah, maybe him holding onto it was for purely sentimental reasons. Jake had to admit he had briefly considered whether upgrading the item was even worth it, but...

"How exquisite," Fairleigh said as he looked at the necklace. "Truly ancient craftsmanship, incredible attention to detail, and that stone used... I am amazed someone would choose to give that to someone of such a low grade."

Even if the vampire could not see the description, he was still an ancient vampire in S-grade. He looked at it a bit more before nodding. "Finding a suitable crafter should be possible; we have some very talented jewelers among our ranks. Do note that unlocking the full potential of the gem will not be possible with your current strength and the necklace being Soulbound."

Jake nodded. "Just seeing it improved is all I hope for. Also, just to check, I want to make sure there are no risks of breaking it if I choose to improve it?"

Fairleigh smiled as he chuckled. "If I can find a D- or C-grade capable of breaking that item, we would have our new Patriarch or Matriarch in the making. You seem to not fully comprehend. That item was made by someone far above C-grade, and was then directly modified by the system to be in its current form, sealing the Records and power within. An incredibly rare thing that is not worth doing.

These items can also only be obtained from system events. Well, in your case, I assume it was a tutorial Challenge Dungeon?"

Jake nodded once more. "Yeah, I was lucky to find one associated with alchemy and got this at the end."

"Just alchemy?" the vampire asked inquisitively.

"More or less," Jake said, shutting down the topic.

Fairleigh smiled again as he took out a token. A moment later, he dispelled it again. "The young lad who brought you here has been tasked with fetching a suitable jeweler I have in mind. Now, tell me, you went to a realm known as Yalsten? I must confess it is not a name I am familiar with, but we had many such worlds back then, and if it was hidden as you claim, it was customary to keep it secret to limit leaks. Did you happen to obtain any valuables from there besides this token? Ones related to our race?"

That was when Jake remembered. During all of his fights with the Counts of Blood, Jake had entered their chambers. All of them had been preserved and filled to the brim with valuable-looking and expensive objects. Furniture, paintings, candle holders, chandeliers—pretty much all of the fancy stuff the Yalsten vampires loved. For some reason, Jake had decided to just gather all of the fanciness, because why the hell not? He'd needed furniture for back home, and it had looked good. Now, that seemingly random choice appeared to have been an unexpectedly wise one.

Jake waved his hand, and a dining table appeared in front of him along with eight matching chairs.

Fairleigh looked at it, and his eyes opened wide. "This... Did you obtain this in Yalsten, too?"

"Yeah," Jake answered. "It was in a chamber of sorts that looked to have been preserved."

"This dining set dates back dozens of eras... As old as the token?"

"It is at least from before the Eighth Era," Jake said. Based on the Monarch of Blood, the Viper had not yet gone into isolation when Yalsten fell, and Jake knew Villy had done that during the Seventh Era. So, naturally, this item had to stem from before then.

"Truly?" Fairleigh asked. "I will have to have a chronomancer confirm the exact age, but we would be more than willing to buy this set if you are correct. We would naturally pay handsomely."

"I got more," Jake said, not wanting to miss the opportunity.

"Oh?" Fairleigh exclaimed, letting a bit of excitement leak out. "Can you show me?"

Jake looked around and noticed how most of the floor space was already filled. "We're gonna need a bigger room."

Vilastromoz was busy as always, multitasking and doing all sorts of important things. Having your mind split and being in many places at once was helpful, but he nearly always kept one part of himself reserved on observation duty, also known as Jake-watching.

However, today he wasn't alone. And no, it was not Duskleaf visiting either.

"Katherine, I do wonder why you don't simply choose to reveal your presence to your kin," the Viper said to the woman sitting with him, sipping on a wineglass filled with a red liquid a bit too red to be wine.

"I will in due time, but not now," the vampire goddess said. "I am more intrigued by your choice of Chosen. I have been observing, but so far, I truly cannot see why you have picked him. His Bloodline does seem peculiar and powerful, but even if it was utterly monstrous, I see little reason to bless a lowly F-grade as you did and not wait for him to at least reach B- or A-grade. The chance of him dying without giving a return on investment would be far lower if that was the case."

Vilastromoz turned to her with a raised brow. "Are you questioning my decision-making skills?"

"No, of course not; I am merely perplexed and unable to comprehend the reasoning behind the choice," she said, quickly backtracking —and failing to realize the reaction she'd just had was a big part of the reason Vilastromoz liked Jake.

He would have remarked that the Viper did have a shitty track record and probably even included a self-deprecating joke about how the Viper had fucked up by blessing him.

"Keep trying to comprehend. I personally fail to comprehend your sense of secrecy, but then again, I guess you would prefer not to get tracked." The Viper shrugged.

Katherine, also known as the True Ancestor of the Nalkar lineage, was the most powerful vampire of the Nalkar line. Sanguine had experimented much to make different kinds of vampires, and Katherine was the first vampire of the Nalkar line that had ascended to godhood, giving her the title of True Ancestor. She wasn't actually the first Nalkar vampire, but many believed she was. It was the kind of rumor that appeared and that no one bothered to correct.

She had left during the Seventh Era to protect her kin elsewhere, as those that remained in the Order had been safe due to the presence of Snappy. Back then, they had not been official parts of the Order, but more like the local branches of Dragonflights. Closely tied to the Order, but not members. Something that, in retrospect, had probably turned out to be a mistake. Once Sanguine fell, the vampires had become unassociated with any factions and unable to decide on joining one, instead trying to stay independent. By the time they'd realized they needed to be part of something bigger, Vilastromoz had already entered isolation.

Today, Katherine and many other vampires, including the closest thing the vampires had to a pantheon, now resided in a hidden realm that not even Vilastromoz knew the location of.

The Holy Church and Risen didn't know either, as if they did, the Viper reckoned they would have already attacked. These vampires had nothing to do with the Order and were not at all under its protection.

This led to the question of why Katherine had visited, and the old snake god had his suspicions. A suspicion that would prove correct as the vampire spoke.

"What are the future plans of the Malefic One? I am aware that the True Ancestor of the Balnar lineage has already made contact, but so far, he is tight-lipped. We are aware of the movements that have recently been happening, and the council has had discussions but has yet to—"

"Ask the real question," Vilastromoz interrupted as he looked at her sharply.

"Is the stance of the Malefic One the same as it was back then?"

"Have I ever said otherwise? When did my word stop mattering?"

He smiled as Katherine finally asked, "Will the Malefic One allow the six clans to fully join the Order of the Malefic Viper?"

"Five clans," Vilastromoz corrected. "The Balnar have already sworn fealty."

Katherine looked surprised before she stood up and bowed. "Then may the Nalkar be the second clan to do so. I shall return to the council and relay the information."

"Just a second," Vilastromoz said as he raised a hand. "How many of you are there now?"

"A hundred and eleven, including us six True Ancestors," she answered.

"Not bad... More than one an era." Vilastromoz nodded. "Bring them all before me, and we can continue this conversation."

Katherine nodded enthusiastically. "As you command."

Vilastromoz watched as she disappeared and smiled a bit to himself. Yet another batch of gods was ready to join him. He knew the vampires had struggled for many eras and had latched onto him as a lifeline. In fact, he felt like the entire multiverse was much more consolidated into enormous factions than back in the day. So, perhaps it wasn't too stupid for the Order to also become more than it had always been. To truly expand it and make it into a multiversal force to be reckoned with. A faction that controlled territory and dominated more than just a few small pieces of land spread throughout the multiverse for their small branches.

Adding nearly every vampire left in the universe to his faction would be a good start. Of course, the Holy Church, Risen, and probably a few dozen—if not hundreds—of factions wouldn't approve. This was why no faction had ever allowed them to join them despite their relative strength.

Sadly for them, Vilastromoz didn't really give a shit.

CHAPTER 15

VAMPIRE HOARDERS

"This one too?" a large vampire asked as he lifted a coat hanger very carefully.

"Definitely that one," Fairleigh said, nodding.

"Where to stash the tablecloths?" another vampire inquired.

"Set the tables like they used to be on the seventeenth picture."

"Understood," the attendant said as she began carefully using telekinesis to move the tables and chairs into the exact positions shown in some old picture.

A second vampire joined in only to double-check all the dimensions and distances were absolutely correct. A third came to put down the forks, knives, smaller forks, tiny spoons, large spoons, medium spoons, and other kinds of different and utterly superfluous fancy-ass tableware.

Jake just stood back and watched all of this happen. At first, he had just thought the vampires were eccentric collectors of old items, but by now, he realized... they were just straight-up hoarders. Organized hoarders with relatively fastidious taste, but hoarders nonetheless.

Fairleigh, the S-grade Patriarch, even personally chose to oversee as the many vampires worked to recreate a dining hall exactly as it was shown in one of the pictures Jake had found. It wasn't even something from a painting, but a picture in a book on proper table manners.

Not that Jake chose to complain. In fact, he was currently just waiting for the jeweler to arrive along with his agreed-upon goods being collected and prepared for him. The Alchemy Token had somehow ended up not even being that big of a deal. The paintings of old vampires from Yalsten, the books from the library telling their history, and the many random items Jake had swiped turned out to be far more valuable in the eyes of the vampires.

The reason for this was ultimately simple: The Alchemy Token was not truly an item of the Nalkar vampires, but merely a gift they'd received from the Order. It was an item nearly identical to many tokens still created today, and had little to do with the culture and history of the vampiric race.

Jake couldn't help but consider what would have happened if he had shown up with the divine artifact the Sword Saint had gotten. In some ways, he was actually happy he hadn't gotten that necklace, as he feared the level of insanity these vampires would show upon seeing it.

The negotiation process had already been a lot as it was, and Jake had no idea if he'd gotten scammed. Though, to be fair, he felt like he was the scammer, selling off old furniture and mundane items he had no use for and would probably have just given away or used for a fun-time bonfire or something.

After looking on a bit longer, Fairleigh finally turned to him. "I just got word the crafter is ready to help with the necklace. Are you prepared to leave, or do you wish to stay and observe the recreation some more?"

"Upgrading the necklace takes priority," Jake said, not having the heart to tell the ancient vampire that he really didn't want to see a group of powerful vampires set a table as if their lives depended on it.

"Very well," the Patriarch said, looking only slightly disappointed as he teleported the both of them.

They appeared in what looked like an area of the city Jake had first arrived in. Except this place was clearly part of the commercial district, as Jake stood before a massive shop.

The C-grade vampire that had initially brought him to the Patriarch was already there waiting. The Patriarch gave the young lad a nod before he teleported away, leaving Jake with the vampire called Alcor.

The vampire seemed a lot more respectful now than the last time they'd met as he motioned for Jake to follow. "Please follow me; the mistress has already prepared all the suitable materials for the crafting session."

Jake nodded as he was led into the shop. He noticed how the street was devoid of people, and Alcor clearly noticed his confusion. The only people he saw were himself, Alcor, and a single other person currently within the shop.

"We cleared out the area in preparation for your visit so as not to have any of the livestock gawking during the crafting session or causing disturbances," Alcor explained nonchalantly.

"Livestock, huh," Jake commented.

"I am aware they can be annoying, but sadly, they are necessary." Alcor sighed, clearly not understanding Jake's comment.

"You know," Jake said just as they entered the shop, "I once fought what happens when livestock reach a breaking point and get the power to resist and fight back. It doesn't turn out pretty for the oppressors."

He was clearly talking about the Minotaur Mindchief. The circumstances back then had been very different, and Jake would argue the vampires were running a far greater risk. Then again, what the hell did he know? The vampires had managed to persist for eras.

"I think it can turn out quite well," he heard a female voice say. "I didn't kill anyone when I received the gift. I did have a few who needed to be put in their place, but now we are all family."

Jake looked over and saw a female vampire standing there to welcome them. She had long black hair, the usual red eyes, and the equally commonplace beauty he had come to expect from all vampires. In fact, all vampires he had ever seen took the whole "look better with every evolution" concept to an entirely new level.

Not that she wasn't more than just pretty to look at. While she didn't feel that powerful, Jake still sensed a strong aura, making him relatively certain right off the bat that she was a pure crafter. One at the cusp of C-grade.

[Vampire – lvl 199]

As for the words she spoke?

"I take it you were a Blood Disciple?" Jake asked her.

"Correct," she said, clearly showing pride at that fact.

It was probably for a good reason, too, if she had managed to get recognized and gain access to vampirism through her own efforts. Considering she was the jeweler Fairleigh had brought Jake to see, he didn't doubt that she had been recognized and given "the gift" through merit.

"This is Mistress Rubylake, one of the most talented jewelers of this generation," Alcor introduced her. "And yes, she was formerly a human but has since ascended."

"Ascended is a strong word," Jake commented again as he shook his head.

Insulting the jeweler he wanted to help him probably wasn't a good idea, so he cut it out there. Instead, he just took out his necklace and presented it to the woman called Rubylake. Jake assumed it was some kind of title, or maybe just the naming convention of where she came from.

"This is the necklace in question," Jake said, noticing her eyes were already trained on it.

"May I look at it closer?" she asked. "I only got descriptions, so I will need to inspect it myself to see if I believe I can do the job."

Jake nodded and handed it over. He felt his connection to it slightly fade as it left contact with his body, making him unable to use the spatial storage. He still had the stats, but he innately knew he needed to touch the necklace to use the storage.

Rubylake looked at the necklace as she took out some weird box. She placed it inside and began infusing blood energy into it. She looked almost in a trance as she sometimes nodded, other times frowned, and finally looked elated.

"This item... it qualifies!" she said with extreme delight.

Alcor, standing with Jake, also smiled from ear to ear. "Congratulations, Mistress."

"Qualifies for what?" Jake asked, more than a little confused. He assumed it was good, but he was more wondering why she didn't say that *she* qualified, but that his necklace qualified for some mystical objective.

"Apologies," Rubylake said. "This item qualifies for my Evolutionary Quest, and I just failed to hold back my excitement. I have been looking for an opportunity for a few years while making preparations for this day."

"Villy... what the hell is an Evolutionary Quest, and please don't tell it is something incredibly basic and common knowledge I have somehow entirely missed?" Jake quickly asked the Viper mentally, as he had a strong feeling asking the vampires would make him look like a moron.

"Gotta do some questing to advance to C-grade along with usual requirements. This is indeed pretty basic knowledge—so basic that no one actually bothers writing about it—and the quests are individualized, so it isn't like telling people about it matters. You will learn more about it later, so stop worrying your pretty little head about it and instead get that bling upgraded. Maybe she can turn it into a giant gold chai—"

Jake began ignoring Villy as he followed suit in congratulating her, not wanting to look like an ignorant idiot. Or a rude one. "Congratulations are in order, then."

"Thank you. It is still a bit premature, as I have yet to succeed, but I have a high level of confidence. Now, do you have any questions? Don't worry—there are no requirements of you besides allowing me to modify the Soulbound item."

Jake nodded in acknowledgment. He was aware that, as it was a Soulbound item, he had to give consent before any modification could take place. He was ultimately still the master of the item, and he merely allowed another outside force to modify and hopefully improve it.

"How long will it take?" Jake finally asked.

"I should be able to do it within a day, maybe one and a half. I have made too many preparations, and the magic circle is already fully charged... If I take any longer, it will likely result in failure."

"What are you planning on doing, if I might ask?" Jake further asked. "If you won't answer, it is fine. Trade secrets and all that."

"No, I will gladly explain. My primary objective is to awaken the Space Heart—the name of this type of Spacegem. Currently, only a small part of the full space is utilized, and its powers are generally sealed. Once I awaken it, I can pull on the Records and energy to forge and awaken latent energy in the rest of the necklace, and while there will probably be no cosmetic changes, the item will improve significantly if I succeed. Just so you are aware, I aim for a legendary rarity for my own quest. It is not a true craft, but to perform an upgrade at this level of complexity should qualify."

Jake nodded in understanding. "I assume you will want peace and quiet during the crafting process?"

He knew he tended to want to be left alone while crafting.

"That would be preferable. However, I will need you to still stay close. There is a waiting room next door you can choose to stay in, but as long as you stay within a kilometer or so, it should be fine."

Nodding once more, Jake decided to just go next door and wait for something else: his alchemy ingredients.

He said his goodbyes and was led by Alcor into the building next door. It was a large lounge room with not a single other person in sight. There was still no one within his sphere either. As he was next door, he could still see into the store of the jeweler. She had gone down to the cellar and activated a lot of wards and formations to hide, but of course, none of that mattered to Jake's Bloodline-powered Sphere of Perception.

Jake saw her carefully place the necklace on an altar as she prepared several ingredients in a magic circle around it. He looked on a bit more before he stopped, choosing to respect her privacy. He also had no idea what she was doing.

Jake spent the next ten minutes or so in meditation. Alcor was not talkative, either, just quietly standing in a corner with his eyes closed, waiting. After those ten minutes, Jake spotted movement outside the building as he saw Fairleigh appear, holding two crystals in his hands.

Fairleigh entered as Jake looked up, identifying the two crystals before the old vampire walked over and had a chance to speak.

[Alchemist's Bloodgem Spatial Storage (Rare)] – A gem containing a spatial storage that is especially suited to any blood-affinity herbs and natural treasures. The energy of the gem is slowly leaking, giving it a severely limited lifespan.

[Memory Crystal (Common)] – A crystal containing infused information.

One was a gem no doubt containing all the herbs and such they had agreed upon. The other was something a bit more unexpected, and Fairleigh quickly explained, "I took the courtesy of creating a Memory Crystal from the input of a talented alchemist from the family who is specialized in Hemotoxins. It contains his insights into the agreed-upon materials as well as some tips and tricks. I hope this addition is a welcome one." He smiled. "And, of course, the ingredients you requested. It took quite a dive into the gardens to find them all, especially in such quantities and all suitable for D-grades, but we managed to do so. I once more took a bit of liberty and placed them within this Bloodgem for you to transport the ingredients while making sure they lose none of their potency. It is far worse than a true Alchemical Spatial Storage, but it will make do. Just know it will only last a few more decades."

Jake nodded in acknowledgment. "I have no plans of taking that long before using the ingredients. The crystal is also more than welcome." The vampires had treated him pretty nicely so far, even if they did have some inherent cultural issues.

"Now, I would offer you one more thing, but I guess I already know your answer?" Fairleigh asked in a not-very-hopeful tone.

"No, I have no interest in becoming a vampire," Jake said, shutting it down.

"A shame. Truly a shame. You would fit right in." Fairleigh sighed but was not truly disappointed. Clearly he'd had low or no expectations to begin with.

"Why would you reject such an offer?" Alcor suddenly butted in, genuine confusion in his voice. "Would it not be purely better? It would allow you to focus solely on either a class or a profession without sacrificing strength, solidifying your Path."

"Child," Fairleigh said as he turned to Alcor. The young vampire froze in fear as Jake felt a bit of bloodlust leak out of the old vampire. "When a gift is rejected, you graciously accept the other party's decision. Anything else is unacceptable. Do I make myself clear?"

"Yes... Patriarch," Alcor said, barely getting the words out as he looked like he could barely breathe.

"Temper your arrogance," Fairleigh said with a sigh. "We vampires are not necessarily superior. No enlightened race is. For all, vampirism is a choice, and if the Hunter does not deem vampirism part of his Path, we should never claim to know better or falsely believe ours more powerful."

"I understand," Alcor repeated as he stared down at the ground. Jake, however, felt that the guy didn't entirely agree.

"Enough of that," Fairleigh said as he smiled again and sent the crystal and Bloodgem floating towards Jake.

Jake caught them both and didn't hold back as he inspected the spatial storage gem, a large smile forming on his lips.

He was about to have a *bloody* good crafting session.

CHAPTER 16

HEART OF THE ALCHEMIST

Jake had asked for alchemical ingredients with hemotoxic properties as well as those with blood affinity. Most blood-affinity ingredients were easily translated into products with hemotoxic properties, making it an ideal material to use. The other function of the blood affinity was in making Blood Potions, which vampires very much enjoyed. As well as quite a lot of beasts that could actually use them as natural treasures to gain experience and levels.

This led to the vampire clans cultivating these herbs in spades. Hemotoxin was also a preferred poison of the vampires, as it synergized with many of their skills. An ability that thinned the blood of a foe and made it more difficult to control one's vital energies just worked incredibly well with blood magic for rather obvious reasons.

So Jake had high expectations. He had asked for the good stuff, but had not been overly specific besides mentioning a few herbs he knew he wanted. Jake was not foolish enough to believe Fairleigh wouldn't know better than him, and Jake was also confident in the vampire not wanting to scam him too much. Even if he scammed Jake a little, it would be fine, as Jake already felt like a scammer after pawning off so much useless shit from his spatial storage.

However, when he peeked into the gem, he realized he had indeed miscalculated: Those damn vampires valued their old antiques more than he had believed. There were fifteen different kinds of herbs and natural treasures, with six of them at rare rarity or above. All of them were exactly the kinds he had hoped, and more surprisingly, Jake actually knew about all of them from prior research and the classes he had taken on Hemotoxins. Well, it probably shouldn't be that surprising, considering the vampires were a major supplier of Hemotoxin materials for the Order.

Scanning through these six high-value items, Jake was very pleased.

[Crimsonwood Ash (Rare)] – Ash of a burned Crimsonwood. Even if much of the potency has been lost, the ash still contains some qualities of the Crimsonwood. If the ash is inhaled, it will enter the bloodstream and cause internal damage as it binds with the blood of its victim, making it incredibly difficult to dispel. If too much is inhaled, the individual will combust, spreading even more ash.

Jake had read a lot about Crimsonwood Trees. They were an entire categorization of trees, but this one came from one of the more valuable types. The Blood-Combusting Crimsonwood was a tree that quite literally set itself on fire to spread its deadly ash and kill everything within huge areas around it. The weaker ones could level entire ecosystems, while the more powerful Blood-Combusting Crimsonwoods were known to wipe out all Vitality-based life in whole solar systems. Of course, the materials of such a tree would be used by A or maybe even S-grades.

The ash that was left over and found close to the trunk of the tree was rare by itself, and as far as Jake knew, any part of the actual tree would be ancient or maybe even legendary rarity. However, it made no sense to kill these trees, as the ash itself was valuable. Jake assumed the vampires had a few of these stashed away and fed them beasts or something like that to make them self-combust and leave behind ash. It was good stuff.

The next three were all also good stuff but considered relatively commonplace. Yet they did still stand out due to the high quality and rarity of the specimens with which Jake had been provided.

[Spikestalk Root (Rare)] – The root of a Spikestalk. Spikestalks are plants that hide under the earth and strike any that get too close with blood-draining spikes. This blood energy is then deposited into the roots, where it is further refined into a liquid containing large amounts of life affinity. Has many alchemical uses.

[Bloodshade Flower (Rare)] – A flower growing in the soil of the freshly slain. This flower has absorbed large amounts of blood from

Vitality-based lifeforms and has evolved to what it is today. To better feed, it exudes pollen that will make any Vitality-based lifeform it comes into contact with bleed from any orifice. Has many alchemical uses and a potent hemotoxic nature.

[Red Moss (Rare)] – *Mutated moss that has become red due to being in an environment with potent blood-affinity mana. The energy within has potent hemotoxic qualities but can also be used in restorative potions. Consuming the Red Moss in small quantities will temporarily grant resistance to Hemotoxins, while large amounts will lead to an overload, causing hemorrhage.*

They all more or less did as their descriptions said but had no interesting qualities beyond that. The only reason these were even rare rarity was due to how old they were and the amount of energy each of them contained. Red Moss, as an example, was just mutated Green Moss and was relatively simple to make if one had a cave with arrays to constantly pump in blood mist or placed it among many Bloodshade Flowers. The stalk was just one of many carnivorous plants that liked to eat people. This one just did it by draining all their blood, a bit like the Indigo Fungus Jake had fought so long ago.

These were all the rare herbs Jake had gained. Next up was an item that wasn't a herb but was nevertheless extremely valuable.

[Crystalized Blood Essence (Epic)] – *The crystalized Blood Essence of a powerful C-grade vampire. Contains an incredibly potent blood-affinity energy. Consuming the Crystalized Blood Essence as a vampire will restore Blood Energy, while if any other race consumes it, it will act as a Hemotoxin. Has many alchemical uses.*

One thing that was common for all living creatures was that natural treasures would often be condensed when they died. For vampires, it was often their heart and their blood, and for someone like Jake, it would probably be his eyes that would be infused with his Records. The Crystalized Blood Essence was one such treasure as it had come from a dead C-grade vampire.

There were some discussions to be had about using the blood of a brethren to do alchemy, but the vampires had no qualms. In fact, they viewed it as respectful to make use of the corpse of someone who had died. Across the multiverse, many who closed in on their deaths made wills concerning what they wanted to be done with their bodies. Thinking about it, it was a bit like organ donation before the system.

Anyway, this Crystalized Blood Essence was a great material and could be mixed into most Hemotoxins to make them better. Each Crystalized Blood Essence could also be used dozens of times in crafts before it would run out of energy, making it suitable for alchemy.

The final item was the most interesting, and the one Jake knew the least about.

[Crimson Dawn Lotus (Epic)] — The lotus spawned after a Crimson Dawn. Contains incredibly potent blood-affinity energy mixed with time-affinity mana. Has many alchemical uses but is incredibly volatile.

Blood and time. An incredibly potent combo, and Jake was a bit surprised this had even been included, considering he hadn't asked for it. He had briefly come across the mention of Crimson Dawn Lotuses during one of the lessons, but it was only related to how they only spawned during a Crimson Dawn. Jake had no idea what a Crimson Dawn was.

Luckily, he had a vampire right there with him.

"What is the Crimson Dawn?" Jake asked Fairleigh.

The old vampire smiled a bit as he pointed upwards to the huge red celestial object hanging above. "What you see above is an ancient artifact crafted by the True Ancestor of the Nalkar Clan many eras ago. It allows vampires to not feed as much and empowers us in every way while under its crimson light. However, as with most objects, it does not hold infinite energy. Every millennium, there is a single month where the Blood Moon is down, and we have to perform a ritual to reawaken it. Once the ritual has been performed, it will rise again, bringing about a Crimson Dawn as its light washes over our lands. These lotuses only bloom during a Crimson Dawn, so they are quite valuable. The ones you have are from three hundred years ago but have been fully preserved."

Jake nodded in understanding. "Thank you for the trade."

"No, thank you. I am not blind to us taking advantage of you by having a young talent use your necklace as an opportunity to complete her Evolution Quest even after you have given us so much. I hope the alchemical ingredients are at least acceptable, and please, do not hesitate to visit again. I have permanently unlocked your token to allow you access." Fairleigh smiled. "Now, if there isn't anything more, I sadly have other responsibilities to attend to."

"Alright. I may stop by again at some point," Jake said, nodding as the vampire disappeared in a puff of red mist.

Only a few seconds passed before the other vampire in the room asked, in a rather odd tone, "How do you do it?"

"Do what?" Jake asked, confused.

"Speak to the Patriarch so casually," Alcor said, seeming genuinely interested. "You show such little care and—no offense—lack decorum and grace. Is it truly to do with your Bloodline? Something about being a hunter?"

"Something like that. It allows me to ignore the suppression caused by their presence."

"Even so," Alcor protested, "do you not realize your way of acting could be viewed as disrespectful? That if you cause someone of such a higher status even the mildest level of annoyance, they could end your life with a touch... no, a single thought?"

"Sure I do." Jake just shrugged.

"Then why act with such... arrogance?"

"Why not?" Jake just smiled. "What's the worst they can do—kill me? Man, you really think too little of those more powerful. Just don't be an outright dick, and things should be fine, and if they kill you due to being some butthurt cry-babies, well, it is what it is, and I will at least go out like a champ."

Alcor just stared at Jake in disbelief as he grinned without elaborating. What he said was once more the truth with some tiny modifications. Jake didn't solely rely on being lucky to not meet a powerhouse that would kill others just for looking them in the eyes. He relied nearly solely on his intuition and sense of danger.

If he did meet someone who would go apeshit if Jake treated them as an equal, he would probably get a sense for it and just keep his damn mouth shut. Of course, if the person began acting like a pompous asshole, then Jake could potentially risk failing to hold himself back and get swatted into the river of reincarnation—or, more accurately, the Truesoul Recycling Center, if Jake's understanding of life after death was correct.

Anyway, considering Alcor just sat back, Jake decided to inspect the Memory Crystal for some advice and tips on how to use his newly obtained ingredients. Once he infused energy into it, he felt a wave of information enter his head, and he quickly became aware that Fairleigh had heavily downplayed it. The one who had infused knowledge into the crystal was an A-grade alchemist who specialized in Hemotoxins and had not held back at all with including tips relevant for a D-grade.

Jake dove right in and began devouring the information. At some point, he felt a small poke on his soul, and knowing it was Rubylake needing his approval to improve the necklace, he just accepted and kept studying. Before going to the vampires, Jake had planned on taking a few more lessons on Hemotoxins and some other minor subjects, but as he sat there going through it, he realized that wasn't necessary. At least, not for now.

The knowledge within focused on utilizing only the fifteen alchemical ingredients Jake had received. It was a hyper-specialized course on making basic hemotoxic potions with a whiff of an improved version Jake was very interested in attempting.

He even considered if he shou—

"Hunter, I believe the mistress is done," Alcor suddenly said. However, even before Jake heard him, he was thrown out of his state of concentration. Something had changed.

He felt a connection to something just on the other side of a few walls and down in a cellar. At the same time, he felt like he had just leveled up many times, as he experienced an influx of stats through that same connection. Rubylake had succeeded.

Without even thinking, Jake held out his hand, and on his palm, the necklace appeared, looking just like before. It was still made of platinum-like metal with the green gem faceted on a beautiful chain. The design was relatively simple, but Jake felt it practically humming with power. He had even somehow managed to summon it to himself through its innate space magic and his Soulbound connection.

Jake saw Rubylake rush out of the cellar through his sphere, and before she had even made it to the waiting room, Jake had inspected his new necklace.

*[**Heart of the Alchemist (Legendary)**] — Once merely proof you were a prodigy, now even more as you have shown you have the heart of an alchemist. An ornate creation of high craftsmanship made of metal attuned to the space affinity, holding a Space Heart Gem in place. Innate power still dwells within the Records of the necklace yet to be uncovered. Allows the user to store items in a medium-sized pocket dimension found within the gem. Due to the nature of the gemstone used, living, non-sentient entities can be stored without harmful side effects in temporal*

suspension. Allows the user to directly deposit beneficial products into their own bodies with a slightly improved effect (can only be used once an hour). **Enchantments:** *Alchemist's Spatial Storage. Innate Consumption.* **+500 Wisdom, +450 Willpower, +400 Intelligence.**

Requirements: *Soulbound.*

Jake carefully studied every word of the improved description. There were a few changes, but the overall item was the same. The storage said it was no longer small, but medium-sized. It had thrown in some more cryptic stuff about more Records within, and it had even added a new ability of sorts to directly consume things like potions through it for improved effects. Moreover, it gave an absolutely massive 1350 total stat points from one item. It felt utterly insane, especially considering it also had all the other effects. He had thought the Altmar Signet was amazing for giving 1000 total, but that was also all it did.

Then again, this was an item he had gained at a far higher level. And as Rubylake stormed into the waiting room and saw Jake holding the necklace, she also shed some more light on the upgrade.

"I did not expect you to be able to summon it! Such a strong connection despite your still-young age. I am impressed." Rubylake nodded in approval, a huge smile on her face. "I was actually afraid it would become too potent, but I felt no resistance or like it burdened your soul at any point. Hard to imagine anyone not already peak D-grade being able to use it."

Jake just returned her smile. His level was still hidden, so she thought he was level 183, making it even better than she imagined. "I can see the craft succeeded. Did your quest too?"

Rubylake's grin grew even more. "I am evolving just after this."

Alcor, who had been silent after Jake had summoned the necklace, also seemed happy. "Congratulations, Mistress! What are your expectations?"

"High, but time shall tell if they are met," she said, returning her attention to Jake.

"Some things do still confuse me... The time it took was not as I expected," she said, and Jake also checked how long had passed as he frowned.

Only a bit over five hours had passed despite her saying it would take at least a day.

"How come?"

"I... Everything just felt right? The materials resonated with the necklace nearly right away, the energy was effortlessly absorbed, and the Records and energy within the necklace seemed almost primed to be awakened. Have you had it attempted before?"

"No." Jake shook his head. "You are the second person ever to lay a hand on it besides me."

"Any idea who originally made it? Or if it was used by someone before it was transformed into what it is today?"

Jake just kept shaking his head. "I got it as a reward from the system."

Rubylake frowned a bit but eventually just sighed in resignation. "Oh, well, it doesn't matter. Just... take care of it, okay? That necklace is no simple item."

"Of course," Jake said. "And thanks for your help."

"I should be the one thanking you for giving me the opportunity. There is no way I would have succeeded this easily without you bringing such a wonderous item." Rubylake bowed as she took out her token, and Jake felt his own within the necklace in his hand resonate. She had put her contact information into it. "Simply call me if you ever need a jeweler."

"Sure thing," Jake said as he returned the favor and also gave her his contact information. Mainly because if he wanted to contact her, it would be a bit awkward if she couldn't answer. Wait, maybe she could answer? He wasn't entirely sure how the call feature of the token actually worked, now that he thought about it

"Anyway, good luck with the evolution," Jake finally said as he felt like he had gotten all he had come for.

After a few more pleasantries, Jake put on his necklace and fused it with his body once more. He then promptly headed back to the mansion, and after a brief exchange with Meira, he dove into the laboratory.

He had no plans of exiting any time soon. Because if there was any question if Jake had been scammed, the answer was a resounding no. The true value of the ingredients didn't lie in their rarity alone, but in the sheer quantity of what he had received.

That's right—Jake was about to waste an absolute shitload of expensive materials.

CHAPTER 17

MOMENTUM + WEALTH = PROGRESS

Meira went over some material from her latest lesson as she gazed towards the mansion. Sir had said he would be around less, but she believed he had insinuated he would leave the Order to return to his own universe, not this.

He had entered the laboratory and then just stayed there after giving Meira the task of handling anyone who came looking for him. He had even ensured that everyone who tried to contact him through the token would instead reach her, making Meira more than a little uncomfortable.

She'd had to tell off a newly advanced C-grade vampire, the succubus in charge of his group from the 93rd Universe, and dozens more who wanted to speak with him and had somehow gotten his contact information. Meira knew the fact that he had a Bloodline had leaked, and it seemed they all wanted to discuss it with her master, but the only one they would reach was her.

Meira had to steel herself every time the token activated, and she had to answer only to inform them that her master was in seclusion doing alchemy. The only lucky thing was that everyone accepted this answer, and coupled with no sightings of him anywhere, they had no reason to doubt her.

She herself was still busy going to lessons every day and learning. Meira was honestly still unsure of the reason why she had been tasked to do it, but she naturally would try her best. She did realize that with every day, her value increased, and she began to have the pet theory that he was actually nurturing her into a long-term slave. That he wouldn't discard her but keep her around.

This was also confusing in its own right, though. It was normal to get new slaves once you advanced a grade to have more useful subordinates. Of course, you couldn't have slaves beyond your own grade, so real talents like the Chosen naturally had to switch out often, as there was no way for a slave to keep up in levels, much less be able to have the same level of Records to keep advancing.

Maybe he was planning on having her serve his descendants? It could also just be that he was eccentric and wanted to see how far she could go. If that was the case, Meira would certainly do her best, and hopefully, that would be good enough.

However, for every day that passed, she actually began doubting if he had just stopped bothering with her. She had originally hoped for this scenario before meeting her new master, but now it gave her conflicting emotions. It wasn't that she truly believed he had forgotten, but that small tinge of doubt never left, no matter how logical she tried to be. It was true that he was in seclusion, after all. The problem was that his way of doing it was a bit abnormal.

It would be fine if it was only in there for reasonable periods when he entered seclusion. When it came to alchemy, a highly intense type of crafting that required a high level of focus, it was normal to at most be in seclusion a week or so at a time while in D-grade, take a few days to rest, and then go back into the laboratory. This was to renew focus and get rest, as many couldn't properly relax within the laboratory.

This was the normal way... and him doing alchemy in seclusion was normal... The problem was that he hadn't taken a single step out of the laboratory for over two months.

The entire area was tinged red as the scent of blood dominated the air. Most Vitality-based creatures in early D-grade would find themselves bleeding from every orifice if they entered this dense cloud of crimson mist, truly turning it into a domain of death.

Luckily it was contained within a shielded room. A room where only a single alchemist sat in the center, unbothered by the mist. No, the opposite of bothered. He reveled in this environment as it fueled his regeneration.

This was naturally Jake, who was sitting within his alchemy lab. He had been busy crafting Hemotoxin after Hemotoxin, going through the net worth of some D-grades every single day as he spent the valuable materials he had received from the vampires.

To Jake, gaining levels was very easy when compared to others due to his overwhelming amount of already-accumulated Records. He could spend a few weeks within a forest and probably get a dozen class levels just killing more powerful foes and taking advantage of all his class bonuses.

This was relatively normal, as most everyone could quickly gain class or even race levels by slaying those of significantly higher levels. Jake did not doubt this was how the King had gained so many levels so quickly. Of course, one should do this with moderation to not hurt one's Records, and it also came with the inherent risk of death, but sometimes a burst of potential was truly what one needed.

Crafting like Jake did, splurging on materials with no care for cost in the face of progress, was in many ways similar to hunting far more powerful enemies in quick succession for levels. Rather than necessarily needing to be perfect when he made a poison, the value of the ingredients alone could help uplift the rarity.

Within the first week of Jake's isolation, he had already gone through hundreds of rare materials and even more common and uncommon ones. Yet he kept pushing on without the slightest care, feeling progress like never before.

He instantly understood concepts that would have previously taken him far longer to grasp. When he encountered a minor problem, he would often have a eureka moment, remembering something mentioned in lessons, skimmed in a book, or recalled due to Sagacity and Palate. He was truly harvesting the fruits of his labor.

He had not truly crafted anything since coming to the Order. He had barely gotten any levels, instead just fortifying his fundamental abilities, and now it was time to build that damn tower higher. Jake had chosen Hemotoxins as his method of doing this because he wanted something that would be effective when hunting beasts. Necrotic Poison also helped, but Jake knew Hemotoxic Poison was better in prolonged combat. Besides, he already had uncommon-rarity Necrotic Poison, which was pretty good.

Jake also used his blood in every creation, which was more potent than ever before, boosted by all the stats that just helped with everything. Things had just gone so smoothly, and after the first week, his experience and talent in crafting Hemotoxins rivaled his previously best kind of poison, Necrotic Poison, as he crafted an uncommon-rarity version.

You have successfully crafted [Potent Hemotoxic Poison (Uncommon)] - A new kind of creation has been made. Bonus experience earned

[Potent Hemotoxic Poison (Uncommon)] - Greatly increases bleeding on infected entities and makes any injuries significantly harder to heal. The poison must be introduced directly into the bloodstream to have any effect. Spreads throughout the body of the inflicted foe nearly instantly, making it even harder to dispel.

To most alchemists, using several rare ingredients and even the epic Crystalized Blood Essence to further improve the process only to then end up with an uncommon-rarity product would be viewed as an utter failure. But what had Jake done? He made another batch. And then another.

He just kept pumping out concoction after concoction with no regard for wastage as he rapidly improved. When he got tired, he slumped over and slept. When he was in doubt, he entered Serene Soul Meditation to calm his mind and refocus on his task. No outside inter-ference got in his way, and even Villy seemed to understand, as Jake had not heard the god ever since he had entered the laboratory.

Weeks quickly passed, and he had barely noticed when it had been more than a month since he entered seclusion. Yet he didn't feel tired at all. He kept pushing, still finding new inspiration and improvements every day—no, every hour. He even recalled the times he had fought the vampires in Yalsten and some of their blood magic. Especially the magic of the Monarch of Blood. He remembered when he had bitten and consumed the blood of the ancient revived vampire. Blood that had now mixed into him with Palate, as it qualified as toxic simply due to the level of sheer life energy it had contained.

Every day was just great, and he produced piles of Potent Hemo-toxic Poison. One good thing about the Order was the limitless supply of glass bottles. He had thrown a buttload into his new and improved spatial storage already, with it barely taking up any space.

On the sixty-third day after Jake entered seclusion, he was crafting his most difficult creation yet. It contained the Crimson Dawn Lotus and pulled on the insights he had gained so far as well as his understanding of the concept of time. This was far from the first try, but he had a good feeling, as he was becoming more and more familiar with the concept due to his class skills and further improving his level of comprehension by researching the lotuses.

By researching, he meant eating them for Palate—something he had done with all of his obtained herbs.

If others saw this, they would be spitting up blood, but Jake didn't care. He knew he was wealthy, and he knew he could earn back his wealth again. Hoarding materials without progressing made no sense. And progress Jake did, as on that day he finally managed to succeed— just around the two-month mark since entering the laboratory.

You have successfully crafted [Accelerated Hemotoxic Poison (Rare)] - A new kind of creation has been made. Bonus experience earned

[Accelerated Hemotoxic Poison (Rare)] — Time heals all wounds, or so the saying goes, but to some alchemists, time can become yet another weapon. Greatly increases bleeding on infected entities and makes any injuries significantly harder to heal. The poison must be introduced directly into the bloodstream to have any effect. Spreads throughout the body of the inflicted foe nearly instantly, making it even harder to dispel. Forcefully speeds up the flow of blood within the foe, accelerating the effect of the poison and making it deal damage faster over a far shorter period.

Seeing the notification had put a massive smile on his face. The poison was exactly what he had hoped and avoided one of the biggest weaknesses of the Hemotoxic Poison, which was the slow-acting effect. By mixing in some time affinity from the Crimson Dawn Lotus, the process would be sped up and make the poison even better. The ash from the Crimsonwood tree would then make the poison bind with the blood more thoroughly, making it even harder to get rid of. It was one nasty poison, and one Jake was very happy about making. Especially as it was followed by another system message.

[Concoct Poison (Uncommon)] - While most focus on the aspect of giving life through their craft, others prefer to take it away. Allows for the concoction of uncommon-rarity poisons and below. Must have suitable materials and equipment in order to create poisons. Adds a small increase to the effectiveness of created poisons based on Wisdom.

-->

[Concoct Poison (Rare)] - While most focus on the aspect of giving life through their craft, others prefer to take it away. Allows for the concoction of rare-rarity poisons and below. Must have suitable materials and equipment in order to create poisons. Adds an increase to the effectiveness of created poisons based on Wisdom.

When he gained the upgrade, Jake was more than elated. He had wanted Concoct Poison to reach rare before he evolved to C-grade. He had evolved it to uncommon rarity in E-grade and now rare in D-grade, so he had to keep the streak going, right? He knew this was already far better than the average, making him smile as he read the changed description.

As expected, it was much of the same, just pointing out he could now make rare-rarity poison. The only other benefit was that it increased Wisdom scaling, now making every poison he created slightly better. More than anything, upgrading a skill like this was a feel-good moment and not a purely practical one... Okay, it apparently did have a great impact on Records and potential profession evolutions, but Jake had a feeling he would be fine in that department either way.

Speaking of Records, there was finally the big one. The one other goal Jake had held when he entered seclusion: to get some goddamn levels. And levels he got.

'DING!' Profession: [Heretic-Chosen Alchemist of the Malefic Viper] has reached level 153 - Stat points allocated, +10 Free Points

...

'DING!' Profession: [Heretic-Chosen Alchemist of the Malefic Viper] has reached level 168 - Stat points allocated, +10 Free Points

'DING!' Race: [Human (D)] has reached level 153 - Stat points allocated, +15 Free Points

...

'DING!' Race: [Human (D)] has reached level 160 - Stat points allocated, +15 Free Points

Sixteen levels in his profession in only a bit over two months. It was roughly one level every four days, which quite frankly was insane and proof of how many materials he had burned through as well as the level of progress he had made. He knew this had been him building off the momentum he had amassed for the last few months before the crafting sessions, but during it all, he'd also realized how much he'd had to pull on for knowledge even before he went to the Order.

One had to remember Jake had undergone the Trial of Myriad Poisons. He had been injected with—as the name suggested—myriad poisons, and even if this didn't help much in his daily life, it allowed him to more easily understand things when he came across them. He got a sense of deja vu whenever a poison he had previously consumed popped up. As with most knowledge, he didn't just remember everything; the knowledge only appeared when in the right context.

With the levels also came two other benefits. One was Path of the Heretic-Chosen getting another charge, and the second was skill selection. To cut a short story even shorter, Jake picked the best skill of the bunch.

[Advanced Core Manipulation (Ancient)] – To touch upon a core of pure energy and Records is to touch upon the broken shell of a soul. Allows the alchemist to far more easily manipulate cores and the Records within the broken soul shells with the goal of refining them. Refined cores will, in most cases, be more effective, and you can also choose to amplify certain effects. Having taken it further, you have learned that the layers of souls can be malleable in some circumstances, and applying this knowledge, you have learned to fuse cores containing similar Records and even change their nature in some circumstances as your own soul influences the core. Adds an increase to the effectiveness of Advanced Core Manipulation based on Wisdom and Willpower.

The reason he had chosen this skill was twofold. First of all, it was something he felt like he needed, especially as he had decided that it would soon be time to awaken the Pollendust Bee Queen. Okay, Jakesoon, as he still didn't feel even close to ready. Additionally, he also knew that core refinement did not work very well with Touch of the Malefic Viper, as that was more core corruption. After all, touch did not really "improve" something; it just changed it. He needed a dedicated skill, so when he saw the option, he was instantly intrigued.

This was clearly an upgrade to the rare Refine Core skill he had been offered at level 120. Back then, he had skipped it due to its low rarity, but also because he didn't have any immediate use. Both of those things had now changed.

As for the skill itself, well, as far as he could tell, it pulled a lot on his experience with Shroud of the Primordial. It had something to do with soul shells or something, and to be fair, Jake was not entirely sure what it was talking about. Either way, he had a strong feeling the skill would be very useful, and it would also offer him more diversity when it came to alchemy. Oh, and being able to fuse the thousands of insect cores he had would make the ritual to awaken the Pollendust Bee Queen way simpler and likely also more effective. The skill also came with a lot of innate knowledge, giving him confidence in using it.

Anyway, that was the first reason he had picked it: because it was good. The second reason was that everything else offered was shit. Like, so shit he didn't even want to think about it. Every single one of the four other options was related to Jake being either a Chosen or a Heretic. All of it was about Jake being back at the Order of the Malefic Viper, offering him a leadership skill, a skill granting knowledge of the Order, a skill to grow dissent and make more heretics, and some fourth bullshit skill Jake would never pick in a thousand years. He would've rather picked the goddamn geology skill at inferior rarity.

And this more or less was Jake's progress over the last two months and change. He had kept crafting a few more rare poisons until the evening of the same day he had made the first one. That was when he was finally contacted by the one person he had allowed.

"Carmen contacted me a while ago and asked me to inform you she was on her way to Haven and would arrive within a day or two. She found clues on where her family might be and a trail to start following. More details to follow when you get back."

The moment Jake heard the message, he also felt like now was a good time to stop. He hadn't entirely burned through all his momentum, but it was best to stop now anyway. He had reached his goal, and besides, he was tired.

So Jake sent back an affirmation as he prepared to leave seclusion for the first time in over two months. On a side note, Miranda had known he was in seclusion, and for that reason, they had skipped their agreed-upon meetings. They had shared a small talk before he entered seclusion and agreed on her giving him a debrief once he returned to Earth.

At the same time as he exited the laboratory, he also reached out to the Viper and got confirmation: The snake god had made a better method for Jake to return to Earth.

That settled everything, and finally, it was time to return to Earth. He would not return to the Order until after the next system event, but he would have to hunt down a Prima before that—something he had also made prior preparations for with the help of Miranda and a little-known mad scientist called Arnold. He also had to help Carmen, so he had plenty of things to do. Things he wanted to do.

Jake smiled to himself as he smelled the fresh air outside the laboratory, happy with everything he had achieved and even happier as he thought about visiting Earth again and finally getting in some good stretches by killing something.

CHAPTER 18

UNEXPECTED NEW PATHS

Before returning to Earth, Jake needed a proper method to travel back and forth that didn't rely on being in Haven. Luckily, he had already talked about this with Villy quite a few times and knew the snake god was on it. They both wanted to give Jake the possibility, as there were still many things to be done back on his home planet and in his home universe as a whole.

So, a quick telepathic phone call later, the snake god popped into his living room. Meira was away at a lesson, with Jake not even having talked with her since exiting his little isolation session.

"Had a nice time doing alchemy?" Villy asked when he appeared, smiling.

"Pretty good, if I say so myself—lots of levels, skill upgrade, a new skill, Hemotoxins for days. You know, all the good things in life."

"Nice to know my dear Chosen at least enjoys what I am known for. Well, known for in at least a semi-positive light." Villy flashed his own cheeky smile before continuing. "I remember you mentioning you took a skill for rituals, right?"

"I did," Jake confirmed, as he had a suspicion about why the Viper asked.

"Well, that entire travel-between-universes issue will require a bit of ritual-making from your side to function," the Viper explained as he fished out a crystal he promptly tossed to Jake. It was similar to the one the vampires had given him and contained knowledge.

Jake quickly scanned it and saw it was a guide for some kind of ritual or array. It didn't take a genius to figure out what the Viper was asking of him. "I need to set up my own teleportation circles?"

He did not like the sound of that. Jake had no experience with magic circles at all, and even if he now had a skill that helped a bit, he had no confidence in setting anything complex up without a long period of practice first.

"Yes and no. You do technically need to make a magic circle, but not a teleportation circle per se. What you will need to do is make a subordinate circle to the primary teleporter placed in the city. Think about it as a receiver with the monument in your city as the sender. You just need to tap into the signal and remote-activate the monument, and off you go through the void between universes."

Jake nodded a bit as he kept scanning the Memory Crystal. It really didn't seem that complicated, but Jake could still see setting up the circle would take a bit of time, not making the teleportation anything instant.

"Thanks, man, this should come in handy," Jake said as the snake god also threw him a bunch of stones, as well as an odd green orb.

"Use those stones to activate the circle and feed it power together with your own mana," Villy said. "As for the orb, give it to that little verdant witch of yours. It is a gift from her Patrons."

Jake inspected the two items he had been given right away and frowned a bit.

[Energy Stone (Common] – *A stone containing energy.*
[Verdant Orb (Unique)] – *An orb made to be used only by those compatible.*

It was one of those cases where Identify did nothing. He was a bit surprised at getting common-rarity stones from Villy to power the circle, but then again, what the hell did he know?

"Anything else I should bring back?" Jake asked.

"Now that you mention it, I do have this nascent plague I would like to ask for you to spread and then report back on the general deadliness." Villy grinned.

"I could take it and just eat it with Palate," Jake commented.

"Funny that you mention it... That is actually quite a normal tactic. A specific poison or disease designed to kill anyone and anything, while being especially weak against Palate, making all those with the skill survive." Villy said all this nonchalantly.

"Is that actually something people do?" Jake asked, not sure if he wanted the answer.

"Plague theory is not really a big branch of the Order. If I am perfectly honest, it is due to its generally low level of power. It is only good at killing those significantly weaker, and even then, it is often easily thwarted by talented healers and others finding ways to combat it. But yes, it has been used. More by the Risen than the Order, though, as it is a good way to clear life-affinity energy from an area to kill off all the weak critters, turning it into a land of death. Now, if you really wanna kill a planet without having to kill everything by yourself... Ah, never mind, we'll save that one for another time. Just know you already possess the necessary tools, even if you lack the power to pull it off."

"I will not mind, no, as I have no plans of destroying any planets." Jake shook his head.

"Yet," Villy foreshadowed with a cheeky smile.

"Anyway!" Jake said, switching the topic. "How the hell do I get back to Earth?"

"Oh. Yeah. That. Well, I already installed the teleporter in your secret sealed-off basement room."

"I have a secret sealed-off basement room?"

"As of ten minutes ago, yes," the god said as he motioned for Jake to follow him.

They went over to the library, where the god pulled on a book that made a bookshelf swing open, revealing a stairway. One that had definitely not been there before.

"A little basic," Jake commented.

"What can I say? I am a fan of the classics." Villy shrugged.

"You just infused mana into the entire shelf, didn't you?" Jake asked, having felt the flow of energy.

"Oh, yeah, totally. The book is just for show. The activation mechanism is bound to your mana—well, and mine, but mainly yours. An array covers the entire place, making even most gods unable to locate this area." The snake god led him down into a small chamber with an intricate teleportation circle in the middle.

Jake looked at it for a moment, then at the scripts that covered the wall. "I take it you facilitate the teleportation from this universe and back to the Ninety-Third entirely?"

"Precisely. You just need to step on the platform, put a bit of mana in, and off you go. It even works with others, but only up to a dozen or so at a time. More than that, and, well, some might get stuck in the void mid-teleport."

"AKA, a bad time." Jake nodded.

"Well, not really an anything-time, as it would just mean ceasing to exist, but that is another conversation my poor little D-grade Chosen is too young to have. By the time you are ready to enter the void yourself, you won't even be my Chosen anymore." Villy smiled. "Now, better get going."

"Aight. Thanks for this time, and see you soon," Jake said as he got on the teleporter. He infused mana into it as he, at that very last moment, remembered... he had forgotten about Meira.

Sadly, he was already swept away before he could stop it, disappearing from the First Universe and heading back towards Earth.

Back on Earth, the planet had experienced what many would classify as a second renaissance after the system had arrived. The system event that allowed individuals to revitalize themselves and find a new path had passed, bringing about incredible change.

For many, the event didn't affect them personally. Individuals like Miranda, Jacob, Carmen, Neil, and his party—any elite, really—weren't affected in the slightest. This event was not for them. No, the true change was found in the level 30 construction worker who had not received a level in months. The warrior who'd discovered he wasn't suited for fighting beasts in close range, the mage who'd learned he was not talented in magic, or just those who had never truly found a Path.

To these people, the event was a second chance. Classes and professions were changed, people found new hope, and a sense of life enveloped every city as progress returned to many. Simply finding a new Path and doing the event had also resulted in Records, allowing those who had changed to get an initial period where they almost sprinted, fast getting stronger and more assured in their choices.

For some who were stuck, this event led to no changes—not because they had failed, but because they were already set on their Path, even if that Path was a mediocre one. The small restaurant owner who was satisfied with his life, the smith that enjoyed just working a few hours a day and then relaxing the rest with his family. These people had chosen a Path, even if it wasn't one to power.

Nevertheless, this led to growth across the planet. The average level of humanity grew, and more and more D-grades appeared as the native humans got a second wind. To make it even better, these people who had just gained another chance could potentially also participate in the next event less than a month away. If not the Path of Myriad Choices, then at least in whatever Seat of the Exalted Prima was.

The cities that benefitted the most were naturally the large ones. Sanctdomo had a massive spike in power, but the fringe groups like the Court of Shadows and Risen also got a boost few had expected: realignment of their citizens. Many had picked professions and classes during their tutorials with no knowledge they would end up working with shadow assassins or the living dead, but now that they got a chance to change? They adapted.

Among the Risen, that meant necromancers, death mages, crafters specialized in death-attuned materials, and even people who'd decided during the event they wanted to become Risen. For the Court, the same was true, as many became more specialized in what the Court needed, with a similar thing playing out all around the planet.

Haven didn't actually experience that much growth overall. Most who went there were already settled in their own Paths, so while some did make use of the event, the vast majority of them didn't. However, there was one large exception.

Miranda sat in the office and drank some coffee with the man in front of her. The last time they had spoken had only been a week ago, but he had grown significantly yet again. Back then, he had just reached D-grade, and now he was already level 110. However, more surprising than anything was that the man had been stalled for so long beforehand.

"You are looking better than ever, Phillip." Miranda smiled at the former military man and leader of the Fort.

"It sure is a strange time," the man said as he also took a sip. His face no longer looked sunken, and he was no longer a tired man at the end of his rope.

Miranda had come to understand him quite well with time and come to realize that while he'd been strong for his level when they first met, it wasn't because he really wanted to be strong.

He had been part of the military. He had been the leader and sent into a tutorial with people from his camp, and they had all turned to him for guidance. When he got out of the tutorial, he had appeared in the old base camp, and yet again, all had turned to him for guidance, as he was the highest-rank commanding officer present.

Out of a sense of responsibility, he had accepted. Then they'd found a sanctuary, saved citizens, made the Fort a fortified settlement, and he'd just kept going because he had to. But then Jake had turned up. A magical bird had rebuffed a force he and his men would've been slaughtered by. Miranda had come and helped take over the management of the Fort. Suddenly he no longer had any responsibilities and was lost.

Phillip had, by all accounts, retired. He'd been a middle-aged man before the system arrived, tired of the constant pressure and expectations. His sense of responsibility was so ingrained in him that he kept working even after he'd "retired" as a representative of the former soldiers and those who stayed at the Fort. Not that they needed a representative; he was just the kind of man that couldn't sit still.

And then... then this system event came. Miranda had expected a lot of people to find their Path through this event, but Phillip was not one of them. He didn't seem to have the drive anymore, but it appeared she had miscalculated.

The man before her could barely be compared to the old Phillip. No longer was he a man constantly wandering around with his rifle to look "official" or with a profession to lead the troops and defend the Fort. Instead, he sat there with well-defined muscles, skin that had an odd semi-metallic tinge to it, only wearing a thin shirt and normal pants. He wore no equipment at all, yet Miranda felt his body brimming with power.

Alteration Mage. No, to call him a mage was perhaps incorrect. He was more a fighter than a mage, even if he did use magic as his primary tool of combat. The difference was that the only target of his magic was him and his own body. His profession had also changed to be some kind of enchanter. Miranda was not privy to the details, but she knew he was no easy opponent, especially not after reaching D-grade.

"Are you sure you want to fully step down from *all* of your positions?" Miranda asked to confirm. Phillip had still been a part of many endeavors but had slowly phased them out. Now he came to get entirely uninvolved with everything Haven and Fort-related.

"I am." Phillip nodded. "I have done enough for this place. For others. From now on, I will focus on myself and myself only. I plan on leaving soon to travel around a bit after the event, but before that, I want to get enough levels to properly do the dungeon beneath the city."

She also liked how he looked when he talked about exploring the planet. He looked happy, perhaps for the first time since she'd met the man over a year ago.

"It is your choice," Miranda said approvingly.

He smiled in response. "For the first time in a long time... it truly does feel like it is."

Jake was still making his way to Earth.

He felt himself flow through the void once more. He closed his eyes and tried to seal off his Sphere of Perception to not be overwhelmed by the odd sensation the place gave him, hoping for it to pass quickly.

However... it didn't.

It took longer than before. Jake suddenly felt like a gaze landed upon him, and he sensed himself stop. At the same time, he felt an overwhelming sense of danger for a fraction of a second before it disappeared just as it came. At the same time, Jake's sphere no longer felt overloaded... In fact, it felt like whatever space he was in had suddenly turned stable and un-void-like.

Jake opened his eyes and saw the pitch-black darkness of the void as cold sweat appeared, and an innate fear swelled up from deep in his soul. He saw only the darkness that high enough Perception could perhaps one day pierce, as he had no idea what or who was watching. He was unsure what was happening, as he felt something besides Villy just staring, with Villy's attention on him being far weaker.

He was nervous when, suddenly, a single eye appeared within his vision. A human eye with an odd, multi-colored iris. Then another. Then ten eyes, a hundred, a thousand, a million. The entire void was replaced by a rainbow of colored eyes before they all merged together and formed what could be described as a malformed head that appeared small yet filled his entire field of vision.

"Deliver. Gift."

The voice echoed in his head, made up of a mix of distorted tones, as blood began pouring out of his ears and eyes. Jake had to grit his teeth as he slowly felt his consciousness slip away, as if his mind was shutting down to protect his psyche. Something impacted his chest, and he began blacking out while floating through the void again.

The final thing he saw before slipping out of consciousness was the entire void suddenly gaining a dark green tinge as a familiar presence descended.

CHAPTER 19

ORAS

Vilastromoz made sure Jake had safely passed through the void and back to his planet before he regarded the being before him. Today had been a stark reminder that even with all of his preparations, there existed beings in the multiverse that could circumvent them.

The Viper had used several methods to hide Jake traveling through the void. The biggest one was, of course, Shroud of the Primordial, but the teleportation itself should also help hide him. These preparations should have been unnecessary anyway, as locating anything traveling through the void in such a brief period was beyond even the Viper himself. Finally, why would some ancient and powerful being even bother with interfering with someone teleporting through? Trillions went through the void every moment, so what was one in so many?

Yet none of that mattered before the being in front of him. It was the same being that had originally spotted Jake when he traveled to the Order. The fact he had been spotted the first time around was no surprise, as the being saw most everything that ever passed the void, with the only surprise being Jake noticing the gaze. Well, not a surprise to Vilastromoz, but probably the creature.

"Snake Who Holds Forgotten Knowledge, you seek compensation?" the voice of the being echoed as the ever-shifting reptilian eyes moved before him.

"I first seek answers," Vilastromoz said, not minding the title the being had assigned him.

"Traveler of the void, passing the veil of the new world," the Void Dweller answered as cryptically as ever. *"A gift given to be delivered to that which I gaze upon."*

The Viper frowned at the answer. For the Void Dweller before him to gaze upon someone was just a fancy way of saying it had blessed them. Normally that would be whatever, but the situation was different when dealing with beings like this. A god's Blessing would affect the target, yes, but the Blessing of a Void Dweller, much less one like the one before him? The effects would be significant. Merely seeing a Void Dweller could make mortals lose their minds and have their mental faculties irreversibly corrupted, so it was no surprise a Blessing did even more.

"What did you ask to be delivered?" the Viper asked.

"Gift. Knowledge. Power."

"And who is it supposed to be delivered to?" Vilastromoz kept pressing.

"He Who Commands The Many Eyes That Dwell Within the Soulless Vessels of Metal and Lightning. Seeker of knowledge like I." The Void Dweller didn't much seem to care about the overly long title.

Vilastromoz finally turned his gaze towards Earth and quickly did a scan. He had never bothered to scan the ones around Jake much, only paying them cursory attention. He had assumed none could hide from his probing, but upon a deeper inspection, he noticed there was indeed one person with a Blessing he hadn't noticed before, making him frown even more.

"You could have asked before making my Chosen a mule," the Viper protested as he stared into the many eyes.

"Yes... decision made in haste. Apologies, Keeper of Lost Knowledge. Compensation will be made." The Void Dweller's eyes shifted a bit in apology. Vilastromoz could read this particular Void Dweller, as it wasn't one of the mindless beasts that usually roamed the endless void, but one most gods of any repute had found themselves in contact with several times in the past.

"What do you offer me?" he asked.

"To the Primordial? None shall be given. Compensation for He Who Hunts. An equal, is he not? Nascent seeds will be planted, more futures planned. Outcomes predicted falsely before. Corrections required."

Vilastromoz just sighed as the eyes kept shifting. He felt movement from afar as he stood in the middle of the void, the attention of more beings gathering in response to the Viper letting his aura flare. "Fine. Just don't have this repeat itself. Even if you want a favor from him, ask through me. Finally, why are you playing with the minds of mortals? I never figured you to be the kind of being to break a weak mortal like that."

"Interpretations infinite, minds of unlimited variations. Comprehension of He With Eyes of Steel, mortal yet mind untouched. Corruption minimal, patterns recognized; seeks only knowledge. Compatible."

He understood the answer, as most of the communication did not come in words, but in shapes and expressions made by its body. The Viper didn't ask further, just looking at the Void Dweller and the ever-flowing ocean of eyes it consisted of. It was a physique not like any other creatures in the multiverse, and these Void Dwellers could only reside within the void. Well, most of them anyway.

"I shall trust your discretion, then." The Viper nodded. "May your gaze land upon all of existence, Oras the All-Seeing."

"May your will shape reality, Malefic Viper of the Primordials."

With that, the eyes all disappeared, and Vilastromoz sighed again. Oras was a difficult one to deal with. A creature as ancient as could be, a true god of the void, unlike the majority of its void brethren.

Speaking of Void Dwellers... the Viper chose not to leave right away. He felt the many creatures closing in on him, their auras dominating the vast nothingness, every single one of them able to slay gods like were they children before men. The weakest Void Dwellers in the void were a match for a newly ascended god, with the ones closing in on the Viper being far above that level, able to slay Godkings and Godqueens easily.

Predators of a domain that should not be threaded by those belonging to the universes. The mere aura of a god attracted them, as they sought to feast and grow from the slaughter of energies not of the void.

Vilastromoz had to admit he felt angry. So far, he had predicted most things, and those he had failed to predict, he had at least had a sense would happen, or they had led to positive outcomes above expectations. However, someone like Oras was not predictable. VIlastromoz did not understand the Void God like he understood his fellow Primordials. Something that annoyed him severely.

Hopefully, the deaths of the approaching Void Dwellers would quell that anger just a little bit, also giving him a chance to get a good stretch in.

. . .

Jake woke up with a start as he quickly oriented himself. The entire area around him was filled with his own mana, and he found himself in a defensive position. Instinctually, he knew that he and everyone else had gotten lucky that nobody had entered his laboratory, where Jake had returned to upon arriving on Earth.

As he observed his sphere, he noticed something out of place. On the floor in front of him lay a small black cube with magical patterns on it and what looked like eyes marking its surface. He instantly recognized the faint energy it gave off as corresponding to that of the creature he had encountered in the void.

Just thinking about that thing made his head hurt, and he groaned in pain. He tried to find out how long he had been out of commission instead, and found he had been knocked out for well over an hour. He checked his status and saw he had lost health, mana, and stamina from the encounter, indicating soul damage. Soul damage from just looking at the damn thing.

The box on the floor suddenly caught his eye. Where had that come from? It had the same energy as the being he'd seen in the void, and—

A headache assaulted him again. Without thinking, Jake pulled off his cloak and threw it over the cube on the floor, making his headache instantly subside. At the same time, he remembered everything far more clearly. That damn box was able to make him forget it even existed? What the actual fuck was it?

"Villy... what the fuck is going on?" Jake finally asked. A few seconds passed before he got an answer.

"You met a Void God... again. Oras, as it is known. An ancient creature born of the void." Villy sounded a tad annoyed.

"How did he spot me with Shroud? Also, are you okay? I remember seeing you appear just as I blacked out..."

"I am fine. Oras spotted you because the Shroud, and everything else I do isn't good enough to hide you when in the void. Not from Oras."

"What the hell does that thing want?" Jake asked, even more confused. *"Something about a gift? Who for?"*

"Traveling through the void isn't easy. Going out of the 93rd Universe is especially hard, and going back in? I reckon only a few can even facilitate this return trip. Oras spotted you and decided to have you bring something into the 93rd Universe. The gift you received is not for

you, but the one Oras has 'blessed.' I use that word very carefully, as the usual result from someone getting blessed by a Void God is a cult that makes the Order of the Malefic Viper look like the good guys in comparison. Luckily, Oras cares little for anything besides knowledge and seeing new things... at least as far as I can tell. I don't fully understand the creature."

Jake nodded in understanding. "So, who is this god-forsaken box a gift for?"

"Arnold."

Hearing the name, Jake's eyes flashed for a moment. For some reason, the answer didn't surprise him, even if he did find it confusing why some being from the void would bless Arnold, a guy who liked making machines. The Viper clearly detected this confusion.

"I don't know why Oras blessed that man. That is for you to discover, but in my experience, the logic of a Void Dweller is not worth trying to comprehend. However, it does seem like Arnold is mostly unaffected... I would look into why that is. His mind seems to accept the Void Dweller, which is quite peculiar."

"So, should I deliver the box?" Jake finally asked.

"Go ahead. Oras said you would get some kind of compensation, and while I do not understand the creature, it somewhat understands mortals. So his compensation should be worth it."

Jake nodded again, and after a few more words, they ended their conversation. He felt that the Viper seemed somewhat distracted during their talk, but that wasn't anything new. What was new was the Viper actively using the name of another mortal. This indicated that Villy actually viewed Arnold as someone with some level of importance now, showing that this Oras was a big deal.

Wanting his cloak back, Jake closed his eyes and pulled it off the box. Luckily, he could look at the box using his Sphere of Perception without feeling like his head was about to split open. He took out a black piece of cloth from his inventory and wrapped the box in it before putting it inside a wooden barrel he normally used for water. The entire thing was only about the size of a shoebox, and when he tried to lift it, he noticed it didn't weigh anything. That wasn't an exaggeration either; the metal-looking box with eyes on it literally didn't weigh anything. It was honestly just creepy.

At least he could put it in his spatial storage while still in the barrel. Jake proceeded to walk up to the lodge above and over to the pond, where he quickly washed the blood that'd come from his own orifices off his face. He wasn't in a hurry to deliver the box and decided to get a few things done first.

To start, he checked in on the troll down in the cavern. Rick, as he had been named, was still just chilling with what was now a sprawling garden down in the biodome. His kids were also there, having grown a little since the last time he saw them.

Next up, he headed for the city center of Haven and met up with Miranda. They had a good talk, with Jake getting updated on recent happenings in the city. He even remembered to give her that Verdant Orb Villy had handed him—primarily because she reminded him to.

He wasn't entirely sure how to feel when he got told that his absence hadn't really had any impact, and that most assumed he was just in the valley doing alchemy or out hunting or something.

The city itself had grown even more since the last time he was there. He was informed that the Fort had expanded yet again as more and more sought the larger settlements. He learned about the outcome of the first system event and how many had begun progressing again, including Phillip. Jake honestly didn't care overly much, even if he was happy that others were finding their own roads to power.

Their meeting was interrupted about an hour in when Jake suddenly felt a gust of wind enter through an open window. The next moment, a bird was standing atop his head. Jake had felt her coming but didn't react, allowing the hawk to get her small moment of triumph as she screeched and flapped her wings happily.

Jake raised his hands and lifted the bird off his head to give her a hug. "Hey, Sylphie. Long time, no see."

The hawk looked up as she snuggled against him, Jake just stroking her small head. He smiled, yet he had a somewhat mixed feeling when he used Identify and saw her level.

[Sylphian Eyas – lvl 163]

For the first time since her birth, she had surpassed him in levels. Jake would be lying if he said it wasn't somewhat expected. Sylphie was growing rapidly and was still just identified as an Eyas, meaning that even if she just slept and did nothing, she would keep leveling. Combined with her Blessing from Stormild, her connection to Jake, and her own efforts, it was no a surprise she had kept progressing so fast.

As he held her, she made some cute chirping sounds. Jake nodded along, getting the gist of what she was saying. She even summoned a medal of sorts with the same symbol on it as Jake's Altmar Signet, meaning his little hawk had also gotten the highest evaluation—or at least been evaluated to be impossible to evaluate.

One thing also quickly became clear: Sylphie was not back in Haven just to say hi to Jake, but because Carmen was coming. Jake was totally fine with the two-person journey to track down Carmen's family turning into a three-person trip.

"I will always be amazed at the growth of Sylphie," Miranda said as she looked at the hawk.

Jake nodded but didn't really think she was one to talk, seeing how her level had also grown significantly.

[Human – lvl 158]

She was nearly at his own level. Jake knew a large reason for this was her profession leveling damn quickly, but she also clearly farmed some class levels here and there. Had Jake not just gotten a lot of fast levels, he would've been way behind. He was also certain Carmen had to have surpassed him in level by now.

Not that Jake was worried. In fact, he found the sentiment exciting. He had never feared not being the strongest, and if everyone else got more powerful, didn't that just mean he had more people to fight?

Sylphie felt his thoughts and squirmed herself free as she screeched in approval. He felt her intentions, and he was more than happy to oblige when the time was right.

"She is a real talent, isn't she?" Jake said to Miranda as he smiled, Sylphie once more letting out a ree of agreement. "I am going to head over to Arnold now to check what information he has gained on the locations of any Primas and the route to this port city."

"Have a nice journey. I will remain here in case Carmen shows up. Not that I doubt we won't both notice her arrival; she isn't exactly the stealthy type." Miranda chuckled.

With that, Jake got up and headed off to the Fort. He teleported together with Sylphie, who had decided to stay with him, and reached the now buzzing city within a few minutes of leaving Miranda's office. The teleportation circles had been moved yet another time, Jake noted as he looked towards the central citadel and saw that the metal sphere had expanded not just in width, but also height, as the mad scientist had obviously noticed he was running out of horizontal real estate.

As he looked towards the metal sphere, he faintly felt the odd box that had been forced upon him vibrate within his necklace, dispelling all doubt that Arnold was truly related to it. Jake just had a hard time figuring out how the many-eyed freak of a Void Dweller was related to a mad scientist. Well, besides the entire theme of madness.

Oh, well, I guess I can just ask him.

CHAPTER 20

COMPREHENDING THE
INCOMPREHENSIBLE

"So, Arnold, what made you decide to get blessed and enter a pact with some sort of otherworldly being of the void that usually turns people insane merely by laying their eyes upon it?"

Jake had barely entered the sphere of metal and made his way to the mad scientist before he popped the question burning in his mind. He hadn't even taken out the creepy cube yet. Jake had just been invited in by Arnold's assistant and walked into his workshop, asking about his Void God pal without delay.

Arnold, to his credit, didn't get fazed or even look up from his workbench as he answered, "By all estimates, being blessed by a god is superior to not being blessed by one, and the offered benefits outstripped all other offers at the time."

It was the kind of answer Jake had expected, but he still pressed further. "But... have you seen this god?"

"Naturally." Arnold nodded, still unbothered as his hands kept working.

"And? No comments on the appearance of a floating thing of infinite eyeballs?"

"The appearance of Oras shifts according to the observer." Arnold shook his head. "I saw not an eye, but a string of numbers. All perceptions one can have are related to the act of observing. You saw a representation of a visual organ, while I saw a language able to relay what is observed."

"Are you trying to tell me you see the world as being made up of numbers, or what?" Jake asked further, wondering if Arnold thought he lived in a simulation or something.

"No. Just that all can be reduced to numbers. Even the system itself." He soon stopped his work and looked up at Jake. "I do not believe you have come here to discuss divine alignments?"

"No, I came to ask about something else... Okay, just one more question. Do you talk to Oras?" Jake couldn't hold himself back from asking.

"Talk? No. Communicate? Yes. Conversation through spoken words, such as the one we are having right now, is a severely limited and highly inefficient way to relay information from one source to another. The communication thus happens through images, arrays, patterns, and formulas, which is far more efficient and helpful."

Jake couldn't help but imagine the two biggest nerds in the multiverse talking with each other by using goddamn formulas to spell out stuff. But... Jake began to understand how Arnold could deal with Oras. "Okay, final question. What is Oras to you?"

He had a hunch and wanted to confirm it.

"Unknown as of yet." Arnold shrugged.

"What is your best guess?"

"Knowing when you don't know something is knowledge in itself. I don't need to guess when I know I can't comprehend something yet. I still have many steps to understand before I can comprehend a being such as Oras, making my lack of comprehending the creature a natural conclusion. The human mind is limited in scope, and we must accept there are some things we are not meant to understand. However, that doesn't mean we can't try to comprehend them and observe the impact they have on phenomena we can see. Through those observations and evolution brought upon us by the system, perhaps one day we can transcend our current limits. But that day has yet to come."

Jake nodded along, kind of getting it. He remembered talking to an old acquaintance from school during a reunion who was studying physics at the time. The guy had talked about quantum mechanics and how there were so many things we simply didn't understand. Concepts that just seemed beyond the human mind to comprehend.

Yet he'd also talked of tools to measure what these incomprehensible things did. He talked about how humans tried to make theories and formulas to explain what happened, even in situations where imagination had long conceded.

Jake didn't really get it... but he did get the simplified explanation Arnold gave.

"Humans couldn't see ultraviolet light before the system, yet we could make devices that could. We couldn't see gravity, but we could measure what it did. That has changed now, as the body has evolved to, in many ways, become the best measuring device in existence, and the mind the best computer to simulate hypotheses and confirm theories. I have already become able to understand flows of energy, comprehend patterns not understandable to the human mind before, and I am certain you are the same. Your senses now also encompass mana. You can feel the flow of energies within your own body, and even metaphysical concepts are now understandable—something we couldn't even observe before the system. In due time, even a being like Oras will be understandable as our scopes expand."

It was the most Jake had ever heard Arnold talk, and he actually heard some passion in his voice. Jake felt like he had gotten a far better understanding of Arnold during this brief talk and, in concert, also understood Oras a bit better.

Arnold was just a damn nerd, and Oras was a nerd-loving knowledge seeker, AKA also a mega-nerd. Simple as that. At least, that is how Jake chose to summarize it.

"Anyway, I brought this for you," Jake finally said as he pulled out the weird box the eldritch abomination of eyes had given him.

Arnold stared for a while, then said, "I am uncertain why you brought me a barrel."

Jake quickly reacted by opening the barrel and pulling out the bundle of cloth containing the box. "I would advise you to close your eyes or something. Looking at this thing is highly unpleasant."

He followed his own advice as he began unwrapping the bundle. Arnold reacted by taking out a pair of spectacles and putting those on. Jake was anticipating the man to fall over or grasp his head in pain when the box was revealed, but he just stood there and looked at it.

"Ah. A puzzle box. Thank you." Arnold went right over and took it off Jake's hands.

Jake himself just stood there with closed eyes as Arnold carried it over to a glass container and put it inside.

"I have contained it now," Arnold said, making Jake open his eyes, and instinctively he looked towards the box.

He saw it clear as day, as it was within a display case of sorts. It looked like only a thin layer of glass separated the cube and himself, yet he felt no headache, allowing him to inspect it freely. The box was black without any patterns on it, and there were no shifting eyes or weird energy surrounding it. It was just a black box, with its only extraordinary feature being how black it was.

Jake kept staring at it a bit as he just put it out of his mind, seriously not wanting to bother with it anymore. "So, Primas."

Arnold nodded and moved his hand, and a large screen appeared on one of the walls to display a map. Jake instantly saw a few familiar markings on it. Haven, Skyggen, Sanctdomo, and several other cities he recognized were labeled, as well as some noticeable landmarks such as the Insect Plains and the large mountain Jake had passed on the way to Skyggen, now dubbed the Frostpeak Mountain.

Waving his hand again, the scientist made a few areas light up. At the same time, the map drew attention to a small mark on the far side of it, right at the edge of a large mass of nothingness—the ocean, Jake assumed.

The lit-up areas were all on the way to this marking, and based on the distance, Jake saw it was about four times as far as his journey to Skyggen had been. Luckily, there appeared to be other settlements along the way, but the final stretch looked like it had to be passed by foot.

"The highlighted areas are ones where the energy signatures corresponding to Primas have been detected," Arnold explained. "This indicates they either live there or have lived there previously. Based on the signals and times of death of the eagle Prima and the monkey you have slain previously, we have a rough estimate of this Prima energy half-life. Primas all give off unique energy, same as races such as humans or elementals of specific affinities."

Jake nodded along, knowing this already. Every single living thing had an energy signature entirely unique to themselves, but the same races also shared some common traits. This was all tied to Records, and needless to say, all humans had the Records of being humans. In the same vein, all Primas had the Records of being Primas, making that the thing Jake would use to track them down.

"I have also marked zones with creatures of interest and the fastest routes to follow," Arnold further explained.

Looking at the map and the level of detail, Jake couldn't help but ask, "How did you map this? Satellites?"

"No. I have attempted launches, but the upper layers of the sky have proven impossible to break through with my current methods.

Even that is secondary to making anything able to survive in space for a prolonged period without getting destroyed. This map was done with drones flying approximately ten kilometers in the air, just below the dense cover of clouds."

"Must have been quite the operation," Jake commented.

"An ongoing one," Arnold said as he motioned for Jake to follow. "I have also worked further on the requested weapon. However, as of yet, it isn't ready."

Arnold opened a container to reveal a slick Nanoblade. It was just the blade, but Jake could practically feel the energy infused into it. It was as thin as ever, too, and Jake wondered what it needed to be ready.

"The blade is mostly done, and the box you brought should help me finalize the product," Arnold said. "We both share the fact that Perception is our primary stat, and I aim to infuse the Nanoblade with abilities taking advantage of that."

Jake nodded along, but when he heard Arnold mention the box, he got a very bad feeling. Wouldn't that mean Jake would eventually run around with a cursed blade seeking to consume all of existence in one hand, and a blade forged using methods passed down by some eldritch monstrosity in the other?

Actually, on second thought, that sounded pretty cool. "It looks damn impressive already. Keep up the good work, man."

Arnold nodded and handed Jake a tablet of sorts, not unlike one of the ones Arnold normally ran around with. "Within this tablet is general information of the areas you will encounter on your way, such as settlements and noteworthy territories of certain creatures. The map is naturally also included, and if you hold onto the tablet, it will track your location on said map. Any further questions?"

"Any advice on the journey?"

"Avoid the red zones or explore them carefully. Those are areas where I have detected C-grades. However, you will have to pass such an area to reach the port city. This place is known as the Grand Mangrove River, and it does contain Primas. Plural. However, I would suggest quickly passing, as it also contains C-grades. Once more, plural. Flying over is not an option either. The reason for this should become rather obvious when you get near there."

Jake checked the map and did notice a river-like area that seemed to cut through the terrain between the city closest to the port and the port itself.

"Got it," Jake said. "Do you need me to bring you fragments from

Primas too?" He hoped Carmen had all hers, as it could get a bit tight on time if he had to—

Arnold shook his head. "No. I shall acquire all I need in cooperation with the City Lord."

"Wait, Miranda got three already?" Jake asked, surprised. She hadn't mentioned that even after they had spoken for so long. He knew Sylphie had two fragments, but that Miranda had three?

"No, we have four between us. The last two are already in the process of being acquired at this very moment." Not explaining further on that topic, he continued, "Also, head towards the east for the Ambermill settlement. A powerful individual is currently passing through with an energy signature matching that of a member of Valhal. You intend to go with that woman, correct?"

To preserve his pride, Jake didn't ask about the Prima fragments further. From the last sentence, he could also see Arnold really wanted him to leave by now, so he didn't want to overstay his welcome more than necessary.

Once outside of the big metal dome, he met up with Sylphie again, who hadn't wanted to go into the dome. Apparently, she had tried to sneak in and cause havoc in the past, and Arnold had somehow managed to throw her out using some built-in defenses, impressing Jake. He still got the feeling Sylphie could have broken out and caused destruction, but neither party wanted that. This had inadvertently led to Sylphie really disliking Arnold but also kind of respecting him.

Another reason she respected him was explained as he got outside and saw her. Jake found Sylphie eating out of the hand of Arnold's assistant, who had kept an eye on her in a small building outside. Arnold was smart, after all, and knew bribery with food was a true and tested tactic when it came to placating powerful beasts.

"Sylphie, are you ready to head out?" he asked the hawk that was happily snacking away.

"Ree!" she answered with enthusiasm, flapping her wings. After a quick screech at Arnold's assistant thanking her for the food, Sylphie flew up and landed on his head again.

"Arnold found Carmen, so how about we go meet her on the way?"

That got another happy flap from Sylphie, and the man and bird headed towards this little place called Ambermill.

. . .

Once his visitor was gone, and he was alone, Arnold activated all of the interior barriers to seal off the dome. At the same time, the entire laboratory shifted as the sensitive devices were retracted into the walls, leaving only himself, a single worktable, and a display case with the gift from Oras within.

Bringing the case to the center of the room, Arnold activated a small laser and cut off the top of the light-refracting glass. A hole just large enough to put a finger through would be enough. He moved back as he took out a chair and sat down in it, risking losing his balance with what happened next.

On the ceiling, a single laser appeared and fired down onto the cube, and the very next moment, it was as if Arnold had been transported into an entirely different world. The light reflected off the cube distorted all senses and made him perceive reality as different from what it was. Yet even if it changed, a pattern remained.

As he sat there, finding himself surrounded by lights with millions of colors and shapes he did not even know the name of, he began to decipher whatever mystery his Patron god had left within the cube. It was the type of mystery that perhaps didn't even have a solution, but merely attempting it would lead to newfound discoveries. Or, perhaps the conclusions would be based solely on the eye of the beholder.

Either way, there were patterns, and a theory adequately explaining this pattern could be made. There was meaning somewhere in the madness, and if there wasn't, then Arnold would just have to refine his theory until it was correct anyway.

Such was his Path. There was always a pattern, always a formula to describe reality, always an answer. With the system, everything was possible—even understanding the system itself.

CHAPTER 21

AMBERMILL: A QUAINT LITTLE TOWN

There were few kinds of people in this world Carmen hated. Scratch that—there were a lot of people she hated, but some she hated far more than others. Towards the top of the latter list was anyone who reminded her of a certain someone. Someone who relied solely on their status, their family or backing, or whatever other vain bullshit to lord over others. In fact, she just hated people who liked throwing their weight around to have others do what they wanted if they couldn't even back up their words.

Carmen had entered Ambermill like any other small, Pylon-less settlement. It was relatively large for not having a Pylon, and due to its proximity to Haven, there weren't many strong monsters around. This made Ambermill a popular place to settle down. She didn't get why they didn't travel the rest of the way to the Fort, but oh, well.

She saw no problems with any of that. No, the problems came later.

Carmen had been on the road for around three days without any rest and seriously needed a goddamn shower before making it the rest of the way. It would take her only an hour to reach Haven from Ambermill, so she decided it was a good place to get all the things done to not look like a hobo when she finally made it there.

The first thing she noticed upon entering Ambermill was the presence of several people wearing what looked like police uniforms. Way too many of them. She considered whether they maybe had some problems with crime, and in the beginning, they seemed nice enough. Carmen had gained a ring that helped hide her level, and she was just asked to not make trouble as she entered. One of them even pointed her toward a motel.

So far, so good.

She had barely managed to settle down and get a room when she noticed some commotion outside. Looking out the window, she saw several people being rounded up by the police from a nearby house in what looked like the slum quarters. Carmen naturally failed to hold herself back, and without even taking a shower, she went to investigate. However, the owner of the motel stopped her and said curfew was in place, asking her to please return to her room until morning.

So Carmen slipped out a window instead and followed after the people from the house, and when a police officer saw her, he yelled at her to join the group. She complied to figure out what was going on, blending into the crowd. Something she did easily, as she was still wearing a dirty cloak and hadn't had time to clean herself up.

They were all led to a large building. Carmen tried to talk to some of the other people, but they looked at her like she was insane for just attempting this, and the police officers also gave her a stern warning that talking was not allowed before they made it to the hall to "not wake up the ones sleeping."

Who the fuck still slept?

Carmen found this ordeal incredibly fishy, and she instantly concluded that some nefarious cult or something like that existed in this small town. Looking at the other people with her, she noticed it was primarily women and children, with a few young men also present.

For some reason, the mood did seem generally positive despite the secretive methods. Carmen decided to not act out as they all entered a large hall. Then the door was closed, and she felt isolation barriers being activated.

"Welcome, everyone," a suited man said as he went up on a stage. Everyone around looked at him with mixed feelings, and she detected outright hatred from some of those present. Plenty of killing intent, too —something she had gotten very sensitive to due to her heritage. So, not a popular figure. Got it. "I apologize for bringing you all here on such short notice, but we just got word that Haven and Sanctdomo opened up their borders once more, and we have been allowed slots to send people there."

Many in the crowd sighed in relief.

"We had to do this secretly, as the slots are limited, and I am not blind to the struggles of those less fortunate. This is an opportunity for those deemed worthy of joining a powerful faction to finally get a stable and safe home with wealth and comfort. Representatives of Sanctdomo and Haven are both here, so please, apply if you are interested in this opportunity."

Needless to say, all this shit was getting shadier as fuck by the second. However, the people around her seemed excited, making her doubt herself.

"Hey... this is my first time hearing of this—is this for real?" Carmen asked a woman with her young daughter right next to her.

The woman smiled and answered, "It happens once a week or so, and always secretly. An open secret, I guess. I heard it is to not cause too much dissatisfaction or something, as normally only women and children are allowed to join the powerful factions. I do find it mighty kind of them to help us."

"Can't you just go to Haven or Sanctdomo without getting a slot or whatever?" Carmen asked, a bit confused.

"No, of course not; you need to be invited, or you will get rejected at the gates. That is why they send these representatives out to other smaller towns." The woman shook her head. "Don't worry, though; I am sure you will get selected."

Carmen nodded, just going with the flow as people were brought to interview rooms one by one. A few people returned dejected, while some didn't return, having been selected, according to what others said. She just stood around, and soon enough, an officer came over to her.

"It is your turn. Good luck."

Curious, Carmen walked into the interview room and saw a man and a woman sitting at a table with a few chairs in front. Looking about, she saw that three other women were there together with her— all around her own age, from the looks of it.

She took a seat as the man at the table began talking, first introducing himself as a representative of Haven, and then asking them to please take off their robes and get comfortable.

Carmen found it weird but did as asked. The others did the same, and they all took a seat. The man and woman talked a bit amongst themselves and asked some basic questions about which classes and professions people had, family and friends in the city or among other factions, and their ages. Again, just basic stuff.

Nothing was really that weird until the two spoke between them again, using some magic to hide their conversation. The woman then said, "I am sorry—numbers three and four, please leave."

Two of the other women exited the room, dejected, leaving only Carmen and a blonde woman. Carmen did note how they were the two who said they had no family or friends around. Curious.

"Congratulations on getting selected," the man said with a bright smile. "Please follow me to the others."

By now, Carmen knew something was off. The man in front of her was level 121, with the woman level 114, making them both solidly in the D-grade. Meanwhile, the woman with Carmen was only 32, and Carmen had lied, saying she was level 101, but only due to her profession, as she had given up on her class.

She followed troop and did as she was told. They went out a back door, and she felt the magic on the other side before even going through it. The blonde woman chatted with Carmen excitedly, all smiles, until the moment they stepped out the other side of the door, and both instantly felt the shift.

They had walked into another large room, and the doorway behind them instantly got sealed off by a barrier as a large, shirtless man stood up from a stool in a corner. "New batch, eh? Two young ones?"

"Excuse me, what is going on?" the blonde woman asked nervously.

The man smiled. "I am going to take both of you to somewhere much nicer than here. We just need to sign some paperwork first."

"Paperwork?" the woman asked.

"Just a tiny little slave contract. No biggie." The man kept smiling. Carmen saw him clearly enjoying himself, but she herself tried to look neutral.

"Haven has slaves?" the blonde woman asked with fright, her eyes wide open. Okay, perhaps Carmen gave the gal a touch too much credit for her ability to read the situation.

"A bit of a dumb one, but I am sure some people like that." The man shrugged, then turned his attention to Carmen. "A fiery-looking silent type? A personal favorite of mine. Let me make it clear: You two don't have a choice, and if you are good and obedient little girls, I will be sure to get you nice brothels. Any questions?"

"Left or right?" Carmen asked.

"What?" the man asked tauntingly.

"What arm do I rip off first? Actually, never mind."

The man didn't even have time to speak before Carmen stood right in front of him. Despite him being level 118, he couldn't even react as Carmen ripped downwards, tearing both his arms off at the shoulders.

"Argh!" he yelled as his eyes opened wide in despair. Carmen caught him by his skin-shirt before he could fall back onto the floor. "Now tell me... What the actual fuck is going on here?"

Jake and Sylphie flew through the air towards the small town of Ambermill. Studying the tablet a bit on the way, it looked like Ambermill was a small town of about five or six thousand, but it had a steady flow of new citizens who were looking to enter either Haven or travel further for Sanctdomo.

It was neutral and didn't have any teleportation gates connected to it, making it a little isolated but otherwise safe. The leader was some level 120 dude who had been the first to stumble upon an old mill. That mill had been transformed into a natural treasure, and since then, he had taken it as his home, using it to harvest and generate wind-affinity crystals. This was also the primary export of Ambermill and where the name came from, as the wind crystals looked like they were made of amber.

A quaint little place, Jake reckoned. This is why he was confused when he got closer and saw smoke in the distance. The mill that stood atop a hill was broken in half, and Jake felt intense energy emanating from the town. As he got closer, he began to smell blood, too, and he activated his tracking skill instantly to search for Carmen.

Something that turned out to be utterly unnecessary, as he felt her familiar aura without having to use any skills. Jake swiftly got a look at the city from above and saw dozens of broken buildings, more than a hundred corpses wearing what looked like police uniforms, and Carmen punching a bunker-like construct. Every punch sent shockwaves through the town that had already shattered every single window in the vicinity and cleared out the area.

Well, then, Jake thought as he headed down, followed by Sylphie, who also seemed interested in exploring these odd happenings.

He quickly detected people hiding inside houses and a general sense of panic in the city. The entire central square and what looked like the mayor's office were utterly ruined. Corpses were smashed to pieces in the rubble, and in the center of those ruins was what Jake assumed was a panic room that Carmen was currently punching.

Jake landed a bit away, Sylphie perching on top of his head.

Carmen instantly turned around, still on guard, but stopped when she saw them.

"Why the fuck are you here?" she asked, clearly annoyed. "Did this fucker really call you?"

"I tend to not have fuckers on speed-dial, so no. I came looking for you." Jake shrugged. "Why? Did whoever you are trying to kill make up some bullshit?"

The people hiding within the bunker also heard Jake, and one of them quickly yelled out from within, "Lord Thayne, you are here! This maniac began to—"

"Who are you?" Jake asked, cutting him off.

"Ah, we have never met in person, but I have—"

"Why are you trying to kill this guy?" Jake's interruption was directed at Carmen this time.

Carmen looked at Jake a bit suspiciously for a moment, but a screech from Sylphie seemed to dispel her doubt. "This entire fucking town is just a front for slave trading."

Jake frowned as he looked at the bunker. "Explain?"

"Please, it is not just me; we were all forced to assist them! They had D-grades and people far more powerful than us. What were we supposed to do?"

Looking inside the bunker with his sphere, Jake saw a total of five people. The guy who spoke wore a ruined business suit, while the four others had full combat attire on. He also saw one of the four working on what looked like a magic circle.

"If you want to talk, get out with your little friends and tell them to stop trying to put down a teleportation circle to escape," Jake said casually. He didn't actually know it was a teleportation circle, but he seriously doubted anyone inside that little bunker wanted to fight a pissed-off Carmen.

Within the bunker, he saw the mage stop for a second and look back at his comrades. The one who appeared to the leader—not the suit guy—motioned for him to continue. The suit guy also looked at this leader and nodded after they exchanged a look.

"Alright, but it takes some time to deactivate all the wards, and we will also need some assurance of safety before we—"

"Have it your way." Jake shrugged as he went over to the bunker.

"It is sturdy as fuck," Carmen warned.

"To your attacks, sure. But if you know the right spot to poke..."

Jake activated Touch of the Malefic Viper, and what looked like dark green lightning spread all over the magic barrier. "It isn't that hard."

Within seconds, the barrier broke down as Jake successfully ruined what kept it together. What? It was a basic defensive formation, and Jake had studied enough about anti-mana poisons to know what worked well against such barriers.

This was clearly not the expected outcome for those hiding within, as Carmen flew forward and shattered the entire bunker with a single punch, sending debris flying and revealing the five occupants. The guy in a suit looked absolutely horrified, but the four others moved fast to toss four attacks Carmen's way.

She ignored all of them, and within ten seconds, three of the four were dead, and the last one—the leader—lay broken in the middle of the square with both his legs missing. It all went relatively fast, and Jake honestly had no skin in the game or impulse to interfere. Why would he? This was Carmen's crusade—and a justified one, it seemed.

The legless man on the ground managed to get his bearings somewhat, even with his friends dead, as he turned to them. "Do you have any idea what you have done? The people that back us?" He said this as a threat, trying to puff himself up. "Even if you two manage to survive, what about your cities? Families? If we reach some agreement, I am sure I can make all this go away."

He spoke to both Jake and Carmen, and Jake did believe the guy had some pull. He had a high level, after all.

[Human - lvl 139]

Carmen turned to Jake, but Jake just shrugged.

"Please, do tell, who exactly backs you?" Carmen asked the guy.

"Slaves are in high demand all around the planet for various means... Someone needs to provide them, and we are those people."

"Ah, gotcha." Jake nodded. "So, people we would also kill if we came across them."

"I second that," the still-bloodthirsty member of Valhal said.

"Please wait!" the guy in the suit suddenly yelled before Carmen could crush the legless guy's skull. "If he dies here... we..."

He stopped talking as Jake and Carmen both stared him down.

"Hah," the legless guy said as he turned to the suit guy with a devilish smile. "You were the one who came to us first. You were the one who offered those useless people in the slums in exchange for cash to expand your little settlement. You enjoyed quite a few of the women, too, didn't you? At least die like a man with some pride intact."

"Says the guy who begged for his life a minute ago," Carmen rebutted.

"Fuck off and just kill me already," he said, scoffing.

Something Carmen gladly did. She kicked his head so hard it exploded in blood and gore.

The suit guy looked absolutely horrified. He began to open his mouth to explain himself, but before any words came out, his chest separated from the rest of his limbs and head as it flew into a nearby wall, splattering all over it.

"I already knew he was a shitbag," Carmen muttered as she looked at Jake.

Jake, in turn, looked around the place and scratched his head.

"What?" Carmen said defensively. "Got any complaints about how I handled things? Every single motherfucker had it coming."

"Nah, not that." Jake shrugged. "I was thinking about what to tell Miranda."

"Just tell the truth," Carmen said with a deadpan face.

Miranda was working in her office when a walkie-talkie on her table suddenly rang. She saw it was Jake and instantly responded. "Hey, Jake, I heard you went out to meet up with Carmen. How did it go?"

"Know Ambermill?" he asked.

"Yeah?" Miranda answered, perplexed. Ah, had she stopped by there? That made sense to—

"Well, apparently they were running a slave business, Carmen found out, and she may or may not have killed the entire leadership structure and pretty much every single member of their local law enforcement. Oh, and left the town in ruins."

Miranda was silent for a moment before she just sighed. "I will send some people…"

CHAPTER 22

FRIENDLY ADVICE & COMPETITION

S ultan stood in the old ruins of what had once been Ambermill as he looked at the departing former citizens. Four large barges able to accommodate every person had been brought from the Fort and would help transport them all back to the settlement.

He had been asked by Miranda to go to Ambermill together with a crew of others to handle the situation. She had heard slavery was going on, and people had been forced into contracts, so she wanted someone with knowledge of slave contracts to go and hopefully help annul those already signed as well as track down potential leads. The first one he had gladly done, but the second job was a bit more... complicated.

"I did tell that idiot this was too close to Haven," Sultan said, smirking as he shook his head. He had known about the operations going on in Ambermill for quite a while but had naturally kept quiet. It wasn't anything that affected him, and he had already left the entire slave-trading scene for good. That didn't mean others had, though.

As he stood there alone, a person slowly became visible after exiting the shadow of a nearby house. "Libra took it too far, attempting to take advantage of the gap in the market left by Haven and Sanctdomo, both cracking down on slavery. I do agree it was wise to take him down a peg."

The shadowy figure soon became fully visible. He wore a dark cloak and was enveloped by shadow magic Sultan naturally recognized.

"I am surprised the Court of Shadows didn't try to defend one of their clients," Sultan said with a teasing smile.

"We are, by giving him the advice to not fuck with this area and hiding all evidence of Libra's involvement in this shithole," the assassin sneered. "The other constellations have already requested an emergency meeting. Have you been informed?"

Sultan nodded. "Naturally."

"Great, then my job here is done," the assassin-turned-instigator of town destruction said with a smile. "Now for my pay."

Returning his smile, Sultan transferred the sum as per the contract for a job well done.

If Carmen had been there, she would have recognized the cloaked man as the same police officer that had brought her to the town hall. The same man who had coincidentally chosen a house right outside the motel Carmen was staying in as a great place to round up potential slaves. The same man who had "screened" Carmen as being part of the slums.

Sultan had predicted Carmen to raise a ruckus, but it had become a bigger issue than expected, more or less leading to the end of the entire town of Ambermill. It wasn't really a big deal, though, as with the biggest asset of the town destroyed—the mill—it no longer held any value.

However, more importantly... he'd managed to toss out a competitor from his very own backyard, and if things went well, he'd possibly get rid of him entirely in the near future.

"Pleasure doing business with you, as always," the assassin said as he slowly faded back into the shadows, his presence disappearing completely.

Sultan summoned his small black book and circled a name in it as he nodded. With his work done, he summoned his ship to travel back to Haven—after a little detour and a covert meeting, of course.

"Do you seriously just do that every time?" Carmen asked Jake as the two ran leisurely through the plains.

They had already returned to Haven, teleported a few times, and were now running from a smallish Pylon city with a teleporter in it. It was the settlement closest to the port city, and thus they had to run the rest of the way.

The problem was that Carmen kept giving Jake grief over Miranda's response. When they returned to Haven, Jake, Sylphie, Miranda, and Carmen had met up briefly for them to exchange greetings and for Jake and Carmen to explain the situation in Ambermill more in depth.

Carmen found it hilarious how little Miranda seemed to actually care or be surprised. Miranda had then made it worse by telling her about all the times Jake had forgotten things, been late or nearly late to events, and how he just kept doing unpredictable stuff. Case in point, when they'd gone and said hello to Rick because Carmen really wanted to know if they were just pulling her leg when they talked about the "troll gardener."

What was so weird about a troll gardener?

"Ree?" Sylphie asked with a confused screech, coming in with the clutch assist.

"As Sylphie said, I wasn't the one who did anything this time," Jake shot back. "You were."

"She did not say that."

"Ree!" Sylphie huffed.

Carmen looked at the bird. "Touche. How the hell do you even understand Sylphie? Like, I can get general intent and stuff, but not anything even halfway complex."

"I did hawk language courses when I went to college. Damn those unrelated electives..."

"With how fucking useless college was for all my friends, I could believe that was an actual thing," Carmen said, scoffing. "But seriously, how? We both got that language translation skill, but I don't think it translates anything that isn't considered an actual language."

"To be honest, I have no idea myself. It's mainly guesswork and just intuition as well as reading the intent, as you said." Jake shrugged. "It helps when you spend a lot of time around the other person. Sylphie and I also have a weird contract, and a connection of sorts due to said contract."

Carmen looked sharply at Jake. "What kind of contract?"

Jake instantly knew what she was thinking about. Beast tamers—which Valhal had plenty of—used contracts or forced bonds to pretty much enslave beasts for use in armies. Not that some beasts didn't also willingly join these tamers, but the fact that they were bound to a master was still a thing.

"A Union Oath, and it wasn't even me who initiated it, but Sylphie," Jake answered.

"Ree!" Sylphie confirmed as she happily flapped her wings and circled around the two running humans a few times, faster than the both of them by quite a bit.

"Good." Carmen sighed in relief.

They kept running a bit more in silence as Jake considered their merry band. It did come as a bit of a surprise, but Carmen had not surpassed him in level as he had thought. She was level 153, seven levels below himself, and the explanation for this was the same as his: She was consolidating her Path.

She had focused on her profession, as her class had gotten too far ahead, and she had pursued improving other aspects of herself, such as forging her fists through weird rituals and magic—something she still did. She said that she had to take a few hours every week and submerge her hands in some golden concoction she had brought with her to forge her hands. Jake was very much looking forward to seeing this process.

This did mean Sylphie was the highest-leveled among them, and damn, did she flex it. She flew around them in circles and made noises to taunt them, and she sometimes sped ahead and then laid down on the ground, pretending to be asleep until they caught up. All juvenile things that Jake and Carmen both found absolutely adorable.

Sylphie had only grown faster, and was naturally also the fastest of the bunch. Her sprinting speed had always been extreme, but even her normal flying speed now exceeded Jake's by a large margin, and while he could keep up with her by using One Step Mile, he would be far slower in actual combat.

Not that he could use One Step Mile, as Carmen didn't have any long-distance movement skills to travel with. Flying up in the air also wouldn't be faster for either of them, as the energy expenditure was far larger doing that. So they were stuck running with Sylphie enjoying herself by flying around them.

The little feather ball did help them a bit, as they always ran with a tailwind and a refreshing breeze blessed their way forward, giving them a bit of speed and reducing their energy expenditure.

Jake kept an eye on the tablet given by Arnold and tracked their movement, and about two days after departing from the small town, they came to one of the areas marked with orange and a P. Orange meant there were high-tier D-grades, and the P meant the energy signature of a Prima had been detected.

While taking a small break before heading into the orange zone, Jake said, "I never got to ask... Do you have a full key for that Seat of the Exalted Prima thing and the system event?"

"I had a key..." she said, though she seemed oddly reluctant to talk about it.

Jake quickly caught on. "Had a key?"

"Well, Sven came out of the dungeon that he had been stuck in for a long time right around when I left... Three members of his party died, and he was in shit condition. He would've had no chance to get three fragments by himself, and I had easily gotten my key, so I thought I would just hand him mine."

"Wait, then why the hell didn't you focus on getting another one?" Jake asked, perplexed.

Carmen shook her head. "It just isn't that important to me, I guess?"

Jake raised an eyebrow as he looked at her. "Bullshit."

"Whatever," she said with another scoff. "Why do you even care?"

"Well, I just wanted to know if we are collecting one or four more fragments. It seems we are going for four, so it may get a bit tight on time, but I am sure we can manage. There should be several Primas in and around this Grand Mangrove River." Jake shrugged.

"I said I don't care about getting a key," Carmen insisted.

"And yet you will. Why are you afraid of the system event?"

"I'm not fucking afraid. I just don't need it."

"Neither do I, but I will sure participate anyway for whatever rewards it may give. You should do the same."

"We are back to asking why you even give a fuck," Carmen said, still being combative. "I don't want to get told how much I fucked up my life already and how I could have been way smarter in retrospect, or suddenly be forced to choose some other class or something, wasting all the effort I have put in so far."

Jake looked at her and thought for a moment before he just shrugged. "You like punching stuff, right?"

"Duh," she said, almost offended.

"Then just keep punching stuff and keep walking a Path where you punch stuff. Heck, I can see myself being shown a Path during the event telling me I am an absolute moron for choosing to use a bow, but I like my bow, so that event can fuck right off. I will instead just use what I learn to improve what I currently do. You should do the same, and fuck what is optimal or considered the best. Just pick what you like the most."

"Sounds like a good way to end up stuck at early C-grade, if you even manage to evolve." Carmen shook her head.

"Quite the opposite. You know Valdemar, right?"

"Alright, now I am just assuming you are purposefully being an asshole," Carmen said, glaring at Jake.

"Dumb question, sorry. Anyway, Valdemar was, well, just a dude who liked swinging his axe and apparently didn't think too much about stuff, but he still ended up reaching godhood in a time where it was far harder than now. All he had were balls of steel and a drive to get stronger."

Carmen now looked at Jake with quite a glare. "Valdemar was a warlord who managed to lead countless battles and dictate the rise and fall of entire intergalactic empires. He was a hero who managed to unite the enlightened races and bring them recognition in a time where humans and most other enlightened races were struggling to gain a foothold."

"Being that and a hardheaded dude who likes to swing an axe aren't mutually exclusive," Jake pointed out.

"Are you trying to start a fight, or—"

Carmen suddenly stopped talking and stood with a blank stare for a few moments. Jake wondered what was going on, but Carmen quickly snapped out of it. "Well, fuck me."

"What happened?" Jake asked.

"Valdemar's fucking wife just laughed and said you were right on the money," Carmen said in disbelief.

"See?" Jake said triumphantly. "So just do whatever feels right."

It looked like the god who had blessed Carmen—Gudrun—spoke to her again, as she stood there with a blank stare. Jake saw a faint hint of gold in Carmen's eyes and noticed how she was pretty much in a trance. Like she wasn't really there.

A few seconds passed before she "woke up" again and shook her head, groaning. "Fucking hell..."

"What?" Jake asked.

"Just... nothing," Carmen said, having clearly been told something by the god she didn't want to share. "Fine. Let's collect those damn fragments already. Let's go."

"Ree!" Sylphie agreed, obviously bored of their, in her mind, boring conversation.

Jake was the slowest to react, as he suddenly got a few system notifications he had not in any way expected.

'DING!' Profession: [Heretic-Chosen Alchemist of the Malefic

Viper] has reached level 169 - Stat points allocated, +10 Free Points*

'DING!' Race: [Human (D)] has reached level 161 - Stat points allocated, +15 Free Points

At first, he had no idea why the hell he had just gotten a level out of nowhere, but he quickly connected the dots: Legacy Teachings of the Heretic-Chosen Alchemist.

Jake hadn't really used the skill for anything before, but had clearly just done *something* related to it during his talk with Carmen. Which had to mean Jake had taught her something. On accident. Something related to his unique Path of being blessed and, at the same time, a bit of a heretic.

Shaking his head, Jake followed after Sylphie and Carmen, who had already run into the tunnel in front of them. As he ran, he focused on his tracking skill together with Sense of the Malefic Viper, fishing out one of the key fragments to get a feel for the energy signature.

Shortly after, he caught up to the woman and bird.

"I can definitely sense a Prima somewhere," Jake said, somewhat surprised at being able to actually detect anything.

"So you do know how to track stuff," Carmen said with a nod, a touch of relief in her voice.

"Kind of. And I have a feeling tracking down a few Primas will help make me better than just kind of being able to track stuff. For the record, I sense the energy in the center of this very tunnel—right in our path, if we keep going straight."

The tunnel was carved into a mountain chain and was the fastest way to their destination. Arnold had marked that they could take another path through a smaller passage, but they decided to go straight through, considering they needed to hunt some Primas anyway.

It was a huge tunnel, several hundred meters in diameter, and had a rather winding path and several sub-tunnels leading in all directions. Jake managed to really put his tracking skills to the test as he followed the energy down certain paths, slowly closing in on their target.

Five minutes into the incredibly long tunnel, they both noticed the lack of any other life. Not even plants. It was just blank stone walls on all sides. At the same time, the level of earth-affinity mana in the air also spiked with every passing step, making the conclusion obvious.

"Earth elementals," Jake said.

Carmen nodded, with Sylphie trying to mimic her nod, just looking a bit silly.

Jake soon felt some subtle movement down below. It was not an attack, but instead felt like something traveled through the earth to get behind them. With deeper probing, he noticed presences—living beings, to put it simply. Earth elementals.

"I feel them below," Jake said. Carmen once more nodded in acknowledgment, and they both put together the plan of these elementals.

Taking advantage of the terrain, they would attack from both sides while at the same time using the tunnel walls themselves as weapons against Jake, Carmen, and Sylphie.

The three of them soon stopped as the earth in front of them rumbled. Behind them, the tunnel was cut off as a large wall of earth sprang up, and vaguely humanoid forms began emerging from the ground, walls, and ceiling. Jake identified a few of them quickly, getting a feel for what they were facing,

[earth elemental – lvl 179]
[earth elemental – lvl 178]
[earth elemental – lvl 181]

Carmen had clearly done the same, and the two of them exchanged a look. Sylphie also joined in, looking between them excitedly.

"Most kills wins?" Jake asked, getting a smirk and a "ree!" in response before all three of them made it absolutely clear that these earth elementals had just seriously fucked up.

CHAPTER 23

EARTH ELEMENTAL PRIMA

Martial artists had a long history of chopping down on stones or tiles to show off how strong they were. Now, this wasn't actually the martial artist having tougher hands than the tile, but just taking advantage of physics and generally weakly constructed, brittle tiles to make themselves look cool. Some did it with bricks, too, even though that also didn't make sense, as these bricks were not constructed to resist force applied to the edges, making them rather brittle too.

Lots of tactics were applied to do this, the simplest of which was always making sure there was a small gap between the surface and the object before hitting. This increased the force applied significantly, as the object was smashed down and thus broken more easily—which explains why there were always small gaps between stacked tiles.

All of this is to say that, before the system, actually smashing rock with your hand wasn't going to happen. No martial artist could break a normal, everyday rock with his or her bare hands. What would break instead was the hand of the person. The reason for this was basic damn physics. For every action, there is an equal and opposite reaction and all that.

This law of physics was also mostly true after the system. There were magical ways of making it not really a thing anymore, but when punching someone or clashing using weapons, it mostly existed. There were some examples of martial arts being able to circumvent these laws, such as when the Sword Saint had blocked Jake's weapon back during their duel and more or less nullified or fully redirected the force.

Carmen clearly didn't have any such skill. Neither did the earth elementals. With how the system worked, one would also think that the bodies of the earth elementals were, on average, more durable than the exposed fists of a human.

But... well, looking at what was currently happening, Jake wasn't so sure—at least, not when the elementals were compared to Carmen's fists.

She flew forward and smashed her fist into an elemental, sending it flying back as shards of rock flew everywhere. It rapidly regenerated, and the tunnel itself seemed to attack her with dozens of spikes erupting from all sides.

They all hit a golden set of phantasmal armor as Carmen kept up her attacks, utterly annihilating the earth elementals. Jake had to admit that she was a lot better than him at melee fighting—not only due to her higher Strength, but also her superior technique.

Some blows were large and flashy, but others were far more complicated. When an elemental charged her, Carmen countered by landing three quick jabs that each left microcracks on the elemental before she followed up with a straight to shatter the entire central part of its body.

Jake, for his part, wasn't slacking off either. He teleported and sometimes floated through the tunnel as he fired off arrows, went into melee, used magic attacks, and generally switched it up for whatever was appropriate. Needless to say, he couldn't use his full power when with others and in an enclosed space. If he was alone, the entire area would already be filled with poison mist and arcane explosions.

However, the one who was thriving the most was a little murder bird who was like a tornado of razor blades just shredding the elementals one by one. Sylphie flew around faster than the poor elementals could handle as they were cut to pieces.

As for the elementals themselves, they were a lot like the cloud elementals Jake and Hawkie had fought. They were pretty slow, but incredibly durable and annoying to put down for good. They kept reconstructing themselves until they ran out of mana, and the only good way to kill them was to just break them repeatedly.

Offensively, they were a bit meh, primarily manipulating their surroundings to strike at their target or just hitting with their huge, bulky bodies, which consisted of stone and soil. They weren't a threat to anyone in the party of three and were, on average, very low-tier creatures. The same as most common natural-spawning elementals, actually.

Elementals were a bit interesting in how their races worked. Basic elementals like fire elementals, earth elementals, wind elementals, and even cloud elementals could vary pretty widely in power even within the same level. The way the race gained stats per level could vary, and one earth elemental could gain 100 stat points per level while another got twice that. This was more or less always tied to the area in which they were born and resided, and sometimes maintaining this growth required them to remain where they had spawned.

Measuring the strength of an elemental was still pretty easy, even without Jake's instincts. You just had to measure the mana levels they gave off and compare that to their level. As mentioned, these earth elementals were on the weaker side, making the three of them do quick work.

They began diving deeper and deeper into the tunnel as they killed anything in their path. Another general trait of elementals was their lack of intelligence, making them little more than environmental hazards with a bit of instinct tossed in. Needless to say, elementals were often the prey and not the predator. The cloud island was a great example of this, and the only way they tended to survive long was if they dominated an area like the tunnel Carmen, Jake, and Sylphie were currently tearing apart.

Soon they were practically sprinting, barely bothering to finish off the annoying elementals. They took too long to kill and would keep chasing anyway, so they just let them pile up and then took down bigger groups. When they got further in, the entire tunnel also expanded to a large cavern with several pockets in between narrower tunnels. Carmen began making a few stops, having Jake and Sylphie follow to loot some precious metals and other natural treasures she needed for her profession.

Jake was all good doing this, as these open spaces where the precious materials existed were also ideal hunting grounds for Jake. It allowed him to get more distance, bombard the elementals with explosive arrows, and even begin testing some things on them, primarily with Touch of the Malefic Viper.

He didn't have any poisons that were good against earth elementals. Heck, he didn't have anything good against most elementals. Lightning poison was pretty decent against many elemental types, but following pocket-monster logic, electric-type moves didn't work against rock and ground types. Of course, the poison type didn't work either, following this logic, but luckily poison in this new world wasn't quite as restricted as before, and Jake soon began making some progress as he used the poor elementals as test subjects.

Honestly, what worked best against them was perhaps what one should have expected: corrosion. Stones were durable and steadfast, but also slow at adapting and expelling energy. A stone could not easily change shape or shake off acid, and the elementals were always forced to take solid form in some way or another. Of course, if he just doused an earth elemental in acid, it could just shear off its outer layer. This would still do some damage, true, but it would be minor at best.

But what if you spread the corrosion into the body of the elemental? Infecting not only the physical body, but the mana itself, with the power of corrosion? Jake didn't have any good anti-rock corrosives he had any experience with, but he did know a few basic types from lessons, all of which proved somewhat effective.

Sure, it was less effective than just using destructive arcane mana, but Jake still found it worth his time to learn and improve this aspect of his profession. It wasn't like these elementals would put up a good fight anyway, and Carmen was damn slow at times getting the metals she needed, as the extraction processes weren't always as simple as just smashing the ground and grabbing whatever gave off the most mana. It was a bit like collecting some herbs, though Jake tended to swipe them up swiftly anyway, even if it lost some efficiency.

Ah, who was he kidding? He just scammed ancient vampires with antique furniture whenever he needed stuff.

"You good?" Jake asked as he finished off the last elemental that tried to stop Carmen from slowly getting the small gem out of the stone. She had carefully taken it out after rubbing away the surrounding stone with her palm like was it made of sandpaper.

"Yeah, I got it," she said. "Last push for the Prima?"

Jake nodded as he sensed the air and took a deep breath, practically smelling the unique mana of the Prima. "It's up ahead... One, maybe two caverns. Honestly, hard to tell with how dense the mana is."

"Ree!" Sylphie complained as she puffed herself up in anger. She really didn't like the heavy earth affinity in the air hampering her wind mana. Jake knew she had to spend more mana than usual—something Jake luckily didn't have to do, thanks to his arcane mana being so closely connected to affinity-less mana, which there was still plenty of.

"Alright," Jake said. "We make the push, then. No breaks till the Prima is down." That got quick confirmations from the others. None of them were tired out yet, and Jake had naturally shared his potions with the group, being a good team player and all that.

Two minutes later, they departed for more earth elemental slaughtering and to reach the Prima. Many orbs containing pure earth mana were collected along the way, making it not entirely a waste of time, even if the experience was subpar.

As Jake had guessed, the first cavern they reached was devoid of any Primas, making them swiftly move through. By now, the areas were getting pretty big, and it especially began opening up when they got closer to their goal.

"It is right up ahead," Jake said with great confidence.

His words were proven true as they reached an expansive new cavern. However, this one was different from the others. The occasional crystal lined the walls, giving off a faint light, and in the middle was a pillar of crystals that seemed to hold the ceiling of the cavern up. It was humming with power, and Jake instantly recognized the pillar as a natural treasure similar to the lightning tree on the cloud island. The tree did give off more power, though, and Jake was certain the tree was a better treasure. The giant elemental that was currently siphoning off its energy certainly didn't help it either.

The Prima itself looked like a large, bulky golem with blocky but faintly humanoid features. It was more than fifteen meters tall, standing with both its arms on the pillar, and was practically pulsing with power. Jake and the others used Identify on it, and it was indeed the strongest thing around and had the Prima tag.

[Earth Elemental Prima - lvl 185]

Jake tossed Carmen a look, and she just snickered as she knelt down and pressed her fists to the ground, giving Jake a nod as he also began to prepare his opening attack.

He did so as he whipped out his Bow of the Apex Hunter and began charging his Arcane Powershot. Sylphie also began glowing green, a small whirlwind revolving around her. Their actions truly got the attention of the Prima as the entire cavern began moving. Dozens of elementals emerged every second, and the Prima itself reached out a hand to attack.

It wasn't a fully charged Arcane Powershot, but it was good enough. Jake let go of the string as he exploded with arcane power, and at the same time, Sylphie flew forward with speed matching his arrow.

"Sacred Battleground," Carmen spoke, and a golden pulse went through the entire cavern. She stepped forward and blocked a barrage of stone fragments heading for Jake, who was already charging his second Arcane Powershot while at the same time beginning to condense an Arrow of the Ambitious Hunter within the special space in his quiver.

Two things impacted the Earth Elemental Prima a second later. One of them was an explosive arcane arrow that sent shards of rock flying, and the second was a hawk that just pierced straight through, surpassing the power of Jake's arrow by quite a bit.

However, the elemental healed almost instantly, pulling power from the central pillar. Its outer shell also began changing and taking on a crystalline form, at which point Jake noticed the many shards embedded in the walls of the cavern give off energies similar to that of the Prima.

Some kind of resonance? Jake asked himself. One thing was clear: This entire cavern was the domain of the Prima, and would make it a lot harder to—

Jake then saw Carmen make a weird hand sign as she punched the ground. A shockwave traveled all across the surfaces of the cavern, and within an instant, thousands of crystals exploded, taking away a large part of the elemental's home-field advantage while making crystal dust rain down.

The pillar in the middle still stood strong, as the Prima displayed a level of intelligence Jake was not used to seeing from elementals. It retreated by sliding up the pillar, sending the many regular earth elementals after Jake and Carmen as it focused on Sylphie.

An endless barrage of rocks went for Jake and Carmen, making her unable to fully defend Jake, and forcing him to fire his Arcane Powershot to blow up a few elementals. Meanwhile, Sylphie engaged with the Prima that had begun changing its form. It transformed into a long, snake-like creature instead of its humanoid form as it coiled around the crystal pillar. It opened its mouth and sent out sharp barrages of rock, each one of them the size of a human forearm.

Sylphie tried to attack, but her smaller attacks had a hard time breaking the crystalline outer shell of the Prima, while the larger ones were instantly healed anyway. Jake kept an eye on everything as he and Carmen killed the elementals one by one. He didn't see them losing, but if the situation continued, it could get tricky... The pillar more or less seemed to give the Prima infinite energy to absorb. It was a situation Jake had seen before, and he knew just the thing to fuck the Prima up.

"I need a path to the pillar," Jake said as he flew next to Carmen.

"Got it." She nodded and smashed her fists together, making her entire body glow golden. She stormed forward and began clearing a path that Jake quickly went through, switching position with Carmen so she covered his back while he went for the pillar.

"Cover me," he said as he went up to the base of the pillar.

He also sent a mental message to Sylphie, and she reacted by beginning to fly around the pillar. Jake felt the wind pick up all around him as a whirlwind of green energy formed, covering his form and keeping the projectile attacks of the elementals away. The only way for them to actually attack him was to come with their true bodies, but Carmen had that covered.

Jake placed his hands on the pillar as Touch of the Malefic Malefic Viper activated along with Arcane Awakening in the balanced state. He focused his energy on the pillar while pulling out two items he quickly began consuming to aid the process. One of them was a rare-rarity Refined Dark Orb from a powerful dark elemental that had been refined into a catalyst for dark-affinity magic, and the other was an all-purpose amplifier for transmutation magic called a Transmutation Stone.

[Transmutation Stone (Uncommon)] — An uncommon stone used to aid in the transmutation process, functioning as a catalyst. Using a Transmutation Stone makes harmonically fusing energies easier.

It was the kind of item that Villy would describe as "a crutch" and wasn't good to use under normal circumstances, but it did make the process slightly faster.

Jake's attack on the crystalline pillar was quickly noticed by the Prima absorbing energy from it, and it promptly reacted. The ground beneath Jake began pulsing, but Jake was ready as he stomped down, sending a wave of pure, stable arcane mana through it. The mana lingered, making the elemental unable to manipulate the earth, buying him time.

Sylphie also picked up the pace and began attacking more viciously, even trying to pull the Prima away from the pillar altogether. It didn't work, but it brought Jake even more time as he worked fast.

Both his items were rapidly consumed as Jake pumped mana into the pillar. Dark cracks began spreading as the dark mana consumed everything it could, and Jake happily helped it along, giving him flashbacks to his days with the Quintessence in the boar dungeon with the lake.

Back then, it had taken him many hours for a lake with far less energy than this pillar to be corrupted... but the Jake of back then was not the same as now. The cracks from his mana began spreading several meters up the pillar every second, and when the Dark Orb cracked, it reached the Prima coiled around the pillar.

When it did, the Prima knew it was screwed. It rapidly uncoiled itself as it tried to flee to the ground, but Sylphie managed to create a wall of wind that sent it tumbling down in Carmen's direction. Jake also stopped what he was doing and went on the offensive again. The pillar would no longer help the elemental, and it knew it.

The Prima changed shape again mid-air into a panther-like form as it met Carmen's fist with a claw. They were both blasted back, but before the Prima had any chance to stabilize, it was attacked by Jake and Sylphie. One was an archer that fired explosive arcane arrows that broke the outer crystalline defensive layer, and the other was a hawk that attacked and sent what may as well have been air shotguns into these exposed areas.

It kept trying to retreat, but they simply didn't give it a chance. The Prima kept struggling, but when Jake pulled out and landed an Arrow of the Ambitious Hunter, it seemed to know its days were numbered. Its form had reduced significantly, and with reluctance, the Prima suddenly flew towards the central pillar again. Jake, Carmen, and Sylphie had placed themselves to stop it from fleeing away from the cavern, not run towards the very center of it. This meant none of them were able to react as the elemental smashed into the pillar. It seemed to almost merge with it, and Jake felt his corrupted mana being affected within the pillar... but it wasn't getting weaker. No, it was being purposefully fed as it grew in power.

Jake's eyes opened wide.

"Defenses, now!" he yelled as a huge surge of energy erupted from the pillar, making it explode into millions of shards as cracks formed all over the cavern walls.

A huge rumble shook the ground as Jake and the others got notification of the Prima's death. it had consumed itself in an attempt to take down its attackers...

By bringing the entire fucking mountain down on top of them.

CHAPTER 24

THE GREAT ESCAPE

W as it a sign of intelligence to willingly kill yourself to try and take your would-be killers down with you? It was undoubtedly a sign of ego, and proof the Earth Elemental Prima had been no simple-minded creature. Calling it smart would perhaps be a bit too much, but it certainly did have some level of intelligence not found in its regular brethren. They just died when they ran out of mana and fought the same way from the beginning till the end. They simply didn't have the mental faculties to display desperation.

They displayed this as, even with the entire place coming down, they kept attacking Jake, Sylphie, and Carmen, putting extra pressure on them while they tried to reach one of the tunnels leading out of the cavern.

"Blocked off here!" Carmen yelled.

"Here too," Jake noted as he quickly surveyed their surroundings. "Fucker managed to direct the force to collapse the entrances first."

He also sent out a string of mana as he tracked the mana of the fragment dropped by the Prima. It was currently falling to the ground along with the broken pieces of the pillar, making it easy enough to snatch along with the orb dropped by the Earth Elemental Prima.

"Plans?" Carmen asked while smashing an elemental to pieces as she looked up at the rapidly cracking ceiling, clearly knowing it was only a question of when, not if, the entire mountain would come down. "I have an escape talisman, but it only works for me."

Jake, too, looked up as he held down and destroyed another annoying elemental. "We break out of here."

"How?" Carmen asked with exasperation. "While I don't see myself dying, it will take a long-ass time to dig myself out of this fucking place, and if these elementals survive and keep attacking, it could get dangerous."

Sylphie agreed as she kept killing elementals, clearly waiting for Jake to decide what they were going to do.

Jake held out his hand, and a transparent flame appeared. "Trying to trap an alchemist under a rock without any will of its own is pretty dumb; that's all I'm gonna say."

He manipulated the flame as it revolved around him and shot it off towards a nearby wall. It simply seemed to remove a part of the wall, confirming his theory. Jake had taken lessons in using his Alchemical Flame, and he still vividly remembered the one about Soulflames and properly merging your flame and your will. Jake was far from that stage, as the dragon back then would have just snapped and made the entire mountain disappear, but he could at least manipulate his flame well enough to dig them out.

Above, a large section of the cavern ceiling cracked, and a massive boulder fell down, causing a chain reaction as everything began collapsing at once.

"To me!" Jake yelled, and the two complied, disengaging from the elementals still causing them trouble.

In an act of irony, the elementals were crushed by boulders falling down on them, making them lose their forms and become unable to assemble themselves again. Jake spread out his hands as he manipulated his Alchemical Flame and formed a barrier of transparent fire around them. A rock fell down on top of the barrier and was consumed as it made contact with the fire, draining Jake's mana in kind.

"Let's go!" Jake said as he moved to the wall and began walking into it, creating a new tunnel with his flame.

The stones weren't that tough, and he had managed to burn through the incredibly durable stone back in Yalsten to steal the doors. This mountain couldn't even hold a candle to the mountain towers back in the hidden vampire realm.

Even within the newly formed tunnel, the cracks kept spreading, and it kept collapsing upon them.

"Can you keep this up?" Carmen asked as she cradled Sylphie to her chest and walked close to Jake, who had been forced to make the bubble of Alchemical Flame smaller to reduce mana expenditure. They were practically huddled together as Jake and Carmen slowly moved forward.

"That fucking Prima did something... or maybe the pillar was just holding this entire mountain up," Jake muttered, annoyed. "Depending on how deep we are, I may run out of mana."

"Got it—say if you need any help," Carmen said, nearly hugging him from behind as they moved forward.

They soon began going at a bit of an upwards angle, and Jake closed his eyes and focused on not only his magic, but also his mana sense and intuition. He went for where the earth mana became thinner, meaning what was closer to the outside.

Jake's flame didn't give off any light unless he used it to heat up an object and set it on fire. However, what he was doing currently didn't really utilize any heat as he infused his flame with destructive arcane mana. The malleable flame accepted it without complaint or resistance.

In complete darkness, they walked. Jake could still see due to his high Perception and his sphere, but it was clear that Carmen had a hard time. Sylphie managed by not having to move at all, just relaxing in Carmen's arms.

Forty minutes passed, and Jake took out a potion with the new special enchantment of his necklace, allowing him to consume it right away. The way it worked was a bit... off. Jake literally had a bottle placed in his stomach, as far as he could tell, but the bottle disappeared instantly once consumed, allowing the mana potion to rejuvenate him.

This forty-minute figure became critical. It was the time it took Jake to consume the full amount a potion could restore, meaning he was constantly losing mana. As the hours passed, Jake's mana pool slowly dwindled, and they began to discuss alternate strategies.

"We could punch and blow ourselves out?" Carmen proposed.

"Potentially," Jake said. "But if we do that, we need to spread out. The shockwaves you send out would end up causing issues for Sylphie and me, and will surely cause cave-ins. This is also assuming the new tunnel or path you make is in any way stable. At least now the ceiling is collapsing at a slow and steady rate."

This collapsing effect was why Jake had to consume soil falling from above, but as they kept moving forward, it wasn't as bad. However, if he began making big moves, it could make everything above collapse and put intense pressure on them. No, the only good way would be to more or less slowly muscle themselves upwards, practically trying to "swim" through the stone, which would take ages.

"Why are none of you a space mage..." Carmen muttered, and Jake couldn't help but smile a bit himself. If Neil was there, he would have just teleported them all out or created a spatial bubble and then put down a formation to get them out.

"Ree!" Sylphie complained, incredibly offended. This earned a quick apology from Carmen, who made it clear she was complaining about Jake.

"I do agree we need to speed this up," Jake said, unbothered.

He had actually hoped to improve his efficiency and thus speed, but he didn't get any worthwhile progress using Alchemical Flame, and a skill upgrade was definitely out of the question. He would just have to keep going and hope they got out in time, but it was looking grim.

Taking a break would mean the tunnel collapsing down on them and slowly drowning them in soil and stone, so that was out of the question. Jake could stabilize the surroundings with mana, but what was the point of that if the entire purpose of the break was to regenerate mana?

"Ree?" Sylphie suddenly asked.

"Say that again?" Jake replied.

"Ree! Ree!" Sylphie repeated.

Jake nodded along at her suggestion as his eyes flashed. "That... could work... definitely..." he muttered, deep in thought.

"I feel left in the dark here," Carmen said, sighing. "In more ways than one... I can't see shit."

"Carmen, are you up for doing something incredibly risky but also potentially cool as fuck?" Jake asked as he shared the idea with her. The woman had a look of utter disbelief at first, with her mouth wide open, and then it just turned into a huge grin.

"That sounds so fucking dumb. Of course I am up for it, and if it fails, well, I guess we will manage."

Jake snickered. "Sylphie. Fire it up!"

The lizard stalked the small rodent that was hiding within its burrow. Both were merely early-tier E-grades, but on this desolate mountain, no other predators existed. The lizard was only the size of a house cat, with the rodent being nothing more than an overgrown hamster. Both were able to utterly slaughter a pre-system human, but in this new world, they were weak, and they knew it.

Sneaking forward, the lizard used its sleek form to enter the burrow. It had barely gotten halfway down when, suddenly, everything began shaking. The burrow collapsed from the tremors, and the lizard rushed out in panic.

It looked around with fright as its instincts told it to run. Without hesitation, it stormed down the mountain as a huge explosion sounded out behind it, and a tornado of earth, wind, and transparent flames erupted from the mountain. It sent the lizard tumbling and rolling down the mountainside as it just tried to escape with its life intact from the three monsters that had appeared. One of them even yelled something with great vigor, making the lizard even more scared.

It definitely wasn't going to go rodent-hunting on this mountain again—that was for sure.

Why hadn't they done this from the beginning? Well, the reason was partly that they hadn't thought about it, and partly that Sylphie had been low on mana when they began their escape. The biggest reason was the lack of thought, though. Also, it was kind of stupid and risky, but it wasn't like that had ever stopped him before.

As for what they had done?

"This is the drill that will pierce the heavens!" Jake yelled the moment they erupted from the mountain, getting an eyeroll from Carmen, who flew up alongside him.

"Ree!" Sylphie screeched as she got free from Carmen's grip and took to the air, flexing her wings.

"Seriously?" Carmen asked the moment they were down on the ground again.

"Are you saying the Sylphie-Jake Wind-powered Mountainpiercing Drill isn't a great technique?" Jake asked, faking offense.

"Ree?" Sylphie screeched sadly as she landed on top of Jake's head.

"No, I..." Carmen said as she looked at Sylphie, who was giving her sad puppy-hawk eyes. Carmen finally gritted her teeth as she made a strained smile. "It was a great idea..."

"Ree!" Sylphie happily flapped her wings at her own genius. Jake had to admit she was a smart little hawk. She had actually been observing Jake's flames and had managed to analyze them. She'd noticed that his flames didn't work against types of mana with intent, or, more Sylphie-accurately, "person mana."

So she'd asked why Jake didn't just make a lot more fire, and then Sylphie would just make it rotate super fast like a tornado to burn away all the stone. As Sylphie's mana was filled with intent, Jake's flame wouldn't work against it, and Sylphie had good enough mana control to not accidentally fight the flame. Then they could just travel upwards and ignore everything else until they would finally get out.

And worked it had! They were finally out, and it had taken like six or seven times longer to use the shortcut tunnel than if they had just moved over or around the mountain. It was totally worth it, though, as they had yet another Prima fragment, making Jake now able to form a key.

"Take a break?" Carmen asked.

"Yeah... I am spent," Jake said. And he really was. The amount of mana he had pumped out during their escape was insane, and Jake was down to less than five percent when they finally made it out.

"Alright." Carmen nodded. "Did you happen to grab the orb from the elemental?"

"Yeah?"

"Do you need it, or can I have it?" Carmen asked a bit nervously. "I will compensate you for it, if that is the—"

Jake took out the orb and tossed it to her. The orb was epic rarity, so it was a pretty good one, but not one Jake was desperate to keep. Heck, Jake had kept the Prima fragment, so this was only fair.

"Thanks," Carmen said, nodding with a smile as she took out two candles and a small altar. She placed the orb on the altar and knelt before it. "I tribute this victory and bounty to Valhal."

With those words, the orb turned to golden dust and disappeared, and for a fraction of a moment, Jake felt some kind of divine presence that disappeared just as it came. Carmen got up and re-deposited everything back into her spatial storage as Jake looked at her with a questioning gaze.

"Part of my profession," Carmen answered. "Dedicating battles and loot helps me in various ways, the most obvious of which is experience gained, but it also gives some other bonuses. It allows me to have 'recognition' within the halls of Valhal, which empowers many of my skills. Honestly, it is more that I fuck myself over without any tributes."

"Huh, you learn something new every day." Jake shrugged. "When I meet up with my god, he is usually the one who brings tributes in the form of beer."

"You and the Malefic One have a fucked-up relationship—you know that, right?" Carmen asked with a deadpan face.

"Funny." Jake chuckled. "I think we are the only ones who have one that isn't fucked up."

Carmen just shook her head. "Weren't you supposed to be meditating so we could get moving again?"

"I was," Jake said, smirking. "I guess it would be too much to ask you to carry me like Sylphie?"

"If you allowed me to first squish you down to be her size, sure," Carmen shot back.

Jake just chuckled as he closed his eyes and entered meditation to regenerate. He still kept an eye out with his sphere, and he saw that after a brief rest, Carmen and Sylphie began playing around. It was a mix between play-sparring and actual sparring, but they didn't use any skills or serious magic. It was more like playing "block the bird peck."

A few hours and potions later, Jake was in pretty good condition again, and with the two others also chugging down some potions, the three of them were ready to head out again.

They grouped up as Jake pulled out the tablet Arnold had given him. He brought up the map, and they all studied it. "Okay, so if we go down this mountain this way and pass this small patch of forest, we only have that plain left, and we reach the Grand Mangrove River. After we pass the river, we only need to cross a few flood plains, and we are in the port city of Changhul."

"Are we going for that orange zone?" Carmen asked.

"No P," Jake pointed out. "AKA no Prima. I think it is better to aim for the Grand Mangrove River for Primas."

"How many Primas do you think there are? Not just in that Mangrove place, but on Earth in general?"

"Arnold says that, based on his algorithm made from data on all the Primas he has surveyed so far and locational data of how far spaced out they are, there should be around eleven hundred within human-occupied land on Earth. He did say it is a bit shaky due to many beings underground or high up, but it shouldn't be too far off. If these Primas exist all over the globe... well, it wouldn't surprise me if they were in the tens of thousands at least. Knowing the system, the number of fragments and keys likely correspond somehow, so maybe thirty thousand? It has to be something that can be divided by three."

Carmen nodded along. "So, there are quite a lot of Primas. Got it. Now let's go kill some."

"Already looking forward to it," Jake said, smiling as they set out towards one of the few red danger zones identified by Arnold—a place where Jake was certain he would find a good fight.

Maybe even a C-grade or two.

CHAPTER 25

GRAND MANGROVE RIVER

Earth had developed some damn beautiful vistas after the system arrived. Grand forests with multi-colored trees, endless, sprawling plains with groups of deer jumping across them, passing tens of meters with every single leap.

Jake, Sylphie, and Carmen traveled through this land at a good pace. They didn't get into any fights for the next two days, as none of them saw any need to bully far weaker creatures. Even the playful Sylphie had an instinctive repulsion to killing anything below herself in grade and level. A usual thing, as killing a bunch of E-grades while in D-grade could apparently have negative consequences on your Records based on the circumstances it'd happened under. Mainly in the sense that it could bring you in a bad direction evolution-wise.

This meant it was a peaceful time where they mainly just chatted about different things, and Jake also finally got to see Carmen "forge" her fists. She did so by making a golden liquid that seemed to almost have acidic properties, but Jake didn't sense any poison from it. When Carmen submerged her hands, this golden liquid would slowly drill itself into them, and based on Carmen's gritted teeth during this entire process, it was in no way pleasant.

Afterward, she told him that she had to control the energy and use it to form runes of sorts into her very Soulshape. It was incredibly complicated magic tapping into many different concepts, and Carmen also made it clear she only knew what the outcome of the rituals were and not how anything actually worked. However, she did say this golden liquid also had to do with the tributes, as the unique energy gained from doing them helped the forging ritual along.

It was interesting magic, that was for sure, but nothing Jake could use or even gain any real inspiration from. It required things Jake simply couldn't get, and he also learned that forging her hands led to some changes Jake would not be a fan of, such as the inability to channel mana through them. Something that didn't matter at all to Carmen, considering she didn't even have mana, having converted it all to stamina.

The two of them did have some interesting discussions regarding the application of stamina, and Jake found out that Carmen really had no idea how to properly manipulate her own Soulshape or even properly perceive it. She just used the methods she had been taught.

She likened it to when she was training to be a boxer. She was no nutritionist or and had no education in biology or physiology, so she just did as she was told and saw the results. Carmen said she didn't need to know *why* something happened, just what she had to do to make the outcome she wanted possible. Rather than learn what lifting weights did to muscles, she would just lift weights and build the muscle.

Jake disagreed with this approach somewhat. He had always been all about feeling the changes on the deepest level possible. Even if he didn't know all the biology about building muscle, he would still understand the process by feeling it. He would feel the muscle fibers break down and rebuild themselves, feel the nutrients and protein feeding his muscles to make them stronger and faster.

Comprehending concepts was also essential to upgrading skills. While it was possible to upgrade them without learning how they truly worked, it would never be to your own upgraded versions. Carmen would only be able to follow the teachings of others and upgrade through a linear Path defined by whoever trained her. Jake was very much the opposite, at least when it came to his class. He did follow the teachings of the Malefic Viper, especially with Path of the Heretic-Chosen, yet his way of learning wasn't by following a training regimen, but instead by comprehending and understanding the skills. The true versions of these Legacy skills were also just so all-encompassing that borderline anything Jake learned using them was already an aspect of the "true" version.

This all resulted in an interesting dynamic where they each had something to teach the other—Jake teaching her a bit about Soul-shapes, and Carmen teaching him a bit about fighting.

"You have the most unbalanced melee fighting style I have ever seen," Carmen said as she looked at Jake after they had a brief spar. They had decided to take a break, but their breaks often didn't include as much rest as they probably should.

"How so?" Jake asked, but he already had an inkling himself.

"Well, first of all, you suck at attacking," she said curtly.

"A bit harsh," Jake muttered.

"No. Not really. Come at me, try to land a hit. You can use your swords and daggers and all that too."

Jake complied as he shot forward, Eternal Hunger and Bloodfeast Dagger ready. He swung, and Carmen dodged to the side but didn't counterattack. Jake swung again and tried to pin her down, but Carmen just kept dodging and weaving in between his hits, not even trying to strike back a single time.

He kept pushing as he picked up his pace, but he somehow couldn't land a hit even when he was faster than her. Jake kept swinging until, finally, Carmen leaped back, making Jake stop.

"You are good at dodging," Jake said, nodding.

"No, not really. I am decent, sure, but the primary reason is how utterly predictable you are. It is like fighting a beast. You don't fucking think. You are just swinging your weapon towards the nearest vital area. No feints, no baiting, no combos... nothing." Carmen shook her head.

"Is it really that bad?" Jake asked. He'd had this conversation before, and he honestly felt like he had gotten better with Fang of Man. It was true the skill didn't actually give him any fighting experience; it just allowed him to properly use any weapon he did pick up. There were no techniques or anything. Jake felt like it was fine, as overcomplicating things just seemed dumb.

"It is." Carmen nodded. "You have no technique at all."

"Shouldn't that make me less predictable?" Jake muttered.

"No, it just makes you suck. You know how to use your body and your muscles. Every swing is powerful and would be potent if it hit. You just have no way to make it hit." Carmen shook her head.

"Any advice?"

"I am not good enough to give any. I am a pugilist. I can teach you how to punch things and be a boxer, but I don't know shit about using a blade—or any weapon, for that matter. No, it is better you find someone more qualified. You got a lot of the things down that most find the hardest, like proper footwork and efficient movements, so you just need a good teacher."

Jake nodded in understanding. It seemed like he would actually have to get some lessons in proper fighting when he returned to the Academy.

"But... just one thing—how come I did manage to land hits on people before, then?" Jake asked, still a bit confused.

"Well," Carmen began, "because while you suck at attacking, you are a fucking monster defensively. Attacking you is a nightmare, and that will inadvertently lead to exposed weaknesses you take advantage of... I don't get how you don't understand this? Actually, don't answer that. I don't wanna know."

Jake just nodded. "I get it... I will find someone to give me some pointers."

He actually felt somewhat bad, as while Carmen did give some serious advice, Jake couldn't actually give anything proper back. Explaining how to "feel" something related to your Soulshape wasn't really easily described, but they did make some progress. Jake advised her to try and feel the stamina moving through her body—something she already had experience with—to map out her Soulshape and slowly imagine it.

Sylphie also chipped in by asking what a Soulshape was, at which point Jake learned that Sylphie didn't have one... Well, she did kind of have one, but not really. She had several "states" of Soulshapes, as far as Jake could tell, but honestly, it was all a bit too complicated for him. Sylphie's own explanation was that she could just be windy and not windy, so that was very useful.

On the third day, they finally made it to the red zone known as the Grand Mangrove River. They had seen the mangrove forest much earlier, and Jake finally understood why Arnold had said flying over it wasn't possible.

"How the fuck is that even possible?" Carmen asked as she stared at the sight before them.

"Magic, system fuckery, and probably a bit more magic," Jake answered, also staring.

"Ree!" Sylphie explained very accurately.

What they saw was indeed a mangrove forest. The trees of which it consisted had large root nets and crowns that began rather far up. This meant that above the surface of the river, there was space between the many roots to move. The problem appeared further up, where the crowns of the many trees were.

The many branches had formed an impenetrable wall that shot into the sky further up than Jake could see. It was a barrier of pure greenery that seemed to extend infinitely, and Jake quickly formed the personal theory that the mangrove forest after which the Grand Mangrove River was named connected to something up there. Potentially another cloud island.

From what Jake could see, the only way to pass the river was at the bottom and through the net of roots. At least there was a lot of space there. The roots had different sizes, with some being as thin as a finger and others nearly four meters in diameter. At places, the roots were also well-spaced out, and with how much they wound and bent, traveling on top of them and avoiding the river below was entirely possible, if not kind of easy.

"This seems like such a shitty place to travel through," Carmen complained.

"No other way." Jake shrugged. "The river cuts off everything. According to the notes in the tablet, this mangrove forest even makes teleportation incredibly difficult, explaining why no network has been established with the port city."

"Has anyone made it through before?" she asked.

"A lot. If you go straight, use stealth skills, and just generally try not to cause a ruckus, it shouldn't be too dangerous, as the local denizens shouldn't be *that* aggressive. That is, if we want to stick to the safest path."

"Which we don't." Carmen nodded. "Oh, well. Just to check, how are you in water?"

"I can swim," Jake answered.

"I mean fighting in it...." Carmen said, taking a deep breath. "Does your archery work underwater?"

"No, not really. I would definitely prefer to stay out of it. How about you, Sylphie?"

"Ree!" Sylphie screeched.

"She isn't a fan of water either?" Carmen asked. She had an oddly hopeful gaze as she waited for Jake to confirm or deny.

"Yep, something like that," Jake said, getting a small cheer out of Carmen as she triumphantly celebrated her increased ability to understand Sylphie.

"Ready?" Jake asked as he checked the tablet. "We are heading straight for a Prima that should be the closest to our side of the river."

Carmen and Sylphie nodded and flapped their wings respectively as they headed into the danger zone.

Jake scanned his surroundings as they dove under the canopy of the many mangrove trees. It didn't turn dark, and he noticed how sunlight seemed to some-fucking-how still make its way through the many-kilo-meter wall of leaves and branches. Perhaps it was absorbed somehow and then released at the bottom? Jake could feel the sun-affinity energy coming from the leaves, and he reckoned they somehow emitted it for the river below. Likely to feed its own roots and underwater plants to not kill the ecosystem in the river.

"Ree! Ree, ree, ree," Sylphie suddenly chirped.

"Okay, I did not get any of that," Carmen muttered, disappointed, but Jake realized how the sunlight reached them.

"She said that she can feel the wind pass down from above... meaning the sunlight reaches us through a net of reflected sunlight," Jake explained, having understood and confirmed this himself by inspecting the structure of the leaves.

"How the hell is that possible?" Carmen asked. "Are you telling me these trees all agreed to set up a huge net of reflective leaves or what?"

"No." Jake shook his head as he inspected some of the trees very carefully. "There is no need for agreement... This entire mangrove forest is one single plant, or at least this section is."

Carmen just looked at him. "That is just—"

"Left!" Jake yelled as his danger sense warned him.

A few spears of wood flew straight toward Jake and Carmen both. Carmen just caught one with her hand, and Jake dodged the others easily as he saw where they had come from.

A small, lithe form was sitting on a root and looking towards them. It was surrounded by five of its brethren, all of whom just stared. Jake recognized the creature as he sighed. "Really?"

[Mangrove Monkey – lvl 140]

The monkeys seemed to have heard him. They bolted off, fright-ened in the other direction. Sylphie screeched towards them, making the monkeys pick up their pace even more.

"I thought you said the wildlife wasn't that aggressive?" Carmen asked as she snapped the small, sharpened wooden spear she had caught.

"Monkeys are assholes," Jake said, shaking his head as he motioned for them to move on.

His assessment did prove to be correct, and luckily the monkeys didn't make Jake commit another monkey genocide. They weren't attacked at all for the next hour or so as they slowly made their way through the Grand Mangrove River, though they did have a few times where they had to diverge from their path.

The biggest danger wasn't in the roots or hidden in the lower layers of the canopies, but could be found down in the river below. Incredibly powerful beasts roamed down there, but they luckily seemed to primarily compete amongst themselves.

Jake had taken out one of the Prima fragments again. He hadn't merged his three into a key in case it made it harder to track the energy signature of Primas. He wondered if he would find another monkey, but he and the others hadn't encountered any of the fuckers besides in the outer perimeter of the Grand Mangrove River.

By now, they were perhaps a third of the way to the center of the danger zone—a sixth into the river as a whole—and the levels had already grown significantly. Jake saw several beasts around level 170 in the waters below, and he could feel the presence of a C-grade somewhere further in. Maybe more than one.

"Are we avoiding C-grades?" Carmen asked.

"Do you have confidence fighting one?" Jake countered.

"Alone? No. But with you and Sylphie, maybe we can take one down if it is on the weaker side."

"In that case, I am up for giving it a shot," Jake said, nodding. He did believe they had a chance, and Sylphie seemed to also agree.

As they kept moving forward, Jake felt several presences five hundred meters or so in front of them. "Be careful. Potential ambush ahead."

Carmen's face turned more serious, but she didn't change her pace. Jake and Sylphie also followed with their guard up. Soon enough, they reached the area Jake had noticed, and his guess was confirmed.

A torrent of water fired out from the river below, making Carmen block as she was blasted up into the leaves and branches above. At the same time, Jake was forced to dodge a pink appendage shooting towards him. It barely missed and smashed into a root, breaking it into splinters before retracting again to its source.

Sylphie also dodged her attack as Jake saw the beasts that had attacked them. Three large and fat frogs were hidden just a bit below the river's surface as they launched their ranged attacks again, and Jake barely managed to Identify them.

[Acidtorrent Frog – lvl 191]
[Pummel-tongue Frog – lvl 194]
[Acidtorrent Frog – lvl 192]

Two green and one brown frog. Jake checked on Carmen and saw her skin had been seared by the acid, but she didn't seem to care as she shot down at one of the frogs. Jake also pulled out his bow and prepared to engage.

This would prove to be the first fight of many, as clearly, the natives of the Grand Mangrove River didn't see the three of them as anything but prey, all trying to turn this mangrove forest into a man-grave.

CHAPTER 26

BEND!

Frogs in all shapes and sizes, birds that ambushed with pecks nearly as fast as Jake's arrows, and a plethora of other annoying animals hounded Jake, Sylphie, and Carmen as they made their way deeper into the mangroves. The first frogs they encountered were a good indicator of what they would face.

They were all specialized creatures adapted to their unique environment. They all made use of the many ambush possibilities offered by the dense branches and leaves above or the river below. Granted, Jake was the worst kind of opponent for them, as the current him would never fall into an actual ambush, but some attacks were difficult to deal with even if you knew they were coming.

The mangrove forest was also more than a little annoying fighting in, especially for an archer like Jake. The creatures made full use of the winding roots for cover or hid away underwater to avoid his blows. Sylphie didn't care much and was able to maneuver well enough to sometimes even take advantage of the environment herself. Carmen could do the same, just hiding away behind cover until her opponent was forced to get close or give up.

Jake still managed pretty well with melee attacks and could land some arrows here and there, but the deeper in they got, the more his archery fell off. When they reached their first target within the mangroves, his archery felt borderline useless.

The first target was a Prima Arnold had already scouted out. It wandered with a small flock in this part of the mangrove forest and was a terror to most wildlife. When Jake finally saw it, he could get why. It was a bird with incredibly long and slender legs, a smallish body, a long neck, and an even longer beak. Identifying it, he confirmed it was indeed a Prima.

[Spearbeak Ibis Prima – lvl 190]

Its most notable feature was the beak. It was long, almost to the point of looking impractical, but Jake soon saw why that didn't matter. The Spearbeak Ibis Prima's flock consisted of seven more ibises, each of them around level 180.

"Same tactic as always?" Carmen asked before they engaged.

"Will try," Jake said, a tad miffed at how it usually went.

He felt like his opening salvo of Arcane Powershot often ended up just missing or being fired way too early, as the opponent either noticed him or was just moving already, and with cover never more than ten or so meters away, most beasts could quickly escape his arrows.

The opening attack did go as expected, but Jake was forced to switch his target to one of the followers of the Prima since the damn ibis walked behind a large root just before he released the string. The arrow tore off one of its legs and made it fall into the river below. Sylphie attacked the Prima with Carmen, but they were pushed back when it was almost instantly joined by the others in its flock.

This was also when Jake learned the reason for the long Prima beak. Rather than fight, it escaped behind a root, but it still pecked forward, its beak simply bending around the root and pecking Carmen in the shoulder, sending out a shower of blood.

Jake and the others had fought one other group of ibises before and knew they were all fast and had powerful attacks, but they had hoped to take advantage of their low durability. The ibises walked on water like it was nothing and could even run and kick off roots to launch themselves around at incredible velocity, using their wings for further speed and maneuverability while in the air.

The Prima took this to an entirely new level, as their group of three fought a foe that had truly made the environment it lived in its own.

There was never a moment when it was exposed, as the Prima switched between the trees and dove under the roots all the time. The bird was only about two and a half meters tall, but the beak could extend to be more than fifteen meters when it pecked forward, truly proving the name Spearbeak.

"I can't get close," Carmen said as they all retreated behind a mangrove tree. "I go for the weaker birds?"

"Alright," Jake said, nodding as he looked up at some of the branches above where Sylphie was hanging upside-down. "Help Carmen finish them off. I will try to handle the Prima for now."

"Ree!" Sylphie agreed.

"Sure that is a good idea?" Carmen asked. "If I can't get close, can you?"

Jake shook his head. "Maybe... but that isn't why I want to handle the Prima alone. I see an opportunity."

Carmen stared for a moment before nodding firmly. "Got it."

She understood the sentiment even without Jake having to explain.

The words Carmen had said about him sucking at attacking had echoed in his mind all throughout their travel in the mangrove forest. He honestly didn't notice it when he fought the beasts... at least, not before now. Usually, he would get changes to counterattack or at least use Gaze to get an opportunity, but this damn ibis didn't give him the chance to.

In some ways, the ibis fought similarly to Jake when he used archery. It always tried to keep itself at a distance and employ ranged attacks. The difference was that the ibis had solved one of the biggest issues: line of sight. Arrows could only fly in a straight line for obvious reasons, and a peck could also normally only go straight... but the Ibis Prima clearly didn't subscribe to his logic.

Jake observed the beak bend at impossible angles as it pecked forward. Every bend was uniform, and that somehow allowed it to retain all its power. One would think a strike curved into a crescent would be weaker when it hit, but for the Ibis Prima, it clearly had no negative effects.

In order to get a good one-on-one fight, Jake summoned dozens of arcane orbs and exploded the area to force the Prima away from Carmen and Sylphie as he pursued it. The long-legged bird didn't seem to care; it allowed Jake to chase, perhaps happy itself to finally get rid of Sylphie, who had managed to land a few scratches with her superior speed.

Jake shot off arrows as he chased, missing every single one. At the same time, he was forced to block or dodge the spear-like beak repeatedly. Their fight was incredibly basic, with one person just shooting arrows and the other pecking while dodging and flying through the mangrove forest.

Seeing the Ibis Prima had given Jake inspiration. The beak was a solid object, yet it seemed so everchanging. He didn't actually want to make his own blade somehow long and bendy... No, it was the concept behind what the Prima did that intrigued him.

Soon enough, the two of them were several kilometers from Sylphie and Carmen. Jake kept trying to land a hit and accomplish what he was attempting to do, but something was missing. Missing what, one might ask?

Controllable arrows.

It was something Jake had theorized a long time ago. He could do telekinesis, so why couldn't he control his own arrows mid-flight? The problem was that arrows in flight tended to be quite resistant to being affected by, well, anything.

Jake trying to influence the trajectory would often just result in him forcing it to slow down. This would make it not hit as hard, if at all. Slower objects were obviously easier to dodge.

He had even looked up some books on archery while in the Order. He'd seen several guides on controlling mana bolts and tried a few of those out, but it always came with the caveat of reduced power for any piercing attack.

There were methods, but none that Jake found fitting. Some didn't work simply because Jake found himself in quite an unfortunate situation with his arrows in particular: They liked to destroy stuff due to his arcane affinity. This included any "strings" of mana Jake wanted to attach to the arrows.

He had also tried to change the arrow design, but that hadn't worked either, as his arrows just flew too fast. The passive destructive abilities of his arcane arrows also helped alleviate the effects of wind resistance—or any other resistance, for that matter. This was awesome for making arrows go fast and straight, but not that good if you wanted them to do anything else.

Other books recommended simply bending space or manipulating time to make the arrow's flight unpredictable, but for obvious reasons, that wasn't quite doable for the current Jake. No, he would need to find another way... because there had to be a way.

The fight with the Prima continued, and finally, something happened that changed the situation. Jake jumped away from a beak spear as another suddenly flew for him. He managed to bend his body, but he was confused because the first peck hadn't fully retracted yet.

Then a third came, but this one was too fast. Jake was pecked in the chest, sending him flying back with a hole through his right lung about the size of a fist. Jake just stared, as he had no idea what had just happened. How could it have two beaks at once? Three?

Despite his surprise, he still managed to stabilize himself and avoid any follow-ups. The Ibis Prima had entered open space to pursue him, and now Jake truly saw how it attacked. Before, he had thought the beak actually extended, but it wasn't quite like that. In fact, he seemed to have misunderstood the creature entirely.

Every time the Ibis Prima attacked, it pecked forward and sent out its beak at such a speed it fired off a mirror image of sorts that looked like the physical beak... a mirror image so "real" it actually appeared like a physical object in his sphere and to all his senses.

Before every attack, the Ibis Prima slightly shifted its head, and Jake felt the sheer level of focus that went into the attacks. The beak was extended and curved, always at a consistent angle based on the starting position of the Prima's head. There was never more than one bend either.

He finally understood why he had taken inspiration from it. It was a beautiful technique. He saw the straight beak aim towards him once more, but it suddenly seemed to bend as it came from an angle, forcing Jake to dodge away. Not before he loosed an arrow to counter, though.

The arrow floundered as it flew at an odd angle and crashed into a tree. Jake was not deterred. He shot again, with every arrow just harmlessly hitting roots or falling into the river below. The Ibis Prima had already hidden away again and used the cover of the trees to counter as Jake shot his arrows into said trees.

By now, Jake was fully focused. He analyzed the Prima's every move, trying to mimic what it did in his own way.

Bend, Jake thought, and his arrow bent mid-air and cracked into small crystalline pieces.

Bend.

The arrow flew off to the side even if he had fired it right in front of him, smashing yet another innocent root.

Bend!

As the string moved, the arrow seemed to slightly turn, but as it was loosed, the arrow lost its course and once more did nothing.

Bend!

Jake's eyes opened wide as he focused. He released his arrow but, at the very end, also infused a large wave of Willpower into it, filling the arrow with a bit of his intent. It merged with the arrow and bow effortlessly, just like all his prior attempts. When the arrow was pushed forward by the string, it seemed to bend until it was finally let go and did exactly as Jake intended.

In a glorious crescent, it traveled around the massive root the Prima was hiding behind, and he heard the beast cry out in surprise as it was hit on the right wing.

Jake had tried to do it like the Ibis Prima but found it impossible. The Ibis Prima retained that connection between itself and the beak all throughout the attack—something Jake could not do. No, he had to find a better way.

His attempts had made him realize that fully controllable arrows weren't something he could do. He would lose momentum if he tried to control them too much... so what if he didn't guide them? What if he just gave them a slight nudge and changed their fundamental trajectory, still making them fly "straight," but defined that as a "straight arc?"

Or, the easiest explanation: He changed the trajectory before he even shot it. He redefined what a straight line was using his own Willpower, just like the Prima had. Rather than try and "program" the arrow to follow an advanced trajectory, he just infused this one intent, making it shoot at a certain angle and follow a simple vector.

The blow was still predictable... and it bent predictably. This did perhaps seem like a flaw, but it was quite the opposite: It preserved speed and momentum.

Jake smiled as he heard the notification that signified he had progressed his archery skill, but he saved looking at it for later. For now, he had a Prima to kill. The beast quickly adapted as Jake began whipping arrows around the roots at awkward angles.

What was perhaps most surprising was the lack of any magic or mana involved in the process. To any outside observer, it looked like Jake was just firing normal arrows, but they all flew at different angles and bent around the roots. Granted, this did result in them traveling a further overall distance, increasing the time it took to hit the target. This would be a flaw under normal circumstances, but in this kind of environment? Well, there was a reason why the level 190 Ibis Prima could dominate any opponent it found.

Getting his spirits up, Jake attempted to fire an Arcane Powershot and used the same technique. The arrow did bend slightly, but when he released it, it only diverted by a few degrees and passed the root the

Prima hid behind, flying into the distance before it exploded upon impact with another mangrove tree.

Okay, doesn't work with Arcane Powershot.

The attack was just too fast and too powerful. Jake could not infuse enough intent into the attack to make it do as he wanted... but he did have an attack that would work.

Jake dodged around as the Ibis Prima began adapting and counter-attacking. Neither party was ever within the line of sight of the other even as they exchanged blows. Jake was attacked several times while he did the mental calculation and fired his bow once more.

A single arrow bent around a root, but just as it did, it split into five. Jake repeated this, firing another arrow from the opposite side, and it also split. The Ibis Prima tried to retreat, but was still caught in the blast that came from ten explosive arcane arrows colliding.

Jake took this opportunity to sprint forward and give chase. He shot off two more arrows as the Ibis Prima prepared to jump away, but suddenly it stumbled when its foot hit the water, making it get hit by another arrow.

The beast looked confused and then terrified. It had clearly been too distracted to notice what had happened to it. That first arrow Jake had landed hadn't just been another regular stable arcane arrow, but one thoroughly soaked in Jake's new and most powerful Hemotoxin.

Wounds had accumulated on the Ibis Prima. Wounds that would typically have already healed. It had noticed too late. Jake was upon it, ready to deliver death.

Jake jumped to the right as he shot to the left, making the arrows curve around to hit the Ibis Prima. In mid-air, he charged Arcane Powershot, and when he made it around the network of roots and landed his sights on the bird, he used Gaze of the Apex Hunter.

The Ibis froze, fighting to barely move again. It tried to block the Arcane Powershot with its beak, which sent it reeling back and bleeding from its head. Three more arrows had also hit it from Jake's curved shot, and by now, the Ibis Prima only thought about escape. Something Jake wasn't going to give it.

It was time to finish this, so Jake finally pulled out his final weapon. Arrow of the Ambitious Hunter emerged from his inventory, and the Ibis Prima instantly fled. Jake just looked as it escaped behind a net of roots, uncaring, then released the finisher.

The arrow bent around several trees and struck the Ibis Prima that had already lost its senses. It fell forward into the river as Jake got the kill notification.

You have slain [Spearbeak Ibis Prima – lvl 190] – Bonus experience earned for killing an enemy above your level

Jake flew forward and quickly swooped up the Beastcore and the fragment the Prima had dropped, simultaneously checking to confirm he had gained levels. Plural.

'DING!' Class: [Avaricious Arcane Hunter] has reached level 154 - Stat points allocated, +10 Free Points

'DING!' Class: [Avaricious Arcane Hunter] has reached level 155 - Stat points allocated, +10 Free Points

'DING!' Race: [Human (D)] has reached level 162 - Stat points allocated, +15 Free Points

Jake was surprised at seeing two levels. He wondered if it had to do with the skill upgrade, but skill upgrades didn't tend to give him class experience. The fight had not been overly dangerous, even if Jake did have a few holes in his body by now. In fact, he would say that overall, this Prima was on the weaker side, being a one-trick pony.

It was also entirely possible he had been mega-close to a level-up already and now just barely passed the threshold to gain two.

"Got what you needed?" Carmen asked as she finally came over with Sylphie.

Jake knew they had been observing from afar to not interrupt his fight and take away his chance to get the inspiration he had been seeking.

"Yeah, thanks," Jake said.

"So?" Carmen asked.

Jake just smiled and nodded as he checked out his newly upgraded skill.

CHAPTER 27

THE DEPTHS OF THE GRAND MANGROVE RIVER

Jake's attachment to archery didn't exactly stem from anything logical. Sure, one could argue that his Bloodline giving Perception made it an obvious choice, but Perception was a stat highly beneficial to nearly all classes and professions. Heck, Arnold had said himself that Perception was his highest stat, and he didn't even use a gun... or any weapon, for that matter.

Many types of magic were also based on Perception. Jake could become a melee fighter with a focus on the stat, too, or do so many other things. Some would maybe even be more effective, as there was a dissonance between his Sphere of Perception and the fact that he preferred to stay at long range to land arrows.

So, why did he focus on archery anyway? Well, because he liked it. It had been the first sport he had gotten into. It was linked with many positive memories of his life. Times he'd gone to tournaments or the archery range with his father, memories of his brother cheering whenever he hit a bullseye. When he'd been introduced to the system, he had instantly known he wanted to do archery once more.

This didn't mean he wouldn't also do other things. He was fully aware he was a bit of a Jake of all trades, but archery was still a centerpiece of those trades. With all of that in mind, it only made sense to upgrade his archery skill, even if said archery skill also pointed out Jake's vast toolbelt of fighting methods.

[Archery of Vast Horizons (Rare)] - An Archer's best friends are the bow in his hand and the arrow in his foe's heart. Unsatisfied with merely

becoming an expert, you have sought beyond mastering common bowmanship, and do not shy away from using magic to enhance your technique. You seek to cross all horizons with your arrows, and your target shall be pierced, no matter the distance, no matter the means. Adds a small bonus to the effect of Agility and Strength when using a ranged weapon. Adds a small damage bonus to all arrows based on distance traveled and Perception.

-->

[Archery of Expanding Horizons (Epic)] *- An Archer's best friend is the bow in his hand and the arrow in his foe's heart. As your horizons expand, you realize flaws and build upon a foundation to make that expansion everpresent. You do not shy away from mixing archery with magic and making your arrows arbiters of your will. Your arrows will cross all horizons and bend over any obstacle to pierce your target, with only your own will limiting the possibilities. Allows you to apply your will to control the trajectory of arrows before releasing them. Adds a small bonus to the effect of Agility and Strength when using a ranged weapon. Adds a small damage bonus to all arrows based on distance traveled and Perception. Arrow trajectory control based on Willpower.*

Jake read over the improved skill a few times. Out of all the ones he had, this one had quite a bit of flavor text, which probably made sense, considering its role as a general archery skill. When he had gained the skill, Jake had also surprisingly gained some instinctual knowledge, making him more aware of how it truly worked.

When he fired a bending arrow, Jake infused it with a small pack of Willpower along with the usual energies he threw in. This pack of Willpower would work on the arrow to effectively nudge and push it in a certain direction with a constant force, making it follow the trajectory Jake intended. This was also why something like Arcane Powershot didn't work well with it, because the pack of Willpower he would have to infuse into the arrow was above what Jake could do at his current level of power.

Due to the Willpower being a part of the arrow upon firing, this also meant he could copy it with Splitting Arrow. The packet of Willpower would remain within the arrow even when it was split. Looking at the skill, he also became more and more certain... True arrow control was a possibility in the future. Guided arrows. Just thinking about it, countless ideas entered his head for future improvements, but all of those were for the future. For now, they had more targets to hunt.

Jake briefly explained his upgrade to Sylphie and Carmen, got his congratulations, and then they took a quick break to chug down potions before moving on.

The map given by Arnold stopped giving any useful information about a third of the way into the mangrove forest, meaning the entire central part of the Grand Mangrove River was a complete mystery. The central part was also the most dangerous.

According to the map, the entire river was about two hundred kilometers wide and didn't have any significant places where it became more narrow. In fact, it was wider in most places. There were also safer places to pass than others, but the mangrove forest was everpresent, showing how utterly massive the ecosystem was.

This did perhaps seem overly huge, but one had to remember that the forest Haven was placed on the outskirts of extended for thousands upon thousands of kilometers into the distance. Arnold hadn't even been able to map a small part of it yet, and it was likely the largest forest in the region of the planet humans currently occupied.

"Are there more Primas nearby?" Carmen asked Jake as their group took a small break up amongst the branches and leaves of the mangrove trees.

Jake had a fragment in his hand as he searched for similar energies but shook his head. "There was one, I think, but the energy is faint. It either moved or was killed. One thing is for sure: It is no longer in this area."

"Ree?" Sylphie asked.

"Yeah, it could be connected," Jake agreed.

They had noticed a general lack of beasts in the area, at least above the river. Down in the deep water below, an entirely different world still existed, separate from everything else. Some creatures did live on the edge, such as the frogs that dove below water or other beasts that used the river to ambush foes, but these were not considered part of the true river. No, those creatures lived deep beneath, likely kilometers down.

"Do you think a C-grade swept through?" Carmen asked, a bit concerned.

"Doubtful... I don't feel the lingering aura of one," Jake said. "That doesn't make it impossible, though, as it could just be one that is good at hiding its presence."

"Guess all we can do is move on," Carmen said, sighing as they did just that.

By now, they had already agreed to just try and make it through the Grand Mangrove River as peacefully as possible if there were no more Primas. It wasn't really a good place to hunt, even with Jake's archery upgrade. Some annoying opponents also fled underwater if they got in trouble, betting on surviving the deep-river creatures over facing Jake, Carmen, and the little murderbird.

As they kept going forward, the general mana level in the air grew. An extreme level of nature, water, and wood affinity also dominated the air, putting them all a bit more on edge. It was normal for the mana density and affinity to grow and change based on the environment, but this case was out of the ordinary.

It far surpassed what was found within the tunnel with the earth elemental Prima. High mana density didn't really mean much for humans besides affected mana regeneration and sometimes slightly stronger or weaker attacks based on the affinity of said mana, but one type of creature it did affect significantly was monsters.

Sylphie seemed to enjoy being there, at least. Mana density could help beasts level faster merely by absorbing it, and it would also lead to beasts and other creatures naturally spawning at a higher level, including anything born from eggs or even living births—hence why rituals were often used to nurture eggs and pregnant animals. It also resulted in more natural treasures appearing, and those that did appear were stronger and would grow in rarity and power faster.

Most notable was perhaps the "level" of the treasures and materials spawning. Two flowers could be uncommon rarity, but one would be far more suited for E-grades and the other for C-grades. They could have the same name, but the amount of energy contained within the one for C-grades would be far higher.

It worked like this for all kinds of natural treasures and herbs. A D-grade would not benefit from treasures in low-mana areas suitable for E-grades unless it consumed ludicrous amounts. In the same vein, then, a C-grade would also not benefit much from treasures suitable for D-grades. What did this mean? That an area's mana density could often be used to determine the level of creatures one would find there.

In all ways, beasts benefitted from areas of higher mana density, which is also why they loved being in them, and the stronger the beast got, the more this became almost required to keep progressing for all the reasons stated above. Hence, high-mana areas tended to be dominated by, and become the territory of, powerful monsters.

And the mana density in this area of the Grand Mangrove River was enough to support not just D-grades... but something above that. Jake could feel that there were C-grades ahead. He could not pinpoint them, but he felt their presence, and soon enough, they would enter an area where he knew there were some.

"Careful," Jake said. "And if you have any stealth skills, use them. If not, just try to stay low-profile. If we are going to get into fights, let's be the ones starting them."

Carmen and Sylphie both agreed, and Sylphie quickly asked Jake if he wanted her to make a big whirlwind to hide them. She only sulked a little when he said no.

They snuck through the mangrove forest quietly. At times, they heard noises off in the distance and felt the reverberations of energy as powerful entities clashed, but they tried to ignore it and moved slightly away from that direction. Jake would've checked it out if he was alone, but with Sylphie and Carmen, he didn't want to take the chance.

Facing C-grades shouldn't be done half-arsed, and if Jake had to face one, he didn't want it to be within this mangrove forest. Any C-grade able to make the Grand Mangrove River their home had to have adapted to the environment, a master of using it to its advantage, making fighting them there too reckless, even for Jake.

So they wanted to just pass by. Humans had passed before, according to Arnold. C-grades shouldn't bother with a small group of three... but Jake had made one miscalculation. They maybe didn't bother with humans, but if there was one thing other beasts enjoyed, it was consuming Beastcores... especially from more powerful beasts. Killing a D-grade wouldn't give a core worth much, but what if it was a beast of an even higher tier that simply hadn't grown up yet?

The Records contained in the core would lack quantity, but the quality would be supreme. Hunting these beasts was common, which was why dragon hatchlings were protected by their brethren, and beasts of powerful heritages were so tight-knit.

Jake and Carmen weren't currently traveling with a dragon hatchling, but something that was perhaps even more precious to an ambitious C-grade: a Sylphian Eyas.

That was when Jake saw it. Almost a moment too late.

"Dodge!" he yelled as a thin line of water suddenly moved across the mangroves.

They all somehow managed to get some height as the needle-thin wave of water passed. Jake's eyes went wide upon noticing that, behind and in front of them, thousands of roots had been severed in two by the water cutter, the mangrove trees now only held up by their branches.

And this was only the beginning.

Bullets of water rained upon them from off in the distance, most of them aimed at Sylphie. They all dodged back as several trees were shredded, and Jake didn't hesitate for a moment as he went all out. Arcane Awakening fully activated, as he had already spotted their attacker more than two kilometers away through the path it had created with its own rain of bullets. It was hidden well, but not well enough... Not that Jake was sure it mattered when he managed to land an Identify.

[Torrent-Tongue Frog King – lvl ???]

It was a full-fledged C-grade. Jake communicated this to Sylphie, and Carmen clearly already knew, as she also activated several boosting skills. The frog in the distance fired off a few more attacks, but suddenly the strikes stopped.

The frog had disappeared below the surface of the river, but Jake had managed to use his Mark on it the moment he saw it. He sensed its activity as it moved at a ridiculous speed underwater towards them.

"Below!" he yelled again as they all spread out and sought up towards the branches of the mangrove trees for cover.

He used Pride, Scales, and Wings, triggering every single skill he could. Jake quickly began charging an Arcane Powershot and fired where he believed the frog would emerge—a guess that was right on the money.

The frog leaped up from the water just as Jake fired. It got hit by the arrow but didn't seem to care as it went straight for Sylphie, ignoring both Jake and Carmen. They were not the food it wanted.

"Ree!" Sylphie screeched, summoning a green shield and firing a blast of green wind to counter the frog leaping towards her, trying to gobble her up.

Together with Jake's arrow, it managed to throw the frog off course. It smashed into the branches above, but their relief was short-lived.

The entire body of the frog exploded and sent bullets of water flying out, striking the three of them. Jake managed to rapidly form a barrier of mana, and combined with the natural barrier from Arcane Awakening and Scales, he shrugged it off and fired another a barrage of arrows.

Once more, he was ignored as the river below seemed to come alive. Torrents of water flew up and enveloped Sylphie in a bubble of water as the frog kept attacking her. Jake flew forward but was smashed back by the frog shooting a blast of water his way, making him fall into the river.

Jake got out of the water, bleeding from his chest, as he went for the frog again. The beast was nearly upon Sylphie when Carmen appeared at its side and punched it hard, sending it slightly off course. She followed up with a combo, hitting it over a dozen times in rapid succession, but Jake could see it wasn't doing as much as Carmen would have liked.

The frog seemed more annoyed than anything as it released its tongue and wrapped it around Carmen's waist. It swung her sideways and smashed her through more than ten trees before it finally let go and tossed her into the distance.

Sylphie had broken out of the water prison and looked like she was about to go all out together with Jake, but at that moment, they both felt something. The frog did, too, as it froze and abandoned all its current plans.

But it was too late for it.

A white form suddenly shot out of the river below, not giving the frog any time to react. It reached the beast in a second, and Jake watched two shining fangs sink into the amphibian's body. Jake didn't even take the time to think before he made use of this opening to run towards Carmen and mentally command Sylphie to follow him.

They were getting the fuck out of there—that was for sure.

Carmen had been flung five hundred meters away after being smashed through two more trees, and she looked more than a little beat up. She looked relieved when she saw them, but her eyes opened in fright soon after, and Jake knew why.

He stopped on a root as he slowly turned around, seeing the same white form rise out of the river. He also felt the aura of the frog was gone along with the Mark placed on it. It had been killed within only a few seconds. He looked at the beast before him and its familiar form.

[Alabaster Crimsoneye Snake – lvl ???]

The beast had a long and slender body. It looked to be around thirty meters long, with an entirely white, almost albino look, especially with the two red eyes that looked like gemstones. The head was only about the size of Jake's torso, and it truly was a thin animal... but that didn't mean Jake would underestimate it.

Even standing there, he felt it. Within the snake was venom at a level far above anything Jake had ever faced. He was instantly aware that his Palate would offer little help. This was no simple C-grade, and Jake was confident this creature was on a whole other level than anything else he had ever seen, surpassing even the Termite King by quite the margin. It was likely a mid-tier C-grade.

As the snake regarded their party of three, Jake's only focus was on escaping. Carmen was heavily injured, and Sylphie seemed scared and leaned on Jake for support. The thought of summoning the Fallen King using his mask appeared, but before he had to do anything, he heard that seemed to originate from the vibrations of its extended tongue.

"What brings one who walks the Path of the Forefather here?"

CHAPTER 28

MAKING "FRIENDS"

J ake stared up at the white snake that, in turn, regarded him, waiting for an answer to its question. It had mentioned something about a Forefather, and the hamster wheel in Jake's mind spun as he put two and two together... The snake had to be talking about the Malefic Viper. It did confuse him a bit, though.

The snake didn't have a Blessing, as far as Jake could tell, and he couldn't see any connection between the C-grade and the Viper at all. Well, besides them both being highly venomous snakes. Also, why had the snake come to begin with?

One thing that did put his mind at ease was the lack of hostility. The snake had helped them and now seemed friendly and curious. Considering that was the case, Jake decided it would be wisest to be honest about what they were doing there.

"We are simply passing through and had no plans of getting into any fights, but the frog attacked us," Jake answered truthfully.

The snake regarded Jake and then tossed Sylphie a look. "To bring a young one from such a heritage through this area is unwise."

Jake nodded. "We realize that now." He still had no idea why the snake was so friendly, though. At least, not for the next half a second. Then he felt a certain snake god send down a message.

"Divine teacher coming in with a quick lesson, because this isn't really anything taught anywhere, as it is considered pretty common knowledge. I got shit-all to do with this particular snake. At least, not directly. Without going into a lengthy explanation, I am in some ways connected to nearly every single snake in existence due to how Records

work, and while I may not know of this snake, it clearly knows of me simply due to its heritage. Beasts have heritages like humans do, and this one may walk one related to me. This all leads back to how we ancient beasts more or less raised the Records of our entire races and hence became known as Forefathers. So, yeah, the snake can see you walk a similar Path as herself. Good luck making a new friend!"

Jake got the entire message from Villy within a few seconds, giving him a better understanding of what was going on. Currently, Jake still had his scales summoned and his wings out. He didn't look very human, and the snake potentially didn't even think he was one.

It was a bit risky, but he wanted to dispel that illusion right away, so he dismissed his scales and wings, returning to being more human. Normally you could barely see the scales, but Jake currently had quite the gnarly wound on his chest, with his armor entirely tattered from absorbing the blow, revealing his upper body.

When the scales and wings disappeared, Jake felt the snake's surprise as she moved her head closer.

"Human?" she asked, perplexed.

"I apologize for any misunderstandings, but even if I am human, I too walk the Path of the Viper—your Forefather," Jake explained to the female snake.

He wanted to make it clear he was still her "kin," so to say, as he really didn't want the snake to turn hostile. Jake was unsure if he could escape himself and certain Carmen would be unable to unless she had some item to help her. Sylphie was also a big question mark. No, better to try the diplomatic approach for now.

Also... the snake had yet to turn antagonistic, and she even seemed disinterested in Sylphie despite clearly being aware of the hawk's heritage.

"I was merely surprised," the snake answered. "I sensed the blood in the river and came as I feared one of my own had been attacked, but I see now it was you. It is interesting to see a human with the blood of the Forefather... Are you a descendant of some sort? No, you are a pure human... Tell me, how do you walk the Path of the Forefather?"

Jake's mind blanked for a while, as he had just discovered a giant gap in knowledge. He had believed himself to be the ignorant one—in his defense, he usually was—but clearly, the snake before him was also unaware of many things considered common knowledge. She didn't seem to have any experience with Blessings and possibly even the way humans worked with their classes, professions, and races. Which... well, it made sense she didn't.

If he assumed the Alabaster Crimsoneye Snake was a native of Earth and had only awakened true sapience in C-grade, how would she have learned? Jake did know that when an animal awakened, sapience was deeply related to their prior intelligence. Reptiles tended to need C-grade at the very least, while some smarter animals would awaken it far earlier. Hawkie had already been damn smart at E-grade, and Sylphie had been a smart little bugger from birth. He also knew beasts had inherent knowledge based on their Lineages. This was likely how the snake even knew of the Viper, but that knowledge hadn't covered this, it seemed.

"Are you familiar with the concept of Legacies and Blessings?" Jake asked the snake.

The snake looked at him with her deep red eyes before answering, "Legacies... yes. Heritages and Legacies are closely related, correct? I have heard of Blessings, but I am uncertain of their effects. A competitor of mine speaks of possessing a Blessing, so I assume it is beneficial?"

"They are, but they also come with some expectations. Tell me, what do you know of your Forefather?" Jake wanted to make sure they weren't speaking past each other.

"An ancient snake who rose to unrivaled power and sent echoes throughout existence as he embraced eternity. I am not certain what more you expect me to know?"

Jake could sense a bit of annoyance, but also expectation. He just smiled as he manipulated his Shroud of the Primordial. His Blessing that was otherwise suppressed to the level of a Lesser Blessing flared as it grew to that of his True Blessing. He had a hunch that proved true as the snake recoiled a tad, staring.

"What are you?" she asked with fright, but also an even stronger sense of curiosity.

"Gods have the ability to give out Blessings to those they want, creating a bond between themselves and the blessed individual," Jake explained. "This usually just resolves in the blessed one getting access to the Path related to the god, and the gods themselves gaining a presence among mortals as well as some other benefits I am not entirely clear on. In my case, I am very closely related to the god that blessed me. Said god naturally being the Malefic Viper, also known as your Forefather."

The snake seemed to take a moment as she absorbed the knowledge, giving Carmen time to also chip in. She had been hanging back and clearly on guard in case things went south. In fact, Jake saw now that she was holding some golden medallion of sorts behind her back even as she spoke.

"What Jake said is true. Gods bless all kinds of creatures and races, and Jake and the Viper just happened to be highly compatible, so the Malefic One made Jake his Chosen. Ah, a Chosen is like a prophet or something, and is the highest level of Blessing possible, more or less making Jake the most important mortal in existence from the viewpoint of the Viper."

Jake could feel her nervousness. He understood why, as the C-grade was far above what any of them could handle. Even Sylphie was hiding away. In her anxiety, she had just opened the floodgates and spoken, wanting Jake to look as good as possible without really thinking much.

For the first time, Jake felt a tinge of hostility from the snake.

"Most important? A human?" the snake hissed as she raised her head a bit. "A D-grade human being deemed more important than any other snake-kin in existence? I only came here out of curiosity, not to be made a fool of."

Carmen froze. "I just meant that—"

"Hey!" Jake interrupted Carmen as he stared up at the snake. "Is that really so hard to believe?"

The snake sneered once more as she stared him down. "The Forefather would never view a human as more worthy than any of his kin. On account of you carrying some part of his Legacy, I will let you go, but don't believe I—"

"Are you calling me a liar?" Jake cut in, getting a frightened look from Carmen, who had just begun to look relieved after the snake said it would let them go.

Jake released his own presence as he stood in opposition to the snake. She glared at him and subconsciously retracted her head from his Bloodline-powered aura. However, he wasn't done yet.

"Villy. Beam me a Blessing."

"Jake, I can't just go around casually giving out Blessings to any random creature you meet," Villy promptly answered. Jake had known the god had looked on with interest, and now it was time to make himself useful.

"Yes, you can," Jake shot back.

"True. Alright, I guess this little one isn't so bad."

"Get your head down here," Jake commanded. "You did help us, so

I guess some kind of compensation is only right."

"What are you planning?" the snake sneered as she showed her fangs. Jake felt the venom within them and got even more sure that he would probably be in for a very bad time if any of that entered his body or even touched his skin.

"Repaying the favor and setting the record straight. Why, are you afraid some measly D-grade human can harm you?" He believed he had read her right, and he turned out to be correct as she reluctantly lowered her head, her curiosity winning out over her cautiousness.

Jake placed his hand on her snout as his hand glowed green. He had asked Villy about giving the Blessing before, but he vaguely felt that he didn't need to when he began infusing his energy. Need to ask, that is. He felt a connection form alongside his ability to give a Blessing without Villy's consent or input. He could only give a low-level Blessing, but it opened up possibilities and implications that Jake wasn't quite sure what to think of.

He didn't need to use this new discovery this time, as he felt Villy bless the snake by using him as the conduit. A pulse of power went through his hand and entered the snake, and he saw the crimson eyes flash dark green for a moment as the snake froze and just looked dumbstruck.

A second turned to five as Jake just stood there with his hand on the snake. None of them moved, and only a good six or seven seconds after it turned awkward, the snake finally reacted by pulling her head back in a sudden yank.

The more than thirty-meter-long C-grade snake just looked down at Jake as she swayed slightly, and Jake saw what he could only interpret as an embarrassed blush as she spoke, "Please don't be mad..."

Meira went through the library as she searched for a specific book she had been asked to find. Well, she needed to find a book with a topic she had been asked about. She was sure she had seen it before—she just wasn't entirely clear on the name—and she had skimmed its description briefly a few months ago.

As she was looking for the book, she saw one of the tables in the library and the books that lay scattered all over it. She hadn't touched it because it had been left like that by her master. He was a bit messy, but she remembered hearing a teacher of hers explain how some people were able to comprehend chaos and didn't need order. Perhaps her master was the same and simply didn't need to put things in boxes and organize them in order to remember things.

Meira finally located the book she was looking for and checked the index. She soon enough found the section she had been thinking of and quickly went towards the entrance hall again, where she activated the gate. She walked through it and appeared inside a small study, where a group of three was already waiting for her.

"Took your time," Nella said once she finally saw Meira.

"Apologies—it took longer to find than expected," Meira said as she handed over the book.

"Don't make dallying a habit, or your sponsor might drop you," Nella said, scoffing as she took the book and opened it.

"Chapter eight," Meira added, getting an annoyed scowl. She didn't mind; it was normal. Nella was a true member of the Order, after all, along with the two others.

"Don't be so hard on her," Izil commented.

Meira liked Izil. She was even nicer than the others. It was probably because they were both elves, though Meira naturally couldn't compare to a student hailing from the Altmar Empire.

"Hey, little elf, got any Whispersnite Fruits left?" Utmal, the final member of their group, asked. She was the child of a dwarf and an ogre and identified as a half-ogre. This made her about the size of a regular human or elf, even if she had a very powerful constitution.

"I already began the incubation experiment with half and planned on using the rest in case it fail—"

"Wait, I'm confused," Utmal interrupted. "Did I ask? I don't care—just don't fail and give me yours. I ain't spending Credits on more than what we were given."

Meira was a bit uncomfortable but agreed nevertheless, summoning the three uncommon-rarity fruits and giving them to Utmal, who swept them up while shaking her head and muttering something about Meira being slow. She was slow sometimes, so that made sense.

"Shouldn't have rushed into the experiment and ruined your own fruits," Izil commented.

"Now, let's not fight," Nella said, stopping the two before they began bickering. Meira was glad she did, as she didn't like it when the two got into fights, especially not when they were related to Meira herself.

Nella was the leader of their group and the one with the greatest background. She was also the sole scalekin of their group and had two B-grade parents. She had been born at D-grade but still needed to study to build up her foundation, and would likely reach C-grade within not that long simply by growing up fully. It still took half a century to grow to be a full-fledged C-grade, but at least she wouldn't need to do anything besides just reaching the threshold and doing the Evolution Awakening.

She had a good status, and Meira wanted to be sure to get on her good side. Izil was the one with the second-greatest background, as she came from the Altmar Empire. Meira didn't know who her parents were or anything, as she didn't talk about it like Nella did, but she had to have a good status if she had come to the Order, right? In any case, she couldn't offend them and make trouble for her master.

"Meira, you should make your sponsor give you some more Academy Credits to pay for the next level of this course," Nella suddenly added.

Meira somewhat meekly answered, "I have not been given permission to use the credits for anyone but myself."

"I am sure you can figure something out." Nella smiled. "If not, just ask for some actual Credits or contribution points and treat us to something nice to compensate, alright?"

"That would be hard..." Meira said as she tried to explain herself without revealing anything about her master. She already felt a bit bad about lying about having a sponsor, but technically her master was a sponsor, so it wasn't really a lie, right?

"Oh, come on," Utmal sneered. "Just spread your legs a bit wider, and I am sure your sponsor or whatever will gladly reward his little who—"

"Utmal!" Izil butted in.

"Fine," the half-ogre said as she raised her hands and continued ignoring Meira.

Meira threw Izil a thankful glance, but all she got in return was a helpless look and a shake of the other elf's head. Meira wasn't sure how to respond to that... but at least they weren't fighting anymore, and for the next half an hour, no one really said anything bad. In fact, they didn't even talk about or with Meira at all. Meira knew that the situation was a bit strained, but she would keep doing her best, and she was sure she wouldn't give her master trouble when he returned. She just hoped she was doing okay in the meantime.

This was her first time making friends, after all.

CHAPTER 29

PORT CITY CHANGLUN

C armen knew she had messed up when she accidentally spilled a bit too much to the snake and ended up offending it. She'd been ready to use the talisman she had prepared to hopefully temporarily distract the snake enough for them to make an escape, but she'd been relieved when the snake said it would still let them go.

And then Jake had decided to piss off the C-grade even more by acting all offended himself. She'd nearly wanted to smack him over the head and drag him away while apologizing, but a few moments later, she could only stand there, dumbstruck.

She knew people who had high-level Blessings or a class or a profession related to their Patron could give Blessings with the help of their gods, but this usually only happened after a long process. Not just casually, such as when Jake decided to one-up the snake by proving himself through giving it one.

The situation after that only made it worse. Carmen still didn't get at all how they had gotten to where they were currently.

Jake, Sylphie, and Carmen were sitting on a small wooden barge as a large brown snake that had to be well over a hundred meters long dragged it across the Grand Mangrove River. Now, this would usually be hard due to all the roots and trees and whatnot, but the snake got around all this by just fucking bulldozing through and creating a path.

How did it do this, you ask? By being another goddamn C-grade. After Jake had given the snake the Blessing, the white Alabaster Crimsoneye Snake seemed to have an entire shift in personality and began acting all shy and careful. The damn snake had then nervously asked them if they wanted an escort and transport through the rest of the river, which Jake had accepted.

The C-grade had then somehow summoned not just one, but five goddamn C-grade snakes, leading to their current situation of sitting on a barge constructed by a C-grade snake able to manipulate wood while being escorted by a total of six C-grades.

But this wasn't even the worst part...

"Are you sure?" the snake asked nervously as she swam alongside the barge.

"You already apologized enough, and this is more than enough to repay the misunderstanding," Jake once more tried to assure the C-grade.

He had to admit that he hadn't expected what was currently happening to take place. It turned out the Alabaster Crimsoneye Snake wasn't a sole operator, but had a small crowd of C-grade snakes following her around—likely the kin she had talked about earlier.

"But—"

"I said it's fine," Jake repeated as he tried to calm down the snake. "I was the one returning the favor for the save from the frog."

"Okay..."

Jake had made quite a few miscalculations. He had thought the C-grade Alabaster snake had to be some kind of old entity, probably at least the age of someone, well, adult, but it appeared he had been a tad off the mark. The snake had just been acting all mature before, and only now did Jake realize he was dealing with an overgrown teenage C-grade snake.

She had found and consumed a natural treasure that had allowed her to rapidly grow, and, at the same time, accepted a quest of sorts. A quest that clarified a lot of things when she finally described the details of it. Jake had known these special natural treasures had appeared on Earth, allowing beasts rapid growth—Mystie had found the Mystbone, a far less potent special natural treasure, after all.

These more special natural treasures also came with limitations. It had allowed some of the creatures of the Grand Mangrove River to reach C-grade but at the cost of limiting them to the river and ocean beyond. This limitation was only temporary, and she didn't know when it would end. All she knew was that the natural treasure she had consumed was still being digested, and if she left the restricted area, it would begin acting up, and if she was outside it too long, the treasure could potentially end up killing her.

This explained why no C-grades had attacked any cities or caused any true trouble so far. Jake knew the system had restricted them, but only now did he know the details. This was perhaps also part of the reason why the Termite King had not pursued Jake more than it had—it had gone beyond its restricted zone.

"Excuse me again?" the snake asked Jake after only giving him roughly a minute of silence.

"Yes?" Jake really didn't wanna be mean to the snake... It felt like a teenager talking to her favorite pop idol.

"Is there, like, anything I can do to help? Even if I am a bit restricted, I can maybe sneak out and—"

"No. Just no. Focus on yourself. Remember, the Path of the Malefic One is about embracing freedom and striving for more power through your own Path. Rather than thinking about how you can help me, think about how you can help yourself and gain more power. Then, when the restrictions lift, you will be able to expand your horizons even more. By then, you can decide for yourself what you want to do in an open multiverse of possibilities. And the more power you have, the more possibilities."

"Actually acting like my Chosen for once," Villy said, unable to help himself.

"Hey, this is as much my philosophy as it is yours," Jake countered.

"I had it first and called dibs before your universe was even born," Villy joked back.

Jake just smiled at their brief exchange, as the Alabaster snake seemed to have gotten his message.

"Okay, I will keep doing my best and improving," she said with conviction.

At least he thought she got it, but she seemed a bit... too determined? Either way, it wasn't bad to want to get stronger.

Their party kept traveling through the Grand Mangrove River as the snake asked some more things related to the Malefic Viper, and Jake also knew the other snakes were listening in with interest. He hadn't spoken directly to any of them, as the Alabaster snake had said they weren't that good at speech yet. Jake was pretty sure they were just shy, though. For every second he spent with them, he became more and more assured they were just a bunch of C-grade teenagers with all the teenage angst. At least socially. When it came to their abilities as beasts?

They ran into two C-grades when they passed the midpoint of the river, which allowed Jake to see two birds more than twenty meters tall getting ripped apart by four C-grade snakes, their barge-dragger and the Alabaster snake hanging back. The Alabaster snake explained how they didn't really spend much time at the surface due to most stuff being weak outside of certain areas.

Besides that, nothing bothered them, and the rest of their trip through the danger zone was a breeze. It turned out that being escorted by a group of C-grades, including a mid-tier C-grade considered one of the most powerful in the entire Grand Mangrove River, meant not many beasts dared make a move.

When they reached the final parts of the river, the Alabaster snake had them all stop as she looked at Jake with some regret. "We can't go much beyond here without leaving the restricted area... I can go a bit further, but—"

"You have done enough," Jake said as he smiled at her. "Thank you for the assistance once more."

"Ah, uhm, my pleasure!" the snake said, embarrassed. Jake knew she still felt bad about questioning his identity and all that, even if Jake was long past it.

The other snakes also all bowed their heads, seeming almost scared of Jake. Even the one who had been dragging their barge using vines bowed. It hadn't looked back at him even once throughout their entire journey and even now had its head halfway hidden underwater. This made it look a bit silly when it tried to bow gracefully like its brethren.

Jake smiled at them all once more, offering a final farewell before heading off with Sylphie and Carmen, with Sylphie giving them a "ree!" in thanks too. Carmen was quiet but did nod in their direction as they took off.

They had been dropped off at the outskirts of the Grand Mangrove River, and it only took them twenty minutes to reach shore once more, exiting the danger zone altogether.

Only when they were out of the mangrove did Carmen speak. "That was... something."

"Hey, it went pretty well, and we got out of the mangrove forest ahead of schedule," Jake said jokingly.

"We nearly got killed by a C-tier snake," Carmen shot back.

"Nah, we were never in danger. She was a real softie, that one."

"The first thing the snake did was kill something when we met."

"Details, details," Jake jokingly said. "In all seriousness, yeah, it got a bit risky. I think we should avoid any danger zones. At least ones with unfavorable environments."

"Agreed," Carmen said. "Let's reach the port city already?"

"Let us," Jake said.

They took off once more, traveling towards the port city of Changlun. On the way, Jake kept the Prima fragment close and tried to scan for any energies but found nothing. Only a bit over a day later did they reach Changlun, and Jake had to admit, he had underestimated the place.

Jake and Carmen stopped atop a hill overlooking the plains leading up to the city, and both just stared. In front of them was plenty of farmland with large crystal pillars spread throughout for kilometers leading up to the city itself.

The city had a wall more than twenty meters tall surrounding it, and from the looks of it, this wall even extended into the ocean, defending them from any maritime threats. When Jake had first read about Changlun, he'd thought it was a small place, but seeing it in person made it clear this was no minor settlement. There had to be at least hundreds of thousands living there.

"Damn," Carmen said. "This is quite something."

Jake nodded as he more deeply considered the placement of the city. Changlun was quite an isolated city. To one side, it had the Grand Mangrove River that cut it off from everything else, with the river itself leading into the ocean. Due to the layout of the shoreline, there wasn't even that much land area to the other side. It was like Changlun was placed in its own little cut-off plain.

"It looks like it goes on forever," Carmen continued. Jake was confused for a moment, then realized that she wasn't speaking of the city, but what lay beyond it. The vast ocean.

"Yeah." Jake nodded once more.

With his Perception, he could see all the way to where the water fell below the horizon with not a single thing in between. It just kept going for thousands upon thousands of kilometers. The oceans had covered around seventy percent of pre-system Earth's surface, and he had no reason to believe this had changed. With how big Earth was now... it was hard to imagine just how humongous the body of water truly was.

Much less to imagine the creatures dwelling within. The Alabaster snake had said that the oceans were entirely open to all C-grades, and it made sense. There were no enlightened species to protect, making the open oceans a true hunting ground for all. There had to be so many C-grades dwelling deep beneath. Heck, he felt like there were even C-grades pretty close to the shoreline. They still seemed to keep a safe distance, though, probably due to the aforementioned restrictions.

"Ree?" Sylphie asked.

"Yeah," Jake repeated.

"Ree, ree?"

"There was a teleporter in Changlun, right?" Jake asked Carmen to confirm Sylphie's question.

Carmen looked zoned out, taking a moment before answering, "Uh, yeah. There should be. Just two jumps, and we should make it to the other continent. We need to stop by an island about halfway before teleporting all the way due to the distance."

Jake nodded. He was aware of many of the intricacies with long-range teleportation gates and knew that even with the favorable conditions offered by the ocean, a mid-way point was probably for the best. In the same way that a barrier like the Grand Mangrove River could disrupt teleportation, then a path without any obstructions—such as over an ocean—would offer no issues and make the process far more manageable.

"Let's head in," Jake finally said after they had stood there for a good while.

They barely managed to get down the hill before Jake sensed someone approaching. A second later, he felt several gazes land upon them, making it clear they had triggered some kind of security measure. Jake was surprised he hadn't detected it, but then again, he was certain there were plenty of ways to make trip alarms he didn't know about.

"Incoming," he said casually, getting a nod from Carmen.

Moments later, Jake spotted three cloaked figures approaching. The one at the front was a bearded middle-aged man wielding a bow, instantly making Jake think he couldn't be that bad of a guy. He also had a decent level.

[Human – lvl 142]

The man stopped together with his two companions a good hundred meters away as he regarded them. "Lord Thayne and Miss Carmen, I assume?"

"That would be correct," Jake confirmed, not really that surprised they knew they were coming. Them going wasn't a secret, and Jake knew both people from Valhal and Haven had been in talks with them about when the teleporter was up and running.

"Aight," the man said. "Just one thingL The boss said he wanted to invite you for a visit before you head off."

Thinking it would be the polite move, Jake agreed, and Carmen didn't care. There was just one thing. "Before that, can you point us in the direction of a hotel or something? I need a damn shower after spending days within a damn mangrove forest."

The man nodded. "Aye, just follow me back, and I can show you some of the fancier places."

Jake and Carmen followed the man as he led them through the plains and farmland towards the city, getting a brief history lesson on the way.

"Changlun was founded by a party of five from the tutorial," the man explained. "We began recruiting everyone interested nearby while fortifying the city. Ah, why build so close to the ocean? Because while that big puddle is a bit dangerous, it is also filled with good stuff. Parts of powerful beasts sometimes wash up on the beach, natural treasures are plenty in the coral reef just a few hundred meters out, and the ocean is also like a big, infinite mana battery able to power all the stuff the crafters need."

Those were just the major points, but it was clear Changlun had not been made without thought. After they entered, they saw the well-paved roads, clean streets, and modern-looking buildings. It did look a bit industrial, but otherwise, everything looked nice. The main building material was a kind of white limestone brick, giving the city an interesting color scheme.

They were led into a hotel, where they quickly booked rooms and got washed up. They naturally got separate rooms, and Jake had fun playing with Sylphie in a bathtub since the little featherball loved splashing him. He did toss her out as he showered, though, as it wasn't proper for a young lady to be present.

After that, he met up with Carmen and had some food before they headed back to the hotel again and decided to have a good rest while arranging for the archer to meet them the next day. Jake and Carmen agreed on getting a good rest before heading to the other continent as they settled in, and for the first time in a while, Jake got a good night's sleep with a bundled-up bird lying on his stomach.

CHAPTER 30

CROSSING THE GREAT POND

J ake woke up the next morning to a bird nipping at his hair. Sylphie clearly hadn't been able to sleep as long as he had—assuming she had slept at all—and had gotten bored. He shook his head to get her off, then scooped her up as she put on a fake struggle.

"You're a little bully, aren't you?" Jake teased with a smile as she looked up at him.

"Ree!" she answered defiantly.

"Excuses." He chuckled as he let her go.

She flew a few rounds around the room as Jake used his spatial storage to get on all his armor. Just in time for Sylphie to finish her morning exercise and land on his shoulder. Apparently, she had decided that today was not a bird-on-head day.

Being up and about, Jake knocked on the wall to Carmen's room, quickly getting a knock in return. They had no plans of staying in Changlun more than that single night and promptly headed out to meet the boss their escort had mentioned. Jake was intrigued, as the presence of a boss contradicted the narrative of a party of five founding the city.

However, as Jake and Carmen met up with the escort and went toward the waterfront, Jake began to understand. He and Carmen were led into a pretty well-sealed-off room—half of it was water, with an underground connection leading straight into the ocean.

"Seems like we will be meeting more C-grades," Jake said with a chuckle, getting a surprised look from both Carmen and their escort. The escort due to Jake figuring it out, and Carmen due to, well, surprise. The archer, knowing the gig was up, said his farewell as he headed out.

The surface of the water within the sealed-off bunker suddenly churned, and Jake saw a figure rise from it. A humanoid form of pure water soon took shape. Jake used Identify but got nothing in return. This was just a summon of sorts, or perhaps remote manipulation.

"I welcome you, Malefic's Chosen and warrior of Valhal," the creature that Jake assumed to be an elemental said.

"Hello there," Jake said, wondering what the presumed elemental wanted.

Carmen just waved, equally restrained. The amount of mana he felt from the apparition wasn't extreme, but it did carry the faint aura of a C-grade. It only seemed to be early-tier, though, not quite matching up to the Alabaster snake or even the Termite King.

"I apologize if I disturbed your travel plans, but I believed it would be a waste to not at the very least make your acquaintances," the elemental said. The more the elemental spoke, the more Jake became certain it wasn't any usual elemental, primarily due to its level of intelligence.

Elementals were notoriously stupid, and even if they awakened some sapience, they tended to be a bit on the juvenile side, often having the mental age of a child at most. Not in the same vein as Stormild, who just had a childish nature, but more like Sylphie and her general naivety due to her genuinely young age.

So, if an elemental displayed high levels of intelligence, it often stemmed from it either being a powerful variant or related to an affinity that naturally lent itself to high intellect. Assuming this was a water elemental of some kind, Jake assumed it was the former option.

"It's all good," Jake answered.

They didn't really get to say anything more as Jake felt six people enter the bunker through his sphere. It was the archer from before walking with five other men. For a second, Jake wondered if this was some poorly planned ambush, but he didn't feel any sense of danger coming from them, and they clearly didn't even try to hide their approach.

Carmen and Sylphie also noticed them, and the three turned around. The five men all looked to be in their late thirties to early forties, with the one in the middle wearing a white robe. Jake vaguely felt the space affinity float around the man, making it clear he was a space mage like Neil. His level was also pretty good.

[Human – lvl 151]

The four with him were also all between 145 and 150. It didn't take a genius to guess this was the party of five that had founded the city of Changlun.

"I believe it is only proper we also greet the Chosen and the warrior of Valhal," the space mage said as he bowed. The others mimicked the motion, and Jake nodded in acknowledgment. "I am sure you have questions about why we are working with a C-grade monster, but I assure you it is nothing malicious."

"No, I really don't," Jake said, shrugging, to the group's surprise. "But let me guess: The elemental helps protect the city and gives you natural treasures and materials from the ocean, and in turn, you assist the elemental through a variety of means. Probably things such as giving land-bound treasures the elemental can't get due to the restrictions C-grades are currently imposed with."

In fact, he would argue this fit pretty well with the entire Unusual Unions theme from the World Congress. Of course, to Jake, this wasn't really unusual, just logical. Why would humans and monsters not work together when it was mutually beneficial?

His deduction also seemed to prove correct as the elemental responded, *"It appears we underestimated the insight of the Chosen. I apologize for our hubris; we merely wished to avoid any misunderstandings, and I would personally prefer to not get a mark on my back, instead retaining my and my follower's friendly relations with humanity."*

"Ah, no worries," Jake said, dismissing it. "You just keep doing you, and as long as you don't act like an asshole, I don't see why we would have trouble. Well, some humans might dislike you, but I am sure you and your pals can handle that."

"I can't really speak for all of Valhal, but we wouldn't just begin hunting down an ally of an ally without reason," Carmen added.

"I thank the Chosen and the warrior for their honesty," the elemental said. *"In that case, I shall not delay your travels any longer. Godspeed."*

With those words, the summoned elemental was dispelled as the water collapsed and became one with the rest of the ocean once more. Jake wasn't sure if this entire conversation had been necessary, but he assumed the elemental was just the careful sort.

"Lord Thayne?" the space mage said. "I just want to clarify once more that we are allies with the elementals, and my companion here even shares a Patron god. I believe that such an alliance can bring great benefits to humanity and Earth in the future. Even if we are not directly aligned with Haven or the Order of the Malefic Viper, we have no desire to stand in opposition to you. No, we wish to try and remain neutral and friendly with all, no matter what happens."

"I said it is fine," Jake said. He hadn't noticed the shared god, but now that he scanned a bit, he saw one of the men gave off a faint aura similar to the elemental. It didn't have to mean they shared a Patron, just that they shared some parts of the same Legacy.

Carmen also seemed to honestly not give a shit. They had never planned to make this into any kind of diplomatic mission, so this entire thing was just a sidetrack. This did turn the situation somewhat awkward until Jake broke the silence.

"You have made a nice city," he said, doing the most cliché thing you can when visiting someone: complimenting their home.

"Thanks," the space mage said with a smile. "Now, let me lead you to the teleportation chamber."

They happily accepted, and the space mage led them through the city while making small talk. This particular teleportation chamber was placed underground and quite far toward the sea. The mage explained it was for safety reasons and because they used the powerful mana of the ocean to power the teleportation. In fact, the type of space magic deployed by the mage wasn't the same branch of space magic as Neil's.

No, the City Lord of Changlun somehow mixed water and space magic. This led to travel over water being far faster and easier, even potentially allowing underwater cities with working teleportation gates. He even said it would be easier for him to teleport to an underwater settlement through water than teleporting through the air.

The island they were supposed to teleport to was roughly a hundred thousand kilometers from Changlun, making this the longest teleport they would ever do. This was only possible due to the unique talents of the space mage to borrow the water-affinity mana given off by the ocean.

Meeting this man and hearing his explanations was a reminder of the hidden talents all over Earth. He clearly had his head on right and was, without a doubt, a far more talented mage than Neil, at least from a technical standpoint.

When they got to the teleportation chamber, they saw there were only three circles active. One to the island and two leading to smaller cities inland in the direction opposite the Grand Mangrove River. The man did explain that he hoped to get past the blockage that was the mangrove forest, but currently, it was beyond his abilities.

"Thanks for the talk, and good luck with everything," Jake said as he, Sylphie, and Carmen stepped onto the teleportation circle.

"It was my pleasure," the man said just before the party of three teleported away.

Jake felt his vision shift, and for a moment, he felt like he was one with the water all around him. An image of the endless ocean flashed in his mind before he suddenly found himself standing on a new teleportation circle. The teleportation had gone more smoothly than expected except for one thing.

"Why are we wet?" Carmen asked.

"Ree!" Sylphie complained as she shook her feathers to get the water off her.

Jake was also surprised, as they were all utterly soaked from the teleportation. As he began considering if it was a side effect of the type of space magic used, he had it confirmed.

"I apologize for them still not having fixed the issue with the teleporter," a female attendant said as she entered the hall they had been teleported into. She was only E-grade and didn't seem to recognize them at all. "May I know your business on Saint Helestras? It is unusual for visitors to come outside of the travel window."

The travel window she mentioned was something that had been established to avoid constant people coming through. It was to make administration easier, and there was an hour each day for people to use the teleporters, with it being off-limits at all other times besides special circumstances.

"We are merely traveling through and heading to... What was the place called again?" Jake asked Carmen.

"Pebblerock or something," she answered.

"Puddlerock?" the attendant asked, a bit confused.

"That one." Carmen nodded affirmingly.

"I will still need to know your order of business, fill out a visitor's pass, and register your arrival," the attendant said apologetically. "This is all following basic protocol and for the safety of everyone."

Jake sighed inwardly, as he knew this was obviously just a half-truth. If the name of this island—Saint Helestras—didn't make it clear, this city was one established by the Holy Church. The fact that the Church was in charge of an island that was fast developing into a central travel point between the two continents was a bit concerning, but it was the kind of concern Miranda would deal with.

"No need for that," Jake said, in no mood for some annoying screening process.

"I must insist on performing the required interviews, or—"

"No," Jake once more said. "And tell the guards to stop hiding. What are they doing anyway? Trying to cosplay the Court of Shadows? Doing a real shitty job if so."

He had already felt seven people hidden within a side room behind a barrier and some fancy-ass light magic that naturally didn't work versus his Sphere of Perception. They realized hiding was useless when he called them out and exited the room with their guards high. Not that it mattered... Jake didn't even need to use Identify to know none of them were even halfway a threat.

"Comply with regulations, or we will have to take you into custody and—"

"Mate," Jake cut in, "rules apply only to the applicable. Now point me in the direction of the teleportation circle to Puddlerock and stop wasting my time. We will be gone before you know it."

"Sir," the attendant said, "these rules are imposed by the United Cities Alliance, and we have to follow them or—"

"Actually, no need," Jake interrupted again as he began walking towards a teleportation circle. They had tried to hide it, but Jake had seen them toss it a look when he mentioned Puddlerock. He knew how the teleporters worked already. As he went towards it, he felt the guard take out a token, but Jake tossed him a look, and the man froze due to Gaze of the Apex Hunter.

"I wouldn't," Jake said as he and the others stepped on the platform and activated it.

To the bewildered looks of those present, they were whisked away, and the group of three finally made it to the other continent across the great pond.

The teleportation was as smooth as the last one, and they appeared even more drenched in seawater within the port city known as Puddle-rock. A downright terrible name, but what could be expected of a city part of the United Cities Alliance? Even Jake didn't like the name and found it too damn generic, and that was coming from a guy naming a hawk Hawkie and his own city Haven.

Jake and Carmen were once more approached by people the moment they appeared. A man and woman, both wearing what looked like police uniforms very reminiscent of what actual officers wore presystem.

"May I see your travel passes?" the man asked.

"Ain't got any," Jake said as he and Carmen began walking out of the teleportation building. Jake saw this one was also relatively isolated and had plenty of barriers defending it.

"Sir, I need you to cooperate," the female officer said.

"Never been good at that one." Jake shook his head as he turned to them. "Fine, I guess we do need some directions. Carmen, where to next?"

"Well, there should be a guy called Clinton who used to travel with the people we are tracking," she answered.

"Clinton. Got it." Jake nodded as he turned to the officers. "You guys love your administrative stuff, so where can we go look up where this guy lives?"

The two just stood there, frozen, both incredibly tense due to the hawk sitting on Jake's shoulder and menacingly staring them down. Luckily for them, they didn't need to do anything, as Jake felt a new presence approach rapidly.

The man teleported into the room and appeared right between the two officers with a bright smile on his lips. "Welcome to Puddlerock! Excuse the silly name; I wasn't the one who decided on it. A pleasure to meet all three of you."

The young man wore silver armor and had two blades strapped to his back. He smiled confidently as he stood there, and Jake could see why. He was level 157 and didn't look like a chump at all. Moreover, Jake was certain the guy was blessed by some god. It was just a feeling, but a feeling was good enough for Jake.

"Hi there," Jake said. "I take it you got some clout in this city?"

"Considering my old man runs the place, yeah," he answered as he looked at the officers. "Shouldn't you two be leaving, or at least show some respect? We are in the presence of quite the personages."

The officers looked frightened as they bowed before nearly running out of the teleportation hall. By now, a few more people had also appeared in the lobby that housed over a dozen teleportation gates.

"Go somewhere easier to talk?" the silver-armored young man suggested.

"Sure," Jake agreed, and they headed off towards some public office. Jake and Carmen got a quick look at the city but had little interest, as they were focused on the task at hand: tracking down Carmen's family.

And probably a few more Primas along the way. Just for good measure.

CHAPTER 31

CITY-HOPPING

Jake and Carmen stood outside of the small brick house. It looked cheaply built, which made sense, as this was squarely in the slums of Puddlerock. Apparently, many of those who lived there had been exiled from Saint-something Island due to breaking some of their stupid Holy Church rules. Or maybe they just had a bit too much independence to fit in.

"This is the place?" Carmen asked as Jake checked the paper in his hand.

"Definitely looks like it." He nodded. "How did you find out about this Clinton guy anyway?"

"The Holy Church isn't the only faction with people able to divine stuff. Valhal has Rune Seers and stuff like that. I just got in touch with one of the better ones, and she used my Records to track my family by linking me to them. This is how she found this guy, too, as his karma is deeply tied to theirs."

"I see," Jake said, nodding. He still wasn't clear on how Carmen wanted him to track her family, considering he had yet to see anything to go from that wasn't just good-old detective work. For the Primas, he could use their energy signatures, and he would need something similar if he was to track humans.

"Why are we stalling, by the way?" Jake then asked.

"I wasn't," Carmen said defensively as she raised her hand to knock on the door. She hesitated slightly before she finally built up the courage.

She knocked two times, and the two of them waited. Jake wasn't worried about no one being home, considering he could already see the man inside sitting in a chair and reading a book. He was on the older side, probably in his late fifties to early sixties. Also, inside the house, Jake had already spotted a lot of fishing gear, and overall the guy called Clinton just gave Jake the impression of an average retired man who liked to fish.

When Carmen knocked, the man looked up, frowned, and placed the book on a table as he went to open the door. It didn't take long before he was there, but he didn't open it right away.

"Who's there?" he asked carefully.

"My name is Carmen... I am looking for some people you used to travel with, and I heard you could provide some information," the warrior of Valhal said somewhat nervously.

The man instantly responded. He opened the door slowly at first, but was surprised and swung it open rapidly when he saw her. "Who are you?"

Carmen looked a bit surprised herself. "I already told you my name."

"Your voice just reminded me of someone else... Sorry. Ah, where are my manners? Come on in. I hear you are looking for someone?" The man called Clinton seemed to finally be calming down.

Until he saw Jake wearing his mask and the hawk sitting on his shoulder, that is. He stared at them as Jake raised his hand to give a friendly wave, Sylphie mimicking him by raising her wing to also wave.

Cuteness won out, as the man couldn't help but smile at the sight and was further calmed by Carmen's explanation. "He is a tracker I work with to help me find the people I am looking for."

Clinton nodded once more as he invited them in, and after the usual pleasantries of being offered a drink and politely declining, they finally got to the main topic.

"I can already guess who you are looking for... You look just like her." With a light smile, Clinton asked, "Your mother is called Marcia, right? Your father, Antonios?"

Carmen frowned as she nodded, but Jake also felt a faint sense of relief. Whether it was because of the use of present tense, implying they were still alive, or the confirmation the man named Clinton knew about them, Jake wasn't sure.

"They were also traveling with several others from my family, right?" Carmen asked.

"Oh, yes, quite a few. I think it is lucky that an entire family could enter a tutorial together. I remember your father mentioning you and saying how you were away at college at the time and therefore weren't present at the annual dinner. It must have been tough."

"Unlucky... yeah," Carmen muttered as her gaze turned colder. "I am currently looking for them and heard you know more. But before that, how come you left their group?"

Clinton sighed. "While it was a very cohesive group, there was also a lot of... drama. Being an outsider, I had no influence, so when I finally came across a safe settlement, I chose to make it my home. I also must apologize, but I am not sure exactly where they went, just that they went towards the western city of Longchester."

Jake finally decided to enter the conversation. "Do you have something related to any of them? An item they crafted or used that hasn't been bound to someone yet, or maybe something similar?"

"Hm..." Clinton frowned, not questioning why Jake asked for it. "I may have something. Let me look."

The man got up and went to check in another room. Jake had decided to butt in for two reasons. First of all, because it needed to be asked, and secondly, because he saw how hard Carmen was clenching her fists below the table. He found it a bit weird, but had still decided that briefly changing the topic would be for the best.

Jake had no idea why Carmen was even looking for her family. He had never asked but had assumed it was similar to his own reasons. Having no plans to pry into her personal business, he would just let her handle it, and even if there was some bad blood between her and her family, it was for her to deal with. All would come to light if they found them anyway.

"Ah, here it is!" the man said as he brought out a wand. Jake looked at it and instantly felt a mana signature from it. "This wand belonged to Antonios. He got a better one when we entered this city, and I didn't have a high enough level to bind it to myself at the time... When I finally did, I realized I had no plans of fighting anymore."

With a string of mana, Jake floated the wand over and scanned it. The mana within was faint, but Jake was sure of it. It belonged to a person that wasn't Clinton. Carmen was looking at him, and Jake nodded as she sighed in relief, muttering something about the Rune Seer not scamming her.

"How much for it?" Carmen asked Clinton.

"You can have it," the man said, smiling. "Your father and mother helped me out a lot in the tutorial, and I owe them at least that. It was your father's anyway, so returning it to his family only seems right."

"Alright." Carmen nodded with mixed emotions.

"If you do find them, please give them my greetings. I hope they are doing well." Clinton leaned back and took a sip of coffee.

"Just one final question... Was there a woman called Beatrice with them?" Carmen asked in a serious tone.

"Of course!" Clinton said with a cheerful smile. "She was such a nice young woman. Beatrice is your cousin, right? You are about the same age, but I hear that you drifted apart due to some differences. I hope you two can reconcile. After all, family is more important than ever in this new world. Do say hi to her for me, alright?"

Carmen frowned but nodded. "I will be sure to greet her when we meet—that I can promise you."

"You guys ready to go?" the silver-armored warrior said as he escorted Jake, Carmen, and Sylphie to the teleportation chamber once more. He had actually been way more helpful than Jake had first thought, having more or less stalked them ever since they entered the city.

The man had even handed him a map of quite a large area that had been created by the United Cities Alliance. It was a lot like Arnold's map, just about a hundred times worse and less detailed. A lot of it was rough estimates with no proper identification of where dangerous beasts resided. This did partly make sense, as to the United Cities Alliance, an area filled with level 160 monsters was viewed as pretty much the same as one filled with C-grades, marking them all as danger zones.

It did give some insight into areas worth investigating, though. But before they would have time to head out and check the danger zones— hopefully finding two Primas on the way—they would head off to this Longchester place and continue their tracking mission.

There was just one minor problem... The young man in silver armor *really* wanted to come with them and had even made a decent case for why they should bring him along. He was well-known and had knowledge of all the areas they were heading to. With his reputation alone, he would remove all potential barriers to their travels just by being present.

"You sure you really wanna come?" Carmen asked skeptically, with Jake getting why. The guy looked young, probably barely in his twenties. He also just struck Jake as a bit green, even if his level was high. He was too... cheerful. But then again, Jake wasn't the best at reading people if they were good at hiding their emotions.

"I can carry my own weight," he said, smiling. "Trust me, I will be of use, even in a fight!"

Jake just shrugged. "Just know we aren't your babysitters."

"Naturally not." The warrior kept smiling.

After a bit more convincing and the man even pulling out a small satchel with snacks for Sylphie, their group was convinced. If nothing else, he was a damn good planner. They continued their journey, which had rapidly turned from a three-man journey into a four-man one.

This did change the dynamic quite a bit, as Jake and Carmen were the kinds of people who could run through the plains for twenty hours straight without exchanging a single word. But this guy? It was like he had a condition that would make him explode if he shut up for more than ten minutes straight.

Anyway, this guy was called Peter, the kid of the city leader of Puddlerock. At first, he'd seemed a tad... well, dull, but the more the guy talked, the more Jake's opinion changed. Even Carmen seemed to shift her perception.

Peter had originally been a member of the Holy Church. The plan had been for him to get good relations with the massive faction on the planet to help out his father—and because he genuinely wanted to make Earth a better place. The Church had been present on both continents from the start, with its influence spreading from the beginning.

At first, the young man had fit in well. His affinity for light magic was high, and he'd quickly been recruited as a potential paladin. He had risen through the ranks, gained power, had his own elite party, and generally just been a real asset. He'd actually enjoyed his time there and thought the Church a force of good... until something happened.

Peter had been part of the Treasure Hunt. He had left pretty early on due to getting into a scuffle with vampires a bit above his own league, but some members of his party had stayed behind. One of them was a mage that the young guy clearly had a crush on despite not admitting it, even with all his blabbering.

She never returned.

This in itself was not that suspicious. Many had died during the hunt. Peter had kept going as normal for months after that until one day, he had coincidentally met up with her parents and heard them talk about how much of a hero their daughter had been. Peter had agreed, but when they talked a bit more about her, he found out that she hadn't died in a fight or anything like that. She had sacrificed herself in a ritual to create a sword.

Jake remembered the Sword Bertram had used on the Monarch of Blood. He remembered the power Bertram had displayed, but only now did it make sense how they had managed to create it.

Peter had been distraught, and he'd only felt more messed up when no one around him thought it that weird. They'd praised her sacrifice and said she was just in the Holy Land now. He had even been brought to speak to her spirit... but still. She had explained how she had reached the end of her Path and had trouble gaining levels, and she had gone out doing what was best for everyone.

Even if Peter could see the logic, he just didn't like it. He had heard about it happening, but, like an idiot, never believed it would happen to someone he cared about. His faith was broken, and it was almost as if his progress stopped from one day to the next.

When the system event of Unusual Unions arrived, he'd participated and become what he was today. He had even renounced the god from the Holy Church that had blessed him. This had all led to some fallout between Puddlerock and the Holy Church, and honestly, Jake put two and two together pretty quickly—Peter's old man hoped to create good relations with Valhal and the Order of the Malefic Viper through Jake and Carmen, as the bridge to the Holy Church was more or less burned.

Since the event, Peter had progressed more than ever and begun leveling again. He was not associated with any faction besides the United Cities Alliance and was more or less a lone wolf. Now, for the final question: How was he in a fight? Well, that was yet to be determined, as none of the guards or officers they met as they teleported around wanted one. And boy, did they meet a lot of guards.

The next days were spent teleporting to a city, going to the public office of the city, and then tracking down Carmen's family in the records. Luckily they were a group of nearly thirty people, making them stand out quite a bit, but it was still damn annoying.

Peter helped immensely by cutting away all the red tape and giving them instant access. It still took a while to get around and put together everything, but finally, they got confirmation after visiting city number eleven.

The family was found.

They were in a city without a teleportation circle in it and had lived there for about two months. Now, while this city didn't have a teleportation circle currently, that didn't mean it had never had one. It had been deactivated about three weeks back due to what an official described as "political differences" that were "currently being resolved."

Talking to a merchant who had been there recently, things became clearer.

"Eh, they had some issues with the guy running it not wanting to contribute taxes or something, last I heard... or maybe it had something to do with all the workers. I honestly don't know, but the place is a damn mess and keeps raking in money. I would generally stay away."

"Why?" Jake asked.

The merchant looked at Jake and shook his head. "The place is just a bit messed up and serves a certain clientele... but hey, if you are into whores, gambling, and doing some messed-up stuff, you may enjoy it. I sure know I ain't going back. If I did, my wife would kill me."

For some reason, Carmen smiled upon hearing this description. As for Peter, he just frowned, clearly not aware of the place. As for the name of the city... well, it had the most on-the-nose name Jake had ever encountered:

Paradise.

CHAPTER 32

TRACKING & DANGER BIRD

Paradise. A city with a rather apt description for certain kinds of people. It was the kind of place that the United Cities Alliance didn't truly recognize as a member but still wanted in their circle. A necessary evil, so to say, where all the weird and controversial shit could be done. A center of debauchery, wealth, and whatever the heart desired—and that came from its own marketing.

Peter had gone and gathered all the intel he could on the place. Considering what he got was clearly a watered-down version of the actual place, Jake was impressed the "civilized" United Cities Alliance hadn't denounced it yet. They didn't exactly promote or endorse it, instead just acting like Paradise didn't really exist, and their stance had led to some recent trouble, resulting in the teleportation circle being cut off.

This meant they would have to travel there on foot, which the clerk heavily advised against. Apparently, one would have to pass quite the dangerous zone where these gazelle-like creatures roamed, and they were known to be rather aggressive towards anyone invading their territory. Hearing this, Jake naturally knew they had to check it out.

There was still one thing bothering him, though.

"Any idea why your family would choose to settle down in that kind of place?" Jake asked Carmen the second they were outside the city.

She looked to be thinking for a moment before answering, "I don't really want to know, but if I had to guess, then it is because they thrive in that kind of environment. My aunt and uncle made their fortune by running a casino, and I know my grandparents were heavily involved in the medicinal industry, so producing drugs or shit like that is right up their alley. As for my parents, they probably just followed whatever my grandparents, uncle, and aunt wanted."

"Sounds like a pretty messed-up family dynamic," Jake commented.

"Yeah," Carmen said simply.

"Whatever the case, I hope they are safe," Peter tried to comfort her. It didn't seem to work very well, as Carmen just ignored the guy.

While Jake did believe Carmen wanted them to be "safe," he had an odd feeling about why she wanted that. She seemed to carry a lot of animosity, yet she also clearly wanted to meet them again. Jake knew he wasn't even halfway qualified to try and figure out what was going on, but he did know that Carmen certainly didn't come from a typical family.

"Let's just get moving," Carmen said, making them drop the topic as the four of them headed off.

Jake took out the Prima fragment to inquire with Peter. "You killed any Primas or gained any fragments?"

The young man sighed and shook his head. "Yes to the first one, no to the second. While I was still with the Church, we killed a Prima, but the fragment was given back to the leaders. I haven't killed or even come across any since then."

Jake nodded in understanding. "Alright. Just gonna say right now that we still need two for Carmen, so even if we come across any, she has them reserved."

"Naturally," the young man agreed.

Jake didn't detect any hint of disappointment from him, so he nodded as they headed forward with great speed, only slowed down by Peter a little bit. Being a warrior with light magic, he was actually relatively fast, but his movement skills were more focused on instantaneous movement than long-range travel.

Sylphie helped as always with her wind magic, and only now did Peter seem to truly take notice of this small hawk. Jake hadn't really thought much about it, but he now realized that most people probably just viewed Sylphie as an extension of Jake. An animal companion or something akin to that.

"I don't think I ever properly introduced you to Sylphie, did I?" Jake asked, way overdue.

Peter just smiled and said, "I do not believe you did."

"Well, Sylphie is Sylphie, a pretty young little hawk and probably one of the strongest creatures on the planet at her level, with less than ten humans alive able to fight her."

The young man froze a bit as he chuckled and looked at the hawk. "Nice to meet you."

"Ree!" Sylphie answered, slightly offended. Even she was able to detect his lack of belief in what Jake had said.

"I am not joking," Jake said in a serious tone. "She is higher level than both Carmen and I, and she is a high-tier variant."

"Yeah, I'm gonna be honest—I would probably lose in a fight." Carmen shrugged. "She is faster than any of us, incredibly elusive, hard to pin down, and has incredibly potent attacks."

Sylphie began circling them, and Jake could feel how much she enjoyed being praised and spoken highly of. Peter looked at the cute little hawk with newfound respect and a touch of fear, as he seemed to finally understand they weren't joking. It did help that Sylphie was circling them faster and faster and created a small hurricane that they were in the eye of, even while running at high speed.

The guy also finally didn't speak for more than ten minutes, as more than an hour passed in silence. He and Jake ended up opening their mouths at nearly the same time as they reached the outskirts of a grassy plain.

"I feel a Prima," Jake said.

"We reached the territory of the gazelles."

Jake and Peter exchanged gazes, and Jake smirked. "Well, then, seems like this won't be a waste of time. I am a bit confused, though. How come no one has bothered hunting down this gazelle?"

"It and its pack moved in—"

"A group of gazelles is called a herd," Jake corrected him.

"It and its herd moved in only a month or so ago, and they are fast and difficult to track down while also being rather powerful," Peter explained correctly.

Jake nodded as he felt for the Prima. He knelt down and sensed the faint energy left in the air by the Gazelle Prima as he and the others began making their way into the plains. While usually referred to as a mana signature, it was more accurate to call it an energy signature, as even someone like Carmen without mana had this identifiable trait. It was tied to the soul, and even with evolutions, it remained more or less the same. In many ways, it could be viewed as the DNA of the Truesoul.

There were ways to obscure it, and for the first time, Jake felt something like that. The trails of energy left by the Prima were muddled. It was like the beast had gone in both directions at the same time while also giving Jake a hunch it had actually gone in neither.

This was one way to hide trails better: making false ones. Jake's stealth would hide his energy signature, and most stealth-related skills worked like that. Due to the way energy was related to the body, it was effectively entangled with the soul, meaning that when Jake used a stealth skill, it hid all the mana in his surroundings, even the traces he had passively left, before going stealth.

What the gazelle did was far more complicated than merely hiding. A false trail combined with stealth skills would mean the gazelle could easily create ambushes and whatnot while never itself falling into a trap. Moreover, when Jake felt the presence of other, non-Prima gazelles, he noted their trails were identical to the Prima's.

"This thing is good," Jake muttered.

"What is it?" Carmen asked.

"The Gazelle Prima is able to mask its tracks and lay down false ones..." Jake turned to the young man. "Peter, have other people tried to hunt it?"

"Yeah, quite a few, but they never find it or never return," he said worriedly. "That is also why we didn't even know it was even a Prima."

Jake nodded. He inspected the energy signatures but simply had no way to properly distinguish them and track down the gazelles using them. Usually, this would be where Jake was fucked, but there was one more thing he could do.

He waved his hand, weaving strings of arcane mana that cut away some of the tall grass in front of him. He went forward as he scanned the area with Sphere of Perception until he finally found what he had been looking for.

"Please stay back," Jake said to the others as he carefully condensed mana under his feet and went forward, avoiding stepping on the grass. With the strings of mana, he cut away more grass as he finally found what he had been looking for: physical tracks.

Tracking in the new world was quite a bit different from old-world tracking. Tracking in the old world relied on spotting actual tracks, analyzing feces, and just looking for any physical evidence left behind by the traveling animal. A lot of these methods were made harder with the system. One such example was the fact that trampled grass was far more resilient and would simply make itself stand again, regenerating with a bit of mana mere minutes after being trampled.

However, the ground below did not even itself out. It became covered by the grass, but Jake could still see the earth below had been dented. Hoof marks had been left, and using them, it became clear the gazelles had gone through there. Unsurprisingly enough, there was no trail of energy despite them clearly running there, but one leading off in another false direction.

Now, it would be a difficult thing to determine where the tracks were pointing. Physical tracking was rarely done, and Jake could only really do it due to his incredibly high Perception allowing him to see minute changes coupled with his Sphere of Perception, but even that did not grant him the knowledge to read and analyze the tracks. This is where Jake had one final card up his sleeve: He used to really like binging those TV shows about guys drinking their own piss and walking around in the wild while explaining stuff.

"One has larger hooves than the others... but is lighter," Jake muttered. He followed the trail a bit and became more and more sure this one was relatively recent. The soil would still smooth itself out with time due to the grass and when it rained and whatnot, and he could see the absolutely minuscule smoothening of the hoof marks by only traveling half a kilometer or so. "That way for sure... and recent. Hm..."

Jake closed his eyes and took a deep breath. No matter how good the gazelle was, it was only D-grade like him. Even if it had a powerful skill and was talented, Jake had something even better: a high-as-fuck Perception stat.

Releasing some of his own arcane mana, he introduced stability into his surroundings. Everything seemed to almost freeze as Jake scanned the mana in the air and around the tracks. He discovered what he was looking for down inside the hoof-print he had been looking at —or, more accurately, embedded in the soil. It was just a faint wisp of energy that did not belong there. But it was enough. Once thoroughly scrutinized by Jake, it revealed itself as the kind of energy he had been looking for.

That of the Prima.

It was like the entire technique made to hide the Prima unraveled as he found this. The false tracks now correctly appeared false in his mind, and a true track emerged, leading into the distance.

"Got you."

[Hunter's Tracking (Uncommon)] - *The Hunter does not sit silently* *in his lodge but actively hunts for his prey. Unlocks proficiency in tracking down prey based on limited clues left behind. Also allows the Hunter to more easily identify characteristics of the game, including mana signatures and aura. Adds a small bonus to the effect of Perception while tracking.*

-->

[Traditional Hunter's Tracking (Rare)] - The Hunter does not sit silently in his lodge but actively hunts for his prey. Unlocks proficiency in tracking down prey based on limited clues left behind, including both magical and physical ones. Also allows the Hunter to more easily identify characteristics of the game, including mana signatures and aura. Allows the Hunter to more easily distinguish and analyze physical tracks. Adds a bonus to the effect of Perception while tracking.

Jake smiled as he got the upgrade. This one came as no surprise. He knew the tracking skill was a lot like the weapon skills or even the stealth skill. Abilities with identical names could have different effects, and Jake knew he had gone in a rather mundane—or traditional—direction with his tracking by using conventional methods, but it clearly had been good enough. Others would mix in odd stuff like analyzing space or the two perhaps most popular paths: karmic analysis and time magic.

Those were a bit too fancy for Jake to dabble in quite yet.

"You got it?" Carmen asked.

"I got it." Jake smiled as the party of four took off to kill themselves another Prima.

The silent wind swept through the plains as a group of three people stood there, gazing upon their handiwork.

"Well, that was a disappointment," Jake muttered.

"Are you sure this was a real Prima?" Carmen asked.

"It dropped a fragment, so... yeah?" Jake said, equally perplexed.

Peter stood and stared all around him at the scattered body parts. Sylphie was busy plucking out all the Beastcores and even eating a few of them as snacks.

"You gotta do that ritual thing?" Jake asked.

"I only do that for good fights," Carmen said, scoffing. "This barely, if at all, qualified as a fight."

"Fair," Jake said, nodding as he managed to swipe up the core of the Prima before Sylphie got to it.

Anyway, it turned out the Gazelle Prima was weak as fuck. It'd been fast and good at hiding itself, but considering Jake could track it and they had a hawk that was even faster than it had been, the fight had been over in less than a minute. The Prima had also only been level 139, making it so weak that any one of them could have taken it in a one-on-one, even Peter.

"This does explain why it hid away when strong parties came looking," Peter mumbled.

"Yep." Jake nodded.

"Ree!" Sylphie said, and Jake had to walk over and pat her on the head.

"Yeah, you did well!"

She really had. She had managed to cut off one of the legs of the Prima, then proceeded to slice and dice it about fifteen times before finally decapitating it with a flyby to cut through roughly ninety percent of its neck. Then it just took a pair of talons penetrating the skull of the Prima, and a good yank later, the head was off.

The poor guy Peter hadn't really had a chance to show off, just killing a few of the normal gazelles part of the herd. He also looked at the small hawk with new eyes, as he clearly thoroughly believed Jake had not been joking about her being a little ball of cuteness and death.

"Ree..." Sylphie screeched faintly as she acted all worn out, looking up at Jake with begging eyes.

Jake knew the spoiled bird just wanted to be cuddled and praised as he picked her up and held her like a cat, much to her pleasure. He kept stroking her as she nuzzled up to him, and he looked at the two others.

"Anyhow, with all that done, let's get to Paradise."

CHAPTER 33

PARADISE

"It looks pretty normal," Jake said as he looked down at the city known as Paradise. "Very well-defended too."

"The question is if those walls and barriers are to keep monsters out or the people in," Peter said with a frown.

"Perhaps a bit of both," Carmen added.

They were all currently standing on top of a cliff, looking at the city below. It was defended by many natural barriers and had tall cliffs on nearly all sides. Finding it had actually been a bit difficult due to how well hidden the city was, and one of their defensive barriers also had a stealth component. It was pretty crap compared to what Skyggen had, but it was likely good enough to fool most people and beasts.

"Just saying, we've been spotted," Jake said as he noticed a presence lock in on them. Well, to call it a presence was not entirely accurate, as when Jake looked around, he noticed a crystal embedded in a large boulder not too far away. It was from that the gaze originated, and Jake assumed it came from some magical surveillance system.

Jake turned towards the crystal and looked at it to make it clear he knew. He wasn't sure if the crystal could also communicate audio, so he waved at it once as he waited.

"What if they attack us?" Peter asked, a bit concerned.

"Then we show them why that would be stupid," Jake answered with a shrug.

He did not feel any presences within the city that he felt especially concerned about. Though he had to admit, he felt far more powerful auras within than he had expected.

The city of Paradise was a well-built city with large houses and mansions of stone and wood. It had one of those mixed styles between medieval and modern, but it was clear this place was far more wealthy than most other cities. The houses were incredibly high quality, and the builders had even added many cosmetic touches to make the mansions look more expensive.

There were still a few less-than-fancy buildings scattered about. They looked a bit like apartment complexes, and Jake guessed this was where the workers lived.

In the center of Paradise was the largest of all the buildings. It was a tall stone building, probably about fifty stories high, and with far more fancy construction than any other place. It was massive and dwarfed every other building in its surroundings. It was surrounded by several other high-rises, all about twenty stories with similar styles.

"This looks like one of the places where my dad used to own a vacation home," Peter mumbled.

"Yeah..." Carmen said as she stared, lost in thought. "Jake, when we go in, can we try to be a bit... subtle? I want to take this slow and not raise a ruckus right away unless we need to, okay? I want to find out what is going on before my family knows I am here."

Jake threw her a glance and nodded. "Alright. I want to investigate this place, too, so we probably shouldn't just start blasting. Also, incoming."

Over a dozen cloaked figures were rapidly approaching them, and Jake at first thought they were perhaps related to the Court of Shadows due to the dark magic used by one of them, but on closer inspection, it was just regular dark magic and not the special branch of shadow magic used by followers of Umbra.

While their stealth skills were far from good enough to hide from Jake even before they entered his sphere, it was clearly good enough to fool Carmen and Peter. Sylphie seemed to have also noticed them only a bit after Jake, but he knew she had her own weird Sylphian methods.

The figures appeared around Jake and the others a moment later, with only five of them revealing themselves. Nine others spread out in the area surrounding them. They kept a safe distance and stayed in stealth, ready for if Jake or the others turned out to be antagonistic.

"Quite the welcome party," Jake said the moment the five figures appeared.

All of them wore dark cloaks and entirely black masks with only holes for the eyes. They were not that much different from Jake's own mask aesthetically, aside from the color and wooden texture. Jake obviously used Identify on the man at the front right away and got a not-that-unexpected response.

[Human – lvl ???]

The man looked at Jake and the others for a moment, but his eyes lingered on Jake. Finally, he smiled and removed his mask, revealing the face of a man in his thirties. "I apologize. We were not informed or aware of the Malefic's Chosen visiting Paradise."

Jake wasn't surprised they knew who he was and had honestly been more busy looking at the guy until he finally got around it. *There we go.*

[Human – lvl 141]

It was a bit like Phillip way back in the day. Jake had just needed an extra moment to circumvent whatever the person used to hide their level. Considering the guy was at a lower level than himself, it wasn't that hard.

"I didn't exactly announce my travel plans anywhere," Jake quipped back.

"Understandable," the formerly masked man said. "May I ask your purpose in visiting Paradise?"

Jake tossed Carmen a glance, and she nodded as she spoke up. "He is here with me. I am looking for some people that I heard reside within the city."

"Hm," the man said. "I am not able to share any personal details of any residents per the law of Paradise—not even if the ones you are looking for do indeed reside there. Do not misunderstand; it is not that I am unwilling to share, but unable. We simply do not collect any information, as subtlety and anonymity is a cornerstone of the city and a necessity due to the clients we serve."

"They are in the city," Jake stated.

He could feel the mana signature similar to Carmen's father's wand somewhere down in the city below. Jake was unable to pinpoint where in the city due to the barriers defending the place, but he was certain he got a response from there. In other words, Carmen's father was there.

"There you have it," Carmen said.

"I see," the cloaked figure said, sighing. " May I know what your business is with these people? Needless to say, we would prefer to avoid any issues or disruption of daily operations."

Carmen shut down the line of questions by saying, "No."

The man looked a bit troubled, but Jake just waved it off. "Are you going to show us the city or what?"

"Very well," he finally relented as he took out two masks from his inventory. "Here, have these free of charge for your two companions. Using masks within Paradise is customary, and they assist in hiding your energy and identity. They even have an enchantment capable of blocking out most mundane Identify attempts."

Jake swept them up with a few strings of mana. He inspected them briefly and found them working as advertised before tossing them to Carmen and Peter. Both of them put on the masks after also briefly examining them.

"May I know what kind of role the hawk serves?" the man also asked.

"What do you mean?" Jake asked, already ready to get angry at the man calling Sylphie a pet.

"Just merely if it is a companion capable of combat or a pet of some sort. I assume it is the prior due to the hawk's power. In either case, the hawk will be bound by the same rules as everyone else, but be advised there are certain... *activities* beasts are unable to partake in."

Jake had no fucking idea how to respond to that. Carmen looked mortified after putting two and two together, with Peter looking a bit confused.

"Ree?" Sylphie asked, equally if not more confused.

"Nothing," Jake said before throwing the cloaked man a glare.

He seemed to get it, as he backed down and continued, "Please follow me, if you will." As they followed him down the cliffside, he explained, "Paradise offers all kinds of amenities for those willing and capable to pay. Please let me know if there is anything in particular you are interested in."

"First, show us a good place to stay," Jake said. "We plan on being in Paradise for a bit."

This seemed to put the man at ease. Jake could see why, as he was probably wondering what the hell the Chosen of the Malefic Viper was doing visiting this city so far away from Haven. Unannounced, even.

"Naturally." The man nodded gladly. "Just a few things for when inside Paradise. Murder, thievery, extortion, and violence of most forms are not allowed unless consented to. Besides that, expect liberal rules and the ability to do whatever you wish. I do not doubt the Chosen is well-off, so you will find most of the city more than willing to welcome you with open arms."

Jake just nodded, pretty sure there weren't that many things Paradise offered that he was interested in. Well... there was one thing, but that was only if they had time. He would have to discuss more with Carmen once inside, as he wasn't entirely clear on her plans. Though, to be fair, he had a feeling Carmen wasn't either, instead just making things up as they went.

Making it into the city was easy with the five cloaked figures escorting them. The other ones who had been hidden had just slipped away without revealing themselves. Their entrance did get a few glances, as it was clear new people didn't usually enter through the front gate.

"I heard you had some teleportation issues?" Jake asked once inside. From what he knew, Paradise was a city sustained by visitors, so he assumed the lack of teleportation to the city would cause issues, but from the looks of it, he was a bit off.

The streets were some of the cleanest he had ever seen. People walking on the road were well-dressed, and the storefronts and large buildings were immaculate. He was sure that things were not as rosy in the poorer residential areas, but clearly, the buzz was still on.

"Heh, sure, they like to say that, and the hypocritical United Cities Alliance did cut off the teleporters... The public ones, that is," the man said with a smile as he pointed towards a large building in the center of town squished between the high-rises. "That is the teleportation station. While many cities cut off the public teleporters, there were often backups placed elsewhere, or simply ones hidden and reserved for the elite. Those, they sure didn't bother to cut off. It is all just empty posturing."

Jake would lie if he said this information surprised him. People in power acted like absolute assholes, and politics had been a shitshow before the system, so why would giving people superpowers change that? Shit, wouldn't adding personal power on top just make it worse? And speaking of worse, Jake had one thing he wanted to check.

"What kind of wares does Paradise offer? Of the more... controversial kind."

The cloaked figure looked back at him and shook his head. "If you are asking if we sell slaves, then no. I cannot speak to if any slaves exist or if such deals occur under the table, but there is no public trade, and selling and purchasing slaves is officially banned. Now, if you are looking for drugs of any kind or even people willing to sell their services for special experiences, we have those aplenty."

Jake narrowed his eyes a bit at the response. *Is Sultan somehow involved in Paradise? Or the people who run it?*

The response clearly communicated the guy knew Jake's stance, which he had only really discussed with Miranda, Sultan, and a few others. It was also possible he was just aware of the rules of Haven, but Jake had a feeling it was more than that.

Following the man, they got a quick tour of the city and were introduced to several establishments. As expected, the three primary industries in Paradise were drugs, prostitution, and gambling. Below that were the high-tier hotels and other forms of entertainment, such as a circus, something akin to a theater, and even a cinema. Jake had thought the cinema a bit silly until he discovered something interesting... They had actual movies from before the system. Primarily older films.

When the system had arrived, it had wiped out most technology, but film rolls had apparently survived. Jake also learned that day that the film industry had used film rolls a lot longer than he had expected, and it was only barely a decade before the system that the industry had fully phased them out.

It was interesting hearing and seeing the city, and Jake didn't know if he should be surprised or not by the lack of any so-called "fucked-up shit" so far. Sure, they had passed a few strip bars, stores openly selling recreational drugs, and plenty of casinos, but that was it. There was no one openly propositioning people or being tortured on the streets or anything like that.

Finally, they made it to one of the biggest buildings in the entire city. A grand tower of expensive marble and glass. Jake could see it was expensive and extravagant just by looking at it and staring into the lobby. There were even two security guards outside, and Jake was sure this was the equivalent of a five-star hotel in the old world.

It was a hotel... and a casino. Of course it was also a casino.

"We shall take our leave here," the masked figure said. "For transparency reasons, I must inform you that the leadership of Paradise has already been made aware of your arrival and where you are staying. The Chosen will likely be contacted during your stay."

Jake nodded, having already expected something like that.

The cloaked men disappeared after that, and the four of them made their way into the casino-hotel hybrid. Jake actually found it a bit refreshing that his accommodations were not just given for free or covered by the leadership of the city. He paid for them all as he booked three adjacent rooms on one of the highest floors, and they made their way up the elevator.

"This feels so... normal," Peter said, frowning as they ascended.

The elevator was far slower than just jumping or flying themselves, but hey, it was a fun novelty and reminder of the old world. Thinking about it deeper, the last time Jake had been in an elevator was the day the system arrived.

Quite a lot has happened since then, huh? Jake thought.

When they made it to their floor, they walked through the well-lit and decorated hallway before making it to their rooms. Each room had a keycard, but rather than chips inside, they each had a small array and used the mana signature of the person with the card. Once more, it was kind of well-made and smart, proving the people behind Paradise had some real talents among them.

The four of them decided to enter the room Jake and Sylphie would share as they closed the door and took their seats at a table. Jake decided to swipe some bottles of alcohol from the bar in the room, knowing full well he would get scammed by how expensive it was. He ignored the pills and powder also on offer.

Carmen took out a small token of sorts and was about to activate it when Jake shook his head. "No one is listening in or observing us, and the room is enchanted quite competently."

"Are you sure?" Carmen asked skeptically.

"Yeah. I am also a bit surprised, but it seems like Paradise at least sticks by its own rules of respecting anonymity." He paused, then added, "So, what are your plans now?"

They were there for Carmen and her business, after all.

"I think I just want to look around alone for now... as long as you can show me where they stay," Carmen answered as she looked at the mask she had placed on the table. "I doubt they will recognize me, and I want to meet them without them knowing it is me."

Jake nodded and looked at Peter, who, after some thought, answered, "I guess I will go scout out the place a bit. I know nothing of Paradise, and I am sure my father would be more than interested in knowing how it operates."

"What about you?" Carmen asked Jake.

Jake just smiled. "It's gambling time."

CHAPTER 34

GAMBLING TIME

Ah, gambling.

Who doesn't love gambling? Well, okay, many people don't like gambling due to the innate predatory nature of the practice and its proneness to exploiting and preying on those with addictive personalities. So, in fairness, gambling was actually more an epidemic that ruined lives and split up families. But there was one crucial aspect required to make gambling a negative experience: losing.

Gambling was designed to always favor the house. There were ways to cheat the system, so to say, like card counting or even just straight-up cheating. Jake never really thought card counting should be viewed as cheating, as that was just someone not purposefully sabotaging themselves by not thinking while playing. Then again... casinos would prefer if people didn't think, which explained why they happily handed out drinks left and right.

To summarize, gambling was a loser's game. Because it was designed to make you lose. Anyone going into it should do so with the expectation of losing all or most of what they put into it. You went gambling for the experience and the fun of it, not to make money. Making money was a lucky coincidence, but never an expectation.

The way casinos always made themselves the winners was just simple statistics. They tipped the odds in their favor. Roulette was a great example of this. Let's say you choose to bet on either black or red, so that should mean a fifty-fifty percent chance to win, right? Except no, because there was the added zero option. Some casinos even added double zero as an option to lower the chances even more. This made it close to fifty percent... but not quite. And by the law of large numbers, the casino would win big in the end. So what if someone won once in a while when there were far more losers? The casino needed these winners to make everyone think they could be the next one to hit the big jackpot.

Gambling in the system worked pretty much the same as pre-system. In fact, some could say it was fairer in some ways than before. Jake had gone to check out the casino after guiding Carmen and seeing Sylphie and Peter off for their own exploration, and he was honestly impressed. He saw people play roulette, and one would think that with magic, stats, and all sorts of skills, it would be easy for either party to cheat... but it wasn't. The explanation for why that was lay in one of the fundamentals of the new world:

System fuckery.

The system recognized gambling and gave skills to facilitate it. It was like a system-bound contract defined every single interaction done during gambling. Cheating simply wasn't possible in most cases. One such example was playing cards. Each person would get their cards just like usual, but each person would only be able to view their own cards and those laid out by the dealer. The face would just be blank to anyone but the owner of the cards, making it look a bit weird when Jake saw people sitting there with face-up cards while playing blackjack, only for their cards to be revealed once it was time.

Jake had to admit that it was an elegant and easy solution by the system. It still allowed some forms of tipping the odds in your favor. In the end, it was still people playing the games. If you played poker and wanted to bluff or read your opponents, nothing stopped you. Jake was sure some mental skills and social skills could help here, but it was also a double-edged sword, as people learned how to fake responses.

People clearly realized this, and the place was flooded. Hundreds were there, people at every table and dealers working overtime. They even had goddamn slot machines and nearly everything Jake would expect from an old-world casino. The entire atmosphere was also spot-on. Jake had only been in a casino once before in his life during a company outing, and back then, he had only played the slots.

Now, to bring the topic back to why gambling is bad... all the system-imposed rules and regulations only made this more obvious. Someone could set up a lottery that was one in a thousand, and sure enough, it would truly be one in a thousand that would win. The same was true if a slot machine was designed with an eighty-percent payout rate for over a hundred thousand games... It would truly have that payout rate. It limited risk, making it a sure win.

There was no way around this. The rules of the system in this regard were absolute. You just couldn't use any skills to cheat besides perhaps the aforementioned social skills. Skills were all blocked...

Skills.

Jake didn't use any skills.

"He does it again!" the dealer yelled as Jake tapped his cards, revealing a straight.

The seven other masked players at the poker table groaned as the dealer pushed their chips over to Jake, who was grinning from ear to ear as he stocked up on Credits.

Another hand was dealt, and Jake checked the cards. Average at best, but better than his last hand. The flop came, and his cards were still good. One pair, highest card. No straight possibilities, but two spades.

Jake thought a bit as he raised. Most had already folded, but big blind stayed in together with one other guy. He still felt like he had it and was keeping a poker face as the two called. Then the turn then came. Hearts. Low card. Not a threat; still no straight possibilities either quite yet.

He looked at the two others. Both looked stoic, and Jake did not have the slightest chance to read them. Luckily he didn't need to read them to know what he would do. A slight feeling welled up in his stomach, but he stayed in even after one of the others raised with only big blind.

Then came the river. Two pairs for Jake, but also another spade. The only thing that beat him was a flush, but...

Jake instantly knew. No one at the table told him, but he knew. As Jake had been small blind, he decided to check. The big blind checked. The last guy raised the pot by double. Jake looked at him for a moment... and knew he would lose this hand. Now he could either choose to fold, call, or raise. Jake looked at the relatively small pot and decided to do what any good cheater would do: He made himself not look like one. Jake called as big blind folded.

Both revealed their cards. The other guy had a flush, just as expected. The man cheered as the others padded him on the back for taking down the big evil Jake. Jake, in turn, just mulled to himself, acting all dissatisfied.

Another hand was dealt, Jake thoroughly enjoying himself while making some money. He liked poker, as even with his abilities, he didn't instantly know if he would win or lose. Roulette was too easy, as Jake knew the moment the ball began spinning, but for poker, he would only know in the moment.

It allowed nearly all the excitement to remain. Now, how did he do it?

His sphere did nothing, as the cards were blank even to that. Likely because the display on them was entirely magical. He could not really use it to read the other players either. Danger sense only went off a few times when another player really looked like he or she wanted to smack Jake.

No, it was all intuition. All gut feeling. To fully get the gut feeling, he would have to be right at the moment things were decided. Jake had a theory that the deck of cards only "decided" what card to deal the moment it was dealt. This did mean burning cards was just for show, but hey, it made the experience authentic.

Jake kept playing a bit more before he saw a very well-dressed man approach. He also felt an aura from the man that actually gave him pause and made him turn his head. The newcomer was wearing a white suit and tie. He looked like a clean-cut man in his mid-forties and was flanked by a man and a woman, clearly acting as bodyguards. Not that Jake believed the guy needed it.

[Human – lvl ???]

He could not see his level, and even when he tried to get around the obfuscation, he failed. The presence the man gave off was the most powerful Jake had felt from another human he didn't already know about. He was stronger than Peter or anyone else Jake had met on his travels, but he still fell behind Carmen... At least, it appeared like that.

Jake felt like he should not fight the man. Not within Paradise. This made him quickly reach a conclusion. *A domain-type fighter.*

It was the same as Miranda. Someone not necessarily supremely powerful in regular combat, but fighting them within their own domains was an uphill battle. Jake scanned the man a bit more, and it was clear he was the City Lord of Paradise just by feeling how in tune he was with the atmospheric energy.

"I see the Chosen is enjoying my establishment," the suited man said as he went over to Jake, who stayed seated.

Jake felt the dealer tense up as the game paused. The other players at the table also looked on with wide eyes as their gazes darted between the City Lord and Jake.

"Please, keep playing," the man said to the dealer and players.

"Yes, sir," the dealer said as she began dealing a new set of cards.

Jake looked at his and just folded right away before turning to the man. "It has been a while since I had a good game of poker."

"And yet you do indeed seem to be an experienced player," the man said with a smile. One thing to note was that he was one of the only people not wearing any mask, though his bodyguards did. He was clearly not interested in hiding his identity.

"I have dabbled," Jake explained as he waved his hand. He wasn't lying either. He had utterly annihilated his family in poker several times in the past during family game nights to the point of them never wanting to play with him anymore.

"Under usual circumstances, I would accuse you of cheating after your display at the roulette earlier, but as I am unsure how you did it, I shall refrain," the man in the suit said with a big smile. "I just hope you are satisfied with your winnings for now and perhaps have time for a more private discussion? I would love to get to know the Malefic's Chosen a bit better."

"I guess I got some time." Jake smiled as he got up from the table while swiping up all his chips. "Been a pleasure playing with you, ladies and gentlemen."

Pleasure ripping you off, Jake thought as he smiled to himself. All the people in the casino were clearly loaded. Not a single E-grade was in sight—not even the dealers. Jake had no shame ripping them off, even if they knew who he was. What would they do, go complain that the Chosen of the Malefic Viper had dared rip them off in a poker game? Shit, it would probably just be a cool story for them to tell.

Jake followed the suited man as he spoke, "I must say, I do appreciate you chose to play against other visitors and not the house directly. Limited our losses."

"Do not misunderstand," Jake said curtly. "I didn't do it to spare your wallet. I just wanted to play some poker." He felt the bodyguards didn't appreciate his disrespect, but he wasn't too worried about it.

They walked through a few hallways as all the employees bowed toward the suited man. A swift elevator ride later and Jake found himself within a spacious office.

"You may excuse us," the man said to his bodyguards, who both bowed and went to stand guard outside. He went over to a small bar and looked at it. "Any preferences?"

Jake shrugged and somewhat cheekily said, "Whatever is on the house."

"Bourbon it is, then." The man nodded as he poured two glasses. "Ah, I also believe it is due time I introduce myself. I am Renato, owner and City Leader of Paradise. Follower of Dyonsy, God of Debauchery, and a proud member of the Golden Road Emporium."

The man called Renato brought over Jake's glass and sat down on a couch across from Jake.

Jake took a swig and quickly concluded it was good stuff. "So, Renato. A bit on the nose for a god to classify themselves as being of debauchery, isn't it?"

"Ah, but what is debauchery if not merely indulging in one's desires and embracing one's Path? The world is cruel and relentless. Is it not far crueler to then also deny others the freedom to truly express themselves?" Renato's answer gave Jake the feeling this was another guy who believed he had Jake all figured out. Why did everyone assume he was some guy who didn't really care much about what others did?

Well, probably because he was that kind of guy. For the most part.

"I do not believe you invited me here to discuss your ideology," Jake stated.

"Indeed, I did not. I am sure you are familiar with the Golden Road Emporium, correct?"

"Remind me," Jake said. Why the hell would he know that?

"Surprising... Sultan has not spoken of his Patron? The leader of the Golden Road Emporium?"

Jake looked at the guy as, suddenly, things made a lot more sense.

Carmen spied on the mansion intently as she sat in a small cafe not too far away. Jake had shown her to the mansion in which her father lived, and it had only taken a minute or two before Carmen saw someone she recognized. It was a cousin she hadn't seen in more than half a decade... before Carmen had a "falling out" with her family.

Soon after, she saw more familiar faces. It also quickly became clear that they owned the place. It was a large mansion, four stories tall, brick construction, with a massive garden. All of it was surrounded by a fence and a gate, both enchanted.

The fence was the type where everyone could look in. Carmen

expected nothing less from the narcissists. They wanted to show off their home and their wealth. They wanted everyone to know they were of high status. Usually, Carmen hated that, but today, it was welcome. It allowed her to just sit there and observe who went and who came. She had yet to see any of the people she was truly looking for, but she was confident they were there.

But more than that, she saw a lot of women come and go. Dozens every hour entered the mansion and left again. Most of them were not the most dressed, and none of them wore masks, indicating they were workers or residents of Paradise. Probably workers.

Carmen had figured out black masks were for the ones in charge. The important people. Her family members she had seen so far all wore black masks or no masks at all, while it seemed like employees did not use them normally, and when they did, they had white masks on.

As she was putting things together in her head, Carmen saw her. She suddenly tensed up, and the glass in her hand was squished so hard she managed to compress it. Yet she didn't notice, as her eyes were trained on the person that had just exited the mansion.

She was wearing an expensive one-piece red dress, hair styled perfectly, with not a single speck of dust on her body. She walked in high heels down the pathway leading out of the mansion as all the employees bowed to her. Her posture was immaculate. Four men wearing black masks flanked her, too, signifying her importance.

But more important was her face.

A perfect, unblemished face with not a single scar or deformity left. No signs of what Carmen had done to her. What had landed her in prison. Not a single fucking mark. Her cousin was back to her perfect self... No, she was even more perfect now.

Beatrice... Carmen thought as she held herself back. *No... be calm... be rational for once in your fucking life... Figure this shit out first.*

CHAPTER 35

THE IMPORTANCE OF KEEPING UP APPEARANCES

J ake had not talked that much with Sultan recently. He knew the merchant was still busy and operating out of Haven while making liberal use of the teleportation network. In fact, he had been a pushing force to integrate more cities into the network and establish more connections with factions like the Holy Church and independent cities.

Miranda had been the one keeping Jake up-to-date on this, but clearly, she had no idea about everything the shady merchant was up to. Jake was already aware the guy had a Blessing due to earlier conversations, but Sultan had divulged no details when it wasn't necessary. It also didn't seem like something worth bothering Villy over.

"I do not tend to pry in the personal business and work of the citizens of Haven," Jake answered Renato. It was the truth and also a way to not just make himself look more ignorant than he actually was.

"An understandable and respectable position. I have already shared more than I perhaps should, then." Renato sighed. "Oh, well. In for a penny, in for a pound. Sultan and I both belong to the same organization, and both have ties to the Golden Road Emporium. I guess you can call the Emporium a Pantheon of sorts, even if it is merely merchant gods banding together in a mutually beneficial alliance."

"And Sultan is blessed by the leader of this Emporium?" Jake asked with raised eyebrows.

"Midas, the Golden God," Renato answered with clear respect in his voice.

"Midas, huh," Jake mumbled as he shook his head.

"One of the cases where the Records of the multiverse bled into our unintegrated universe, a bit like Valhal and many other such cases. Our world's connection to a mercantile system and focus on wealth and capitalism no doubt only strengthened this bond and resonated with the Path that Midas and other merchant gods followed. Of course, this is merely my interpretation, even if it is one I am confident about. Please do enlighten me if the Chosen has other insights."

"No, it seems reasonable," Jake agreed. He did know that the multiverse as a whole had affected their world. Shit, just looking at all the mythical creatures should be proof enough. Dragons, phoenixes, and entire races of monsters that had already been legends before the system. That was too much to be a coincidence.

Renato nodded as he smiled. "I do hope that today and this visit can lay the groundwork for a long and mutually beneficial relationship. While you may not be a fan of some of the things we do here in Paradise, do know we are no slave traders. We merely have a more liberal and open market than anywhere else, allowing those who offer more questionable services to find clients."

"Through my initial exploration, I did not find much... so do share. What kind of controversial services? And please hold nothing back. I came back from the Order of the Malefic Viper recently. Don't think anything we Earthlings get on will surprise me." He wanted to make himself appear more like the Chosen than he probably had to, and sharing his ability to travel to the Order and back was also very deliberate.

"It is no secret that we have no set rules besides the obvious ones you have already been informed of. As long as the cornerstone of consent has been reached, we do not interfere. Even if one party consents to get killed by the other. As for some anecdotal examples, we have some individuals with certain interests. Fantasies they like to carry out. Before the system, carrying out these fantasies would involve some rather unfortunate consequences, but now, with healing magic and the human body being far more resilient, they can indulge.

"One frequent client enjoys the fantasy of assaulting and killing women, something he, to my knowledge, carried out even before the system to great cost and inconvenience. Another is a woman who has specific fantasies related to a concept called vore, I think, or perhaps we should just call it cannibalism. She likes to eat the member of her partner after intercourse.

"These are just some of the sexual ones. Others simply want to experience beating someone beyond recognition or torturing others. For some, Paradise is merely about being themselves and partaking in whatever drugs they so desire. With overdose being no risk with a good healer and an alchemist with an antidote on hand, you can imagine how many substances they can experience at once."

Renato held nothing back as he continued talking about Paradise. He also added on his justifications for the city needing to exist. The powerful tended to also be the unique, and unique people would have very varied tastes. Any Path could legitimately lead to power, and staying true to yourself was fundamental to avoid stagnating. Renato viewed himself as nothing more than a businessman who facilitated a required service under the best conditions possible.

Jake knew he couldn't argue about some points. There were many fucked-up people within the Order of the Malefic Viper, and Jake had no interest in being an arbiter of justice. He was not interested in making the world a better place... At least, not all of it. As long as his small world—himself and those he cared about—could live a good and comfortable life without the negative influence of others, he was fine.

His and Renato's conversation was somewhat enlightening, and he knew the man did have limits for what he allowed. Jake was not particularly happy learning that slaves did exist in the city, as the law only prohibited selling and buying them. The rule did also extend to slaves being unable to offer services and be pimped out to others, meaning they could only act as personal servants. Jake was repeatedly assured every individual who worked there did so with consent... even if he did admit some did so out of desperation and to get some semblance of safety. Others were just as fucked in the head as the clients they served.

This was the kind of place Jake didn't like but also wouldn't actively move to get rid of. It did not interfere with him at all, and Jake had a feeling this was exactly what Renato wanted to make clear. Paradise was no threat to him or his interests, and he would prefer if Jake just left them alone.

This brought them to the principal topic of this conversation.

"I am aware you are here together with Ms. Carmen from Valhal," Renato said. "I do not know the details, but I want to know if Paradise can expect any... trouble coming from this visit?"

Jake shook his head. "I don't know. All I know is that she was looking for people; I am uncertain what her intent is once she finds them."

It was a half-truth. Jake did know who she was looking for, but he truly didn't know her intentions. That was for her to decide... It was her family, after all.

Renato sighed at Jake's response. "I will not get in the way of you or the Runemaiden, but I will ask a favor. Please inform me before anything violent happens. Just a bit before or right when it begins, and it should be fine." Jake raised an eyebrow as the man further explained, "Paradise exists in its current form because my employees and I have created a balance. We are the ultimate authority that none dare stand against. If my base is shaken and a seed of doubt is sown, it can mean the end of my city. So, if the unfortunate happens and killings take place, it will need to look like these are approved and accepted by Paradise. In other words, I will justify whatever actions you choose to take. Retroactively, if I have to."

That was... not what Jake had expected him to say. He had expected him to maybe ask them to take it outside of the city, try to be subtle about it, or even outright tell them to leave if they planned on killing anyone. There was even the possibility the man would choose to oppose them. It turned out he would just sweep things under the rug while acting like Jake and Carmen were just cleaning house and doing Paradise a favor.

"Even if it is high-status allies and friends of yours?" Jake asked.

Renato shook his head. "You misunderstand. Sultan and I have many disagreements, but one thing we share is that we do not have friends. If people other than you and the Runemaiden had come for the same reason, I would have already mobilized everything to kill the both of you. However, as it stands, there is none within the city I value enough to face the consequences such a confrontation could bring."

Jake nodded in understanding. He was also not dumb enough to not recognize the jab against Sultan, more or less telling Jake they were not really allies but just temporarily partners of convenience. But oh, well. Such was the world of merchants, and Jake already knew. Everything was a calculation of risk and benefits, viewing people and personal relationships the same as a business would view deals and partnerships. In many ways, life was just cheaper now.

"Fine," Jake agreed.

"Thank you," Renato said as he tossed over a small device. It looked like a pager of sorts—the kind they'd used before cellphones were a thing. "Merely activate the device when something happens. It will briefly scan your surroundings and send it to my chief of security. After that, we will analyze it and come within a few minutes."

"Got it," Jake said. They had more or less been granted a free pass in the city to do whatever they wanted. Which also meant...

"I will head back to the casino, then." Jake smiled deviously. "I think I have some time before Carmen is done for the day."

Renato surprisingly smiled. "Naturally. Do note we have recently changed the rules to have maximum betting amounts and limited games allowed per hour on all house-run games."

"I feel like this is targeted," Jake protested.

"I apologize if you feel that way," Renato joked in kind. "Perhaps sticking to poker would be preferable? I am certain many rich folks are more than willing to play a few hands against the Chosen of the Malefic Viper..."

Jake looked at the man before he just shook his head and decided that ripping off rich folk who probably also had some messed-up hobbies was acceptable.

Peter scouted through the streets as he made sure to fulfill the task he had been granted. He held a small crystal in his hand that took in his surroundings and recorded everything. He went towards the seedier areas as a few members of security spotted him, but they left him alone once they recognized who he was. He could only smile, knowing they did not actually know him and had purposefully refrained from investigating him further to not incite the Chosen.

All they knew was that he had come with the Chosen and Carmen, the warrior from Valhal. Peter did feel a bit bad about deceiving the two of them by just acting like a follower, but he had a job to do. Paradise had long been growing beyond what was healthy. As he scouted around, he confirmed it had indeed grown—not only in size, but also in power. Below the cobblestones on every street were runic circles and formations. The walls were immaculate too.

He had a feeling that even if an early C-grade attacked, the city of Paradise would be fine. The defenses were just that powerful. It was lucky he had been let inside with open arms, and from the looks of it, everyone assumed he was working for the Chosen as he did his job. The ignorance and apathy of the Chosen were truly beyond what the United Cities Alliance had expected based on the intel.

Peter snuck inside a larger mansion, using his magic to hide. Light refracted around him as he became invisible, and his epic-rarity stealth skill activated to make his footsteps, aura, and everything else disappear.

Nobody noticed him as he recorded everything. People got careless when they thought they were safe and removed their masks without any worry. Within ten minutes, he already had recordings of over a dozen individuals that surely would prefer to not have anything made public about them.

He swiftly left and made it to more places spread around the settlement. This was an opportunity the United Cities Alliance could not miss. Peter praised their luck and the guy who had given them a tip that the Chosen and the woman from Valhal were coming towards Paradise to track down those people. It had given them the perfect opportunity to integrate Peter into the group as a guide no one would suspect.

With the woman busy dealing with her own matters, the Chosen occupied in the casino, and the hawk out of the city flying around to scout the surrounding wildlife, Peter could do as he wanted without suspicion. Even if he was caught, he could just claim he was working for the Chosen.

Peter's next hours were spent collecting information on hundreds of individuals. He saw sights he would much prefer to do without, but his task had to be done. Even if taking down Paradise entirely was not an option, they could use this against the ones who had been there.

More importantly, what would happen if recordings from all over Paradise spread? The trust in the anonymity and integrity of the city would be broken. It would hurt Renato significantly and weaken his position when negotiating with the United Cities Alliance. Removing Paradise was not preferable. No, they just wanted it to be controlled.

As for the Chosen... well, making him their ally was never the purpose... No, it was not even a possible goal. At most, they could hope that he simply left Earth to never return. That would be the optimal outcome. Luckily for them, it appeared he had already gone to another universe before and would leave again soon, based on what he had talked about with Peter and Carmen.

Wanting him to leave was the official stance of the United Cities Alliance. Peter actually began to see the Chosen as more than just his reputation. He was surprisingly normal and easygoing and didn't at all seem as their intel implied. This did make Peter feel a bit bad about the deceit.

While he had spoken many lies, his history was not one. He had been part of the Holy Church, but not in any regular party. Like any organization, the Church needed those acting covertly. Assassins, scouts, and rogues handling the dirty business. Peter had been good at this, which was also why he'd felt genuinely betrayed when one of his party members decided to selfishly sacrifice herself.

It'd thrown off many of his plans and derailed him emotionally. She had joined the Church together with him. They were not meant to truly fall for the promises of the Church. At the time, he had been genuinely unsure what to do. Split between two camps. One was ruled by his father... and the other was ruled by someone Peter had always looked up to. Yet now, he found it hard to truly recognize him. He looked the same, and his demeanor was similar, but he had changed.

Peter didn't blame his brother, though.

His brother had always been one to easily convince himself something was the right thing to do. He was steadfast once his opinion was made and loyal to a fault at times. He wasn't a bad person... but he would do bad things for the greater good. Something Peter understood from a logical standpoint but didn't agree with.

Something like the Holy Church was like a cancer on Earth, the same as every other major religious faction. Everyone knew each and every one of them wanted to conquer the planet. Assimilate everyone forcefully, if they had to. Earth's culture and history would be wiped out, and Earth would become nothing more than a single planet in the endless line of planets ruled by the Holy Church. An unacceptable fate.

The purpose of the United Cities Alliance was to preserve the identity of Earth. Peter's goal had been to join the Church and figure out if it was possible *with* them. It was not... that much was obvious. Even if Peter's father had hoped it was. For his family.

Ah... one other thing Peter had not been entirely truthful about. Peter's father was indeed quite high in the hierarchy of the United Cities Alliance. In fact, his family seemed to have a tendency to always reach the top.

Especially his father, Arthur, leader of the United Cities Alliance.

CHAPTER 36

THE SALVENTO FAMILY

Jake and Carmen sat on the balcony and looked out over the city. Jake saw the mansion in question as Carmen also stared intently. Due to the enchantments placed on the construction, everything was vague, and he could only barely see some people moving within. When he didn't focus, that is. A bit of squinting, and he saw around the formation to perceive the large lawn and even in the windows clear as day.

Peter and Sylphie were still out, with Sylphie being on a super-secret special assignment, as she wasn't interested in gambling, drugs, or sex. She was too young for all those, too, and Jake was glad to keep her away from the degeneracy. If he didn't, he was sure Hawkie and Mystie would somehow find a way to kill him.

"I saw most of them," Carmen muttered as she also looked down at the mansion, even if it was still blurry to her. "They looked so... carefree. Like everything was fine."

Jake just kept silent as she talked.

"My grandparents, aunts, uncles, cousins, parents... Everyone was there. Just one big, happy family. And... my cousin—the one I told you about... She was just so fucking perfect. Again. Not a single mark, like nothing I did ever mattered. To any of them."

When she returned that day, Carmen had been a mess. Jake had done nothing more than just allow her to vent as he learned everything that had happened. How Carmen had grown up in a toxic family that cared more about reputation than not being shit people, how her cousin had always been perfect and pretty much bullied Carmen, and how no one had ever done anything to address this.

How Carmen had finally found a calling, only to get that dream shattered when her cousin decided to just straight-up assault her. How the legal system had failed. Jake had to admit he was unable to hold back a small smile when Carmen told him about the day she had smashed in her cousin's face so hard the other woman had nearly died —and on her wedding day, no less.

Then came the fucked-up prison where Carmen had managed to make it by fighting even more. Even guards. They'd all left her alone as her hand only got worse from her using it to pass out beatdowns. She even confessed she had just considered ending it all at times. Her future had been one where parole was something that would likely never happen with her family's influence, and if she had made it out, she would've effectively been disowned.

She had been saved by the system like so many others. Finally, she could confront her family. She talked about how she had been looking forward to seeing them all struggling. None of them were fighters, just socialite assholes. They had to have suffered, right?

But no, they were thriving.

"The one thing that kept me going every day was that at least that bitch Beatrice was also suffering. But now... now she is just healed. No, better than healed. You saw her, right?" Carmen turned to Jake.

"I did," he admitted. In fact... Carmen didn't even have to point her out.

"And?" Carmen asked with a fiery glare.

"She looks like the kind of person an army of rich, middle-aged men would pay top dollar to make their sugar baby," Jake said. He wouldn't lie... She was one of the most attractive humans Jake had seen. However... "But... meh, I doubt looks will get her that far in a few years."

While she was hot, Jake had seen more than what Earth had to offer. Irin and Meira both had her beat handily if Jake went by pure looks. Personality, too, if even a fraction of the things Carmen said were true. This was, of course, disregarding people of higher grades.

Carmen nodded but still looked down with an empty gaze.

"What is the plan?" Jake finally asked.

It was the part she had never addressed. He could not figure out what she actually wanted. Revenge? Justice? Just to mess them up a bit, or the full nuclear option? Maybe even some kind of reconciliation? No matter what, Jake could see she was conflicted.

"I don't fucking know," Carmen sneered. "Why does everything just work out for them every fucking time?"

"You know, we could just leave," Jake proposed. "Within a few minutes, we could be through a teleporter and in another city, never to return. You could forget all about them forever."

It was only a half-honest proposition, as Jake, more than anything, just wanted Carmen to think about what she wanted. He had no real advice to give, because what the hell did he know? This sounded like something a therapist was needed for—something Carmen had never tried, as her family "didn't believe in therapy," whatever the hell that meant.

"And just let them get away with everything?" Carmen asked, staring daggers at Jake.

"Get away with what?"

"Fucking... everything. Being the scum of the Earth who can just go about their day unbothered. How the hell do they still do so well, even now? How the fuck is my aunt D-grade when her only talent is to be a stuck-up bitch and a terrible person?"

"She must be supremely talented at being a stuck-up bitch, I guess." Jake shrugged.

Okay, he was legitimately unsure if the system recognized that as a Path. Being a manipulative person who used others for her own gain... Now, that was probably something you could gain plenty of progress with.

Carmen just fell silent again as she kept looking down at the mansion. One moment she looked like she wanted to go pummel the place into dust, and the next, like she just wanted to leave. She clearly didn't know what she wanted. Carmen's planning and strategy had ended upon seeing them... and Jake had a theory.

She had wanted to see them be utterly fucked. She had wanted to see them living a terrible life while she had managed to rise up again and gain power and status. To experience their situations being reversed. But what she had instead gotten was them still being wealthy, privileged, and everything just being fine and dandy. However...

"Must be pretty miserable being them, huh?" Jake mumbled.

"What?" Carmen asked, confused.

"They have nothing worth anything." Jake just shrugged. "All they have is their social clout. Take that away, and what are they?"

"A bunch of rich bastards who are nearly all still D-grade?" Carmen shot back.

"To be more accurate, they would be a bunch of weak D-grades with just wealth, which will do them no good when faced with a superior force. Have you seen a single fighter among them worth anything? I haven't during all this time sitting here, looking at them come and go. So how do they survive? By them being viewed as valuable enough to be kept around by the City Lord or other backers."

"Right, but why the fuck does that matter? Do you think the City Lord will just throw them to the wolves for no reason? They may be fucking assholes, but they also know what they're doing when making connections."

"Funny," Jake said. Due to how this entire flow of conversation had gone, Jake had no time to explain what he had been doing. Including his meetings with Renato. "The City Lord seems to not care about them at all."

"Explain," Carmen said.

Jake smiled as he told her about his talks with Renato. Carmen seemed to have a hard time believing it.

"So you are saying I can just do whatever I want?" she asked skeptically.

"Essentially, yeah." A tad teasingly, Jake added, "Renato clearly doesn't want to go against the Runemaiden of Valhal."

"Or the Chosen of the Malefic Viper," she shot back.

"Well, of course not. I got a big, angry snake with really nasty poison backing me, but you also got an angry guy with a really big axe as well as all his drunken god friends behind you, so I think we are both pretty damn scary."

"None of which are in this universe at all and won't be for a long-ass time," Carmen argued.

"True, true. But they will be one day, and people like Renato are in this for the long game and have godly backers themselves. If he pisses us off, it reflects badly on his backer. So do not question the fact that when it comes to status, you have them thoroughly beat."

She still looked skeptical, but Jake kept piling on with, "Also, in personal power, you are far beyond them. They can't touch you in any way. They are forced to comply with what you want or face the consequences. They have no one to complain to or seek justice from. Not now or ever, as you will keep getting stronger.

"Think about it like this. Positive thoughts. You will reach C-grade and beyond, and in the meanwhile, they will all grow old and rot away while you live on and gain more and more power. By then, they will be nothing but an annoying memory of your younger days."

A few moments of silence followed as the warrior from Valhal just took in the words. She had a personal struggle to overcome. Minutes more went by before she finally seemed to have made up her mind.

Carmen took a deep breath and looked down. "I will meet them and confront them. If I just leave and act like nothing, I will beat myself up over it forever. I... I want to hear them out... or at least hear something from them. Closure, maybe... before they die of old age, you know."

Jake smiled as he asked, "Want me to come with you?"

She looked at him and slowly nodded. "Yeah... just promise me one thing."

"What?" he asked.

"Let me do the talking, and if things get weird, give me a reality check, okay?"

Jake nodded once more. "Sure thing. Want Sylphie around too?"

"No." Carmen shook her head. "Let her continue doing whatever she is doing... Wait, what is she doing anyway?"

"Oh, I asked—or, well, bribed—her to keep an eye on Peter, as the guy was acting shady, and so far, it seems like he is indeed up to some shady stuff. Went all stealth mode and began running around with a crystal. Probably recording or scouting for the United Cities Alliance or something. I will probably talk with the guy later and figure out what he is up to." Jake shrugged.

"Wait, he was shady?" Carmen exclaimed, surprised.

"Oh, yeah, for sure. Not sure exactly what the deal is with Peter, but he did seem genuine in most things, and honestly, what he is doing doesn't seem like my problem. Renato can figure that one out, and even if he arrived in the city with us, it isn't our fault if everyone decides he is somehow the fourth guy among the Three Musketeers."

"We are the Three Musketeers now?"

"Look, it was the fastest analogy I could get on with three people," Jake said, laughing. The mood was instantly lightened as they sat there just a bit.

"We should go now, before I chicken out," Carmen finally said.

"Let's get a move on, then. I'll send a quick message to Renato and update him on the way, so no worries if you see some shady cloaked figures around." Jake smiled and practically dragged Carmen out of the hotel before she had time to change her mind.

Jake knew whatever Carmen was dealing with could be bad in the long run. The Viper had told him that being hung up on things could lead to stagnation and issues. His fellow Primordial, known as the Daofather, had dubbed this kind of thing a heart demon or something like that, which just sounded like a metaphor for having doubt or insecurities by someone trying to sound more profound than they actually were.

Either way, Carmen would do best by confronting it. No matter how things turned out. All he could hope for was that things didn't end too badly.

Who knows—maybe they had turned into at least marginally less shitty people than Carmen described them to be? He knew she was a biased source, and they couldn't be that bad, right?

--

"The Salvento family... Why?" Renato asked himself in a confused tone once he got word from the Chosen who they were going to visit. His chief of security was also there with a slightly worried look.

"I am uncertain, but it was clear that was their target. No other place fits the description." The man wore a worn-out police uniform a looked a bit sloppy, but he was nevertheless one of the strongest people in the city.

"But out of everyone, why them?" Renato asked, still concerned. The reason was simple... Out of every faction, they were one of the ones Renato preferred not to make an enemy. Not because of the family itself, but who they had managed to bring into their fold through the age-old strategy of deploying a honeytrap.

That woman Beatrice had him wrapped around her finger, making him little more than a loyal dog, even if he was incredibly powerful and used a tricky kind of magic Renato would prefer not to get involved in.

"Maybe it is some moral mission?" the chief of security chimed in. "It seems like this is for the Runemaiden, not the Chosen."

"Perhaps, but it is still odd they chose them out of everyone. It also feels personal. The Runemaiden sat outside the mansion for nearly an entire day just scouting it out with a frown on her face, and now they decide to go. Who are these people to her?"

"People who wronged her? Wouldn't be a first; the Salventos aren't the most popular." The other man shrugged.

"No... no, if it was that simple, she would have just attacked."

Renato kept pondering the issue a bit more. He did have some theories, but none that could be confirmed, and it was possible they had simply wronged her. The Salvento family had done everything under the sun, including slavery, before they entered Paradise. They currently ran several brothels and high-level escort services—not just in Paradise—as well as produced nearly a third of the entire drug supply of the city, and that was the part that wasn't exported. They had a major influence, but also a horrible reputation, for one simple reason...

They treated everyone they viewed as below them like absolute shit and had a triple-digit body count of people who'd "offended them."

Carmen stood around the corner and stared at the imposing gates of the mansion. They felt so much larger than the last time she had come there and looked utterly indestructible. She felt nervous and had second thoughts, but when she looked around, she saw Jake, who was judgingly staring at her behind his creepy mask. Well, she also wore a mask while in Paradise, so it was fair.

She felt more assured seeing him there, so unbothered and relaxed. She quickly composed herself, and with Jake in tow, they silently walked towards the gates.

Carmen didn't truly know what she wanted. She had fantasized and dreamed for years about what she would do. While in prison, she'd dreamed about getting out and somehow making it big to then return home in an expensive car to make her parents and family look at her with recognition and pride. To view her as good enough.

It was stupid. No matter how many times they'd put her down and ridiculed her, she still wanted to get their approval. She only had a handful of memories where she thought her family actually felt proud of her. All of them in her youngest years. After she entered her early teenage years, it was all downhill from there.

They had wronged her so many times. They'd made her life hell. Made her want to kill herself several times, took away any little joy she found, and never acted like she was worth anything more than dirt. Dirt to be pushed into a corner when guests came over. When she went to prison, it was like she was dead to them. No visits or calls, with the only thing she ever got being a card from her father saying he was disappointed while also outlining how she had been taken out of all wills and barred from any inheritances.

And now, even with the system, it seemed like they had just written her off. If they let it slip that she existed, they could just lie. Clinton seemed to believe she had been off to college, and it was implied she had probably just died due to that. That part was likely true... They did just assume she was dead. How could they possibly think the useless Carmen could survive?

So... what did she want? Did she want them to see how far she had come? To be impressed that she was now a Runemaiden of Valhal, a high-ranked warrior? Did she want them to praise her and welcome her back with open arms and apologize for their past actions? Say she truly was family after all? For her father to say that he was proud of her?

Did she just want to brag? Show them how wrong they had been and then make them know she was so above them that they weren't worth her time? To look Beatrice in the eyes and say she would enjoy watching her die of old age as she would forever stay young? Call them all out for the shitty people they were before walking off, now their superior?

Or... did she just want to kill every single last fucking one of them?

CHAPTER 37

PEAK FAMILY DRAMA

Jake walked with Carmen towards the large gate with two guards out front. The two guards had clearly already seen them and noticed the black mask on Carmen and Jake's own rather unique mask. Both were identifiers that they were guests of Paradise and likely wealthy individuals, which also meant the guards took a polite demeanor by default.

"Good afternoon, sir and madam," one of the guards said courteously. "May I know your purpose for visiting the Salvento residence?"

Carmen looked at the man for a moment before just saying, "Tell them that Carmen is here."

The guard looked confused and exchanged a look with his partner. They didn't argue back and just decided to do as asked. Jake felt the other guard keep an extra eye on him, making him guess the guy probably had some way to gauge people and how strong they were beyond merely using Identify—an ability similar to that of beasts, making them know who not to mess with.

A few minutes passed and a few more guards made it out of the house before, finally, Jake spotted someone that was clearly a member of the family. It was a man wearing a tailored tan suit who walked beside a woman in a relatively modest dress. Both looked to be in their forties to early fifties, and looking at Carmen's conflicted reaction to seeing them, he had a good guess who they were.

Her parents.

Jake didn't know what he expected, and neither did Carmen. He just stood back as they observed. Carmen looked at the two of them as they came closer, with the man clearly not in a good mood.

"Who are you?" he asked the moment they were within earshot. "What the hell do you want? Money? How dare you use the name of my dead daughter to—"

Carmen didn't hesitate to rip off her mask and stare daggers at the man. "Who the fuck is dead?"

The man stopped with his mouth still half-open. His expression was odd, but the woman—Carmen's mother—had the kind of reaction Jake would have expected from someone finding out their daughter was still alive.

She brought her hands to her mouth as she ran over and past the security guards, tears in her eyes. "Carmen? Is it really you?"

Carmen had no idea what to think. She saw her mother run over without any hesitation while crying like she was actually happy to see her. Meanwhile, her father still just stood there, dumbstruck. She hadn't seen or heard from her mother since her last court date. Sure, her mother had also been crying then, but she hadn't visited her a single time in prison. She hadn't even once made a call or sent a letter or done anything. How did she dare to suddenly act like she was happy to see Carmen after willfully not going to see her for nearly two years?

"What, surprised I am not dead?" she sneered at the both of them.

Her mother stopped a few steps away as the tears just kept streaming down. "I... I'm so sorry... about everything. I..."

"You what?" Carmen shot back.

"Carmen, do not speak to your mother like that," her father said, as he had now composed himself. "Stop making a scene and come inside if you want to talk."

Glaring, she shot him a look as she felt her anger build. "What the fuck are you going to—"

She then felt a slight tap on her shoulder. She whipped her head around and saw Jake, who was just shaking his head. Carmen looked into his eyes for a moment before taking a deep breath. *Don't get too emotional... You are in control here.*

"Fine. Lead us inside," Carmen finally said. Her mother seemed relieved and her father nodded, still looking deep in thought.

The two security guards just stared as she saw her father raise a hand. "Hold it. Who is this man, and why are you bringing him along?"

"I am a companion, and I am coming along, no discussion," Jake answered. "I have been hired to and have no intentions of shirking on my promises."

His answer was short, but it seemed good enough, as her father only looked at him briefly before ignoring him. The moment he had said that he was hired, Carmen already knew that her father had passed judgment and now didn't see him as anyone worth anything... He had always been an ass to service workers, but it had clearly only gotten worse.

Yet her mother seemed so happy. She wouldn't stop crying and looked like she wanted to just give Carmen a hug. *What the hell is up with... everything?*

Man, if this wasn't peak-level family drama. Jake could see Carmen about to lose it right away, but he noticed quite the discrepancy. Her father did indeed look like an utter asshole, but her mother's relief and emotions felt incredibly genuine. Moreover, the glances the man tossed his wife were proof he wasn't happy with how she acted.

Carmen had asked Jake to help ground her and give her reality checks, so he would do that. Jake had the lucky advantage that he quite frankly didn't give a fuck about what happened to any of these people. All he cared about was Carmen not making a kneejerk reaction that she would come to regret. She was effectively holding a loaded gun at all times, and a single moment where she lost control could kill either one of them—something they clearly weren't aware of.

Wordlessly, they were escorted inside as Carmen walked beside Jake, her mother a bit off to the side and her father at the front. The woman looked like she wanted to say something or at least get closer, while Jake saw the man with a deep frown on his face that he probably believed none of them could see, as he had his back turned.

Jake exchanged a look with Carmen, who just had a stony face. He tried to give her an assuring look, and she nodded a bit stiffly. For now, they would let her family take the lead and see what they planned on doing. Jake took his time to scan the mansion with his senses and quickly noticed a vast underground complex. He also felt someone powerful in the house... but it was odd. Like, the aura was powerful, but it also felt almost fake? Now Jake was also curious.

Once inside the mansion, her father exchanged some words with a servant of sorts before leaving, practically dragging his wife along. Jake and Carmen were then led into a lounge room of sorts, where they sat down.

Jake took the initiative by summoning a barrier of stable arcane mana, isolating them from the outside world entirely.

"What the fuck is wrong with them?" Carmen instantly shouted at Jake the moment he was done with the barrier. "And why did you stop me? Do you understand any of this shit?"

"No, not really... but your mother seemed genuine. There is definitely more going on than you know." Jake shook his head. "I think hearing out their side can be beneficial. Not for them, but for you. If you don't figure things out, you may discover something in the future that will make you look back at today with regret. If they prove to still be absolute assholes, you will always be able to turn the situation around to your advantage. Remember, you are in the right here. You decide what happens today, not them."

Carmen finally sat down and stared at the expensive-looking coffee table. "What will you do if things turn bad?"

"Depends on what you want me to do." Jake shrugged. "Ah, but I did place a Hunter's Mark on each of your parents to keep an eye on them. To be safe, ya know?"

She just shook her head and smiled a bit. Jake knew she still had no idea what she wanted to happen, and that it all depended on what her family chose to do. It was all a complicated reason, and Jake was just happy nothing was really up to him. He would just do his simple task of making sure Carmen made choices with an at least partly clear mind.

Minutes passed as they sat there, just chatting. Carmen decided now was a good idea to discuss how many people undervalued good form while in the gym and how important it truly was when building muscle, especially when focusing on building specific muscles. Jake had rarely seen someone so obviously just talking about a random topic to take their thoughts off things, but he nevertheless listened and engaged.

It took more than twenty minutes before anyone even addressed them aside from the first servant. Jake had noticed many attempts to probe them and observe or listen in, but Jake's barrier was too good for their bad scouting attempts to work. This wasn't only because Jake was good, but because the attempts were half-arsed at best.

The door to the room opened, and in came another servant. "The family will receive you now," the woman said courteously.

This choice of words was not lost on Jake, but Carmen didn't seem to care much as she just got up. Jake had dispelled the barrier when he saw the servant approach and followed her out. Their welcome so far had been less than welcoming... They weren't even offered tea and cookies.

They were led through the grand mansion and into what Jake guessed was a banquet hall. Jake already saw the gathering of people in the hall before the double door was opened. "Prepare yourself—it looks like they are pretty much all there," Jake said, infusing his voice with a bit of Willpower to only let Carmen hear.

More than fifty people were gathered. Around thirty of them wore suits or dresses and other such fancy clothes, while twenty were guards or servants. It was quite something. Jake saw Carmen steel herself as the doors were opened, revealing the entire hall and the many people gathered. It reminded Jake of the most intimidating job interview imaginable, with all of them just staring at the maskless Carmen.

Now, Jake had expected many opening questions... but not even he could predict this one.

"Child, what on god's Earth are you wearing?" a woman who looked to be well in her seventies with frilly hair and a baggy dress asked.

Carmen was wearing her combat outfit. Cured leather, metal bracers, heavy combat boots. Generally, she looked ready for a fight at any moment. The only skin she revealed was her face and bare hands. Meanwhile, every other woman in the room wore dresses or other "elegant" clothes.

"Mother, cut her some slack," another woman cut in. "She must have had a hard time traveling all this way."

"Doesn't excuse her lack of proper etiquette," a third woman cut in.

"Also, who is this man?" one of the male residents chimed in. "And look at those... things on his feet. Do the servants not vet any random homeless person who wanders in?"

"Now, now, let's all calm down," a fourth woman finally said as she raised her hand.

Jake recognized her instantly as the woman Carmen had mentioned was her hated aunt, the mother of her most-hated cousin, Beatrice. To note, Beatrice was not present in the room currently, but Jake saw her in another room off to the side, clearly observing them through some monitoring device. With her was a relatively thin and nerdy-looking man with glasses. He was currently giving her a shoulder massage as she looked at the confrontation between Carmen and the rest of the Salvento family.

"Carmen, it truly is you," the aunt said, all smiles. "I cannot tell you how much of a surprise this is. We had feared the worst when we failed to get in contact with you after so long, and I cannot tell you how happy we are to see you return to us. I am sure that if you work hard, our family can find it in our hearts to forgive you and move on. With the world in such turmoil, isn't it a great opportunity to give new chances?"

To her credit, Carmen didn't lose her shit but just stood with a steely face. "That's it?" she finally asked after a good five seconds of silence.

"Carmen! Be respectful, and do not make this more difficult than it has to be!" her father yelled from across the room. He was red-faced, and Jake noticed how Carmen's mother was just standing all the way in the back, looking down with tears in her eyes.

"Nothing is difficult here," Carmen shot back.

"She is right," the aunt agreed. "Now, Carmen, I must know, why did you come now? Why come at all?"

The mixed messaging could not be more clear. The aunt was simultaneously welcoming her back with open arms and yet questioning why she would come back as if it was obvious she wasn't welcome.

"I felt like I had to," Carmen answered truthfully.

"Daft as ever," the old woman—Carmen's grandmother—said. "After all the trouble you caused, you dare show your face like this again? You dare show up covered in dirt, ignoring all etiquette and social norms by just barging in the door? Without a single apology? You should be on your knees begging for forgiveness from your aunt and your cous—"

"Enough!"

Jake had expected Carmen to be the one yelling, but while the voice was similar, it wasn't her. Her mother broke out of the crowd and ran towards Carmen as she stood in front of her. "This is... enough!"

Carmen stared at the woman's back, confused. While it made a bit more sense to Jake, he chose to stay silent as he curiously observed.

"Maura, what in god's name are you doing!?" Carmen's father yelled. He looked both worried and infuriated at what was happening.

"This isn't right or at all what we agreed! You promised—"

"Maura," the aunt cut in, staring down at Carmen's mother, "think very carefully about what you want to do or say next."

The woman hesitated, and Jake decided to get a little involved. He infused his voice with a bit of Willpower and whispered into the woman's ear, "Just speak. Do not underestimate your daughter, and share the truth. Have no doubt that the side you now stand on is the superior one."

No one but her heard his voice, and she looked bewildered for a moment, but it seemed to have given her the confidence. She gritted her teeth as she practically screamed, "Why should I trust anything any of you say!? I already lost my daughter once, and I will not do so again! You promised me she would be out of prison within a year and be back with us! You swore you were doing everything, and that as long as we kept our distance, we would be fine! You never did anything!"

"Maura, shut your mouth right now and apologize! Get back here and—"

"No! I am not leaving my daughter again!"

The situation had turned tense a lot quicker than expected. The woman called Maura had only managed to share a few details, but Jake could see Carmen was shaken. She looked unsure of what to do, and Jake placed a hand on her shoulder to calm her down.

Carmen looked up and collected her thoughts. She seemed to make a decision as she stepped forward. "I think there are some things I need to know. Mother, please follow me so we can—"

"Dear, I will need you to stay so we can talk this out," the aunt interrupted her, and Jake saw the guards move to cover the door. "Having you and your mother simply leave like this will just cause issues no one wants, wouldn't it?"

Jake just sighed internally. *What a fucking moron.*

And, of course, they just *had* to make it even worse as the side door swung open.

"Now, what is all this ruckus? Is my retarded little cousin causing a ruckus again and in need of another lesson?"

The cousin entered, and with her was the nerdy-looking man that gave off quite an odd aura. Finally, all the related parties were gathered in one room for the highest-stake game of family feud imaginable.

CHAPTER 38

A ONE-SIDED FAMILY FEUD

Jake's attention was firmly on the two newcomers, especially the scrawny-looking man. He was thin, pale, wearing glasses, and even in D-grade, he still looked like someone who hadn't left his basement for half a year. Yet he did have an aura of confidence, and Jake could see why.

[Human – lvl 165]

He was actually higher leveled than Jake himself, and it wasn't spoofed or anything either. However, even so, Jake got weird vibes from him. His aura was oddly inconsistent, and his mana signature had an odd, well, signature. It was a bit familiar to Jake, but he wasn't entirely clear where he had felt it before.

The other newcomer was the woman called Beatrice. She wore the kind of dress Jake would expect out of a high-society gala, and she clearly cared a lot about her looks. Jake also felt an aura from her as well as a domain of sorts. His senses heightened, and he quickly noticed how the subtle domain only affected Jake and the other man that stood next to her as well as all the male guards. Somehow, it excluded family members and women. Jake did recognize this kind of aura, as he had seen a familiar one before, though that one had been far less potent and controlled. It was a seduction aura of sorts, and Irin, the succubus, had a similar one.

Her level was also quite a bit lower, to say the least.

[Human – lvl 131]

Carmen looked at the two of them, and Jake saw her one hand slightly shake. Jake did not do anything to interfere, preferring to let things play out how they should. Whatever happened, he would just follow Carmen's lead, and from the looks of it, there was also her mother around now, who had far more insight into who was a bastard and who wasn't.

With impressive calmness, Carmen looked at her cousin and scoffed. "You're still as big of a bitch as back then, huh? Nice guy you got yourself there, by the way. I see you are still at least good at whoring yourself out."

The nerdy-looking guy instantly turned aggressive, but Beatrice held his arm and shook her head. "No need to get mad, babe. She is just jealous. Look at that pathetic guy she managed to drag along."

Okay, why am I getting attacked? Jake questioned but still chose to hold his mouth.

"I understand that the concept of having a man around and not fucking him is foreign to you. Oh, wait, is that why you're so popular in the family? It wouldn't surprise me to learn you fucked half your cousins and uncles you—"

"Do not utter another word!" a man Jake recognized as Carmen's uncle screamed as he turned to her father. "How dare someone like you come in here and act like this!? Didn't I tell you you shouldn't have married that bitch and had a devil spawn like her!?"

Jake saw Carmen begin to shake more and more before she finally just stopped. She took a deep, audible sigh as she looked at her mother. "Mom, who here would you prefer not to see dead?"

Maura looked bewildered before she turned afraid. "Please, let's just leave; I am sure that if we send a message to the authorities, they will—"

"They already locked down the room," Carmen said, sighing. "They don't plan on letting any of us leave. So, tell me... who do you prefer to leave alive?"

Maura didn't answer, just looking dumbstruck as she stared up at the rest of her family. Jake saw the cold gazes they sent in return, and Jake honestly found it impressive. The sheer level of cohesion in this family was insane. Even her own husband, Carmen's father, looked back with disappointment and anger.

"At least you realize the situation you are in," the aunt said with a smile. "Now, we aren't heartless enough to kill our own family. But house arrest is certainly the least of the consequences you will face. Beatrice, dear, do you have any ideas on how we can involve little Carmen more in the family business?"

The cousin just smirked. "We always need more little whores. We can even take the mother."

"No," Carmen's father finally spoke up. "I shall handle my own wife."

Jake saw Maura shake as she backed away. Honestly, looking at this entire situation... Yeah, these people had a seriously lacking ability when it came to probing others. Jake took out the beeper he had gotten from Renato and sent a message, more or less making it clear that murder was going to happen.

"You are all fucking insane," Carmen sneered, "and equally fucking delusional to think you can in any way tell me or anyone around me what to do when I am here."

"Heh," Beatrice laughed when she saw Carmen clench her fists. "Are you still doing that silly boxing thing? Think a little girl like you can fight? I thought you had learned your lesson the first time around, but it seems like you need another one? Ah, I just got a nice little idea for where you can work; we just need to chop off those useless arms. I am sure we have plenty of clients looking for a little para-play."

Jake saw Maura look horrified, with Carmen's father also frowning deeply, but the others barely reacted. He decided to finally get a little involved, as he felt Carmen was about to make her move.

"Excuse me, what am I to do?" Jake asked. Carmen threw him a look, but he just tossed her a glance, and she seemed to get it.

A few people finally looked at him, though they barely seemed to register him.

"You are trespassing and are not family," the aunt spoke. "Guards, apprehend him already and put him in the dungeon for dear Alberto to play with." Jake instantly guessed the guy with Beatrice was Alberto, based on his creepy smile.

The guards reacted, and Jake threw Carmen a look. She just nodded, so Jake smiled as two men flanked him on each side.

Two heads fell to the ground before anyone else in the room reacted, as Jake now stood with a black blade in his hand. He could have just blown their heads off, but Eternal Hunger hadn't been fed in a while, so why not use this opportunity?

His display instantly stopped them in their tracks. Carmen's mother stared at Jake in disbelief as Carmen just laughed out loud, getting the attention of everyone. "Fine. You attacked first."

Carmen stepped down and flew forward with incredible speed. She appeared right in front of her aunt a moment later and mercilessly chopped down on her shoulders. Blood erupted as two arms were severed, and she screamed bloody murder.

Not a single other family member moved to help, instead running away as some of them took out expensive-looking items to defend themselves. Carmen showed no mercy. She moved again and kicked her uncle so hard in his stomach that her foot went through. With a whip, she tossed him away and into a wall, blood flowing down the pristine marble.

"Alberto!" Beatrice screamed, and the man reacted.

That was when Jake learned why the aura of man felt familiar yet also fake. He instantly lit up with red energy as power flooded the room and five summoning circles appeared. He saw that deep below, similar circles appeared, and five creatures were teleported from below.

They all looked humanoid and wore armor and wielded weapons, but Jake felt nothing human about them. The reason why he found the energy so familiar was because he had felt it before—demonic energy. He Identified one and found them all around the same level.

[Demon-Possessed Human – lvl 164]

Now he knew his fate if he was to be captured. He had a fully fledged warlock on his hands, it seemed. It was a class Jake had become faintly familiar with. The demons that were summoned moved for Carmen right away, and Jake remained in place. Alberto kept an eye on Jake, also not moving from Beatrice's side. Jake, in turn, stayed to protect Carmen's mother.

Carmen was surrounded by demons in a moment as Beatrice yelled, "Tear that bitch apart!"

Carmen scoffed. "Fucking idiots." Golden runes lit up on her body, and Jake knew she had finally activated just a few of her boosting skills. "Do you have any fucking idea who I am?"

Golden light erupted as she moved. A possessed human chopped down with an axe, but Carmen just caught it and proceeded to punch the man so hard in his chest it exploded, sending him flying back. Dodging under another blow, she landed a low kick, put another off balance, and punched him so hard that his head was embedded in the stone below.

It was an absolute slaughter. They were simply not on the same level, and Alberto knew this. Jake was aware the man would make a move as he went over to Maura. "Apologies."

He tapped her head and sent in a bit of Willpower, instantly knocking her out with a mental attack. He had a feeling it was better he got involved now. Of course, he still had to ensure Carmen's mother was safe. And, well... that was a task for the third musketeer.

From above, what looked like a green bullet fell. A section of the roof collapsed as the hawk smashed down and cut one of the possessed humans in two from head to groin before swiftly flying over and joining Jake. Jake had communicated with her the task she had been given as he left Carmen's mother in the hawk's care.

Beatrice, to her credit, seemed to notice things had gone south. She looked at Jake and backed away, with Alberto taking a defensive position in front of her. Jake felt that the man had already gathered some energy within his body and could release the prepared skill at any point. Moving to attack would be smart, but... this was not Jake's fight. It was Carmen's privilege to kill them.

"Hey... hey, how much is she paying you?" Beatrice asked. "I am sure we can figure something out." She then released her seduction skill at full power, all of it directed towards Jake. He felt the level of mental influence, and it was at quite a high level, if he had to say so himself. Still useless, of course.

"I don't believe you can offer anything I want," Jake said, shooting her down. " And if I wanted a prostitute, I would go to a brothel."

Beatrice looked shocked, but Alberto was furious. He should probably have expected it, but his comment triggered the man enough to also make his own move. It was a bit premature, as Carmen had only barely gotten done killing the second-to-last possessed human, which was actually respectably tanky with potent regeneration skills.

Jake felt the man's aura flare as he knelt down and pressed his hands to the floor. The magic responded, and Jake felt a gateway open. Jake briefly felt a connection being established with something far more powerful than anyone in the room as the man fully activated the trump card of most warlocks.

"Demonic Transformation!"

His body bulged with muscles erupting on his body. His skin

turned red, and Jake saw a faint mirage behind him of a similar-looking demon. A true demon.

Demons were a rather unique race in the multiverse due to one of the racial skills possessed by all demons in C-grade and above. The Demonic Contract. It was the ability to make a contract with those significantly weaker than themselves, allowing the contractee to pull on their power and, in extreme cases, even allow the demon to possess them or someone else for a limited time, making them far more powerful. This was a very common path to power for demons, and these contracts could take many forms.

That was a simplified version, but Jake had no time to go through all the information in his head right now, as the transformation was complete. He'd gone from a small and scrawny nerd to a three-meter-tall demonic mass of muscles with an axe of bone.

Feeling the bellowing aura, Jake understood why even Renato was careful around the guy. Warlocks were notorious for being powerful at their levels due to the nature of their Path. It was a Path that had plenty of drawbacks, too, but none that mattered at the current time.

Jake dodged as the axe swung down, and he retaliated with Eternal Hunger, getting a good stab in. The bulky demon barely cared, still swinging wildly, every single axe hit tearing up the hall. A few shockwaves even reached the family members of Carmen and Beatrice, ripping them apart.

Carmen swiftly finished off the last possessed demon and charged over. Jake graciously bowed out and allowed Carmen to have her fun with the demon guy. At the same time, he made sure no one else left the room—including Beatrice, who had managed to flee into the room she and Alberto had entered from.

He followed her and appeared in front of her with One Step Mile in an instant. "And you folk talk about etiquette. Isn't it rude to leave in the middle of a party without notice?"

"What the hell do you want!?" she screamed. "What has that witch given you? Who even are you?"

"Lord Thayne, Chosen of the Malefic Viper and perhaps the most powerful man on Earth," a familiar voice said as Jake saw the man in his white suit teleport into the room.

Renato quickly glanced about and saw the carnage, then frowned at the fight between Carmen and the demon. While the demon probably had Carmen beaten in pure Strength, Alberto clearly had no idea how to fight, and it didn't look like he knew the Demonic Avatar skill to have the demon actually possess him. Carmen rapidly wore him down as her fists fell like rain and sent blood flying.

Beatrice stared at Renato and actually looked relieved. "Mr. Renato! I am so glad you are here; these lunatics came in here and—"

"Shut it," Renato cut her off with a death glare before turning to Jake. "Lord Thayne, thank you for informing me of the decision you and the Runemaiden reached. I have already made the necessary preparations, and the Salvento family will be punished according. If you and the Runemaiden choose to leave any survivors, that is."

"That will be up to her." Jake shook his head, waved his hand, and sent out strings of mana to tie up Beatrice, who was once more trying to sneak away. She fell to the ground and struggled, her stats pathetic for a D-grade. Jake had also tied her mouth shut for good measure.

The situation was firmly under control. The family members who had survived were huddled up in a corner, Carmen was beating down the only fighter worth a damn, and Jake had Sylphie bring over the unconscious Maura, who Jake entrusted to Renato.

And then he just observed the fight between the large demon and Carmen. He saw how she didn't really use any skills but was just pummeling the transformed man. Jake felt how she let out all her frustrations and anger by using him as a living boxing bag, and honestly, good riddance.

Jake only knew a bit about what went into creating demon-possessed humans, and it wasn't nice. It required you to completely break down someone enough to have them willingly take in a demon, effectively killing themselves to come hosts. Currently, he could see a lot of what was beneath the mansion, and it appeared like it had primarily belonged to Alberto and housed his workshop.

"Should send some men to the cellar," Jake said to Renato. "And bring some healers."

The man nodded gravely as Jake just stood there and kept watching Carmen let out all the pent-up emotions. Sylphie also joined him, just letting her do her thing before the demon finally died a slow and probably very painful death.

CHAPTER 39

CATHARSIS

Carmen stood over the body of the demon. Blood dripped onto the floor from fists that didn't even have a single scratch on them. She breathed heavily as she kicked the corpse in frustration at the fucker dying so fast. She knew it wasn't all fair that she had let out everything on a man she had only met less than an hour ago, but from the looks of it, he was a fucking asshole. Fit right into the family.

At least he had been worth more than her pathetic uncle and aunt. They could barely handle anything, and she was relieved to see at least one of them still alive despite her injuries. They were still D-grade, after all, and anything short of blowing up their entire torso or ripping off their heads wouldn't lead to instant death, which is why it was maybe overkill to tear her uncle in two, though that shouldn't have killed him instantly.

Anyway, it was good the demon guy had at least been a bit durable to let her vent, considering the rest of her family was too pathetic. And they were pathetic. She wanted to kick herself for being so scared before coming that day. These people were nothing more than bottom feeders.

She looked into the room and saw Jake standing with the shady City Lord Renato, but she also saw her mother lying there unconscious. Jake gave her a nod to make her know she was okay, and even Sylphie mimicked him, making her smile a bit internally. Finally, she saw the tied-up Beatrice.

I'll save her for last.

Carmen turned her attention to the other family members in the room. As she looked at them, her anger flared again. *No... they deserve worse than death.*

"Get the fuck over here!" she yelled at them.

"Little Carmen, please, this is all a big misunderstanding!" her grandmother, who had managed to survive, cried out. She even had the gall to use the name she used to call Carmen when she was like five.

"I told you all to get the fuck over here," she said again. It seemed to get the message across the second time around as she also pointed at her aunt. "And drag that bitch along. If any of you are healers, fix her up too. At least enough so she doesn't die too quickly."

They did as ordered without another complaint or word spoken. Only now did Carmen truly recognize how fucked up their sense of authority was. The moment she had the upper hand, pretty much everyone just rolled over and did as told. It was pathetic.

Jake and Renato then walked over, with Jake dragging the bundle of mana strings containing Beatrice. The woman was wriggling, trying to get loose as she looked up at Carmen with fright.

Carmen had to hold herself back from just stomping on her head then and there as she turned to Renato. "Is this all of them?"

"Everyone from the Salvento family present in Paradise, yes," the man confirmed.

"And you really have no issues with everything that happened today?" she also asked.

"I have major issues with it. I lost a major source of income and an important part of our infrastructure. Your family—or former family— were at least decent at their jobs, and it will take a long time to find suitable replacements." He then added, "However, this is a preferable outcome to dealing with the fallout of making you an enemy. More- over, it was only a question of time before they tried to reach beyond their station, and would've no doubt gone for the position of City Lord eventually. So, truly, good riddance."

Carmen just sighed as she wondered what to do next. She consid- ered if she should just kill them all, but then she saw her mother. Still unconscious. She gritted her teeth as she sighed and looked at Renato and Jake. "Can you help me contain them or something? I think I need to have a talk with my mom."

Jake nodded and smiled as he tossed her a few potions. "Good luck."

"Thanks." She smiled as she went into the other room with her mother and shut the door, trusting Jake to make sure no one escaped. Even if they did, she had confidence he could track them down again.

Jake stood in the large central banquet chamber and saw it all torn up and destroyed. Renato stood silently at his side, seeming happy everything was contained within the mansion and that nothing spilled outside to impact the rest of the city.

"You allowed them to get away with a lot," Jake finally said, both men knowing what he was referring to.

"A balance is required," Renato just said in defense of himself.

"They have a fucking dungeon full of prisoners. Human experiments. I am pretty sure this goes against the so-called rules of Paradise."

Renato sighed. "I was aware of some of it. Slaves were brought in from the outside. While slave trading is illegal, owning them is not... and even if it is frowned upon, we simply didn't have the means to investigate and—"

"Bullshit," Jake said. "You just didn't think it was worth it."

"As I said... a balance is required." As two of them stood in silence, he added, "But do know that I shall strive to improve things."

"I hope so," Jake said.

And hopefully, whatever Peter does will light a fire under your ass and make you get your shit together.

Hours passed.

Carmen had woken up her mother and heard the whole story. Between sobs and apologies, Carmen became a bit more clear on what had been going on back then. When Carmen gave her dear cousin a good pummeling and was charged criminally, her mother had fought for her with her father also kind of supporting her.

However, due to the pressure from other family members, they were told to back off. Her mother was finally promised that Carmen would say incarcerated for a year or so before they would agree for her to get out. With the family's power, she hadn't doubted it was possible, but the promise did come with some limitations.

First of all, they could have no contact with her during this time, and her mother had agreed. Carmen did learn that some things did not line up. The letter disowning her was news to her mother, making her cry even more at learning that it had indeed never been their plan to let her out.

Her mother also said that things got worse after she went to prison. Her father got more aggressive and short with his wife, and her freedom was limited. Her father and mother had apparently been threatened to be cut off from the family entirely, and at that moment, her father had chosen the family over Carmen and his wife. It was a fucked-up situation, which just led to the ultimate question:

"Who of them is worth keeping alive?" Carmen asked her mother.

"I..." her mother said with hesitation. "Carmen, we shouldn't stoop to their level. Please, enough people have died today. Don't make it worse."

Carmen just sighed at her mother's naivety, yet it also made her a bit glad. She also decided that she wanted another perspective on this, so she dispelled the barrier in the room and said, somewhat louder, "Can you come in here? I need some common sense."

Jake was not a good person to ask for common sense, but nevertheless, he entered the room where Carmen and Maura were sitting. The woman looked like a mess, and Jake greeted her with a wave. He took the initiative and made his own mask invisible when it was just the three of them.

"Not sure you want me for common sense," Jake commented.

"You are the best I got," Carmen said, scoffing with a smile. "You have been keeping an eye on my 'family'—any thoughts so far?"

"They are trying to figure out who to throw under the bus, but it seems like they all agreed on the uncle, aunt, and Beatrice as well as that grandmother of yours. A few more, too, probably. They are all kept in the room, so you can figure out what you want to do with them."

"What do you think I should do? No... what would you do?"

Jake took a moment to think. Would he kill them all? Maybe. It seemed like a waste of time to do so. Would he let them go? Fuck no. But if he wasn't going to let them go...

"I don't think I am the best to ask. I don't know them well enough... but think about it like this. What are the consequences of leaving them alive, and what do you want out of their deaths? Remember, this is not about them, but you. If you genuinely believe killing every single one of them will make you feel better, do that. That would also remove all karmic ties and potential future issues one of them could bring. If you believe that leaving them alive—and that they are no future threats—will make you feel best, do that." It was an honest answer. He did not know what he would do if he was in the same position. He would just go by his gut in that situation.

Carmen looked like she considered her words before asking her mother, a tad coldly, "Do you want your husband alive or not?"

"Your father—"

"He is not my father," Carmen interrupted, "and I am not a part of that shitty Salvento family. They lost the privilege for me to recognize them long ago."

"He... I don't know." Her mother shook her head.

Jake sighed as he saw the woman so... lost. Her entire life had been upturned in just a few minutes, and all the conditioning would take far longer to fade away. It was a difficult situation, and Jake could only watch from the sidelines as, luckily, Renato entered the conversation.

"Ms. Carmen, would it perhaps be best we find a peaceful place for your mother to rest for now?" he asked. "We have plenty of healers and individuals with experience dealing with injuries not necessarily of the physical nature."

Carmen hesitated before finally nodding. Maura didn't even try to argue, but she did say one last thing. "Please don't kill your father... even with all he did..."

With that, she was led away, and Carmen looked at Jake and Renato for a moment. Jake understood at that moment what she had decided. "Have everyone leave the hall," she said, with Renato complying by ordering his men out.

"Meet you back at the hotel?" Jake asked.

"Yeah." Carmen nodded as she closed the gate and entered the central hall.

Carmen wiped her hand with a cloth. It was still red even after she cleaned it, but with a bit of water and soap, it should come off. Around her lay more than twenty corpses of people she had once called family. Once. She realized that forgiveness was just not in her heart. Carmen was not going to justify anything to anyone. She killed them purely out of selfish revenge, and fuck her, did it feel good.

Now there were only four left. Her chair moved a bit as her dear cousin struggled. She really was a sucky chair.

"Pipe down," Carmen said as she grabbed Beatrice's thigh and let her fingers sink into the flesh, causing the woman to release muffled screams.

The other three people were her aunt, grandmother, and father. Sadly, her uncle had died during the fight with the demon, leaving only four of her primary targets. None of them spoke, and with good reason —they all lay on the ground, every single limb broken.

Her grandmother had not even reached D-grade, and it was a miracle she still lived. Carmen stood up and made sure to do a back-kick into her cousin's stomach as she walked over to the vile old woman.

Carmen squatted down in front of her. "Never imagined this day would come, huh?" she asked as she held up the woman by her frilly white hair.

The woman only glared back as she muttered, "Devil... spawn..."

"A bit hypocritical, considering your favorite granddaughter's boyfriend literally summoned demons," Carmen sneered. "Not that I would argue. Devils are demons who have reached the realm of godhood; did you know that? No, probably not, based on how fucking ignorant you have shown yourself to be. Either way, I shall take it as a compliment, so good riddance."

With that, Carmen simply extended a finger and poked the woman on her head. Her finger penetrated the skull and sank into the old hag's brain. Her eyes opened wide before going blank and lifeless.

"And now for my favorite aunt," Carmen said as she sprang up and walked over. "For you, I really have no grand speech. I always fucking hated you. You are a coward and an utter failure as a parent and a person. The mere fact you managed to pop out that cousin of mine is a sin worthy of death alone, so I am giving you just that."

The woman struggled, but Carmen had already ripped out her tongue and broken her jaw, as she hadn't stopped yapping on, begging for mercy earlier.

Carmen turned and looked at her cousin as she dragged her own mother over to her by her hair. "I wondered for a while if I should kill your own daughter in front of you... but honestly, I prefer it the other way around."

She stomped down with her foot while keeping hold of the long hair on her aunt's head. All the hair was ripped out as the woman was smashed down. Carmen had actually planned on ripping the head off, but oh well.

Another good stomp later, and all that remained of her head was a mass of blood, skull fragments, and brain matter.

"Now the finale. Beatrice, oh, Beatrice. Do you have any idea how long I have looked forward to this day? I am actually a bit sad I wasn't better back on that fateful day. If I was as skilled then as I am now, I would have killed you in time. I did try to kill you, you know?" Carmen stared down at the crying woman—who naturally also had her tongue ripped out.

"Ah, wait, here, let me help you answer." Carmen pulled out a potion and fed Beatrice. She instantly healed from the head down, and within less than a minute, a new tongue had regrown.

"You psychotic bitch," Beatrice screamed. "You absolute fucking psycho! You are never going to get away with this!"

"Get away with what? Fixing a minor family issue?" Carmen scoffed.

"I hope you get raped to death, you—"

"And tongue privilege is revoked," Carmen interrupted her as she ripped it out again. "You really don't know when to shut the fuck up."

Beatrice kept trying to scream as Carmen just took a deep breath and closed her eyes. She put a hand on each side of her cousin's face and lifted her up. Opening her eyes, she stared straight into the eyes of Beatrice and saw only defiance meet her.

Carmen began squeezing, and soon the eyes changed from defiance to pain and then finally despair. Gradually, she increased her power, as she didn't lose eye contact for even a second. She wanted to make sure Beatrice suffered until the very last moment.

"Goodbye, and may you rot in whatever hell a bitch like you ends up in," Carmen said as she increased the pressure and, like a melon, Beatrice's head exploded, splashing blood all over Carmen.

Carmen couldn't help but smile, as she, for some reason, felt relieved. Yet she also felt tired, like she had just won a fight against her most powerful opponent ever. She looked at her bloody hands before she was brought out of her thoughts by the muffled cries of the final person left alive.

She turned to him and scoffed. "Be lucky my mother asked to keep you alive. That is the only reason you leave alive today. Don't fucking ever contact me again, and if you do, I will not be as nice, even if it goes against my mother's wish."

The man didn't even answer, as he looked to be in a state of shock. He just kept screaming.

Carmen ignored him and threw the corpses a final look before leaving the hall. Outside, she saw the same guard that had first escorted them into Paradise.

"Ms. Carmen," he said, bowing.

"I am done."

"What are we to do with the survivor?" the guard asked, unbothered.

"I honestly don't care, as long as he doesn't die," Carmen said dismissively.

"Very well. What will the Runemaiden do now?"

Carmen thought for a second. "Well, first of all, I need a damn shower."

"Honestly, that saying is just bullshit," Carmen said as she took another shot. "Revenge is never the answer, my ass."

"But an eye for an eye makes the whole world blind—didn't you know that?" Jake teased her as he also took a drink.

"Well, I can live with that; I got confidence in my self-healing," Carmen joked in return.

It had been a few hours since everything had ended. Renato was doing clean-up, Peter was nowhere to be found, and Sylphie didn't like sitting around in a hotel room, so she had decided to scout out the surrounding area of Paradise.

Jake and Carmen had met up in the hotel room and were currently liberally emptying out the minibar while chatting about everything that had gone down. Carmen was now just sitting in a bathrobe with damp hair as she drank, her clothes still full of blood after the happenings earlier today, with Jake having also switched into something more casual.

"It's weird," Carmen said as she stared up at the ceiling. "Based on all the movies and TV shows and whatnot, one would think only some hollow feelings would remain. You know, how it is often shown where some guy gets their revenge and then they just become empty husks without purpose. I feel just the opposite. It was cathartic. Like finally, I am free... Am I a bad person for that?"

Jake shrugged as he took another drink. "Good or bad... I don't know. Is it really worth thinking about? Freedom is what allows you to be and do whatever you want to. So what if others think you are a bad person if you and those you care about don't?"

She was silent for a while. "Do you think it makes me a bad person? Killing them all, I mean."

"No, not really. It was merely a consequence of their own actions. They lived their lives killing and taking advantage of others while never even being willing to risk their own hides. It was just a matter of time before reality caught up to them, and they pissed someone off they shouldn't." Jake shook his head. "Not sure about others, but I may have done the same. I truly don't know."

Carmen smiled and nodded, just staring around the room for a while. She adjusted her hair and took another drink as she drew a deep breath. "You know, for nearly four years, I have either been stuck in a fucked-up women's prison or been busy running around, killing things by myself for the most part. I know I have major trust issues... I don't like others having my back. Sylphie was the first living thing I think I ever really trusted, and that was just because she was so cute and innocent I couldn't see her backstabbing me."

Jake kept silent, letting her talk.

"I don't like all the pressure Sven put on me, or the importance people place on some stupid title like Runemaiden," she continued. "Shit, I ended up going through several gods before I found one I stuck with, more due to my own damn insecurities than anything else."

"I get it," Jake said. "Trusting people sucks. In my tutorial, I was naive and trusted people, and that nearly got me killed. But at the same time, you need to trust some people, or life just gets too miserable. I guess I did get lucky with who I met."

Carmen smiled and looked at Jake. "I guess I could have been more unlucky with who I met."

The two of them fell silent and just drank. Carmen finally sighed, leaned forward, and grasped Jake by the collar as she muttered something about Jake being dense under her breath.

She looked him straight in the eyes. "Wanna hook up?"

Jake's brain short-circuited for a moment before he nodded and was promptly thrown towards the bed.

CHAPTER 40

THE MORNING AFTER

When fighting, Jake liked to be in control and dictate the momentum. He liked when he decided what would happen next, and the flow went as he predicted.

That night did not feel particularly in control, and if he was candid, he was totally fine with it.

Not that he didn't also seize the momentum here and there as the battle continued, making it a big back and forth.

After their battle, Jake found himself lying on the bed as he relaxed, with Carmen leaning against the headboard next to him, still stark naked. He looked over and saw her relaxing. Her short blonde hair was a bit more unkempt than usual, and her defined muscles, especially on her stomach, were still visible even as she relaxed them.

She noticed his gaze and didn't bother to hide anything as she said, "I guess I should make it clear this doesn't mean we are getting married or anything."

"And here I was just thinking about picking out a good ring and wondering if Sylphie should be a bridesmaid," Jake joked back in return as he also sat up in the bed.

Okay, Jake had to admit, he could be a bit dense at times. He had not at all expected what happened to happen, but he wasn't averse to it. He just went with the flow and would be a damn liar if he said he wasn't a huge fan. If this was pre-system, he would definitely classify Carmen as someone way out of his league, especially factoring in the aesthetic improvements from evolutions.

"Don't get me wrong," Carmen further clarified. "I do like you, but there is no way I am looking for any kind of relationship right now, okay? So let's just keep it casual."

"I didn't expect anything else," Jake said, nodding. Life was too complicated for both of them, and they each had too much of their own stuff to deal with to get into any kind of meaningful relationship. A relationship would mean either or both parties had to sacrifice something to make it work, and Carmen and Jake were too selfish to want that.

"That doesn't mean this has to be a one-time thing," Carmen said suggestively.

"Technically, it already isn't," Jake said, smirking in return. Carmen threw him an even more suggestive look, but Jake sadly shook his head. "While I would love to, I have already had to make five excuses to Sylphie about why we were busy, and by now, she seems to think we are performing some grand ritual."

"Too bad." She shrugged as she jumped off the bed and had armor appear on her body. "What are your plans now? I will stay in Paradise a bit to sort things out. I still need to figure out what to do with my mother. Taking her back to a settlement belonging to Valhal would be best, but getting there isn't that easy right now."

"You could always wait for the teleportation gates to be fully established. I am not sure how long it will take, but it shouldn't be that long with how fast the space mages are progressing. It may also be possible for me to help by doing a bit of roundabout teleportation by first going to the Order and then back to Haven, but I'm not sure if I can even do that."

"No need—I will figure this out myself, but thanks for the offer." Carmen went over and gave him a kiss, adding, "Still only friends."

"With benefits." Jake smiled as he promptly got a chop on top of his head.

He also decided to finally get up, and was dressed in moments through the power of his spatial storage. As he put on his clothes, he also took out an item. It was a Key of the Exalted Prima.

[Key of the Exalted Prima (Unique)] – *A key to the Seat of the Exalted Prima. Allows entry to the Seat of the Exalted Prima.*

"Here, take this," Jake said as he tossed Carmen the key.

She caught it and looked at the key with a frown. "Don't you still need another fragment? The only reason I didn't have a key is that I gave mine to Sven, so it really isn't your problem."

"I just gave you loot priority for the three Primas we killed." Jake shrugged. He knew Carmen wasn't a fan of charity. "And I plan on spending the rest of my time before the system event just exploring this continent. I am sure Renato has some good information on nearby spots with dangerous foes, which will likely include a Prima or two. Even if he doesn't have a map, I still got Peter's."

"Sure you trust that guy? Didn't he disappear after doing some shady shit?"

"Eh, trust or not doesn't matter; the map is at least legit, based on what I can see," Jake said, shaking his head.

"You aren't angry at him lying to our faces this whole time?" Carmen asked with a raised eyebrow.

"Thinking about it, did he actually lie? We never asked, did we? Sure, one could argue he lied by omission, but by that logic, we also lied to him about the nature of why we were going to Paradise. As far as I know, he didn't do anything against either of us and will only cause trouble for Renato, which I quite frankly don't give a damn about."

Carmen thought for a while. "I guess you have a point, and it isn't like Valhal or Haven is allied with that city alliance either."

Jake nodded as he went over to the balcony. "Okay if I let Sylphie in now?"

She shrugged. "Go ahead." The bedroom was still a bit of a mess after their nightly battle, but it didn't matter much.

Jake opened the balcony door, and the moment he did, a green form flew in and quickly circled the room. She zoomed a dozen rounds before finally landing on a table, knocking over a bottle.

"Ree!" she shrieked.

"Yeah, we discussed the situation," Jake said, nodding with a serious expression.

Sylphie looked at Carmen suspiciously.

"Eh, yeah, we finished the discussion," Carmen played along. "Adults only, you know?"

"Yep," Jake reiterated. "Carmen will stay here for a while to handle the rest of her matters while the two of us can head out for a bit of hunting. We will meet up at the system event anyway, so—"

"Ree, ree, ree?" Sylphie asked.

"I guess?" Jake said, somewhat surprised as he turned to Carmen. "Can Sylphie stay here with you until you got everything handled?"

"Why?" Carmen asked, confused.

"Well, according to her, she found some sky-anomaly around twenty kilometers up, hidden above the other clouds, and she wants to eat it." Jake shrugged.

"Eat it?"

"Yep. Sylphie's words, not mine. Well, her insinuation, not mine."

"What is this anomaly?" Carmen asked curiously.

Jake turned to Sylphie, who made a few more screeching noises.

"A very windy one," Jake explained very accurately.

Carmen seemed to understand she would not get a proper answer, and Jake had also given up. From the sounds of it, it was perhaps some kind of natural formation or jet stream or something. Sylphie seemed to want it, so the rest didn't really matter, as he trusted her instincts for what she could and couldn't absorb.

Anyway, it seemed like Jake would have to head out alone. Sylphie and Carmen both had their own Prima keys, and Jake only needed one more fragment to form his own. He had over two weeks to get that done and also get some great hunting in.

Before he left, he went by Renato's and talked to the man to clear some things up. First of all, he washed his and Carmen's hands of Peter by making it clear they didn't know the guy, and he even managed to come out looking like the good guy by "warning" Renato about Peter once Jake claimed he couldn't find him.

The visit also gave him some good information about the surrounding area. Renato had mapped out some areas where his elite was hunting, and more importantly, areas his elite avoided, as it was too dangerous for them to hunt in. Jake also learned that the man didn't even have a single fragment himself and was fully aware he would not get a key. He was running a full-on turtle strategy, which meant hunting wasn't something the man was skilled in.

With everything in Paradise done and dusted, Jake headed out for a danger zone about a day's travel away. For Renato's men. Jake could probably get there within a few hours.

Once he was outside, it finally came. Something he had waited for since last night. A presence descended as Jake heard the voice.

"I am so proud of my Chosen," Villy's voice echoed in his mind. *"To lay with a Runemaiden from Valhal? Truly my man. Tell me, who's next now that you have finally abandoned your days of celibacy? You know it is entirely possible to—"*

Jake tried to ignore the god as he ran, but he finally felt compelled to answer after Villy began talking about setting up blind dates with other influential women from other factions.

"You are way more invested in this than I thought you would be," Jake mumbled.

"Oh, I am not; I just like to make fun of you. Good for you to finally get some tail, even if your partner in question didn't have a tail. Ah, but just to make sure, you didn't, you know, go for making more mini-Jakes?"

"No, and if you keep asking, I will from here on out live a life as a eunuch," Jake said. Okay, he wouldn't. That was too big of a sacrifice to make, even to spite Villy.

"That would include you cutting it off, you know? But okay, okay, I'll leave you be. Just one piece of advice—don't get too attached to anyone, alright?" More seriously, he added, *"You are both only D-grade, and if I am being frank, then chances are not a single person you have met from your own universe will live as long as you. The amount of talents who have fallen due to sentimental reasons isn't few, and being able to live with seeing everyone around you wither and die is a requirement if you want to go all the way."*

"I know," Jake answered, the god bringing down the mood. "But that sounds like something I will consider when it becomes relevant, not now."

"Just remember to prepare yourself mentally," Villy reiterated.

Jake nodded as he kept running. Not wanting to end the conversation on such a somber note, he smirked and took a jab of his own. "I am impressed you actually stopped being a peeping tom."

"Alright, I am many things, but a voyeur is not one of them, especially not when it is my mate. That would just be weird, man." In jest, he added, *"Well, unless I am part of the deed, in which case, seeing things is unavoidable, you know? It is a possibility, depending on how free-spirited and open-minded you are."* At least, Jake *hoped* that was in jest.

The two of them chatted a bit more about random, somewhat unrelated things before Villy had to get back to "work," as he called it. It appeared that Jake having a nightly escapade made Villy decide that now was a good time to have a status meeting with the three Witches of the Verdant Lagoon—for entirely unrelated reasons, Jake was sure.

Checking out his map, Jake went towards the closest danger zone worth looking into. He also pulled out a fragment to scan for any Primas. He had spent the last while with others, and honestly, Jake was a bit glad Sylphie had found something that made her stick around Paradise, allowing Jake to go off solo.

With only a couple of weeks till the system event, Jake smiled as he looked forward to some solo hunting and hopefully some more class levels under his belt. He had noticed the lack of experience gained when with others and was relatively sure by now that he got a lot less experience when fighting with others than by himself. Even less than the usual penalty of shared experience and the battles being made easier as a result of partying.

Who knows... if the hunt was good, maybe he could even find a "weak" C-grade worth killing.

It was shortly after the Second World Congress.

Casper checked the Magiscript one final time. A vast tapestry of runes and symbols revolved all around him as he scanned it for any flaws or missing parts. He had already messed it up a few dozen times by now and had to debug what was effectively ultra-complex computer code. His many years working before the system in research and development with software came in very handy, as he was more or less just coding in a magical language infinitely more complex than any computer code humans could ever invent. Something only made possible by his now superhuman abilities.

Taking a deep breath, he activated the testing core and ran the simulation. It started up as expected, and soon enough, the entire structure stabilized. The energy flow was up to the hoped-for standards, with the density even surpassing what he had calculated prior by about half a percent. Casper grinned as time passed, and half an hour later, a perfect equilibrium had been reached.

Having confirmed the result, he took out the real thing. The unique item hummed with power, and Casper knew he was in possession of something even peak-level factions would go far to acquire: a real dungeon core.

*[**Intermediate Dungeon Core (Unique)**] – A Dungeon Core offered directly by the system due to Earth's performance during the Treasure Hunt event. This Dungeon Core is of the intermediate level and can support monster spawning up to low-tier C-grade. Must have a suitable environment to activate and spawn the dungeon. **Requirements:** Soulbound.*

After looking at it for a while longer, he went to the prepared cavern. Several guards were in place, and when they saw him, they knew. Priscilla was notified and sent a communication to Casper asking if he was ready. He confirmed as he entered the cavern and made everyone else leave the area.

He would need silence and focus to implement the core and create a true dungeon. Casper sat in the middle of the cavern and took out the core, and the moment he got the go-ahead to initiate, he began infusing his Magiscript. The entire cavern responded as the process started. Beneath him, another ritual was also going on as hundreds of D-grades fed a ritual that supported him and the cavern with energy, all led by Priscilla herself.

Casper had begun preparing this cavern the very day the city was founded. He had worked on the scripts and directed thousands of workers to assist him, and out of everyone in the city, if not the world, he had been the one to use the most resources on such a singular goal. Casper had even been trained by an S-grade Archlich specializing in Magiscript and dungeon-making. Heck... he even had pointers and was blessed by a Primordial to do this job.

There was no room for failure.

Days passed with Casper in a constant state of focus. The walls were slowly filled with scripts as the cavern expanded. Space was distorted, and a week in, only Casper and the area a few meters around him remained stable. On the outside, the cavern was about two hundred meters in diameter, but in there, it had expanded to tens of times that. Anyone trying to go inside would also swiftly find themselves rebuffed, as a barrier had been made by the dungeon core itself.

Casper had lost count of the number of potions he had consumed, and even time itself. Lyra's encouraging words helped keep him awake and keep track of everything as she fed him energy through their connection. His body had difficulty enduring the process, but Lyra began defending him and healing his wounds.

Two weeks passed. Three weeks. A month.

Casper was haggard, but he knew he was nearly done. The script was perfect. He had only found a few minor flaws to perfect. He had worked with this kind of thing before... He'd been a damn talented computer scientist before the system, and now he did not doubt he was a damn proficient user of Magiscript.

Day thirty-three, it happened. The core was fully stabilized, and suddenly Casper's vision shifted as he felt himself overseeing an entire space. He felt like he was a god in control of his own world, but he quickly pulled himself back to reality to not lose himself as he disconnected from the core.

When he opened his eyes again, he found himself with his legs crossed in front of the entrance to the cavern, a white, mist-like barrier blocking the way inside. He broke out in smiles as Priscilla arrived behind him.

"Did you...?"

Casper just grinned. "Damn straight, I did."

He went to stand up but found himself stumbling. His mind was still in a daze as he focused on all the notifications he had gotten, with them being the last thing he saw before he passed out from pure exhaustion.

'DING!' Profession: [Blight-Touched Dungeon Architect] has reached level 172 - Stat points allocated, +8 Free Points

'DING!' Profession: [Blight-Touched Dungeon Architect] has reached level 173 - Stat points allocated, +8 Free Points

...

'DING!' Profession: [Blight-Touched Dungeon Architect] has reached level 189 - Stat points allocated, +8 Free Points

'DING!' Race: [Risen Human (D)] has reached level 154 - Stat points allocated, +21 Free Points

...

'DING!' Race: [Risen Human (D)] has reached level 162 - Stat points allocated, +21 Free Points

Title acquired: [Progenitor Dungeon Master]

Title earned: [Progenitor Dungeon Master] – *A master of reality itself, you have created your own little world. For doing so while still in D-grade and within three years of the integration of your universe, you have shown yourself to be a true Progenitor Dungeon Master. Increases your ability to create dungeons and manipulate self-created world spaces.*
+25 all stats, +10% all stats.

CHAPTER 41

JUNGLE HUNTING

Each step bent space as Jake ran through the landscape. It had already been a day or so since he left Paradise, with nothing especially interesting happening so far. A few mediocre D-grade areas had been explored, but nothing worth hunting.

He checked his map and saw he was approaching a new area marked as a danger zone. This particular area was exactly the kind of environment Jake loved to hunt in. It was a vast swath of greenery with tall trees dominating the horizon and dense foliage covering the ground, making it impossible to see far. It was not a forest, but something even more filled with nature mana: a jungle.

While some areas of the forest Haven was placed in the outskirts of could qualify as jungle-like, this place was on another level. Jake checked the intel from Renato and even double-checked with what Peter had given him—both had mentioned this place, as it was both a danger zone and a very popular hunting spot.

Reading the intel, it seemed like a great spot. In the very outskirts, a few E-grades could be found, but just a bit in, D-grades began dominating. This was still only talking the outer ten percent, as none of the intel mentioned what was further in, just that it was dangerous. Renato's information did note the risk of C-grades, so that was positive.

The opponents one could expect ranged from beasts to plants to a few scarce mentions of elementals—primarily water elementals, due to the high humidity. Nature elementals weren't a thing, as far as Jake knew. Nature mana tended to just seep into living things attuned to the affinity instead of coalescing into elementals, creating monster plants or treants and stuff like that.

Jake felt satisfied after studying the notes and headed in. It didn't take him long to notice several beasts and creatures all around him through his sphere. All of them E-grades, hiding either in bushes, in trees, or even below the ground. There was a high level of verticality to the jungle, with plants and trees reaching hundreds of meters into the air, even in the outskirts.

Needless to say, Jake did not care for these E-grades, so he swiftly ran forward. He didn't cut a path but just dodged through the dense vegetation, taking this opportunity to practice his stealth. He also pulled out the Prima fragment once more and didn't get any immediate response when he tried to search for the energy signature. Then again, the mana in this area was dense, making it difficult unless he got really close. His newly upgraded tracking skill also didn't work, as, well, it wasn't like he knew what kinds of tracks Primas left behind. Scanning every track for signs of the Prima signature sounded like a nice way to spend his two weeks before the event accomplishing jack shit.

About half an hour later, he finally encountered his first D-grade. It was a ferret-like creature that hid in the underbrush, and while Jake did scan it briefly, he did not engage. In the area ahead, he found dozens of these creatures hidden, making it clear this was their territory.

As he got further in, the space did begin to open up a bit. Not because there was less nature mana or plant growth, but because of what was happening there. Fights between D-grades didn't always leave the environment intact, and entire areas were often torn apart.

Due to the high mana density, new plants would grow back within days, if not hours, but the sheer number of beasts meant entire caverns within the foliage were formed. Jake spotted a cat-like creature battling a large mantis-like monster, both rapidly dodging and weaving in between trees, only for a third opponent to interfere and kill them when they were weakened.

Jake's hopes were heightened as he finally felt something. A gaze upon him... an unfriendly one. Finally, a beast had been able to see through his stealth and decided to make him the target. Acting like he hadn't noticed, Jake kept going, waiting patiently for his foe to strike. He didn't need to wait long until the creature entered his sphere from above. He saw it was a snake-like monster, but it was made up of vines, bark, and plant parts rather than flesh, blood, and scales.

It stalked him from above and waited to strike, but Jake didn't give it a chance. He turned around mid-jump, pulled out his bow, and fired a barrage of explosive arcane arrows, tearing up the surrounding greenery.

The snake was startled but still continued its assault. The head didn't actually have a mouth but was shaped like a halberd of sorts, allowing it to sweep and stab. Jake dodged away as he fired another arrow into the creature and continued bombarding it with arrows, not allowing it to ever get close before it died. It had only been level 150, meaning it didn't even give experience.

Despite the fight, he had kept pace as he traveled inward, and that first snake would prove to set the example of what was to come. Ambushes happened frequently, but it was nothing Jake couldn't easily handle. He did begin putting in a little more effort and even used poison on his arrows when the levels grew to above 160, and especially when he started to get experience.

For the first time in quite a while, Jake began to have a feeling well up inside him. He had spent long periods doing events, going to the Order, traveling, and being in cities. He had been around others all the time. But now... now he was alone.

It was almost like his senses sharpened, and he stopped thinking about anything irrelevant. He felt more comfortable than he had for months. There was only himself and an environment filled with things wanting to make him their prey.

An environment he would show exactly who the real hunter was.

A small smile crept onto his lips as he dodged the attacks of two treants trying to seal his movements. Jake moved on the offensive, bombarding the treants with explosive arrows and, with a beat of his wings, sending a cloud of miasmic poison down towards them. They struggled for a while before Jake finished them and moved on, but he barely got a hundred meters before he was attacked again.

Few predators moved through this area, and those that did, these creatures knew about and did not attack. They didn't know Jake, making them all attack him if they felt like they were at a higher level than he was. This resulted in a path of destructive arcane mana being carved into the jungle as he traveled. Nature would fix it soon enough, but for now, only destruction was in his wake.

Two primary types of enemies dominated the jungle around him: beasts and Vinewood creatures. Vinewood creatures were like the snake before. It was more often than not just a plant lifeform in the shape of a beast, given life due to the dense and potent nature mana, making them effectively nature elementals. The beasts were... well, the usual beasts one could find in jungles.

One type of enemy could bleed and die to Jake's poison, and the other could be destroyed by the power of arcane mana. Jake had no poison dedicated to plants like the fungicide he had made back in the day, but his blood did a banger job anyway. While he had learned how to make an inferior-rarity poison during his studying just to shore up his foundation, the poison would be way worse than his blood, even against weak foes.

Weak foes who slowly grew stronger as the days passed, and Jake continued his hunt.

You have slain [Vinewood Viper – lvl 166] – Bonus experience earned for killing an enemy above your level

You have slain [Deathfang Sloth – lvl 169] – Bonus experience earned for killing an enemy above your level

You have slain [Vinewood Mongoose – lvl 175] – Bonus experience earned for killing an enemy above your level

You have slain [Spiketail Lizard Devourer – lvl 182] – Bonus experience earned for killing an enemy above your level

As his foes grew stronger, so grew the difficulties of the fights. In the section he had just entered, primarily the Vinewood creatures existed, with all beasts daring to roam there at a high level themselves. Vinewood creatures did not attack one another, meaning the chances of being ganged up on were high.

With the increased difficulty Jake faced also came levels. Each individual kill did not give much experience, but over the course of the next week, he slew hundreds above his own level, not a single one of them yet able to put up an equal fight.

'DING!' Class: [Avaricious Arcane Hunter] has reached level 156 - Stat points allocated, +10 Free Points

...

'DING!' Class: [Avaricious Arcane Hunter] has reached level 159 - Stat points allocated, +10 Free Points

'DING!' Race: [Human (D)] has reached level 163 - Stat points allocated, +15 Free Points

'DING!' Race: [Human (D)] has reached level 164 - Stat points allocated, +15 Free Points

Jake felt himself grow in power and familiarity with the foes he faced. Even as he enjoyed himself in the euphoria of the hunt, he stayed calm enough to remember his primary goal for going hunting besides leveling.

A goal he met in the beginning of the eighth day as, finally, his Prima fragment got a response. Jake's eyes lit up as he stalked towards the Prima. It quickly became clear what kind of foe he would face, as he saw no regular beasts for nearly fifty kilometers of the jungle while running towards the energy signature. It was all Vinewood creatures dominating and basking in increasingly dense nature mana.

Soon enough, he even began seeing traces of his prey. Torn up ground, dried blood of beasts that looked like they had been dragged, and even a few pristine bones with every single trace of blood and flesh already devoured. Jake wondered what he was dealing with, but when the energy signature of the Prima felt like it was right in front of him, his prey entered his Sphere of Perception.

Vines... wood... the usual stuff, but rather than an animal, this just looked like a large bush. It slowly crept across the area with small roots dragging it forward as its body wrapped around the trees and larger plants while simply devouring and assimilating smaller ones. Jake used Identify on the Prima right away.

[Oakwood Brambleshrub Prima - 191]

It was more than forty meters across and ten meters tall. The huge mass of shrubbery was more like a moving mini-jungle than an actual creature. Jake stalked it for a bit as he prepared to make his move. He would use his blood as his poison of choice and keep a safe distance due to its low mobility.

Jake placed his Mark on the Prima as he scouted out the immediate area to make sure no other powerful creatures were nearby. Jake had noticed that Primas tended to be surrounded by those of their own race before, so he was a tad careful. However, this one seemed to be a solitary one, meaning it was likely also on the stronger side of the spectrum.

After checking out the area and finding no other living things, Jake wondered how to get a good vantage point. Due to the dense foliage, being more than a hundred meters away would obstruct his arrows, and even if he could now curve his arrows, it didn't really work that well with Arcane Powershot. He would need a clean line of sight and—

Wait, why not just...?

Jake looked upwards, summoned his wings, and jumped to quickly emerge from the dense jungle. As soon as he got above it, he grinned. Large trees and some plants still emerged, but the jungle itself was only really a few hundred meters tall due to its high density, and due to the jungle constantly regrowing, each plant was not as powerful as, say, the trees around Haven.

The creatures of the jungle were still well protected down there due to having a "roof" over their heads, obstructing vision and functioning as a barrier to many types of attacks. Moreover, there was much cover inside the jungle if an opponent attacked from above.

That last point only really mattered for beings able to actually move and dodge. A category the Prima squarely did not fall into.

He flew up nearly two kilometers but didn't go any further, staying below the faint clouds floating about and dodging the flocks of birds sometimes coming by. He would prefer not to get interrupted. As he was up there, he did notice some other predators clearly also using the jungle as their hunting ground. One of them was a touch close to him —a silver-colored owl with large eyes that stared at him for a moment.

[Silvernight Owl – lvl 188]

Jake stared back before the owl decided to fly off, showing that owls were indeed pretty smart birds. He shrugged as he pulled out his bow and focused on his Mark of the Avaricious Hunter below. Arcane Awakening activated in the destructive state, boosting all his offensive stats by 50% to give him some extra firepower. With a mental command, he activated Pride of the Malefic Viper and began condensing dozens of explosive arcane bolts in the area all around him. They were not made with the intent of actually doing damage to the Prima, but merely removing the upper barrier of greenery.

The Prima was still moving slowly below, oblivious to what was about to happen. Jake nocked a stable arcane arrow with some of his blood poured on it, his quiver already full of pre-prepared arrows. He began charging Arcane Powershot and, at the same time, launched his arcane bolts. He didn't do so with much power, but more or less just let them all down towards the jungle as he charged his attack.

He held nothing back as he infused energy into Arcane Powershot, and dense arcane power soon swirled around him. Nearby clouds distorted and were dragged in as Jake focused on the shot. He charged the attack for nearly fourteen seconds with his entire upper body searing in pain before finally releasing it to an explosion of pure power.

Half a second before he released the arrow, the arcane bolts reached the jungle, and an explosion that would put nearly all pre-system bombs to shame rocked the jungle. Each bolt sent out destructive arcane mana for hundreds of meters around itself, and with more than fifty of them hitting at once, a jungle area of several square kilometers suddenly found itself with a large part of the upper foliage destroyed.

The Prima below reacted as it was hit by remnant arcane energy, but none of it was strong enough to harm it. Jake had focused on destroying the jungle and not actually killing anything, after all.

The same thing could not be said about the next attack.

Parting the arcane energy, a single arrow descended along with a storm of destruction that tore a hole straight through the massive, bush-like creature before impacting the ground below. Jake heard what sounded like an angry roar, but had already released the follow-up. The explosive arcane arrows rained down, courtesy of Splitting Arrow.

Another carpet-bombing session was initiated, and even larger sections of the jungle were destroyed with the Prima right in the middle. While it didn't feel like he did much damage due to its large size, his Mark of the Avaricious Hunter made him aware he indeed did, as the Arcane Charge was building fast.

Jake fired off a few more barrages until, finally, the Prima seemed to have pinpointed its attacker. Before he could shoot again, he had to dodge to the side to avoid tens of wooden spears shooting at him. This was followed by hurled stone and boulders in massive numbers, the Prima's tendrils just tossing everything they could find in his direction, including entire damn logs.

Not that any of these had a chance to hit, as Jake kept his distance and dodged while releasing destructive arrows. The Prima tried to defend by intercepting his shots but found itself unable to, as the arrows curved in unpredictable directions

Come on, pal... you need to have more than that, Jake thought as he dodged the many projectiles. Each of the spears would pierce deep, but they simply didn't have a chance to hit.

Below, the destruction continued as the Prima defended itself while counterattacking as well as it could. Jake did notice how little damage he seemed to do and noticed it was constantly absorbing energy from the soil below. Lower parts of the jungle hundreds of meters away that had survived began wilting as the Prima absorbed energy to rejuvenate itself, but Jake quickly cracked down.

He took flight and swiftly flew in a circular pattern around the Prima, spreading poison mist to kill the plants and make the creature unable to heal. Jake didn't stop attacking either, but as he got closer to the ground, the Prima did find more ways of fighting back.

Vines shot up towards Jake as he dragged the fight out and just built up damage. He did get a few minor cuts as the bramble part of the Prima's name was shown. Each vine did not aim to merely wrap him up or stab him, but was lined with sharp thorns that would rip anyone apart like a chainsaw while draining their blood.

Jake managed to build his advantage for several minutes before the Prima made its move, clearly aware it was losing badly.

His sense of danger reacted, and he was forced to quickly flee upwards as more than a hundred tendrils emerged from the soil below. Jake released a blast of arcane mana to destroy some tendrils, then suddenly realized how useless that was.

Out of the corner of his eye, he noticed another tendril rise in the distance. Then another, followed by ten more. A hundred more. Like the jungle itself was rising towards him, thousands of tendrils reached towards the sky and tried to catch Jake—and he had no delusions that being caught would be a good time.

As he flew upwards, the cloud of poison bathed the many tendrils chasing him. Some of them began withering but were rapidly replaced by others, forcing him to repeatedly release arcane explosions behind him.

Somehow, the tendrils kept chasing even as he reached a kilometer high, but clearly, the Prima was running out of ones long enough. Jake took the chance and rapidly moved to the side to dodge away and nock an arrow. Arcane Powershot charged as the tendrils came again, but Jake just tossed them a glance with Gaze of the Apex Hunter, making them eerily freeze mid-air. At the same time, his sense of time slowed due to Steady Aim as he focused intently.

The nearly entirely purple arrow he had nocked was larger than any of the others, as it looked more like a spear, and pulsed with power. With the Prima infected with his poison, he had rapidly gained an understanding of it good enough to condense an Arrow of the Ambitious Hunter.

Jake released the arrow down towards the defenseless Prima and saw it sink into the creature just as it became able to move again. It writhed in pain, and the many tendrils swayed in mid-air as they seemed to lose strength. With a mental command, Jake activated the Arcane Charge from Mark of the Avaricious Hunter that had been charged more than Jake had ever done before.

For a brief moment, a flash lit up the world.

The swaying tendrils all began to wither, and the Prima below slowly turned black as it fell apart and began crumbling to ash.

You have slain [Oakwood Brambleshrub Prima - 191] – Bonus experience earned for killing an enemy above your level

'DING!' Class: [Avaricious Arcane Hunter] has reached level 160 - Stat points allocated, +10 Free Points

Jake stayed in the air as he gazed below. An area several square kilometers wide had been utterly decimated and left bare, with remnant arcane energy still lingering here and there. Without further ado, he flew down and quickly located the loot, which included the expected Prima fragment and an odd seed of some sort. He tossed the seed in his inventory for further inspection later, but for now, he had another matter to attend to.

Avaricious Arcane Hunter class skills available

CHAPTER 42

SKILLS, STATUSES, & A STEALTHY FUTURE

Finally, it was skill-selection time. It had been a good while since he had last selected a class skill. Shit, the last time he'd picked one was when he got Steady Focus of the Apex Hunter during the Treasure Hunt. It felt like ages ago. Since then, he had gone to the Order and mainly focused on alchemy, so his class had really been put on the backburner. Not that this time spent hadn't also benefitted his class. Through his profession, he had gotten a lot stronger, especially when it came to his magic and energy control.

Jake did not know what he wanted from this skill selection. He considered if he needed a good melee skill but still wasn't entirely certain on what Path he wanted to walk there. Not that what he wanted necessarily mattered anyway when it came to what the system offered... Well, it did to some degree due to Records and all that, but for the most part, it was down to what he had done and experienced, not what he wanted.

So, without further ado, he opened the menu and, as was customary, saw a disappointing first offer.

[Looping Arcane Bolt (Epic)] – The only thing better than one arcane bolt is two arcane bolts. Allows the Hunter to summon a large arcane bolt that will passively drain mana to recharge itself and release arcane bolts every few seconds towards any designated targets. The large arcane bolt can be detonated at any point, releasing destructive arcane mana. Adds a bonus to the effectiveness of Intelligence when using Looping Arcane Bolt Arcane Orb.

Arcane Bolt, but now self-firing or something? From how he understood it, he could summon a bolt that would then shoot more bolts, allowing Jake to set up remote towers to bombard people. He liked the idea... if it summoned a bow that shot arrows, that is.

True, this could have some practical applications here and there, such as the fight he'd just had with the Prima, but it wasn't like he needed it, and he viewed it more as a bit of direction for what he could do by himself without getting a skill.

As it was, this skill was just proof Jake had continually improved his mana control enough for the system to unlock this skill. Something the next skill also did.

Arcane Lance (Epic) – *Just a bigger Arcane Bolt. What did you expect?*

Yeah, that wasn't actually what the description said, but it was exactly what it was. A big Arcane Bolt that was now an Arcane Lance that took longer to charge but did a lot more damage. Jake could already do that and sometimes even did, and considering he had no interest in gaining the extra stat-scaling from having it as a skill, he moved on.

[Twin-Fang Whirlwind Strike (Epic)] – *May your fangs embrace the wind as a whirlwind is born from your strikes. Allows the Hunter to infuse both weapons with potent wind mana and perform a circular strike to create a whirlwind that cuts and rebuffs all foes around you. Twin-Fang Whirlwind Strike can be repeatedly performed to further empower the whirlwind and persist for a small period even after the skill is no longer performed. Adds a small bonus to the effect of Agility, Intelligence, and Strength when using Twin-Fang Whirlwind Strike.*

Three epic skills in a row... but this one did not include anything related to arcane energy, something Jake more or less felt used to at this point. No, this was pure wind magic, a school of magic Jake hadn't really dabbled in at all outside of that one bow he got in the tutorial, and that had just been an item. So the question was... how did he get it?

His first guess would be that his class just liked to offer some melee skills, and Jake had the affinity, with his second guess being that a certain green murder bird was the cause. In any case, the skill itself looked interesting and clearly took some inspiration from Fang of

Man. However, it didn't really click with him. It required him to be in melee, and when Jake fought in melee, it was usually against foes he overpowered or when he did so defensively. This skill did have some defensive applications, but it struck him more as a skill that affected a large area and needed some charge-up to work, which was not the kind of melee skill Jake wanted. He could already imagine himself beginning the spinning to use the attack, only to get smacked away.

So, yeah. Jake was not keen on it, and thus moved on to a skill that was a lot more interesting.

[Arcane Stalker (Ancient)] — A true artisan of stealth, you stalk your foes as they remain none the wiser to your presence. You find it easier than ever to blend into the environment, making your presence, mana, and nearly all traces of your existence hidden as you move stealthily. You are hidden from nearly all forms of magical scans, and when standing still, your arcane mana will automatically create a barrier, making you appear one with the environment, even to the sense of touch. Adds a bonus to the effect of Agility, Perception, Willpower, and Intelligence while successfully remaining undetected.

WARNING: *This skill is unlocked by, and will serve as an upgrade to, your existing Arcane Stealth.*

Jake had already made some progress with stealth himself, going from a sucky inferior-rarity skill to a rare one, so for the system to finally recognize it and offer him a skill was no surprise. The skill itself also clearly built upon what he had already done before. Currently, he could make himself invisible when standing still and actively focusing on using his arcane mana to hide, but this skill would make it all more automatic. It was without a doubt a good stealth skill... but...

He didn't know why, but he didn't like it. Logically, he knew the skill was good, but something made him think picking it was a bad idea. Jake frowned as he closely read it a few more times, but he found nothing that indicated to him it would have any downsides compared to what he currently had. Yet the feeling remained.

For a moment, he considered asking Villy, but ultimately decided not to. His gut feeling told him to not take it, and he would trust that even over the advice of a god. He did consider why he felt as he did, and he only had one real guess.

I got the other upgrades myself...

It was comparable to if he was offered an archery skill. Jake seriously couldn't see himself picking a skill during the selection that upgraded his archery proficiency skill. He did remember some conversation with Villy about wasting skills by choosing to upgrade one in the past, so perhaps this was also part of it. Picking a direct upgrade would also inadvertently result in the skill not being as familiar to you compared to a skill you upgraded yourself, hence making it less powerful in nearly all cases. Finally, maybe this would lead him down a Path of stealth Jake shouldn't walk.

Anyway, he didn't feel like picking it, so he moved on to the final option. He saw the legendary rarity right away... and then the rest.

[Thousand Voices, Million Eyes, Single Mind (Legendary)] –
Resist and perhaps even channel the whispers of the void as your soul finds serenity in madness, solace in the unknown.

Sometimes you came across a skill you kind of understood why you'd be offered, but also noped the fuck away from. This was one such skill.

It didn't take a genius to figure out why Jake had been offered this. Even so, it did surprise him. It didn't make much sense to him that merely meeting a creature of the void would warrant unlocking a legendary skill. If that was so, wouldn't peak factions just have a god bring an entire army to gaze at one for a bit before leaving? Then again, would this skill fuck people up somehow? Or was it rare to get it offered? Did he gain the skill offered by not losing his mind?

Jake had many questions but only one answer: fuck no. He got a headache just remembering Oras, and the skill itself also had some shady-ass wording, making him believe it had a great chance of having... unforeseen effects. His guts also told him to stay the hell away from it.

To summarize, there were five skill options. Two related to arcane magic fitter for mages than Jake, one melee skill, one stealth skill that did seem great but made him apprehensive, and one with fuck-no void-stuff. None of them were skills he wanted to pick up, which begged the question... what would he pick?

He decided to scroll up through the list and checked skills he had considered prior but skipped for better options. One that quickly came to mind was one he had skipped at level 140 in favor of upgrading his Hunter's Mark: Barrier of the Avaricious Arcane Hunter.

[Barrier of the Avaricious Arcane Hunter (Epic)] – Stability is a cornerstone of your arcane affinity, making barriers an obvious application of your arcane. Allows the Avaricious Arcane Hunter to summon a barrier of pure, stable arcane energy, blocking out all kinds of direct attacks that attempt to pass through—both physical and magical alike. Mana or stamina will be consumed depending on the nature of the blocked attacks. All concepts not deployed by you will be significantly weakened within your barrier. Adds a small bonus to the effects of Wisdom and Endurance when using Arcane Barrier.

Currently, Jake did not have any real defensive skills. It also had the concept-suppression effect, which Jake found interesting. The thing that made him a tad reluctant was how much his own barrier magic had already progressed without any skills. Also... a pure magic skill like this just didn't feel like it "fit" with the rest of the skills for his class. All the ones he currently had—at least, the ones gained in D-grade—were related to archery in some way, while this one would have no relation. Sure, that was only two skills so far, not counting the ones gained from the evolution itself, but even those he had from his earlier grades all fit a hunter "theme" more than an arcane barrier would.

Also... the big reason... Jake felt like he could do what the skill did himself with practice. His mana control was improving every day and had especially taken a jump after he went to the Order. As he got more familiar with his arcane mana, he would learn all these things soon enough, same as the many Arcane Bolt skills.

Due to that, Jake kept looking through the list. A few interested him, but he also noticed some had disappeared, such as the Basic Nature Affinity offered all the way back at level 30 and the mental defense skill from level 40.

As he scrolled through the list, one suddenly jumped out at him. A skill Jake had skipped over back at level 50 in exchange for Bestial Survival Instincts—a skill that instantly became Moment of the Primal Hunter.

Perhaps he had not thought much about this skill back then due to how curious he had been about what would happen if he picked Bestial Survival Instincts... but... wasn't this skill damn good? Like, really fucking good?

[Stealth Attack (Common)] – The strongest blow is the one not seen coming before it is too late. Increase the power of the first attack made on

an otherwise unaware foe. Works with both ranged and melee attacks. Adds a bonus to the effect of Agility and Strength when using Stealth Attack equivalent to Arcane Stealth.

It was only a skill at common rarity. That alone was usually enough to make Jake skip it outright, but this one felt different. While it seemed like a super simple skill—Stealth Attacks do more damage—he now knew far more than back then. While on paper it seemed simple... it truly was not. While it wasn't some fancy or showy skill, it had something even more important: conceptual power.

Like his Mark of the Avaricious Hunter, it did something theoretically possible to do without a skill, but it would be so hard that Jake had no chance. Anything that gave direct damage or directly increased something without any drawback was naturally useful, and this one was an all-around improvement to Jake's repertoire.

He could also often strike when unseen due to his high Perception and ability to locate his foes with Mark and his sphere, making it immediately useful. There were only so many ways to make his Arcane Powershot more powerful, and this was one of them.

But equally as important, it could be upgraded. Jake's stealth skill had been shit when he got it. His archery skill had also been at inferior rarity yet was now epic. While he right now had no idea how to upgrade it easily... he had time.

Villy had told him a long time ago how valuable skill slots were, and having some kind of stealth attack was something Jake was certain he would one day want. To get it at common rarity meant he could mold it, and it would likely be a better skill for him at whatever rarity he upgraded it to than one he just picked up at an already-high rarity. That was no doubt one of the reasons why his Arcane Powershot was arguably still his most powerful offensive skill despite being only at epic rarity.

Having convinced himself, Jake picked up the common Stealth Attack skill. A bit of knowledge entered his head, but it was damn minimal and just made him aware that only the first attack would ever count, as it would count as if the foe was "aware" of him after that.

With it picked, Jake cracked his neck and took a deep breath. He checked his status for the first time in quite a while to see his progress so far.

Status

Name: Jake Thayne
Race: [Human (D) – lvl 164]
Class: [Avaricious Arcane Hunter – lvl 160]
Profession: [Heretic-Chosen Alchemist of the Malefic Viper – lvl 169]

Health Points (HP): 35682/46250
Mana Points (MP): 39888/72825
Stamina: 19369/33750

Stats
Strength: 3279
Agility: 6133
Endurance: 3375
Vitality: 4625
Toughness: 3358
Wisdom: 5826
Intelligence: 4703
Perception: 10243
Willpower: 4936
Free points: 0

Titles: [Forerunner of the New World], [Bloodline Patriarch], [Holder of a Primordial's True Blessing], [Dungeoneer VII], [Dungeon Pioneer VI], [Legendary Prodigy], [Prodigious Slayer of the Mighty], [Kingslayer], [Nobility: Earl], [Progenitor of the 93rd Universe], [Prodigious Arcanist], [Perfect Evolution (D-grade)], [Premier Treasure Hunter], [Myth Originator]

Class Skills: [Stealth Attack (Common)], [Basic Shadow Vault of Umbra (Uncommon)], [Traditional Hunter's Tracking (Rare)], [Arcane Stealth (Rare)], [Enhanced Splitting Arrow (Rare)], [Arrow of the Ambitious Hunter (Epic)], [Arcane Powershot (Epic)], [Big Game Arcane Hunter (Epic)], [Arcane Hunter's Arrows (Epic)], [Archery of Expanding Horizons (Epic)], [Descending Dark Arcane Fang (Epic)], [One Step Mile (Ancient)], [Fangs of Man (Ancient)], [Mark of the Avaricious Arcane Hunter (Ancient)], [Moment of the Primal Hunter (Legendary)], [Gaze of the Apex Hunter (Legendary)], [Steady Focus of the Apex Hunter (Legendary)], [Arcane Awakening (Legendary)]

Profession Skills: [Path of the Heretic-Chosen (Unique)], [Herbology (Common)], [Brew Potion (Common)], [Alchemist's Purification (Common)], [Alchemical Flame (Uncommon)], [Craft Elixir (Uncommon)], [Toxicology (Uncommon)], [Cultivate Toxin (Uncommon)], [Concoct Poison (Rare)], [Malefic Viper's Poison (Epic)], [Soul Ritualism of the Heretic-Chosen Alchemist (Ancient)], [Advanced Core Manipulation (Ancient)], [Blood of the Malefic Viper (Ancient)], [Sagacity of the Malefic Viper (Ancient)], [Wings of the Malefic Viper (Ancient)], [Sense of the Malefic Viper (Ancient)], [Touch of the Malefic Viper (Ancient)], [Legacy Teachings of the Heretic-Chosen Alchemist (Legendary)], [Palate of the Malefic Viper (Legendary)], [Pride of the Malefic Viper (Legendary)], [Scales of the Malefic Viper (Legendary)], [Fangs of the Malefic Viper (Legendary)]

Blessing: [True Blessing of the Malefic Viper (Blessing - True)]

Race Skills: [Endless Tongues of the Myriad Races (Unique)], [Legacy of Man (Unique)], [Identify (Common)], [Serene Soul Meditation (Epic)], [Shroud of the Primordial (Divine)]

Bloodline: [Bloodline of the Primal Hunter (Bloodline Ability - Unique)]

As usual, it had expanded—not only in length, but also, naturally, in numbers. Jake liked it when numbers went up. He had gained a lot of profession levels since his last check and upgraded his necklace, so he had especially gained a lot more Intelligence, Wisdom, and Willpower. Skill-wise, he had gained some upgrades here and there, such as his tracking skill and archery skill. Fundamental hunting skills, really.

On the topic of Free Points, since the last time he took a good look, Jake had invested 200 stat points in Agility, 200 in Strength, and the rest in Perception, as he still had to put some points in it. Investing in Agility and Strength did not feel super good, but Jake kind of knew it was necessary at this point. Having Strength as his lowest stat wasn't that bad, as it was still high compared to many other humans his level due to all his bonuses and Fangs of the Malefic Viper, but he still felt "weak" against pretty much every foe he faced. That was fine in most cases, as he could beat them with Agility and magic, but he still wanted some more Strength to not bottleneck himself too hard.

Closing his status, Jake flew up into the air again as he looked out over the jungle. He smiled to himself and continued this hunt.

This time with a focus on stealth.

More accurately, Stealth Attacks.

CHAPTER 43

COVERT WILLS

Jacob sat in his office and stared at the item lying on the table in front of him. He picked it up and felt its metallic surface. Their smiths had already tested the metal and found it completely unrecognizable. Even those who had Patrons said they were unable to identify the metal, meaning it either had to be new to the universe or made by the system specifically for this item.

[Key of the Exalted Prima (Unique)] – *A key to the Seat of the Exalted Prima. Allows entry to the Seat of the Exalted Prima.*

The key belonged to the Church, as most items of value did, and Jacob was the current safekeeper. He stared at it for a while as he considered... well, everything.

The upcoming event was all about different Paths if one had made different choices. Jacob had made many choices that he questioned himself about, all the way back to the day the tutorial began. Shortly after entering the forest, Jake had shot a boar that attracted a larger level 10 boar that had attacked them. While Jake had killed the beast, Joanna had come away crippled.

Back then, Jacob had admonished the man for his decision. He had blamed Jake, and Jacob believed that decision had been what initially tore a wedge between him and the rest of their group. Then, when Jake had defended himself and killed three men... they'd all blamed him again.

He couldn't blame Jake for leaving the group and going off on his own when confronted by Richard. If he had stood up for Jake then, things would have been different, but Jacob's bad decisions didn't end there.

Jacob had been used by Richard, fooled by Caroline, and ultimately tricked by both to lead Jake into an ambush... He had stood by and done nothing worthwhile as all the people he felt responsible for had been killed one by one. He had been cowardly and stuck by his own rules of non-aggression... He had decided the fate of so many people.

That had "rewarded" him with the class of Augur. A fate Jacob was quite comfortable with. He liked who he was now, for the most part, but he still couldn't help but wonder: What if he had done differently?

What if he had pushed Caroline and maybe started an uprising against Richard? What if he had tried to keep Jake close? What if he had killed William when he had the chance?

He did know that even if he'd ended up killing William back then, it would only have led to everyone dying later on due to a beast tide when Jake eventually progressed far enough in his quest to defeat the King of the Forest. However, would that truly have killed them all if they had done all they could to progress and fortify their settlement?

So many doubts haunted him, and they had for a long time. He couldn't even claim that he now only did what was best for the Holy Church. He made decisions not necessarily beneficial for the Church, but for his own personal feelings. Jacob had warned Casper about the goals of the Church and that plans were being made to crack down on the Risen. Needless to say, sharing such information was clearly not in line with the goals of his faction.

Jacob even had to do so during the World Congress, too, as it was only there the gods could not peek at his conversations. He was fully aware there was already much scrutiny on him from several internal factions due to a number of factors. His friendship with Casper was just one of them, but that he still stayed relatively close to Jake was even more of an issue to many. While the Order of the Malefic Viper was not an enemy of the Holy Church, they were definitely not allies either. They were more of a faction that the Holy Church ignored and left alone—an approach they had wanted Jacob to take with Jake, too. Add to that the fact that the Holy Church was losing more and more influence on the planet and their ever-falling chances of becoming the World Leader... Things were rough.

What if I had made different choices? Jacob repeatedly asked himself.

Chances were he would be dead. He was reasonably sure he would be dead, actually. That wasn't the most important thing, though. It was a question of if the planet would be in a better state if he had died. Without him, the Holy Church would still be there, but he knew they would be far smaller. He at least gave himself that much credit.

The work of the Church had also only become easier in recent times. The former King of the Forest seemed to have reined in the wild beasts quite well, and attacks on settlements had practically dropped to zero. The system event of Unusual Unions had also helped immensely, with many beasts and monster factions now even working with human settlements. There was still conflict, and many humans did not want monsters in or too close to their cities. Attacks on settlements also still happened here and there, but such was unavoidable. In the same vein that humans could attack beasts in their habitats, so did humans have to accept the fear of being attacked in theirs.

Feeling the key in his hand, he considered using it. He knew he could. He found it a bit hypocritical that his job was to guide others to their ideal Path while he so often questioned his own... but perhaps that was part of it.

No... I have made my choices.

A future had been realized partly due to his choices. Jake had become a Progenitor, Casper was an influential figure of the Risen, and Bertram still lived by his side. Even his own survival mattered, as he knew things that would be beneficial due to his class. He knew that undercurrents were building and that the independent factions were preparing something. Something big.

Putting the key down on the table, he decided it would go to Maria, the strongest fighter in their city—possibly excluding Bertram —even if she was only a mercenary and not a member of the Church. It would benefit her the most. She had been part of the hunting teams for one anyway, and Jacob knew she wanted one. Bertram had already made it clear he had no desire to get a key himself.

It was probably a decision that would once more bring scrutiny upon him. Nothing would be said or done openly, just small whispers in the corners questioning him. He could seek to silence it, but he saw no point. No, he would stop questioning himself and begin reaffirming himself. He closed his eyes and sighed.

I know my task.

To choose the best Path for Earth. The best Path for the most people.

Even if that Path did not include the Holy Church.

As a Malefic Dragonkin, Draskil had killed his first C-grade when at level 173 or 174. Needless to say, Jake wanted to beat that by killing one even earlier. While Jake wasn't entirely confident he could beat Draskil even if they were the same level, he had a large advantage when fighting higher-level foes due to his class and even his profession. Alchemy allowed him to often come out on top in drawn-out fights—something any bout with a C-grade was bound to become—and his entire class was about punching above his weight class.

With his new Stealth Attack, he had even more confidence. Not right away, necessarily, as he planned on spending the next few days practicing and trying to improve it. He checked the time for the event and saw he had nine days left till the system event with the Seat of the Exalted Prima began.

Nine days of hunting.

Thus, his journey as a stealth archer in practice began. Before, when Jake hunted through the jungle, he would tear up a path and kill everything that attacked him, but now he went slow. He would slowly stalk through the greenery and always stay hidden.

Each time he struck, he did so unseen. His senses made him know if his foe was aware of him, allowing him to more easily land Stealth Attacks. Except, he quickly ran into one issue.

Danger sense was not something necessarily unique to Jake. Honed warriors and nearly all beasts also had some form of danger sense, and even if it was far weaker than Jake's Bloodline-empowered ability, it was still there. This meant that the moment Jake released his attack and his arrow headed towards the beast, the beast would be aware, canceling out the effects of Stealth Attack.

That sucked. Big time. At least Vinewood creatures seemed to have no proper danger sense, allowing Jake to easily land sneaky attacks. He did notice that he could get stealth hits in melee for beasts, but only if he struck when they were right next to him. He managed to barely land a Stealth Attack on a pig-like beast that wandered right next to a Jake hidden with Arcane Stealth.

Also, magic attacks did not count as ranged attacks. Only physical blows did, which the scaling with Agility and Strength had quietly hinted at. Funnily enough, throwing a rock would trigger Stealth Attack, but a stable arcane bolt would not. Ignoring the absurdity of that, Jake quickly found more and more lacking aspects of the skill. Then again, what could he expect from a common-rarity skill? He did not doubt it would have been way better back at level 50 and E-grade in general, but it was pretty damn hard to use in D-grade.

However... when it did hit... Jake did not know what he had expected when he picked it up. Maybe damage a few percent higher? Five to ten percent seemed fair enough to him. Oh, boy, had he been wrong.

Stealth Attack effectively increased damage by a third when it was triggered. Thirty-three fucking percent damage bonus from a common-rarity skill. Sure, it was hard as hell to actually land a Stealth Attack, and it was limited to one a fight, but it was so much more powerful than he could have ever expected. He did regret not picking it up earlier in some ways, but then again, he had not really picked any skills he didn't like. A few had fallen to the roadside, like Descending Dark Fang, but he was confident he could improve them with time. Shit, it even had fang in the name.

Now, thirty-three percent was great, but landing an Arcane Power-shot with it triggering was borderline impossible. The energies it gave off just made it too easy to notice for anything with halfway decent senses, making it only applicable against foes such as elementals. And even if it did land, Arcane Powershot was partly magical... so, yeah.

Needless to say, Jake would work on improving that. To do that, he first had to figure out what Stealth Attack did, exactly. Not what its effect was, but why there was an effect at all. Jake quickly bit onto the fact that he did not expend any extra energy at all, but that did not mean there wasn't anything extra added to his attacks.

There was... something. It was subtle. Jake would not quite call it energy; it was more like all the energy already in the attack was affected subtly. The energy did not truly change, but was somehow "primed" to work as a Stealth Attack. Jake reckoned this was done by the concept behind Stealth Attack.

These were the things Jake could swiftly discover himself, but it was only the first step. Even if he saw changes, he also needed to know what happened with these changes when actually used. How could this changed energy and concept suddenly disperse the moment a creature was aware it was being attacked?

Not just aware of the attack itself or its nature, but just that *some-*

thing was attacking it. Jake was lucky and found two foes fighting, where he confirmed that his Stealth Attack did work, meaning the foe just had to not be aware of the attack *he* launched.

The next day was spent experimenting even more, as he killed quite a few beasts and Vinewood creatures, but his hunting speed had definitely slowed down compared to the week prior. Not that his time was fruitless, as he finally got a good idea of what to do with the Stealth Attack skill. A skill that truly was limited, making the entire common-rarity tag make more and more sense.

So, Jake had several goals and avenues of improvement.

First of all: magic. He needed his stealth skill to work with attacks of a magical nature. Right now, what was considered a magic attack or not was highly arbitrary. Arcane Powershot was only partly physical, but his explosive arrows were not at all. Hence, the explosion didn't benefit from Stealth Attack; only the small initial impact of the arrow did.

Secondly, he needed some kind of consistency against different foes. He needed it to trigger even if the opponent became aware of his attack, as quite frankly, the current form of the skill was just useless against some enemies, like beasts. There were two ways of doing this: obfuscation or a change of trigger requirement.

Changing the trigger requirement was simple enough in theory. Jake just had to ensure that even if the enemy was aware of *a* blow coming, it had to know more of the attack or attacker than the current rules required, either by requiring it to know that Jake was the attacker and maybe even locating him, or by making sure that Stealth Attack worked as long as Jake fired the attack while the foe was unaware.

Obfuscation was trickier. The goal here would be to hide Jake's attack until the moment it hit. Jake knew a thing or two about danger senses, as he had quite a potent version himself, but that didn't make his danger sense fundamentally different than others. For the danger sense to trigger, some part of you had to be able to sense it. In Jake's case, it was primarily with his sphere picking it up or his even more overpowered intuition warning him. Most often, these two worked together along with all his other empowered senses, and that resulted in his overpowered danger sense. For beasts, it was much the same.

Perception-related abilities were not rare at all, and Perception as a stat allowed most creatures to sense things around them, especially mana. Everyone could sense mana in their environment, and Jake firing an arrow that disrupted energy within his foe's "Sphere of Perception" would make them aware of his attack, rendering Stealth Attack useless. So Jake would have to hide it somehow.

This did not deal with the intuition part. Many actual danger sense skills used intuition, even if it was considered far less reliable. The description of Bestial Survival Instincts back then had even said, "has a small chance to feel a distinct sense of danger from any attack," which was, as the name suggested, a common ability of beasts.

Naturally, an ideal solution would be to change both the trigger requirements of Stealth Attack and hide the attack for maximum effect. The issue was just figuring out how to do that, as well as allowing it to work with magical attacks.

One thing was certain: It had to do with the odd sensation of concept he got from his attacks. The invisible concept was something only he could see and feel. His first issue was figuring out how to actually engage with it. It was untouchable to energy, and no matter how Jake tried to somehow affect it, he failed.

Yet he did not give up, instead trying different approaches. He figured out more and more nuances of the skill, such as how the blow did not count for his poisons at all, but only the initial impact, and the one time he managed to land an Arcane Powershot from stealth on a Vinewood creature that seemed to be in meditation while hidden in a tree canopy, he saw how the damage amplification was a lot less than it should be, according to his "adding a third" assessment, confirming his prior theory that Arcane Powershot would be limited. This made Stealth Attack increase overall damage by way less than a third—not because the amplification did not scale, but because of how much "magic" was involved in Jake's archery by now, especially with poisons mixed in too.

Another day went by, Jake using his new skill repeatedly. He did not consider much other than merely figuring out how to improve Stealth Attack. How to apply the concept to the magical aspects of his fighting style or how to make it more reliable. He used it on different foes, sometimes failing, sometimes succeeding, and he did get a sense of improvement and a feeling his success chance had increased.

His only method of improvement was to simply use the skill over and over again to observe what *he* did when the skill was used. One had to remember that the user was the cause of every skill. The originator. This meant Jake was the one who infused the concept into his physical blows, and as long as he could figure out how and why he did that—

something the skill currently did without Jake consciously noticing—he would be able to control it.

The breakthrough came in an unexpected way. As Jake was hunting a boar-like beast while in deep focus, he sat hidden with Arcane Stealth and nocked an explosive arcane arrow. He was so focused on drawing his bow and trying to observe the process as the Stealth Attack concept was applied that he didn't even notice himself mutter under his breath before it had already been done. He muttered his so-far unspoken hope towards the arrow.

"Be stealthy..."

CHAPTER 44

STEALTH ARCHER TRAINING

Willpower.

Out of all the stats, it was the one Jake understood the least. Intelligence made him a bit faster at calculating stuff and probably helped with other mental things while making magic more potent. Strength made him stronger. Wisdom made it easier to remember things and increased his mana pool.

All of them made sense and had some form of scaling in combat. Perception was also a difficult stat to understand at times. It increased all his senses, even if he suppressed most of them the majority of the time, as knocking yourself out from every bad smell seemed like a bad idea. But... Jake knew what it did, improving his reaction speeds and such. Jake also sensed a very noticeable correlation between high Perception and increased energy control. However, another factor for energy control was Willpower.

Willpower as a whole was weird. Every single action someone performed included aspects of Willpower. Of the more tangible aspects, It also increased mana regeneration, but Jake would definitely say the primary benefit of Willpower was assisting in controlling energy. Alongside Perception, it was the primary stat when it came to controlling pretty much anything. That was why when Jake used the domain part of Pride of the Malefic Viper, he could summon far more magic in his immediate area, as his Willpower was "buffed" inside the domain, so to say.

This was a very overt and obvious application—the conscious use of Willpower as Jake actively tried to control something. However, when Jake was merely swinging his weapon or firing an arrow, he did not actively infuse Willpower into the process, but just went through the motion. As these motions were willful, Willpower would naturally come into play and enhance the effects. It was subtle, but Willpower more or less made everything done more powerful, as long as the action was done intentionally.

Then there were Words of Power, the absolutely most direct use of pure Willpower there was. It was when you only used Willpower and a bit of energy mixed in to make something happen. You quite literally imposed your will upon the world and made your words law to make it obey. Forcing something to move or ordering an entire planet to explode—both things were possible, depending on how much Willpower an individual had and their ability to apply it.

Words of Power were to speak your will to further amplify and focus it. It was incredibly standard, and the most common use of Words of Power was when speaking the name of a skill or an incantation related to one. Some skills even required one to speak to muster enough Willpower to make it possible. The Sword Saint was a good example of this, as many of his skills made use of Words of Power. This did not mean speaking the skill was a good idea every time. Jake, as an example, had no skills where it would help with anything, and Words of Power also had the downside of increasing the cast time of skills. Also... it would look stupid if Jake went around screaming "Arcane Arrow!" every time he shot one.

The one place where it made sense for Jake to use Words of Power was when he was practicing using his Willpower or ordering a pen to fly to his hand while working. This incident happened to fall into the first category, albeit accidentally, as Jake finally found the trigger for Stealth Attack.

One so simple it was stupid.

He just had to will for it to happen. To actively infuse his Willpower into an attack to make the Stealth Attack concept appear. He did this instinctually with physical attacks due to the common skill, but not with magic skills. Jake naturally tried and willed for his magical attacks to work with Stealth Attack, but it was not enough without him actively focusing on that aspect. It was not a matter of stats either, as influencing more energy naturally required more Willpower.

However, the concept was reinforced when he spoke—no, ordered —the explosive arcane arrow to work with the skill. Not just the small physical impact, but the entire arrow was thoroughly infused with his will and intent for it to be a Stealth Attack.

He saw it fly forth, the concept remaining strong until it finally hit the unsuspecting Vinewood beasts that looked like a mix between a bear and a horse with long, thin legs. The resulting explosion was more powerful than any explosive arcane arrow Jake had ever landed before without using Arcane Powershot or Arcane Awakening.

About a third more powerful.

The Vinewood Beast was enraged at being attacked, but Jake was not in the mood to play. Arcane Awakening activated at 30% as he engaged and quickly finished off the level 172 creature. Then he retreated and once more returned to being a stealth archer.

He searched for his next foe and nocked another explosive arcane arrow. This time, he did not speak but merely focused on the arrow, as there was no way he would make speaking a habit when trying to be stealthy. That would be utterly moronic and look very, *very* stupid.

And a little bit funny... but mostly stupid.

Jake focused on infusing his Willpower into it as he spoke and willed in his mind for it to work. He soon enough felt the same sensation as before. He released the string the moment he did, and as the arrow flew forth, a notification appeared.

[Stealth Attack (Common)] -->
[Enhanced Stealth Attack (Uncommon)] – *The strongest blow is the one not seen coming before it is too late. Increase the power of the first attack made on an otherwise unaware foe. Adds a bonus to the effects of Enhanced Stealth Attack dependent upon the nature of the attack. This effect is further improved by the level of Arcane Stealth.*

An explosion sounded out once more, with Stealth Attack working exactly as he intended. The word intended was crucial here. As with all skill upgrades, it had to come through conscious thought and not just happenstance and accident. Of course, there were some cases where it was arguable if something was truly intended, but the system did what the system did.

Jake smiled as he flew forward and finished off his prey before properly looking at the upgraded skill.

The upgrade seemed like the most straightforward kind there was, just adding an enhanced tag. All Jake had done was add magic, but from reading it, he now guessed it was *all* attacks, no matter what kind they were. It also changed the scaling of the skill to depend on the nature of the attack while still retaining the tie-in with Arcane Stealth.

Usually, people would be happy and lay off a bit when getting a skill upgrade, but Jake felt the exact opposite. He was already so engaged in upgrading and analyzing the skill that stopping now would be a complete waste of momentum. While he would test the new version and confirm his theories, he would also move on to the next task:

Making it more consistent. Now that Jake had added power to the skill, he needed it to actually work. More power didn't matter if it remained useless against beasts and enemies with even halfway decent senses and Perception. Using his newfound discoveries of the importance of controlling and infusing this "stealth concept," he began the next step.

A step that included the wanton slaughter of foes more than a dozen levels above himself as he enthusiastically tried to find a path to an upgrade.

The Vinewood creature rapidly moved on its four legs as vines and thorns spread out to attack the group, but several barriers sprang up to block the ranged blows. Most of the barriers broke, but the hunting group managed to hold on through collective effort.

Arrows, spells, thrown weapons, and even non-projectile ranged attacks rained down on the Vinewood lizard. Individually, only a few of these attacks would deal noteworthy damage, but together they proved highly effective. The creature was forced to retreat, allowing the group leader to make his move.

Sterling pushed his palms together as magical scripts revolved around him. Space compacted into spatial bindings that suppressed the Vinewood creature, allowing the melee strikers to launch the final assault.

A man and a woman, each carrying a massive sword, attacked with their blades raging and burning with deep red flames as they smashed the creature. Fire damage was highly effective on Vinewood creatures, and though the lizard struggled, nobody in their group let up before it was dead for good.

"Good job, everyone," Sterling said as he nodded at his group.

Taking down a level 171 beast with their group consisting primarily of individuals between 120 and 130 was an achievement, even if he was 143 himself. There was a total of twenty-two in this party, quite a lot more than the customary five, but Sterling had always found the number five needlessly arbitrary. As long as you avoided dungeons, it was better to have more people.

He watched as the scavenger began taking all the useful parts of the Vinewood creature for their alchemists back in the city. His brother was the City Leader and had emphasized the importance of keeping their progress and power up. The United Cities Alliance had a lot of internal competition, and even if Sterling was highly valued due to being a space mage—not to mention a central figure in the largest hidden project of the United Cities Alliance—he could not slack off. In fact, he had to keep progressing to keep that position, as their success would have a huge impact on deciding their planet's fate.

After they were done cleaning up and relaxed a bit, they moved on. Two archers functioned as scouts, and a few minutes later, they found their next foe. It was a large, sloth-like beast at level 179—a touch above what they usually went for—that was lazing around in a tree.

"Alright... prepare to strike," Sterling said, as everyone knew what to do. The archers had their arrows enchanted, the mages prepared spells, and the melee folk got into position.

However, just before he gave the order to engage, something else happened.

A pillar of powerful energy descended from the heavens and exploded the entire tree, with something impacting the sloth itself. It was smashed onto the ground as the ground shook from the impact. The beast managed to stand, but another pillar fell, and the sloth nearly lost an arm trying to block.

Several more attacks fell as the beast tried to flee, but the attacks kept finding it no matter where it went. Sterling finally managed to spot the attacks and saw... arrows? They bent around the trees and struck from unexpected angles from above, making the sloth utterly unable to escape. Moreover, he saw the sloth bleed far more than usual, and the repeated self-healing he would expect from a beast did not happen.

Sterling just stared and made his group pull back. Only he and the two warriors remained as the sloth finally succumbed to its injuries. The moment it died, a figure descended. Black wings of death and a body burning with powerful energy akin to the arrows landed right before the sloth, his presence alone making Sterling fearful.

The space mage instantly knew who it was. Sterling froze and took a few steps back as the man turned towards them. Beastly yellow eyes stared Sterling down as he bowed and retreated fully, cold sweat running down his back. The warriors did not hesitate to follow suit. As he ran, he failed to hold himself back from taking a peek. He saw the man penetrate the body of the beast with his hand and pull out the bloody Beastcore. Though barely audible, he felt like he heard the man speak to himself under his breath.

"Still not there yet..."

Jake had felt it that time. For an incredibly brief moment, less than a hundredth of a second, the Stealth Attack concept had persisted even after being discovered. It was such a short time, but it was there. Jake would not fault anyone for believing their senses had merely been off, but Jake wholeheartedly trusted he was on the right track.

He threw a quick glance at the retreating hunting party as they hastily ran. He didn't bother with them, but he did judge them a little, as he found that hunting in a big crowd like that was highly inefficient. Five was the sweet spot for a reason, and having more than twenty was just overkill outside of wars. Okay, to Jake, the optimal number was one, but he did recognize some did better in parties. Still. Twenty was not a party, but a goddamn rave.

Turning his attention back to his failed Stealth Attack, he finally believed he was onto something. It would soon be a week since he upgraded the skill to uncommon rarity, and while that seemed like a long time, his growth had been meteoric when it came to improving the skill. He had even figured out how to time attacks to hit two Splitting Arrow shots within the same moment for both to benefit.

Yeah, that part was not that useful.

What Jake had also learned was that the stealth concept was very... fragile? Ephemeral was probably a better big-boy word for it. Few potent concepts would just disappear like that, but this one clearly did not matter what he did. However, there was some progress, as he did discover that the Stealth Attack did linger for such a short amount of time that even he could not notice the concept disappear when the beast became aware. That it was not instant meant that he had a path. He just needed it to linger longer.

Jake had tried many things to do this. He had infused more of the stealth concept and tried to make it more prevalent but found that useless. Many other methods had even been attempted, like trying to somehow "copy" his Arcane Stealth effect to make the arrow not look like an attack and meld into the environment, and while that seemed possible theoretically, it was not something Jake could figure out in any short amount of time. It would probably be easier to upgrade Arcane Stealth somehow, when he thought more about it.

He kept trying out things, but during a brief round of Serene Soul Meditation, he remembered something. Arcane Barrier.

It had talked about suppressing concepts. Jake did not want to suppress a concept, but he did want to influence it, and clearly, his arcane affinity could. Concepts and affinities were heavily interlinked, after all. Jake's arcane affinity could also be called his arcane concept, and within that concept were primarily two parts. Destruction and stability.

And what did Jake's Stealth Attack need, if not a bit of stability?

With that idea in his head, he got to work. His recent kill was proof it was possible to extend the Stealth Attack for a fraction of a moment without losing any of the effects, so he would just need to do what he did best:

Continually smash his head into a wall until it worked.

It was a bit like mixing a concoction or an alchemical brew. Jake needed to find the right mix and achieve balance for him to avoid "washing away" the stealth concept. At the same time, he had to make sure the Stealth Attack got enough stability to do what he wanted. Now, mixing two affinities outright was not easy, but the Stealth Attack did already contain some stability within. It had to.

Stability as a concept was in no way unique to Jake's arcane affinity, and he had to truly separate it from his affinity before it worked. He needed to reinforce the stability of the Stealth Attack and not try to mix in anything more related to his arcane affinity. It did take some time to truly figure it out. He just had to really get the infusion of Willpower down. With every try, it got slightly better, until finally...

Jake took aim at the owl that sat on a tree. He was once more flying above the jungle, with the owl marked so he knew where he was aiming. He had perfectly remembered its surroundings, and now took aim as Arcane Powershot charged. The concept of Stealth Attack appeared automatically due to the skill as Jake mobilized more Willpower to try to stabilize it.

The moment he felt it was good, he let go of the string. Before it even hit the target, he knew, and the following fight was just a slaughter. The owl lost a wing from the initial impact—an impact that was fully empowered by Stealth Attack despite the beast noticing the attack just before it hit.

Another upgrade in the bag!

> ### [Enhanced Stealth Attack (Uncommon)] -->
> ### [Superior Stealth Attack (Rare)] — *The strongest blow is the one not seen coming before it is too late. Increase the power of the first attack made on an otherwise unaware foe. Has a brief grace period between the foe being aware and the effect still triggering as long as the foe is still not conscious of the Hunter's position or the nature of the attack. Adds a bonus to the effects of Superior Stealth Attack dependent upon the nature of the attack. This effect is further improved by the level of Arcane Stealth.*

Jake looked at the skill upgrade and smiled. Once more, it was viewed as a more or less straightforward upgrade, and he was totally fine with that.

In less than two weeks, he had managed to bring the rather useless skill from common to rare, now making it a powerful and reliable skill that suited him nicely.

A skill-upgrading journey that had also resulted in quite a body count as he had found unwilling test subjects.

And a big body count meant experience and levels.

CHAPTER 45

PHANTOMSHADE PANTHER

Jake decided to find a nice tree and take a seat as he opened his notification window to go over the last few days of hunting. There were many kill notifications, all of them giving experience, as a stealth archer was naturally always the one engaging, and why would Jake choose to engage lower-leveled foes?

As for levels... well, it was pretty good, as his hunting speed kept picking up, and in his fervor to upgrade the skill through trial and error, he probably ended up hunting faster than before. Especially when he considered the ever-growing level of power of his prey.

Checking it out, he was at least satisfied.

'DING!' Class: [Avaricious Arcane Hunter] has reached level 161 - Stat points allocated, +10 Free Points

...

'DING!' Class: [Avaricious Arcane Hunter] has reached level 164 - Stat points allocated, +10 Free Points

'DING!' Race: [Human (D)] has reached level 165 - Stat points allocated, +15 Free Points

'DING!' Race: [Human (D)] has reached level 166 - Stat points allocated, +15 Free Points

Jake looked at the notification and saw his level. 166. He'd gained four class levels and two race ones from that. *This has to be enough, right?*

He believed it was. Draskil had done it at 173.

That's right...

With a bit over a day left till the system event, it was time for this stealth archer to take down his biggest prey yet.

It was C-grade hunting time.

Now the issue was just finding one. No, not just finding one, but finding one suitable to hunt. One Jake was good against would be preferable. This meant it needed to be flesh and blood, probably a beast of some kind, and if it was not on the more durable side, that would also be nice. He wanted to avoid prey with healing powers if possible, as Jake knew that he would risk running himself dry. Fighting any C-grade would require Arcane Awakening to be active from start to end, putting him on a timer, so facing a foe able to turtle down and wait him out would suck.

The reason it needed to be flesh and blood was naturally his rare Hemotoxic Poison, his most potent toxin to date. He had made it with C-grade hunting in mind, so finding an elemental or something like that would be inadvisable.

His other requirement would be a good hunting ground, but honestly, the jungle was fine, if not downright great for him. He had a lot of space to kite, and he had already tried and tested the effectiveness of striking from above to land Stealth Attacks with excellent results.

With all of that in mind, he set out on his hunt.

--

The Malefic Viper had naturally observed as always, nodding as he saw Jake's recent skill upgrades. Nothing was overly unexpected so far —not because what Jake was doing was normal, but because Vilastromoz had gotten used to it. Pointing out the fact that it could usually take months of deep meditating to identify and become familiar with the conceptual changes brought on by such a skill would be a waste of time. Jake's level of perception was truly disgusting, and the Viper was not just talking about the stat.

He had a policy of never giving Jake direct advice on picking skills or upgrading them. Doing so would only lead to adverse effects down the line. Perhaps it would help him upgrade it now, but the next upgrade would only get more challenging, and the god fully expected

Jake to one day reach godhood on his own anyway. Trying to "help" would only risk hampering that.

Vilastromoz failed to hold back a small smile as he recalled his old days. A skill starting at low rarity was just that—a starting point. While getting one that was higher rarity was all fine and good—in most instances, the preferable choice—there were also cases where it was not. Stealth Attack was a case where picking it was clever. The Viper had never wanted to ask or question Jake about getting the skill, and he had to admit seeing Jake pick it was a pleasant surprise.

Back in his day, he hadn't picked up quite a few skills... One he had skipped for a long time had been called Scale Armor. Instinctually, the Viper had passed it back in F-grade before he even had anything close to sapient thought. Back then, it had been useless, as the Viper had been small and an ambush predator. Chances were, if caught and hit, he'd have lost anyway, so running away was better, making more robust scales useless.

Naturally, it was skipped in E-grade and D-grade too. The useless inferior-rarity skill was ignored, and the Viper had already gained other defensive means. The Malefic Viper had always been a magic-focused beast, so getting magical defenses just made sense. Who needed stronger scales with a powerful mana shield and a cloud of miasma warding off any foes daring to engage in melee?

His thinking on that hadn't changed until C-grade—late C-grade, that is. His decision-making then had spawned from interacting with some humans who had theorized these low-rarity skills could be worth it. As he'd had no other skill choices he truly wanted at the time, Vilastromoz took a gamble and picked up the weak skill. The day he got it, he'd been disappointed, as it did nothing besides making his scales a bit tougher to physical attacks... but he recognized something in it.

A concept spawned by the system. Simplistic damage reduction. A flat damage reduction on every blow, that is. Its effect was so weak right when he got it, but it got stronger and stronger as time progressed. He adapted the skill, made it his own, fused it with Dragon Scales when he reached B-grade and refined it more... until one day, it became a skill known to many alchemists and followers of his:

Scales of the Malefic Viper.

It was quiet. Incredibly quiet. Far more so than in any other areas of the jungle. Rather than encountering beasts or Vinewood creatures every few minutes, Jake now barely saw any, and those he saw were all towards the peak of D-grade. Jake hunted a few, but they were not his target, and even the stronger ones didn't offer a good challenge.

None of these foes were beings born of struggle or created from extraordinary circumstances. They had just grown up in an environment with high mana density, making them grow powerful just by time passing and hunting each other. Nothing compared to genius-level beasts like Sylphie or the hydra Snappy had been back in the day. They were just regular beasts... and so were the vast majority of C-grades.

Jake was not looking for a powerful C-grade. All C-grades were already powerful to him, and he knew he didn't stand a chance against something like the Termite Hive King. No, he needed a lower-tier C-grade, and after spending the next many hours searching, he thought he had found one.

He had seen several already: A massive treant that towered above the jungle and made all the greenery sway and wave in its wake. An owl that looked to be made out of metal and used light magic that Jake did consider as a target, but it had taken off before he got a chance to properly assess it. A third had been a Vinewood Elephant that was also utterly massive and looked to be made entirely out of bark. As he did not want to fight a being that was not of flesh and blood, he quickly moved on.

Finally, he'd found his current target, which he had been tracking for nearly an hour.

The beast was no larger than a regular specimen of its species. Its entire body was black and covered in sleek, fine hair. Four paws soundlessly hit the underbrush as it hunted peak D-grade beasts and creatures, consuming their cores or other natural treasures, with Jake covertly observing from a distance.

Identifying it, the name fit.

[Phantomshade Panther – lvl ???]

Jake had been keeping an eye on it to get an idea as to how powerful it was and what it was capable of, and he had to say... it was weaker than expected. It was undoubtedly a C-grade, but the fact that it hunted peak D-grades was evidence enough it was struggling to fight others of the same grade. Compared to the three other C-grades he saw, it was far behind. Still stronger than any of the peak D-grades, but still.

In an hour, he had seen it kill three opponents of the Vinewood variant. It seemed to use a mix of dark and space magic, coupled with incredibly high Agility, to take down its foes. The Panther was a bit of a glass cannon, though, and he saw it take a few minor wounds here and there. Even if these did rapidly heal, the mere fact that these D-grades could hurt it was a testament to its relative weakness.

He did find it peculiar how its flesh, even beneath the hair, was black... and how it bled entirely black blood. The way the wound healed also looked weird, but who was Jake to comment on what kind of physique made sense for a C-grade?

Checking the time, Jake had around eleven hours left till the system event. He smiled a little, knowing it was enough time, and made all his preparations. He marked the Panther and kept tracking it as he took to the air. It had just engaged a beast to fight, and he would wait till the moment it stopped to relax after the kill—something it had done every other time.

It did not take long before the Panther had won, and Jake felt his Mark stop moving. He could not make an Arrow of the Ambitious Hunter, as he had yet to understand its physique, but he could still land quite the opening blow. He had already prepared his arrows with his rare Hemotoxic Poison and now pulled one out. He activated Arcane Awakening in the offensive state and began charging Arcane Powershot.

The Panther was still unaware as arcane wrath descended upon it. It reacted only a moment before impact by rapidly dodging, but the arrow was too fast. The beast was hit in its side, opening up a deep and nasty wound. Stealth Attack naturally fully triggered.

Jake followed up, but his next attacks were dodged as the Panther instantly locked on to him. He had just nocked an arrow when his danger sense exploded, making him stop what he was doing and step down just in time.

A claw emerged where he had just been as the Panther teleported right up to him. Jake quickly stepped down again as the beast rushed him with anger in its eyes. Space distorted in the wake of its charge, bending everything between them as a dark streak cut across the sky.

Luckily, Jake was far gone and managed to land a potshot before rapidly flying upwards to get some distance. He glanced back at it, and just before it charged, he turned and shot an arrow again while using Gaze of the Apex Hunter, finding it worked even better than expected as the Panther froze for a moment. His arrow, already in the air, hit the Panther, infecting it with even more poison.

Come on, you can do better than that, Jake thought.

The Panther stared at him for a moment before it began to emit black smoke. The smoke absolutely obscured the form of the Panther as it charged once more. Jake smirked a bit when it entered his sphere, and he easily sidestepped the beast, pulled out Eternal Hunger, and managed to stab the C-grade in the side before he stepped down, teleporting away once more.

He teleported, but the Panther seemed to have read him and followed a moment later. Jake blocked the paw and found his arms buckling as he was pushed back. Another swipe left a nasty cut on his arms, tearing his bracer apart, but before it could land the third blow, Jake used Gaze once more and, with a Descending Dark Arcane Fang, smashed the Panther down towards the ground.

Before it could stabilize, Jake fired a barrage of Splitting Arrows that exploded in a torrent of arcane energy, sending it tumbling down even further. Four black crescent waves were sent in return as a swipe tore up space itself, but Jake managed to dodge between two space tears while firing an Arcane Powershot rapidly charged through the use of Steady Aim.

The beast tried to dodge, but Jake had predicted its movements. The Powershot slightly curved and smashed into the Panther's stomach, sending it barreling down towards the ground, creating a crater on impact.

His foe had taken great damage, but there was no way a C-grade would go down that easily... no matter how weak it was. And damn, this one was weak. The mere fact that Jake had time to properly consider how weak it was during the fight was proof of that. It reminded him a bit of his first "true" D-grade kill against the giant lightning bird.

It was disappointing.

However, he would not let his guard down, and now he pressed the assault. The Panther was already healing, its black flesh wiggling, but the Hemotoxic Poison clearly did work. Its speed was incredibly impressive, and it could make itself invisible and attack stealthily—skills Jake already knew about from observing its prior fights. All things Jake could easily deal with.

Finally, it did something new.

He faintly felt space around him being affected, though the Panther did not move from down on the ground. Jake shot several arrows but found them all bent away from the Panther as it stared up at him. Looking back, he met its gaze, and the moment he did...

Everything went dark.

No, he was not knocked out, but all his senses were thrown for a loop. His eyesight disappeared, all sound was gone, all smells. Even Sense of the Malefic Viper was entirely cut off. Dense black energy had invaded his very soul, and Jake rapidly began cleansing it, but it was not something he could get rid of instantly. Even so, Jake did not panic. He still felt the space around him bend through his sphere, and he quickly adapted and made a plan. Acting as if his senses were all gone, Jake began flailing helplessly.

The Panther took the bait.

Jake felt the same charge attack as before. In an instant, the Panther appeared right in front of him and cut down with its paw to shred him into several pieces. The moment it committed to its attack, Jake stopped acting. He dove forward under the paw of the beast and got below the Panther before stabbing Eternal Hunger upwards and penetrating the Panther's belly. He then firmly held on with one hand as he placed his other on the beast and activated Touch of the Malefic Viper.

His senses returned just in time to hear the Panther hiss in pain as it tried to get him off. Something made even more difficult by Jake pulling out strings of mana to wrap around the beast as it tried to stretch its body and bite Jake, who just kept pumping poison into the C-grade. Fang of the Malefic Viper was naturally fully active on Eternal Hunter, pumping venom into the beast from the inside, and Touch pumped it in from the outside.

Finally, the beast managed to muster enough energy. Jake swiftly disengaged as the Panther's body exploded with space magic, leaving hundreds of small scratches on Jake's body from the torn space. The Panther looked spent as it stared angrily at Jake.

Let's finish this.

Jake stepped down and teleported to dodge a blow as the Panther tried to attack. The Panther teleported away when it failed to land a blow, but Jake was ready and stepped down once more to appear above the beast. With a blast of arcane mana, he sent it tumbling down, and an Arcane Powershot blasted it into the jungle below once more. Explosive Arcane Arrows then fell like rain as the jungle, along with the Panther, was torn apart.

Looking down, Jake felt disappointment when he activated Mark of the Avaricious Arcane Hunter. The Panther that was already on its last legs flashed with arcane light before it finally succumbed and gave him a notification. The beast rapidly began decomposing, and within a few seconds, its entire body turned to black smoke. Jake frowned.

He flew down and landed where he had killed the Panther but did not see any signs it had ever been there. No loot, no nothing. He got a feeling something was very off as he checked the notification.

You have destroyed [Phantomshade Panther Clone – lvl 204]

Wait, what!? Jake thought as his eyes opened wide.

Before he could properly grasp the situation, he suddenly felt more presences nearby. In the clearing created from the fight, Jake stood as four figures appeared. Four identical Panthers surrounded him on each side, and his frown changed into a serious expression as realization struck him.

He had only killed one of five clones.

Arcane Awakening fully activated a moment later as all four Panthers charged.

CHAPTER 46

IN THE JUNGLE

Jake launched himself into the air to avoid the charge of the four clones, and just in time, as the space he had just occupied imploded from the impact of four paw-swipes infused with potent space magic.

He pushed his wings to fly faster as he felt the approaching beasts. Twisting his body, Jake turned and shot off blasts of arcane mana while also landing a Mark of the Avaricious Hunter on all four of them. Not for the damage, necessarily, but also to keep track of them.

Four forms flanked him during his ascent. A part of Jake had hoped they wouldn't bother chasing him, but clearly, they were out for blood. Two usual responses would appear in this kind of scenario: fight or flight. Jake's survival instinct was by far his most potent one... and not a single doubt was in his mind at that moment.

Fight.

Blasting arcane energy to one side, he propelled himself into one of the Panthers and took it by surprise. In mid-air, he took hold of its pelt and tossed it towards another of the beasts as he began flying sideways, his wings leaving poison mist in his wake. Taking out his bow, he fired arrows directly ahead of himself, away from the beasts. The arrows flew straight for a while but soon began bending as they did a one-eighty turn and flew back in Jake's direction... while splitting into five each.

Jake flew between several arrows while the Panthers chasing him were hit by arcane explosions. They blocked them, but it bought him enough time to properly turn and shoot a well-placed Arcane Power-shot into one of the clones.

It hit the beast, and right away, the poison entered its body. When it did, Jake quickly noticed a difference... These clones were stronger than the one he had destroyed earlier. Not by overly much, but probably around ten percent.

Clones... split power somehow?

Jake wasn't sure, but what he did know was that the Panthers were done playing around. Before, they had chased him rather cautiously, which indicated they did not have a proper measurement of Jake... which furthermore probably meant there had been no shared memory or memory transfer from the clone. All they knew was that he had killed one.

However, even so, it was clear that the clones could communicate, at least while in close proximity.

Space around Jake suddenly seemed to shrink, as he didn't really move forward as he flew. Dark mana began collecting all around him, and black bolts appeared in the warped space—none of which Jake had time to address. He had to rapidly dodge to the side as a Panther teleported in front of him, only to find another one trying to take advantage of the opening. He barely managed to dodge between the swipes of two beasts by twisting his body and creating a platform of mana to step off.

He tried to get away, but the dark bolts bombarded him, and as space constricted even more, he found it difficult to move as he wanted. In melee, the two Panthers continued their assault. Jake was on the backfoot, not getting any chances to retaliate.

Need to get distance, Jake thought, gritting his teeth as he tried to break out of the contained space one of the Panthers had created. Both melee weapons had appeared at this point, and he managed to land a few minor wounds on the two beasts, but they also managed to hurt him by marring his body with several claw marks.

In a gamble, Jake dove forwards between the two Panthers. He spun around as arcane edges expanded from both blades to try and scare the Panthers away. It worked on one of them, but the one he tried to scare off with Bloodfeast Dagger simply swept the edge away and attacked instead.

Jake ducked at the very last moment, turning his body to block with one of his wings. The Panther tore up the flesh on it and promptly bit down on the joint. The teeth sank into the flesh, and pain ran through his body. The Panther bit down even more, ready to rip off the wing entirely. He knew the wing was a lost cause, so he decided to make use of it.

Stamina and mana both flushed the wing as Arcane Awakening was directed to overflow it with energy. In a flash, it began burning with pink-purple energy before promptly exploding in a blast that sent both Jake and the Panther flying away.

Blood sprayed all over the Panther and into its mouth, complementing the damage caused by the explosion itself. Jake himself had lost a wing, and if that was all, he would be ecstatic at the outcome of the exchange... but sadly, he was not fighting a single opponent.

The second Panther went in for his neck, and Jake barely blocked with an arm that he pushed into the feline's mouth to avoid the sharp front fangs. It still hurt like hell, but scales covered his arm just as he blocked to lessen the damage.

With his other arm, he managed to make a barrier of arcane mana to protect himself from dark bolts bombarding him. He did so long enough for the Panther currently biting down to begin shaking him violently, trying to rip off his arm entirely. He was tossed around, but he managed to not lose the arm, as the Panther eventually let go due to the poisoned blood soaking its throat. It tossed him towards the jungle below, with several dark bolts bombarding him on the way down.

With a tattered arm and a lost wing, he blocked the bolts as best he could while falling. On the positive side, he had gotten out of the compressed space, but on the negative side, he had taken a lot of damage. He had managed to also do some damage to the Panthers and had infected all but one with poison. However, the winner of this first exchange had clearly been the clones.

He took notice of how one of the clones stayed back, not engaging him at all. It had just done some space magic, with the one using dark magic being the one he'd injured earlier with Arcane Powershot.

Jake landed on the ground below, and before the Panthers could follow up, he sprinted into the dense jungle. Fighting them up in the air had been a terrible move, as it quite frankly gave him too much space. He had no natural obstacles he could use to block and was just surrounded up there, while in the jungle, he had the advantage.

One had to remember... Jake was now a stealth archer as well as a hunter.

Using his Marks, he kept track as they all followed him. Jake would honestly accept the result if they chose to disengage, but he failed to hold back a faint smile when he saw them chase. His body was hurting, and Arcane Awakening was still burning his energy and health away at a steady pace, putting him on a timer. That is why he didn't wait long before he went back on the offensive.

Taking a lot of ninety-degree turns, he managed to get them off his track for a moment. Enough for him to enter stealth once more as they lost track of his position. Jake had already noticed earlier how they needed a moment to locate him whenever he had teleported, proving they clearly didn't have a good tracking skill or particularly high Perception. This was fixed by them fighting together and one being at a distance to observe, but such was not the case right now.

Sneaking around, the Panthers were tracking him and had split up a fair bit, with one of them still flying in the air far above. The uninjured one. It had not moved but stayed far up, nearly at the clouds. At that distance, not even an Arcane Powershot would reach before it could dodge.

That left three in the jungle, all spread out in a triangle pattern as they searched. Pulses of dark mana passed over him, but his Arcane Stealth managed to keep him hidden, as he stood still whenever such a pulse came.

Just as another pulse had passed, Jake found an opening. A Panther had found an unsuspecting D-grade trying to hide and had decided to rip it out of the ground and tear it apart. Jake took the chance and fired an Arcane Powershot from behind.

The Panther reacted too slowly. It was blasted in the back and sent flying through several trees with an arrow now stuck in it. The moment he attacked, all of the Panthers became aware of him, and without hesitating, he retreated into the dense foliage again.

Just as he retreated, he found himself forced to lay flat on the ground as a ripple of space passed over him. Less than a second later, a black crescent wave passed, followed by several more as the Panthers tore up the area to find him. Jake just lay there, Arcane Stealth active as he blended in.

Clearly believing he had escaped, the Panthers assaulted another area, only for Jake to pop up again and land another Arcane Powershot on an unsuspecting Panther.

The best part about all this? Stealth Attack bloody worked every time they completely lost track of his position.

Once more, he tried to retreat, but clearly, the beasts were not interested in being made fools of three times in a row. All three charged him at once, ignoring their wounds and the poison running through their bodies.

Jake knew fighting them straight on was a losing battle, so he tried to dodge as he ran. Pride of the Malefic Viper activated for the first time and began condensing mana in his surroundings. Repeated arcane explosions sounded out in his wake, but the Panthers ignored them all to keep up the chase.

He tried to shake them off, but he was chased by one and flanked by two others. Out of the corner of his eye, he spotted a faint distortion in the air. Jake jumped just as a Panther appeared. He managed to get over the attack and condensed a platform of mana to stop his momentum just in time to dodge the second beast.

Flooding the platform with destructive mana, Jake exploded it and sent himself launching backward towards the chasing Panther. Taking it by surprise, Jake managed to land a cut with Eternal Hunger before fleeing once more. However, just as he thought he would get away, he suddenly spotted a problem.

Fuck.

In front of him, space was already distorting, and it became clear he had once more been trapped within some kind of spatial seal. However, this one was far more of a barrier to keep him from escaping than the space seal prior.

With reluctance, Jake was forced to change direction, but that resulted in him not being as fast as he should have been. A Panther teleported, and Jake barely managed to block as two more appeared. The second one he dodged by the skin of his teeth, while he was forced to simply take the hit from the last one, ripping up his back. His cloak and armor, together with the passive shield of Arcane Awakening, managed to take much of the blow, but his equipment was shredded, with five deep gashes still left behind. Jake managed to capitalize on the situation by stabbing a Panther with Eternal Hunger as he froze another with Gaze. Using all his strength, he spun around and used the impaled beast as his shield so the Panther that tore up his back couldn't strike again.

He was forced to let go of his weapon, jumping back and landing on the ground just as he teleported away. The clones chased him quickly, and different spells flew all around him. Jake gritted his teeth as he repeatedly teleported in tandem with the Panthers, always a single step ahead.

Pulling out his bow, he began firing arrows in all directions. One right in front of him, one a bit to the side, one above, and so on. The arrows curved around to hit the Panthers, with most of them missing but a few landing as intended here and there. The Panthers adapted swiftly and grouped up to make a barrier, rendering his assault useless.

Eternal Hunger had already been ripped out of the one Panther's body and left behind somewhere on the ground, but Jake suddenly felt its call. He didn't think but just wished for it, and it appeared in his hand. *It could do that?*

Not bothering to ponder it, Jake manipulated the shape of the blade slightly to make it a larger and firmly two-handed weapon. He then dismissed it, ready to summon it again when it was time.

From behind, a dark pulse went through the jungle, followed by a wave of black smoke that seemed to drown out everything. Jake could barely see through it, and it even absorbed sound. However, even more importantly, Jake noticed the smoke infiltrate his body.

It was poison.

Dark poison.

This kind of trap would surely work on many types of foes. A black mist that blinded them and weakened their senses, as well as poison seeping into their bodies to amplify this effect further. A real nasty combo, actually.

Well, except for Jake, who failed to hold back a grin. All he felt was his mana regeneration spike. He did notice that the Panthers also absorbed some of the mist to counteract the Hemotoxic Poison and other toxins he had infected them with, but it was far from enough.

The Panthers waited a dozen or so seconds for Jake to lose his senses. Which he did. His vision was blurred with dark spots, his hearing muffled, and even his sense of touch was all off. To really sell it, Jake began firing arrows into the air, having already noticed that the odd spatial seal didn't affect his arcane arrows. It was likely just meant to seal living beings in, and not all energy, as that would make the cost skyrocket.

While Jake found himself satisfied with the result, a beast him. He purposefully reacted just in time by blocking with his bow, the legendary weapon more than durable enough. Jake was smashed back and into a tree as the same Panther followed up. Two more hung back, with one of them expelling the mist and the other seemingly trying to speed up its healing.

He took a few more blows that he barely blocked before he made the Panther smash him into a large tree. The idea appeared, and he instantly executed. As expected, the beast charged him, and just as it leaped, Jake used Gaze of the Apex Hunter, barely still able to see the Panther through the mist due to his insane Perception.

It flew through the air as Eternal Hunger appeared. Using the tree as a counterweight, the Panther smashed into the sword head-first, impaling itself entirely. Instantly, the other Panthers reacted, but Jake was too fast. Bloodfeast Dagger appeared, and he rapidly stabbed down on the skull of the beast dozens of times before finally breaking through. The moment he did so, the entire beast just turned to black smoke.

Two down... three to go.

Jake felt like he'd just had a major victory, but then he noticed how little the Panthers seemed to truly care. The one who had been healing still waited for the one pumping mist to stop, realizing it was useless. Instantly, the poison mist began dispersing, and he saw the two injured beasts stare at him as his Eternal Hunger changed back to its regular shape again.

A two-second staredown later, Jake decided it was a good time to return to being a stealth archer, so he stepped down and teleported back. He had just appeared when the two Panthers followed him, and instantly he noticed...

Faster.

A swipe hit him from the side, and as he blocked, he found himself sent flying away even more than before.

And stronger.

It was confirmed. For each clone he killed, the others got stronger. It was only a little... but it wasn't good. Far above still was the third Panther, clearly still not interested in joining, and Jake could only begin to imagine what would happen when it was down to the last one.

Kind of exciting, wasn't it?

CHAPTER 47

THE MIGHTY JUNGLE

Clones... Jake knew a bit about them. Making a clone was something many, if not most, would learn to do eventually. In most cases, making a clone was more or less cutting off part of yourself to act autonomously. It could also be to just create a copy that shared all senses and that you still had to somewhat control, but these were often classified as puppets instead.

This varied further from illusion or mirages, which were entirely fake and often only existed for brief periods, while many clones could persist permanently. Illusions and mirages did not need to be intangible, either, but could often interact with the world around them to some extent. Naturally, they were usually far weaker than the main body, but they could help.

What the Phantomshade Panther did was a high-level cloning technique. Each clone could exist independently, and from the looks of it, the Panther used them for hunting on their own, indicating shared experience. It was pretty much just one beast split in five for improved hunting speed and to consume five times as many natural resources. Brilliant optimization, even if each copy was weaker.

Splitting in five did not necessarily mean equally splitting power five ways, though. Each could easily retain half or more of the primary body's power from before the split. Considering how much stronger they had gotten after he killed the first and second one, Jake reckoned each had around seventy percent of the true body's strength... maybe closer to sixty. High-level clones did also mean they were far harder to form, and it likely took a long time to make just one for the Panther.

Either way, considering just killing one clone was a pain when there were five, it only got worse with three. It was limited, how much synergy four or five beasts fighting together could reach—even if they were the same creature—simply due to the limitations of the jungle and the need to avoid hitting each other. It wasn't like one was a support Panther and the other a ranged attacker. In fact, their pure magic kind of sucked.

But... reduced to two fighting purely in melee, they no longer had to care as much. With the two of them now even more powerful in addition to this, Jake soon found himself pressured more than before. Their level of recklessness had also increased, as they chose to sacrifice their own bodies to try and injure Jake.

Jake was continuously pushed back by two aggressive felines swiping and biting at him, space warped all around. He held Eternal Hunger and Bloodfeast Dagger tight, but his arms were hurting from blocking, and he got no indications of the Panthers stopping their assault. Nor did he see a path to escape.

He tried several times to disengage, but every time he did so, space around him contracted, and when he used One Step Mile, he teleported a far smaller distance than he wanted with the two cats still hot on his trail.

Worse yet was that even if he handled these two, there was still the one flying in the air above the jungle. A completely uninjured copy, and with the energy transfer from the clones, Jake understood why it did this. Wounds did not heal when a clone died, so if he had managed to damage all of them heavily and then killed them one by one, he would win far more easily. By saving one clone, the Panther would always have a spare to absorb everything and return to full power.

As for if it had a sixth one hidden somewhere, Jake was certain it didn't. He had spent enough time interacting with them to feel the subtle connection between them. It was faint, but it was clearly there, and he only sensed the three remaining ones. There also had to be some limitations to using clones and the energy transfers. If not, why would the Panther have even shown up with all its bodies and not kept one far away? Even with his senses, he could not rule out the connection was only there due to their proximity... but his intuition told him he was right.

This won't work. Jake still gritted his teeth as he was pushed back by a Panther. He dodged its next attack and managed to stab it before he was hit on his shoulder by the second one and knocked away. A nasty gash was left there, but Jake had accepted that to get a chance.

He and the beasts had exchanged many blows, and while he was winning the battle, he was losing the war.

When he landed, he instantly jumped, resummoned his wings, and flew upwards. The Panthers chased, and Jake barely dodged one as the other teleported right next to him. He chose to take the hit as he kicked it hard.

That backfired, as the beast rapidly reacted and bit down on his foot the moment he kicked... and that was where the poor cat fucked up. Some things were not meant to be chewed. The saying that something was like chewing leather when it was too tough did not come out of nowhere, and when the Panther bit down, it encountered an impossible opponent.

Jake's old leather boots.

With incredible pressure, the Panther bit down, and Jake felt incredible pain as the bones in his foot broke, but at the same time, he heard something else break. One of the long fangs of the Panther had snapped in half when it failed to penetrate the leather, making it yelp in pain.

Without even a moment's hesitation, Jake swept up the broken fang with a string of mana and caught it in his hand. He kept flying upwards, the beast refusing to let go, so he tossed the fang he had already made into a weapon with Fang of Man. He hit one of the Panther's eyes, finally making it let go as he managed to get some height. The second Panther was already hot on his heels when he made it out of the jungle to the open air above, where he headed straight for the uninjured Panther.

This was clearly an example where injuring or killing all opponents at once would be the most effective. Classic boss mechanics. The two other Panthers were already heavily injured and were infected by quite a lot of poison. Taking them down was not too difficult. The problem was the final one. If he killed those two, he would be left with one fully powered and uninjured Panther, leaving him in a far worse position.

So he wanted to at least get an edge now before he would have to face it. Maybe he could even goad the Panther into engaging him with the two remaining ones. Jake flew towards it with great speed and saw it just standing still in the air far above him, staring down.

Two Panthers flanked him as they teleported, but Jake himself began running vertically upwards, every step hurting like shit on the injured foot. He even managed to inject the two cats with even more poison and get some distance by activating both their Marks, making them flash with arcane energy and roar in pain.

About halfway up, the Panthers suddenly stopped. Jake took two more steps before his danger sense suddenly spiked. Spiked intensely. Not realizing why, Jake took out his bow and drew an arrow as Steady Aim activated, slowing down his perception of time significantly. He did not necessarily do this with the intention of shooting an arrow... He just needed the time.

With everything slowed down, he perceived it. Space was contracted and was cut off all around him. A cylinder-shaped path had been formed between the Panther up in the air and the two chasing him, no more than five meters across. When within it, Jake didn't even notice it. Not even his sphere picked it up, as space didn't even distort more than what usually happened with continued teleportation.

He also realized that power was building up both behind and in front of him. Jake was, at this point, forced to release his arrow as his senses returned to normal. There was no more time. He understood what was about to happen at that very last moment, and his eyes opened wide as he roared.

Space magic colliding never led to good results. The backlash on the caster was also absolutely immense... which would've mattered if the casters suffering the backlash in this situation hadn't been clones. From below, small black tunnels of dark magic and space formed before each Panther. Ahead of him, the uninjured one prepared itself.

It all happened at once.

Something cracked.

The sky was torn as if a plane of glass had been cut down the middle. A black, bullet-like form was the cause of the crack, and as reality shook, a second crack formed that shattered the horizon, caused by a second bullet. A cross-shaped rift in space tore the entire airspace above the jungle asunder for dozens of kilometers in all directions, a winged human figure caught in the middle.

The remaining two Panthers were dead. Two clones had been sacrificed to create a technique that could prove lethal or at least heavily damaging to many mid-tier C-grades. The remaining Panther stared down at the cracked space before it, the rift perfectly torn in a straight line. The only remnant of the human having ever been there was a single arrow fired just before the collapse. One that flew harmlessly by the Panther.

However, as seconds passed, the beast clearly noticed something was wrong. There was no notification or sign of the human's death. The beast realized this a moment too late.

A tear in space was cut open, and Jake suddenly appeared right in front of the Panther, space reforming right behind him. He stabbed forward and left a nasty cut on the beast's face as it recoiled and retreated, disbelief in its eyes. On the other hand, Jake just stared at it as blood bled from his eyes. His entire body was filled with cracks, blood seeping out of them, with scattered broken scales spread throughout his skin. One of his arms was gone and several holes marred his chest, some of them even cutting straight through him so you could look through his body. His wings had naturally also been torn off.

As he stood there, he quickly used the ability of his necklace to summon a healing potion into his mouth, then consumed it for extra effect. He also activated the Second Wind enchantment from his pants. His body was flooded with vital energy as he began healing, his mind still racing from what had just happened.

Scrolling back a few seconds, Jake had found himself in deep shit.

Space around him had suddenly become incredibly rigid. Then, without any warning, a Panther had teleported up right next to him. It hadn't even attacked, its entire body burning with black flames as space distorted around it. The beast had blown up the very next moment, costing Jake an arm, and everything around him had begun shattering and falling apart.

Then a second Panther had appeared and done the same to his other side. He'd been caught between two collapsing spaces within a rigid space tunnel that also collapsed. Everything had imploded and shattered down upon him as he felt like he was about to be torn apart... and then time had slowed down.

Moment of the Primal Hunter.

Reality had seemed to freeze. Jake had felt like he was in the most extreme maze of mirrors imaginable. Like his own remaining arm was several meters long. Like his body was not truly solid, but merely made up of many small fragments with holes in between. Nothing had made sense... but it hadn't needed to.

Jake had just needed to survive. He hadn't needed to understand, just to trust his judgment and not hesitate.

So, he'd stepped down. Space had seemed to warp once more as

Jake forced the skill by pouring in all his energy. Stable arcane mana had enveloped his body to keep himself whole as scales also appeared. Pride had helped stabilize what space he could... enough for him to see it.

No matter the situation, reality was still there. If it was not, it would be the Void... something no C-grade could bring forth. And as long as there was reality, there was some space to travel through. His step had landed as his body unraveled. Holes in space—small vacuums —were unavoidable. It'd felt like he was riddled with bullets as holes formed all over, and yet none were lethal. His body had swayed, moved, and dodged through a reality his mind could barely comprehend, but with everything slowed down and his survival instincts at the highest they had perhaps ever been, he'd managed to minimize the damage.

His Sphere of Perception had fed information about the path, his danger sense had made him angle and dodge the most dangerous vacuums, and his intuition had made him aware this was the only way. The only path forward hadn't been "out" of the spatial tunnel, but through it—straight towards the Panther.

This path would normally have been nearly impossible to find... but Jake had had a guide. A single arrow that had been fired. One soaked with poison that had made it out of the most tumultuous space and was ahead of the tunnel collapsing. It became his guiding light as he found his way out, and the moment before time resumed to normal, he'd pulled out Eternal Hunger—a weapon that not even the collapse of space could harm. He'd cut through the final barrier of space and entered stable space once more, right in front of the Panther.

This brings us back to the present. Jake stood in front of the beast with only one arm, the blade pointed forward. His bloodshot eyes still bled, and he was a mess, but his gaze was firm. The Panther stared back in disbelief and took a few moments to collect itself, allowing Jake to take advantage of his potion and Second Wind.

The Panther got out of its stupor and, for the first time, looked at him with new eyes. Rather than indifference and a hint of disdain, he now only saw respect. Jake returned the gaze in kind.

He had believed the Panther a C-grade on the weaker side. An assessment that was clearly off. The C-grade frog he had met in the Mangrove River was nothing compared to the beast before him. He'd been confident beating it back then, even in an unfavorable environment.

Mutual respect was given. They both knew they faced another

predator and that neither of them had any intention to back down or retreat.

And after showing respect, the Panther did not give its opponent any more time to regenerate before it attacked. Jake was finally facing the beast at full power.

CHAPTER 48

THE HUNTER SLEEPS TONIGHT

Jake did not have time to consider anything but the battle in front of him—not even the notification he had gotten after he escaped the collapsing space tunnel. His body was marred with wounds, and the only injury on the Panther was a single cut left by Eternal Hunger. A cut that had benefitted from Stealth Attack, as he had been hidden in the folds of space.

A swipe came from the right, but Jake managed to block. A follow-up from the left forced him back as the beast rapidly pushed its advantage. Lacking an arm made fighting incredibly difficult, especially considering the foe he faced.

Stronger. Faster. Every single speck of the Panther had been heightened. However, he was certain of one thing: It lacked energy. While the Panther had not fought in melee, it had used large-scale magic, especially with that final attack. Additionally, chances were it had portions of its energy reserved due to the clones, and even if it gained its stats back, that didn't mean it also gained mana, stamina, and health.

That was why it didn't use any complex magical attacks right away, coupled with a potential adaption method. At least, Jake guessed that was why as he was smashed downward by a swipe. His left arm was rapidly regenerating as he focused on his vital energy to make it happen. The holes covering his body would have to wait for later, and he managed to stop the bleeding by blocking off the wounds with the passive barrier of Arcane Awakening.

Jake fell down as the Panther charged him. A swipe sent crescent waves of dark space mana towards him, making everything vibrate. Jake stopped his fall as he stepped down on his one good leg, teleporting away. He found himself traveling further away than usual, but he didn't question it, as he quite frankly didn't have the time.

The beast did not have any interest in letting him escape and teleported in pursuit. A pulse of dark mana was emitted, but Jake felt no sense of danger from it. The pulse somehow hit the fabric of space itself, and several small cracks appeared out of nowhere in the middle of the airspace.

Tendrils of dark mana emerged and lashed at Jake, forcing him in specific directions. He knew the Panther had planned this but was forced to comply. A spatial prison was slowly formed around him... yet he didn't feel like it was an issue. Jake stepped down and, with no fanfare, teleported straight past the spatial lock and out of it.

This was clearly not a part of the Panther's plan, and Jake took the chance to fire off a blast of mana to accelerate himself towards the ground. Picking up on what Jake intended, the Panther gave chase. Another pulse and more cracks in space appeared, sending tendrils out to stop him. Jake looked down and saw the ground half a kilometer away, tendrils blocking his path. Without hesitating, he stepped down and appeared below, once more passing any obstacles.

One Step Mile definitely upgraded, he thought as he jumped forward, dodging a blast of space mana that blasted a several-meter-deep hole in the soil. Jake got below some trees and attempted to hide and give him more time. His arm was slowly regrowing, but he was no Eron and couldn't just instantly regenerate. He needed a few minutes, and fighting while healing was a bad idea. Any half-arsed attack on the regenerating arm would set him back, just wasting the vital energy.

Jake sprinted, every step hurting like hell, but he could not slow down. A pulse passed, and just as it did, he stood completely still and used Arcane Stealth to hide. It worked, and he began running again, but then a figure suddenly entered his sphere.

The Panther ran a bit off to the side of him and would luckily pass, so as long as he stayed sti—

A second Panther entered. Then a third. And a fourth. Dozens of Panthers appeared and scouted the jungle, and Jake was in disbelief... until he finally felt their energy signatures. It was weak. Each of them was barely tangible as they scoured the greenery for him.

Rather than clones, these were illusions or mirages. At first glance, and even to his sphere, they appeared real, but they were effectively just energy constructs. But even if that was the case, Jake knew they weren't harmless... especially not with so many of them.

Even if they couldn't hurt him—which he was certain they could—their presence alone made hiding nearly impossible. They scouted around, and while Jake was confident in his Arcane Stealth when standing still, he did not believe himself infallible.

Something that was proved correct as an illusion approached. It sniffed the ground and moved past him at first, but it stopped just as it did. It turned around and walked towards Jake, lifting its paw to swipe at the stable barrier covering Jake with suspicion.

Jake did not give it a chance as he stabbed forward. Eternal Hunger penetrated the illusion, and instantly the construct turned to black smoke. As he "killed" the illusion, he felt the true body of the Panther above instantly lock on to him. It was prepared, and Jake's sense of danger exploded as he used One Step Mile.

He teleported only fifty or so meters, as even with its upgrade, he was in a jungle filled with trees and other greenery. Fifty meters would usually be good enough, but in this case, it wasn't. The Panther had fully locked on to him, and Jake noticed a small mark left by the illusion just a moment before the beast struck.

Everything around him shimmered. Space itself seemed to contract as a tunnel was formed. The very next moment, a Panther was before him with its claw bathed in dense black energy. Jake tried to block but was sluggish from the odd movements of space. He had no time. The beast went straight for his neck to sever his head, but in the final moment, he leaned forward.

A paw smashed into his face. Jake felt bones in his neck crack, and he was only saved by the impact also knocking him back. His entire head would have been carved apart if not for the wooden mask on his face that allowed him to survive.

Jake smashed into a tree, but he quickly landed, teleported away again, and fled. He didn't think, just going in the opposite direction of the Mark indicated where the Panther was, navigating with his sphere. Using his eyes was not an option, as even if the mask had blocked the impact, the eyeholes were still there. Eyeholes that had allowed the dark space energy to utterly annihilate both his eyes and much of the flesh surrounding them.

His Gaze of the Apex Hunter had been removed as an option, but luckily he only needed a bit more time. Flesh wriggled, as most of his left arm had reformed by now. The Panther attacked once more, and

Jake was forced to face it with his right side to protect the left, resulting in him getting knocked away with yet another gash.

Without the healing earlier, he would likely be dead by now, but he held on. His skin was flaying more than before due to Arcane Awakening having been active for so long. He was in an incredibly precarious situation as the beast kept up the constant assault until, finally, he was ready.

Jake blocked a blow as the Panther tried to take advantage of his weak left side. Instead of meeting no resistance or making Jake dodge, the paw impaled itself on a dagger. A newly formed arm held it, the skin being covered with scales as they fought.

When it recoiled for a moment, Jake took the chance. He stepped down and appeared several hundred meters in the air above, and with a second step, he teleported to the side as he spun in the air, taking out his bow. He managed to only get a single arrow off before several figures leaped out of the jungle towards him.

The remaining illusions summoned earlier.

Not wanting to give them any chance, Jake's empty eyeholes opened wide as Presence of the Malefic Viper intensified. An arcane barrier was formed that instantly exploded, destroying all the illusions. Something that proved a wise decision, as all of the illusions also exploded upon destruction, functioning as Panther suicide bombers.

His primary target was still below. Jake did have the minor issue of no eyes, but he could still track it with Mark and his sphere, and he felt the poison ravaging its body. The Panther seemed to believe he was unable to find it, as Jake felt dark magic move below, but his Sense and Mark both got obscured partly. While he could not see it, he imagined the beast had created a dark mist or something to cover itself. It appeared that it wanted to deal with some of the poison while charging up another deadly attack.

Sadly for the Panther, it had made one mistake. While it had clearly analyzed his sphere and many of his abilities to some extent, it had failed to realize how bonkers his Perception stat truly was. The winner was clear in a battle where it tried to hide from his Mark that scaled with Perception.

Jake charged and shot an Arcane Powershot, tearing up the jungle below. The Panther was surprised and partly hit as it jumped away and teleported into the air. Jake felt some of his poison infect the beast and followed up. Curved arrows blanketed the air as he consecutively activated Splitting Arrow to try and catch the cat.

It teleported away from most of them but was hit by a few exploding ones here and there, as it seemed to have a difficult time differentiating between exploding arrows and the stable ones. The unpredictable curving didn't help either.

Teleporting back a few more times, Jake tried to keep a distance as he attacked. The Panther chased and teleported too, trying to lock him down, but his upgraded One Step Mile seemed to primarily be about breaking through such restrictions, letting him escape again and again.

Their battle quickly moved across the sky, wayward blows tearing up the jungle below. Jake even got a kill notification at one point as an Arcane Powershot missed and struck something else. Naturally, he had no time to check it as he pressed his momentary advantage.

The Panther knew it would lose a ranged battle, so it picked up the pace. Jake felt its body suddenly burn with energy as mana impacted his body. He suddenly felt like his sphere was full of stuff... Mana. It brought him back to the first time in the Forgotten Sewers rat dungeon. He reacted a bit slow when his danger sense warned him, resulting in him getting blasted back by a space bolt of sorts.

Adapting quickly, Jake analyzed the domain unleashed by the Panther. Shortly, he saw a cat-like figure charge him from the side, and he reacted promptly. Believing the Panther did not expect him to adapt so quickly, Jake swiftly dodged under the claw and stabbed Eternal Hunger upwards, penetrating the head of the Panther.

Which proceeded to explode in his face.

Jake was tossed back, his right arm filled with wounds, and his chest burned with black spatial energy. Five more figures then appeared in his sphere as the beast reverted to using exploding illusions. All of them were shrouded by the domain of black mana, making Jake unable to distinguish between them.

Five charged, and Jake sent out stable arcane bolts towards each after failing to summon a barrier like before. Four dodged, while one was hit and exploded. The remaining ones closed in, and Jake tried to release more attacks, only getting one before the last three were upon him.

One of them is real, Jake thought. His intuition was clear: All three of them attacked from different directions, and it was a pure matter of chance... he would usually think. Because he also felt something else that conflicted with that thought. No matter which he chose, he felt like he would be wrong.

Jake gritted his teeth and stepped down to teleport away. A Panther managed to follow him, and Jake blocked, sent tumbling back by what had to be the real one. Another of the three illusions then came, but Jake once more blocked, as that too was real. He realized this when he tracked not only Mark of the Avaricious Hunter, but also his poison. It was moving.

It can swap between them, Jake instantly realized. Likely another benefit of the domain.

An incredibly annoying ability that put Jake on the backfoot as more wounds covered his already-mangled body. The Panther was not doing that well itself, poison ravaging its body and the many blows Jake had landed during some of their scuffles doing work. Jake was certain he had been right about it lacking energy. It'd had low health points, stamina, and mana from the get-go. Contrary to Jake, it also had no potions to swiftly regenerate a bit.

Illusions closed in once again, but this time Jake was ready. He had gotten some distance, so he instantly drew his bow and nocked a special arrow. He had plenty of time to condense an Arrow of the Ambitious Hunter by now, even if the stamina and mana consumption to summon it was intense.

Jake knew he had to hit as he drew his bow and charged Arcane Powershot. He had only one shot, as his resources were dangerously low.

His perception of time slowed as three figures closed in, now with a cautious approach. The Panther knew this attack would be powerful, and Jake constantly felt it shift, with the beast not just charging in but keeping its distance to dodge. One in three... No, lower. It would no doubt be dodged in the final moment. So he would just have to stop that.

Gaze was out of commission, but he had one more method to lock down an opponent for a moment's time. His presence flared as it blanketed the sky. For a moment, he pushed back some of the domain, and Jake focused everything on the illusion the Panther was currently in. Pride of the Malefic Viper was on full display as Jake attacked the psyche of the beast. He had begun to feel its desperation as it repeatedly failed to kill him, and now he capitalized on it. Jake made it feel the full brunt of his unshakeable confidence that he would win.

It hesitated for less than half a second.

His string was released, and the arrow flew forward. The Panther reacted only a moment too late. The attack sank into its body and sent it blasting back. It had done good damage, but not enough. Rather than retreat or do anything else, the Panther unhesitantly used Jake's elation to strike.

It swapped places with a copy close to Jake and warped space as it charged, the other two illusions disappearing as the Panther dedicated all its energy to killing him. Jake was indeed taken by surprise and tried to block with his left arm. Bloodfeast Dagger was caught between two claws, and with a tug, it was ripped out of his hand and sent falling to the jungle below.

Striking again, Jake felt the claws sink into his newly regenerated arm. It cut to the bone, but he didn't wait to strike back. Eternal Hunger swept in from the right and cut the leg of the Panther before it could fully separate the arm from the rest of his body.

He swung again but found his blade blocked. He retreated a few steps in the air, trying to get more distance. The Panther once more struck, and Jake swung Eternal Hunger down. Rather than dodge, the Panther angled its head and did something unexpected: It caught his sword in its mouth and bit down tight, trapping it. It then yanked its head to disarm Jake.

Jake didn't hesitate. He simply let go of his blade and moved in closer. He jumped forward with both arms spread out and wrapped his arms around the neck of the Panther. Jake got to the top of the beast and held it tight in a neck hold as Touch of the Malefic Viper activated.

The Panther tossed his sword away as it roared. Jake refused to let go, and the Panther responded by sending itself flying downward while trying to get him off.

They both smashed into the ground, Jake taking most of the impact as the beast landed on top of him. Rather than let go, he wrapped his legs around the Panther's body and held it tight, poison pumping into the C-grade.

Its body began burning with dark mana as Jake's scales and passive barrier fought against it. The two wrestled on the ground, the energy invading his body and ravaging him from within, but he refused to let go.

He was smashed into several trees as the beast roared and scrambled. The fur around his hands fell off, and the flesh began rotting. Yet no matter what the beast did, it only made Jake hold on tighter. It was a death grip that would end when either he or the beast ran out of breath.

It would have, at least, but Jake had one more option. He used his head as he bit down on the neck of the Panther, pumping in his venom using his canines. At that moment, it would be difficult for an outside observer to tell who the real beast of the fight was.

Jake felt his own body losing strength as it began giving up. He knew he was soon out of time, but he had one final thing. He activated Mark of the Avaricious Hunter, and the arcane charge triggered. The Panther roared in pain, and Jake let go with his hands and his mouth as the beast froze. He held up both hands, and Eternal Hunger—which had been tossed away earlier—appeared, Jake sitting on top of the Panther holding it in both hands.

Roaring in tandem with the Panther, he stabbed down through the neck of the beast, driving Eternal Hunger into the ground below. The beast struggled a bit but finally fell limp to the ground, Jake collapsing on top of it as he got the notification.

Arcane Awakening finally deactivated as Jake's broken and battered body stopped burning with energy. An insane wave of weakness invaded his mind, and for a moment, he feared his body would give in, but the tenacity of his physique was not that easily overcome.

Jake managed to form a faint smile as he was still lying on top of the Panther. He didn't even have the energy to push himself off the corpse as he lay there, covered in blood with a happy expression. He'd won.

Tired as fuck, Jake closed his eyes and took a well-deserved nap.

CHAPTER 49

A STEP FORWARD FOR THE UNIVERSE

An annoying ringing sound reminiscent of his old alarm woke Jake up from his nap. With a start, he sat up, only to groan in pain. His body still hurt like hell. He wondered what was going on as the alarm kept blaring in his head until he finally found the cause.

"Villy... are you cosplaying as an alarm clock?"

"I was going more for a phone alarm with the most annoying option selected, actually," the god answered.

Jake was about to ask why the god was doing that, but he instantly realized the reason, and Villy also gladly reminded him.

"Let us just ignore the fact that you effectively just demoted your own Patron—a Primordial—to a damn alarm to remind you of your own damn scheduled system events," Villy said in a half-joking, half-scolding way. *"Not that I am surprised. In fact, I am beginning to see a pattern here. Do you just like hunting dangerous prey while under time pressure? Either way, you got ten minutes till it begins, so get going with all the stuff."*

"If it is worth anything, then you are the best alarm clock I have ever had," Jake said with a smile as he stood up.

He had been using the now rapidly decaying corpse of the Panther as a bed, and he was a little bit dirty. Not to mention how his armor was shredded, his body filled with holes that were still healing.

"It is not," Villy said. *"Now go on with what you have to do. We will talk more after the system event. If my guess is correct, this one will be like*

the others and not necessarily only concern Earth. Good luck with it all... and good fight, mate."

Jake nodded in appreciation, a smile still on his lips. He hurt all over, but he felt elated. Killing a C-grade was not easy, and the Phantomshade Panther was not a weak C-grade either. Checking his notifications, he saw that while the beast had been C-grade, it was only barely. Also, the clone level had been right.

You have slain [Phantomshade Panther – lvl 204]–Bonus experience earned for killing an enemy above your level

'DING!' Class: [Avaricious Arcane Hunter] has reached level 165 - Stat points allocated, +10 Free Points

...

'DING!' Class: [Avaricious Arcane Hunter] has reached level 169 - Stat points allocated, +10 Free Points

'DING!' Race: [Human (D)] has reached level 168 - Stat points allocated, +15 Free Points

'DING!' Race: [Human (D)] has reached level 169 - Stat points allocated, +15 Free Points

Jake had gained five levels from that one fight. Killing a level 199 didn't even give him a full level anymore unless it was a particularly strong specimen, so seeing how much he got truly demonstrated the difference between D- and C-grades.

Jake turned his attention to the beast in question and began using Alchemist's Purification to remove the last of the remnant poison lingering behind. Once done, he checked for loot and found a C-grade Beastcore attuned to dark and space affinities... and something even more interesting.

It was a black fang that hummed with intense energy. Jake frowned as he looked at it, but he quickly realized what type of item it was.

[Partly Digested Phantomshade Fang (Unique)] – A
Phantomshade Fang granted by the system to the newly integrated 93rd Universe. Contains a vast amount of energy and Records that will allow

*any compatible beast that consumes it to grow far faster and gain
magical skills and abilities related to dark and space magic. This fang is
already partly digested, having only a bit of the original energy left.*

It was something like the Mystbone that Mystie had absorbed to
quickly reach D-grade, but a far more potent version... perhaps one
good enough to push a beast to C-grade. It had clearly helped and
forged the Path of the Panther.

Jake picked it up and put it in his inventory along with the corpse
of the fallen beast. The pelt was not worth much, but he still wanted to
take it with him and not leave it rotting on the ground. A C-grade
corpse had to have some innate value, and this one had even been
strong.

After his looting, there was just one more thing. When he had
escaped that spatial tunnel with Moment of the Primal Hunter active,
Jake had managed to go above and beyond anything prior, thus
upgrading One Step Mile. With great excitement, he saw the notification.

[One Step Mile (Ancient)] – *A single step is sometimes enough to cross
vast distances. It is said that the very space between the user and their foes
shrinks with every footfall. By drawing on the concept of space, this skill
allows the user to cross far longer distances with every step than otherwise.
Note that there must be a clear path between you and your target. Grants
a noticeable bonus to the effectiveness of Endurance and Agility when
using One Step Mile.*

-->

[One Step, Thousand Miles (Legendary)] – *A single step is
sometimes enough to cross vast distances. It is said that the very space
between the user and their foes shrinks with every footfall. By drawing on
the concept of space, this skill allows the user to cross far longer distances
with every step than otherwise. Note that there must be a path between
you and your target. Grants a noticeable bonus to the effectiveness of
Endurance and Agility when using One Step, Thousand Miles.*

Jake had to have a few takes as he looked at the descriptions... where
nothing had changed. Okay, saying nothing was not accurate. One fucking
word was gone. It had gone from "there must be a clear path" to "there

must be a path," which was so damn minuscule it barely counted. Was that all his improved ability to pass through barriers and such boiled down to?

But... the rarity had upgraded along with the skill name. Jake wondered what was up with that and quickly pinged the Viper, knowing the god was still watching.

"Hey... One Step Mile, or, well, One Step, Thousand Miles, as it is called now... What is up with that skill?"

"What do you mean?" the god gladly asked in return.

"It just upgraded, but nothing really changed?"

"Isn't it better now? What did you expect to change?" Villy wasn't speaking in a teasing tone, but a very serious one.

"I am just used to skills kind of, you know, changing when upgrading. This one just got a bit better, and nothing else." Jake shrugged, but he began to understand what the Viper meant. What would he expect to change?

"I believe I have mentioned this before, but the One Step line of skills is far more powerful than you give it credit for. It is a skill known to pretty much anyone of power and influence, gained by far more individuals than you would expect. It is simple, elegant, and a core skill that has been around since... forever. It is a skill with a clear upgrade path all the way to a rank I have never heard of anyone reaching."

"So, it is a bit like your 'of the Malefic Viper' skills?" Jake asked.

"Yes and no. Those are Legacy skills bound to me and my Records. One Step is a skill that originated from the system itself, as far as I know. It is not bound to any individual or any Path; it merely is. The skill is one that you can keep upgrading and using all the way to the pinnacle, going from simply stepping a bit through space for a few meters to, with a single step, appearing anywhere in existence you so desire. However, fundamentally it will never change, and will always be about the simplest of actions and concepts—to take a step, moving you towards your destination."

Jake nodded along at the explanation and began to appreciate the simple skill even more. Thinking about it, didn't it fit him quite nicely? It was simple and easy to use and understand, just the way he liked it.

"Thanks for the exposition on the deep lore of my movement skill," Jake thanked the Viper, only half-joking.

"No problem. Goodbye again. For real this time. You got like five seconds."

"Yep," Jake said, having already seen the timer, and as it expired, the quest Jake already had updated.

Quest Updated: The Call of the Exalted Prima

As the world progresses, the Prima Watcher of Earth has been observing. Soon the Seat of the Exalted Prima shall appear on Earth and invite in all those who have managed to form keys to allow their entry. Anyone entering the Seat of the Exalted Prima can participate in the Path of Myriad Choices event, as well as gain access to the other benefits offered within the Seat of the Exalted Prima.

Beware, however, for the Seat holds dangers that the current warriors of Earth may not be ready to face yet. Should they unleash this danger and come out victorious, it shall reward the entire planet, while should they fail, it may fall to ruin.

Having obtained a key, you shall be allowed entrance into the Seat during its opening hours. May fortune be with you, and may your world come out stronger. The Seat of the Exalted Prima will remain open for one week.

Objective: Using the Key of the Exalted Prima, enter the Seat of the Exalted Prima that has appeared on Earth.

Jake took out the key from his inventory and used Identify on it once more. He had expected it and was proven correct when the description updated.

[Key of the Exalted Prima (Unique)] *— A key to the Seat of the Exalted Prima. Allows entry to the Seat of the Exalted Prima. Use the key to open a portal only a Prima Key Holder can use, leading to the Seat of the Exalted Prima when it is available.*

One thing was sure: This event was different. Jake was not just teleported to it after accepting a system prompt, but could now choose to teleport there. Nothing said he had to go right away either. Oh, but he would.

Jake deposited a healing potion into his mouth and, looking like someone who had just survived a fight to the death with an incredibly powerful opponent, used the key. A portal opened up in front of him, and feeling no sense of danger, he stepped through.

It was finally time to find out what all of that Prima stuff was all about.

Caleb stood in front of the two people who had managed to get keys along with himself. Nadia, the sniper, and Matteo, the second-in-command, had teamed up and hunted down seven Primas together, with Caleb naturally taking care of his own key.

"According to Umbra, this event has a high likelihood of allowing us to meet or even potentially pit us against individuals from elsewhere in our universe," Caleb explained to them. "This quest is far from unique to our world, and other planets have also been tasked with hunting down Primas to gain keys. All of this is to say, do not engage with anyone not from the Court. While we may be viewed as at least a little influential on this planet, we should not ever underestimate what other monsters may lurk in a near-endless universe."

The two of them nodded. They'd had this conversation before, but he believed it prudent to reiterate.

"As for the Myriad Paths event, simply do as you see fit—though I would prefer if you don't come out the other end ardent followers of the Holy Church after truly seeing the light." Caleb's joke got a chuckle out of Matteo.

He smiled at them and nodded as they all took out their keys, and he opened a portal.

"Let's go, then."

Miranda had to admit things had gone a lot more smoothly than expected when it came to collecting keys, and was honestly amazed at how many people from Haven would go. Herself and Arnold made sense, as they had teamed up, but Sultan had also managed to get one. Neil and his party had only gotten a single fragment, but that had been put to good use... kind of.

Sultan had also gained three fragments and thus a key. Rather than hunt for them himself, he had simply bought one from Neil and his party along with fragments from two other independent parties. This meant that, counting Jake and Sylphie, five people from Haven would go, matching if not exceeding many of the major factions.

They did not have any plans going in like the other factions, as they were effectively five independent people who just lived out of Haven.

Arnold and Sultan were very much their own men and not people Miranda could tell what to do in any capacity. Sylphie and Jake were... well, Sylphie and Jake.

Let us hope this event offers something valuable, she thought as she went through her own portal, Arnold and Sultan no doubt also going through their own.

Carmen looked at the key and smiled a bit. She turned her head to her mother and gave her a nod. Things in Paradise had stabilized, and Carmen had spent the time since parting with Jake hunting in the surrounding area and making sure everything went smoothly back in the city. Her mother had taken over operations and the employees her family had controlled before, all with the blessing of Renato, who gladly offered a helping hand.

Not that Carmen cared particularly much about the family business. She cared much more about the upcoming event.

"You ready to go?" Carmen asked the green bird currently lying flat on the bed.

"Ree!" Sylphie answered, with Carmen naturally not understanding at all.

Sylphie had been busy doing... something up in the air and had come back very happy, so Carmen assumed she had succeeded in whatever she was up to.

Carmen just smiled and summoned the portal.

"Take care," her mother said.

Carmen nodded in response and said her goodbyes as she and Sylphie went through the portal.

All over the planet—and even on other planets—individuals had collected keys and entered their respective portals. Rather than an event limited to a planet, it was one involving the entire universe. Future overlords of the world, leaders of the largest factions, and champions of their time would enter their own respective Seats of the Exalted Prima.

It was an event that would be the start of much conflict and lay the foundation for alliances to come. It was the first opportunity for factions to potentially meet up with members from other planets. For trade relations to be formed. Grudges to be born. Friendships to form.

And fated enemies having their very first meeting.

CHAPTER 50

SEAT OF THE EXALTED PRIMA

Bright light entered Jake's eyes as he stepped through the portal. He instantly felt several powerful auras all around him, recognizing most of them. They came through their own portals, which rapidly appeared and disappeared all around him within what he found to be a large, spherical room.

Metal plates covered the walls and floor, with nothing of note visible anywhere besides the people. That is, until Jake noticed that the room was split in two by a large, fully transparent panel of glass. All of the humans were on one side, along with Sylphie and the Fallen King, but on the other side, Jake saw other beings appear. All of them were beasts or monsters of various forms, with there being no rhyme or reason to what appeared. One was a large elemental crackling with lightning, and another a rabbit-like creature only a bit larger than Sylphie.

Speaking of Sylphie... the little murder hawk flew over to him once she located him, and Jake quickly found Miranda and Arnold, who both stood together. Sultan also walked over as they all met up.

"Been a while," Jake said with a smile as they gathered and had some small talk to quickly catch up.

All around them, members of other factions also found each other. Jake did notice how a lot of people he would expect to be there were noticeably absent. Jacob was nowhere to be found, and neither was Eron. The Sword Saint and a few people from the Noboru clan were there, but one thing quickly became clear: this was no factional event.

No faction had more than a few people each. Casper and Priscilla were the only Risen, the Sword Saint was with three other people, his brother had come with two from the Court, and the King had appeared alone. Carmen and Sven were also the only people from Valhal. Most powerful people from independent factions had appeared alone, and the only faction with more than ten people was the Holy Church. They just had so many people it was possible. From the looks of it, around a hundred fifty people had entered this event, meaning close to five hundred Primas had been killed.

"Lord Thayne," Sultan greeted Jake as he regarded him, "I take it you came straight from a battle?"

"Yeah," Jake said, not wanting to elaborate further. Too many people around. "Good job getting keys, everyone. Anyone figured out more about this event?"

Nobody had an answer, let alone time to answer, as something finally happened. A fluctuation in space caught Jake's attention, and he whipped around as a new figure appeared. A floating orb of metal had teleported into the room, getting the attention of everyone.

The orb looked like it was made out of polished aluminum and had no noticeable traits except for a glowing blue eye-like fixture. Jake felt nothing but a bit of energy coming out of it as he used Identify.

[Prima Watcher of Earth - ?]

It only had a single question mark as level. Jake did not think this was because its level was in the single digits, but quite the opposite. It was strong, yet Jake felt no danger. As he thought this, he suddenly got a quest notification.

Quest Completed: The Call of the Exalted Prima

Reward Received: Key of the Exalted Prima has been upgraded and become Soulbound. One entry into the Path of Myriad Choices event granted.

He quickly skimmed it, something it looked like everyone did, considering they all stared blankly for a moment. A few kept their attention on the floating orb, clearly ready for a fight. Yet it just floated there for a solid ten seconds before addressing them.

"Welcome to the Seat of the Exalted Prima, located within the Milky Way Galaxy. To both the Prima Slayers and surviving Primas. All

Prima Slayers have been awarded a single entry into the system-tier Path of Myriad Choices event. Following will be some basic information pertaining to the Seat of the Exalted Prima and your stay.

"All violence is strictly forbidden while within the Seat of the Exalted Prima. Breaking this rule will lead to instant expulsion and a temporary ban from the Seat, along with the deactivation of your key. All Seats are managed by the Exalted Prima, and events can only be entered if the user has permission and meet the requirements. The Seat of the Exalted Prima will only remain open for one week in this initial trial phase."

The orb spoke in a very mechanical voice that was neither male nor female. Jake looked at the thing as he saw many frowns all around him. The orb attracted way more attention than the bloody and savage-looking Jake, so in some ways, that was lucky.

When it stopped speaking, Jake also got a new quest. Something he once more assumed everyone did.

Quest Received: Seat of the Exalted Prima

Entering the Seat of the Exalted Prima, you find yourself with opportunities before you. For collecting a key, you have been granted a semi-permanent key able to conjure a portal and enter the Seat. Additionally, an opportunity to enter the Path of Myriad Choices event has been granted. But hurry, for the Seat is not available to visitors forever.

Objective: Participate in the Path of Myriad Choices event.

Time limit: Until the Seat closes.

The quest once more cemented that this entire thing was different than any event prior. It was clear that Jake could enter and leave this Seat of the Exalted Prima if he wanted to and return once more. The portals made by the key went both ways and only seemed to have a short cooldown time between uses. There was also the fact that the quests and general information so far were lacking. He got way more information from prior quests, and something like the Treasure Hunt had a whole slew of rules.

Meanwhile, this Seat of the Exalted Prima seemed not to be a system event, but rather a place that simply housed one.

"Excuse me," someone Jake did not recognize said. The orb turned towards him, the glowing eye focusing on the poor dude and clearly intimidating him a bit, but he still went through with his question. "What kind of opportunities does this Seat of the Exalted Prima offer, and can we be given any more information regarding the Path of Myriad Choices event?"

It was a question many no doubt wondered about, but no one had asked.

The orb more or less instantly answered with the same mechanical voice as before. "The Seat of the Exalted Prima is a satellite station established with a direct connection to the Exalted Prima. All opportunities offered by the Seat will take place within simulations of reality performed by the Exalted Prima. Opportunities vary depending on their nature, and a single fulfilling answer cannot be given. The Path of Myriad Choices offered is a simulation of reality wherein a different Path resulting from a choice not made earlier in life is shown. More details will follow upon engaging in the event. Additionally, for safety and privacy concerns, all outside communication is limited or entirely cut off both ways while within the Seat."

Everyone listened, with Jake being a bit surprised. Simulation? A station? Looking around at the walls and the glass panel and the weird orb itself, he kind of understood. This was some kind of high-tech facility created by the system, or at least brought there by the system, right? At least, that was his first guess.

"What is this Exalted Prima?" someone else asked.

"The Exalted Prima is the core directive consciousness of all Seats of the Exalted Prima spread throughout the universe," the orb said without offering further details.

"If I may ask, what are those monsters doing here?" a third person also inquired. He referred to the many beasts behind the glass panel, all of which were acting relatively calmly.

Weren't they Primas? Jake asked himself before the orb answered.

"Two ways of entry to the Seat of the Exalted Prima were provided. One method was through the integration of a Prima Fragment by a monster found compatible with the core directives, and the other was collecting three fragments and forming a key. Those creatures are Primas, and all Primas shall be offered a unique opportunity separate from those who obtained keys."

Jake nodded along. It seemed like the Primas had effectively been given a quest to survive long enough with their fragments to enter this place. It was a trade-off, a classic case of risk and reward. On the one hand, they got a target on their backs, and on the other, they were offered an opportunity.

Before anyone else could ask any more questions, the Watcher spoke, "Introduction has been completed, and the facility shall now open up. Once more, violence is not allowed within the Seat of the Exalted Prima. More information can be found within the facility where deemed a necessity."

With those words, the orb disappeared. Jake barely felt the fluctuations of space as it teleported. He turned to the others around him. Most of them were taking in the information, with Miranda looking deep in thought. However, the one he took most notice of was Arnold, who had his tablet out while nodding.

"Did you discover anything?" Jake asked the man.

Arnold glanced up after looking through a few more things and nodded. "We remain within the 93rd Universe but have still been cut off from the outside world. System-imposed, I would presume, even if the Watcher claims it is caused by the Exalted Prima. Indicating this Exalted Prima is a conjuration of the system."

"Are you sure?" Jake asked with a frown.

He could not feel Villy at all, true, but so had it been during all events. But all those events had taken place in a separate space that none could truly locate, not just somewhere in their universe.

"My conclusion is within a critically significant margin of error, making me certain, yes," the scientist said. "I cannot say where we are, but I would assume, based on information provided, it is within the Milky Way Galaxy."

Jake nodded in response.

He began to have some idea what this entire place was more and more. If he was right, this whole Exalted Prima thing was bound to be significant not just for Earth, but the entire 93rd Universe. Not just for one system event, either, but for a long time to come. Perhaps this place would even hold significance for the multiverse as a whole.

A few moments passed as everyone discussed. A few began to get impatient as a segment of the wall began opening up, leading into an even larger area. On the other side of the glass panel, the Primas were led somewhere else too. Jake had spotted a few of them out the corner of his eye that got into conflict, and he noticed how the moment any one of them tried to attack another, they instantly just disappeared. He hoped for their sakes that they had the same rules as those with keys and weren't just vaporized.

People began walking towards the opening, and Jake followed with the others. Carmen threw him a glance from across the room, and he gave one back. Silently, all the humans and the two monsters—Sylphie and the Fallen King—exited the large, dome-shaped room.

Jake had expected a portal leading into some other room where these simulations would happen or something in that vein, but instead found himself in a large lounge that looked incredibly casual. However, more than anything, he stared at what truly lay before him—and above him.

The lounge had no roof. All Jake saw when he looked up was a sky full of stars, planets, and an endless world spreading out before him. Others also stopped and gawked at the expanse above. Jake stared for several seconds before looking to the side, where he saw several similar hemispheres to the one they were currently inside in the distance. Looking behind him, he saw they had exited a small box with an opening in it, the entire thing no bigger than a large elevator. Spatially expanded for sure.

Each of the hemispheres surrounding their own was at least a kilometer in diameter and of equal size. The inside was filled with furniture and several screens that no one seemed to know how to control, their purposes equally unknown.

Nothing immediately caught Jake's attention as he got a feel for the place. It was clearly just a meeting area of sorts. Likely a place for those who came from Earth to meet up and enter through. Looking at another hemisphere, he saw what looked like a wire hanging from it. Their own also had a wire, he was sure. All of them did.

Jake walked forward with the others and went to the edge of the hemisphere, where it felt like he stood at a cliff leading down into the infinite vacuum of space. Only a thin barrier, barely a few millimeters thick, blocked him from being in space. Not that Jake feared such a thing. First of all, he felt relatively certain he could survive there, and secondly, that no one present could destroy that barrier. Or if anything could, for that matter.

"This is quite something," Sultan said as he stared out.

"Yeah," Jake agreed.

Others had also joined them and looked out. Even after all the progress Jake and others had made, all their levels and all their power, there was a feeling of powerlessness in standing there. There were stars and planets in the distance so far away that Jake was certain he would die of age before even getting halfway to one if he decided to fly. It was such an impossibly large scope it was hard to imagine. Yet he knew that to gods, all of this was nothing. With a thought, anything within his field of view could be reduced to ashes. It was power out of this world. It was hard to picture Villy being that powerful, even if Jake knew he was.

Yet it was also exciting. To see such a vast world of possibilities. An infinite world. And this was just part of one universe... No, part of one small galaxy out of billions of planets. The multiverse was so vast and filled with things to explore that Jake couldn't help smiling. He caught himself and dispelled the thoughts.

You got a long way to go, Jake. You barely beat a damn cat just a few hours ago, he reminded himself.

Turning his head to the side, he also finally got a look at what these wires from the hemispheres connected to. It was a floating, cylinder-shaped structure. Jake saw nearly a thousand wires connecting hemispheres and the cylinder that he assumed was the actual Seat of the Exalted Prima. This entire setup was a massive structure in its own right.

He then saw some people go over to what looked like a metal disc with complicated scripts on it. Jake didn't recognize them and didn't have time to use Identify before the group disappeared. *Guess I found the teleporter to the actual Seat.*

Seeing no reason to wait, he began leading his group towards it. Tossing a final look at the endless expanse, he stepped onto the platform and was teleported into the true Seat of the Exalted Prima.

CHAPTER 51

UNREALISTIC PLANETARY STANDARDS

Jake found himself teleported onto an identical metal disc within a small hall. Sultan, Miranda, Arnold, and Sylphie appeared together with him shortly after, and just as they stepped off the teleporter, it activated again.

A familiar figure appeared, and Jake turned and gave the Unique Lifeform a look.

[Fallen King – lvl 196]

The level of the King was approaching peak D-grade. Unique Lifeforms were truly cheats... Then again, the King only had his race to progress while Jake had both profession and class. Furthermore, the Unique Lifeform had been busy, as far as he knew, forming an entirely new faction on their planet as well as doing his fair share of hunting. Not everyone liked being ruled, after all.

"You have been busy," Jake said.

"So have you, little Hunter. I feel the remnants of a C-grade signature upon your soul. A very recent one. Perhaps the cause of your unsightly state?"

Jake was once more being reminded he was wearing tattered clothes and still had quite a bit of blood on him. To be honest, that no one had commented on it yet was kind of crazy.

"Your assumptions would be correct," Jake said with a confident smile. The King had sent his telepathic communication wide and had regarded them all. Therefore, Jake also responded openly. The next thing, however, he said to the King using telepathy.

"You are approaching peak D-grade," Jake simply stated to the King covertly. *"Won't you be kind of fucked by me being behind?"*

"You worry needlessly," the King dismissed him. *"I am in no rush for C-grade and see no purpose in sabotaging myself for temporary gain. I have been D-grade for over a century already, but most of that time was spent doing nothing worthwhile. This King also needs to fully comprehend his new reality. So no, I am not in a rush. Just don't make me wait another century."*

Jake sent a mental nod in return as he ended their secret conversation. It was good to know even Unique Lifeforms had shortcomings they wanted to square up before evolution.

"I am wondering what kind of Path you are looking forward to seeing," Jake told the King. "Though I do have at least one guess..."

"A guess I would presume you correct about. In fact, I have two prominent possibilities in mind. One is if I never chose to participate in the tutorial but stayed on my pathetic homeworld instead. The other—the one I presume you guessed—is if I had chosen to kill a certain little hunter and not died due to my own folly."

That certain little hunter smiled and joked, "Live and learn. Or die and learn, in this case."

"A lesson I have taken with me, and a reason why I am in no rush."

A few more words were exchanged, but their conversation quickly drew attention. The tree-like willow form of the Unique Lifeform and the hunter wearing tattered armor and covered in blood did stand out a bit. Heck, Sylphie and the King stood out by themselves quite a lot, being the only two non-humans from Earth that had keys.

The unwanted attention made them move on, but not before Jake fixed up his state. He went to a corner and summoned a stable arcane barrier and even used Arcane Stealth to stay undetected as he deposited all his armor in his inventory. He quickly stirred his energy to clean the blood off, releasing a wave of destructive mana that ran across his body. He was still not in top condition after the fight with the Panther and still felt pain from all over, but at least he was mobile and could function normally. Fighting was not the best idea, though.

Feeling adequately clean, Jake put on his non-combat party outfit from the Order. He had worn it at the World Congress too, and it was certainly better than his other things. Or being naked. In time, all his equipment would be repaired within his inventory, and those that required some extra help, he helped.

Dispelling the barrier, he saw the others had waited. He hadn't even taken thirty seconds, so it wasn't like he had made them stand there for long. Jake did notice the King had left, not one to wait around for others.

"What are you guys planning on doing?" Jake asked the group once he went over. "I personally intend to go and do this event right away. Who knows how long it will take, and we only got seven days. Also... I am curious."

"I do believe it is wisest to go now and do it," Miranda agreed. "If this is truly a possibility to meet those from other planets, I have no doubt some diplomacy will be carried out, but the event is a priority for sure."

Arnold just nodded, seemingly not in a rush. In fact, he seemed more interested in their surroundings. Then again... it was Arnold, and it wouldn't be that surprising if he found the space station more interesting than a system event.

"Ree!" Sylphie also agreed.

Jake looked at her and gave her a good head rub as he wondered what kind of event the hawk could even be offered. She wasn't even a handful of years old yet, so how many big choices did she have time to make? Maybe choosing to be blessed by Stormild or not was one? Or choosing to leave Jake and Haven altogether at some point? Who could say? He would have to ask her when both of them were done.

"Let's go, then," Jake said with a smile.

While he did want to talk with his brother and the Sword Saint, it seemed like both had already left towards where the event would be held. At least they had exited the small entrance area belonging to Earth with the teleporter in it.

The party from Haven moved onwards and soon enough exited the room. They found themselves on a large platform—or perhaps balcony would be a more accurate word. Jake curiously went forward to the edge of the balcony and saw they were probably a few hundred meters up. More platforms were below them and above them.

The entire tower that was the Seat of the Exalted Prima was built like a circular atrium with several hundred floors. Looking straight ahead, he stared onto another balcony and saw several people standing there too. None of them were quite human either. They all had a greenish tint to their skin but otherwise looked mostly human. Well, okay, the four arms were a bit different than humans. Using Identify, he saw a race he had not seen or heard of before.

[Kolbar – lvl 131]

He checked out several of them and got the same race response. The man at level 131 stood in the front of all the others, and Jake saw his level was the highest of them all. This man also saw Jake and stared back with two odd eyes. One of them held two pupils and the other none at all.

Jake nodded, but the man did not seem to understand his gesture. Looking around again, Jake saw so many different races, most of which he had never heard of, but nearly all of them humanoid. There were also elves, dwarves, beastfolk, and all the usual suspects, along with two very interesting groups that only consisted of Risen and other undead creatures. Did they hail from undead planets, perhaps?

Miranda and the others—besides Arnold, who was busy checking out the metal on the railing—all looked around curiously. This was truly a clash of cultures, with over a thousand different civilizations holding their first meeting within an atrium in a space station.

However, Jake also noticed something else. Something odd.

Why are they all so weak?

He had only seen one or two above level 150. That was incredibly low, wasn't it? Jake knew he had been slacking off a bit too much with levels and had only begun to get back on track recently. That is why he was so confused... Wouldn't people who rushed levels or had cities level faster? Jake wouldn't be surprised if someone like Jacob was already peak D-grade by now, close to C-grade.

Miranda noticed his frown, and Jake felt a mental probing as she tried to speak to him telepathically. Jake allowed it in.

"You are surprised by their average level, right?" she asked.

Jake threw her and glance and nodded. *"A bit. Did Earth have special opportunities or anything like that for us to grow? You know, something more than everyone else?"*

She shook her head and smiled a little. *"Answering that is a bit complicated, I think. I have been to the Verdant Lagoon many times with my dream skill and talked to many people, and I have come to realize Earth is truly a special place. Not because of what, but who. Records have a way of congregating and building off each other. So I would say that in some ways, it had special opportunities by having the possibility of interacting with individuals on a level far above the norm."*

"Can it really be that simple?" Jake asked skeptically.

He already knew there was some truth to it, but it was hard to believe the only reason so many strong people had appeared on Earth was that other strong people appeared. It reminded him a bit of the old catch-22 where you can't find a job without having experience and can't get experience without finding a job. Just in this case, a lot of strong people would only appear if there were other strong people, yet you needed strong people to get truly strong yourself. Okay, not exactly the same, but close enough.

"Probably not that simple, no, but at least it is a partial explanation. Jake, I want you to remember that you are used to interacting with figures far above the norm. To become a member of the Order of the Malefic Viper already makes someone a supreme genius in the eyes of the average resident of the multiverse, while I am sure you view the average members of the Order as not worth much.

"Heck, take me as an example. I was no one before you spontaneously wanted me to be City Lord for you. It is questionable if I would even have reached D-grade without that happening—assuming I even survived that long. Me being near you and working for you changed my Path entirely. I got a Blessing and was taught by gods. I got artifacts I could never dream of. All because of you making that one choice that day... and I am certain that is something I will be shown in the upcoming event what would have happened if I had rejected becoming City Lord back then."

Jake listened without interrupting, not completely agreeing. He frowned, as he didn't feel like it was entirely fair to give him all the credit.

"While I may have helped, that was only in the beginning," he sent to her encouragingly. *"Since then, I have done close to nothing, and it feels like what I have done often just creates more problems for you. You have run Haven more or less alone, and those you found to help you were selected and trained by you. I know nothing of your magic and barely understand how your class or profession works. Don't sell yourself short; you are plenty talented in your own right."*

Miranda smiled at him but shook her head. *"It is odd, isn't it? Why can I figure out this magic when who I was before the system should in no way allow me to? Why do I understand things I shouldn't? I have come to believe that it isn't always those with talent who get Records, but that Records can birth talent... You know, like how one says a child can inherit the talent of their parents, so can you benefit from the talents of others. Nurturing it, of sorts. The Witches of the Verdant Lagoon have mentioned something like that but never truly confirmed it. Either way, this is all a sidetrack. Just know that Earth is special and that you cannot judge other planets using ours as the standard. But that doesn't mean we are at the peak... You never know which monsters may be out there."*

"That, we can agree on," Jake answered. Their conversation had been telepathic and taken far less time than using words, but a solid ten seconds had still passed. People were still curiously observing others, and he himself got quite a lot of attention... Wait, no, it was Miranda who got it.

Her level was the highest of anyone around. This also made Jake realize why no fighting was allowed. Chances were the ones arriving from Earth could massacre most other "powerful talents" from other planets in their own galaxy, instantly wiping out much of their potential future competition.

Jake looked down towards the bottom of the atrium and saw hundreds of people gathering there. From the looks of it, all of these balconies and floors of the Seat of the Exalted Prima were merely for those from different planets to enter, and the true Seat was at the bottom.

"I will head down," Jake said.

Being not the most patient person, Jake merely stepped forward and teleported several hundred meters down to appear on the ground floor. A few surprised and frightened gazes landed on him, but luckily the King was also there and took the attention away from him.

Not even when Sylphie swept down did they get attention. Then again, a Unique Lifeform above level 190 was bound to attract attention, especially as the King didn't even try to hide his level. Jake was damn sure he could, considering he was an expert in soul magic, which meant he chose not to. Probably to show off.

Oh, well. That was all well and good for Jake. With Sylphie on his shoulder, he made his way past the crowd that tried to suck up to the King. In the center of the atrium was a pillar that Jake saw several people walk into like it wasn't there, and Jake noted several complicated scripts on it. As well as words.

Seat of the Exalted Prima Simulation Room

It was clear this was the entrance. With his sphere, Jake saw this metal pillar registered as just one huge mass of mana. Danger sense was also silent as he went over and, not wanting to make any queues, walked straight into the pillar like everyone else.

He phased through it without even feeling anything, and only whiteness met his eyes. At the same time, he felt his connection to Sylphie disappear, with the bird now gone off his shoulder. Jake stood there for a moment before a menu popped up in front of him.

Welcome to the Seat of the Exalted Prima

Due to still being in the early stages of the 93rd Universe's integration, simulation options are limited.

Options available:

-

System-tier events:

Path of Myriad Choices

It was the most barebones menu Jake had ever seen. Had they been offered an early alpha version of the Seat of the Exalted Prima or what?

Oh, well. Not wanting to delve too much into the questionable actions of this Exalted Prima, Jake selected Path of Myriad Choices.

On one of the top floors of the atrium, another teleporter activated. A figure appeared, followed by over a hundred more. All of them stayed behind their leader, not a single one daring to walk in front. These were clearly part of a single force rather than a collective of individuals who participated in the event.

The leader was a man with deep orange skin with blue tattoo-like patterns running across it. He wore an intricate red robe and equipment that would put most others to shame. His face had near-perfect features that made him look androgynous yet also inhuman.

This figure, leading his entourage, exited their own hall as he looked down towards the bottom, ignoring all of those staring at him and his followers with wide eyes. He smiled upon seeing the Unique Lifeform he knew as the former King of the Forest.

He failed to suppress a smile when he also spotted several other figures of interest. How could he? There was so much to look forward to. So many things to do and such interesting stories to be told.

Soon... Soon it would be time to meet his fellow Chosen and begin the first chapter of their legend.

Chapter 52

Path of Myriad Choices

J ake had selected the only thing possible, and a new menu popped up, finally giving him a better idea of what the event was all about and how it would work.

System-tier event: Path of Myriad Choices.

Simulation Description: The participant will be shown a minimum of two and a maximum of six choices made prior that significantly impacted their current Path. This simulation allows the participant to see a potential reality wherein that choice was not made. Dependent on the results of the simulation, the participant may be offered rewards related to the actions of the simulacrum of the participant during the simulation. The scope and length of all simulations vary but shall never simulate past current Realtime.

Note that no actions can be performed during the simulation outside of observing or ending the simulation. Only one choice can be selected.

Rewards may or may not be gained from this event. All participants are encouraged to take inspiration from the simulacrum and a potential Path other than that which they currently walk.

Initiate Path of Myriad Choices?
Y/N

Jake read the description carefully before entering. The Watcher had not given much information, but this sure shed some light on things. It truly was a simulation, and considering the system-tier event tag, Jake reckoned that the simulation would not be anything simple.

It seemed insane to think that the system would more or less create an entirely different world and show it to the participants. How much had to go into that? And how accurate could it be? Jake was sure as hell curious as he accepted the prompt.

Instantly, changes happened. Within the whiteness, four scenes appeared out of nothing, simply existing there in the space contained within rooms of sorts. One of the "rooms," if it was even correct to call it that, depicted himself walking through a dark tunnel. Jake instantly recognized it as the one he had found during the tutorial after splitting up with his colleagues.

The one leading to the Challenge Dungeon.

The second scene was one that came quite a lot later. It showed Jake and the King of the Forest standing before one another. It was before the fight had begun.

But... from there, it got weird. The two other scenes were not at all what Jake expected. The first one was of him standing before his compound bow back in his parents' old house. Back then, he'd been a teenager with big dreams of going pro with his archery, and from the looks of it, this was before his accident. Through that, he'd ended up tearing several tendons, suffering severe damage to his shoulder, and being told by a doctor that he could no longer practice for over a year. That had made the dream impossible, as it had put him out of the competition for so long and resulted in him studying more and ultimately going to university.

The fourth scene was something Jake did not get at all. He didn't even remember it. It showed who he assumed to be himself standing in the entryway of a house he barely remembered as being the one his parents used to own. The one they'd moved out of when he was five years old to get closer to a better school and for his dad's job.

Jake was nothing but a toddler in the scene—less than three years old for sure, as his mother was heavily pregnant with Caleb. Jake was clearly throwing a tantrum in the scene, and his father and mother were frantically trying to calm him down as his grandmother, who had probably come to babysit, stood confused in the doorway.

I don't get it, Jake thought as he looked at it. What choice had he made back then? Sure, he kind of understood the others, but what decisions could a damn toddler make? Luckily for him, the system of the Seat had more options available. He saw that four options had appeared before him, each with a small description attached. Treating it like a skill choice, he started from the top.

Choice 1: Turning back and never entering the tutorial Challenge Dungeon, resulting in you never meeting your Patron god or obtaining your current profession.
See preview?

This one was straightforward, and Jake pressed the "see preview" button with interest.

The moment he did so, the entire world around him changed. Jake watched himself stand in the dark tunnel before cursing, shaking his head, and turning around.

It shifted again and showed Jake looking at Jacob and the others in Richard's camp. Jake kept an eye on them and noticed William and Richard meet.

Next, he saw himself shoot an arrow through the head of Richard, killing him. He saw himself surrounded by dark magic as he did so.

The next image was of Jake killing the Nest Watcher—the third of four dungeon bosses before the King—and barely coming out on top moments before the tutorial ended. A brief flash was of him standing with more of his old colleagues, with Jacob still an Augur and most having still died.

What followed was almost a montage. It showed Jake making it to Skyggen, meeting his parents, and formally joining the Court of Shadows, also making it clear Jake had accepted the Blessing of Umbra. It showed him and his brother hunting through several flashes, fighting beasts together, entering a different system event than the Treasure Hunt, and generally just Jake being a lot closer to his family than before.

The preview ended there. The room turned white again, only showing the four scenes. The entire thing had taken only a minute or two and shown Jake snippets, but damn, was it interesting. So many things changed.

Not wanting to dwell on it too long, he saw the next.

Choice 2: Choosing to not fight the King of the Forest, but instead bowing out and leaving the tutorial there and then, thus not ending the reign of the King of the Forest and allowing him to return to Earth for a rematch one day.

See preview?

Jake selected it, and the simulation changed once more. This one proved a lot more boring than the old one. It was just Jake leaving the tutorial and many of the same things happening as before, but everything was just... lesser?

He had killed a D-grade later, gotten fewer levels, from the looks of it, and had just been far less impressive. Haven was also far more boring. Towards the end, Jake barely paid attention as he just shook his head. He knew why this one sucked.

Him backing down back then was backing down from everything he was. Surrendering like that was not in his nature and a rejection of his Bloodline. The only result of not fighting the King would be Jake not becoming a Progenitor and being far weaker. He would lose several titles and get worse skills from the Tutorial Store. Overall, just seeing it made Jake annoyed at watching such a version of himself.

It was especially hammered home how much this version sucked when he saw the King and the Sword Saint fight to a standstill as he could only support from behind, not quite at their level.

Yeah, fuck that.

Next option.

Choice 3: Choosing to not practice archery that day but instead staying home, thus never suffering any injury and allowing you to continue practicing.

See preview?

The third simulation... was weird. The preview was weird. It showed a few flashes of Jake doing archery, him standing with a trophy, him in an entirely different tutorial—one with Caleb also in it. Jake saw a brief flash of himself standing before what he assumed to be Umbra, but her form was obscured. It showed him becoming the Judge and returning to Earth.

Jake was surprised at many things that happened, but one of them more than anything else. It showed Jake killing Bertram before forcing Jacob into a teleporter that took him off the planet.

It also showed him fighting the Sword Saint, but the moment the man realized his Transcendence, Jake was demolished and saw himself be saved as several members of the Court gave their lives to allow his escape.

It ended with Jake somehow teaming up with the Sword Saint and fighting the King of the Forest, who stood side by side with William of all people.

"What the fuck did I just watch?" Jake asked himself as he stood there and stared at the scenes still flashing before his eyes. The simulation room had returned to normal as it waited for his next input.

No, seriously, what the fuck did he actually just watch? There were so many things to take in. Him the Judge of the Court and, from the looks of it, an utter beast with the bow. Sadly, Jake saw no details, just clips. The Seat wasn't giving away any juicy stuff, just showing possibilities. Fighting Jacob and the Church... losing to the Sword Saint... So much to take in.

However, this weirdness did make it an attractive option. A chance to see the possibilities of mixing dark magic and archery. There was the issue of Jake being pretty damn committed to his arcane affinity by now, but he could still learn a bit for sure.

Shaking his head, Jake decided to give the fourth preview a shot.

Choice 4: Obeying your parents and choosing to let them leave.
See preview?

This one was barebones. Jake frowned a bit as he began the preview. He instantly remembered that day as the first scene played out. It was odd he remembered, with Jake still too young to truly form memories back then, but now he remembered it clear as day. He remembered the emotions, at least.

His parents were leaving to go to a hospital check-up for his mom. Jake had gotten a horrible gut feeling when they were about to leave and had stopped them by throwing such a large tantrum, so they'd had to stay and reschedule. It was something Jake did not even remember... but was that decision really that big?

As the simulation began, he realized it was.

He had chosen to ignore his gut and let his parents leave after only a bit of placating. The next scene was of Jake at a funeral, followed by him living with his grandparents, who soon passed away also. Then a foster home, another foster home... The scenes just kept changing rapidly, and all that stayed constant was Jake getting older.

Then... everything became almost incomprehensible. A scene

showed Jake in his early teenage years standing over a body. The next of him with a knife covered in blood and wearing a hoodie. Then him in a jungle-like environment, fighting other humans.

It kept repeatedly changing, and nothing made sense until it reached a scene where he finally saw something familiar. The same tutorial Caleb had gone to, and one Jake had also been participating in during the third preview.

But things were very different this time around. The version of himself Jake saw was different to a level where Jake could not recognize him. Moreover, there was no bow to be seen anywhere. This version of himself was so different from who Jake was today; that much was obviously clear from just the preview.

The preview ended almost prematurely, shortly after Jake entered the tutorial, showing him fighting several shadow beasts.

Being done with all the previews, Jake needed a moment to process everything. Because damn, was there a lot. Watching a movie of yourself doing things you never did was just fucking weird, man.

Ultimately, these previews were lackluster and only allowed one to form an idea of what it was about. Jake considered all four of them and quickly filtered out the second version. That one was just a more cowardly version of himself who didn't become a Progenitor.

Next up, he filtered away the first choice. He wasn't a fan of it; it included Jake doing much of the same, but with more dark magic and no poison. It did have the bonus of Jake spending more time with family, but... that wasn't exactly something Jake could learn from. Okay, he probably could, as he really needed to go visit more and be a better son and brother.

That left the third and fourth, and of them, there was really only one option.

The fourth one was just too impactful and the one Jake understood the least. The Path was so different from who Jake was today. It was a Jake who fought entirely without a bow or poison. Moreover... the vision had ended shortly after he entered the tutorial. Did that mean he would die, according to the simulation? Or was it something else? Curiosity alone made him feel forced to pick it.

However, before he did that, some considerations should be made.

One thing was clear from all these previews: Even without showing him anything substantial, Jake could infer some things, and the constant relation to the Court of Shadows couldn't be a coincidence. Even when his entire life was different from childhood, he ended up there. Yet now, Jake had no relations to it besides through his brother. He didn't even use his dark affinity for much.

That should maybe the initial takeaway, Jake noted mentally. *My dark affinity is excellent, and I should be able to make some use of it.*

There was also one very notable absence, a choice Jake would have expected—what would have happened if he had become a Malefic Dragonkin? It was such an obvious one Jake was surprised it wasn't there. Why had it chosen these four? It couldn't be due to how significant their impact would be, could it? All Paths ended up somewhat similar—either with the Court or Villy—and there wasn't a choice where Jake even went with a third god, as far as he could see.

So, why was it? Jake had fought a version of himself back then. He knew he could have absorbed the power back then and changed significantly. Why was he not shown that? System limitations? No, that was out of the question. It could show even pre-initiation events, so thinking it couldn't figure out how to show him as a Dragonkin was moronic.

Wait... ah... Yeah, that is possible.

Jake landed on a potential explanation. These choices he had been offered had one thing in common: the lack of knowing their impact before making the choice. The only one that one could argue he did know was the one with the King and leaving the tutorial, but did he really know? He had no frame of reference for what was good or the true reward for victory.

So maybe it just showed choices one could have made that would have had a significant impact without you realizing it. If not, wouldn't all the options offered be evolutions? It was a given that if Jake had chosen a different class or profession during evolution, it would've changed his Path.

It was just a theory, but it seemed kind of right. Either way, he had no way to confirm or deny this theory, not that it truly mattered. Jake had four choices and had already picked one mentally.

Without hesitating anymore, Jake chose the fourth option. The second he did so, a new message appeared.

Initiating simulation of Choice 4. All simulated content will be curated, and low-impact events and actions will automatically be filtered out or swiftly passed over.

With that message, the entire world changed. Jake found himself standing in the old entryway as if he was truly there, staring at a toddler version of himself throwing a tantrum.

"No!" little Jake yelled as he refused to let go of his dad's leg.

"Just stay with grandma, okay? We will be back soo—"

"*No!*" Jake yelled again, tears in his eyes as he yanked the leg.

Jake remembered it now, clear as day. He had kept it up long enough for them to stay... but this time, it was different. He saw this version of himself relent, abandoning his trust in his instincts in favor of obeying his parents. He had let them go, despite feeling something bad would happen if he did.

Two hours later, a phone call came. A major car crash.

Less than a week later, the funerals—both his parents dead. His brother never born.

When Jake was five, his grandmother died, and he now no longer had any family he was still in contact with, meaning Jake became an orphan. Time quickly passed, but one thing was different from the start: He was no longer growing up in a loving family with parents and a little brother, but in an underfunded and apathetic system where children were more often than not viewed as burdens.

Jake more than anyone. For there was one major difference between this child and Jake from back then. Something separate from the trauma and hurt. As he grew, it only became more apparent.

He had never suppressed his Bloodline... Instead, he had embraced it.

CHAPTER 53

A VERY DIFFERENT LIFE

J ake looked on as the life of the other Jake progressed at a steady pace, far more detailed than before, and it even included sound now. In fact, it was as if Jake himself was present and standing in the room and could even move around.

Many of the first memories after simulation-Jake—or sim-Jake for short—went into the foster system were of him being thrown into new environments, surrounded by other children in equally unfortunate situations.

Such children tended to not be the best. They were emotionally underdeveloped and immature and often had no way of handling their situation besides acting out. So when a new kid entered a foster home of twelve kids—one younger than many of them—it was natural to make him a target.

A scene like this was one of the first major things that the simulation deemed an impactful event.

Sim-Jake, no more than seven years old, stood surrounded by children between the age of seven and ten. There were six of them in total. Jake was smaller than all but one of the other kids.

"Give!" one of the larger kids screamed as he reached towards sim-Jake's toy. It was a foam dagger that Jake remembered his grandmother getting him before passing away. It appeared that it was a gift he would receive in both the simulation and real life.

Sim-Jake pulled away but didn't say anything. But Jake saw the eyes of the other version of himself. He was ready. The larger kid moved in closer and pushed the far smaller sim-Jake, sending him stumbling backward. The other kids just laughed at the bullying as sim-Jake fell to the floor. Another kid came over to try and take the foam dagger while the large kid walked to Jake and prepared to kick him.

Now, even children have some kind of natural limiter on them. Grevious injuries when children were in scuffles rarely happened, as even when so young, they understood not to do it—be it out of a fear of getting in trouble or inborn empathy, or perhaps a limiter imposed by society and early nurture.

Something sim-Jake clearly did not care about.

Out of nowhere, a dinner fork appeared. The kid trying to take the foam dagger didn't even have time to react as he was stabbed in the arm, making him scream out in pain. Rolling up, the far smaller sim-Jake caught the leg of the bully and stood up, making him fall backward. Most would end there, but the small Jake ran over and stomped the ten-year-old kid in the head repeatedly until he started crying.

It only took a few seconds before a disheveled woman came into the room yelling and dragged Jake off the kid. Even as he was pulled away, sim-Jake held the foam dagger tight and stared daggers at the kid nearly twice his age on the ground.

As the scene was about to end, Jake noticed that the small version of himself seemed to almost look in his direction. *Hm?* Jake questioned, but the scene had already been completed.

A few more scenes appeared after that of Jake growing up. Each scene was of a different foster home, and all of them were of others trying to make trouble for Jake, and Jake using what could only be described as excessive force in self-defense.

Where usually a kid would shove someone, Jake tackled them to the ground and began punching. Where one would punch someone, Jake broke an arm or a leg. His violence landed him in repeated trouble... but it was also effective. One instance was all it took, and no other child dared cause trouble for him.

Jake—the real one—had to admit he related to a few of these things. He didn't remember exactly when he began to truly suppress his Bloodline, but he still had it in some parts of his childhood. Even after it was suppressed, some of the effects were also still retained but far weaker. However, rather than slowly suppressing it more and more, this version of Jake embraced it. He grew into it.

Scenes continued, and the next most noticeable scene was of a fifteen-year-old sim-Jake. Rather than being in a foster home this time, he lived in an old abandoned warehouse. Homeless, most likely. Maybe the authorities had given up on him, or maybe he had run off himself, but either way, he was clearly out of the system.

Jake first noticed the body of this version of himself wasn't what one would expect of a homeless fifteen-year-old. He had more muscles than kids of that age and looked more like an athlete in training. In the scene shown, he was also doing push-ups as two men walked over. Both looked to be in their thirties and were not happy.

"Hey kid, get the fuck up," one of the men sneered.

Sim-Jake barely reacted and kept training as he just turned his head. "What do you want?"

"I heard you made trouble for our boys," the other man said more calmly.

"Funny, I remember it being the other way around. Them trying to rob me." Sim-Jake finally stopped training and stood up. He was smaller than the two men by quite a bit, but not a trace of fear was on his face.

A teenager before two large men would usually be viewed as a foregone conclusion. Facing little more than a child, the adults naturally didn't take sim-Jake very seriously as one of them reached towards him.

"Listen here, ki—"

Sim-Jake grasped his wrist and looked him in the eye. "I am listening, am I not?"

The man did not take kindly to this. He wrested his arm free and took a swing. Sim-Jake effortlessly dodged it and took a step back to avoid a follow-up. The man looked like he had some minor boxing experience, but it was far from good enough.

Sim-Jake caught his arm as the man made a wide swing and twisted it. The attacker yelled in pain as sim-Jake just pushed him away, making him fall to the ground.

"Just fuck off already, man," sim-Jake said, annoyed.

The other man, who had yet to attack, looked at his fallen comrade. "Kid, you stole thousands from us. We aren't leaving." Sim-Jake raised an eyebrow and frowned as the other party pulled out a switchblade. The man raised it threateningly and added, "Stop being an idiot."

The real Jake saw his simulated version take a clearly defensive stance. The man with the switchblade looked like he had hoped to just intimidate. No one wanted to kill someone and potentially land themselves in legal trouble over what could not be that much money. Yet when the man saw Jake clearly wanted to fight, he sneered and jumped. Sim-Jake dodged the blade, but one thing quickly became clear:

Sim-Jake was fighting someone with actual experience.

A cut landed on sim-Jake's arm, and he was forced to back away. He began retreating more and more as he took several wounds. When he made it behind a pillar, the man with the blade followed... only to have a rod of rebar smash towards him.

The man leaned back and dodged, once more showing he was no pushover. The first man had also gotten up again and pulled out a knife of his own.

"We really doing this?" sim-Jake asked as he stood there with his rebar rod.

Neither man answered, but they had clearly decided to kill him. It was answer enough. The simulated version of Jake dove forward, taking the men by surprise and managing to hit the guy he had injured earlier on the arm.

Sim-Jake tried to swing again as the man dropped his blade, but he had to stop and jump back to avoid getting stabbed in the gut. The second man came at him again, and sim-Jake managed to keep him away with his metal rod.

Jake—the real one—looked on, noting how mundane the battle was. It was almost weird seeing three people who were just average humans go at each other. His simulated version was in many ways at a disadvantage, but despite being younger and smaller, he held his own.

The situation changed when sim-Jake managed to tackle the second man, and they rolled to the ground. Sim-Jake got up but was bleeding from his thigh, while the other man... didn't get up. He was lying there with the knife stuck in his own chest, straight in the heart, with a look of disbelief on his face.

This took the two remaining survivors by surprise. It was clear sim-Jake had not done it on purpose. The real Jake also saw how it was just "luck," if one could call it that. Sim-Jake had tried to block while the man tried to stab and had hit Jake on the thigh, but it hadn't cut properly, and he'd ended up falling on his own knife.

"You! Fucking cunt!" the first man said, but he did not engage. Instead, he began retreating. The man was not the fastest, but neither was sim-Jake.

He just stood there for a moment and stared at the corpse... before something clicked.

He looked at the fleeing man and picked up the metal rod from before. With an impressive toss, he hit the man on the knee as he tried to flee and stormed over, his wounded thigh leaving a trail of blood behind him. Sim-Jake picked up the fallen rebar rod again as he went to the fallen man.

The man stared back as sim-Jake lifted up the rebar rod, yelling another curse just before sim-Jake swung down and hit him in the head. A few more blows sealed the deal. Sim-Jake then dropped the weapon and wheezed. He looked at his hands and started shaking.

"Fucking fuck. Shit... Just... fuck..."

The real Jake noted how they both had the habit of cursing a lot. He also understood the frustration... This was his first time killing anyone. The simulacrum, that is. But... it was a necessary kill. If he hadn't done it, things would have no doubt ended worse. They would have been back with reinforcements. Taken revenge.

Jake saw his simulated version limp away, still cursing and looking incredibly panicked. For some unknown reason, he also kept looking nervously around, primarily in the direction of where the real Jake was standing within the simulated space. The scene ended there, and everything changed once more.

The next scene was of sim-Jake sitting in a room, clearly older now. An older-looking gentleman in a suit handed him a picture. Sim-Jake looked at it, nodded, and handed it back. He then got up and left.

It switched again, now showing Jake standing over a dead body with a knife in his hand. He cleaned the weapon with a cloth before sheathing it beneath his clothes and walking out of the decrepit apartment building like nothing had happened.

At least he tried to, as there was movement in adjacent rooms.

The real Jake felt everything. Even in the simulation, his sphere was fully functional and showed him the world as genuine. He could see an actual world for hundreds of meters in every direction, and from the looks of it, his simulacrum also had this ability.

He stopped at the door and waited, clearly sensing someone walking through the hallway. The person stopped at the door and knocked. "Hey, boss, one of the corner girls was caught trying to stiff us again. Want us to handle it as usual?"

Yep, this entire joint was clearly a hidden brothel of sorts, and it appeared like sim-Jake had just killed the boss of the establishment. Real-Jake honestly felt a bit relieved that if sim-Jake was a killer, then at least he killed assholes.

The guy outside the door knocked again before finally opening the door a bit nervously. "Boss?"

He barely had time to step inside before sim-Jake snuck up from behind and slit his throat while covering the guy's mouth. He fell limp to the floor as sim-Jake shook his head and went out the door casually, wearing a black hoodie.

This version of him was probably eighteen or nineteen tops.

Similar scenes repeated, and it quickly became clear what kind of person he was. He was not necessarily a contract killer but just a mercenary for hire. There was even a brief stint overseas where he worked for an arms dealer but left soon after.

Throughout these scenes, Jake came to realize there was a lack of guns. Not used by the other side, but by sim-Jake. He used it overseas but quickly discarded it. Instead, he tended to use knives, wires, improvised weapons found at the location, or just his body.

He would sneak past police with his supernatural Bloodline abilities every time. Like a ghost, he would enter, kill, and leave again. Gradually, he moved up the food chain and went from killing low-life pimps to high-rollers in the criminal world. He even took out a corrupt judge at one point.

Real-Jake observed and went along for all these scenes. Weeks had passed for him, but time moved differently within the simulation room. Some of the scenes were incredibly impactful, while others were just more of the same. What they all had in common was an ever-growing Jake in skill, physique, knowledge, and just overall ability. Compared to other humans, he seemed borderline unstoppable. He was the type of person to bring a knife to a gunfight and utterly annihilate the other side.

The most impressive scene was one of the times sim-Jake was in legitimate trouble. He had been in a motel room but was clearly restless. He was on the run from the goons of a recent target and had chosen to lay low. Yet he felt like they had found him.

It turned out that the one who'd hired him had decided to try and get rid of sim-Jake and had informed the goons of his location. Knowing showing up in force would not work, they had simply placed two snipers focusing on the room's exits.

Sim-Jake exited one day to move to the next safe house. He looked semi-aware of what was happening.

For a bit of trivia... sniper bullets before the system traveled faster than the speed of sound. Many modern firearms did. This meant that one would not hear the gunshot before the bullet had already hit the target. Realistically, there should be no way to react or know it was coming.

Which is why the sniper was surely bamboozled when sim-Jake swayed to the side and avoided the bullet before taking cover and eventually making another miraculous escape.

Jake had to admit... this version of himself was so different from who he had been. From a university-educated financial worker to a top-tier assassin and killer. Comparing the two was like night and day.

Yet it did not feel foreign. To the current Jake, this made sense. This version of himself just embraced what made him, well, him. He became a hunter, and Jake was certain sim-Jake did not only choose targets based on money or prestige... He did it for the challenge.

He was a Primal Hunter, after all.

It was odd, knowing this could have been a version of him. Assuming the simulation was truly as accurate as it seemed to claim—and it did seem like it was so far—wasn't this version of Jake just... superior?

There was a lot to think about. He would just have to see what happened as the simulation progressed.

A new scene soon appeared. One Jake could not see the significance of right away. It was just a hotel room with his simulacrum sitting on a chair in a bathrobe, drinking some water. He had a tablet at the side, and the entire place looked expensive as hell.

What skin was showing made the life of this version of Jake clear. Even with his abilities, injuries were unavoidable. Sometimes one had to take a hit to avoid a lethal blow, and this had resulted in dozens of scars covering his body, from knife wounds to bullet holes.

From the looks of it, this was happening not long before the initiation would begin. Real-Jake peeked at the tablet and saw the date displayed, nodding when he realized it was around two months off. It would be exciting to truly see how he would handle that.

But.... then something weird happened.

Something very weird.

Sim-Jake looked deep in thought. He stared at the ceiling before finally sighing, steeling himself, and then looking straight at where Jake was.

"I do wonder who or what you are, oh, silent observer."

CHAPTER 54

UNDERSTANDING THYSELF

Odd. The world was odd. Jake hadn't noticed it much—at least, not to begin with—but as he grew up, it became more and more apparent. It was as if someone was watching him. Not all the time, mind you, but this observer appeared at important events. That feeling of a gaze and a feeling of wrongness. It was also only in those moments where he felt observed that he truly felt this oddness of the world.

It was no security camera, no satellite locking in on his position... It was as if the observer didn't truly exist, yet could observe him. Jake chose to ignore it for the most part, as his instincts told him he could do nothing about it, and so far, this observer had had no impact on his life.

Perhaps it was a guardian angel given to him after his parents died? Or was it a god? Some extraterrestrial being? A creature existing in a world separate from his own? Many theories dominated his mind, especially as the gaze felt so familiar. Familiar, yet different.

As time passed and he grew older, this silent observer seemed more and more familiar. He even began wondering if it was his unborn brother's ghost. It would make sense if his brother would have been like him, right? That he would have the same abilities and be born with the same innate talents?

Sitting in a chair within the extravagant hotel room, he stared at where he faintly felt this apparition was. He shook his head and spoke out loud into the room, expecting nothing in response.

"I do wonder who or what you are, oh, silent observer," Jake muttered randomly.

And surprisingly enough... it felt like this apparition had heard and understood him.

Jake stared at his simulacrum for a moment as he felt the familiar yet foreign man stare back.

"Wait... did he just talk to me?" real-Jake said. Then he shook his head. "Nah, it shouldn't work like that."

"You understand me?" sim-Jake asked, equally confused.

Two Jakes stared at each other. Both were in utter disbelief. The real Jake because his simulacrum, an apparition of the system or the Seat or the Seat of the Exalted Prima, was suddenly aware of him. Sim-Jake because he was talking to what he probably assumed to be a mere delusion that gave him the sense it understood his words.

"What or who are you?" sim-Jake asked as he stood up and went over to where Jake was standing. He moved his hand, and it passed straight through Jake. Yet when it was around his heart, his hand stopped for a second, and he frowned.

Jake also felt it. A recognition or resonance of sorts. Sim-Jake removed his hand and backed away as his frown only grew deeper. "You're like me?" he asked almost with a look of realization. He then smiled before he started laughing. "I fucking knew it. I now know why this all feels so damn wrong. I'm not meant to be here, right? What the hell happened? Did I get thrown into a separate dimension or universe or some shit? Am I even human? Are you?" His questions were full of excitement.

The real Jake stared as he considered the questions, deciding to answer despite the other version not being able to hear him. "Eh, I guess I am not meant to be you? But there was no accident, just a different choice. And yeah, you are human. We both are. Just more human than anyone else, perhaps." Inside, he was asking just as many questions as sim-Jake.

Firstly... how the fuck was this possible?

This was a simulation. The system was clear on that. Which just raised even more questions. This other version of himself had everything Jake had, including his Bloodline. He was Jake in every sense of the word, even to the level of being aware he was being observed by an outside force he should in no reasonable way be aware of.

Jake knew that the system itself had made this simulation—it had to—and that it could be considered a real world for everyone in it. Maybe the system did just go above and beyond, straight-up creating a parallel universe to simulate what would have happened.

Then again, would that even be going above and beyond? For an omnipotent force, was there truly a difference between creating a speck of dust and a universe? Omnipotence was omnipotence, after all. One or a trillion was equally insignificant before something infinite.

So... if it had just made a new world to simulate that one choice, why not do it perfectly? And a perfect Jake would know he was in a simulated world if he was. Well, he wouldn't know-know, but he would be aware something was off and that he was being observed.

Villy had mentioned that the system did not create Bloodlines, but he'd never said it couldn't. Just that it didn't. Actually, that wasn't even entirely true, as if the system controlled everything, wasn't it also the system "creating" new Bloodlines when two people with Bloodlines had a child and their Bloodlines fused, making a new one? Or at least it allowed it to happen.

Jake shook his head as he considered all these questions he would perhaps never get a straight answer to. Even Villy made it clear he didn't know. All he knew was that the system didn't create new Bloodlines outright but recycled old ones for some system events, so for it to copy a Bloodline temporarily for such an event was not overly surprising.

What was a bit surprising was that this Bloodline in question allowed the other copy to recognize the event itself.

Recognize the "real" version of itself speaking to it.

"I'm... wrong?" the copy said. The ambiguousness of Jake's answer about them both being humans and in the right places still seemed to confuse the simulacrum. Especially considering he didn't actually hear any answer but had to go by pure intuition. "No, not entirely," sim-Jake concluded. "Alright, yes and no questions. Hm... how to confirm answers..."

The real Jake got an idea for this. He began moving back and forth while keeping an eye on sim-Jake. He, of course, noticed and picked up on it instantly. Jake knew he would. They were both Jake, were they not?

"I understand. To confirm, can you move to the left? My left."

Jake did so.

"And right?"

Jake did so too.

"Alright, method of communication with a creature from a separate dimension established," sim-Jake joked. Real-Jake knew he would have made that exact same joke.

"A step to my left is no, and to the right is yes, alright?" sim-Jake said, beginning the "conversation."

Jake stepped to the right to confirm.

"Okay. First of all, are you human?"

Once more, Jake confirmed that, yep, they were both humans.

"And so am I?"

Yep.

"Hm. But we are different, aren't we?"

Confirmed.

"Odd. Very odd. Are there others with abilities like mine?"

Jake thought for a second. Well, there were others with Bloodlines, but not others with his Bloodline. So... yes, but also not really? Not knowing what to say, Jake just stood unmoving as his simulation waited for him to decide.

After a good five seconds, the simulacrum frowned and asked, "You don't know?"

Jake chose to say yes to that one.

"So you do know?"

Yep once more.

"But yet you will not say there are others like me. Us. Hm..."

The next few minutes passed with sim-Jake asking questions and Jake trying to answer as best he could. It was damn weird having a conversation with himself, but it was also way smoother than it should be. Jake naturally understood his own logic, and even with how differently they had lived and grown up, he understood his simulacrum. Perhaps that was telling of how much the Bloodline truly had worked on forming him... or it was an argument that nature mattered more than nurture.

Either way, he ended up properly communicating that while there were others who were special, there were only those two who were Jake-special. It was also a bit awkward when sim-Jake asked if they were related somehow. Jake had chosen just to stand still and give a "maybe" to that one, as he wasn't sure people would consider what they were as related. He knew he would not, so of course, his simulacrum wouldn't either.

The questions eventually turned away from the question of "who" and moved on to the question of "why."

After a few preliminary questions where Jake confirmed he was unable to actually interact and influence the world outside of the communication they were currently having, his simulacrum began to understand.

"So you are here to observe me?"

Big yes to that one. It was all he could do.

"But you are only around at certain times... Do you choose when?"

An equally big no there.

"Is someone else dictating what you are allowed to see?"

Eh, a no to that one. It wasn't someone, and his simulacrum quickly picked up on his answer.

"A set of rules, then?"

Yes.

"Hm... okay, so you are here to observe me according to a set of rules. Which means you are here to see something specific about me. Considering that you mainly appear in or before combat situations or at other major events... is the reason related to our shared special ability?"

Maybe for that one. Yes and no. Jake was there to observe everything he was, and his Bloodline was certainly part of that.

"So partly, I guess. Is it related to combat?"

Also a maybe, as that too was only partially right.

"Not combat either? At least, not fully? Is it related to my targets somehow?"

Nah, it wasn't. Jake didn't really care who he killed, only how he did it.

"So it is only related to me?"

Big yeppers.

They went on a bit further as they narrowed it down. Dozens of questions later and a conclusion had been reached that Jake could confidently answer yes to.

"You are here to observe me passively to learn—not necessarily from me, but about me. Who I am, why I do as I do, and pretty much just see my life and how I develop and who I become?"

Jake answered yes to that clarified summary.

"I think I kind of get it now. Okay, not really. But you do say this will be beneficial to me?"

Jake confirmed that. They were the same person, after all. Help me, help you, which is actually me. It made sense.

"I don't get the feeling that is a lie either... Alright. Let's go from here, then. You want to learn about and from me about who I am? Well, let me teach you without holding anything back. You have seen everything anyway, so the more information, the better, right?"

Which was once more confirmed by Jake. His simulacrum was about to open his mouth and say more when the scene then skipped forward, much to the frustration of Jake. The next scene was of sim-Jake in a dark, forest-like area with lights in the distance leading up to a remotely located mansion.

The moment he appeared, sim-Jake noticed and smiled. "Been a week since our last meeting. I was beginning to wonder if you were done."

He was in a camouflage outfit, and his mouth was covered as he spoke incredibly softly. During their questionnaire, they had already confirmed that sim-Jake could speak in the lowest of whispers and real-Jake could still hear it. Not due to simulation stuff, but just because Perception was the best stat.

His simulacrum then began to speak. Almost rantingly. "You know, I never really liked humans and found it a bit disappointing when you said I was one. I felt like I could never relate to other people. Not truly. They were all so different from me from the get-go. They were stupid, made moronic decisions, and their instincts were so pathetic it disgusted me on a fundamental level. I was superior to every one of them. Granted, I am not the smartest when it comes to books, but hey, you don't judge a fish by its ability to climb a tree, and you don't judge an apex killer by his ability to discuss philosophy. Besides, all that shit is just needlessly complicated, you know? I always manage with the same plan:

"Make things simple... and take the complications as they come."

Jake's eyes opened a bit wide at that sentence. The sentiment. It was something he often thought to himself and was almost a motto of his, once more making it clear they were indeed one and the same.

"Anyway, this all makes me dislike other humans more," sim-Jake rambled on. "I hate working with them and being around them. They want plans or strategies, and if something—anything—goes wrong, they fucking panic and do nothing useful. Even if they are trained and don't panic, they still don't adapt. Not properly. Not like we do. I guess another way of looking at it is that I feel like I am a wolf living amongst sheep.

"None of them are aware of me or other dangerous entities around them. Perhaps I envy their ignorance, as they can die with a simple shot to the head or a knife in the neck before they even notice. Perhaps I envy that they can belong somewhere and not always be the odd one out. It may sound narcissistic of me, but I do think I am better than everyone else. Not at everything, but at what I am and what I do. Overall, this does make me superior. Makes me more than human. Perhaps the next step in evolution or simply the apex of what humanity can reach. It isn't even a guess anymore. I know I am objectively superior from the core of my being. Even when I try not to feel superior, I feel disdain towards those weaker than myself... which is everyone. It is worse with those who don't even try."

Jake listened on. His simulacrum whispered beneath his breath as he snuck forward and passed over a fence. Security cameras were covering most spots, but sim-Jake picked up a small stone and, with a piece of cloth, launched it towards the one covering his entrance point, breaking it instantly. He then quickly ran over and tossed a dead bird at the base of the mansion as he ran across the side of the large building.

"Don't get me wrong—I also like to laze around once in a while and do nothing, but how can you live a life doing that? How can you not improve yourself? More than anything, how can you live with yourself standing in a crowd, knowing the majority there could end your life if they so desired? Would that realization not make you strive for power more? I know, I know, this doesn't apply to them. They don't feel the inherent danger others can pose. They just embrace their feeble safety given by others. Maybe that is why I like what I do."

Guards reacted to the broken camera as they made their way to investigate. Sim-Jake easily took advantage of this and scaled the building on another side to reach an already-open window. Clearly, the one living there feared little. It was located in a remote forest, with Jake counting more than forty guards total and a top-of-the-line security system. Not expecting someone to climb four stories in less than half a minute with absolute ease was also reasonable.

"A lot of the 'powerful' in this world are just the opposite. They are weak. Feeble old men are elected leaders of countries, institutions, and large, influential companies. Even leaders of cartels and criminal enterprises tend to be on the older side. They are viewed as the brains of the operation, or maybe they are just leveraging who they used to be and their reputation. Logically, I understand. You want the one in charge to know what he is doing... but does he really need to be at the top? Why is he at the top when a simple reality is clear?"

Sim-Jake had small breaks in between whispering as he hid from guards who patrolled. They found the broken security camera and noticed the dead bird, perhaps concluding that it had flown into the camera and destroyed it. In the midst of night with low visibility and nothing else going on, this was an easy and frankly lazy conclusion.

Jake's alternate version finally made it to a door guarded by two men. Thinking quickly, sim-Jake retreated a bit and quickly dispatched one of the patrolling guards. Once the man was silently eliminated, sim-Jake pulled on his clothes, which included a nice pair of night-vision goggles perfect for hiding your face.

"They like to hide away. Use others as shields. They live in a reality that simply isn't true, and they hold a worldview I love to shatter. They think they are the superior ones. I feel it. They genuinely believe they are better than everyone else. That they are apex humans who are untouchable."

Sim-Jake walked casually towards the two guards who lazily stood there, not really commenting on the approaching disguised figure. Only when sim-Jake was within striking distance did one of them notice something was off, and by then, it was too late. A knife was thrown, and another man was stabbed in the neck as they both fell to the ground, unable to even resist.

Inside the room was only a single man sitting at a desk with a computer. He looked up as the door opened and saw sim-Jake, who had already taken the mask and night-vision goggles off. He smiled at the man, his clothes splattered with blood.

He spoke the last part out loud to both Jake and the man who stared at his approach. "Even with all their wealth, all their influence and their grand reputation... they are still weak, feeble humans."

The man behind the desk finally reacted by pulling out a gun and aiming. Sim-Jake just smiled as the man shot; he had already dodged the bullet before it was even released from the chamber.

"Weak, feeble humans that, despite everything they have..." Sim-Jake dodged the final bullet of the chamber and now stood before the scared-shitless old man. He tried to speak, but a single fist hit the side of his head as he fell, his eyes glazed over. "... still die by my hand. Because that is true power."

CHAPTER 55

A LONELY EXISTENCE

Jake watched on as his simulacrum made yet another miraculous escape by leaping out a window and rapelling down four stories before swiftly making it over the fence to the forest. The guards were a bit distracted by the gunshots from their boss earlier and had, of course, gone to investigate, only to find the man dead.

Back in the forest, sim-Jake kept running as he spoke once more, a smile on his lips. "I wasn't even paid for this one, you know? I just didn't like the guy. He tried to hire me a year or so ago, and when I refused the job, as the target wasn't my kind of thing, he threw a hissy fit and tried to have me killed. Naturally, he failed, and I killed the people he sent, and the idiot probably thought that was the end of it. Or not, based on the guards, but hey, I enjoy the added challenge. Sometimes you got to sneak a bit, as not even I can survive the barrage of an entire squad of gunmen. Too many bullets. Even if I can feel the trajectory of every one of them, it would be like trying to dodge the rain itself."

He talked about himself more and explained things that Jake, of course, understood. Ah, but the rain was dodgeable; he just had to get strong enough. If it wasn't, Jake would have been torn apart by the Sword Saint.

As for the philosophy of his simulacrum... Jake also understood. Understanding and agreeing were not the same, though. He himself had felt similarly, and still did at times. His Bloodline was, in the end, partly about being at the peak of the food chain, and looking down on others was just inherent to him. Be it an unwanted side effect or a necessary part of his ability to ignore presences, it was there.

Jake could only imagine how it must have been to grow up with his Bloodline on full display. The real Jake had at least met actually powerful individuals after he fully awakened his Bloodline to get some perspective. People so strong he would not be able to land a single injury on them no matter what methods he deployed. Those so powerful they could wipe him from existence with a mere thought. Looking down on those individuals was something not even Jake could do. However, that was still different from recognizing them as superior. To Jake, someone being stronger than him was just a temporary state of things. One day, he would stand at the top, or he would die trying with a smile on his face.

Sim-Jake did not have that kind of perspective at all. It was entirely possible he was the strongest individual on the planet. That there truly was nobody he couldn't kill. Jake could understand why that could be... boring. But, something else was also readily apparent:

This Jake had way less empathy than the non-simulation Jake, and damn, Jake was not the most empathetic person to begin with. Never had been. But his family had ensured he had some "humanity" in him. He could confidently say that he truly loved and cared for his brother and parents. His simulacrum had never had anyone that he judged worthy of recognizing as worth caring for. Especially not if he'd disconnected himself from humanity early on. Jake had seen no signs of lovers or even friends in any of the visions he had seen. Sim-Jake was always alone. In some ways, it was a bit sad.

"I sense a trace of disapproval," sim-Jake said. "Why? I know you understand. Don't get me wrong—it isn't that I like to kill humans for sport. There is no sport in committing a senseless murder. It would be like a pathetic loser sitting back with his rifle to shoot a rhino. There is no danger, no challenge... no meaning in such an action. I also do have some rules. I will not kill people I believe genuinely contribute to making the world a better place, or if I believe their deaths will cause too many issues for too many innocent people. The last rule is the reason why I haven't killed nine out of ten politicians." The last part was only half a joke.

His simulacrum ran through the forest a bit more before making it to a boat at the edge of a river. He jumped on and started the surprisingly silent motor, then sailed the thirty-odd meters to the other side.

"You may ask if I couldn't look for my challenges elsewhere... and I did," sim-Jake further explained, somewhat defensive. "Underground fighting rings, hunting in the wild, or even fighting animals. None of it was able to truly scratch that itch. Sadly, I could never do anything official or even try to perhaps compete with the peak of humanity in sports, as I have not been viewed favorably by the law since I was a teenager. I don't even think I am officially alive anymore. And even if I competed in sports, it would all just be too fake. A challenge without consequences is just not as good, and fencing competitors don't want to use real swords during combat. What true combat I could find, such as in the underground fighting ring, was not interesting either. They were too weak, and even their rules ruined the fun. Ah, I did have a handful of life-and-death fights, but after four opponents, no one wanted to fight anymore. Understandable, I guess."

Getting off the boat, sim-Jake went up a hill and into a camouflaged getaway vehicle.

"I would never claim to be a good person, but I would not call myself a bad one either. I am just me. I don't kill without reason, but I also don't spare those I find undeserving. I have rules I abide by, even if they conflict with what society believes I should do. I fight, I kill, and I try to challenge myself. I do what I want, eat the best food I can get my hands on, and go wherever and do whatever I want. So let me ask you..." The simulacrum then turned to Jake, who sat beside him on the passenger seat, flying along since he couldn't actually sit on the seat. "Why do I feel so fucking miserable? Why does this world feel so utterly meaningless? Why do I feel like I am just waiting for something to happen? For true meaning to appear? Tell me, oh, silent observer... will things ever change, or am I doomed to live in this meaningless reality, surrounded by weaklings till I die of boredom? I do not expect an answer. I ju—"

The real Jake had already floated in front of sim-Jake by this point. As the simulacrum drove the vehicle, Jake appeared in front of the window. Jake then moved to the right to answer a confident yes. Jake saw his simulacrum smile through the windshield with relief as the scene changed abruptly once more.

Jake saw himself standing within an entirely white room that he instantly recognized. A humanoid figure that wasn't quite human sat in a chair with sim-Jake right in front of him.

It was the Introduction. This was the very moment the integration began, and the tutorial was about to begin. Sim-Jake seemed to instantly notice and turned around. He looked at Jake, but Jake was more focused on the apparition of the system that ignored him entirely and directed sim-Jake to select a class or profession like Jake had—minus the possibility of a profession. But his simulacrum instead asked the system,

"Are you aware of someone other than us in the room?"

The system construct answered instantly, "Yes. Now please select a class or profession."

"Was this the change you spoke about?" sim-Jake instead asked Jake. Jake moved to confirm, and the man smiled. "You are telling me life gets better from here?"

Once more, a solid yes.

Sim-Jake turned to the system construct again. "I choose light warrior."

With that, two daggers and a set of basic armor appeared on the table just as the scene ended.

As the transition to the next scene began, Jake noted the first major difference in the tutorial. Firstly, he could pick either class or profession —something the real Jake could not do in his. Additionally, his simulacrum had chosen light warrior, which made sense based on his prior fighting style.

The new scene appeared soon after: A huge hall, filled with individuals wearing their starting gear, with dark elves and other high-level individuals scattered around. Jake instantly realized this was the tutorial he had seen in the preview, and the one Caleb was meant to be in. This was further hammered home when he saw the two people Caleb had entered the Seat of the Exalted Prima with—Matteo and Nadia, if he remembered correctly. What he did not expect was the next scene.

A circle was formed. A circle around a certain individual. Jake had been told this tutorial included a lot of former assassins and contract killers. Criminals. It also seemed like people quickly realized who he was and backed away as the Organizer of the tutorial stepped up on a platform overseeing them all. Jake was amazed at feeling the presence of an S-grade there, and when the aura of this entity bathed the area, all of the assassins were affected by it.

This was clearly a moment to establish dominance. No mere newly initiated G-grade could stand against even a fraction of an S-grade's presence, and everyone was forced to their knees.

Everyone except for one.

Sim-Jake stood tall, surrounded by over a thousand kneeling or squatting individuals. Even all the dark elves were pressured, leaving only two entities in the entire tutorial standing at that moment.

The S-grade stared at sim-Jake as sim-Jake just looked back and made a toothy grin. Jake felt the excitement. One he had felt himself. However, his moment was when he'd seen the Malefic Viper during his vision from the mural back in the dungeon.

It was an emotion born from standing before something so much more powerful than yourself you couldn't truly comprehend it. It should lead to a feeling of powerlessness or inadequacy, perhaps humility, but to both Jake and sim-Jake, it meant only one thing: a new goal. A new mountain to climb and a peak to shatter. Jake could imagine his simulacrum thinking, "I want to beat that person one day."

"What are you?" the S-grade asked as it looked at sim-Jake, all attention gathered on them.

Sim-Jake just kept his smile as he answered, "A hunter."

The scene ended a mere moment later, sim-Jake not even acknowledging Jake in this particular scene. Then again, it'd been a relatively short, if impactful, one.

A brief flash showed the next scene: sim-Jake standing before who he assumed to be Umbra. No words were spoken that Jake could hear, but he saw sim-Jake extend his hand as the being of pure shadows humored him and shook it. The scene ended just as sim-Jake turned around to look at Jake.

As the scene changed again, the environment was very different. Sim-Jake stood in a dark cave, with the dark mana almost palpable in the air. Monkey-like creatures hid in the crevices as sim-Jake turned his head towards where Jake had just appeared.

"It's been a while," he said, smiling. Jake could already see the changes. His smile was far more genuine, and he looked much happier than before. "In case you are wondering, this is about a month into this tutorial. You truly did not lie. Tell me, is your presence here related to this system and the multiverse?"

Jake smiled a bit himself as he did his old dance routine of stepping to the right to confirm.

"I see." Sim-Jake nodded. "Are you a god?"

That one, Jake had to deny. He wasn't a god. Not yet, at least.

"I kind of figured you weren't, based on not even that god Umbra being able to detect you despite being quite impressive according to, well, everyone. Which must mean the system is directly involved. Am I right? Ah, by the way, no one is watching or listening in right now, but I reckon you already knew that. I made it clear to Umbra I knew and shut that shit down instantly."

Another change. Jake felt the level of distrust from his simulacrum was as intense as ever, and from the looks of it, he was hunting alone. Nothing wrong with that, but Jake had a feeling this Jake was always alone. Again, solitude was nice, and Jake liked his alone time, but that didn't mean he never wanted to interact with others.

Sim-Jake was the opposite. He distrusted everyone else heavily, which was a bit odd, if you thought about it. His Bloodline offered him an intuition that allowed him to quickly get a gut feeling about others, so shouldn't that help him trust people a little more? Sure, Jake had been wrong about people, but he had also been right often. Miranda had given him a good feeling, and he felt like he had hit the jackpot there.

Meanwhile, he did not see his simulacrum ever forming a city. At least, not without being the City Leader himself and ruling it with an iron fist. He would also no doubt be shit at running the city, as he didn't trust anyone, so he wouldn't delegate and, of course, wouldn't do stuff himself, as he was too busy hunting.

Such an existence had to be lonely, as Jake had noted before. Lonely but also limiting. Jake had gained a lot from talking with Villy, sparring with others, and fighting people like the Sword Saint. Would sim-Jake also learn a lot through fighting? Yes... but he would not have an enlightening conversation afterward with his opponent.

Sim-Jake would also be far less receptive to feedback and would have probably just ignored all he had been told during the D-grade test dungeon in the Order of the Malefic Viper. A lot of issues could crop up from that... but it would also lead to something unique. Sim-Jake would perhaps forge a far more unique Path, and at least it did seem like he took pointers of some kind or at least embraced the skills of Umbra, based on his aura.

Anyway, Jake confirmed the question of the system's involvement, making his simulacrum nod in understanding. "Is this part of some test or something?"

Hm... Jake thought. It wasn't really, but then again, it kind of was? Maybe? The system event description wasn't very clear on that, and Jake was unsure if he could describe what happened as a test. So he stood still.

"Partly, huh? Odd. But the objective stays the same, right? Observe and learn about and from me?"

Jake confirmed that one.

"Well, then... let me teach you," sim-Jake said. Dark mana began revolving around him as Jake watched dark veins appear on his skin. "No, let me show you my Path."

CHAPTER 56

PROFESSION??

From all the things Jake had seen so far, his simulacrum wasn't that much better at fighting in melee than him. He was better for sure, but it was more from experience than pure fighting technique. One could say that to beat other humans, sim-Jake didn't need to learn anything advanced. He just needed to attack with one quick blow and end their lives.

With the system, enemies did not go down as easily. Especially not foes above himself in level. Even a blow to the brain didn't necessarily mean instant death, so Jake finally got to see his simulacrum in extended combat against several foes. From this, Jake truly understood... this version of himself was far superior to the current Jake in melee combat. Far, far superior.

Jake followed sim-Jake for days as his other version went through the dark caverns, ascended a set of stairs and entered a grand hall, fought there, and then ended up within a decrepit old village after going up another set of stairs. Jake was a bit confused until sim-Jake explained the tutorial a bit.

"I am in what is called the Shadow Trials, which is the combat grounds. It is split into several floors, and I am currently on the twenty-fifth floor. I have killed two bosses of sorts so far, but neither have been that hard. As you know, I was blessed by the god known as Umbra and offered the Legacy of some god known as Tenlucis, who died or something like that. Quite potent, if I say so myself, even if I do find it questionable to accept the Legacy of a god weak enough to have died, but oh, well. I will take what I can get, and I do get the feeling Umbra is worth working with. For now." He said all of this rather casually.

These were borderline blasphemous words that most other mortals would scoff at, if not scream at him for. Not only did he offend a dead god, but he also put himself on the same level as Umbra by insinuating they worked together and that he was no follower. Naturally, Jake expected nothing else, and from the looks of it, Umbra was also fine with it. Jake was not told what level of Blessing his simulacrum had gotten, but he knew he was not a Chosen. Potentially a Divine Blessing.

Dark lightning began revolving around sim-Jake as he recognized some of the abilities Caleb had. It was a bit odd, seeing a version of himself surrounded by that same black lightning. Sim-Jake dove forward toward a zombie-like creature. It lunged towards sim-Jake, but he hit it through the head with a dagger before it had time to do anything. It struggled and tried to strike sim-Jake, but every attempt was foiled, and it soon died.

He then stepped back and seemed to sink into the shadows. Jake still saw him with his sphere, but it was like sim-Jake melted into the shadows to anyone else. He ran over to the next zombie that didn't notice him before getting stabbed through the head. Flailing around, the zombie used its claws to tear at the ground and collapse the building it had been hiding in, but sim-Jake was already out of it and proceeded to throw a bolt of black lightning at the collapsing house, making it explode.

Everything shown so far had been simple and easy like this. Sim-Jake dominated everything he'd so far encountered. This made Jake initially think these foes were just low-level monsters... but no, they were all several levels above sim-Jake himself. In fact, sim-Jake was many levels ahead of where Jake had been about a month into the tutorial. In Jake's defense, he had focused on alchemy for nearly all that time, but Jake also soon noticed something else.

Through the days Jake observed his simulacrum, he didn't see him do anything that was not fighting or meditating to prepare for another fight. Jake frowned at this and began moving back and forth to get his simulacrum's attention.

"Hm? What?" sim-Jake asked. "I must say, this is the longest you have been around so far, so I guess this entire combat thing is quite important. Is that why you are moving around? Do you want me to explain more of why I fight like I do and such? Sure, I guess."

"Well, no, that wasn't what I meant," Jake said out loud, continuing to stand still. What? He still wanted him to explain more. Sometimes telling was just better at delivering information than showing, especially if one wanted to learn the intent behind something.

"Not right, huh? Or only partly?" sim-Jake asked as he proceeded to take out a potion. Jake saw it and rapidly moved back and forth, making sim-Jake stop just before drinking it. "What?"

Jake tried to move a bit more, as he wanted his simulacrum to just give him some damn information on his profession. He was really curious by now what this version of himself would do, as he honestly had no idea. He had ended up becoming an alchemist to not die, and had come to like it only after getting the profession. What would this version have chosen? Any kind of social profession was out of the question, so it had to be crafting-related, right? What interests did sim-Jake even have besides fighting and killing? Maybe something to make things that made that easier?

"I am blanking here. Something to do with the potion?"

Stopping his movement, Jake stood still to confirm that was partly it.

"Is anything wrong with drinking them?" sim-Jake asked. "Hm, I have theorized that they are too good to be true and may have some long-term demerits that I have yet to notice, so—"

Jake quickly denied it. Potions were awesome, and he was almost offended at his super-distrusting simulacrum talking shit about them.

"Good to drink? Then does it have something to do with this particular potion?"

Jake stood still.

"Is it the effects?"

Nope.

"Where it comes from?"

Yep!

"I traded it with an alchemist fo—"

Jake began moving quickly again the moment he said the word alchemist.

"What? You want to know about this alchemist?" sim-Jake asked, looking genuinely confused.

They went through a few more questions before sim-Jake finally asked a question Jake could work with.

"Are you asking if I am an alchemist?"

It wasn't actually what he wanted to ask, but that question would lead to a natural follow-up, so Jake answered yes.

"No, I am not. Oh... yeah, I should have understood this way earlier. Of course. You are here to learn about me and my Path, so it is relevant. You want to know what my profession is, right?"

Yes! Finally!

Sim-Jake just smiled and shook his head. "Why the hell would I have one? Sure, the stats would be nice, but that just isn't me."

Jake froze at that. What?

"I know, I know. I have been told plenty of times I need to get one, but I ask again, why the hell should I?" Passionately, he continued, "They want me to sit on my ass making swords, or, what, pick up painting? Make magic formations and spend hours on making something that is still fucking useless to me as I am currently? Become an alchemist and sit with a stupid pot like some second-rate cook who only knows how to make fucking soup? No, fuck all that. I am a goddamn hunter, not a good little craftsman making my masters happy. I am the damn master. They can spend their time learning how to make things, and I can spend mine using their creations to get stronger and do what I was born to."

Now more than ever, Jake saw the difference between them grow. The thing is, Jake did not disagree with much of what he said—besides his words on alchemy, which he forgave sim-Jake for, as he knew it came from ignorance. He'd had a hard time imagining himself doing any profession when he first entered the tutorial. He'd just wanted to hunt. If he had not found the dungeon, he would have waited a long time before getting one, and if he had gotten one early, he would have half-arsed it.

The only reason Jake had appreciated alchemy in the beginning—after using it to not die, that is—was because he'd seen its usefulness. He'd seen how it made him stronger. The skills related to the Malefic Viper were skills that did have alchemical effects but were also combat skills. Sure, Scales of the Malefic Viper could be used to touch toxic substances and resist fumes and such, but its true value was in combat. Villy knew it, Jake knew it, and the system also knew but allowed it.

Not having a profession this early also wasn't an end-all, be-all. Sim-Jake was only a month into the system. Sure, it would make him lack some easy race levels early on, but he could always get a profession that would fit him later. There were near endless possibilities, so—

"Just to reiterate, I don't plan on ever getting a profession. The lack of instant gratification through easy levels is a sacrifice I am willing to make to follow the Path I have chosen for myself. It may sound stupid, if not outright moronic, but I believe this is truly the best decision. Even if I can somehow get a profession that fits me well and doesn't feel like a waste of time, I wouldn't do it. But I have a plan. One I even discussed with Umbra. And while there was some disagreement, you, of all people, should know that those like us can be stubborn. What I plan to do is evolve. To evolve out of this pathetic human form and become more than I am now. I need the class still, but there are enlightened races that only have either-or of class and profession. I want one such race. Till then, I shall walk a Path of purity. One of pure combat and dominance. Also... while I said I may sacrifice instant power, it isn't like I have encountered anyone worth fighting amongst humanity quite yet, and the multiverse runs on a timescale far different than our pathetic old world."

Jake stood with his mouth open for a while. When he'd heard the first part about never wanting a profession, Jake thought his other self was indeed a moron, but... could Jake really say sim-Jake was *that* wrong? At least he had a plan, and what he planned was entirely possible. So far, Jake had already had the possibility of evolving into a vampire or a Malefic Dragonkin, which would allow him to only have a class or profession, so who was he to say sim-Jake would not get similar options down the line? Even if he did not get any of these extraordinary evolution chances, there was a good chance he would get one for his D-grade evolution.

Now, to make one thing clear, Jake still thought his simulacrum was being stupid. Clearly, he had some inborn hatred of being human —one Jake did not have at all. In fact, he thought being human was pretty darn awesome. Also, after seeing Valdemar tear Villy a new one, how could he ever proclaim that humans weren't great?

"I still sense disapproval, but my mind is set," sim-Jake said. "I may crash and burn and ultimately adapt my Path, but I doubt it. Now, come. The boss is ahead."

Yet just after he said that, the scene ended. Clearly, the upcoming fight was not viewed as at all impactful by the system. He then saw a few brief scenes. Sim-Jake was fighting in nearly all of them, where he faced different, progressively stronger monsters and eventually had duels with humans. Jake saw him easily beat both Matteo and Nadia in duels, making it clear he was the strongest in the tutorial. Even without his profession to gain race levels, he stayed ahead of the curve, and what levels he did have were probably more valuable due to a powerful class.

Jake watched on, and it soon settled on a scene once more. Sim-Jake noticed him the moment he appeared and smiled at him.

"Not just popping in briefly this time, eh?" he asked with a light smile.

His equipment had entirely changed since the last time Jake saw him. He wore dark leather armor now of high quality and even had a spatial item, from the looks of it.

"I guess it makes sense... We are at the end of this tutorial, after all. With a day left, we stand before the final fight." He laughed a bit as he looked at what was on the horizon.

Jake followed his gaze and saw a spider-like creature sitting on a massive web. He instantly knew it was a D-grade. Looking at sim-Jake, he wondered if he was up to the task... but quickly realized that it wasn't even a question.

He was level 66. If he still had no profession, it meant he had pushed his class all the way to the cap at 99 and then kept getting experience to level his race about a dozen more times. In a bit over two months. It was a speed that completely put Jake to shame in every way.

Moreover, this Jake was not facing a King of the Forest but a regular D-grade. He also didn't seem to have any special items; even if he did, Jake knew sim-Jake would not use it. He simply didn't have to. One had to remember that Jake had been around level 80 when he had killed his first D-grade back on Earth, but that fight had been rather easy. And while this version of Jake was not as strong as Jake was then, he could surely put up a big fight.

But before he engaged in the fight, sim-Jake turned to Jake with an odd gaze. "You know... I always felt something was off about this world. I believed for a long time it was simply due to my uniqueness. Then I thought it was due to your presence. Finally, I believed it was due to the initiation not having happened. But even now, things just feel slightly off." He smiled at Jake.

"Yet I choose to ignore it. I choose to suppress that emotion even now... so please observe as always. From the very first time I laid my eyes on this creature, I wanted to fight it, and now that I stand before my goal, I will reach it. I will prove my Path to you, and after I win, we can discuss... everything." His smile turned melancholic as he added, "If I survive, that is."

Dark magic began revolving around him as weapons appeared in both hands. At first, Jake thought they were daggers, but at a closer look, they were more... fist-blades?

The weapons had an H-shaped horizontal hand grip that rested against one's knuckles. Each weapon had one blade, which was wide, triangular, and straight—roughly forty centimeters, making them rather long.

"These are called katars. Classified as push daggers, they are highly efficient stabbing weapons. However, they are also usually rather impractical in battles and inferior to a dagger or a sword, much less a spear. However, they do also have advantages. First of all, using them is very natural and similar to punching. Secondly, you can put your whole weight behind every hit. They can also be used for slashing, but it is a bit less practical, while the handle itself can help block, albeit not that well. Defensively, it is a weapon inferior to most others you will see. I shall show you why these weaknesses truly don't matter."

With those words, shadows surrounded sim-Jake as he prepared to face a D-grade in the tutorial. No gimmicks. No special quest items. Just a natural predator that had grown through hunting to reach that stage in two months.

And what followed was indeed a display of what that natural predator was truly capable of.

Chapter 57

A Path To Survival

"As we both know, the Bloodline offers abilities that are on a qualitative level at the peak of the multiverse," sim-Jake explained as he flew towards his foe, Jake easily keeping up. "Merely doing by instinct, dodging anything and everything, is simplicity itself, but that does leave one obvious flaw: attacking. Don't get me wrong—the instinct to attack weak points is still there, but such a simple instinct may do more harm than good. When attacking, you are forcing a reaction, not being the one to react, meaning our predictive instincts are far less useful.

"So let me show you how I truly fight. Ultimately, that is what you are here for, isn't it?"

Jake didn't confirm, as they both knew the answer. He stopped a bit away from the spider-like creature that had already noticed the approaching human. It was sitting on a massive web with hundreds, if not thousands of eggs beneath it. Its many eyes were shining purple as it looked at sim-Jake, but it didn't do anything until sim-Jake stepped his foot onto the web. It was likely due to a system restriction of some sort, or maybe it was just a territorial creature.

"One word," sim-Jake added under his breath as his body exploded with power, the sky above darkening and thunder rumbling. "Counter."

A spider several times faster than sim-Jake descended upon him. A leg bathed in deep shadows shot forward, but rather than block, Jake dodged under it and stabbed the side of the leg, using the creature's momentum to make his katar sink in deeper.

The spider made a screaming sound as it attacked again, but the same pattern repeated as several blows were exchanged. Sim-Jake was clearly using a very intense boosting skill at this moment, and Jake saw him begin to take damage as the intensity of the dark sky above increased. When the web below began shining silver, sim-Jake did not hesitate to jump into the air away from and float backward. The spider followed him into mid-air, where he finally blocked a blow, but as he was in the air and already going backward, all that truly happened was that he was sent flying.

"Two objects colliding will result in damage from the sum of their speeds upon collision. Two objects hitting each other, each going forty kilometers an hour, is the same as a single object smashing into a solid object at eighty. Simple physics, really, and even if this law doesn't truly apply anymore in its elegant simplicity, it is still a thing. It is hard to stop an attack mid-swing no matter what, and the blow will deal more damage if you hit it mid-swing, as not only will you hit it—your foe will hit itself upon your weapon." Sim-Jake then landed on the ground below. He clearly knew the spider did not want to follow, as he sat down and stared at it, drinking a potion. His boosting skill was also deactivated, but the dark clouds above persisted.

"Winning in a single engagement is naturally out of the question," sim-Jake explained as he regenerated. "This beast is far too durable and even has energy stored inside the web. However, it is also territorial to the level of making it a fatal weakness. It will not leave its net and the eggs it protects unless absolutely necessary. The unique dark lightning I use is a perfect weapon for a situation like this. The dark mana hampers regeneration and lowers its perception while the lightning burns its mana. An additional effect gained from merging these two concepts also means it burns stamina."

Jake looked at the spider and did detect the dark lightning still lingering. The dark clouds above seemed to also pressurize the entire area, which only affected the spider.

Ten minutes later, sim-Jake rose once more. "Second round."

He stormed forward and engaged the beast in yet another bout of melee with his boosting skills fully active. His fighting style was like before—a mix of dodging and then the occasional stab whenever an opening presented itself. It all looked incredibly simple, but the more Jake watched on, the more confused he became.

Wait, that was such a good opening. Why stab there? Wait, did he delay the strike? Why? Now! No? What?

Jake was very engaged in the fight, but he didn't get it. It seemed, well, not random, but arbitrary when sim-Jake chose to strike. He let obvious openings pass and instead went for tiny, tight openings to land a hit.

Yet the result was clear as the spider slowly got whittled down. Sim-Jake retreated several times until, finally, the spider seemed to realize this could not go on. The entire web began glowing and moving as the energy stored within was fully absorbed, making it fall apart.

The spider, with renewed vigor, left the web and attacked sim-Jake. Its eight legs carried it forward at a swift speed, following Jake when he tried to disengage. This forced their brawl onto the ground, where Jake saw how the dynamic instantly changed.

This time, sim-Jake went on the offensive. Power revolved around his weapons as lightning roared forward. It covered the spider, but as a D-grade, it was far too durable to take any noticeable damage. Sim-Jake nevertheless went close to attack with his weapons. The spider retaliated, and suddenly sim-Jake pulled back. He delayed his attack by a mere moment, making the spider miss with a dark lance of magic, allowing sim-Jake to land a blow uncontested.

Once more, the spider tried to attack its attacker, and it missed by a narrow margin yet again. Jake stood there and observed, dumbstruck. The spider was missing, despite its far higher speed and power. No, sim-Jake did not dodge... it was the spider missing. In every exchange, its timing was off. Like they were dancing, following set steps in the choreography, but sim-Jake was almost half a second behind, making the spider off-tune.

The spider was, purely stat-wise, probably three or four times stronger than sim-Jake. It was a wider gap than any opponent Jake had faced during his tutorial besides the King of the Forest. In all of Jake's fights, he had been struggling, he had overcome his limits, and he had come out victorious. Sim-Jake did not need to overcome any limits. He had spent his entire life pushing himself towards perfection, and the system had only allowed him to flourish more.

This did not mean he wasn't struggling. Jake noted his simulacrum was running out of energy and had taken many minor wounds—sacrifices made to avoid more dangerous blows or land a counterattack. Of course, these would build up and, with time, become an issue.

If the spider had simply fought from the beginning and not allowed sim-Jake to constantly reset and consume potions, it would have no doubt won. But... it hadn't. It had allowed itself to be slowly whittled down. Sim-Jake had targeted one leg many times and finally managed to sever it. This led to a chain reaction as it stumbled, only to get another near-fatal stab with the katar into one of its eyes. It retaliated, but sim-Jake turned to lightning, dodged behind it, and stabbed again.

He moved from blindspot to blindspot and landed puncture wound after puncture wound. It couldn't heal due to all the dark lightning, and finally, sim-Jake landed the final blow. He stabbed the katar through the weakened skull of the spider and pushed down, producing the creature's last breath.

Less than a second later, the dark clouds above dispersed like they had never been there. Sim-Jake himself shook for a moment as he spat out blood, then fell onto his back. His eyes were now bleeding, and Jake saw his arms and legs begin to turn purple, along with several dark spots appearing on his body.

"Another tip," sim-Jake whispered in a coarse voice. "Never show weakness and give your prey hope." He then turned his face and looked towards Jake, who stood near the corpse of the slain D-grade. "Thank you for observing what may be my final fight."

With those words, the scene ended. Jake frowned deeply. What? Final fight? Why wou—

Jake then felt something odd. Like a pull was on him or something. A summoning. He tried to figure out what it was, and his eyes opened wide as he accepted.

"Granted."

Jake found himself standing inside the same old familiar white room. The Guide had been the one who spoke, sitting in a chair across from sim-Jake. Confused, Jake looked at what the hell was going on. Him appearing there was not a usual scene transition at all... It was instead as if he had been asked to be there.

"For my third tutorial purchase... I want to reveal and become able to interact with him within the confines of this room until the Tutorial Store expires," sim-Jake said as he turned and looked at Jake. The system acknowledged, and Jake knew his simulacrum got some system prompt that he accepted.

Once more, Jake felt himself be "asked" to approve of this. With a thought, he could reject it, but he chose to accept it once more.

He felt solid ground beneath his feet for the first time in a long time, and he knew...

For the first time, he truly met the eyes of himself—of sim-Jake. He was no longer a mere observer, but a physical entity now within the room.

They stared at each other for a moment, and sim-Jake smiled. "Hey, me," he said in a melancholic voice. "Good to finally meet you... Me. Us."

Jake looked at his simulacrum and nodded in recognition. "When did it click?"

"I guess I always had my suspicions, but it was when I met Umbra I truly understood. We have the same Bloodline. I am a Bloodline Patriarch, which means I am the only one with it... except you. Which means you are either some descendant from the future, or you are me. I still had that tiny sliver of doubt, but just a few minutes ago, I confirmed it using my first of five purchases from the Tutorial Store."

He was calm. Awfully calm, if not too calm. Jake would have been at least a little distressed or, at a minimum, weirded the hell out. Then again, perhaps his simulacrum had already gone through all that before during a scene Jake did not see. Or he was just that much calmer than Jake.

Jake had also not seen the usage of the Tutorial Store coming in. Jake remembered the custom option back then could offer anything. Even information, it seemed. There did appear to be some limitations, as it had to ask Jake for permission before bringing him there and making him visible, but that could also potentially just be due to the way sim-Jake made the purchases. Had to be cheaper if Jake went along with it.

"I will be honest; I am unsure how to handle this situation," Jake said. "But I guess an explanation would be a start?"

"Before that, let me ask you a question," sim-Jake said. "Are you stronger than me?"

"Yes," Jake answered.

"But you are also older, aren't you?" he followed up.

"Yeah."

"So... if I had the same time as you, who would be stronger?" he asked with a raised eyebrow.

Jake smiled. It was exactly the kind of question he would ask if he stood before another version of himself. He also knew the answer.

"I would," Jake said with a smile. "But if we switched situations, I am sure the answer would be the same. You are stronger than me in certain areas while I have you beat in others. You have abilities and skills from growing up I do not, but my upbringing also means I have some things you don't."

"And what would those be?"

"Friends," Jake said simply as he stared his other version in the eyes.

His simulacrum, surprisingly enough, didn't protest that answer, instead asking, "Do you trust them?"

"I do."

"Well, I guess that is a stark contrast to who I became. I haven't trusted anyone besides myself since I was a child. Besides you... which should maybe have been a clue too. Trusting you is just trusting myself, after all. Now, if you will enlighten me as to what exactly is going on..."

Jake decided to just be completely honest. "You are in a simulated world, of sorts, created by the system as part of a system event showing what would have happened if I made a different impactful choice at some point in my life. In your case, it was not stopping Mom and Dad from leaving the house the day they died. I did that in my world, and it resulted in me growing up with a family and a brother. Overall, it completely changed my trajectory of life."

"For the better or worse?"

"Better, I would say. Granted, I did end up suppressing my Bloodline to fit in and more or less made myself depressed since I was a child, viewing the whole world with apathy and boredom. So that part did suck, and I never really did form any meaningful relationships with anyone outside of my family, either, but it was sure as hell better than you." Jake laughed.

"I guess we are dysfunctional no matter which choices we make," sim-Jake said with a wry smile before turning a bit serious. "But this does mean I never truly existed, doesn't it?"

Jake shook his head. "I don't know how this entire thing works, to be honest."

Sim-Jake turned to the figure of the Guide, who was still just sitting there, unbothered. "Which one of us is real?"

The system entity looked at them. "Both are parallels of the other and hence both real."

"So, what would happen if I just leave this store like this and go on back to Earth and act like nothing happened?" sim-Jake pressed. "Will I cease to exist one day randomly? Will I just have never been?"

"Negative. Simulacrum will persist in the simulated world until destruction, at which point the simulation will be closed."

"I guess that answers it," sim-Jake sighed. "Kind of pointless, isn't it? Man, living in the simulation, knowing you live in a simulation, does suck. Tell me, is it possible for me to be transferred into the real 93rd Universe right now?"

"Negative. Parallels possess identical Truesoul signatures, and multiple separate copies are unable to exist in the same universe."

Jake heard this and remembered something from quite a while ago. Back when he'd wanted Rick, the gardening troll, out of the dungeon. It was about how multiple versions of the same creature could not exist in the same universe. Remembering this, Jake also knew the answer to the follow-up question.

"Can I then just fuse with my other version?" sim-Jake asked before throwing Jake a look. "I gotta ask. If I can 'survive,' I sure as hell want to."

"Fair enough."

"Negative," the system once more said. "Secondary Truesoul signature shall be automatically delegated and potentially assimilated into the original with no impact on Records."

"Bummer," sim-Jake said as he looked up at the ceiling. "Hey, original, what did you even hope to gain from this kind of event? Was it really as we discussed?"

"I wasn't sure in the beginning, but it was truly just learning from you," Jake answered. "Especially your melee fighting skills, which are quite a bit better than mine."

"Huh. While I would love to give you a crash course, I am pretty much dead, and it seems pretty pointless. Besides, this Tutorial Store business will end semi-soon." Sim-Jake shrugged.

"Sorry," Jake muttered.

"Eh, not your fault. Shit happens, I guess, and as fucked up as it seems, you were the only friend I had throughout my life, even if you turned out to be me." He shook his head. "Besides, I have one more gamble. System, I would like for my fourth purchase to be a method on how to exit this simulation and enter the true 93rd Universe while remaining who I am and staying a unique and separate entity."

"Unable to provide an acceptable result with current funds," the system responded, surprising Jake and sim-Jake a bit.

"What?" sim-Jake asked, confused. "Fuck. I hoped there was a way..."

Jake stood there and stared for a moment, feeling kind of shit about this entire thing. However, as he stared, he got an idea. "Guide is the reason transference cannot happen due to the requirements of unique Truesoul signatures?"

"Correct."

"In that case, is it potentially possible for the Records of this other version to enter the 93rd Universe through some other medium? In other words, making his existence tied to and dependent on our shared Truesoul while still allowing him to remain unique and separate?"

The system paused for a while. Sim-Jake also looked at him oddly before the system finally answered.

"Positive. Transference of Records into a non-living Soulbound entity that is tied to the primary being is possible through storage within a suitable vessel. Additional limitations may apply."

Sim-Jake looked at Jake for a moment as he also understood. One would think another person would be angry or offended at what Jake insinuated, but instead, sim-Jake just shook his head and sighed. "I guess this is a start?"

CHAPTER 58

THE FAINT LINE BETWEEN THE
VIRTUAL & REALITY

There was potential. Jake nodded at the system's answer as he asked to clarify, "What kind of limitations may apply? And what do we need to do to make it happen?"

Monotone as ever, the system entity answered, "Limitations include absolute separation from the material realm and interacting with other entities, limiting the transferred simulacrum to the True-soul. All expression must be made through an inanimate Soulbound object. Requirements to facilitate this process include a vessel able to house the transferred simulacrum as well as expenditure of all other material Path of Myriad Choices event rewards."

"That is the name of the event?" sim-Jake asked. "A bit on the nose."

"Oh, it totally is," Jake agreed as he regarded the system entity again. "Do I have a vessel able to house the simulacrum?"

"Negative."

"Not even this?" Jake asked as he pulled out Eternal Hunger. That had to be good enough, right?

"Negative."

"Okay, then this!" Jake tried as he spat out the Root of Eternal Resentment from his internal storage using Palate of the Malefic Viper, getting a weird look. He had confidence this item could be used, it had housed a curse and was meant to house energy, so surely—

"Negative. An incompatible vessel will result in destruction, alteration, or complete erasure of the simulacrum as well as the vessel. A unique vessel created to facilitate the process is required."

"Do I possess enough Tutorial Points to create such a vessel?" sim-Jake asked. "Also, is it possible to elaborate on these limitations? What does my being limited to the Truesoul mean?"

"All rewards given by Tutorial Points within the simulation are limited to the simulation, and no reward given can be transferred or persist within the true world. Limitations result in absolute non-interactability with the world, with the simulacrum permanently confined to the Soulspace. The simulacrum's existence shall remain permanently tied to the simulation to ensure continued autonomous existence. As such, the simulacrum will continue to exist as a simulacrum only viewable and detectable by Origin."

Sim-Jake looked in thought a bit. "Okay, I am just confused now."

"Wait," the real Jake said. "Will it mean he more or less is just what I am now, but in the real world? As in, he will be a silent and undetectable observer to everyone that isn't me? Like, we turn the situation one-eighty?"

"Interpretation acceptable," the system answered. "Limited manifestation outside of Soulspace potentially possible, but will remain detectable only to the Origin and non-interactive with the world."

"Huh," sim-Jake said with a frown. "So I will just be... what? Unable to do anything?"

"Simulacrum will have free movement and interactability within the Soulspace," the system answered.

"Guess it is about time I ask... what is this Soulspace?" sim-Jake asked, clearly not happy to admit he didn't know.

"Like, a world inside the soul? I am not entirely sure how it works, but I can meditate and enter there and have trapped energies within, including an ancient curse that could probably destroy the planet." Nonchantly, he added, "Definitely could destroy the planet."

"Sounds like you have had quite the fun so far, huh?" Sim-Jake smiled. "But I guess any option is better than just dying. Because the alternative is dying. I can't see myself living within a virtual world I know only exists because I do... It would make it all feel so utterly pointless, knowing nothing I do is real. No, rather have a small impact on reality than dominate a fantasy."

Jake just nodded in understanding. While experiencing a simulation temporarily would be fine, knowing that nothing you ever did would carry over had to be hell. It was a perfect case of "ignorance is bliss," and once the veil had been lifted, there was no going back.

"Besides," sim-Jake added, "we are the same person. So me helping you is helping myself in every sense of the word, isn't it? Also... if I do get transferred into an item of some sort, it won't be permanent, will it?"

The last part was addressed to the system, which confirmed his question. "Resonance and equilibrium may eventually be reached, making the simulacrum and Origin one."

"Hear that?" Sim-Jake smiled. "Who knows, I may even be able to take over your mind and become the real version?"

"Isn't it more like we will eventually just be so similar in every way a natural fusion kind of just happens?" Jake asked, looking at the system.

"Correct."

Jake and the simulacrum nodded in sync. Neither truly understood but were still guessing. All Jake knew was that sim-Jake was looking for some sort of Path to survive, and Jake wanted to help himself—his other self—and potentially even benefit from it.

"Alright. What kind of vessel is required to store the simulacrum?"

"Vessel must originate from the original universe yet contain innate ties to specific virtual universe. The vessel must meet parameters, including, but not limited to, durability, storage ability, non-attunement, energy signature resonance, Record compatibility, and Origin compatibility."

"Wait, will I be able to transform any of my items into a compatible one?" Jake asked with a bit of hope.

"Negative."

Jake and sim-Jake threw each other a look as his simulacrum groaned. "So we just had this entire shitty conversation to say that I am fucked either way?"

Frowning too, Jake considered more until he got an idea. "You got two purchases left, right?"

"Yeah?"

"Hm. Hey, Guide, when will the Path of Myriad Choices end for me?"

"Due to developments within the simulation, the final scene is currently being displayed," it answered.

"And if I leave here, will I ever be able to go back, so to say? As in, could I go back and get my simulacrum out later?"

"Improbably."

"But not impossible," Jake murmured. "If my simulacrum does leave with me to the original universe, what will happen to the simulation?"

"Simulation shall persist as long as simulacrum remains."

"Huh," Jake considered again.

"What are you fishing for?" sim-Jake asked.

"I am getting there," Jake said dismissively. "I happen to be buddies with a god who loves semi-breaking or at least bending the rules of the system a bit, and I guess it rubbed off. Guide, the rewards of the system event are based on the performance of the simulacrum during the simulation, correct?"

The system confirmed.

"Alright, then. Do these rewards include physical items?"

"Potentially."

"Okay... considering this is the final scene, are the rewards already calculated, and how will they be given?"

"All rewards will be given and calculated only at the conclusion of the event," the system confirmed once more.

Jake just smiled and asked his simulacrum, "Hey... for the fourth purchase, how about you buy that your performance will award me a compatible vessel?"

"No fucking way that works." He shook his head and turned to the system entity. "Does it work?"

The system paused for a moment. "Partial consumption of Path of Myriad Choices event reward required."

Sim-Jake froze for a moment as he looked at Jake.

Jake just nodded. "Can the fifth purchase then be for the Records of the simulacrum to temporarily be safely stored within my Soulspace to then be transferred to the vessel upon exit? Without causing any harm to him, that is?"

Once more, it paused for a moment. "Partial consumption of Path of Myriad Choices event reward required. Requires total temporal suspension to facilitate effect. Acceptable."

"Do I have enough Tutorial Points for these two?" sim-Jake asked with concern.

"Vessel can be adjusted to minimum requirements, allowing the process."

Sim-Jake just stared for a moment. "I truly have no idea what the hell we are doing here or why this is even allowed. It feels like we are somehow cheating the system and using an exploit or something, which makes no fucking sense if the system is supposed to be omnipotent."

Jake shrugged. "Eh... listen. Think about it like this: Why are we allowed to do this? Talk like this? This is all due to how you performed during the simulation. Your actions led to this possible outcome. If you hadn't dominated the tutorial or become aware of me and done as you did now, it wouldn't have happened. Remember, we are still in the simulation right now, and even this conversation is part of the event. So... in some ways, isn't it pretty normal to reward a simulacrum, becoming aware it is in a simulation, with a way to somehow find a way to break out of the simulation? For the system to not at least leave a Path? So... yeah. It is allowing this to happen and is within expectations."

Sim-Jake tossed the system entity a look. "I guess that makes sense... Would also explain why the hell nothing has happened despite the time for this Tutorial Store thing having elapsed."

"Yep," Jake agreed despite not actually knowing.

He did recognize the absurdity of the situation that sim-Jake pointed out, but he also vehemently believed in what he had said. The system clearly facilitated these sorts of things. It allowed sim-Jake to be an autonomous person, and thus Jake also believed it would allow him a Path as a reward for his performance. A true Path that he so desired.

"So, to summarize," sim-Jake said, "I will be transformed into a form suitable to be transplanted into an item and deposited into your —our—Truesoul, suspended in time to not disperse and forcefully remerge with the Truesoul, and stay me. Then this event will end, you will be rewarded an item I can merge into, and you will do that fast as fuck before I cease to exist. I got that right?"

"I think that about sums it up," Jake confirmed. He then looked at the system entity. "And, just to be clear, you have never done anything like this before, right? Has anyone?"

"Yes," it answered. "Prior divergent simulacriums have appeared and, through contact with their Origin, merged into the true multiverse."

"Alright, so only semi-uncharted territory. You confident?" sim-Jake asked Jake.

"Believe it or not, yeah, I am. I have to be."

Sim-Jake finally sighed. "Aight... let's get this show on the road. If I don't make it... Never mind. You already know."

Jake smiled. "Let's go."

"For my fourth purchase...

The last two purchases were made. One to make sim-Jake into something capable of surviving the transfer and one to make sure Jake got something to transfer him into. With that, the scene finally ended, and Jake got a few notifications as he appeared in the white room, but he didn't pay them any mind.

As he appeared, so did a new item in his inventory. It was a black, bone-like item, and Jake instantly took it out and did a quick Identify.

[Bone of the Virtual Gap (Unique)] – *A bone created from a human rib belonging to a world that exists yet does not. Specifically made to house the simulacrum of Jake Thayne.*
Requirements: *Soulbound.*

Having confirmed, Jake entered Serene Soul Meditation and appeared in his Soulspace. The moment he did, he saw the distorted human form of pure energy. It looked halfway broken. Jake knew this was because it wasn't meant to exist and was only held together due to the direct interference of the system.

Jake got to work as he controlled his Soulspace. In the outside world, he sat in meditation with the bone in his hands, while in the Soulspace he forcefully collected every single fragment of the Records that had been sim-Jake.

Gritting his teeth, he focused, knowing sim-Jake would only stay together for that long. At the same time, he felt the energy itself almost move to help him. It wanted to be gathered and become one again. The energy that was the simulacrum resonated with the Soulspace itself as he felt everything pulse. With focus, he began collecting faster than before. Soon enough, a foot appeared, then a leg, two legs, a torso, arms, and finally a head. This version of sim-Jake was slightly different than the simulacrum from before but also wasn't a copy of Jake himself. It was instead more like sim-Jake having undergone his D-grade evolution.

When the full form was collected, Jake moved on to the next stage. A black bone appeared in his hand, and Jake did not hesitate to stab the human form in front of him right in the heart, letting the bone sink in deep and take the place of one of the ribs. At the same time, he began infusing the bone in the outside world. He had done something similar with Eternal Hunger, and frankly, this was far easier. Sim-Jake was primed already, and rather than fighting him like the curse energy had when he made Eternal Hunger, this energy actively wanted to work with him. Almost as if it had an instinct of its own.

Throughout this process, he poured energy into the bone and

established a connection between the two. The bone would serve as an anchor to the world, as it still existed partially in the virtual simulation. Some parts of sim-Jake had to always exist there, or he would cease to be a simulacrum and thus his own person.

This entire merging process was complicated, but out of everyone in D-grade, Jake was probably one of the best. Not only had he made Eternal Hunger, but he had consumed and slowly absorbed knowledge from the Root of Eternal Resentment for a long-ass time, learning close to everything he could about it. The Root was a marvel when it came to all kinds of energy, and Jake was certain that if it wasn't because of the peculiarity of the simulation, it would have worked. In every sense of the word, it was a top-class natural treasure when it came to energy transference and storage.

As he pressed on, Jake felt the temporal suspension applied to sim-Jake about to wear out. It was clear that while the system had allowed this entire ridiculous situation to happen, it would not do it for them. If he fucked up, sim-Jake would simply disperse and become one with Jake. All this would do was probably just add some Records with unknown effects later down the line, perhaps just adding a skill option or two—something he obviously didn't want.

Stabilize, Jake thought as sim-Jake's body was fully assembled. It looked complete, and the bone had fully merged with his body. Jake gritted his teeth as, suddenly, the temporal suspension completely expired and something went wrong. The arm of sim-Jake suddenly disappeared, and his entire body turned transparent and began leaking.

"Fuck," Jake muttered as he pushed his Willpower to the extreme.

A barrier of pure arcane mana covered a huge portion of his Soulspace as he compressed it together to keep the energy in. To his relief, the dispersing energy that was about to be reabsorbed by the Soulspace was slowed down, and he managed to force back most of it.

His entire Soulspace began shaking as he expanded the barrier even more to try and put back all he could. Every piece of Records had to be there, or sim-Jake would not be sim-Jake. In the outside world, blood began dripping out of his nose as he strained every fiber of his being.

Finally, something fell into place. The energy that had begun dispersing collected once more and formed around sim-Jake, but... some had been lost. His body was slightly transparent compared to before, and Jake cursed himself inwardly. There was no more energy to collect, and the entire Soulspace fell still. Nothing happened as Jake stared at the figure that still had his eyes closed, yet to wake up. It was stable... but what the hell did that help if what he had made was just an empty husk of a simulacrum?

"Come on, man... don't let this all be a waste."

Jake stood there, nervous, until the figure in front of him abruptly opened his eyes. Yet what Jake saw was not the gaze of sim-Jake, but something far more... primal. The figure moved before Jake could react, and the next thing he knew, his arm was gone. Yet he did not react, as his danger sense had yet to make even a single peep.

The arm reappeared instantly since he was within the Soulspace. The arm taken by the simulacrum was absorbed into the figure as his body rapidly turned far more corporal.

Jake stared as he understood. "It replaced the Records with mine..."

One had to remember that Jake and sim-Jake shared a huge percentage of their Records. All that was innate to them was shared... and it appeared that although some parts had been lost earlier, they could be replaced.

Jake smiled as the simulacrum blinked, and he finally saw familiar eyes.

"Welcome to our Soulspace."

Sim-Jake stared a bit at his hands as he clenched his fist. He looked up at Jake and smiled. "Is this where I declare my intent to take over your mind and become the true owner of our body?"

"Sure, just after I throw you into a trashcan," Jake joked back, though he was inwardly incredibly relieved. He felt the same relief from his simulacrum... but also noticed something else.

A bit of knowledge had appeared in his head... and a few memories he did not quite recognize as his own, even if they did feel like his own. His simulacrum also seemed to have noticed.

They both looked at each other with understanding.

This entire thing was temporary... They were one, after all. As time passed, they would slowly meld into one another until one day, there would only be one Jake left in the Soulspace. A bit had already leaked during the formation, and chances were it would continue to, had there been issues with the process or not. Of course, this led to the question: Who would he become? The original? Sim-Jake, if he managed to somehow exert influence?

Or was it a question that didn't even matter, as there was no real division? Perhaps they were naught but two parallel Paths that had briefly split up after making a choice and would always one day rejoin to form their true Path.

The Path of the Primal Hunter.

CHAPTER 59

INTERNAL DEVELOPMENTS

However... even if the two Jakes would someday become one again, that day was not today or any day in the near future. For now, they were quite different. One thing they did agree on was a bit of quick experimenting, though. The first item on the list was the bone in the real world. Jake had already confirmed that sim-Jake could see everything Jake could and shared all senses, but it appeared that sim-Jake couldn't talk to him in the outside world, so all communication had to go through the Soulspace.

All detailed communication had to, at least. Jake still kind of knew what sim-Jake was thinking, and it was honestly a bit weird, as most of his thoughts were the exact same as Jake's. However, one thing they did not agree on right away quickly appeared when the bone began ever so slowly warping and growing. Minutes passed as Jake decided to let sim-Jake do with his new "body" as he wanted, deciding that they would talk about it later.

Instead, he would get a look at the system notifications he had delayed checking. The first of which was the good-old flavor text.

Congratulations on fully experiencing the simulation of Choice 4!

Due to the exceptional performance of your simulacrum, you have earned the highest-level award. Not only did your simulacrum excel before the initiation, but it also managed to become Progenitor in the tutorial, similar to Origin, despite different prior choices that resulted in significant divergence. Finally, the simulacrum managed to realize its existence within a simulation and successfully partially remerged with Origin. Each Path you walk is truly unique and powerful, making you a true Progenitor of Myriad Paths.

Rewards Gained: 1x **[Bone of the Virtual Gap Unique)].** **Title Earned:** Progenitor of Myriad Paths.

Jake read it all over carefully and nodded. The system recognized everything that had happened and seemed totally fine with it. No, more than fine; it had rewarded him for doing what he had done. Though, to be fair, Jake should not really be surprised. The system had also rewarded him back when it helped make Moment of the Primal Hunter and by giving him the title for making a legendary skill, even if he had cheesed it. It'd been somewhat similar to when he made Eternal Hunger, which was only possible because Jake's Soulspace was ridiculously powerful—something also primarily caused by his Bloodline.

He saw that he had received just two things from the event. The system had told him material rewards would not be given due to making the bone, but it appeared that he still got a title. With quite a bit of excitement, Jake checked it out.

*[Progenitor of Myriad Paths] – A Progenitor through and through, you are born to walk unique and powerful Paths. You have earned the recognition of the Watcher attached to Earth and thus the Seat of the Exalted Prima. All bonuses gained are dependent on the simulacrum during the Path of Myriad Paths. **+100 Agility, +100 Strength. +5% Agility, +5% Strength.** Recognized as a potential Administrator Candidate for the Milky Way Seat of the Exalted Prima.*

Jake had added yet another Progenitor title to his portfolio. It was beginning to compete with the prodigious tag and seemed to be of a generally high-to-peak tier when it came to titles. The details of the title were also a happy surprise. Jake hadn't had many speculations on potential rewards, but a title was certainly one of the best. Moreover, it gave percentage increases along with just a pile of pure stats. The only difference from what he usually got was that everything was added to Strength and Agility.

It didn't take a genius to figure out why they gave these stats. This reward was based on sim-Jake, and sim-Jake had been a melee fighter focusing on Strength and Agility. In all honesty, it was pretty good for him to get some points for both, and considering the bonuses he already had, the 100 in each stat actually added 150 to Strength and 160 to Agility. That wasn't even counting the new percentage increases. Even with just five percent more in a stat, with more than 6000 Agility, it translated to more than 300 free stat points, equivalent to several levels.

Then there was the second part of the title: "Recognized as a potential Administrator Candidate for the Milky Way Seat of the Exalted Prima."

Now, Jake naturally had no clue what this was actually about, but he could infer some things and quickly formed a theory. This Seat of the Exalted Prima was not just some system event location or something spawned and created just for the new initiates. It was something far more... and something one could come to influence.

Additionally, it was not limited to Earth but their entire galaxy. Candidates would come from all sorts of races, and Jake would compete with not just a few billion other Earthlings but potentially hundreds of billions, if not trillions of sapient creatures spread across the Milky Way Galaxy. Also... one more thing. The existence of a Milky Way Seat of the Exalted Prima indicated that other galaxies with life also had Seats. If that was the case, was there somewhere or something that controlled it all?

Perhaps this Exalted Prima itself. Perhaps some headquarters that commanded millions of Seats of the Exalted Prima spread across an entire universe. If it truly was like that, Jake knew what to talk to Villy about when he exited. Well, that, and about his new best friend in sim-Jake. Jake was truly a Prodigious Progenitor in everything, even being his own friend.

Jake smiled a bit goofily to himself and closed his notifications, satisfied with what he had gained. The bone he was holding was still slowly molding itself, and it looked like changing the shape would take a while. Popping into his Soulspace, he saw sim-Jake in deep meditation, as he had immersed his consciousness in his new "body."

Guess I will just wait here to make sure, Jake thought. The space he was in was clearly the meat of the Seat of the Exalted Prima. Looking around, he wondered how one was supposed to exi—

Do you wish to leave the simulation room? Possible destinations:
Simulation room entrance cube.
Administrator's Terrace.

Alright, never mind, Jake thought. *Also, Administrator's Terrace? Looks new. It must be due to the title.* Still, he already knew where he would go. After sim-Jake was done, of course. For now, Jake would meditate and actually fill up his resources. He was surprised at seeing they were still low after his fight with the Phantomshade Panther—a fight that seemed like it was ages ago.

It appeared Jake had only been in the simulation for half a day or so, even if it had been way, way longer on the inside. Just counting the elapsed time of the actual scenes, Jake had to have seen at least a few months' worth, most of it spent watching Jake fight both pre-and post-system.

Jake meditated for a while, deciding to do so using Serene Soul Meditation to enter his Soulspace to also see when sim-Jake was done.

About half an hour later, sim-Jake opened his eyes and smiled. "All done."

Real-Jake also opened his eyes and finally got a good look at the bone that was now no longer a simple rib. Instead, it had changed into an H-shaped handle with a blade attached.

"This is a katar?" Jake asked inside his Soulspace as sim-Jake summoned an identical copy of the weapon in the real world.

"Yep."

"You do know I use swords and daggers, right?" Jake asked.

"I know," sim-Jake said. "This whole partially shared memory is far from one way... In fact, I would say I got a lot more of you than you got of me. From this, it is clear you have yet to make proper use of our abilities and, most importantly, have yet to actually develop a proper melee fighting style for yourself."

"Well, you suck with a bow," Jake countered.

"Oh, wow, great burn. Very clever of you. I am not even fucking criticizing you; I am saying it in a positive way. It is good you never had anyone else teach you how to fight in melee, because, quite frankly, they all suck compared to what I will teach you. Don't get me wrong—that old swordsman you fought in vampire land is an absolute fucking monster with his sword, to a level you can't even begin to appreciate, but we also both realize we will never reach his skill level. Not that it would even be worth trying for us. I spent years training with people, fighting experts, and it quickly became clear that nothing suited me. Not because they were weak, but because fighting my instincts constantly while fighting would be a fucking pain. No... the style I began developing is not about fighting my instincts but making full use of them."

"Developing?" Jake asked. "From the fight with that D-grade, it seemed pretty damn effective already?"

"Yeah, no. Dude, stop making us look stupid by thinking that was in any way good enough. That stuff was developed in a few months and is just the basics that were built off my experience before the system, and I had only just begun integrating these concepts into a more magical framework. I guess one can say that all the time you spent training magic, I spent training melee combat, but I had a massive headstart due to the lives we lived before the initiation."

Jake nodded. "Am I right to assume the core concept is about controlling the flow of the fight?"

Sim-Jake smiled. "Right on. We are not experts who have trained for a hundred years. We are ultimately little more than beasts in human skin that rely on our instincts above anything else. However, the problem is that while we can use these instincts to survive due to us responding to complex attacks, we cannot form our own complex attacks, which is why I began to question if I even have to? Why not just tab into those god-like instincts and use them to counterattack and control the momentum of the battle from start to end? Anyway, my point is that the katar is the best weapon I found, though I guess if you had become a Malefic Dragonkin, that would have been just as good. Though I get why you didn't get it... Would have been weird with the Viper."

"Hm, any reason why claw weapons aren't good?" Jake asked.

"What kind? The kind where a few come out of your wrist and get stuck in things while cutting, or rip your flesh apart by something getting wedged in between them or someone simply slashing down the length of the extended claw... or the type that is basically a glove?"

Jake scratched his hair. "The glove?"

"Also a great idea. Here, let me just tank the impacts with my hands while believing my weak-ass human finger won't snap like a broken twig if the attack hits slightly wrong. If I used glove claws, I would be a grappler, but that would just be a damn waste. Both types of claws commonly used just don't fit as well and sorely lack the penetrative effect of the katar. Also, they are fundamentally slashing weapons and not stabbing weapons. Stabbing is best in my opinion, and with your poison, I reckon it will be even better." He'd been shaking his head throughout the explanation.

"You know what?" Jake said. "I will leave this up to the expert. When does the training session begin?"

"Not now," sim-Jake said in a serious tone. "I still need to figure stuff out and get a feel for this place. Rather than asking, I would prefer to just absorb the knowledge directly. Also, more than anything, I need to do one absolutely critical thing."

"Take a nap?"

"Right the fuck on once again." Sim-Jake grinned. "Molding that bone I am in was tiring as hell. I will also take this time to observe you a bit to really get a feel for where to start, though I already have a good idea. Also, this just feels fair. You have been staring at me like a creepy stalker for my entire life. Now it is my turn."

"Blame the system, not me. And have a good nap!" Jake snickered as sim-Jake waved him off and moved his hand to summon a bed and a blanket out of nothingness. He got cozy under it as Jake disappeared from the Soulspace and returned his full attention to the outside world.

The first thing he did when outside was Identify the black bone once more... and to be honest, Jake was not sure if he should be disappointed or not. Okay, he was a little disappointed.

[Bone-weapon of the Hunter (Epic)] – A weapon containing the simulacrum of Jake Thayne. Can be molded by the simulacrum. Extremely tough and nearly unbreakable as long as the simulacrum persists. Highly upgradeable.
Requirement: *Soulbound.*

It was... kind of bad? The system had done as it said and made the item only meet the bare-minimum requirements. In every way, it was just a really tough bone that had now taken the shape of a katar, through a process that was both slow and tiring.

However, that was only now. According to the description, the weapon was highly upgradeable, and it was even possible to combine it with something else in the future. Naturally, it couldn't even begin to hold a candle to Eternal Hunger, but it was a start.

Putting it in his inventory, Jake thought about leaving as the option popped up again. He picked the one for the special kids who had done well.

Administrator's Terrace.

He was swept away a moment later, and to his surprise, he appeared standing on grass. He felt the soft soil under his feet and looked around to find a beautiful garden surrounding him. However, rather than a cloudless sky and a sun, he saw cloudless space and a lot of stars.

He was clearly within a hemisphere, but one different from any of the others. Seeing nothing above them but stars, Jake guessed they were perhaps at the very top of the Seat of the Exalted Prima. The air in the garden felt incredibly refreshing, and the mana density was insanely high and extremely pure. He nearly wanted to sit down and do alchemy then and there, but he decided against it. One, because it would be a bit weird and there were still more pressing things to do, and two, because he wasn't alone.

Standing on the grass towards the edge of the hemisphere was a single figure, gazing out into the vast cosmos and clearly admiring the stars. The figure looked over when he saw Jake and smiled. "Ah, welcome. You are the first person besides me to arrive," he said courteously.

Jake gazed at him with some suspicion. He was not human, but had orange skin with blue tattoo-like markings all over it. Overall, he had quite an otherwordly look. Jake met the man's eyes and saw they had no pupils, instead reminding Jake of the stars beyond the faint barrier sealing them in. They did have a faint red tint to them, though, making them stand out even more.

Jake naturally used Identify as he sensed the man also use it on him.

[Nahoom – lvl ???]

He failed to pierce the man's protection from Identify, and Jake knew the other party also failed to Identify him. It was honestly to be expected. Jake felt the man in front of him was strong... real strong. But he also didn't feel threatening in the least. In fact, he gave off incredibly good vibes to Jake and did not at all register as an enemy. He seemed like an even more approachable guy than even Jacob.

Oh, and there was one more important thing about the guy.

He had a Bloodline.

CHAPTER 60

BENEATH THE STARS

The Path of Myriad Choices was an event quite a bit different than any prior. It was not one that was decided by simply being strong or one that could be teamed up and strategized over to beat. All you had was who you were fundamentally and simulations showing you what your choices could have changed.

To some, no simulation shown made them more than what they were. One such person was Miranda. She saw five previews. One where she died because she led them in another direction than where Haven would eventually be founded, resulting in Jake never saving her, Hank, and the kids. Three more were about choices in the tutorial, only one of which ended at least a little happily due to her saving Hank's wife and leaving the tutorial with them to settle down in a small settlement ruled by the Holy Church. That was the one she had selected, as the fifth choice was her trying to take over Haven from Jake and getting herself killed. With all these choices being, well, bad, Miranda did not get any particularly valuable reward. Except for one thing that was perhaps better than any minor item or title.

Confidence. Confidence in her Path and the choices she had made to get where she was. Many had this happen to them, as all they saw were worse or maybe equal outcomes from making different choices. They experienced newfound belief in their own decision-making and Paths, which would no doubt help move them forward. To some extent, Jake was also in this camp.

Then there were the ones who saw only utterly negative options. One such person was the former King of the Forest. All of his choices included him not becoming the Fallen King. He had three options. One where he stayed on his old planet and nothing of particular interest happened for the entire period until Realtime, one where he killed Jake during the tutorial and returned to Earth only to overconfidently try and take over the planet, resulting in death by humanity, and finally, one where he'd fled the fight with Jake during the tutorial, resulting in him still getting hunted down just a year or so later back on Earth. All choices meant a far worse outcome, and the Fallen King despaired at seeing how fortunate it was for him to get killed.

A whole other segment saw Paths that were just... meaningless. Ones where no choice truly had any major impact at all. All the examples were of faintly similar scenes, with only slight variation unless some just led to unfortunate early deaths.

And then... then there was one person who got three options of so little consequence the system should have been embarrassed for even offering them. Sylphie had been given these minimum three, and none of them had any impact whatsoever. Even the one where she rejected getting Stormild's Blessing ended up with Sylphie accepting it the next day after getting a minor bribe from Jake to at least consider it.

Second to last, there was one more person with just outstanding choices. One person who was offered six choices, but all had only minor variations of their Path. It was the Sword Saint, who, no matter what choices he made, would end up with a sword in hand and standing as one of the strongest on Earth.

Finally... there was an anomaly. A person that stood out from the get-go. The thing is, the Path of Myriad Choices event was based on, well, choices. Single events with huge impact. So, what happened if said person had never made a choice without considering everything about it first, rapidly evaluating the outcome and course-correcting? You would get a person who kept realigning his Path again and again.

You would get Arnold.

He and others also appeared within the Administrator's Garden. Soon enough, he was joined by the Sword Saint and a lot of individuals from other worlds. All in all, around two hundred people ended up in the Administrator's Garden, making them Candidates.

"Hm?" the Sword Saint suddenly said as he looked towards the far end of the hemisphere garden and saw two people already there. Talking as they gazed out into the vastness of space, both of them were clearly in an excellent and friendly mood as they chatted away heartily.

--

Before anyone else made it to the garden, Jake and the man sized each other up. After the man greeted him, Jake finally replied, "It does indeed appear I am the second to arrive. I assume you also did the system event?"

"I did," the alien man answered in a friendly tone. "Quite an interesting experience, wouldn't you agree? Did you find it enlightening? I personally found much inspiration from seeing how much impact a simple choice can have on one's entire Path."

"Definitely an experience," Jake agreed as he began walking over. The other man gladly took a step to the side and invited Jake to join him at the edge of the hemisphere.

"I have to ask—is nahoom the name of your race or something else?" Jake asked. It was probably a somewhat rude question, but Jake had never encountered the race mentioned anywhere before.

"We are a rare breed, it seems," he explained. "I have not found any mention of my race in any records either, so perhaps we are native to the 93rd Universe. From what I have gathered, we seem to share most of our traits with elves and the starborne. Naturally, we are not born as powerful entities like the starborne, but we seem to share some affinities with them."

Jake was amazed at the man's willingness to share information and found it only proper to respond in kind. "I assume you already guessed I am human?"

"That one isn't hard. You humans are quite widespread across the multiverse, so not knowing about you would be a challenge." The man smiled and chuckled. "But rather than races, how about names? Ah, I mean no offense if your culture does not use such things."

Jake shook his head at the overly polite nahoom and answered, "Jake Thayne. A pleasure to meet you."

"Ell'Hakan. And the honor is all mine." He bowed, and Jake returned the bow politely. "Now, do tell, what kind of world do you hail from? What exists in the cosmos has already interested me greatly."

"I come from somewhere named Earth," Jake answered. "A quaint little place that got quite a bit larger after the initiation."

"Sounds pleasant. Is it a blue or a red planet? What I mean is if it is a world of greenery and vast oceans, or one of dust and rock."

"Definitely on the blue side, even after the changes," Jake said. "Plenty of greenery too. Heck, I live within a city placed in a forest called Haven. Well, I live there sometimes. I am more the traveling kind and don't really have a set home, I guess?"

"Having a home is important," Ell'Hakan said, disagreeing slightly. "I hail from a planet that is more on the red side. Most of our water is found underground, but we made it work, and I live in a beautiful city myself. One that I also rule, just as you do. Of course, without my companions and friends, I would not be able to handle such responsibility, and it pains me to stand here without them by my side."

"Definitely essential to have good help. I have a friend called Miranda who handles most, if not all, city-related things for me, and I also have several good friends that I made mainly through fighting. At least, I consider them friends. Shit, I even killed one, and we are now kind of on friendly terms?" Jake finished with a chuckle.

"Having friends, especially those that one can trust, is more important than anything," Ell'Hakan said, still using his friendly tone. "I myself try to be as trustworthy and genuine as possible. Though I do have to admit that when I look back, most of my greatest allies right now are there due to our shared Patron. Do tell, are you also blessed?"

Jake definitely got the feeling that the guy was trustworthy just from their brief conversation. He was like a capybara: friend-shaped.

"I do happen to have a Blessing," Jake answered. He considered if he should share more, but it wasn't like he usually bothered hiding it, and Ell'Hakan seemed like a good dude, so why not? "I am blessed by the Malefic Viper. Ah, but don't misunderstand. While he does have quite a bad reputation, we get along very well."

"Judging others solely based on the accounts of their detractors is never wise," he said understandingly. "Better to meet them and reach your own conclusions. My Patron also has unsightly rumors, but I shall not base my own judgment on that, but rather how the relationship we formed ourselves shapes up."

He truly didn't seem to care about Jake's identity at all and didn't view him badly due to it. Yet he also clearly knew of the Viper, which would only make sense if he was blessed by another god. The twelve Primordials were pretty hot topics, as far as Jake knew.

The entire conversation was interesting, and Ell'Hakan was undoubtedly a character worth knowing. Jake definitely got a good feeling from him all around, like he was making an ally for life. He didn't even bother when other individuals appeared on the other end of the Administrator's Garden, and the man in front of him set up a quick isolation barrier. It was a nice gesture.

"Sometimes I wonder why our Patrons chose us," Ell'Hakan muttered out loud after the barrier was formed to give them some more privacy. "Is it our power or our persons? Tell me, how powerful are you? Truly?"

Jake shrugged. He felt like bragging a little, especially as the barrier was now there and no one untrustworthy could listen in. "Eh, I am actually 169 in race, class, and profession level, so that is pretty damn nice. I also got my own fair share of titles adding up further."

"Impressive! Now... this may be presumptuous of me, and please do forgive me if I am wrong, but you are the Chosen of the Malefic One, are you not? I heard from my Patron he chose a mortal from this new universe, and with how impressive you are, I cannot help but wonder if it isn't you?"

Grinning, Jake said, "I am his Chosen, yeah."

Ell'Hakan smiled in return. "Another thing we have in common, it seems. My Patron also chose me to make his Chosen. He has helped me a lot, but I also know it is because of one of our other... commonalities. I have never met anyone else with one, so I may be wrong, but you have a Bloodline, right?"

There was really no reason to hide it. They could both detect it due to how Bloodlines worked, so Jake naturally confirmed. "Sure do."

"As one would expect of the Chosen of a Primordial. I cannot say my own Bloodline is one that offers a lot of power, but I do wonder if yours does. Tell me, what does this Bloodline of yours do?"

"Oh, it is called Bloodline of—"

THUMP!

A pulse went through Jake as he felt his own heartbeat. It stopped him before he could answer further, and with the heartbeat came another feeling. Clarity.

Ell'Hakan looked at Jake expectedly, and his smile only deepened when Jake stopped himself. "Impressive indeed, Malefic's Chosen. Few, if any, manage to regain themselves."

Jake stared at the guy as all of his previous feelings began dispersing. Feelings that now seemed odd and ungenuine to him.

"What the fuck was that?" Jake asked as he clenched his fists. His danger sense flared, as he was about to charge forward to attack—not necessarily due to Ell'Hakan, but the rules of the Seat. He stopped, but he still stared as his fingers dug into his palms.

"A greeting, Jake Thayne. Our first exchange. One made under the stars as we both get to know the other and begin our shared story. It was truly an enlightening encounter, and I must say I look forward to meeting you again under less... let us say, regulated circumstances." Ell'Hakan's smile never changed.

Jake was more focused on analyzing what had happened internally. The question of "what the fuck was that?" was as much to Jake himself as the man before him. A conclusion was swiftly reached: Bloodline. The guy had some weird Bloodline that had affected Jake.

Addressing the words of Ell'Hakan, Jake grit his teeth and said, "Sure you want that?"

"I am most certain I do," he confirmed. "Our next meeting shall be far more enlightening and eventful than this one; that, I promise. And do not worry... it will come earlier than you think."

"If you ever—"

"Jake, do not misunderstand," Ell'Hakan interrupted him. "You are not the one who decides anything here. I do. Your role is already written, and so far, I must say you are a brilliant actor. And with that, my part here is done. Goodbye. For now."

Before Jake could say anything else, the figure of Ell'Hakan disappeared like it had never been there. Jake clenched his fists even harder and punched the ground where the alien fuck had just disappeared from. His level of anger was intense as he just stared at the now broken ground, ignoring the gazes of others directed at him.

What the fuck is that Bloodline? Jake asked himself as he considered what had just happened. His emotions had been affected somehow? Was it mind magic? A mind magic Bloodline? Was it something else? Emotion control of some sort, which would probably also be considered mind magic?

Jake was only happy that he had caught himself in the very last moment before he revealed his Bloodline or any details. However, before that, he had already overshared way too much. He had no idea what he had thought when he just blurted out his damn levels and information on Earth like it was nothing. Okay, he kind of knew... He'd done it because he truly felt in that moment that there was nothing wrong with it and that he was talking to someone genuinely trustworthy.

Well, that was a fucking lie. Jake cursed inwardly as he kept considering the nature of the other person's Bloodline. The only truly good thing was that at least Ell'Hakan didn't know Jake's either. One thing was also for sure: He would have his revenge the next time they met.

Jake shook his head and looked upwards with frustration. He just stood there for a while, staring into the cosmos within a massive space station among the stars—the stars themselves uncaringly staring back at him.

CHAPTER 61

MEETINGS & LEAVING THE SEAT

J ake wanted to punch someone in the throat, as he was still internally raging. More than anything, his lack of understanding frustrated him the most. He hadn't felt anything was off until the very last moment when Ell'Hakan perhaps went a bit too far with his questioning.

He had been complacent... Jake knew others had to constantly watch out when it came to social skills and keep their minds steeled. Jake never did that, as he always felt when someone tried any mind magic shenanigans. Things would feel "off," and his Bloodline would warn him, allowing him to easily ignore or snap out of it. The Minotaur Mindchief was a prime example of this early on his journey and had set a precedent.

However... against another Bloodline, Jake had no defense—at least, not his usual one. Whatever the Bloodline of Ell'Hakan did, it could affect his emotions and make him trust someone for no goddamn reason. Actually, thinking more about it, the man had first broached several topics that he would have mentioned without anything shady going on, such as that he was indeed a human and had done the same event and whatnot. Even asking about his planet had seemed pretty damn normal. Why wouldn't you be curious about what other worlds were out there?

He had slowly eased into more personal questions and asked about subjects Jake would usually keep a secret, yet Jake had, at the time, felt like he was just answering mundane things to a trusted friend. No, perhaps more than a trusted friend, as he would never share details of his Bloodline with anyone, even Villy.

Wait... maybe that is why it crossed a line.

Bloodlines would never be all-powerful. There was no way the guy could just make Jake trust him fully, and even if Jake did trust him fully, he would never share details about his Bloodline. That was the one thing that no level of trust would make him share. So maybe that was it... He could make people slowly trust him somehow?

It felt too simple, but it was all Jake truly had for now. Either way, if that was really what it did, Jake would make sure that Ell'Hakan could trust that Jake would turn him into a pincushion with arrows the next time they met.

Jake was thrown out of his thoughts as the Sword Saint walked over. Everyone had seen Jake punching the ground, and a few had backed away, afraid, but the old man clearly wasn't the frightful type. "It appears you have made a new enemy?"

Sighing, Jake turned to look at the old man. "If you ever see him, watch out. He has a Bloodline with some kind of emotional control, or at the very least one that makes him somehow feel trustworthy. Also, he appears to be the Chosen of some god."

The Sword Saint frowned. "Disturbing to have an enemy with unknown powers. However, the most important thing is to prepare for what may happen. Do you believe he may target Earth?"

Jake shook his head. "No idea, but it seems improbable. He would need some way to get to our planet, and even if we are in the same galaxy, that seems challenging. It is more likely he personally views me as an enemy for some goddamn reason. Probably related to the Viper."

The old man nodded. "I see. Now, do tell—I heard you returned to Earth recently, leaving the Order, which makes me wonder. How is my great-granddaughter doing there?"

Contrary to what many would expect, Jake actually knew. "I checked with the Viper a week ago while hunting and was told she is making slow and steady progress. She isn't in any danger, if that is what you are afraid of. The Order is rather stringent with its rule of not killing other members. As long as she doesn't accept tea from anyone, she should be good."

"As expected, then." The Sword Saint smiled before turning more serious. "Do not baby or even attempt to help her unless absolutely necessary. Reika has always been good at everything, to the detriment of her own development. She always had the best of everything, and I believe she needs to face others who are superior to truly progress."

Jake raised an eyebrow. "A bit harsh. I already think she got a wake-up call, as she didn't do that well in the entrance test, and it seemed to motivate her more than anything."

"Motivation can be a fleeting emotion after what one believes to be only a minor momentary setback," the old man explained in a stern tone. "Reika needs to see others outdo her and chase behind them, feeling like she will never be able to catch up no matter what she does."

"Again, sounds harsh. Isn't that more likely to just make her hopeless?"

"If such a situation is enough for her to despair and surrender, then so be it. With a lacking mindset dependent on comparing yourself to others for validation, she would never reach the top. Reika is one of the smartest people I know, but that does not instantly make her the fastest learner or the best at everything. I firmly believe she can reach far... but she will be slow. Her caution and perfectionism will lead to greatness only if she has the patience and will to realize her potential without believing she also has to beat others in the process."

"Tough love, then," Jake reckoned. He didn't necessarily disagree, and even if he did, it wasn't his place to argue or decide what the old man wanted for his family..

"You can view it like that," the old man said. "Moving on to other topics, are you satisfied with your gains from this event?"

"Oh, yeah, definitely," Jake answered, finally smirking a bit. Sim-Jake was still being a sleepy Jake and would be for a bit, but Jake was really looking forward to a future alongside his simulacrum.

"Then do not dwell on a single negative encounter, but look towards the future. Remember, you are the one who decides how a potential next meeting plays out. If you are stronger, that is." The old swordsman smiled encouragingly.

"True." Jake nodded and smiled. "How about you. Good rewards?"

"Naturally. I must say, this entire event was very enlightening. Did you know that in every single scenario, we ended up fighting? The outcome did change some of the times. The time and place also changed, but we always ended up in a duel." The Sword Saint chuckled. "I am not a believer in fate, but perhaps we were fated to fight."

"Or, more likely, we are just two humans pushed together by system events and relatively close to each other geographically, while both being overly competitive and battle-hungry, making our desire to eventually duel natural."

"But is that not fate? A foreseeable future based on who we are? I would think the Augur would argue that is exactly how fate works. Never a guarantee, but a prediction with high likelihood."

"Maybe, but I really don't wanna talk about fate or any of that crap right now... Reminds me of that orange fucker from before." Jake shook his head. "I also need to get going. I wanna catch Casper before he leaves."

"Very well. Greet the Risen for me, and godspeed. And remember... if any outsider does come to Earth, you are not the only one able to defend it."

Jake said his goodbyes and willed himself to leave the Terrace after also noticing Arnold had already left, clearly not interested in exploring some garden.

He appeared back where he and the other Earthlings had originally entered the Seat of the Exalted Prima. Jake hoped Casper was still around as he began tracking and searching for his old pal's mana signature. Luckily, Risen were pretty darn easy to track down, as all that death affinity made them stand out. It did not take him long to get a scent, and based on how fresh it was, Casper had to still be around.

When he began moving towards where he felt Casper, the scent got stronger. Maybe even too strong. A touch of scanning picked up hundreds of similar mana signatures. *So, the Risen are having a meeting, huh?*

Jake didn't hesitate to walk in, getting a few odd stares as he noticed many others kept their distance. Even in the Seat of the Exalted Prima, the Risen clearly weren't popular. He didn't particularly care and walked into an area belonging to another planet.

When he got closer, he noticed several guards outside. They threw him a look, and one of them raised his hand. "Please do not go any further and create problems. We are merely having a meeting, nothing insidious."

He stopped and Identified the man.

[Risen Elf – lvl 126]

"I am just here to see a friend before he leaves this event," Jake explained. The two guards looked at each other with suspicion as Jake elaborated, "It is to give him something."

"Alright," one of the guards relented. "But please allow one of us to escort you."

"Sure." Jake shrugged. They couldn't fight, so why even have guards? Couldn't people just walk in anyway? Jake sure could have. He was just being polite to not piss off Casper's new pals.

The elf joined him as an escort and led Jake into a room filled with Risen. Priscilla and Casper were both there, along with who Jake guessed were other leaders. Jake's presence instantly drew attention as they all turned to him. Now, they had taken precautions and were within an isolation barrier, but Jake had his sphere, so he noticed their very suspicious looks.

Luckily, Casper acted quick and excused himself as he went outside the barrier. "Jake, I did not expect you to come."

"Having a meeting about how to take over the universe and turn it into a land of death?" Jake asked jokingly.

A joke that did not land. Instantly, he felt everyone within the barrier raise their guard. He saw Priscilla nervously begin to explain and calm the others, but Casper just laughed and went along with it. "Damn, you caught us; I guess I will have to start a zombie apocalypse on Earth now."

"Over my dead body. Wait, no, that would only be playing into your plans!" Jake smirked. "Good to see you again. I don't want to disturb your meeting for too long, but I just came to give you this."

Jake took out the Root of Eternal Resentment and presented it. He had already had it within Palate for a long time and learned nearly everything he could. With the curse energy also absorbed, Jake had little use for it, even if it was a great treasure. He also knew Casper wanted and needed it, so he decided to finally hand it over.

Casper stared at it for a bit before asking, "Are you sure?"

"Yeah."

Casper nodded and took it. Jake saw him scan it magically as he looked at Jake. "You madman, you actually used all of it!? I expected you to use a portion or do a slow infusion or something like that, but everything!?"

Jake scratched his head. "Well, yeah? It was good stuff, and everything worked out well, didn't it?"

"Sure did. Let's not talk about that little incident, right? Anyway... can I see it?"

Smiling proudly, Jake pulled out Eternal Hunger and presented it to a visibly excited Casper. The man moved forward and touched the blade as his eyes widened. "This is just insanity, and very much the sort of thing I would expect from you."

"I shall take that as a compliment."

"It was a compliment; I love it. That weapon is a pure marvel." Casper smiled. "Thanks for the root, man. I promise I will put it to good use. If you get the time, you should come by and visit. I have something new and interesting to show you."

"What is it?" Jake asked expectedly.

"A secret. You can see it if you come," Casper teased.

"Fine, keep your secrets," Jake joked back as he gave his mate a bump on the shoulder. "Nice meeting up. Oh, and I should say hi from the old man. I'm gonna leave you be and allow you all to continue planning for world domination."

"Do begone, pathetic being of life," Casper said, smirking as he waved Jake off. "And good to see you again, Jake."

Jake left the secret undead meeting and went to see a few other people, including Miranda and his brother. He checked in with Caleb to see how his family was doing and, contrary to expectations, was told he shouldn't hurry to visit, but instead focus on himself. His parents understood and were patient, just making Jake want to visit more.

With all meetings done, Jake tried to look for Carmen but found she had already left, so he entered the simulation space once more, where it quickly became apparent the Seat of the Exalted Prima had nothing more to offer for now. Standing in the simulation room, Jake considered if it was time to leave.

Sim-Jake was still asleep, and he had done everything he needed. He sighed as he remembered the talk with Ell'Hakan again, willing himself to leave the simulation room. He then returned to Earth's hall and teleported back to Earth once more.

Jake appeared back where he had entered the Seat of the Eternal Prima from, still standing in the broken jungle not far from where the Phantomshade Panther had been killed. It did not take long for a familiar presence to descend and the expected question to be asked.

"So, had fun at the Seat of the Exalted Prima?" Villy asked a tad teasingly.

"It was certainly something," Jake answered. "I will tell you about it later, but first... do you know of anyone named Ell'Hakan?"

"I cannot say I do. Why?"

Jake proceeded to explain what had happened. How he had nearly revealed his Bloodline due to the other's Bloodline, and how the other party had acted as if everything had been planned out and made threats. It didn't take long before the Viper had an answer.

"Sounds like the Chosen of Yip of Yore," Villy answered.

"So?" Jake asked.

"Yeah?"

"So what the hell is up with him?" Jake exclaimed, somewhat frustrated. "Who is this god? Who the hell is his Chosen and why is he after me, and do you have something, anything, more to add?"

"Jake, what you are dealing with is called a mortal issue, not a god issue. Figure shit out yourself. I will tell you that Yip sees this as a fight by proxy, and as my proxy, I choose to trust you to handle it. The only real piece of advice I will give you is to not let your guard down, as this kind of opponent fights in a less straightforward way than you are used to. Do not expect him to just pop up and fight you in a duel, but something far more elaborate. As the Chosen of Yip, this mortal will clearly be one tricky bastard, but this is where my input ends. Ah, I forgot to add the most important piece of advice. Don't die, alright?"

"I will try," Jake muttered as he shook his head. "Enough about that weird fuck. Allow me to instead introduce you to my new best friend and tell you the glorious story of how we met..."

CHAPTER 62

GREAT WONDERS & WONDERING
WHAT TO LEVEL

J ake narrated his brief trip to the Seat of the Exalted Prima and talked about the event. Villy asked several questions along the way, even some technical ones, about how the simulation worked and what Jake had learned while experiencing it. He was especially interested when Jake got to the conversation he had with the system alongside sim-Jake. Of course, what he was most interested in was sim-Jake himself.

"So, it appears you entered what we call a Parallel World Simulation rather than a Dreamscape Simulation," Villy explained. "*The difference between these is that one is 'real' while the other one is 'fake,' if that makes sense. Parallel worlds are pretty damn rare but do offer more opportunities and are actually accurate, while a dreamscape is nothing more than a fantasy constructed primarily with pieces from your own mind and inaccurate details, all based on the Records of the one who experiences the simulation. This also does mean the simulacrum you have eaten is truly his own person and even had his own Truesoul while in his own universe."*

"I have figured out that last part," Jake said, nodding, "but do you have any experience with what happened? What it may mean in the future, any risks, and what I might gain out of it? Also, can you interact with the simulacrum?"

"Yes, maybe, some, depends, and no. You really need to get better at asking individual questions. I have had experience with other simulacrums from Parallel World Simulations crossing over. Not myself, but people I have known in the past. What you will gain out of it and any risks are ultimately dependent on the simulacrum in question, but

from the looks of it, there won't be any issues there. The worst thing I have seen happen is that someone gained a split personality and suffered extreme delusions and even parallel senses. That eventually led to him going utterly insane and destroying a few dozen solar systems, believing that nothing was real and that he was stuck inside an illusion before finally getting put out of his misery. And one of the reasons why no one could ever help him was because no, I cannot interact with your simulacrum. He does not exist in our world, only within your Truesoul. He is still anchored to the simulation, as without the simulation, he would not exist, and without him existing, neither would the simulation. They are conceptually entangled in every possible sense."

Villy's answer gave Jake quite a bit more insight into sim-Jake and echoed much of what the system had said. "Are there risks of me also fucking myself up?" Jake asked, having latched on to the part about someone going insane.

"Probably not. May this simulacrum slightly affect you? Sure, but not to an extreme level. The primary difference was that in the example, both believed themselves to be the real person and the other the simulacrum. Whenever one was in charge, the other one believed they were possessed and would fight for control, resulting in a fucked-up Soulspace. In your case, you are in agreement on who is real and who is a simulacrum and that one day you will rejoin."

Jake nodded along before asking further, "Are there ways to make my other self persist?"

"Before I answer that, I want to hear why you even consider that something that should be done?"

"Just to, you know, allow him to be him." Jake shrugged.

"Look at it like this. Right now, he is effectively a clone you separated from yourself at a certain point in life. While bringing a simulacrum to the real world is not normal, reuniting with clones is. Some even purposefully create a clone to send them into areas cut off from the outside to allow them to develop by themselves for a while. Then, later on, the real version and clone reunite and merge, gaining from what each has done in the meanwhile. Granted, this method is risky and leaves you weakened while your clone exists, but it is more common than you would think. In these cases, both are fully aware of who is real and who is the clone from the get-go, and remerging is a given. They both want to remerge. No matter what, this simulacrum will not die as long as you live, for he will be you in both body and mind, and he too will want to merge. Your souls

want to be one. To gain all you can for now and benefit for both your sakes."

Good insight, as always, and he finished by adding, *"Just do know there is an innate power imbalance, and it isn't that you will gain all his memories or Records. So training with him is best. Out of everyone, no one understands you better than yourself, so take advantage while it lasts. Also, I gotta add, having yourself as your teacher is the epitome of 'fuck it, I'll do it myself,' and I applaud it."*

"Alright." Jake nodded and smiled a bit at the last joke. Believing they'd had enough simulation talk, he moved on. "So, the Seat of the Exalted."

"Definitely one of the Great Wonders of the 93rd Universe. Well, not this Seat itself, but what links it all together. The true headquarters of this massive undertaking." Rather confidently, he continued, *"Perhaps this Exalted Prima is even a Bound God."*

For some context... While in the Order, Jake had bumped into the mention of Great Wonders quite a few times, and had wondered—pun intended—what they were all about. It turned out that with the birth of each universe came places created not just for the native universe, but the multiverse as a whole. Chances were the Seat, or wherever the Seat led to, was one such place.

Jake knew of a few other famous Great Wonders. The most famous one was Nevermore, where the Primordial known as the Wyrmgod had ended up effectively taking it over and ruling the dungeon, but others included the White Sun, a massive star and one of the largest celestial bodies in the multiverse, or the Mothership of Null, a giant spaceship of sorts where no magic could exist. There were many others, but some disappeared with time, some only appeared at set times before fading away for a period again, and most importantly, most were not aimed at anyone on Jake's level, but at those who had reached far higher. A place like the White Sun would instantly kill even weak gods just by them getting near.

The second thing was Bound Gods. Bound Gods were not living beings with Truesouls, but gods born out of objects or places. They would be real in every way yet severely limited, most often serving a function of sorts rather than possessing truly free will. Many believed these Bound Gods were merely apparitions of the system like the Guide, but others believed they were creatures born by the system to run certain places or even serve as protectors of some zones.

Another reason for a Bound God to exist was also simple enough:

deterrence. Most Great Wonders in the multiverse were claimed and controlled by factions, but those with Bound Gods were often different. A Bound God would often have total control over what they inhabited, so even if they were weaker than a god, they still had the ultimate defense of merely making the Great Wonder useless by stopping its functions. Destroying a Bound God was also impossible unless one destroyed the Great Wonder, and destroying one tended to be a good way to make a lot of enemies. Some had been destroyed throughout history, but it was incredibly rare, as every time one was lost, it was lost forever and considered a major setback for the multiverse.

Of course, this assumed anyone was strong enough to destroy a Bound God. Some Bound Gods in the multiverse were more powerful than even Primordials.

"I do find it probable it is a Bound God of some sort and that it is a Great Wonder," Jake answered. "Having been there, it was clear that it wasn't just made for this one event; it even existed in the universe itself and not some hidden dimension. Moreover, with its competitive element, I believe the plan is for someone to gain at least some partial control of these Seats, and with that in mind, there would have to be some protections in place, or this whole Administrator Candidate business would be useless."

"I second that. It is a massive opportunity to get system-sanctioned partial control of any Great Wonder if it truly is one."

"So... this is one of the reasons why so many gods want to get involved in new universes, right?" Jake asked, understanding a bit more.

"Right on. This event is only open to you natives, and you have a first-mover advantage. Having just some influence will allow one a better position to negotiate and form alliances or even sell off eventual rights."

"So, you want me to try and claim this Seat of the Exalted in the Milky Way?"

"I would recommend for you to at least try—not for the Order, but for yourself. You said you got a title just for doing this event; imagine what you would get for taking control of something even factions like the Holy Church want? Of course, this doesn't mean you have to actually want the Great Wonder. You can always just use it as a bargaining chip." Shamelessly, Villy added, *"Also, for full disclosure, I would one hundred percent benefit from you doing well, as you are my Chosen, so definitely a good idea."*

"Aight... finally, do you think the Chosen of Yip of Yore is a legitimate threat right now? Like, can he come to Earth?" Jake genuinely didn't know. Considering how much they'd struggled with making a teleportation network on Earth, it seemed unlikely, but one could never know.

"Why would the answer to that question matter?"

Jake frowned. "To know if I need to get levels under my belt fast in case it comes to a fight."

"That is up to you. My only advice is that you are truly in no rush for anything. What is the worst that can happen? Either you win, or you should be strong enough to just not engage no matter what you do. Worst case, just leave the planet and go somewhere no one knows who you are. With Shroud of the Primordial, no one would find you. All of this assuming he can go to Earth in the first place and can actually fight you."

Jake considered the Viper's words. He was currently level 169 in both his class and profession, meaning he could focus on either. Focusing on his profession was slower for sure, while he could get quite a few quick class levels if he went hunting for a couple of weeks.

However... the more he thought about it, the less wise it seemed to focus on his class levels at the current time. Recent happenings made Jake reconsider many things, and he knew he would need a lot of live combat to properly learn to fight in melee, which would include a lot of hunting. However, before that, he would need sim-Jake to be ready to teach him, and to probably practice with his simulacrum for quite a while.

It had also been a while since he had been back at the Order and done some alchemy. He had many shelved projects like the Bee Queen ritual he needed to get going, and he could always use more time doing alchemy. If the orange asshole did come to Earth, it wasn't like the planet was defenseless either. Shit, who was he even to think he was the protector of their world? There were many C-grades stronger than him, and even the King had him beat. The Sword Saint had also felt more powerful than ever when they met in the Seat of the Exalted Prima.

To summarize... Jake would just focus on himself and what he needed to do. He wanted power, and he was playing the long game to get it. He would need to get his profession leveled up anyway, so why not now? He could then save his class for when he and sim-Jake began their melee training session.

"I am planning on heading to the Order again, then," Jake said. "Let's hope some good lessons are coming up."

"I will have beer ready," Villy said as the connection faded.

Jake shook his head and began retreating from the jungle. He was lucky to find a hill with a cave in it and promptly headed inside, where he got to work. He pulled out a small pamphlet given by Villy on how to set up the teleportation formation.

Reading it carefully, Jake quickly got the gist of it and began working. With the ancient skill Soul Ritualism of the Heretic-Chosen Alchemist, Jake figured things out far faster than expected, as it filled in the gaps where needed. In less than an hour, the formation was complete. He was surprised when it was done, as it seemed to become one with the environment, and he could barely feel it was even there.

After a bit of testing, he stepped into the middle of it. "Oh, well, here goes. Let's hope no Void Dwellers decide to poke me along the way."

As he activated the formation, he felt Villy assist with energy. Before long, he was teleported away, his final thought before disappearing being about a certain elf he hadn't seen in a while.

I wonder how Meira is doing and if she is keeping up with her lessons.

--

Meira studied the tome carefully to make sure she understood everything properly before she had to go take care of the garden. The book was about the energy circulation systems and physiology of different creatures in the multiverse. It was complicated, but her teacher had insisted that she memorize as many diagrams as she could before the next lesson.

It was a bit harder than usual, as she had to copy down some parts. Nella and Utmal had asked for her to do it for them, and Meira had naturally agreed, as they were friends. She had discovered that the books in her master's library were a notch above what others had publicly available, and many of the tomes were considered of the highest tier. Naturally, she couldn't take out any books of real value, only the most common ones, so she had to copy down anything important to show the others. Nella and especially Utmal had pressured her to just bring the books, but Meira was hesitant, as she didn't have permission.

Contrary to what many would perhaps expect, Meira didn't question her master's absence in the slightest. It was natural that his residence within the Order was but one of many, and she was sure he had plenty of servants and slaves elsewhere. Anything else would just be weird for someone as esteemed as the Chosen of a Primordial. She knew he wanted to keep his identity a secret in the Order, which was why he only had a single slave, but he no doubt had more on his home planet.

She still, of course, hoped he was doing well and that he would return someday. Until then, Meira would just keep up with her studies, and hopefully... maybe... her master would be a bit proud of how well she had done and even that she had made some friends.

Meira smiled at the thought as she finished copying down the final diagram and got up to head towards the garden. On the way, she checked the mansion was in good condition as usual, not thinking much as she opened the door to the living room.

The moment she did, she froze on the spot as her eyes opened wide.

"I am just saying Jake should have stayed longer the first time around, and he needs a good talking to about staying firm and the true importance of alchemy!" Duskleaf, the Grand Elder and leader of the entire Academy, said disapprovingly. "He didn't even get to study any proper ritualism or formation magic. Just look at how slow he is setting down that magic circle!"

"And I am arguing that going back finally got him laid, which is invaluable for his personal development," the Malefic Viper, the almighty Primordial and leader of the Order, argued.

Meira didn't even have time to properly register what they were talking about before she passed out from the sheer presence of the two gods.

CHAPTER 63

NOT BLACKMAIL

Jake stood with his hand covering his face in a solid facepalm as he stared at the chaos that was his living room. Using his sphere, the very moment he teleported into the garden, he saw everything. The trip had been smooth, if a bit nauseating as usual, with no void stuff along the way, and he had entered with expectations of finally relaxing a bit, only to come home and see two honored gods acting like children.

In the doorway to the room lay an unconscious Meira, and on the sofa, Villy was busy arguing with Duskleaf about Duskleaf wanting a "temporary leave of absence" from the Academy to do a minor experiment that would "only be a few thousand years tops," with Villy telling him that he would take away his cauldron if he did. Jake really didn't want to get involved, and luckily they both stopped arguing when Jake entered the house and went towards the living room.

"Should I expect an explanation?" Jake asked the moment he entered the room.

"It is a welcome party," Villy said as he lifted up and showed a can of beer. Lifted from a pyramid of beers made on the sofa table.

"I wasn't gone for that long, only a few weeks," Jake commented.

"Which is basically forever for you mortals, isn't it?" Villy cheekily countered.

Jake shook his head and looked at the plump Duskleaf sitting on the couch, staring at him. "Hey, Duskleaf. Been a while. I didn't take you as the sort to join in for these kinds of things."

Duskleaf looked a touch embarrassed and combed his beard with his hand as he tried to appear wise. "I am not here due to this welcome party, but to discuss your recent commitment issues. I saw you headed back to your little planet not long ago after only being here for a short while, and I firmly believe that was a gross misprioritization of your time."

"Oh. Well, I was asked by a friend to help out, so I had to head back." Jake just shrugged.

"While that is an understandable sentiment, you must remember that alchemy always takes precedent!" Duskleaf argued with great fervor.

"I also needed to head back to gather the necessary items to participate in a system event that may eventually lead to taking partial control of a Great Wonder," Jake added, shrugging again. "But I guess you got a point. Titles giving percentage bonuses to stats, and controlling Great Wonders probably isn't worth my time."

"I..." Duskleaf shook his head. "Naturally, it is healthy to sometimes take a brief break to reflect on recent experiments and obtained data. But that break is over now, right?"

"I am back, aren't I?" Jake just smirked. "Thanks for the concern. I do plan on staying for a while. Now, with all that handled, why is everyone ignoring Meira just lying there?"

He finally decided to address the fainted elf in the room as he went over to her.

Villy shook his head and sighed. "You know that is entirely your fault, right? Suppressing one's aura and presence takes conscious effort, and as I said, it doesn't really work if the individual knows who you are, and no way I will bother making myself invisible when visiting. We have gotten used to not needing to hold back our auras in your presence, so it is one hundred percent your responsibility to make sure she can handle it."

Jake looked over at Villy as he levitated Meira over to a chair and sat her down on it, arguing, "And how do you expect for me to handle it?"

"Well, by either not caring that she faints or by training her not to," Villy answered, giving a surprisingly reasonable response.

Jake wasn't really sure why he hadn't considered using his special "talents" to help Meira train her resistance to presences. It would make life a lot easier if she didn't constantly faint whenever Villy stopped by. Then again, maybe she would still faint, presence or not? Either way, it seemed like something he should do.

"Are you confident that would be wise?" Duskleaf asked Villy. "The elf is commonly known as Jake's, and any development in resistance to presences such as the one he provides is outside the norm. Considering it is also known that his Bloodline offers resistance to presences, it wouldn't be an overreach to conclude others would infer that he can also, at the very least, train this resistance to others if the elf gets it. Right now, only Umbra—due to Jake's brother—and the two of us truly know. A few others may also, but it may spread and become public knowledge if he does teach her. Jake has chosen not to do so yet to hide this ability of his, right?"

Duskleaf asked Jake the last part, and he felt a little bad at seeing the level of belief the old alchemist had in him. Villy threw Jake a knowing smile as Jake just scratched his head and chuckled. "Eh, I don't think it is a big deal if people know? Isn't it actually pretty easy to hide the real truth? I can just say it requires a slave contract or something to share the resistance due to a skill or something."

"That will work until people become aware of your brother," Duskleaf argued.

"Do you really think Umbra will openly share it? I am sure people can form a hundred different explanations as to why he is resistant." Jake shrugged.

"Oh, I do think that would work, except you also helped train some of his people when you went to their city, who now also know." Villy snickered. "The dragon will be out of the egg soon no matter what you do, so I truly don't think it is that big a deal. You may even be able to turn it to your advantage."

"Ultimately, it is your decision," Duskleaf said, sighing.

Jake smiled at him. "Thanks for the concern either way."

He then went over and began picking up some papers that Meira had dropped. Jake did find it a bit funny she still wasn't used to the spatial ring he had gotten her, as he saw the papers all contained rather complex diagrams.

Duskleaf also noticed when Jake brought them over and looked interested. "Oh, are you teaching the girl alchemy?"

Jake nodded. "Well, not really me, per se. You see, I have this plan..."

He explained his plan of making Meira a real member of the Order by properly teaching her and how he had her attend lessons and do her own thing. Duskleaf nodded along and motioned for Jake to hand him the papers. Seeing no reason not to, Jake handed him the diagrams.

The god looked them over and nodded as he muttered mostly incoherent words under his breath. "Shoddy... Acceptable... No... hm..."

Jake and Villy both just stared at him until Villy asked teasingly, "So, is the girl some hidden genius you just have to take a student?"

"Hm?" Duskleaf grunted as he looked up. "No, not at all. Her dedication to detail is respectable, but she made several mistakes, and her notes are all over the place. She does have a healer class, though, doesn't she?"

"Yeah," Jake confirmed, not knowing why it mattered.

"Those are rare at least." The old alchemist nodded.

"Wait, why are they rare?" Jake asked, confused.

"Not rare in the context of the multiverse, even if they are the rarest type of class," Villy butted in. "We are talking about here in the context of the Order. If you haven't noticed by now, we here in the Order tend to be self-serving assholes, so who would waste their class on being a healer? That is for those who even have classes. A lot only have one or the other, and considering they are in the Academy, they likely have an alchemy profession."

"Oh," Jake said. "Makes perfect sense. I assume that gives her some advantages?"

"Some," Duskleaf answered. "Minor, but there is synergy and overlap. Her knowledge of physiology is at a high level, likely from her class and learning how to be a better healer. However, her general skills when it comes to learning, studying, and taking notes are atrocious. I guess you cannot expect anything better from someone who has lived in servitude their entire life. Does seem at least a bit worth training if you think she has the dedication and mindset to progress."

"I see." Jake sighed as he got an idea and tossed Duskleaf a sly look. "Guess I will add teaching her some general stuff to my to-do list, then, along with the resistance training. Going to be a busy stay."

"What?" Duskleaf asked in shock. "Absolutely not. You need to focus on alchemy when here, not messing around. The resistance training is fine, as you can do that passively, but spending dedicated time on teaching her is out of the question."

Jake looked at Duskleaf and tilted his head. "She will have to be taught."

Villy smirked in the background and nearly failed to hold back a laugh as Duskleaf shook his head. "I am not foolish enough to fall for something that childish."

"Man, and here I was hoping I could do some more shenanigans with my arcane affinity and Bloodline in a ritual with the Bee Queen to make another creature like Sylphie." Jake sighed. "I was even hoping to ask you for advice and have you help and naturally observe the entire process."

Duskleaf gritted his teeth and clenched his fists. "Are you black-mailing me?"

"What?" Jake said, acting shocked. "I would never do such a thing. I merely realize that due to my workload, I will have to re-prioritize my tasks and abandon the ritual. Such a bummer. I was really hoping to see what kind of being I could make now. Especially after I have evolved and even partly merged with a simulacrum from a Parallel World Simulation that realized it was in a simulation with whom we, together, reached an agreement by negotiation with a system entity."

"After you did what?" Duskleaf jumped a bit.

"Eh, nothing. I already talked with Villy about it, and seeing how busy you are, I don't want to waste any more of your time talking about such boring topics." Jake waved him off as he made another exaggerated sigh.

"Jake," Duskleaf suddenly said, turning far more serious than before, "trying to blackmail a god will never end well."

"Pretty sure I already clarified I am not blackmailing anyone?" Jake said with a big smile. "And you keep forgetting that acting threatening has no effect when I feel more animosity and danger from the countertop than you."

"Fine," Duskleaf finally relented. He then stood up and took out a green, fist-sized seed, pricking his finger to put a single drop of blood on it. The seed sprouted instantly and, within five seconds, formed a fully humanoid form that looked like an exact copy of Duskleaf himself.

"This is one of those high-level cloning techniques I told you about, Jake," Villy said with a smile from the sofa before asking Duskleaf, "How much of your power did you put into that?"

"Nothing. I improved the seeds," the newly sprouted version of Duskleaf answered. "However, they have a limited duration, as it runs on the seeds alone."

"How long?" Villy asked with a raised eyebrow.

"Around two billion years," Duskleaf answered, looking disappointed. "Takes about the same amount of time to grow one."

Jake listened in, and while some might feel bad about how he'd roped in Duskleaf and even made him spend a seed he had grown for longer than humanity on Earth had existed, Jake was totally fine with it. "So, that clone will stay here?"

"What?" the clone once more answered. "No. While it will be available, I can't waste it too much. It can still display around ten percent of my full capabilities, you know."

"It is as I said," the real Duskleaf said. "I will leave this clone here and teach both the girl and you. Just remember to include me in the ritual."

Jake gave him an affirmative nod before the god teleported away without any detectable spatial disturbance.

Villy just grinned and looked at the cloned Duskleaf. "You can still drink beer even as a little beansprout, can't you?"

"Naturally," Duskleaf—or Sproutleaf, if Jake wanted to be cheeky —answered as he took a seat on the sofa where the real version had been before. Once he was sitting down, he looked at Jake. "And now you tell me everything about that system event and let us go over your plans for the ritual with the Queen Bee."

Jake nodded and smiled as Villy tossed him a beer can. He popped it open, took a swig, and began, "As I said, Villy and I think the event may have taken place in something linked to a Great Wonder..."

Within a throne room on a planet far away from Earth, the servants waited expectantly. At times, some would appear, teleported there by the system itself, as they too joined the other servants in awaiting the return of their king. The grand palace in which they knelt was a marvel of pre-system engineering, created from a bronze-like metal native to their world. A material only allowed to be used by the royal family.

Soon, the room was filled with servants as, finally, their leader appeared. Ell'Hakan was teleported right in front of the throne, and he had a big smile on his face. Minutes passed as he seemed to have an internal dialogue—or a talk with his Patron—before he turned and briefly regarded his subordinates.

"Has everything been delivered?" he asked one of the servants standing at the front—one of only fourteen people kneeling on one knee.

She nodded. "Everything has been prepared, and they signed the agreed-upon contract as expected. They are fast proceeding on their end but will still require some time to fully prime the array. It will be ready in time."

Ell'Hakan thanked her, adding, "We cannot expect too much from them. Even with the guidance of my Patron, there are limits to the competency of the lesser. However, I believe they shall play their role adequately."

The woman nodded. "Even if they are less skilled, they still possess heritages allowing them to do it. Humans are an adaptable breed, after all."

"That they are." Ell'Hakan smiled, remembering his brief encounter with his fellow Chosen. His smile deepened as he looked forward to their next encounter. After assuring everything was as it should be, he headed towards his chambers in the highest tower and the tallest structure on their planet: the Celestial Spire.

The top of the spire was the place closest to the stars, and only the king and his most trusted servants had ever been allowed there.

Standing on the balcony, he waited only a few moments before his most competent and vital companion appeared.

Ash and transparent flames shifted form as the air shimmered from the heat. Rapidly, an elemental-like being condensed out of the ash and transparent flames, taking a vaguely humanoid form. Space shifted ever so slightly in its surroundings as it appeared fully formed next to Ell'Hakan.

"So?" the being asked in a deep, echoing voice.

"Your kind truly does come in all shapes and sizes," Ell'Hakan said simply, adding, "Like you, this creature that wanders the human planet was no doubt more powerful than I or even the Malefic's Chosen. You shall have what you desire."

"That we are supreme is a given, for such are the laws of the universe. Remember your promise, and I shall do as sworn." Then the being dispersed into nothingness, leaving only a faint shimmer in space behind along with a small pile of ash.

Ell'Hakan just smiled and shook his head. He gazed up at the burning red sun above and the two faintly visible moons only detectable due to his post-system improved senses. Some companions were harder to deal with than others, and the Ashen Phantom Devourer was certainly the hardest. Not that it was unexpected.

One couldn't expect Unique Lifeforms to be loyal subjects. They were too prideful, too assured of themselves. One could never truly make them trust another fully. But they were easy to figure out and thus make use of.

He smiled as he gazed upon the cosmos above, enjoying the sight. "I hope you look forward to our next meeting as much as I, oh, Malefic's Chosen."

CHAPTER 64

LEARNING STYLES & INTERNAL STRUGGLE

Meira had a nightmare as she slept, her eyes rapidly darting around below her eyelids. She felt like she had been thrown deep underwater and had constant suffocating pressure on her. At the same time, she felt like she heard the raised voices of others. She tried to escape and swim away in her dream, but she only kept getting pressed further and further down into the deep and overwhelming darkness.

Finally, the pressure lessened, and she began floating upwards towards the sunlight. Meira felt relaxed and comfortable as she slept comfortably for the first time in a while—the last time being when she was knocked out by the previous divine visit. She had many odd dreams during her rest, and everything kind of blended together... but they were generally good dreams.

After having been deep in slumber for several hours, her mind finally stirred as she woke up. She opened her eyes and saw she was lying on the bed in her bedroom. She looked to the side and saw Grand Elder Duskleaf sitting at her small desk, looking in one of her notebooks. Meira turned her head back to the ceiling and sighed. Yeah, she was definitely still dreaming. With that thought, she closed her eyes again, but it didn't work. She felt the pressure. An unsettling emotion. Her eyes shot open again as she stared to the side once more, meeting the eyes of the Grand Elder.

They stared at each other for a bit as Meira tried to comprehend what was happening. She was only thrown out of her stupor when the door to the room opened after a knock. She abruptly sat up in the bed as her master entered with a smile.

"Good morning, sleepyhead," he said casually with a smile. "Sorry about the lack of notice I was returning, but in my defense, I also didn't know those two would invade my living room."

"I am sitting right here," the Grand Elder grunted before turning to Meira herself. She sat there, frozen, and tried to comprehend what was happening as he spoke. "Our first lesson will definitely be regarding proper categorization and organization of information and general note-taking."

The god held up some of her papers, and she spotted the diagrams she had made for her friends. Meira then remembered she had been on her way to meet them before passing out... not that it mattered with what else was currently happening. She wasn't even sure if she should answer him or if that would be disrespectful. She just nodded, unsure how to act.

"Liven up, girl," the Grand Elder said loudly. "I am not going to teach an unresponsive statue anything. Focus and get over here to make sense of this utter mess you call a notebook.""

Meira nodded and quickly got off the bed before the words properly registered. She was confused as she realized and asked out loud on accident, "Teach?"

Jake had attended many classes in university during his studying days and, of course, gone through well over a decade of mandatory schooling. He'd had thousands of lessons overall with kids and adults of all ages. Hundreds of teachers.

But this lesson had to be the most awkward and weirdest by far.

The teacher was overqualified, while the primary student was overly receptive to the point of being non-receptive due to pure nervousness. Jake quickly just became an observer, finding the scene of the alchemy god teaching the poor elf novice far more entertaining than he should.

Duskleaf and Villy had made it clear early on that they would have no impact on Jake's learning method, as neither would ever be able to fully understand how he best absorbed information. Jake was a very instinctive learner and had to learn by doing to fully digest anything, but when he did things, he also caught on quickly. That didn't mean he got nothing out of reading or being told what to do, just that it wouldn't "click" properly in his mind before he actually saw—and more importantly, felt—theory working in practice.

Meira was far more typical in the learning department. She did best with a varied approach to learning and was totally fine just reading and being told something. Naturally, she also needed some practical experience, and luckily—or unluckily, if you considered the emotional damage—had gone through plenty of "learning" with her body. She had built up her resistance to poisons through a long period of exposure where she had to learn to control her own energies to survive, and through this had also gotten to know her own body very well. Knowing her own body's metaphysical shape had then served as a gateway to also comprehend those of other creatures.

However, Meira had something far more valuable than what experience or teachers could teach her. She had a powerful survival instinct. Jake had noticed, after interacting with her so much, that her entire mentality was about survival and doing all she could to keep living a relatively "safe" life. It was odd, in some ways. Jake wanted power to be free, to do what he wanted, and was willing to die on his journey, while Meira wanted to desperately avoid death by gaining power.

Of course, it was natural to not want to die. It was the most basic of all instincts and a primary driver for many to try and get stronger. Each evolution offered a massive boost in lifespan and natural treasures, and created products that increased longevity were incredibly popular and expensive. Many even turned to becoming vampires or undead to live just a little longer... not to mention the entire concept behind the Holy Church and the Holyland.

Meira was not like those who just wanted to live as long as possible. Her instinct was all about immediate survival. To survive till the next day. The next week. Next month. She took it one step at a time, and her long-term plans now revolved around Jake being satisfied with what she was doing. While it was maybe a bit cruel, Jake wanted her to keep this mentality. It had an air of desperation, and for Meira, desperation led to dedication.

Though he would also be somewhat encouraging... and maybe even give her some work to get some practical experience. Currently, she was just doing a bit of gardening here and there for him, but he knew she wanted to do more.

"Duskleaf, there is quite a big crossover between the metaphysical constructs of beasts and Beastcores, right?" Jake asked the god, who had just finished correcting a very nervous Meira.

"Beastcores are ultimately just remnant Records of a beast as well as a portion of their energy, so yes, one can say that." The god nodded. "I assume you are considering its link to core refinement. Core refinement is essentially trying to construct a metaphysical framework within the core to allow it to house and store more Records with the core itself as the base. That is why you had such a profound effect on the Sylphian hawk when you made her. You created a catalyst that housed many of your Records. Though that was only possible due to the Malefic Viper's poison triggering and stabilizing it using the Records of the Viper. If not, you would have probably broken the ritual."

Jake nodded, having already realized these things far earlier. He then turned to Meira. "What would you say to assisting in a project of mine? The goal is to create a Pollendust Bee Queen variant, and to do that, I have a lot of cores gathered. To use them properly, I will need to have them all refined. Trust me, I have a lot of them."

That was something Duskleaf had told him during their talk while having beers. Jake had just gone off the ritual with Sylphie and thought that having as many cores as possible would be best, but the alchemy god had shut that down hard. While there was some value in quantity, the biggest challenge was to make all the cores properly work together.

As mentioned, then, each contained Records and energy. Simply trying to smash it all together in a massive ritual would only result in disaster, so you needed to do something else. You needed to make sure that each core would complement and not conflict with one another.

One had to remember that when Sylphie was born, only a single Beastcore had been used, and the rest were orbs from elementals. Elemental orbs were quite a bit different from Beastcores, as the orbs were pretty much pure mana with no Records that could conflict. So as long as they were all of the same affinity, things tended to be fine.

So, for the ritual to go well, Jake needed to refine every single core to ensure they would resonate. He already had a good start, as each core was from the same kind of insect, and he wanted to use the cores to empower an insect. This removed a lot of conflict in Records already, but each termite had still been slightly different, making refinement a necessity.

There was also the option of first filtering out all the Records from the cores and only using the energy—something that you often did when using cores while concocting—but that wasn't what Jake wanted. After all, he wanted to improve the Records of the Bee Queen to get a variant.

Meira looked at Jake with a bit of confusion as she stuttered, "I... I am not sure I will be of much use..."

Duskleaf also threw him a questioning look and telepathically sent, *"I fully understand if you don't want to spend time refining so many cores, but there are many far more qualified to assist you in the process than she."*

Jake heard him but was already determined as he talked to Meira. "I want you to help. Don't misunderstand—I just think you will be the best because I don't plan on you doing it in any usual way. It will be coupled with presence-resistance training."

Meira looked confused, as he had yet to bring up the idea of resistance training yet, but Duskleaf opened his eyes in realization. "You plan on infusing the Records of presence resistance into the cores to give it to the Bee Queen and thus resonate better with the Records of your Bloodline while also hopefully granting the Queen an innate resistance? Smart to not only seek to implement the concept of resistance, but the process in which it is granted."

"Bingo," Jake agreed. Okay, that wasn't precisely what he had in mind. He had only hoped to maybe give the Queen some increases to aura resistance like Sylphie had if he combined the two by having Meira refine cores during resistance training, but Duskleaf made it clear his idea was even better than he first thought.

Poor Meira still looked somewhat confused as she mustered up her courage to talk. "I... I have no experience in core refinement..."

She spoke in a tiny voice, as if scared she would get scolded, but Jake just shook his head. "No problem. I didn't expect you to. Also, this request is outside of your usual lessons, all of which I still expect you to keep up with. This is just if you have leftover time, as we will have to do the resistance training anyway."

Meira nodded, but Jake noticed something. He had believed he misperceived it earlier, but Meira seemed to slightly shudder every time one of them mentioned resistance training. Jake quickly understood.

"This resistance training we are talking about is resistance to presences such as those of gods," Jake said, assuring her with a relaxed smile. "Duskleaf here is trying really hard to suppress himself, and yet it is still clearly affecting you. I can help you train to be far less influenced."

He saw her nervousness reduce slightly, but she was still afraid. *Oh, well, it will be a bit unpleasant, so I can't lie and say it will be a walk in the park either. Better she is relieved at it being not as bad as expected than lower her expectations so much she gets a rude surprise.*

"I will do my best!" she finally answered with determination.

Jake smiled. "I know you will. And there is no rush; we won't get started yet. You need to first learn and practice core refinement, and I have a few matters to handle before the cores can even be used."

Meira confirmed she understood with yet another nod, but she quickly looked nervous again. Seemingly having gotten some more confidence, she spoke once more, "Uhm... before the esteemed Grand Elder and the Malefic One graced us with their presences, I was on the way to visit some of those I study with... My friends..."

Jake opened his eyes wide, needing to know more. He had no idea Meira had any friends. Okay, that came out very wrong, but he had no idea she had any people she would actively call friends. "Oh, friends? Well, that is nice to hear. So that is why you copied things down from the books? To show your friends?"

She nodded and quietly spoke, "I know it is master's boo—"

Jake stared her down for using the M-word.

"My lord's books... I apologize for overstepping and not asking if I was allowed to copy anything," she said while bowing.

"I was going to say that if you want to look over some books together, you have my permission to ask them over and just look at the library." Jake shrugged. It was Meira's home too, and he wasn't going to tell her she couldn't even have friends over.

Duskleaf shook his head. "Master stocked the library with quite a few tomes not commonly available, and—"

"Duskleaf," Jake interrupted him, "that word is banned in my house."

"I have been calling him that since I was a mortal," Duskleaf protested.

"Well, social norms develop, and things that were acceptable in the past become frowned upon. More importantly, this is my house and my rules, so no M-word," Jake then telepathically added, *I also don't want to make Meira think it is okay. You know, she may begin taking after you.*

"You don't want the elf girl to take after a god?" Duskleaf countered. *"One of the best alchemists in existence?"*

"Oh, she can definitely take those parts, just not the one where she uses banned words," Jake replied, shutting it down with a grin.

Duskleaf grumbled something about Jake being lucky he had

seniority as Villy's friend, but he seemed to agree. "What I was trying to say is that the Malefic One did not put books in your library to be handed out mindlessly."

"I understand that," Jake said, inwardly celebrating his minor victory. "Which is why they will have to come by and look at them in the library."

"Acceptable." Duskleaf sighed, shook his head, and turned to Meira again. "Now, where were we... Also, Jake, are you joining in?"

Jake shook his head. "Nah, I got something else to deal with right now."

"Oh?" Duskleaf raised an eyebrow.

Jake just shrugged. "Yeah, so apparently, a big fight is going on inside my Soulspace, and I should probably check it out."

CHAPTER 65

TWO GENIUSES MAKING PLANS:
ME & MYSELF

The ground shattered as the two beings clashed. Mountains were torn asunder, and space shuddered with every impact as their bout seemed to go through a neverending cycle of change. The larger of the two figures repeatedly adapted and transformed in response to the attacks of its small foe, while the small combatant always seemed able to counter whatever the monster did.

Jake stood back and observed this all as huge areas of the Soulspace were ripped apart. It was a fight clearly far beyond D-grade, and yet sim-Jake didn't even seem that pressed. The level of power Jake could display inside his Soulspace had always been a bit of a mystery to him. It wasn't a real world, but just one created from his Records and his own mind. Kind of. It was real and yet imaginary—a dreamscape.

What sim-Jake was fighting was naturally the chimera made up of the curse energy from Eternal Hunger. The hulking monstrosity of pure energy had an ever-shifting body that constantly tried to adapt and improve to better kill and consume sim-Jake, but even with everything it did, it was a losing battle. Not that it cared, considering it was just pure instincts with not a shred of thought within. It just saw sim-Jake and wanted to eat sim-Jake, because that is what it did. One could almost call it eternally hungry.

The fight finally reached the zenith as sim-Jake vaulted over its massive form and, before it could adapt, smashed his katar down into its head. The blade extended in an explosive way on impact and blasted the chimera into the ground below, where it took a moment to recondense its body. Mind you, no energy was actually lost by either of them, and this battle could truly go on forever or until Jake himself died, thus making the Soulspace disappear.

Getting a feeling it was time to interfere, Jake stepped forward, once more wrapped up the chimera in mana strings, and re-sealed it. Primarily so that it would stop trying to constantly eat Villy's blood, only to hurt itself and actually risk getting destroyed.

Sim-Jake nodded at him in approval once the job was done. "I must say, that arcane affinity is nifty."

"Definitely better than the boring dark affinity," Jake said in return.

"Spoken like someone who never bothered to explore it properly." Sim-Jake shook his head. "Also... an elf slave? Really? How fucking stereotypical can you get?"

"Villy set me up." Jake shook his head in the exact same fashion as sim-Jake. "But I am handling it. More importantly, you seem to be having fun playing with that little bundle of very hungry joy."

"Definitely worth it." Sim-Jake nodded. "It is better at fighting than most beasts I have encountered and is pretty damn interesting in the way it constantly adapts. Forces me to stay on my toes, you know? How come you never trained against it?"

Jake scratched his hair. "I maybe should have... Anyway. How was your nap? Feeling rested and good to go?"

"Adequately rested, sure. I have been awake for a few hours now, just sitting back and watching." Sim-Jake shrugged. "I really don't have much interest in all of that alchemy crap, and based on how clueless I still am when it comes to it, I haven't merged with any Records related to your profession."

"But do you get the attraction?" Jake asked.

"Kind of?" sim-Jake answered, pondering the question. "I get the attraction in the complexity and that it can offer a different sort of challenge, though the lack of life and death makes it a bit less interesting."

"Eh, a bit, but it makes up for it with pure complexity. The field of alchemy is so damn broad, and there is so much to learn and so much to craft. I feel like I would be able to keep doing alchemy forever while still progressing." Jake smiled. "But enough about me. This version of me. What is the lay of the land?"

Sim-Jake sighed. "A mixed bag. First of all, my skills are gone. All of them. This is partly to be expected, but I don't even bloody remember how the skills worked anymore. I tried recreating some, but anything even remotely complex is completely lost to me. I have a feeling the system purposefully did it like this, but I am not sure."

"That sounds plausible," Jake said, nodding. "It probably deemed it too much to borderline hand me a bunch of skills to learn. Sure, they wouldn't be skills, but that level of knowledge would make doing what the skills did a lot easier and make me learn them far faster."

"True. However, there is one exception. After coming here, I naturally lost my Blessing and all connection to Umbra as well as anything related to Tenlucis... but I got a skill related to Umbra very early on. Before I was blessed."

"You mean...?" Jake asked with realization.

"Shadow Vault." Sim-Jake smirked as he jumped backward and used the skill, turning into a shadowy form for a second before fully reappearing. "This one I can still use... but my version was at a higher rarity. As it is, this Shadow Vault doesn't really jell with us anymore."

Jake nodded. He hadn't really used Basic Shadow Vault of Umbra for a long time, and the reason for that was simple: it was prone to do more damage than good. If he encountered anything while using Shadow Vault, he would lose heath, mana, or other resources, and at his current grade, it was hard to travel in a straight line without anything getting in the way. If he had a clear line to where he wanted to go, One Step was just better.

"Any thoughts?" Jake asked, but he kind of knew the answer already.

"We gotta use it with this," sim-Jake said as he condensed a small arcane bolt. "And yeah, I can, of course, use the affinity too. Though I must say, I don't quite understand it... I can just use it. Weird, that one. Like, I get the destructive parts of it, but I have a hard time balancing it with the stability and making it useable." As he said that, the arcane bolt looked a bit unstable and soon scattered by itself. Sim-Jake shook his head. "Anyway, we need to make Shadow Vault work with our arcane affinity, but without losing what actually makes Shadow Vault so great. More importantly, we need to get rid of its connection to Umbra."

"Being a bit harsh towards your old Patron," Jake joked, but he got it.

Having skills related to several gods at the same time wasn't necessarily a bad thing, but it could lead to some conflicts, especially when it came to upgrading the skills. One of the primary reasons Jake so easily upgraded his "of the Malefic Viper" skills was because of his deep connection with Villy, flooding him with Records related to the Primordial and hence his skills. One could say that as his Chosen, Jake was playing life on easy mode in regards to upgrading his Legacy skills. In the same vein, then, the less connection Jake had with Umbra, the harder upgrading it would become.

"I am not being harsh, just realistic," sim-Jake said. "Either way, I have some thoughts in regards to Shadow Vault and will focus on improving it. Or at least find a good direction."

Jake nodded once more. "Now for the main dish. Melee combat. I assume you lost the skill you had made with your fighting style?"

"I never really had one," sim-Jake answered blankly. "I got that starting weapon skill to uncommon rarity, after which I didn't even try to upgrade it anymore. I thought it would be a bad idea to upgrade an existing skill if I wanted to make my own style..."

"That isn't how that works," Jake said with exasperation.

"And I know that now. Major trust issues, remember?" Sim-Jake scoffed, a bit offended. "Not that you should complain. That just means I retained one hundred percent of that knowledge. Again, that was probably helped along and approved by the system."

"What more knowledge have you lost?" Jake asked, a bit concerned.

Sim-Jake fell silent before sighing and explaining, "A lot... but it is more like they are being replaced. I remember taking a university exam despite never going to university, but I do also recall the university itself, as I once followed a target while there. The only things still clear in my mind are all the things after the system and mainly events related to fighting. If I stand here and try to remember details of mundane things, I instead just remember what you did. It is weird, man."

Jake felt a bit guilty, as he knew part of this was caused by him fucking up a little during the infusion process of the bone. Yet he also knew this was an inevitable conclusion to two people with the same Truesoul sharing a Soulspace. Well, that, or being like the guy who'd gone insane that Villy had mentioned.

Nevertheless.

"Sorry," Jake apologized.

"For what? For replacing memories of digging through dumpsters alone while avoiding adults wanting to take advantage of me with new ones of begging Mom and Dad to get fast food at the drive-through? Sure, both resulted in us eating trash, but at least I had a family and a brother in one of those memories." Sim-Jake had started off jokingly, but he now turned more serious. "I am being genuine here. You clearly made the better choices and ended up better off than I did. All I had was being strong and good at fighting. Sure, you are still a broken-ass human with major issues, but you are less broken than I was. Did you know I was a damn virgin? Not due to lack of opportunity, but because I thought it too risky to get vulnerable with another person. How pathetic is that?"

"Dude, too much information," Jake said, trying to lighten the mood.

"Considering I got flooded with very vivid memories of sleeping with a certain Runemaiden, I don't think you have much to say." Sim-Jake smirked. "At least I now have memories that I actually find positive. Ah, the one with Carmen included. I am becoming you more and more by the day, and I fully accept that. The day you learn everything I can teach you is also the day I will finally become a real boy. By becoming you."

"Already beginning to inherit some humor, at least," Jake said, also smiling. They looked at each other for a bit before sim-Jake spoke once more.

"Well, then, enough sentimental bullshit. Come at me." Sim-Jake spread his arms wide.

"Unarmed?" Jake asked.

"That you think it makes a difference already proves how much you suck," sim-Jake confidently said before taking a more relaxed stance. "Alright, the first lesson i—"

Sim-Jake charged forward, barely giving Jake time to block. A follow-up came, but he was able to dodge it. However, as he tried to avoid the third blow, sim-Jake managed to grab hold of his clothes and swing him over his back, smashing Jake into the ground.

"First lesson is to always seize the momentum," sim-Jake said, smiling as he backed away.

Jake stood up and didn't hesitate to attack. He went for a punch that was dodged, and as he tried to land a kick, his leg was caught. Sim-Jake just smirked again as he tossed Jake away, making him land on the ground with a thud.

The entire "fight" had been without either of them really using any superhuman abilities, and even then, the difference was clear.

"As you see, you do way better defensively," sim-Jake said. "It is also pretty stupid to make such wide moves against someone with your instincts. So, let us say the second lesson is to not just go in swinging without thinking."

Jake stood up again and cracked his neck. "Let's go again."

Sim-Jake just laughed. "Man, you are going to make people believe we are into self-harm."

The next half an hour or so was spent with Jake fighting sim-Jake, or more accurately, Jake getting his ass whooped by his own simulacrum. After half an hour, Jake decided he wanted a win, so they changed up the rules by removing all rules.

Arcane explosions, arrows, shadow magic, and all sorts of methods were deployed. The two of them were perfectly evenly matched in power, as they shared the same Truesoul, making it a truly "fair" fight. There were still differences in skillsets, though.

Sim-Jake was very good at dodging arrows, but real-Jake was very good at landing them too, and his curving arrows coupled with magical attacks made it undodgeable even for him. Meanwhile, sim-Jake would come out on top whenever he got close enough to land blows with his katars before Jake could disengage. Overall, Jake won most of the time —which was only to be expected, as he ultimately had more experience due to having lived with the system longer.

Eventually, they both stopped as sim-Jake sighed. "This was actually a little productive, as I have a better sense of your fighting style now. And a newfound hatred for bows. Those fucky curvy arrows are just annoying."

"Guess we still got some way to go before we are perfectly similar," Jake said, laughing at his simulacrum's dislike for bows. Bows rocked.

"Anyway, go back to the outside world," sim-Jake said.

"Is my life that entertaining?" Jake asked jokingly.

"No, not really, but it is the best I got, and I at least find the company you keep interesting," sim-Jake answered. "Don't worry, I will also be busy practicing and maybe having a few bouts with the chimera."

"Suit yourself." Jake shrugged as he disappeared from his Soulspace and opened his eyes in the real world. He was sitting on his bed within the mansion and stretched as if he had just woken up.

"Hey, Villy," Jake spoke out loud, "is the inside of the Soulspace considered a Dreamscape Simulation?"

A small hole in space was opened as a head poked out. "It is a version of one, yep. Took you long enough to figure that one out."

"Oh... I think I get it now," Jake said, nodding. It had been bothering him, but he kind of understood now. "Sim-Jake can keep being a simulacrum because he just went from one simulation into another...

with the difference being that I am running the new simulation. Or, well, my Truesoul is the one powering it."

"Close enough to be true," Villy, the floating head, said. "So was that everything?"

"Yep. See you around."

With that, the head popped back into the hole in space and disappeared. It was just a small realization Jake had reached and wanted to confirm.

Still sitting on the bed, Jake could see the entire mansion through his sphere, including Meira and Duskleaf in the library, still working hard. During their earlier talk, Duskleaf made it clear that while he would teach Jake about formations—only because Jake was pretty much a total novice—he would not touch anything else.

So, Jake still needed regular lessons. With that in mind, he took out his Order Token and began looking through everything that was on offer. He hadn't been gone for that long, but long enough for him to not really be able to follow the old lessons he had been enrolled in. Fortunately, there was never a lack of willing teachers, especially not in the lower grades, making it easy to find replacements.

The next hour or so was spent picking out lessons about concocting poison and brewing potions with a few general lessons about miscellaneous topics mixed in as well as two related to elixirs. Coupled with the lessons Jake would have with Duskleaf and his planned resistance training sessions with Meira, Jake's schedule was packed moving forward.

Looking at the many lessons planned and what they were about, Jake had a feeling he never thought he would ever have...

He was actually happy to be back in school.

CHAPTER 66

A COUNTER+INTUITIVE FIGHTING STYLE

Multitasking. Everyone loved multitasking, and it was one of those great buzzwords people often used when they attempted to do fifteen things at once poorly rather than just doing a few well. Multitasking also wasn't truly doing more things at once. It was just rapidly switching between several tasks or starting tasks that could automatically continue or finish on their own while then spending the meantime on something else. Like an author putting food in the oven that would take forty minutes to cook and then using that time to also focus on writing.

Jake's ways of multitasking were at a level far above this. He had found a way to not only train with sim-Jake but also train Meira at the same time. It was quite honestly genius and not at all an accidental discovery found when Meira walked by his room while Jake was having a fun spar with his other self.

It appeared that when Jake was fighting himself or just straining himself within the Soulspace, his aura flared, as he was effectively having an internal struggle. When Jake also began to purposefully amplify this effect, it became highly effective to the point of Meira barely being able to move. It was just too good not to use.

So currently, Jake was sitting in the library on a pillow in Serene Soul Meditation, while Meira was anything but serene. Duskleaf was trying to teach her as sweat poured down her face, and she was out of breath from the presence. The old alchemist god was unaffected due to the sheer difference in power, but he did admit that it was a very impressive aura when they began this kind of training. He had even added that if Jake was a god, it would maybe have been a little intimidating.

However, as things were, they did conclude that Jake could only do this kind of resistance training with those significantly weaker than himself. There was also some passive resistance to auras gained from just being around him frequently, but it was meager in comparison to a full-on training session where he was just blasting.

Anyway, while Meira was struggling in the outside world, Jake struggled in his inside one. He and sim-Jake had been training for a few weeks now since their first bout, and it was no longer just "fights," but there was some actual teaching going on.

"Don't let it adapt—move faster," sim-Jake said as Jake was busy fighting the massive monstrosity of pure curse energy. "If you let it get used to your patterns, you will be screwed."

You said that ten fucking times, Jake grumbled as he dodged and punched forward with his katar—a weapon he was still very much getting used to. He hit the arm-like appendage of the chimera but was soon pushed back by several spikes claws flying towards him, followed by a whipping tail.

"Momentum is key. Seize it," sim-Jake spoke once more as Jake moved to attack.

He delayed his actions by a fraction of a second, making the tail miss before he truly attacked. He managed to land several blows before the beast could adapt and strike back. Jake was pushed once more and had to find a new way to counter as their endless cycle of switching advantages continued.

Jake had made himself weaker than the chimera on purpose to make it into an actual fight that he could lose. All other times he had "fought" the chimera had been merely using overwhelming power. He had blasted it around and sealed it, never truly engaging in combat.

And now that he did... he concluded that the chimera was far stronger than he had ever thought it would be. It was so adaptable it was insane. Its body would evolve on the fly to counter its opponent, and its instincts were absolutely top-notch to the level of Jake suspecting it tapped into his Records a bit.

While sim-Jake had made the brawl with the monster look simple, Jake was struggling, unable to keep up. Which, in some ways, was a good thing, as it showed how much room he still had for improvements.

The key to the fighting style sim-Jake had developed was all about seizing momentum and using the opponent's own fighting style and instincts against them. Jake had not truly considered it before... but this style was incredibly Perception-centric. It was all about reading the flow of combat, reading your opponent, and understanding the tempo of your foe instantly. It was about reacting, and to react, you had to see and be aware of what was coming. Jake's Bloodline-empowered instincts leaned towards always just avoiding danger and not attacking, meaning that while his instincts could help him read his enemies, it wouldn't help with what kind of response he had to formulate.

Reading your opponent during a fight also wasn't a one-time thing, but something you had to repeatedly do as the fight progressed. The entire concept of controlling momentum and understanding the one you were fighting wasn't anything new either. Everyone did it, and it was the basis of most martial arts. Someone like the Sword Saint was a prime example of someone who was already a master at this, and as Jake recalled their fight, he did notice how the Saint became able to counter and strike him more and more as the fight went on.

"On the surface, a fight can seem simple," sim-Jake had explained. "It's just about hitting the right timing and then swinging your weapon or landing that punch, right? While technically true, it is a harmful oversimplification. One of your other major flaws is overextension. When you see an opening, you pounce on it without considering the next step. Sure, you may land your blow, but won't it just end with you getting smashed in return? I am not saying trading hits can't be a good strategy, but it has to be an intentional choice and not the result of you fucking up and still managing to get out on top.

"Every single move in a fight revolves around making choices. How much power do I use? What angle do I strike at? What will the opponent do? Follow-ups? You always need to consider the fight as more than just that lone exchange. Our Bloodline is a bit limited in that sense. It will make it appear smart to take advantage of an opening, even if doing so can lead to getting screwed five moves later. The same is true for dodging. It is all about dodging every individual move, sometimes a few consecutive moves, but the pre-cognitive danger sense is simply not able to predict far enough ahead. Once an enemy picks up on this, they can begin to take advantage. That isn't really a problem in D-grade yet, as even your flawed style has so many adaptions it would take a peak-level genius to figure it out... like that Sword Saint."

Jake and the chimera kept fighting as Jake stayed close to it, trying to keep up with its ability to adapt and change to better combat what he was doing. It wasn't going perfectly, though, with Jake repeatedly losing out.

"We have better senses and instincts than anyone else... which also leads to my next point," sim-Jake had also added. "It is something I am working on myself, but that you may as well also begin considering. Right now, we adapt and react instinctually and 'stop' the instinctual reaction when we want to counter. This leads to a very small and minor delay compared to merely following along with what our body wants to do. I have been wondering... why does our body dodge the way it does? If you noticed, our ways of dodging are slightly different, and you borderline instinctually form mana barriers and use magic. Something I certainly do not. The cause of this lies in what is essentially the system version of muscle memory. Soul memory, maybe? So imagine if we could train our muscle memory. Actively, that is. Currently, we are still training it just by fighting, which is why battling the chimera is a good way to spend your time. It would lead to an entirely new world where can instinctually make perfect attacks... theoretically."

Jake pushed back the chimera in their fight and got the advantage. He kept pressing and adapting faster than this foe could adapt to him. He stabbed it over a dozen times as he countered its blows before finally choosing to release his power and reseal it.

"That was better than before," Jake commented with a proud smile, looking at the wriggling form of the chimera within its prison of mana strings. It stopped struggling after only a few seconds and just went dormant.

"Yeah, if you weren't us. You got a long way to go before you get on my level." Sim-Jake shook his head. "But you are improving for sure. Fighting our instinct is hard, isn't it?"

Jake nodded. It bloody was. Countering wasn't a natural reaction for him, so he had to always register a blow, want to instinctually react by dodging, stop that reaction, and then counter instead. He would then, of course, need to quickly decide how to counter based on how he had wanted to dodge and what he sensed from his opponent. Jake needed to take in a whole lot of information and decide on it almost instantly. Something made easier by being able to quickly gather that information.

This was, as mentioned, a fighting style intrinsically linked with Perception. It was about not only reading your opponent, but reading your opponent better than they could read you, and if you saw them do the slightest adaption or shift, you had to pick up on it and counter-adapt. Always be one step ahead, never allowing the other side to get an advantage or any momentum.

To summarize the fighting style... it was about always knowing what your opponent did and taking advantage of those moves. It was such a simple concept made complicated by the sheer level of sim-Jake, and now real-Jake wanted to take it. Theoretically, this would be an unbeatable style as long as he wasn't beat handily in stats, but reality was not that simple. There were too many variables in any fight, and often one didn't know the variable before the very final moment.

A hidden skill, a saved trump card, a new item, a boosting skill, help arriving, the environment changing—everything and anything could happen. Sim-Jake had naturally recognized this, which was why the goal was never to know everything—just more than your opponent. Coupled with senses good enough to react to any trump card, sim-Jake believed that the most important thing was to be able to quickly seize back the momentum after surviving the trump card. Needless to say, simply expecting to instinctually survive these trump cards was only possible due to Jake's Bloodline, and honestly, the entire style could only really be called a fighting style due to the Bloodline. It wasn't something Jake could teach someone else, as there were no "moves."

Everything was reactionary. Well, okay, maybe there were kinda moves, but the moves were all based on reactions and tended to be simple, varying from opponent to opponent.

"Any progress on the Shadow Vault front?" Jake asked sim-Jake after discussing melee combat a bit longer.

"Some," sim-Jake said, "but nothing worth sharing. Just trying out some things. It isn't like I can upgrade the skill myself, and honestly, I have a feeling if you just copied the progress I have already made, you would get an upgrade. Don't do that, though. It is still not there, and I don't want it to be a skill with a dead-end or one nearly impossible to upgrade further."

"Very forward-thinking for a simulacrum that will one day in the not-so-distant future cease to be," Jake morbidly joked.

"I will be immortalized through that skill and your melee style," sim-Jake said, waving it off. "I naturally assume you will become immortal. Anything else would just be a fucking embarrassment."

"Maybe I just die to some random critter?" Jake teased back. "Or maybe I find an opponent your super style is utterly useless against, and I get killed."

"Well, that would be all on you for not further developing it, then." Sim-Jake smiled. "Even after I am gone, it will not be done... Remember, I made it with melee and katars in mind. We now have far more methods than that."

Jake shook his head. "One thing at a time."

He knew what sim-Jake meant. All Jake was learning was pure melee combat. There was no use of skills or any other means of combat besides just brawling. In actual combat, Jake would, of course, be different, and he also had some minor adaptions to make based on his use of poisons. While sim-Jake wanted to land a deep wound to do a lot of damage, it was more important for Jake to land a blow that was good at injecting some poison.

"I am just saying," sim-Jake said. "You know, you can even add archery in and make it an absolute god-tier style."

"Or, even better, I can take it one fucking step at a time and not bite off more than I can chew and fuck myself over," Jake said, shooting it down. That was one thing Jake knew he was better at than sim-Jake. While Jake would overextend in combat, sim-Jake would overextend in adding to his own workload, making him stretch himself thin. "Anyway, just keep it up with the melee practice and Shadow Vault. I am going to see Meira now, and I've got a class to attend in a bit too."

"I know," sim-Jake said with a deadpan face. "Remember. Same body, shared senses, partially shared memory. Ah, but do give Meira a thumbs-up from me. She is doing well."

"Already planned on doing that." Jake nodded and smiled as he disappeared from the Soulspace and opened his eyes to exit meditation.

Duskleaf noticed he had woken up, and Meira also breathed out in relief as he stopped openly releasing his presence into the library. "Had a good time? Any good progress?" Duskleaf asked.

"Plenty of progress as always," Jake said. "I have the best teacher in existence, you know? I guess that sometimes if you want a job done well, you have to do it yourself."

"Ma—"

"Hm!?" Jake interrupted promptly.

Duskleaf groaned and corrected himself. "The Viper has made jokes nearly identical to that one nearly every time he summoned avatars, and I was around..."

"Great minds think alike." Jake smiled cheekily.

Meira, for some reason, nodded along with a serious expression like he wasn't joking. Jake turned his attention to her, making her tense up before Jake calmly spoke, "How are you handling the presence training these days?"

"Uhm.... better?" Meira said. "It is difficult, but I am doing my best!"

The sweat on her brow had quickly disappeared after Jake stopped releasing his aura, and she had calmed down a lot. Meira hadn't even noticed that she didn't have any adverse reactions to Duskleaf's presence despite him purposefully leaking out a little. Jake met the gaze of the old alchemist god, and he nodded approvingly.

Jake, fulfilling a promise, gave her a thumbs-up. "You are doing great."

She smiled shyly as Jake exchanged some quick words with Duskleaf before leaving the two be. He went towards the entrance hall and the wall to teleport to lessons. Meira still had some ways to go, and despite it being nearly four weeks since Jake said she could bring friends over, she had yet to bring any. Not from a lack of opportunity, as she had still copied some notes from books for them. Maybe they didn't wanna go?

Jake did see how it could be intimidating, entering the home of another member of the Order of the Malefic Viper due to the rules, so maybe it was them not wanting to go? That explanation would make sense.

Shaking his head, Jake didn't think about it anymore as he used the Order Token to open up the gateway to the lesson hall. This was one of those big lessons only held rarely for newer students, and Jake felt he would see many familiar faces there. It was the first time it had been held since he entered the Academy, and the teacher was also a familiar face.

It was Viridia, the S-grade Hall Master Jake had met briefly way back in the day when he astral projected to the Order by accident. The highest-ranked mortal within the Order of the Malefic Viper.

Well, besides himself, that is.

CHAPTER 67

"SO, YOU WANT TO JOIN THE ORDER OF THE MALEFIC VIPER?"

Some lessons in the Order of the Malefic were limited to certain members. This was one such lesson, limited to individuals who had been in the Order for less than a year. The lessons were also held once a year, making it one you could only attend once. Jake heard that the Hall Master had missed some lessons in recent times due to being away training, but the teacher themselves didn't have that huge of an impact. Rather than teaching much, it was an orientation of sorts, and Jake honestly only attended because it would be suspicious if he didn't. Well, that, and one kind of ulterior motive.

As for the topic of the lesson? How to become a true member of the Order of the Malefic Viper. Currently, they were all members of the Academy, but they were not truly members of the Order. One had to remember that many who attended the Academy came from different factions from all across the multiverse. Risen, who were loyal to the Blightfather and the undead faction, people from the Altmar Empire, or even the Endless Empire of insect-like creatures. That wasn't counting all those from minor factions.

Reika was still a member of the Noboru Clan and loyal to Earth, with no real sense of loyalty to the Order, as far as Jake knew. Jake didn't really know if he would consider himself a true member of the Order, even if everyone else would, for one simple reason: he had a Blessing. That was, to many, a clear indication he was a true member. Even if no such rule existed, those blessed just tended to be. Jake was sure it would be touched upon how easy those like him had it with Blessings from the Viper.

With plenty of knowledge of what he was about to experience, Jake walked through the portal to the lesson hall, and to call this one huge was an understatement. But it was more than that. It was not one of the regular lesson halls, but one clearly specialized for this kind of thing. Carvings of the Viper lined the walls, and at the podium in the center was a massive statue of the Malefic Viper. It was a huge, coiling snake wrapped around a dragon and sinking its teeth into the neck of the larger beast, with the aura given off by the snake far more profound than the dragon. It was almost a statement that the Viper as a snake was superior to dragons.

On the ceiling was an equally impressive mural depicting the founding of the Order. At least, that is what he assumed it was about. It showed the Viper in human form followed by a huge swath of people in robes as he demolished an army of beasts and, with a wave of his hand, created a massive hole in the ground to begin building the mostly underground headquarters of the Order of the Malefic Viper.

The entire hall was pretty much an advertisement for how awesome the Malefic Viper and the Order were. As mentioned, Jake didn't feel like he would get much out of this lesson, but he did also go for one other reason: to see familiar faces.

Being the hunter he was, he used his tracking skill to find the aura signatures of those he was seeking. He quickly spotted Reika with the other alchemists from the Noboru Clan, sitting with a bunch of other people and chatting away already. Jake had to admit that the other alchemists looked a bit haggard, but Reika looked full of positivity as she chatted with a female beastfolk Jake didn't recognize.

Seeing as Reika looked A-okay, he left them alone. Jake scanned the room a bit more and spotted Draskil by himself, as always. By choice, mind you, as there were many who wanted to get close and talk to him. His Divine Blessing was just too effective at making people want to suck up to him and make him an ally or even friend.

Jake looked around and spotted a few more people he had seen or met before, including quite a few with whom he shared lessons. Ultimately, he decided to just go over to Draskil and sit with him.

One had to remember that Draskil had a standing higher than pretty much anyone there. He was no doubt known as a loner who was too haughty to bat an eye when anyone approached, and those he would bat an eye at wouldn't approach him.

So Jake got quite a few stares as he casually walked over and took a seat next to Draskil. It was naturally unoccupied, as no one had dared to sit and risk angering him. The Malefic Dragonkin regarded Jake as he sat down, with Jake taking the lead.

"167."

"What?" Draskil asked, confused, before his eye widened in realization. "Was it a weak one? Barely evolved?"

Jake shook his head and grinned beneath his mask. "It was pretty newly evolved, yeah, but not on the weaker side at all. Wielded both dark and space magic, with the ability to clone itself and a bunch of other tools. Definitely not weak."

He was naturally talking about his successful C-grade hunt. The last time he and Draskil spoke, they had discussed Draskil killing a C-grade while still in D-grade, and Jake had now managed to kill one while a few levels lower. He had to brag about it, and the Dragonkin seemed more than interested in engaging him in conversation. Much to the dismay of many of the observers who probably wondered how the guy with a lesser Blessing managed to get so friendly with Draskil.

"Good!" Draskil grinned as she patted Jake on the back, clearly elated at his kill. With great interest, he leaned a bit closer. "How was the fight?"

"Damn good," Jake said, also grinning. "Man, it had this one attack..."

The two of them kept discussing as the stares of dozens inspected Jake carefully. Not many of those in this lesson were aware of who Jake or even Draskil was before attending. All the get-togethers so far had consisted only of those from the 93rd Universe, and that was certainly not the case for the lesson hall they were in now.

Jake even felt several C-grades present within the hall. Considering the Order recruited and allowed entry of people of all grades, Jake assumed there were separate lessons for them. It usually wouldn't end well to mix B-grades with those significantly weaker, as their auras alone would crush those present. E-grades—which there were a few of —already felt the pressure from the C-grades and stronger D-grades, making them all congregate at one end of the hall.

Soon enough, about fifteen minutes had passed, and it was time for the lesson to begin. Everyone had taken their seats and the gates on all the walls closed. Down on the podium, in front of the statue of the Viper, a green portal opened as a green-haired, human-looking woman stepped out. Her aura instantly blanketed the entire lesson hall, making everyone know she was firmly in the S-grade. But there was more mixed in. It was like her aura carried a concept of authority, more than just something born of power.

Jake did not have a shadow of doubt in his mind. She had an incredibly potent social-type profession. Probably even one called Hall Master or something.

"Welcome, all newcomers, to the Order of the Malefic Viper." Viridia smiled as she regarded everyone in the room. Her eyes stopped on Jake for a second, clearly aware beforehand he would be there. She also lingered on Draskil a little but quickly moved on. "I hope you have all settled in during your time in the Order, or more specifically, the Academy. It is a pleasure to see so many attending, even more so in a time of celebration of our Patron's return. No more words need to be said to fully establish that the Order is not the weak shell it was merely a few years ago; it is now truly a pinnacle faction within the multiverse once more. It is an Order that I must emphasize barely anyone here is actually truly a member of."

A few confused murmurs were heard around the room—primarily from those who hailed from the 93rd Universe, but also some who had merely applied to the Order by doing an entrance test. Jake felt a bit good about others also being clueless about things they should seriously know. Even Jake knew this.

"While all here are members of the Academy," she continued, "that does not make you members of the Order. As students, you are offered temporary membership while within the confines of the Order, but outside our territory, you are not considered one. This lesson today is about your status in the Order, how to improve that status, and how to potentially truly join the Order of the Malefic Viper."

She waved her hand, and a projection of a hieratical structure appeared above her. It outlined the general power structure of the Order in a simple fashion. At the very top was naturally the Malefic Viper himself, and right next to him—but placed a bit lower—was his Chosen.

Beneath that were other gods of the Order, then the Hall Masters, followed by Branch Leaders, and then a bunch more ranks Jake didn't bother to remember before finally getting to the bottom. Temporary outer members. This rank was highlighted as Viridia spoke again.

"For now, you need not consider the top. The Malefic One stands supreme, his Chosen second, especially among us mortals." Jake briefly felt her attention on him, but her eyes didn't even move, nor did she in any way indicate she was talking about him. "No, the ranks you can reach for are those at the bottom. Right now, the majority of you are the highlighted temporary outer members, which, as I mentioned, means you are not truly part of the Order.

"However, this sort of membership also offers benefits. As temporary members, you do not need to formally join or have any true responsibility towards the Order. You can remain part of any other faction as long as they are not enemies of the Order, and we will have no control of your actions or if you choose to leave. Not that we tend to exert much control over our actual members, but some responsibility is expected."

Being a temporary outer member was the end-point for most students of the Academy. Jake already knew that. Not necessarily because someone couldn't join, but by choice. As mentioned many times, factions often sent talented individuals to the Order to study for a time, and these would naturally only be temporary members. While in the Order, these people were formally recognized as members, and their status from their home faction decided how they were treated, making them even sometimes viewed as having a higher status than true members. If the Chosen of the Blightfather chose to attend the Academy, he would still only be a temporary outer member, but his actual status would be far above his rank.

"As a temporary outer member, also know that your membership will end the day you stop attending the Academy or are made to leave," Viridia continued. "If you wish to remain a member, you will have to become a non-temporary outer member of the Order of the Malefic Viper.

"Now, many of you here will easily be able to do this. Simply being able to enter the Academy makes you individuals with some semblance of potential, already making you pass the first hurdle. In fact, I would reckon that becoming an outer member within the week would be possible for the vast majority of those present. If you wish to also take upon you the responsibility membership includes, that is."

This led to more murmurs, and a few were clearly interested. Most knew these things, and Jake kind of knew, but her just stating it outright was something different. Many of those unaffiliated with any faction probably wanted membership in the Order, and knowing that was a possibility was great news. Especially for those from the 93rd Universe... Not.

"Naturally, this near-guaranteed acceptance into the Order does not extend to those who entered under extraordinary circumstances, such as those who recently arrived from the 93rd Universe," Viridia said, making hundreds deflate a bit all across the lecture hall. "Again, to make it clear, nobody here is guaranteed membership even if they want it. Except for one group: the blessed."

Jake knew this part was coming as Viridia lit up the next stage of ranks above outer members. "Anyone who carries any Blessing from the Malefic One will automatically become an inner member if they so choose, and dependent on the Blessing, perhaps even higher. Those with Blessings from gods loyal to the Viper or members of the Order are also automatically offered to become inner members of the Order."

More murmurs, more talking in hushed voices, and more speculation sounded out. Quite a few looked at Draskil, too, as he sat there with his Divine Blessing.

"Membership and your rank in the Order will naturally also bring many benefits. You will gain more resources, more Academy Credits, and some new lessons will become available to you. All that is asked of you in return is to help the Order as they help you. This may include missions, providing materials for the Order, completing commissions, or just assisting it in other ways. We are not a charity, but neither do we expect slave labor from you. We have actual slaves for that." Her joke got a few chuckles from around the room.

"However, more than some resources, you become able to finally claim yourself a member not just within the Order, but in the multiverse as a whole. If you wish for it, you can leave behind a Soulseal in the Order that will detect if anyone slays you, marking your killer. People will fear your very presence, and no faction will dare make a move against you lest they invoke the wrath of the Order. Many foolish forces have fallen through the ages by daring to make us an enemy, and do trust in that—your enemies will become the enemies of the Order. Ah, not to say we will simply deal with any issues for you. That is ultimately still up to you. What it will mean is that someone a few grades above you will think twice before killing you. If you die to someone around your own level... tough luck."

Jake smiled a bit under his mask. That did sound like how Villy would run stuff and pretty much what their personal agreement was. If Jake lost and died to someone around his own level, Villy would not interfere, but if some god decided to kill Jake, he would. The Order would probably not save someone in time, but at least it sounded like they would take revenge. The second-best thing.

"Now, as for the ways to officially become a member. Quite frankly, you just apply with any official through the Humanoid Resources department—you should each have a contact person linked to you—and they can get your application started." Viridia quickly added, "Tests and such will be performed on an individual basis."

Jake, at this point, began zoning out a little as Viridia continued explaining what one could do if they became true members. She took some questions too, but none of it really interested him. Instead, he focused on the statue near Viridia, and as he stared at it, he remembered something.

Wait... whatever happened to that insane sculptor from the Primordial Church back in Haven? I heard he was trying to make a statue of the Viper, but surely... surely he can't still be doing that?

CHAPTER 68

MINOR MISUNDERSTANDINGS & DUNGEON

I t wasn't good enough. It was never good enough. With disappointment in his own incompetence, the sculptor shattered his half-made creation. Only a bit of the material was lost, as he could still use the marble-like rock by refusing it, but some material was gone forever. Fortunately, the City Lord understood the importance of his task and provided him the funds necessary to do what had to be done.

Felix had not left his workshop for... a long time. He wasn't actually sure how much time had passed. All he knew was that nothing was more important than making the perfect sculpture. The only breaks he took were those forced upon him. It was good that he had at least evolved to D-grade so he didn't have to really sleep anymore, allowing him to focus exclusively on his work.

The image was still vivid in his mind. The sculpture displayed by the Chosen of the Malefic Viper depicting his Patron had been nearly perfect. It held meanings Felix could not understand and profound concepts he would not even dare to try to comprehend. He did question the purpose of the bottle and the link between it and the mushroom, but such were not his questions to ask or his task to understand. He was merely the sculptor—a tool to bring about magnificence.

If only he was more talented. Even if his skills upgraded and the system called him a "prodigy," he did not view it as enough. How could it be? All that he created was trash. Poor imitations. Not a single one was even close to being able to house the presence of a Primordial infused by his Chosen adequately. He didn't even aim for perfection... just adequacy.

This was a task given to him by the Chosen of the Malefic Viper himself. Felix knew he had the backing of the entire Primordial Church behind him, and his Patron had even upgraded his Blessing to Divine in recognition of the importance of this task. The Malefic One had not had a statue made by one of their own for a long time... much less had the chance to have the Primordial's Chosen infuse it.

Felix collected himself and prepared to start again. This time... This time, he would surely do it. If not, he would just have to wait a bit and get his level 180 skill in his profession. If that wasn't enough, he would just have to wait for C-grade. Felix was not in a rush. The Chosen had not given a deadline, and he would rather see himself die of age than present a subpar sculpture.

Because if he failed, he truly did believe he deserved death just to make up for a fraction of the sin that would entail.

Yeah, that sculptor guy probably moved on to other things by now or asked Chris about what kind of statue he should make, Jake thought as he stayed zoned out during the boring orientation marked as a lesson. It wasn't as if Jake had actually ever shown that Felix guy what kind of statue to make.

Anyway, refocusing a bit on the lesson, Viridia kept explaining stuff and taking questions, and from the vibe, Jake got the feeling a huge portion wanted to officially join the Order. Those who weren't interested fell into two camps: Those with existing backings or those who were just on the fence.

Jake understood from a logical standpoint why one would join the Order. In the simplest of terms, it offered safety. It was why many factions could function. Even if it didn't lead to someone not killing you, it would make them think twice before doing so.

It was also important to note that many in the Order were faction leaders or at least highly influential figures on their home planets. While returning was maybe not currently possible for them, if they did return in the future, they might want to make their planet part of the Order.

There were, in general, quite a few draws when it came to joining a major faction. Some had likely already applied to become a member. One of which was the guy sitting beside Jake.

"Hey... have you officially joined the Order?" Jake ended up asking Draskil.

The Malefic Dragonkin looked at him. "Of course. It got me free stuff."

Jake nodded at the reasoning of his dragonkin buddy. As Viridia had explained, members would passively just get more things. They got more Academy Credits, had access to certain stores that no one else did, and even got a stipend of sorts to further their own power. All in all, if you had no other obligations, joining just made sense. As a member, you also had a lot of freedom.

Most other factions were largely restrictive of what their members could do. There were high levels of expectations when it came to loyalty, and going to wars for your faction and risking your life was simply a given. The Holy Church was the most extreme example of this, as when you were part of the Holy Church, leaving it again would get incredibly difficult, especially as your entire planet was often part of the Church, and you were born into it.

However, with restrictions also came benefits. The Order of the Malefic Viper would not just shower their talented members with help. They would not assign them teachers or give them all the materials they needed. In the Holy Church, you would never want for anything as long as you stayed loyal and fulfilled all expectations. In the Order, you would get tossed out if it was decided you sucked too much and were a leech.

It all came down to the fundamental difference in ideology. The Order believed in freedom over everything else—in always offering the choice. If the Order wanted something from you, it would be far more transactional. Naturally, the Order would come out on top in these transactions to not fuck itself over in the long term.

Now, it has to be mentioned that this kind of model could only really work with the Order due to how they operated on a multiversal scale. The Order did not engage in wars or choose sides in larger conflicts. Their members could join as mercenaries on either side, and there were several examples of Order members even killing each other on the battlefield. Something the Order of the Malefic Viper naturally didn't do anything about. If you joined a war and got killed, that was on you.

Jake knew all of this just by doing a bit of studying and listening to Viridia's lesson. But there was still the question...

"Did you join?" Draskil also asked.

"Did I?" Jake instead asked the god observing them.

"At this point, no one would believe you if you said no," Villy answered. *"You have acted like a member, got way too many AC not to be a member, and I am pretty sure that when one of the Verdant Witches had you registered in the Humanoid Resources Department, she did so as a member of the Order. Not to mention what happens when you eventually slip up and reveal yourself as my Chosen. Actually, you denying being a member after that happens would be hilarious, so maybe just act like you aren't?"*

So, yeah. He was. Maybe. Jake looked at Draskil. "Yeah, I did. Kind of. It's complicated."

Draskil shrugged at his response. "This lesson is boring. You also think that?"

"Oh, that isn't a complicated answer. Yeah, very much a waste of time with no real information for me or you. But it seems like it is good info for many."

"Hm," Draskil hummed. He fell silent again for a few moments before changing the subject entirely. "What is your real level?"

Jake was still hiding his level and showing it far higher than it actually was, but Draskil had quickly picked up on it being off, especially as Jake had openly discussed a few things to make him suspicious. Ultimately, Jake prioritized a good conversation with Draskil over hiding his true level, and Draskil didn't seem like the type to share it around either.

"169, all three balanced," Jake honestly answered.

"Profession holding you back." Draskil shook his head. Jake faintly felt approval from a certain simulacrum within, but he ignored that guy, as he didn't know better.

Jake just smirked in response. "I don't know... I killed one before you."

"I am stronger now," Draskil shot back.

"Arguably. And even if that is true, I will be stronger than you in the future."

"Bah, I would beat you." Draskil scoffed. "Power is supreme."

Jake smirked. "You never know how a real fight will end."

He actually didn't have much confidence against Draskil, but he was sure he could at least escape or put up a good fight, especially considering his recent advances. One also had to remember that Draskil had not done the system event due to being in the Order, meaning Jake had probably grown more in power simply due to his new title.

Draskil observed Jake a bit more before smirking himself. "Then prove it. You are a member of the Order, so join a mission."

Jake raised an eyebrow. "What do you have in mind?"

The Dragonkin pulled a piece of parchment—yes, old-looking parchment—out of his spatial storage and presented it to Jake.

Jake stared at it for a moment. "I'm in."

He only had to read the first few parts of the mission. It was a dungeon run, but not just any dungeon run: an alchemy dungeon run. Kind of. It was a dungeon designed and created by the Order for their late to peak D-grade members, and considering Jake still needed his fair share of Dungeoneer titles, it would be silly not to use it.

Alright, that was another thing that factions could provide their members: access. Every faction had its own dungeons and general areas. That the Order would have a bunch of dungeons was just to be expected.

Draskil nodded at Jake agreeing to go. "We leave in three days."

"Who is we?" Jake asked further.

"The succubus, me, you, and two more alchemists if we bother." Draskil shrugged.

"What kind of dungeon is it?"

"Combat mixed with alchemy tasks. Unique plants need to be crafted into toxins to pass areas. Maybe potions, too, or other stuff. Not sure. I just needed alchemists."

"Is Irin an alchemist?" Jake asked, a bit confused. He was pretty sure she, as a demon, only had a social profession and her race without any class to speak of. Sure, she could learn alchemy, but—

"No, but she is hot," Draskil just answered blankly.

I guess that is kind of an argument to bring her, Jake thought, laughing a little internally. "Fair enough. Any other alchemists in mind?"

"Can't do it alone?" Draskil asked with a frown.

"Maybe, maybe not. How would I know? But even if I could, wouldn't it be faster to bring more?"

Draskil looked like he hadn't considered it much before nodding. "Okay. You know any?"

"Eh, I can think of at least one," Jake answered.

Wasn't it about time to see how far Reika had come in her alchemy? It would also give them a chance to catch up and do some alchemy together. Jake had glanced at the parchment a bit more, and it very much seemed like a dungeon all about learning and effectively housed puzzles.

Jake still recalled how he had met Reika doing a puzzle in the Treasure Hunt and how well they had jelled working together back then. So why not invite her? Maybe she even had another friend to bring, or they could find another fifth person.

Meira was not an option for hopefully obvious reasons. She was busy with her own stuff anyway, and Jake didn't want to drag her into a dungeon. Especially not with Draskil around. He was a bit of an intimidating guy until you got to know him. Reika should be fine, though.

"Then you find more alchemists," Draskil said, nodding. "You have my contact information."

Jake nodded. "Yeah, just send me the information."

"The succubus will," Draskil confirmed.

Their conversation just devolved into small talk after that until, finally, the lesson ended. Throughout Jake and Draskil's conversation, the two of them had sealed themselves within an isolation barrier made by Jake that made it impossible for others to listen in, but also for others to see them. Viridia or even some of the C-grades could easily go through it, but none had, so that was nice.

It could be argued the two of them chatting during a lesson could be considered rude, but they were far from the only ones. Many barriers had appeared as friends, small factions, and groups discussed potentially joining the Order.

Not long after, the lesson came to an end. Jake was preparing to leave as one of the first ones when he felt a telepathic connection. *"Chosen, may I have a word?"* he heard Viridia ask him. Jake considered for a moment before nodding. *"Thank you. Please simply come to my office once it suits you."*

With those words, Viridia also disappeared from the lesson hall, none of their conversation leaking out. Jake got up, went for one of the gates, and, just like usual, activated his token and stepped through. The difference this time was his destination.

Viridia had sent to him what was essentially an address through the token. Seeing no reason not to go, Jake headed through the gate and appeared in a large, luxurious office. He instantly spotted Viridia already standing in front of her desk, bowing as she saw him.

"Once more, thank you for offering your time," she spoke while bowing, making Jake a little uncomfortable and reminding him why he wanted to keep his identity as the Viper's Chosen secret. If he didn't, everyone would treat him like Viridia, if not even worse.

"No need to be so overly courteous," Jake said, trying to be both dismissive but also understanding.

"I apologize," Viridia still said, but she also had enough awareness to move the conversation forward. "It has been a while since our last meeting, and it is an honor to finally have you within the Order of the Malefic Viper."

"It's been a while for sure," Jake said, nodding. The tutorial felt like it had been ages ago. "Now, why did you want this meeting?"

"Firstly, I wanted to formally introduce myself to the Chosen. As the Hall Master of the Order, I find it only fitting that I make my loyalties clear. Secondly, to ask if the Chosen requires any assistance with anything? I have heard of your current considerations from the Verdant Matriarchs and wish to help as much as possible."

Jake frowned, a touch confused. "What considerations?"

"I fully understand if you wish to keep it under wraps for now. Just know that I will do my utmost to find candidates from within the Order."

What the hell is she on about? Jake thought, now more confused than ever. What candidates? Had she somehow listened in when they talked about the dungeon earlier? No, that should be impossible. He would have sensed it.

"Please be clear what considerations you are talking about," Jake said.

"Ah, my apologies. I am naturally talking of your plans for propagating your Bloodline. To my knowledge, the Malefic One relayed his wishes to the Verdant Matriarchs, and I have been tasked to assist you wi—excuse me, my Lord?"

Jake had already turned around and begun walking towards the gate again.

"Dispel whatever plans you had," Jake just said as he used his token to make a gate. "You are misinformed, and I have no such plans."

Viridia seemed taken aback as she asked, confused, "I apologize if I am overreaching or if there are any misunderstandings... but where is the Chosen going?"

Jake tossed her a final look before stepping through the gateway. "Just gonna have a small talk with my Patron."

CHAPTER 69

OVERSHARING & ONE MORE BEER

Jake stared at the god, who had a rare look of slight embarrassment.

"Would you believe me if I told you that this is all a misunderstanding?" Villy asked a very angry Jake the moment he stepped through the portal and stood face-to-face with the god, who was currently leaning back in a chair with a book.

"Should I?" Jake asked sharply.

"You know, I mess with you in many ways, but this is actually not one of them, I swear!" the god said very earnestly. Jake at least interpreted it as such. "You know I already told you to avoid tossing out any baby batter until you are at a higher grade and when you are really sure it is something you wanna do, didn't I?"

"Explain," Jake said, agreeing that it did seem off.

"So, I was having some fun with the Verdant Witches after you had fun with your little Runemaiden, and I may have said something that made them believe you wanted to... how can I say it... be more out there. Or at least that I believed you should be more liberal."

"What exactly did you do?" Jake asked, piercing daggers.

The Viper then smirked a bit. "You know what? Wouldn't it be better if I just showed you?"

"I am not sure I want tha—"

"Too late!" Villy smiled as the entire room disappeared, and Jake knew he was thrown into an illusion. He still saw the room and everything with his sphere... but what his eyes perceived and his ears heard was out of his control. Even the smells.

And damn, did he wish he could turn off those senses only a few seconds later.

A scene appeared before Jake. Three fully naked women were leaning on and pleasuring the Viper, who was lying on a large bed surrounded by messy silk sheets. All of the green-haired women looked nearly identical, and all were more than eager. Jake had to admit he was momentarily taken aback at how they looked, but he quickly flashed back to reality. Or, well, illusion.

One of them, who was snuggling up to his chest, said in a sultry voice, "It is rare you take the initiative."

"What can I say? I felt in the mood?" Villy smirked, clearly enjoying himself.

"Oh? Did something good happen?" another of the sisters asked as she ran her fingers across the Viper's fine scales.

"You can say that. My Chosen finally managed to have a major breakthrough in the art of not being as dense anymore and got laid." The Viper laughed a bit. "Not that it is anything serious, but some casual fun is just healthy. He should definitely get himself out there more. It should be good for him."

The three sisters looked at each other but didn't say more as they proceeded to get more aggressive. It was at this point Jake would have preferred the illusion to end, but nope, it kept going.

Jake sighed. "Villy, I do not need to see your willy in action."

As if it had never been there, the illusion faded, and Jake was back in the room. The Viper looked at Jake with a shit-eating grin. "Oh, did I misread the situation again?"

Jake shook his head and took a jab in return. "I don't know what is weirder—you needing me to get laid to get it up, or you enjoying making others watch."

"Now that is just a blatant misrepresentation." Villy shook his head. "I like to make you watch because I think it would be funny. I also want you to remember that I used to be a snake and that you humans are the ones who are weird when it comes to copulating. It isn't that big of a deal, ya know? As long as everyone enjoys it and is willing, who cares what others think?"

"I guess I am just not as free-spirited as you," Jake said, shrugging. "And also not as unperceptive, if you didn't even notice the glance they exchanged."

"Oh, I did notice," the Viper said. "But I honestly didn't think they would do anything this fast or make plans with the Hall Master. At most, I thought they would try to push that City Lord on you or make plans behind the scenes to set you up with those they liked. Believe it or not, I am not watching everyone all the time, and even I respect the right to privacy everyone has. Well, unless I have a reason not to respect their rights, in which case I do whatever I want."

"Very noble of you," Jake said. "But can I trust you to shut down this entire thing?"

"Maybe." Villy smirked. Jake looked at the Viper a bit more seriously, making Villy fully capitulate. "Alright, alright, but just be aware that even if I tell them to stop, that is no guarantee. They know you have a Bloodline, they know you are my Chosen, and they know we have a rather unique relationship. They are socially-minded and will want to take advantage of all that, maliciously or not. So they may or may not still do some things behind the scenes that neither of us is aware of before it is too late. Witches are nefariously good planners; you should know that."

Jake chuckled. "If I am perfectly honest, then I don't really know how the witch class even works or how their magic operates."

"Totally fair. I barely get it myself," the Viper said, surprising Jake. Villy clearly noticed and elaborated, "Witchcraft is an entire branch of magic that is awfully separated from borderline anything else. Their rituals follow a logic that nothing else does, and their magic is wholly unique. Sure, they do things that are a bit like curses but are actually called hexes. Oh, but hexes can actually create curses, but only if certain criteria are met. What are these criteria? No one fucking knows. It can feel so random at times. Maybe the trees need to be placed in a certain way, the stars form a certain pattern, or a number of highly specific items need to be in the proximity of the ritual."

"I have noticed they have a lot of... remote magic, I guess is the term?" Jake chipped in.

"Sure. Sometimes. The requirements can once more just be so odd, and even if it is true that they are not as affected by distance, as they use mediums for most of their magic, I wouldn't say it is an inherent trait of the school of magic. Witchcraft can tap into so many other concepts too. Anyway, enough about that. Trying to understand witchcraft—or worse, voodoo—is just a great way to mindfuck yourself and lead you astray on your own Path of magic."

"Got it," Jake said. "But it is a pretty rare school of magic, isn't it?"

"Yep." Villy nodded. "And the best part is that you often won't know you are fighting a witch before the trees around you suddenly turn into spiders, and the sky begins to rain exploding frogs that insult your hairstyle."

Jake laughed. "I want that to be real more than you can imagine."

Villy didn't flinch as he looked Jake straight in the eyes. "It is. I shit you not, the Verdant Witches wiped out a planet solely by the use of exploding frogs that insulted people before going boom."

Jake slowly nodded. *Note to self: Do not piss off witches for any reason and bring back a nice gift for Miranda when you return to Earth.*

"Ah, but don't worry too much. Witches tend to suck in direct combat and rely on hiding and avoiding confrontation. You are close to a direct counter." That gave Jake a bit of relief. "Anyway, was this all you came to talk about?"

"Yeah," Jake said. "Oh, actually, I am going to a dungeon with Draskil soon. Any tips?"

"Eat things," Villy said. "No, seriously. Eat a lot of things. Dungeons are great ways to duplicate ingredients and materials for free, but some of the stronger ones are placed with limitations. I am sure you noticed how things like those Golden Mushrooms from the Undergrowth couldn't be brought outside the dungeon... The same is true here. But what you can do is eat them, and the knowledge gained from Palate is permanent."

"Makes a lot of sense," Jake said, nodding.

He already kind of knew this. He also knew that while it was an "exploit" of sorts to place valuable things in dungeons, it also came with many restrictions, and balancing what could and couldn't be in dungeons was an entire art. Art for the dungeon architects and dungeon engineers to figure out. He did know that the dungeons tended to require some level of combat before one could access the valuables, which was probably why Draskil was still good to have around. That the Order had made a dungeon that mixed alchemy and combat made sense too.

All factions had their own dungeons designed, often specifically to fit their own needs. Shit, Casper and the Risen planned on making a dungeon on Earth that he would no doubt design to be helpful when training Risen.

Villy proceeded to give Jake a few more general tips but not much substance.

"Thanks for the tips and for handling your witches with benefits," Jake finally said, adding on, "You got anything on your mind?

"Eh, just one thing," Villy said. "Can I check out that bone weapon you got from the system event?"

Jake was a bit surprised and couldn't hold himself back from asking, "Why? More specifically, why now and not when I got it?"

"I want to check something. No worries—it won't do anything to your other self. The reason I waited was to make sure it was truly stable before checking, and it clearly is."

"Eh, sure, then," Jake said as he took out the bone katar and handed it to Villy.

The god took it in his hand, and Jake felt that Villy was trying to scan it. He could resist the scan and make it impossible even for the Primordial to see anything—due to system fuckery, of course—but Jake allowed him to scan away.

Villy checked it out for a dozen or so seconds before he nodded. "Thanks, mate. Coming across items like this is rare, and I wanted to make sure of something while also scanning it for future reference."

Jake got the bone katar back and took note of how sim-Jake didn't even seem to have noticed, probably busy fighting or training in his Soulspace. "No problem. Any time."

The two of them had some more small talk and shot the shit before they said their goodbyes, allowing Jake to do the next thing on his list. He pulled out his token and dialed Reika. It didn't take long before he got a response.

"Hey, there, how are you doing?" Jake asked her once she picked up.

"I am doing well, thank you... but what made you decide to contact me?" Reika asked in a confused tone, clearly not expecting the call.

"It is easier to ask in person. Can you give me your address and I can drop by? Ah, I can also give an update on stuff that happened on Earth and with the system event while we're at it."

A few seconds passed before she answered again. "I can, but maybe we should meet somewhere public? As you know, I live in dorms of sorts, and while we do have our own private chambers, I would not want to create misunderstandings by you visiting."

"Eh, it should be fine. I don't care as long as you don't care."

"Alright, fine. When do you plan on coming by?"

"Right now?" Jake asked.

He heard a sigh in answer, followed by a small break. "Alright, but wait at least five minutes, okay? Maybe a bit longer is also okay."

"Sure," Jake confirmed.

Still standing in Villy's room, Jake put the token back into his inventory and looked at the god, who looked back at him. They had already said their goodbyes, but Villy read the situation as two bottles of beer appeared.

Well, I do have five minutes...

Reika hurried to clean up her chamber, as it was frankly a mess. She even called in her roommate, a beastfolk, to help her get it presentable. She regretted saying five minutes less than five seconds after she said it, but it was too late now. With a bit of panic, she stacked the textbooks in a corner before remembering she had a spatial ring and began tossing them in there.

"Will he even care?" Bastilla asked as she helped put away some glassware.

Reika shook her head at her friend. "Maybe, maybe not. Either way, it needs to look presentable if a guest comes over."

"Sure." The beastfolk just shrugged.

Reika smiled. "Thanks for helping."

Bastilla waved her off. "Eh, it wasn't like I had anything better to do, and this guy got gold in the test, right? Sounds like a good guy to get friendly with."

Reika shook her head as she kept cleaning up. Before coming to the Order of the Malefic Viper, she would never have imagined the situation she was in now. She was ashamed to say it, but she'd been very uncomfortable around anything and anyone that wasn't human or at least very close to a human when she first got there.

Elves, dwarves, and whatnot, she was fine with. But Dragonkin? Beastfolk? Demons? Weird elemental creatures? She was very averse to their presence. Reika wouldn't say they scared her, but they were offputting. It took her a while to begin to truly view them as people rather than just... monsters.

Bastilla had been the one to truly open her eyes. Her father was a winged lion-like beast, and her mother an elf. Reika had wrestled with how that was even possible until she learned Bastilla's dad could take human form, and that he'd been in late C-grade when she was born.

Her heritage meant Bastilla had a very lithe form and cat-like features, as well as fine golden hair covering her entire body—even her face. She even had two moth or butterfly-like wings she could summon. She didn't look like the oft-fetishized cat girls of the old world that were pretty much just humans with cat ears, but a true fusion between man and beast. Reika had not liked her in the beginning, as Bastilla was crude, always stared with her beastly eyes, and was generally overly curious. Yet with time, she came to learn that Bastilla was just inquisitive and highly skilled in alchemy. She had a talent for it, and she had a Perception-based build, making her great at analyzing and seeing the crafting process.

By now, they were genuinely good friends, and as they had the same shared living space connected to their personal chambers, they often interacted and even had many of the same lessons.

Reika and Bastilla continued to clean, and Reika saw five minutes had passed. Yet he was not there yet, nor had he pinged her to show he had arrived, so they kept making the space more presentable. Ten minutes passed, and it was close to perfect.

A quarter of an hour.

Half an hour.

Only forty minutes later did Reika get a ping on her token that Jake had arrived at the gate... now standing in a completely spotless room.

CHAPTER 70

SPONTANEOUS DECISIONS ARE THE BEST DECISIONS

Jake hadn't set foot in a dorm for years. Counting time dilation, close to decades. This wasn't the dorms of the old world, with underfunded, shitty facilities and shared bathrooms and only one washing room for several people, and every time you had to wash clothes, all the laundry machines would be taken, and even if they were not taken and you got the rare chance to start washing your clothes, some absolute asshat would stop the machine and take your clothes out halfway through the cycle.

No, it wasn't that kind of dorm, but the dorm for those with bronze tokens. It was significantly nicer than what those with white ones got, as far as he knew, but even the white token ones had to be better than the shit Jake had lived in for a few years back in university. All in all, the Order tended to be pretty generous with accommodations, even if he was a bit biased as a black token himself where he got his entire huge residence.

When Jake first stepped through the gate to enter the dorm, he found himself in a circular room with eight exits leading into long hallways. Each hallway had nearly ten meters to the ceiling and was made of marble-like rock, with bronze engravings and setpieces placed here and there. It looked damn good for dorms—that was for sure.

Many individuals went and came from the different hallways, walking towards the wall with gates on it or into the different hallways. No one took note of Jake as he stood there and tried to figure out where Reika's room was.

Checking the address Reika had given him, he saw it said "4-121," and it didn't take long before he understood what it meant. Each hallway was numbered, and then each room also had a number. It was a simple system.

Going down the fourth hallway, Jake quickly found the right place. It also quickly became clear, as he walked through the hallway, that behind every door wasn't actually a room, but more like a small pre-set gateway. He also felt severe distortion of space, likely meaning that each chamber was spatially expanded. Which they would have to be, considering there were only three or so meters between each door on both sides of the hallway, and with thousands of rooms in each of them, each room would be mega small if not for space magic.

Jake raised his token to the door and pressed the doorbell, so to say. A few seconds passed before it opened, revealing a large living room with Reika walking over to invite him in, a beastfolk woman behind her peeking curiously.

"Hey, glad you could make it," Reika said with a smile as she invited Jake inside.

"I was beginning to think he wouldn't come, considering he said five minutes more than half an hour ago," the beastfolk commented.

Jake got a good look at her and saw that she had some kind of cat heritage. Very shiny golden fur, too.

He was somewhat surprised at the comment, though, as he looked at Reika. "Didn't you say at least five minutes? I got the feeling you kind of wanted it to be more than five, so I stayed a bit longer and had a drink with a friend."

"Ah, yeah, no worries," Reika said, slightly embarrassed.

The beastfolk was about to speak up again when Reika cut in. "So, what brought you here, by the way? A meeting of some sort? What about?"

"Maybe we should talk more privately?" Jake asked, nodding towards the cat lady, who seemed very interested in their conversation.

"Alright," Reika agreed without hesitation. The beastfolk didn't protest, but just shrugged and waved them off.

"Have fun!" she said with a suggestive grin.

Reika groaned, led Jake into her own personal room, and closed the door behind her, activating the seal on it.

Feeling they were isolated, Jake finally spoke freely. "So, how have you been enjoying being in the Order of the Malefic Viper so far?"

Okay, not the most pressing question, but Jake was interested. Reika came from quite a different culture and, contrarily to Jake, didn't have a good buddy who also happened to be running the entire place. She had a far more raw experience without any real help, and Jake genuinely wanted to know how she was doing. The old swordsman had also asked him to check in with her, so it was only right.

"It has been... better than expected?" Reika answered. "Not to be insulting, but I had expected things to be far worse and even less professional, if that makes sense? Everything feels above board. Well, ignoring the fact that there seem to be far fewer restrictions on everything compared to the old world. I also do not particularly enjoy the fact that I have had a dozen people so far try to sell me slaves or questionable organs and body parts clearly belonging to humanoids."

"Does indeed have its issues, true," Jake agreed.

"But overall, I find it incredibly generous that the Order gives so much and demands so little. I have been able to attend lessons with experts I could only ever dream of learning from. All I have given up in return is some labor by selling some things I crafted. I would think this entire setup was too good to be true if I didn't experience it myself. I can only imagine how much better it is for you."

"Well, glad to hear you are settling in nicely." Jake smiled. "And the reason why I came today was actually to ask you if you wanted to participate in a mission with me and a few others, so that should earn you some more Academy Credits too. It is a dungeon run, and I have been asked to look for alchemists to join."

Reika looked surprised when Jake pulled out the paper detailing the mission, but she instantly shook her head. "This one is designed for late D-grades... I am not quite there yet."

"Eh, you are level 154; it should be fine. Your profession is late D-grade, right? That counts. The dungeon itself just requires the one entering to be D-grade, and all we will need of you is your alchemical knowledge." He was already pretty determined that if Reika didn't wanna go, they would just do the dungeon as a three-person team, as he didn't want to spend time getting to learn and work with a stranger.

"Are you sure these other people would be fine with that?" she asked, concerned. "Who are they, by the way? Ones I know?"

"So far, it is me, Draskil, and Irin going."

"Oh?" Reika exclaimed, surprised. "Irin? The succubus? How and why? I would assume she had already completed the dungeon, or has she truly never done it before? And even if she hasn't done it... why go now? She is not an alchemist, as far as I know, nor a good fighter. At least not someone who would be useful with you and the Malefic Dragonkin around."

"I was surprised too," Jake answered, not sharing Draskil's reason why he wanted to bring her along. "And I actually think your how and why are related. Why would she have gone before? The only reason now is because Draskil decided to ask her, probably just to not go alone or make her recruit alchemists to join or something."

"Hm," Reika said, clearly still unsure. "So it will be the four of us? Sure I will be of help?"

"Why not? You have been focused on alchemy and were already pretty good before you went to the Order. I would rather work with you than some random." Jake shrugged. "Draskil also doesn't know shit about alchemy, so I would have to handle everything without you around, and that sounds like a bad and very tedious idea."

"I see." Reika nodded in confirmation, a bit more assured. "It would be my honor to attend, then, as long as all of you are fine with it."

"Great. We go in three days." Jake smiled, not giving Reika time to comment on the short notice. Jake had also gotten short notice, so it wasn't his fault. "Moving on... I see you made a friend?"

"Bastilla," Reika said, nodding. "Yeah, we get along well. She is also an alchemist and rather talented. A bronze token like me, and I think she will upgrade to silver within a few years at most. Where she came from, no one really taught her anything, making her progress fast after entering the Academy. She is a bit like myself in that regard, even if our methodologies vary widely. Her methods are far closer to yours than mine."

Jake nodded as he got a brilliant idea. "Do you think she wants to come too?"

"Come to what?" Reika asked, genuinely confused.

"The dungeon."

"I... Would that be wise?" Reika muttered. "To bring along two bronze tokens... The disparity in the group will be massive."

"Eh, it should be fine," Jake said, brushing it off. "Just try to convince her to come so we fill the group. Not to brag, but I would probably be able to do most of the alchemy myself anyway, so I just need you two to help speed up things by pointing out obvious things I am too dumb to notice."

Reika shook her head and smiled. "Fine, I'll try. Anyway, you talked about a system event back on Earth?"

"Well, not on Earth," Jake began. "It was in this giant space station of sorts, and I think it may even be a World Wonder..."

Jake began recounting the system event and how it had worked, Reika being very interested in the details. He also shared his brief conversation with the Sword Saint and let her know things were fine back on Earth. Reika herself began talking more about her experience in the Order, how she had felt incredibly insecure initially but had begun to find confidence again in her skills and talent, and how she had managed to get along with her roommates. Jake even told her of his bout with a C-grade—not because he wanted to brag or anything. He didn't talk much about his trip with Carmen, as he didn't want to share the Runemaiden's personal details.

It was a nice chat, and he ended up leaving a few hours later and heading back to his own residence. He got quite a few stares from Bastilla when he exited the room, and he saw that other people who shared the living space had also shown up to glare. Jake didn't particularly mind as he headed home for some more alchemy and to prepare for the dungeon dive.

Jake got confirmation less than five minutes after returning to his residence that Bastilla was in the dungeon group. Didn't take much convincing, it seemed. With a team assembled, Jake pinged Irin and let her know.

In what should not be a surprise at all, Irin didn't even know Draskil had asked Jake and was more than pleased to hear he would come along. She also didn't mind the two tagalongs and sent over some more information on the dungeon to Jake, which he then also sent to Reika.

With everything done, Jake got back to work with his usual schedule as he waited for the dungeon run to begin.

Draskil and patience apparently didn't go well together. Jake had barely gotten started on his alchemy when Irin pinged him again very apologetically. She explained that the second Draskil heard Jake had already found two other alchemists, he saw no reason to wait three more days, as the wait was originally for Irin to find alchemists. So he wanted to go... now.

Others would perhaps get mad at this, but Jake's response was a shrug and a quick call to Reika. Now, Reika liked to plan, and when she was asked to spontaneously go to a dungeon only hours after learning about it, she was hesitant, but her roommate Bastilla convinced her.

This is how the group of five ended up meeting only half an hour later within a large meeting room of sorts made for exactly this kind of thing. Draskil had been the first to arrive, impatiently sitting there and waiting. Jake was second, as he didn't have better things to do—or, well, he chose not to begin doing important things. Reika and Bastilla came a few minutes later, with Irin the last to arrive, as she had to prepare some materials and ingredients they would need in the dungeon.

"Everyone is already here?" Irinixis asked with surprise after she stepped through the gate. "Well, that does make things simpler. I know it is on short notice, but has anyone managed to read the supplied material?"

Jake quickly scanned it before nodding. Reika also agreed along with Bastilla, who looked weirdly out of it. Draskil was just staying mute as his tail moved back and forth impatiently. Jake noticed that Bastilla kept staring at Draskil, who didn't even glance her way in return.

He also took note of how the one at the highest level present was Irin at 193, followed closely by Draskil at 190. The dragonkin hadn't gotten many levels recently—probably on purpose to strengthen his foundation before C-grade.

"Okay, then... brief explanation only," Irin said. "The dungeon we are about to enter is made for late-to-peak D-grades and features monsters above level 170 as challenges, up to and including a weak C-grade final optional boss. The dungeon itself contains nine floors total, all of which need to be cleared to battle the optional boss. Each floor has unique herbs, natural treasures, and materials one needs to obtain to craft a required product to pass the floor and move on to the next. All of these aforementioned things are guarded by monsters of various kinds, and often some materials from the monsters themselves are also required in the alchemical process. That is about all. Any questions?"

"How long is it expected to take?" Reika asked. "Also, a pleasure to meet you. I am Reika from the Noboru Clan of Earth."

"The pleasure is mine," Irin said, nodding. "The expected duration is around two to three weeks total, but for this group, trying to go on any averages seems pointless. So the real answer is... I don't know. Ah, but the maximum duration we can spend in there is four weeks before the dungeon itself collapses."

Reika nodded at the answer, and Jake followed up with one of his own. "What kinds of monsters will we encounter?"

"Assorted ones. The floors tend to vary in affinity and design, meaning I once more cannot say. Besides the general design, I do not know the specific details. No one does, due to how these dungeons work." Irin shook her head. "It is only once inside that things become clear."

Jake nodded, guessing there was maybe some element of random generation going on? Either way, with that information, there was just one more thing to say.

Draskil stood up and stretched his wings as he smirked. "Then let's just go and find out ourselves!"

In agreement, the party of two humans, one demon, one drag-onkin, and one beastfolk headed out for their dungeon run.

Jake had at least prepared himself in the most important way for this run:

He hadn't eaten breakfast for weeks and was ready for a feast.

CHAPTER 71

GIRL TIME & GUY TIME

Irin took the lead as she led Jake and the others toward the location of the dungeon. It wasn't as simple as Jake had thought it would be to get there. He had kind of just assumed it would just be another gate, and then boom, they would be teleported straight in front of it.

However, reality was a bit different. They went through a gate and appeared in a small waystation of sorts within an utterly massive, damp cavern, with the gate itself within a structure carved into the stone walls.

"We are currently within the first layer of Primordial-4," the succubus explained once they made it out of the small waystation. "This part of the layer is usually safe in this area, and we shouldn't expect any C-grades to appear. The dungeon itself is placed deeper within this cavern. In case any of you are wondering, then not placing the dungeons in natural environments more suitable for the dungeon in question would just be moronic and waste resources unnecessarily. You need the mana density to reach a certain level, too, for the dungeon core to operate properly. This dungeon is also on the older side, making its placement a bit more inconvenient than usual."

Jake saw that only a single person was present there, inside a hidden meditation chamber of sorts. While he could not be sure, he had a feeling this person was firmly in the C-grade and acted as a defender of sorts.

Not thinking deeper about the issue, Jake followed Irin as they began making it deeper into the cavern. The place was utterly huge, and when they made it out of a small cave system, they came to an even larger, chasm-like cavern where Jake couldn't even see the ceiling. Below them were blue pools of water with beasts and monsters of all kinds everywhere, fighting and bathing in the water.

Jake felt that the water was some kind of natural treasure or perhaps the byproduct of one. Yet this trip was not to collect water or fight beasts, but to head to the dungeon. Besides, the beasts below were only around 120 to 140, so they were not worth his time at all.

"The blue water in the pools may look attractive, but it is actually completely useless by itself when it comes to alchemy," Irin explained once more as Reika and Bastilla looked curiously at the happenings far below. "Instead, we allow the beasts to soak in it and refine the energy so that when they are killed, their cores can be harvested. Ah, but some members of the Order with heritages that allow them to make use of the pools also come by once in a while, so do watch out if you ever go hunting here. Would be unfortunate to kill another member of the Order."

Irin gave a few more explanations of the local environment and what one could expect to find there if one decided to go exploring at one point or another. Jake considered if he should go at some point, but he knew he probably wouldn't.

On the topic of getting to the dungeon, they had chosen to fly there, as that was faster. There were some flying creatures in the cavern too, but none were threats. Hell, none of these flying monsters even bothered the party for one simple reason: Jake wasn't trying to hide his presence at all. The beasts all avoided them, as they instinctually knew not to mess with them. Not that it was necessarily even needed for Jake to be the one to scare them off. Draskil's aura was plenty scary all on its own.

"The dungeon is located at the end of this cavern, pretty much just straight ahead. It shouldn't take us more than half an hour to an hour to get there." Irin smiled. "I do not expect us to meet any beasts or foes that are of any danger to us."

Draskil turned to Jake once he heard this. With a toothy grin, he spoke, "So, how fast is your flying speed?"

Jake wasn't surprised in the least, and he smirked in response. "Are you looking for a race?" The dragonkin didn't even respond as his wings began glowing with energy. Jake, in response, slightly raised his foot and got ready to step down. "No one says it needs to be flying, right?"

Draskil shook his head. "Loser owes a drink."

With those words, he exploded with power and took off. Jake threw a glance at Irin, and after he got a nod in response, he stepped down and warped through space. He appeared over half a kilometer away before stepping down again. Slowly building up momentum, he chased after Draskil, who had a small headstart.

Irinixis sighed as she saw the two of them run off like two children let loose. She had been working in the Order for a long time now and had managed many individuals... but this was her first time getting such important people as two black tokens that even had a Malefic Dragonkin with a Divine Blessing among them.

Quite honestly, it was all luck. Humanoid Resources assigned managerial staff to those from the 93rd Universe; the groups they would manage were chosen entirely at random. Most others who handled groups from the new universe had gotten mediocre to slightly above mediocre groups. Having a few gold tokens would be considered exceptional, and a few of her colleagues had bragged about it.

So when Irinixis had been assigned two black tokens, she was ecstatic. Not to misunderstand, she still was ecstatic to be their primary contact person. This was a huge opportunity for her. There was just the minor issue of feeling completely out of her depth with both of them. She was used to powerful young masters throwing their weight around and caring about face above all else, but these two just did whatever. They were more like children than highly talented geniuses blessed by the Malefic One.

Perhaps their laidback attitudes are part of the reason for their growth, Irin thought, unsure if that could be the case. Either way, understanding Draskil seemed impossible at the current time, but as for the human? She had a great opportunity right there and then.

"So, girls, I guess it is just us till we reach the dungeon," Irin said to the two of them with a smile. "Better get going so we don't make those two wait too long."

"Let us," the woman called Reika agreed. She began condensing a board of ice that she stood upon as a mode of transportation, having just flown using pure mana before. The beastfolk woman followed by priming her wings with energy, Irin doing the same.

The three of them took flight, Irin being the fastest, but not by much. She was surprised at the level of magic deployed by the human, especially considering her limited time to train. *She will advance to a silver token within not that long simply due to her talent in magic,* Irin reckoned. *I should not doubt the judgment of a black token... Jake believed she was worth bringing along and knows things I do not.*

As for her beastfolk companion, she clearly had an Agility-focused race due to her feline heritage, making her on the faster side. She was about as fast as Reika, which in reality was just proof of Reika's talent, considering she was firmly in the mage category.

While flying, there was no reason not to get to know one another, as they would spend some time together in the dungeon anyway. It wasn't like they were in a real hurry, either, as Jake and Draskil could just spend some guy time together while they spent some girl time.

"Man, those two sure are something," the beastfolk woman commented as she looked at Irin. "I am called Bastilla, by the way. A pleasure to meet you. Are you one of those management demons?"

"I am," Irin replied, not thinking it worthwhile to further elaborate.

"Damn. That dragonkin one of those you help manage? What is he, anyway? A gold token like that Jake guy?"

"Neither of them has gold tokens?" Irin exclaimed, confused, noticing Reika looking a bit embarrassed.

"Wait," Bastilla said, glaring at Reika. "You said he was gold, though. With his own residence and all that."

"I... didn't want to... you know..." Reika muttered.

Irin found it slightly endearing. She smiled, fully understanding the situation immediately. "She didn't want to come off as a braggart, and thus downplayed her connections. To clarify, both Jake and Draskil have black tokens and are blessed by the Malefic One, with the dragonkin—as you rightly pointed out—being a Malefic Dragonkin carrying a Divine Blessing."

Bastilla looked weird for a moment before she opened her mouth. "For real? Isn't that like... a big deal? A super-big deal?"

"Anyone with a black token is considered extraordinary and a big deal, as you so eloquently put it," Irin said in confirmation.

"I am beginning to feel the pressure here," Bastilla said, shuddering. "Why am I part of this group again?"

"That, I am not certain of," Irin answered as she looked at Reika, who had some time to collect herself.

"As Irinixis said before, I didn't want to show off, you know?" Reika confessed. "It is also a bit embarrassing he is so much more skilled than me despite us spending an equal amount of time doing alchemy and learning energy control. It is infuriating..."

Irin just shook her head. "Listening to all of you complain is infuriating. That you managed to get bronze tokens is already more than the vast, vast majority of the multiverse can ever achieve, and you are both early on your Paths. So just keep working hard, and you can go far. Meanwhile, I am hoping to make those two black tokens my ticket to C-grade, as, currently, it is still a toss-up if I will make it."

And wasn't that the truth. Irin had been D-grade for close to a century and had only recently gained a single level. The path to C-grade was even harder, and while she did have some confidence, it wasn't a sure thing. She downplayed it a bit to the two girls, but she was truthful that she wanted to make Jake and Draskil—or at least one of them—her ticket to C-grade. It was what her profession was all about, after all. As for if she would also progress her succubus race... now, that was a whole other question.

"Still didn't answer why I was asked to join," Bastilla muttered, making Irin refocus on the conversation.

Reika just sighed. "In all honesty? I think the primary factor was proximity. Jake wanted a fifth, and there you were."

Irin nearly flailed a bit while flying as she heard the reason. *I truly don't understand these geniuses... but I should take the chance to.*

"Reika, I have been wondering about the planet you and Lord Thayne hail from," she began with a smile. "I strive to know more about those to whom I am assigned, so I would love to learn more about you two and your origins."

It was a perfect time to learn about at least one of the two geniuses when he wasn't within earshot.

The two "geniuses" managed to turn what should have taken half an hour into less than a five-minute trip. Jake had used One Step, Thousand Miles, while Draskil had a legendary movement skill related to flying. Jake won out in the skill department when it came to traveling, as One Step was a line of skills used for traveling and not necessarily for combat, while Draskil's skill was more combat-oriented with a focus on instantaneous movement to escape and attack.

However, the level disparity meant that Draskil could make up for it. He was just faster, and Jake failed to catch up in the short time it took to reach the dungeon. Without the headstart Draskil had, Jake could have likely caught up.

Ah, but Jake still won. The race was to the dungeon... and Draskil flew straight by it while Jake picked up the unique mana signature emanating from a hole in the ground. Draskil quickly noticed Jake hadn't followed and put two and two together.

Which led to their current situation.

"I was faster," Draskil said.

"That wasn't what we were competing about," Jake argued. "It was who would make it to the dungeon first. Which I did."

"Who cares about who got here first when I was faster?" Draskil sneered, clearly dissatisfied.

"If it wasn't about who got here first, then why get a headstart? And didn't I slowly catch up to you?" Jake argued further, feeling like he had Draskil cornered.

"Does not matter. I was the fastest to pass by the entrance and won."

"If you run past the finish line, it doesn't count." Jake smirked. "And if it wasn't for me, you would still be flying right now."

"She said half an hour," Draskil said, deciding to blame a third party.

Jake laughed. "Sounds like bad excuses. Just take the loss."

"I didn't lose."

Jake was beginning to believe that this was not an argument that could be won, as the other party simply chose to deny reality. Okay, in some fairness, all Draskil had asked was how fast Jake was, and there were no formal rules, but Jake only found it reasonable that their race was to the dungeon.

Having decided to not pursue it further, he properly inspected the chasm the hole had led into containing the dungeon. The entrance to the dungeon looked incredibly out of place, as it was just a black metal door embedded in a stone wall, and it looked like one could easily break it or take it away. However, with further inspection, it became clear the gates were somehow entirely locked in place.

Jake inspected them with Draskil still moping, proving that he did recognize his loss. He just was just too shy or prideful to admit it. At least, that is how Jake chose to interpret the actions of the dragonkin. Feeling good about himself, Jake began to consider ways to pass the time as they waited for the rest of their party to arrive.

About forty minutes went by before the others made it to the dungeon, and in the meantime, Jake had time to craft a batch of health potions just for good measure. Draskil had also gotten bored and turned to meditation.

"Sorry for the wait," Irin apologized when she made it into the chasm along with Bastilla and Reika.

Draskil just made a slightly dissatisfied noise while Jake waved it off. Having no need to exchange more words, they all went over to the gate, and as Jake laid his hand upon it, a system message appeared.

Dungeon: Nine Floors of the Indigo Caverns
Requirements to enter: D-grade
Requirements to enter met
WARNING: Only 5 challengers are allowed per party attempting the dungeon.
Enter Dungeon?
Y/N

Not a single one of them hesitated to enter the dungeon. Jake felt excitement as he was teleported by the system, but his excitement died instantly when he appeared in the dungeon.

His smile faded, and his eyes opened in horror as he gazed out upon the first floor and what they could expect this dungeon to contain.

"Fuck me," Jake exclaimed out loud, realizing this whole thing was a mistake. Because he saw them.

Mushrooms.

So many fucking mushrooms.

I want to go home...

———

The Primal Hunter will return in Book 8.

Thank you for reading The Primal Hunter 7

We hope you enjoyed it as much as we enjoyed bringing it to you. We just wanted to take a moment to encourage you to review the book. Follow this link: The Primal Hunter 7 to be directed to the book's Amazon product page to leave your review.

Every review helps further the author's reach and, ultimately, helps them continue writing fantastic books for us all to enjoy.

――――

Also in series:
The Primal Hunter 1
The Primal Hunter 2
The Primal Hunter 3
The Primal Hunter 4
The Primal Hunter 5
The Primal Hunter 6
The Primal Hunter 7
The Primal Hunter 8

――――

Want to discuss our books with other readers and even the authors? Join our Discord server today and be a part of the Aethon community.

Facebook | Instagram | Twitter | Website

You can also join our non-spam mailing list by visiting www.
subscribepage.com/AethonReadersGroup and never miss out on
future releases. You'll also receive three full books completely Free as
our thanks to you.

Looking for more great books?

Crimefighting is illegal. Punishable by life in prison beneath the ocean. That won't stop Harrier. Justice—a concept without a universally accepted definition. To some, it means reconciliation, while others deliver it with swift and violent judgment. For me? I just want to not be considered an outlaw for years of serving and protecting New York City. Yep. That's right. Crimefighting is against the law and punishable by life in prison at the bottom of the ocean. It sucks. But that won't stop me from doing what I was born to do: uphold justice and stop good people from being hurt. Even if everyone I once called a friend is against me, I'm not bowing down to the Counter Vigilante Taskforce. My name is Sawyer William Vincent (I know, it's three first names. Think I haven't heard that before?) Once known as Red Raptor, I'm now Black Harrier, one of the world's most famous masked crime-fighters, and this is my city. I think. **From #1 Audible & Washington Post Bestseller Jaime Castle and CJ Valin comes a new superhero universe perfect for fans of both DC and Marvel. Actually, its for fans of anything superhero-related. You're gonna like it. Promise.**

Get Harrier: Justice Now!

The Everfail will rise. His enemies will fall. *Hiral is the Everfail, the weakest person on the flying island of Fallen Reach. He trains harder than any warrior. Studies longer than any scholar. But all his people are born with magic powered by the sun, flowing through tattoos on their bodies. Despite having enormous energy within, Hiral is the only one who can't channel it; his hard work is worth nothing. Until it isn't. In a moment of danger, Hiral unlocks an achievement with a special instruction: Access a Dungeon to receive a Class-Specific Reward. It's his first—and maybe last— chance for real power. Just one problem: all dungeons lay in the wilderness below the flying islands that humanity lives on, and there lay secrets and dangers that no one has survived. New powers await, but so do new challenges. If he survives? He could forge his own path to power. If he fails? Death will be the least of his problems.* **Don't miss the next progression fantasy series from J.M Clarke, bestselling author of Mark of the Fool, along with C.J. Thompson. Unlock a weak-to-strong progression into power and a detailed litRPG system with unique classes, skills, dungeons, achievements, survival and evolution. Explore a mysterious world of fallen civilizations, strange monsters and deadly secrets.**

Get Rune Seeker Now!

The last thing a Necromancer expects is to be brought back from the dead... *After fulfilling the duty all Arch Necromancers are tasked with, the last thing Sylver Sezari expected was to be reborn. He was usually the one reanimating dead things. How ironic. But reborn he was. And after crawling his way back into the land of the living, he finds himself a strange land, a strange time, and with a strange floating screen in front of his new face. Either through plan or chance, he's alive again, and planning to enjoy himself to his heart's content.* **Don't miss the start of this LitRPG Adventure about a reincarnated necromancer growing in power and finding his way in a new world where the rules have changed vastly since he last "lived."**

Get Sylver Seeker Now!

FREEID

[PSYCHOKINETIC] EYEBALL PULLING

[1]

There is no weapon more powerful than the [Psychokinetic] mind. Astrid, a mischievous noble teen, long dreamed of exploring the ancient cities preserved beneath the waves, left behind from a time before the ocean swallowed the world. She's been training all her life to become a magic swordsman capable of doing just that. But when an ancient monster long thought dead assaults humanity's last bastion–a floating ship-city–she awakens her System early. Only, she's not a warrior as expected. She's forced to walk the path of a[Psychokinetic] Mage. With Spawn-infested oceans, pirates looking to plunder, and mysterious monsters that lurk within Bubbled-Cites at the bottom of the ocean, Safety is anything but guaranteed. She'll learn levitation, ovject throwing, eyeball pulling, and more, all the way to the apex of psychic powers. But, what happens when she discovers that her world was a lot larger than she– and the rest of humanity, once thought? **Don't miss the start of this action-packed and often hilarious LitRPG Apocalypse series about a young survivor with a craving for adventure and fighting. Perfect for fans of Azarinth Healer and Eight.**

Get Psychokinetic Eyeball Pulling Now!

For all our LitRPG books, visit our website.

Made in the USA
Middletown, DE
25 September 2023